Sacred River

MODERN
African
Writing
from Ohio University Press
Ghirmai Negash, General Editor

This series brings the best African writing to an international audience. These groundbreaking novels, memoirs, and other literary works showcase the most talented writers of the African continent. The series also features works of significant historical and literary value translated into English for the first time. Moderately priced, the books chosen for the series are well crafted, original, and ideally suited for African studies classes, world literature classes, or any reader looking for compelling voices of diverse African perspectives.

Books in the series are published with support from the Ohio University National Resource Center for African Studies.

Welcome to Our Hillbrow
A Novel of Postapartheid South Africa
Phaswane Mpe
ISBN: 978-0-8214-1962-5

Dog Eat Dog: A Novel
Niq Mhlongo
ISBN: 978-0-8214-1994-6

After Tears: A Novel
Niq Mhlongo
ISBN: 978-0-8214-1984-7

From Sleep Unbound
Andrée Chedid
ISBN: 978-0-8040-0837-2

On Black Sisters Street: A Novel
Chika Unigwe
ISBN: 978-0-8214-1992-2

Paper Sons and Daughters
Growing Up Chinese in South Africa
Ufrieda Ho
ISBN: 978-0-8214-2020-1

The Conscript
A Novel of Libya's Anticolonial War
Gebreyesus Hailu
ISBN: 978-0-8214-2023-2

Thirteen Cents: A Novel
K. Sello Duiker
ISBN: 978-0-8214-2036-2

Sacred River: A Novel
Syl Cheney-Coker
ISBN: 978-0-8214-2056-0

Sacred River

a novel

SYL CHENEY-COKER

ohio university press athens

Ohio University Press, Athens, Ohio 45701
ohioswallow.com

Printed in the United States of America
Ohio University Press books are printed on acid-free paper ♾ ™

24 23 22 21 20 19 18 17 16 15 14   5 4 3 2 1

Library of Congress Cataloging-in-Publication Data

Cheney-Coker, Syl, [date]- author.
Sacred River : a novel / Syl Cheney-Coker.
pages cm. — (Modern African Writing)
Summary: "The reincarnation of a legendary nineteenth-century Caribbean emperor as a contemporary African leader is at the heart of this novel. Sacred River deals with the extraordinary lives, hopes, powerful myths, stories, and tragedies of the people of a modern West African nation. It is also the compelling love story of an idealistic philosophy professor and an ex-courtesan of incomparable beauty. Two hundred years after his death, the great Haitian emperor Henri Christophe miraculously appears in a dream to Tankor Satani, president of the fictional West African country of Kissi, with instructions for Tankor to continue Henri Christophe's rule, which had been interrupted by 'that damned Napoleon.' Ambitious in scope, Sacred River is a diaspora-inspired novel, in which Cheney-Coker has tackled the major themes of politics, social strife, crime and punishment, and human frailty and redemption in Malagueta, the fictional, magical town and its surroundings first created by the author in *The Last Harmattan of Alusine Dunbar,* for which he was awarded the coveted Commonwealth Writers' Prize. Sacred River is equally about love and politics, and marks the return to fiction of one of Africa's major writers."— Provided by publisher.
ISBN 978-0-8214-2056-0 (hardback) — ISBN 978-0-8214-4465-8 (electronic)
1. Africa, West—Fiction. I. Title.
PR9393.9.C5S24 2013
823—dc23

2013041960

To the memory of my dear wife Dalisay,

who read a good chunk of this book and made

some very valuable suggestions on her deathbed.

Very deeply missed.

Author's Note

This is a work of fiction, although some of the events are set against the background of recent political history in the region where Malagueta is located. Any resemblance to actual people, dead or alive, is purely coincidental. Names and characters are all imaginary and used fictitiously by the author. Places, however closely related to any existing geographical entities, are entirely the author's creation. Also, in writing this novel, and as I did in my previous novel, *The Last Harmattan of Alusine Dunbar*, I have made liberal use of the myths and legends of my West African heritage, which is not to be confused with that of writers grouped inside that intellectual humbug called "magic realism."

The novelist's inheritance in much of West Africa is of millions of wonderful narratives and myths about the complexities of our world, and of the existence of another realm, where extraordinary events do happen. We live and thrive in that wonderful intellectual canvas, full of myriad colors, rich in imagination, and, yes, our own kind of *magic*!

Consequently, for anyone to suggest, or even imagine, that my work has something to do with someone else's literary humbug is not only misleading, it shows gross ignorance of the multilayered African sense of reality. Until you have lived in various parts of West Africa for a short time, and have experienced how extraordinarily rich it is in magic, you really cannot put an African novel in another literary domain. African writers really have no use for so-called magic realism because our lives, contrary to other people's misconceptions, have the pulse and sense of the magical on a day-to-day basis.

So, as you read this novel, please remember that you are entering an African book that was conceived in the seminal but complex whirlpool of our narrative traditions and dynamic cultures, and that what might seem fantastic or magical to others is as real to us as waking up and going to sleep again; as splendid and enigmatic as the voice of that ancient African narrator who has been our guide and magical teacher since the dawn of civilization.

Time and the world, money and power belong to the small people. But to the rest of us, to the rest of humanity, belongs nothing; nothing but eternity.

—*Hermann Hesse*

Civilisation has nothing to do with the tallness of our buildings or the size of our grain crop. It is about the quality of the men and women that a nation produces.

—*George Santayana*

Mythic language; and far-off songs, voices woven like strip-cloths of the Sudan. And then, dear lamp, your kindness in cradling the obsession with this presence.

—*Léopold Sédar Senghor*

Contents

BOOK TWO: PASSION AND IMMORTALITY

BOOK THREE: PARADISE, BAD NEWS, THE HOURIS, AND A TURQUOISE OCEAN

BOOK FOUR: LA DOLCE VITA

Prologue

Contrary to what she had assumed at the time of innocence, Yeama Iskander realized that the devil's face was red when she finally encountered him.

One hour before the devil made his entry, Yeama had been listening to some old Dizzy Gillespie standards and watching the waning sun disappear into the embrace of a September evening. It had been a good day: two fowls had hatched, her stray guard dog had returned home, and she felt at peace with the world, a gentle woman unaware that she had a date with the devil, whose likeness she would experience in the vortex of three men that came to the garden of her house near a river. At first she thought they were bandits out to rob her, considering she lived in a lonely part of Malagueta and was not about to stop them looting her house. One look at them, however, convinced Yeama they had come on a more personal purpose. There was something mean and brutal about them: coarseness so inhuman they had the aspect of gargoyles propelled on the devil's wings. Her faithful dog barked and lunged at them, only to be silenced by a violent kick. When Yeama tried to run to a safe corner of the house, they broke the door down and came in, giving off an odious smell, the result of a prolonged march through the war-torn country. Inspired by the devil, they slapped her hard, dragged her out into the garden, tore off her clothes, and pinned her down the way a sacrificial lamb is held to the ground in that part of the world.

"Kill me, kill me," she screamed, convinced that death was preferable to the dreaded idea of being taken by the devil.

One of the men removed a cutlass from his belt and flashed its shining blade in the sun. With a grin so menacing that it sent a chill down Yeama's spine, he made a mock chopping movement on his left scapula, the better to suggest that if Yeama preferred death to being violated, it would be a long, torturous one, needlessly brutal, with blood pouring out of her shoulder.

Trapped in their clutches, she did not try to fight the men off, but steeled herself for whatever the name of the country of shame was that they were about to take her to. The devil's men wore the red bandannas, assorted T-shirts, and jungle fatigues that were the insignia of the rebels fighting against the government of General Soriba Dan Doggo. One pounded the ground with the dull thud of military boots a size too big for him, while the other two moved unsteadily in tennis shoes, proof enough that they were high on some form of hallucinogen. Before that evening, even with the taste of innocence still on her lips, Yeama had come to think of war as a woman's worst period, a time for even the most outwardly decent of men to move ever so closely to the savagery of cruel creatures. Seeing how red the devil's face was, she did not need reminding that she was in the grip of men who were armed with weapons, magnified by the rising tumescence in their loins.

Terrified by the thought of what the men could do, she trembled from the naked horror in her soul and brought a weak utterance of her mother's name to her lips. Even before they had unleashed the devil's spurs, she held her breath and imagined that these men had gone without a woman for a long time. Where was God in all this? she asked. Given his various incarnations—Allah, Brahma, Jehovah, Olodumare, Shang Ti, and so forth—it was obvious that God was a man, which left a woman no choice but to look for deliverance from some other source.

The first man commenced the devil's work with a most brutal harshness; he was hungry, almost insatiable, and Yeama bit her tongue against the needles of her pain. She lay stiff as a dead horse and abandoned her body to the other two men, who huffed and puffed themselves into exertions. Horror and pain invaded her soul as the rapids of the devil tore her apart; she felt like screaming, wanted to ask the devil's men whether they had no sisters of their own, but so intent were they on their thrill that she experienced the longest moment of her life, a violent ocean raging in her. After the men were satisfied, they collected their guns, kicked the dog into a final death spasm, spat onto the ground, and then looked at the waning sun, as if for guidance into some distant land, and began to walk away.

Besides their hungry grunts, they had not spoken a word to her, for they had ceased to need speech, having severed all connection to humanity, gone as they were into the deepest recess of savagery.

Then, as though he had suddenly remembered something more cutting than even the terror that they had just inflicted on Yeama, the most brutal-looking of the men hissed at her, "Stupid woman. You act like civilized Aristo woman, when your mama was a harlot, before dat foolish professor give am respect."

Deeply stung by those words, Yeama began to cry, more for her life than for anything her mother might have been. She felt battered, especially by a terrible sensation that her body did not really belong to her; it was some other being that had lain there, a castaway sullied beyond her recognition. Shamed. Feeling very naked in her soul, stripped, like one of the scorched trees in the yard, she felt drained of her spirit. A deep feeling of nausea overcame her; to be so terribly assaulted made her nakedness a wound more painful than the act of being violated itself, and she couldn't stop shaking. She thought she was going to die but was brought back to a spark of life when she saw one of the men signaling to a boy who had been waiting behind a thicket.

The boy was not more than nineteen and marked by a solitary aspect as he came slowly to her, hesitating a bit, his strides not as bold as the others. He looked briefly at her—such a long anguish it was for her—and then tried to avert his eyes when she glanced at him. Something about his unease suggested that he knew her, and that perhaps they had even been at the same school, she in a higher form, when the country was beautiful, full of hope, before the spasm of war and destruction had set in. Mercifully, he was quick with her but, unlike the others, spoke humanely. "I had to do this or they would have killed me," he said, trying his best to make some connection with her demented mind.

She let him take a few steps away from her before she stretched her legs to relax the cramps. She felt her body slowly waking up, and a great agony shrouded and threw her into a spell when, for a brief moment, she imagined she was languishing between life and death. Only then did she realize that the nearby river had been singing all the time, lashing at the bulrushes, perhaps grieving for her, while she was being assaulted. A little blood had coagulated on her bruised lips, but it was not its dry blot that she tasted, rather the aloes of shame as she was still stung by the surprise of fate. Even then, she did not crawl into the embrace of hate or surrender to self-pity, because, even as her pain continued to pierce her heart, she knew that a test had begun with those men, and that she wanted to leave her choices open.

Book One

The Years of the Barracudas

CHAPTER ONE

The Metamorphosis of King Henri Christophe

ONE EVENING early in his rule, after he had eaten a meal of oxtail soup, rice, goat meat, and spinach, then drunk two shots of brandy to dull his rheumatic joints, Tankor Satani, president of the country of Kissi, whose capital is Malagueta, removed his dentures so that he would not choke on them while sleeping at night. Next morning he spent an hour looking for them, only to discover he had thrown them with some leftovers into the garbage bin.

"Just like my life!" he moaned.

He was unaware of the dramatic changes that were about to happen in his life.

Seventeen years later he would drown in the cockpit of a magic plane, but not before he had wrecked the economy, hanged fifteen men, ordered the killing of a much-respected governor of the Central Bank, and exiled his successor. Even more incredible, in one of the most bizarre and mysterious transformations of human beings, his young, ravishing mistress of seven years would turn out to be a mermaid, and the discovery would stun him that while living with her for so long he had been unaware of the several transformations, admittedly subtle, in her being. The startling color changes of her eyes should have warned him; the moon had always had a noticeable effect on her whimsical nature, and she had a bizarre affection for the ocean, but he had been so taken up with her he failed to read the signs. That he was outsmarted so late in life by someone so young was proof, to the glee of his enemies, that the Houris must have sent her to his bed to avenge the collective suffering of a stifled people. And act she did, with feline cunning, on the night that Tankor Satani was celebrating his greatest achievement: holding a Versailles-like convention in the region, at which he was crowned an emperor.

Nothing in the early days of his presidency had prepared the citizens of Malagueta for Tankor Satani's profligacy. In fact, before he built the impressive Xanadu on the hill overlooking the city, life was far from sweet for him. His mistresses were conniving, especially when money was short and he could not satisfy all of their demands. Sometimes he smelled of the verbena of his dogcatching years, and a stale odor, like that of combustible peat, would hang on him for days. Weighed down with the problems of trying to govern some of the most unruly people on earth, he always looked tired and talked, frequently, of dying "before my time," although he was only sixty-five.

During an obsidian night, soon after misplacing his dentures, he sat in his study as a week-long storm began to rage through Malagueta, threatening to wipe this former ex-slave paradise off the face of the earth and making most Malaguetans feel that such a long fury was nothing less than the vengeance of the dead at the bottom of the ocean for the neglect they had lately suffered.

"What an ungrateful lot we are!" said a very old man.

It had been many years since the government had honored the dead with a public feast at the foot of the large cotton tree where the ex-slaves had held their first thanksgiving, almost two hundred years ago, after they came from the Americas and parts of Africa to start the town. As the storm raged through the town, Tankor Satani thought of rectifying that neglect.

Yet it was while he was contemplating doing something about the neglected dead that Tankor Satani had a dream so extraordinary it canceled out all notions of time and place: Henri Christophe, ex-slave and the legendary first king of a liberated Haiti, had crossed an ocean of two centuries to appear to him.

Tankor Satani recognized the fiercely noble profile of the old king from his image on some mintages in the national museum that the children of the former slaves had built. Although Henri Christophe looked much older now than during his reign, he had a regal bearing befitting a king and wore a tricorn Napoleonic hat to match an ermine-and-gold gown. He held a staff with a brass lion-head top, and his courtiers, slaves, eunuchs, and voodoo priests and his harem of quadroons, mulattos, and black and white women were kneeling at his feet. With the two centuries separating their lives, Tankor was at first afraid of the ghost of the legendary king, but the ex-slave quickly put him at ease.

"Don't be afraid," Henri said. "Why do you think I have changed my image and traveled through the centuries if it is not to come and show you how to run this place?"

"How do you know who I am?" Tankor asked, amazed.

"Nothing is hidden from the dead," came the imperial voice. "As you know, Haiti was the first republic created by ex-slaves; and Malagueta was established by the children of former slaves and recaptives, who had been deprived of their kings. So it is up to you to start acting like an emperor."

"But why me?" Tankor asked.

"Because you are the chosen one: you carry the burden of history. By so doing, you will be completing my work, which was destroyed by my own false sense of grandeur."

Tankor Satani was still not convinced. "But this is a democracy," he objected, although not too emphatically.

"Forget about democracy; that can wait for another twenty years!"

A deep rumbling of thunder shook Malagueta as Henri returned with his retinue to La Citadel, his castle on the Haitian mountain, where, according to legend, he had been living since his death two hundred years ago, visible only to the "chosen eye." When Tankor woke up from his dream, more than the drama occasioned by the fantastic visit, the one thing he was grateful for was that he had been sleeping alone that night in his study, after a tired evening of reading cabinet papers, and thus did not have to explain anything to his wife about his bizarre dream. As far as she was concerned, his esteem had taken quite a drop after he threw his dentures into the trash can. She had begun to worry about the irrational drift of his mind, and would have considered her husband's dream further confirmation that he had finally entered the period of madness inevitable for someone who had spent too many years as a dogcatcher when he was young.

Inspired by the belief that he was about to become an emperor, Tankor Satani began to conjure fantasies about that future. Given all of its trappings, not ruling out self-coronation, he thought about how that would change his life. The first thing he would do would be to build a castle, like Henri's, on the slopes of the densely forested mountain overlooking Malagueta. With an almost demonic fervor, he began to prepare for his perceived grandeur by ordering all the available books about Haiti brought to his office. For the next two weeks, sometimes past midnight, he spent long periods reading in his study, his most startling discovery being that before the time of the Duvaliers, the mountains of Haiti had been as lovely as those in Malagueta—lush, green, full of secret grottos, from which the zombies came out to walk the night's secret avenues. Animals that talked like humans roamed the forests shimmering with quartz and other brilliant colors. Some hardworking peasants who had given up fishing had moved there and had built hutches, then farmed and raised families, protected by the sorcerers among them: men and women who could ward off all kinds of evil and dispense various cures in their sacred argot. It was just the right place for a great king.

One afternoon shortly after his dream, Malagueta now calm after the storm, the dark mist hanging over the forest finally began to lift. Accompanied by a handful of guards, Tankor Satani drove up to the verdant slopes of Mount Agadi thinking of the Xanadu he was going to build on it. With a falcon's concentration, he began to map out the area where it would loom, large like La Citadel, on at least fifty acres, his eyes misting over with the thought of how many diamonds he would have to sell to accomplish his dream. Each stone for the porticoes of his castle would be shaped like a round gem. He thought of how the gates would be embossed with his own coat of arms, and he imagined a driveway lined with aromatic eucalyptus trees imported from Australia, and nowhere else, leading to the castle.

Evening was falling, and the light on the forested mountain was pale violet. Lost to everything but his obsession with immortality, he heard the night-prowling animals coming out and the hooting of a hungry owl. Nonetheless, he stood dreaming about the Xanadu, imagining the trembling surveyors reading the maps' tangled skeins to transform the virgin area. Punctilious engineers who knew how to hold back mountain avalanches appeared in his dream, fighting off the unruly behavior that nature might put in the path of his glory. He let his fantasies assume a most extraordinary zenith as he pictured the columns of laborers hurrying against the coming rain, sweating in the granite quarries to fashion the stones for the porticoes. July's rain had always made the forest impenetrable, but buoyed by his fantasies, he thought he could already hear the saws of the master carpenters slicing away at the heart of the nation's finest mahogany to shape the dowels for the varnished wood to build his library.

A deep sense of filial gratitude rose into his head, and tears welled up in his eyes, for although his mother had been dead a long time, Tankor Satani imagined her standing in front of him, as though telling him how proud she was he had turned out to be a success after she had abandoned him as a disaster soon after he was born. Resplendent in sequins, she thanked him for his recent spate of generosity when he had paid visits to her grave, bringing with him a lavish spread of food for the dead. "Thank you, Son," he heard his mother's voice say.

A bolt of lightning brought him back to earth, and he felt the first signs of anxiety thinking about how some of his enemies might react to his extravaganza: those recalcitrant judges, for instance, who had opposed him.

But he dismissed them from his thoughts and returned to the world of fantasies, convinced that their mouths would tremble with reluctant praise after they had seen his marvelous castle.

"They will see what a former dogcatcher can do," he said with infinite determination.

Building the Xanadu was going to take some time, though, so Tankor Satani set about preparing the elementary steps to carrying out Henri Christophe's unfinished work. Once again, it was the former slave who illuminated for Tankor how to proceed. "Act boldly, consult the masters of the occult, and never make the mistake of believing only what your naked eyes can see in the stars. That is for white people."

Considering that it was not so long ago that he had been mulling over the idea of death, Tankor Satani felt grateful to the spirit of Henri Christophe for giving him the chance to look beyond the present.

CHAPTER TWO

Group Portrait of a Woman

TO BE fair to her, when she was much older but still alluring, Habiba Mouskuda was the severest critic of some of the affairs she had carried on as a young woman with more men than she cared to remember. When she was only eighteen, her father had died suddenly, after which she not only had to fend for herself, but as the oldest of four children was expected to help look after her siblings. Her mother was a hardworking clerk at the government treasury, but given how poorly Tankor Satani paid civil servants at that time, the only recourse open to a young woman like Habiba was to sell her body to the highest bidders, even though she hated doing so in the beginning. Strangely, while Tankor Satani was being carried away into the imaginary world of his immortality thinking about his Xanadu, Habiba Mouskuda was reassessing her years spent in the byways of intemperate loves.

She had grown up in a country that was an African Wild West of diamond smugglers and corrupt officials, to which prospectors, crooks, and schemers flocked, sometimes in the guise of researchers, investors, tourists, and even priests. After she decided to become a kept woman in that climate, she did not have any problem advancing her gifts. In fact, the only problem she had was keeping men away. However, when she met the philosophy professor Theodore Iskander, for whom she would have Yeama, she decided to come clean about her past. "I had to tell you so that no one will have to lie about me!" she said.

Fifteen years her senior, Theodore Iskander was part of what used to be called the intelligentsia in Malagueta and had gone out mostly with women from that circle. When he started seeing Habiba Mouskuda, no one gave the relationship any chance of surviving. For one thing she was a *Coral*: a half-African and half-Arab woman, whose Lebanese father was a member of the much-hated business class that had bled Malagueta dry in cahoots with successive African governments. She was stunningly beautiful, almost six feet tall, with hazel eyes and cinnamon skin that was the result of the most dazzling mixture of bloods, but was nonetheless a woman with a quick temper and a loose tongue, so it seemed all the more improbable that the highly cultured, classical music–loving professor would come to love her, when his friends felt he could have had any woman he wanted: "someone with class." His mother, the redoubtable Irene, had a simple answer for the enigmatic coupling. "It is witchcraft," she decided.

Irene went to church regularly to pray to God to break the couple up. Inspired by her belief in the supernatural, she spent sleepless nights thinking of other ways to achieve her aim, but her efforts proved fruitless because Habiba was a most determined and wily malatta in love, as tenacious as her father's ancestors had been in their conquest of Malagueta's commercial business.

Soon after the freed slaves had built the town, the Arabs mysteriously began to appear from the ships sailing from Syria and Lebanon, dazzling the black pioneers with their colorful clothes and their ability to quote arcane verses by Moroccan dervishes. The Arabs always exhaled exotic perfumes, a good splash of which was needed to dull the smell of garlic and other condiments on their breath. Given their hard-won freedom, the black citizens were initially suspicious of the newcomers, viewing the arrival of these people speaking a barbarous argot as a diabolical plot by the then-ruling English to check the power of a thriving black business class that would brook no nonsense from half-baked colonial officers.

At first the Arabs did their best to avoid offending the Malaguetans, limiting their activities to peddling coral and other beads. Braving the torrential downpours and ferocious dogs, and sometimes almost robbed or beaten up, they went from door to door peddling their wares, all the time quoting the words of the Sufi mystic Rifai on "sublime ignorance," to help convince the Malaguetans that wearing the beads as amulets could drive out the devil, whose existence the Arabs insisted was commonplace in the town. The blacks, who fancied themselves tough pioneers, were not convinced that the devil posed any threats to their livelihood, or that even if it did, coral beads or any other magical amulets could chase it away, so they mostly ignored the Arabs. But it was from those early days that they began to refer to them as "Corals," which in their good humor the blacks pronounced as "Cor-raals"!

By the time Habiba Mouskuda was born, the Corals had come a long way, due in part to their ruthless ability to start a new life anywhere and their pugnacious competition after the discovery of diamonds. The discovery would turn out to be a disaster for most Malaguetans but a godsend for the Corals and a few of their black lackeys, the lure of the diamonds bringing all kinds of speculators to the shallow alluvial rivers where they were mined: good men, scoundrels, and yahoos.

After the Corals had taken control of smuggling the gems to Beirut, Rotterdam, and, later, Tel Aviv, they became a different class of men: bold, arrogant, crudely manipulative, and, worse, insouciant about the country's welfare, as long as they could bribe the British and African officials in charge. Not for them, any longer, the smallest courtesies to people. Rather, they were rude to many of the blacks, who had hitherto laughed at their "Cor-raal" penury. They kept mostly to themselves in their new, rented villas in the Arab quarters that faced the ocean or in the inland ones that they had built with the profits from their smuggling. Most evenings they were seen playing dominoes and smoking hookahs in the splendor of their verandahs. On those enchanting Sundays when the Malaguetans usually went to church and the entire city was shut down, the Arabs would be heard singing the rhapsodically beautiful songs of their origins.

But they soon grew tired of the tempestuous rains lasting for almost six months; and not having women to make them forget about their misery, the Arabs missed the enchanting desert evenings of their youth, back in Lebanon or Syria.

"If we are to survive in this hellhole, we must have women," an old man with a walrus mustache said one night, contemplating their predicament. With their new wealth, he saw the possibility of the Corals easing the lonely hours of the night and of having children.

Their first overtures were to the peasant girls who went from door to door selling peanuts and fruits in the Babel of tongues that characterized life in Malagueta in those days, given its exotic mix of peoples. Eventually won over by the Corals because of the generous swathes of cotton, silk, and taffeta that they offered as bait, some of the women began to frequent their shops, especially on those days when the sun was a boiling furnace. Thrilled, the Arabs would offer the women water from earthen jugs to cool their throats, buying up their entire trays of fruits, always feigning concern for their plight. But it was soon clear to the women that the Corals were desperately trying to entice them to their beds. Such dedication yielded results, and after some seamstress had turned the fabrics into elaborate gowns, the women came, shyly at first, to see the Corals in the evening, quite a daring thing to do in those days. The Corals would suffer a case of the stutters just looking at them.

Soon they were having malatta children, but the Corals, to whom many of the women had surrendered their virginity, had no intention of marrying them. They were merely exotic tropical fruits that the men had enjoyed devouring: sweet molasses on their desert tongues, especially the very dark ones: tall, willowy, mysterious, but still playthings for the Arabs. The girls had been tricked into satisfying their needs until the men could send to Lebanon and Syria for veiled wives, chosen by their mothers, who came hurriedly to live off the profits of Malagueta's diamonds.

It wasn't long before the Corals came to own the best commercial businesses in the town, although in the esteem of most highbrow Malaguetans they did not really amount to much, especially as in spite of their newfound wealth, many of the Corals could neither read nor write.

Habiba Mouskuda was one of the lucky malattas who in her youth had polished herself for a few years in a secondary school, though she was still regarded as a "lowlife" woman by some condescending black women. When she was thirty, and already a *femme fatale*, some very desperate men were still chasing her all over the town. In spite of her age, she was fantastic competition for any woman ten years younger, and had turned out to be so skillful at driving some of her lovers off the roller-coaster of death that not even the law was able to lay anything on her. She felt driven by a compulsion to dominate some of those men and seemed destined to write the tragic scripts of their demise. But even when she was suspected of having a hand in those deaths—the hanging of Colonel Fillibo Mango and the fishbone-choking death of General Augustus Kotay, for instance—other men kept coming, drawn to her fatal allure. So it was all the more surprising that she would confess to Theodore Iskander, when they started going out, how easy it had been for her to dispatch to hell or heaven three of the men who had really loved her.

"It was as if I had been cursed to bring harm to men," she cried.

The first time it happened she was only twenty, sweet like an overripe pomegranate, as people say in Malagueta. Her curvature was proof of what a great artist God could be on his good days, and with her bewitching smile, cinnamon skin, and long legs she numbered among her earliest victims the scalps of some rich boys who merely wanted to be introduced to life. When she was done with them, she honed her skills, bought some new dresses, and, after adding some cheap jewelry to her allure, was ready when Ismael Touré feasted his eyes on her.

He was the government surveyor, and in addition to large acres of land, his job brought him ample profits of office—not a surprise to anyone, given the way he had been moving beacons and land boundaries, even though some of those landmarks had been pegged long before he was born. Family titles to land disappeared from his office, and he saw to it that ownership disputes were tied up for years in Byzantine litigation in the compromised courts, swelling the pockets of lawyers and judges always willing to share his ill-gotten gains with him: blood money with which he sought to win Habiba Mouskuda.

"I am not a cheap woman," she said, trying to ward him off, when he started courting her, "someone you can have for a night or two, just because you are a surveyor."

"For you, I am prepared to stop going to confession," he replied.

Helplessly drawn to her, he wooed her with the remarkable patience of his much older years. At every chance he would watch her go by, standing at a distant corner with his trained eyes, as though he were mapping out a clearing in the forest. One day, unable to bear his torment any longer, he went over to her place in broad daylight to beg her to become his woman. Just thinking about her made it impossible for him to sleep, which finally aroused the suspicions of his wife, who had taken to complaining to her friends that her husband had stopped eating well and that he would drop off to sleep as soon as he came home, tired and worn out every day.

"It must be the humid forest vapors that are making him tired," one of the women said.

Determined to conquer her, Ismael Touré sent Habiba Mouskuda jewelry: onyx, malachite, pearls, and beads made of barracuda bones. On her birthday, he gave her French perfumes that he had bought in the duty-free shops in Abidjan, gift-wrapped with the sweet talk of sending her abroad to study in England, if only she would have him. It was an auspicious beginning for a twenty-year-old, except that after she had slept with him three times, Habiba Mouskuda decided she was not prepared to wait for the attack that she hoped would rupture his weak heart so that she could move on to someone who had more money and was less ponderous as a lover: an uncomfortable mess for a woman, especially if she did not really like the man.

Impatient like a tropical storm, she took fate by the hand and said goodbye to the fat surveyor by the simple formula of overworking him in bed one Sunday afternoon.

When the death was announced, it was with great envy that less adventurous men learned about how the surveyor had met his end. The rumor was that he had done so the way some of them had dreamed of going, beyond the ambit of heavenly pleasure, on top of a mistress, the dead man dying with the satisfaction that the angels had rung their death bells only after they had allowed him the intemperance of making love in the roasted fowl position for an hour, after he had received the Holy Sacraments in church before going to Habiba for some dessert in her bed.

Angels had seldom been as generous to a dying man as they were to Ismael Touré that afternoon. Taking their time, allowing him to indulge in his dessert, they saturated the room with a mesmerizing fragrance before they tapped his chest very gently. Being good angels who did not want to appear capricious right away, they had removed the skullcaps that they usually wore when they were about to execute an immediate death sentence. It was such a cunning fraud that the exhausted man made the mistake of confusing the diastole and systole of his weak heart with the excessive exertion of sexual activity.

Habiba Mouskuda knew very little about the versatility of angels when they chose to appear to lesser mortals, but nevertheless recognized their presence by the celestial air in her room. Alarmed, she tried to steady her nerves when it dawned on her that the angels had come on a death mission, the tremors of Ismael Touré's hands and mouth being so rhythmic that it was obvious the poor man was dying. With practiced skill, she rolled him off of her, calm as if she were removing a quilt whose warmth she no longer needed. When the final tremors of the angels flattened his heart, Ismael Touré was lucky not to suffer too much.

It was in awe at how magical they could be that Habiba Mouskuda experienced the hallucination of seeing the angels leave. When she had fully recovered her wits, she grabbed a dress, hurried into it, and touched the face of the dead man to confirm that he was really gone. Hurriedly, she walked over to the next house, where her friend Victoria lived.

"What are you doing here," Victoria asked with a wink, "when you should be busy serving the Son of Man?"

"You have to come with me to see what fate has done to me!" Habiba replied, breathing heavily.

The angels had been gone for some time, but their pungent perfume was still on the dead man's clothes. He lay in the same undignified position he had been in since Habiba had hurled him off of her chest, and his mouth was wide open, as though he had been surprised by the nature of his death. Habiba, who up till then had really tried to be composed, started trembling, ready to cry.

"Be quiet," Victoria cautioned. "We have to move him out of your room!"

Hurriedly they closed the mouth of the dead man, bundled him into his blue Sunday suit, and straightened his breast pocket handkerchief. The visit of the angels had left him first with a smile, then with a woebegone countenance that bothered the women, but with almost clinical skill they relaxed the tight knots of his brow so that he looked as though he was enjoying his siesta. Except for a few girls hanging their midday laundry out, the neighbors were inside; a relief to the women, whose hearts were throbbing as they hurried with the dead man to his car, holding him as though he was drunk, and a priest would have admired their skill as they slid the dead man into a comfortable position in the front passenger seat. Victoria, who had not lost her nerves, offered to drive.

Less than two hours before coming to the house of his mistress, Ismael Touré had been listening to a hearty rendition of Bach's *St. Mathew Passion* in church, but his date with the angels of death in Habiba's bed meant that he was not to hear the Lord's Prayer that she had started singing for him. In the past, when distressed, she had not sought the comfort of song or even of prayer; but, now, in an enchanting voice, careful not to arouse the suspicion of the handful of late homegoers strolling on Talabi Road, still flushed with the blood of Christ they had received in church, she sought solace in that prayer. She stroked the head of the dead man and thought of how fortunate he had been to die on a Sunday, a sign that he was going straight to heaven. Breathing like wild horses, the two women turned into Bambara Street, where some of the first houses built by the descendants of the pioneers in the late nineteenth century had retained the charmed but decaying elegance of that period, their lush gardens still blooming, the wild bougainvillea and hibiscus luxuriantly cascading over the high cement walls.

The women missed killing a bad-luck cat before they came to their destination in front of the mortuary, which the surveyor had driven past less than an hour ago on his way to his mistress, and it was a beautiful cameo the way they shifted the dead man into the driver's seat, shocked that even for a fat man he was so heavy in death. Aware that they were working against time, they called up all their reserves of strength to create the right subterfuge, making sure he was slumped forward, being very careful that his head should be resting on his folded arms on the steering wheel. So convincing was the effect that Ismael Touré really looked as though he had been assailed by a heart attack or by the excesses of a Sunday afternoon's drinking at his local bar, which was precisely the ruse that Habiba wanted to achieve, just in case someone who knew the surveyor should pass by and see the poor man in his car.

Then it was that the women heard the elegiac notes of piano music coming from one of the houses, where a gifted artist was playing "Un Sonnet d'Amour," the third movement of the *Petite Suite de Concert* by Samuel Coleridge-Taylor. Otherwise, everything was quiet on Bambara Street. In spite of his lofty English name, the composer was a black man whose father was a doctor, born in Malagueta. Clearly in a celestial sphere that afternoon, his long fingers burnishing the black and white keys, the pianist was unaware of what was happening on the street. Besides the few hungry dogs and cats that had witnessed the dead man being taken to his car, Habiba Mouskuda felt no one had seen them when they were moving him. Smiling at the animals, she said a few hurried liturgical lines that she had suddenly remembered from when she was polishing herself at the Catholic girls' school, thinking that such contrition would help ease the passage of the dead man into heaven. Moved by the certainty that this was the last time she was seeing him, she took a quick searching look at him, patted his cheeks, and squeezed them.

The sun had come out and the jowls of the dead man had lost some of their firmness. He had the pallor that Habiba recognized as the first signs of death in a man who had not been taking good care of his health. For the first time since the angel had stopped the heart of her lover, she felt, in the deep resources of her heart, a tinge of sadness for the fat surveyor who had sometimes watered her garden.

Then, as though it was the most natural thing she had ever done, Habiba used a public phone booth to call the dead man's wife, who had been waiting for him to come home to their Sunday lunch, with the news of the disaster that she had always been afraid might happen, given Ismael Touré's cardiovascular condition.

"You don't know me, Madam, but I think something terrible has happened to your husband," Habiba said in the calmest voice she could use under the circumstance.

CHAPTER THREE

Tankor Satani Has Another Unexpected Visitor

NOT TOO long after he returned from surveying the mountain for the spot on which to build his Xanadu, Tankor Satani dispatched a secret emissary with an urgent message to the president of the neighboring French-speaking republic of Bakazo, as though something about the trip to the mountain had convinced him of the need for caution. To the consternation of his ministers and friends, he soon installed two eunuchs from that Islamic nation in the guest rooms of his private residence.

His wife, Sallay, was aghast. "Why have you brought those men wearing talismanic cords on their arms and looking like the devil's disciples to my house?" she demanded.

Tankor's reply was laced with a concern in his voice she had not heard before in more than thirty years of marriage.

"I am a president, and I cannot afford to take chances with my life with so many enemies around. Besides, who would keep an eye on my prime minister, who wants this job so badly before I die that he is acting like a sycophant?"

"But you will die soon, all the same, given whatever is eating you up!" she screamed at him.

Back in Bakazo the eunuchs had been renowned for their abracadabra, which was precisely why Tankor had sent for them. Obviously enjoying the consternation that their arrival had caused, he saw to it that the eunuchs stayed in the cloister of their rooms most of the time, going about their work quietly, and were only heard when their soaring Berber-Arabic poetry would waft through the windows into the courtyard, sending the peacocks running helter-skelter from those alien tunes. Turbaned, with parts of their faces veiled with indigo cloth, they exuded a mysterious air that the guards found fascinating, as the eunuchs did their best to stay out of the way of the president's wife, who did not trust anyone who was not a born-again Christian like herself. Moreover, as far as she was concerned, the vagaries of fate were best left in the hands of men who knew *something* about women!

But contrary to her disdain for the eunuchs, her husband had a lot of trust in the efficacy of their clairvoyance, which was greatly enhanced after they warned him about the diabolism of the book that his amanuensis, Colonel Fillibo Mango, was writing.

"That book will ridicule your mother and put pepper in your eyes, Excellency."

"In that case, I shall have it banned and arrest the colonel!" Tankor Satani said, alarmed by the prospect of the book becoming a best seller.

On the morning the colonel was executed, Tankor Satani lit a cigar with a burning copy of the book and then telephoned his prime minister, Enos Tanu.

"I leave it to you to see that the offending printing establishment is smashed up as punishment for daring to bring out the book," he informed the underling.

"That is why I am your prime minister," Enos Tanu replied effusively.

Tankor Satani's confidence about a rosy future was now greatly increased; he went to sleep every night convinced that his eunuchs would anticipate any threats against him. He felt so confident that he decided to lift the ban on the offering of public sacrifices or *sara*, which were rites sometimes used to bewitch people. Whether by instinct or because of something hard to define about the man, the eunuch that Tankor Satani really trusted was Pallo, who had come to him separately, many years later, and was not installed in the guests' quarters, but had been given a room in the Xanadu after it was built.

Silent as a crab, astonishingly prescient with his sorcery, Pallo began to advise Tankor on whom to include in his cabinet, the choice of ambassadors, and when he should go to the presidential office downtown. Faced with the country's volatile politics and afraid he might be poisoned by some harmless-looking lackey, Tankor appointed the eunuch his sole food taster and asked him to keep an eye on the goings-on in the military barracks.

"I shall know when they are cooking up rebellions, Master, so don't worry. I shall alert you before the gun finds your heart."

The eunuch was to save him from the autumnal follies of old age, such as his passion for malattas. "They might be good in bed, Excellency, but bad for business, because they have too many men."

He did all he could to keep the old man away from those Coral and other "brown-skin gals," who would have wrecked Tankor's presidency in the first three years. In return, all that the eunuch asked for was that he and the other eunuchs meet under the giant cotton tree in the center of town three times a year and dance.

"Anytime you feel like it, Pallo, just let me know," the president was quick to assure his sorcerer.

Tankor Satani was over sixty when he became president. Given Malagueta's glorious beginnings, the sons and daughters of the founders always wore their pedigree with an unmistakable contempt for others, especially the Corals. Cocksure people that they were, the founders did little to control their petulance with servants and were just as injudicious about their dislike of the president. They ridiculed his presumptions and speech making, and called him "too common," for which reason he was sometimes heard to refer to his first three years in office as being in a "snake pit." With the congress packed with lawyers and doctors of the old school, he fought epic battles there, and his honeymoon with the military was brief, a mere two years, during which time, with troops rushed in from Bakazo, he had to put down three mutinies. Afterward, he carried out his first batch of executions of the insurrectionists, exiled their wives and mistresses, and confiscated their properties. Then, to guard against further rebellions, he sealed the national armory so that on ceremonial occasions his soldiers were reduced to performing their military exercises with wooden guns.

"Look at Tankor's soldiers," the kids would laugh; "they are Boy Scouts!"

Before becoming president, Tankor Satani had worked in the mines and had been a dogcatcher, broke most of the time, lonely, but philosophical about the destinies of men, never giving up—a determined young man. Surprisingly, as president he came up against a system more annoying than those dogs, more intractable than death, a civil service bent on destroying him, courts tying up his first bills or sending them back to him with the insult that they were not properly written in the Queen's English. His most implacable critics were the judges, roasting in their ermine and wigs in the tropical courts, who took delight in delaying his injunctions, flooring him with legalisms, making him look like a weakling in the foreign press, whose appetite for scandal was growing every day. Under the pretext that he had not been crowned with the laurel of a law degree, the university council barred him when he tried to name himself the chancellor.

"He did not even go to a proper college!" scoffed one of the professors.

Nor would the Freemasons allow him into the secret rites of their order, where black Englishmen played Scottish fantasies. Some diamond smugglers, illiterate Corals, and thieving lawyers were members of the Order, but the bigwigs insisted on keeping him out.

He felt trapped in the labyrinth of a constitution he had inherited from the British and began to think of ways to establish his order, if need be, by abolishing the courts, but so powerful was the opposition against him he knew he had to take it easy. That was until he received help, once again, from Henri Christophe. As had happened prior to the first visit, the ghost of the old emperor appeared in a ring circle of storm, rain, and lightning, but without his outlandish entourage. Somewhat older than when he had last appeared to Tankor, he said that even for someone capable of crossing oceans at will, it was becoming too difficult for his large entourage to travel, but he had brought his harem with him.

"I always travel with my women, as I cannot live without the pleasure they give me," the emperor said.

"I know what you mean!" Tankor hastened to agree.

"Someone is coming to see you," Henri said. "But don't fret over things you cannot change. Epochs change men, not the other way around. And watch out for a *mermaid.* She is one woman no man has been able to fathom."

Just as he had promised, he sent Tankor Satani help from a most unexpected source: one of the very lawyers who had made a career of opposing him.

Victor Adolphy was the unacknowledged Coral son of an Arab father and a black woman. Like his father he was short, stocky, built like a baobab, but he had the angelic voice of his mother. Widely rumored to have the Corals' habit of avoiding doing straight business and paying taxes, he preferred the dark, smoky rooms where they could bribe politicians. Life had kissed his brow with money, but he wanted *respect!*

His most feared attribute, however, was his rumored secret taping of the rituals of court deals, the conversations of his colleagues, and, most damaging, the contempt that the chief justice had for the president. God, he hated the judges, and saw his chance of getting back at them after they had blocked some of Tankor Satani's bills.

One evening while Tankor Satani was enjoying a gourmet meal of cassava leaves stew, the lawyer was suddenly announced. It was not a good time for visitors, especially lawyers and journalists, whom Tankor did not trust, and his suspicions were aroused, but the lawyer convinced him he was not there to talk about a business deal.

"I have come about your welfare, Excellency."

"Tell me what it is and I shall reward you for your confidence in me," Tankor Satani said to the Coral, gripping the younger man's hands.

Victor Adolphy finished the goblet of French brandy that the old man had offered him and cleared his throat, aware that he was about to cross a great river. "I have found a way out of your predicament, Excellency."

"What do you intend to do?"

"I'll bring you tapes of what the chief justice has been saying about you."

"For that you will deserve an ambassadorship of your choice," the old man said, almost leaping out of his chair.

Victor Adolphy thought about the ambassadorship for a while but realized he was making more money as a lawyer and liked the climate better at home than in some cold, lonely European outpost. An ambassadorship was not for him.

"No, thank you, Excellency," he said. "I am happy knowing that I have helped you overcome the problem of how to ensure that you will rule forever."

He drained the last measure of his brandy, thought of how he was going to enjoy his visit to the Freemasons' club that evening, and extended his fat hand to the president.

Tankor Satani thanked the Coral profusely. "Go with God," he said, barely concealing his glee.

The lawyer left the house as surreptitiously as he had arrived.

Before the ghost of Henri Christophe and the brazen lawyer came to visit him, old age had offered Tankor Satani limited opportunities for happiness. Challenged on all fronts, his presidency had swung between a few bold acts and retractions. Moreover, the currents of his own old inadequacies would sometimes jar his brain as he tried to come to grips with his predicaments, so he viewed the visit by the lawyer as a rare chance to square things up with his enemies. Meanwhile, he would raise the profiles of the Corals in all the commercial business, and decided he might even amend the constitution so they could stand for election to the parliament, which was something that those diabolical courts had fought against.

As soon as the Coral was gone, Tankor Satani poured himself a glass of Georgian brandy and paced up and down in his study, savoring the taste. After a while he began to dance, throwing his arms wide in the air like a nubile girl at a Fulani wedding, drunk with the prospect of revenge on the chief justice. He drew up a long list of actions against the other judges. First he would destroy those expensive monuments to the imperial governors, built with unpaid black people's labor; the judges felt attached to them. Those statues erected to the glory of the missionaries were just as insulting, and so pleased was he that some of them had died of malaria that he had established the Order of the Mosquito in praise of the pests. He stopped dancing to look out the window at the mountain, dark now and covered by thick clouds of mist, but still majestic, where he was going to build the Xanadu. What secrets, he wondered, lay in its bowels?

The years that he had spent working as a dogcatcher—broke most of the time, laughed at because of his suits, growled at and almost bitten by the dogs, his blood running high just thinking of his fate—had given Tankor Satani a good deal of time to hone his skill at trapping the strays with a swing of his club; at being patient. Now, surprisingly, it was about those miserable days that he was thinking as he began to make preparations to show his enemies he was still capable of stealth. He still kept as mementoes a pair of the old shoes that he used to wear. Issued by the miserly colonial administration, they were tough as camel leather and made to last forever. In those days he had gone without the luxury of a radio or even the comforts of a house. Most of the time he slept in a small room, having to put up with the impertinence of the insufferable English, their black lackeys, and the illiterate mulattoes running the place.

Armed with the Coral's tape, he was going to change everything in this godforsaken place. Life had never been so good to him. Yet he had a little regret.

His children had not turned out well, especially his daughters. Alas, they had taken after their mother when it came to the bulge on their bottoms and had married useless men to boot, whose indolence had increased, thanks to his generosity, which was keeping them in style. When he thought of his children, it was with deep pain, and in spite of the promise of a great autumn of his life a swamp of bitterness rose in his heart. It was the despair of a man whose children had made a mockery of their parentage.

CHAPTER FOUR

A Fishbone-Choking Death

SOON AFTER the death of the surveyor, Habiba Mouskuda forgot about him and took up with a new lover, a colonel in the army. He was a man of high birth, principled, and a chess player with an existential bent, who would have preferred a career in the diplomatic service but had been made to follow a family tradition into the military. At twenty-five he had married a fine-boned ebony woman, in whom, after three children and fifteen years of marriage, sex had taken a dry harmattan retirement. It was nobody's business that the colonel kept a mistress, as such dalliances did not appear in the newspapers, not when people had other things to worry about in Malagueta. Nor did it reduce his stock at the country club where he played golf. But that woman was Habiba Mouskuda, whom he housed in a government bungalow to boot, and Colonel Fillibo Mango was unaware that he was sleeping with a woman feverishly desired by his boss.

Two years after he started seeing her, Colonel Fillibo Mango, the amanuensis of Tankor Satani, was arrested on a trumped-up charge of publishing a slanderous book on the president and of plotting to overthrow him with some renegade soldiers, for which the colonel was tried and sentenced to death.

"What did he expect?" his wife screamed after the death sentence was pronounced by the military tribunal. "He dug his own grave not by sleeping with his boss's harlot, but by sleeping with the devil's woman!"

During the entire trial, the colonel had maintained a dignified martyrdom, and was adamant about his innocence. When called to defend himself, he declined. "I prefer to die an honorable death rather than engage in the charade of a confession for a crime I did not commit."

That virtually sealed his fate. While awaiting execution, using ink made from the red clay that was peeling off the walls of his cell and a feather that a wandering crow had dropped on his windowsill, he penned some articles that his wife managed to smuggle out of the prison during one of her fortnightly visits.

"Give these to one of the courageous editors," the colonel said after he had completed the last article. "History will absolve me."

That night he dreamed that a winged cat was flying over Malagueta, disturbing the dead and making some old-timers feel that perhaps, as the first Corals had proclaimed, the devil was indeed prevalent in the town. But while they were speculating on that possibility, Habiba Mouskuda was impervious to the outrage amongst the colonel's friends that Tankor Satani was about to hang an innocent man. In fact, she was asleep, as soundly as a pampered Abyssinian cat, deaf to the furious drumming of his supporters near her house, on the night before the colonel took the jump, wearing a black hood in a prison yard. After the execution was over, she woke up with a yawn to a dull, gray morning overcast with dark clouds, and was as untroubled as she had been on the day the poor man was convicted by a tribunal of civilian judges afraid of the president. Rain had spattered the city during the night, emptying the trees of all the birds; bats, seldom seen flying during the day, were shrieking all over the place; battered by the rain, most of the trees in Malagueta had turned purplish dark in that sad city, but she took no notice of such a bad omen. Looking as fresh as seaweed, and without any sign of remorse, she sat down to a drink while the bulldozers were pushing her lover and seven others into unmarked graves.

One week later, the colonel was nothing more than a piece of official statistics fed to the termites. After his execution, Habiba Mouskuda tried to erase him from her memory as quickly as a bitch forgets her three-month pups.

"He had a mother, you know; one day you could have a son like him," Victoria told her, unable to understand how her friend could treat the memory of such a good man with disdain.

"If that happens, I shall be around to give him some advice about women," Habiba replied.

Three months later, when she thought she had completely forgotten about him, Habiba Mouskuda suffered a terrible shock: the ghost of the colonel had come to haunt his wayward mistress during her troubled sleep.

"I have come to ask you for a glass of water," the dead man said. Such was his disbelief over how she had reacted to his execution that he had difficulty recognizing the woman as the one he had once loved. He told her about how, after he was rescued from the anonymity of an unmarked grave, he had been in the Arcadia of the dead. He stood near her bed looking at her, a painful map on his face. It was white like his tunic, a shepherd's replacement for the soldier's olive-green uniform that had fired Habiba Mouskuda's money-mad heart. He said that the brutality of his death had not only broken his neck but had left him thirsty for water, which was why he had come to her. He showed her the area round his neck where the executioner's rope had found its mark, and asked her to sit down and listen to him. Finally, he begged Habiba to renounce any further association with men and to dedicate her life to doing charitable work.

"Do that for me, so you won't have to go around the world haunted by the faces of other dead men," he pleaded.

Habiba Mouskuda did not allow the dead man to trouble her a second time. Convinced that the shy, lovesick colonel was more afraid of her serpent's tongue than of the loneliness of death, she saturated the house with the smell of burnt onions, camphor, ginger, and wild basil, in the belief that such a potent mix of the sorcerer's art would keep his ghost out of her house. To heighten her exorcism, she waited until midnight, when she thought people in her neighborhood would be fast asleep, opened a window, and let loose her disdain for her former lover.

"Go away, Colonel," she said. "Your time has passed, and you can't keep a good woman down."

The prospect of becoming the mistress of a general, with all of its rewards, was the one thing she had always dreamed about, as that would mean she was really going up in society. When the opportunity came, she cleaned out the bungalow, leaving behind the ghost of the pathetic colonel, and moved into a bigger one rented by General Augustus Kotay, chief of staff of the armed forces, with not so much as two teardrops for her colonel. Three years later, much richer than the philosophical colonel had left her, Habiba Mouskuda nevertheless had her eyes set on the future, because she knew that a kept woman's life was like a schooner's sail hoisted on her young body's mast, but could be discarded later, like a cleaning woman's rag. With her experience of men, she did not need a captain's skill at reading a compass to tell her how to sail on those ephemeral waves of a man's desire for women, men being such fickle creatures where relationships were concerned. Time was of no concern to them—a woman's time, that is. She had to act fast.

Using her considerable skills at palmistry, she read General Augustus Kotay's palms when he was drunk, intent on discovering whether fate had promised the general a life beyond his exploits in her bed. The readings proved ominous for him. As Habiba had suspected, his lifeline was short; given that he was visiting her almost daily, it was obvious he would not survive three years of lovemaking in her tempestuous bed. She pressed her alluring advantage over him, skillfully navigating him through the slippery rapids he had entered. After saturating his ears with her lyric of "Any time you want it, General," she reminded him that middle-aged men had to pay for the privilege of enjoying the delectable pleasures a young woman could offer, but was careful not to arouse General Augustus Kotay's suspicion about her intentions. She bided her time, but after one extremely creative night in bed, she brought up the subject of what would happen to her in the event of a sudden death visiting the general.

"You are just going to have some fun and leave me as dry as banana leaves when you die, General," she cried. "Think of what people will say knowing that I was the mistress of the chief of staff, yet I won't have anything to show for my pains."

"Don't say that again," the general said, "as I have only just started watering your garden."

"A garden without a house is not my idea of security, General," Habiba shot back, draping her legs with a nice wrap of Senegalese cotton.

That was enough to make General Augustus Kotay sit up and listen to her. Thinking that he was about to lose the most ravenous woman he had ever encountered in bed, he tried not to let her know his heart was playing a staccato of fear. He twirled the thick brush of his mustache, and his eyes, suddenly filled with tears, roamed over the not too comfortable space of the rented house where they had been meeting for months. He was prepared to do anything to keep her satisfied, just as long as she was his, trapped as he was in her delicious aura. He felt possessed, his pride sinking, so much so that he finally let her in on something he had been keeping a secret until he was sure she wasn't out to milk him for every soldier's penny he had.

"I have a title deed to a nice plot of land somewhere quiet," he said with a stammer. "One day there might be a house there, like the one I know you are dreaming about. So it is up to you to make me happy."

"You have just saved my honor, Augustus," she cried, "as everyone was saying I am only your plaything, considering you have a wife and children."

"Nonsense," the general replied, "but I have just signed away my own honor."

Habiba did not share his anxiety. Not when the sweet sound of success was so beautiful to her. On the following Sunday, she draped a muslin shawl on her shoulders and went to mass with a celestial air, to pray that the general would not die before he had finished the house. After she had finished praying, she kissed the ring of the priest and put a generous donation in the collection plate. From that day on she began to relish her lover's being at her place with more pleasure than in the past; his needs, not always sexual, now met with a tantalizing look and a fanatical devotion she had not hitherto offered him. Just as she had expected, he went into all kinds of delirium, imaginary swallows beginning to fly from the treetop of his burnished happiness at being so well cared for by his ravishing mistress. During those evenings when the world looked so beautiful, as they sat drinking rum and Coke in her well-tended garden, she even forgot about the trajectory of her objectives. Over the next six months she oiled his worries away with delectable care, treating him to culinary delights she was experimenting with. After his afternoons spent listening to the village bumpkin ravings of Tankor Satani, the general, tempted by her sexual gyrations, always looked forward to visiting her; it was almost as if he was losing his mind.

"I am your desert concubine now, and you don't have to dream about that Arab woman," she would tease him, aware of his propensity to remember the time he had spent serving the UN in the trouble spot of Lebanon.

General Augustus Kotay was soon assailed by the illusion that he had regained his lost youth. Besides the comfort of his office, it was the one thing he wanted to preserve, so he went to the herbal section at the open market and had a wizened apothecary prepare a bottle of an aphrodisiac to stimulate his hot papa of a bull, still thinking of his prime at fifty-five. A large glint of immortality appeared in his eyes as he prayed for more years in the lavender mist of Habiba's passion, after she had spiced him up good and proper with the condiments of love she had copied from her Arab grandmother's recipe. Delectably, she kept him high on St. James rum for another year, skewered him, and ate him with a hot barbecue sauce, never for one minute hinting that behind her smile was the hope, however sinful, that he would leave this earth as soon as the house was completed.

The house was progressing according to plan, its windows being the only things left undone before Habiba would stop the ferocity of her assault in bed. She was so dedicated, the effect showed on the general. He lost his immaculate sartorial bearing, took to dozing off on the job after he had spent a night in her bed, and was lax with underlings, who were aware that he was cutting corners and siphoning off army materiel to his mistress's house. Worse, his advanced years began to show, although, seduced by the spurious notion that he was still young, he resorted to the vanity of dyeing his hair. Soon he was spending more time at the senior officers' club than at the office, more dazed than a mesmerized rabbit. At one time, he was even late going to see Tankor Satani about a trip abroad.

"You don't look too well, General," the president said, giving his army chief a mischievous wink, as though he was aware of the effect that the malatta was having on him.

"Everything is fine, President, sir," he managed to lie. "It is just that I need some more fresh air after all the paperwork I have been doing since becoming army chief of staff."

"Then this trip abroad should do you some good."

A few months later, the house now completed, no one was surprised when it was reported that the general had choked on a fishbone, after a cat mysteriously appeared from nowhere to leap into his lap. Six hours earlier, he had given Habiba the keys to the house, in front of which he had planted an oleander as a sign of his love. Habiba's reputation as a femme fatale was enhanced when the general died that night. Like a small dog cornered by a wild boar, his eyes bulged out of their sockets, and his tongue shot out of his mouth like a loose handkerchief out of a magician's trick hat. As he lay dying on the distant hill overlooking the army barracks, he heard the tormented voice of another dead man, one no longer in uniform but still haunting the grounds of his former military abode, and General Augustus Kotay barely had enough time to recognize the sad, poetic face of Colonel Fillibo Mango before he went to join him in the pathways of the dead. Suspected of practicing the ancient art of witchcraft, Habiba Mouskuda was reviled for a while, especially as everyone felt she had timed the general's death so perfectly as to be able to get away with it. It was as if the wheel of fate had come full circle; as if, in the time-honored belief about predestination, some men were tainted with a brush of death spread by their excessive passion. While drinking the rum of remembrance at the wake for the general, some of the people there would recall that, incredibly, a winged cat had flown over the city on the night before Colonel Fillibo Mango was hanged.

CHAPTER FIVE

A Crepuscular Time for Tankor Satani's Presidency

A GROUP of women, colorfully dressed, went to Mount Agadi early one morning and began to dance the *geledeh.* It was a courtly dance performed only by women, in honor of their worth, who always wore elaborate costumes, false faces, and canvas shoes, and its origins could be traced to the arrival of the Yoruba women in Malagueta in the early nineteenth century. When the women had finished showing off their skills, another set of folk dancers put on a boisterous example of the maringa, which the Maroons had brought from Jamaica at the same time that the *geledeh* had arrived. The construction of the Xanadu had begun.

One of Tankor Satani's eunuchs had been watching both performances. Wearing a splendid white gown trimmed in blue at the neck and with sleeves cuffed with gold lace, he looked very dignified, the embroidery of his gown glistening as he walked around the area after the dancers had finished their acts. It was pleasantly cool, the forest on the mountain shimmering like emerald in the brilliant sun; just a touch warm as hundreds of men—engineers, surveyors, carpenters, masons, laborers, plasterers, and stonemasons—began to arrive in trucks to start the monumental task of building the Xanadu.

Over the next six months they would drive themselves hard, determined to finish the first two floors before June, when the rain would start again and the air would be very humid.

Inspired, no doubt, by the idea of his own immortality, Tankor Satani showed up the next day with the eunuch. In a calm, bold voice, one that he had used for many such rites, the sorcerer-eunuch recited some sacred verses, then plucked leaves from various plants and chewed them into a pulp before spitting the residue out, as a weak wind picked up his piping voice.

"That will keep the evil eye away from this place."

As though he was intent on mesmerizing not only the men, but also the stray dogs that had come to the site, his piercing brown eyes continued to roam all over the place. Still reciting his arcane verses, he poured a libation under an almond tree to invoke the blessings of Tankor's dead mother.

"I can feel her spirit," the sorcerer said to the satisfied president.

But however much Tankor valued the prescience of this sorcerer, he did not let on about how Henri Christophe had visited him in his dreams. In fact, only the night before, still hoping Henri would come back one more time, Tankor had poured a good jigger of rum at the foot of a tree and spent some time talking to the spirit of the old slave.

"I have many enemies," he pleaded. "So don't desert me, now that you have given me the task of continuing your work."

Two days later, the workers were hacking away at some trees when a woman, dressed in the outlandish costume of a wandering Tuareg fortune-teller, came to the construction site in a van painted in the psychedelic colors of a traveling mime troupe. With a delicious smile, she supervised the distribution of bottles of rum, canned meat, beans, and sachets of rice to the laborers.

"It is from Tankor," she said, "so that you will be happy to work for him."

For the big-shot engineers and contractors, Tankor Satani's gifts were small nuggets of gold and tiny gems of diamonds for their wives and mistresses, so that there would be no delay in the construction of his castle. But considering how much it would cost to build the Xanadu, not to talk of the destruction to the flora and fauna, most people felt that Tankor Satani did not really need a new palace. His old house, built from the profits when he worked in the mines, was almost luxurious, save for two things: it lacked a view of the ocean, and the neighborhood had begun to attract some foreign riff-raff, not the least of whom were the Russians who had recently moved into the house next to his. Once every two weeks they would get drunk on vodka, play balalaika music, bring in some classy hookers, and let off enough Slavic ribaldry to disturb the dead. After six months of the madness, they finally got the old man's goat.

"Good diplomatic relations are necessary between nations, but I can't go to sleep with the parade of harlots on my street!" he fumed.

Although the Soviets had always backed him when he was fighting against the hard-nosed parliament, he threatened to break off relations with the Kremlin. It was a bold step because, over the years, they had also been keeping one of his useless sons at a university in Moscow, where, with a rich stipend from his father, he was spending lavishly on the svelte blondes from Byelorussia instead of studying.

The construction workers had been at their task for a year and a half, sometimes in the most unfavorable weather, busily putting the finishing touches to the first three floors of the Xanadu, when Tankor decided to move into them "before I go crazy in this place." Now increasingly critical of most of his actions, his wife was baffled that he had not confiscated the house of Colonel Fillibo Mango, as was his wont to do every time he was displeased with a subordinate.

"Why go to all that trouble to frame an innocent young man for writing the truth about you, if you are not going to complete your job?" Sallay asked her husband.

"Don't bother me, woman. I have a presidential right to do as I please," he retorted.

Tankor Satani woke up thinking about his Xanadu. He went to sleep with the same thought. It was an obsession like no other he had previously manifested. Nothing this grandiose, this vast in conception, had ever invaded his mind, so he had no time for the petulance of his wife. In fact, their marriage, never really one based on true love, had foundered long ago, because Sallay, God-fearing to an extreme, obsessed with the idea of crime and punishment, could not understand her husband's desire to build the palace in his old age; or, as she put it so regularly, his attempt to turn back the "clock of death." To escape from her nagging, he had taken to spending most nights alone in his study, his unlit pipe always dangling from his mouth, before dozing off.

One year after he moved into the unfinished Xanadu and cordoned off a section of it so that the place had started to have the feel of a home, he was in the study one evening, drifting into the languor of deep musical pleasure, while his guards were surreptitiously exchanging pictures of a satyr copulating with a goat. A light wind was blowing, and he closed his eyes, listening to the hypnotic notes of some Arabic songs touching his soul. In spite of his best effort to put an end to the matter, Sallay had not let up hounding him about how upset she was about the death of the colonel, and came to the study to disturb his peace.

"He was a good man, that colonel. And I know he was framed!" she screamed at him.

Tankor Satani's eyes blazed with fire at this interruption to his rhapsodic evening.

"If you don't stop disturbing me, I swear one of us will be going to the grave before God's time, and it won't be me."

There was so much menace in his voice that Sallay beat a hasty retreat from the study, leaving him to his madness.

After she was gone, Tankor Satani poured himself a glass of brandy and said something unprintable about her family. But he soon regained his composure and went back to imagining that he was on a trip to the moon, flying high into the stratosphere, now that his hydra of an account was spreading its arms in the deep vault of a Swiss bank. Going frequently to check on the construction of the Xanadu after his official duties left him very little time to relax, but even presidents were allowed some time off to act like simple mortals now and then, especially when their nest had been feathered, which was another reason why he was listening to the exotic music.

The opiate was a collection of love songs by the Afro-Lebanese singer Salma Aboudi that Tankor had received as a gift from his most trusted friend, the Coral diamond magnate Moustapha Ali-Bakr, with whom he had formed a business alliance.

"Look at it this way, Excellency," the Coral enthused. "This music is the union between two great cultures, just as our business is a combination of two great minds."

Life was going according to plan: Moustapha Ali-Bakr would soon be making a business trip to the Middle East to sell gem diamonds. Through a complex network of middlemen, the Coral had bought, at a discount, a hotel in Cape Verde, ostensibly for the president, although, after Tankor Satani's death, it was discovered that the hotel had really been registered in Moustapha Ali-Bakr's name.

That was not all. The crumbling façade of the Soviet Union was bringing an unexpected dividend to one of Tankor Satani's sons. Although he was receiving a monthly allowance from his father, the young man had been searching for an opportunity to prove to Tankor that he was not a parasite solely dependent on him. With an acuity that stunned the old man, Modu seized upon one of the most promising businesses in Malagueta: bringing in whores from the Soviet republics for some important politicians and the rich Corals. Dreamy-eyed, svelte, mostly blondes from Byelorussia and Ukraine, the girls came to town on the promise that they would get rich on diamonds.

Sallay Satani thought she would go crazy when she discovered that her oldest son was a pimp. "Lord have mercy!" she screamed at her husband. "What have I done to deserve this life? I am married to a man who imports sorcerers from Bakazo, and now I have a son who brings in harlots from Russia."

"Don't trouble your head, woman," Tankor said dismissively. "The boy had to start learning how to be a businessman somewhere, and anyway, it is better for the Corals to sleep with them than with our daughters."

Two years after enduring the heat and the mosquitoes, the promised wealth not materializing for the least enchanting of the Russian women, they soon joined the ranks of the seven o'clock evening women often seen parading near the drinking shacks on the seafront where the cheap tourists went.

Although he was happy about his son's business and, strictly speaking, he had other things to be thankful for, Tankor Satani was worried that his restless generals might be plotting against him.

Moustapha Ali-Bakr was soon back from his Middle East trip and was concerned that the president was worrying about the army. "The only way to control them is to bring some of the generals into your cabinet, Excellency," the half-caste advised.

Tankor Satani forgot about the army for a while. Yet even the comforting feeling that, with the armory secured, he was not destined for disaster was nothing compared to the thrill he was about to experience later that night. It was seven o'clock in the evening, the sky was gray, and a light harmattan wind was blowing. Working with floodlights, the builders were putting the finishing touches to the Xanadu. It was a time of the day when the old man was not to be disturbed, not even if the wind was threatening to blow Malagueta off the map of the world. But it was precisely at this hour that the lawyer Victor Adolphy, dressed in the ceremonial black and white of his profession, arrived to see the old man. The wind had started hitting their bones, and the guards had put away the X-rated pictures of the satyr and gone inside their guardhouse intent on a little tea, when they saw the red Volvo of the lawyer coming up the tree-lined drive.

"You done craze?" one of them asked, and tried to block the car from entering the compound. "Come back in de morning when de wind done stop," he told the lawyer.

Victor Adolphy had anticipated the order. "Make ah pass," he said. With a wry smile he showed the guard the official pass bearing the seal of office, with the acrylic signature of Tankor Satani. Allowed into the compound, he raced to the main entrance, hurriedly parked his car, and after being let into the foyer was soon announced by an orderly. When he came into the study he was breathing like an ox and holding the tape he had recorded at one of the Freemasons' dinners.

Instead of showing any annoyance at being disturbed, Tankor Satani welcomed the mulatto like an old friend from his dogcatching days. "Sit down, my friend, and let us celebrate a promising future together," he said. He switched off the sultry voice of the Afro-Lebanese singer and turned his attention to the lawyer, after first pouring Victor Adolphy a drink.

A tight knot in his neck had been troubling Tankor for quite some time, which was another reason why he had been listening to the music for relaxation. To be more comfortable, he sat in a Hepplewhite chair, and with his arms folded across his belly expelled a round of foul air and waited as Victor Adolphy switched on the tape recorder.

Ten minutes later, Victor Adolphy raised his head and looked at the old man for any change in his expression. What he saw were the same unblinking eyes of the old man, the hard, inscrutable stare, the powdery river in the deep lines of the brow, alternately tightening and spreading over the granite jaws, as Tankor Satani sat listening to what not even his wildest fantasy had imagined.

"Those bastards who should be grateful for what life has given them are crucifying me!" he suddenly yelled, losing his inscrutability.

His pallor had changed, and the lines of his face—tight, veined with a rush of blood—were those of a man who felt his enemies had rubbed his origins in a pig's mud. In spite of his high office, it was obvious that what they felt for him was contempt, for they had scoffed at the way he would read his speeches at the formal opening of parliament and had mocked his petulance and bragging when he spoke on the radio. Contrary to what he had assumed, they knew he was selling off the national treasures, the game parks, coastal waters, and diamond mines, to his Lebanese friends.

Much to his shock, the most insulting jab was reserved for his mother. He had preserved her memory with a school named in her honor, but he now heard her name was pasted on some harlot's hut, after he had put out the dubious claim that he was the son of a respectable teacher. As for his "preparation" for the job, the judges had poured scorn on his intelligence; some cheek he had, claiming he had been to that trade unionist college in England.

Worried about whether he had done the right thing bringing the cassette to the old man, Victor Adolphy tried some damage control. "I am sorry, Excellency," he said, with genuine concern. "I just thought I should bring you what you really wanted to hear."

Tankor Satani managed a smile and fixed the lawyer with an inscrutable look before replying. "You don't understand, my son; only my guardian angel could have sent you to me."

"What is his name?" the lawyer asked, "so that I can consult him in the likelihood that I may be discovered for what I have done."

"Don't worry too much about being harassed by your friends," Tankor said. "Before all of this is over, the only fear left in the country is the one I shall create."

Later that night, Tankor Satani dreamed yet again that Henri Christophe was speaking to him.

"Be tough with your people," the emperor said. "Otherwise they will put capsicum in your nostrils."

CHAPTER SIX

An Albino and Dancing to the Moon

"MY NAME is Habiba Sara Mouskuda. I am thirty years old and I have had all kinds of relationships, but I have a feeling you are the type of man that I can tell anything, so I have decided to take my chance with you."

That was what Habiba Mouskuda said to Theodore Iskander on the very first day she met the man who was to change her life and for whom she would have Yeama. Such an unusual opening—brave, challenging, almost unbelievable, considering the way most women tried to keep their past secret from most men in that town—was bound to convince Theodore that he had met a most remarkable woman. They were complete opposites. While she was barely educated but a ravishing beauty, he was the dutiful son of the widow Irene Iskander, a direct descendant of one of the illustrious sons of Malagueta, the great poet Garbage Martins, who had championed the cause of the original founders of the town against British occupation. Irene had been trained as a nurse but, like so many sons and daughters of the old families, had fallen on hard times after Tankor Satani came to power. Proud, fiercely independent, she had high hopes for her only son, then only fifteen. When all attempts at finding a respectable job in the hospitals proved futile, she did the only thing that brought in regular money and became a washerwoman for the hated Corals. But she kept her incomparable dignity, and would tolerate no rubbish from them.

While Theodore studied at his desk, the dark, long shadows of night in the simple house were those of his mother as she moved her washtub. She filled it with water, sorted out the linen from cotton, separated whites from colors, a long-drawn-out process. But she was glad that she could do something for her son, whose father, God bless his soul, had died when the boy was only twelve.

After years of hard work, she was thrilled when Theodore won a scholarship to Trinity College, Cambridge University, in England. Concerned about his future, she would have preferred his choosing some practical subject—accountancy or law, for example—but did not mind that he had chosen to read classics, and that many years later he had come back mouthing some complicated words by some fellows named Hume, Kant, and Russell. A week after he was back, it occurred to her that his years of eating English scones and drinking Earl Grey tea had not changed him: a note of pride for her; and she could tell, listening to him talk to his less fortunate friends, that his heart had remained African. His skin was the same mahogany gloss that no accumulation of snowflakes on his head had been able to change, and unlike some of the other academics he was not pompous. In fact he was very considerate, even taking time off now and then to help his mother sort out the Corals' laundry, as Irene had gone on working, although not for long, because she did not want to be a "burden on my *pikin*." Not until after "he had put a few pairs of trousers on his bottom."

The most difficult ordeal for Irene, when she started working for the Corals, was having to put up with their children. Pushed to the extremes of tolerance so many times, she went down on her knees one evening to ask God to restrain her hands from strangling the "uncouth barbarians." She put up with the salvoes of vulgarity from their loose tongues, their penchant for dirtying their clothes as fast as she could get them clean, the way they would sometimes spit all over the place. They had been too much for her to bear sometimes, but she had a son to feed. She thanked God those days were behind her.

Although she had retired from that phase in life, she still woke up early and had preserved her original teeth, which she was determined to take back to God, for which purpose she ate only the vegetables that she grew. But she was not yet ready to contemplate her demise. Not until she had achieved her most desired objective.

She ambushed Theodore one evening, when they had sat down to some rum. "Only one thing remains for you to do for me, Son," she told him. "Find a good Christian gal and make me a grandmoder before ah die; do dat for your poor moder. And I know just de right kind of gal for you, Son."

Dark, lovely, with topaz eyes, voluptuous lips, and wide hips, Hawanatu Gomba was Irene's choice for a daughter-in-law. She was willowy, with alabaster teeth beautifully set like perfect gems in gums that had been blackened with rich ochre, in the way the Mandingoes enhanced their beauty. She was quite a gem. Pleasant, reserved, and "well brought up," she hailed from a town not too far from Malagueta and plaited her hair the right way—African, that is—and did not have the city habit of drinking beer out of the bottle, nor did she bleach her skin: just the sort of girl Irene felt comfortable with, considering that the old woman was from a time when modesty was an old-world virtue, and a woman could count on civil men respecting them for possessing that trait. Hawanatu had the broad hips of a mare, which was proof enough to Irene that the younger woman had the right pelvic bones to give her half a dozen grandchildren. If Hawanatu Gomba could not make French paté or surprise her man with spaghetti bordelaise, which the old woman did not like anyway because it looked like worms, it was not important; Hawanatu knew how to cook some great local dishes.

But what stood her most in Irene's favor was Hawanatu's humility. "Ah don't want a daughter-in-law who is going to stand on my *pikin*'s head," the way she had seen some women trying to dominate their men: she was sure of that as she contemplated the future with a prospective daughter-in-law.

She chose the right time to introduce Hawanatu to her son, when he was over for a meal and the young woman "just happened" to be there, talking to the older woman about the magical properties of lemongrass. "Drink it as tea, but also plant it round your house, child, to keep snakes away," Irene was telling Hawanatu when Theodore walked in.

After she had introduced the young people to each other, using as much tact as she could muster, Irene tried to get her son to take an interest in Hawanatu Gomba. A short courtship followed, after which, to the delight of the old woman, the gal seemed destined to make her happy; that is, until Habiba Mouskuda arrived, red-lipped with mischief, to spoil everything.

When she discovered that Theodore was seeing the Coral, Hawanatu Gomba thought it was just a passing fancy. Considering how pleasant she was, she felt that, with time, Theodore would eventually come to his senses and realize that the other woman, that malatta suspected of killing two of her lovers, was a wild gypsy who would bring him nothing but trouble.

But after three months, when Theodore had shown no sign of abandoning Habiba Mouskuda's tempestuous bed, Hawanatu was convinced this was a contest she could not win in that sphere. She threw all pride away, prepared to fight for Theodore with the other skills of enticement she possessed. One evening, when Theodore was a bit drunk, she turned up to confront him over his betrayal.

"Even you fell for her, after what she has done to other men?"

Soon after meeting the Coral, Theodore had been surprised to discover that her green eyes were possessed of such a penetrating magnetism that they could cut and polish diamonds with their mesmerizing power and get a man to shower her with those gems. The art of the lapidary that Habiba Mouskuda had used to trap him to her bed had been so effective, he could not see straight. Now that he was drunk, he was about to commit the unpardonable sin of mistaking Hawanatu for his ravenous mistress, but he soon came to his senses, aware that the woman standing before him did not have the gypsy eyes and sexual magnetism of the malatta, but possessed an earthy blossom that Habiba Mouskuda had lost a long time ago. Moreover, Hawanatu was not as light as the Coral, and she was wearing a muslin blouse and a dark cotton skirt, which were not the kind of clothes favored by Habiba.

The mist left his eyes, and he came out of his stupor and saw, in the purple light of evening, the vestal woman who was offering to cook him the stew of a blissful future; just the sort of woman who would make him happy, it was quite clear to him. He noticed how her plaid skirt was moving rhythmically, and the spasms of her body, which had made his lips tremble in the past, before he met the malatta, almost made him moan. He inhaled her smell of fresh jasmine and longed to touch her, remembering how supple that body was; not as ravishing as the Coral's, but beautiful. He thought of the nights he had spent with Hawanatu dreaming about a house in the country, away from the city, which had grown as noisy as a motor park. But it was useless: his heart had been eaten up by the treacle that Habiba Mouskuda had served him, washed down into his soul with a carafe of potent guava wine.

Although he was forty-five, the caprices of the heart were things he had not previously experienced, and he would have readily admitted that although learned in European philosophies, until he met the malatta he had been as innocent as a choirboy about the wiles some women could use to lure men to their beds. To top everything, his upbringing, under the hawk-like strictures of Irene, had even prevented him from getting laid until after his second year in England, when a redheaded French coed had taken him to her room and made love to him because of his ability to recite the first three stanzas of Baudelaire's *Flowers of Evil* by heart. A dutiful son, he had promised Irene anything on earth, but falling in love always happened on another planet, away from mothers! Transported to a tempestuously magical bed by Habiba's love potion, held captive like a zombie, lost, trapped in that woman's gypsy spell, he destroyed his mother's dream.

"I don't know what to think anymore. Only God knows what is happening to me," he moaned.

Stunned, blinded with despair, Hawanatu fled from the miserable man. As she ran out of the house, the only thought on her mind was how mockery would turn emerald in Habiba Mouskuda's eyes after she had heard about the agony of her rival. The pale light of the moon had turned into the dark blue hue favored by the zombies, and Hawanatu tripped over the last steps of a porch on her way out. Her heart was constricted, she felt wretched, as though she was losing her mind, and did not see the pained look of a dejected Irene, who had been listening inside the house.

A sliver of moon was still visible when she arrived home, and its faint glow was all that Hawanatu needed to drape a red cape, adorned with coral beads, rusty mirrors, ancient coins, the skin of dead lizards, and dry tapioca leaves, on her shoulders. With a deep pain in her heart she went inside her room to prepare herself for the ritual she was about to perform. A blast of wind, unleashed by the mirrors that adorned her cape, winged Hawanatu with osprey feathers so that it was as though she had been transformed into a furious bird of prey, and she began to spread her wings, twisting her giraffe's neck as she raised her head to look at the moon.

In her bird form she headed toward the well-lit quarters of the Corals, squawking as she flew over their houses and bringing such torment to the hearts of the Corals that they rushed to their verandahs to toss out money, thinking that armed bandits were assailing them. But it was an unrelenting bird that they saw flying with a terrible fury above the town, which had turned miraculously bright now. Inspired by lessons from that distant period when she had been instructed by another rejected woman about how to cook the tapioca leaves to punish their rivals in love, she continued to circle over their houses. Lost to everything but her anger, she unleashed the hot winds that she hoped would send the malatta to the flames glowing in the disk of the moon. After circling over the houses three more times, she came back to earth satisfied that she had settled her score with the malatta, and regained her human form.

The wind did not let up throughout the night, and the street dogs went on howling in a way no one could recall in living memory. The wind even put out the light at the power station, and the drunks, cussing, had to look out to avoid falling into the open gutters. Using their arcane argot, some magicians saw a chance to make some money, thinking that after the wind had let up they would put out the word that the bird was the soul of the executed colonel and that only they could appease it.

Long after Hawanatu Gomba had gone to bed, the wind was still howling, and she had a dream: a thousand birds were flying in and out of the houses of the Corals, like a biblical plague; all their houses were suddenly wiped out, but the others were saved. Two weeks afterward, some people insisted they had dreamed similarly about those mysterious birds.

Eight months and two weeks later, hell-bent on trapping Theodore Iskander for life, Habiba Mouskuda felt the liana of childbirth twisting her insides one night. Surrounded by two stout Coral women, who were applying wet towels to her brow to ease the pain, she went into a long labor. As she moved between life and death, pulling out her hair, she felt as though she was about to lose all of her teeth until, finally, the child came out. But when she was shown her baby, her face turned crimson, horrified, because the child was an animal with a skin like a newt's: pale yellow, ugly, stamped with the truth that an albino had found its way to her womb.

With a pained, angry look Habiba Mouskuda rejected the child and turned to face the wall. She pulled at her hair, cried, and cursed her fate. When she was a bit calmer, she said, "I know who is responsible for my bad luck, and I shall hit back."

God must have been listening at that moment, because the child died within a week, after which Habiba buried the evidence of her tragedy under a solitary lime tree, hurriedly, the way they dispatched tragic albinos in the town.

Habiba Mouskuda suspected Hawanatu Gomba's hand in the tragedy of the albino. Twenty-four hours after the freak child was buried, the Corals came out of their houses in an agitated state. As usual they smelled of garlic as they began to curse and scream insults about black magic, bending their verbs and pronouns because they were still trying to master the cadences of the black people's language. With deadly accuracy, they rained stones on Hawanatu Gomba's house, forced her out, and beat loud staccatos of rage behind her on their pots and pans, the most painful insult being when they called her *kakaras*, asshole.

They turned her into an outcast, drove her into exile, and it was not until five years later, during which time Habiba Mouskuda's then famous reputation for killing off her lovers had raised questions about what really happened to the albino, that Hawanatu Gomba was able to return home and wash off the shame of being a "witch," and to begin a new life.

CHAPTER SEVEN

Healing on the Beach

TWO YEARS after General Augustus Kotay choked on a fishbone and went to the soldier's final battleground in the sky, Habiba Mouskuda did not seem the least concerned that she was still viewed as a femme fatale. In fact, she appeared to relish her reputation as a woman whose breasts could torment generals more than an entire battalion of enemy soldiers. But her disregard for public opprobrium was really a mask to disguise the livid terror she had been carrying around for some time: the fear that, like Colonel Fillibo Mango, it was only a matter of time before the ghost of General Augustus Kotay came to visit her. At thirty, thinking she had burned her candles in a slow amethyst at both ends, she decided to take stock of what was left of her adventures in the byways of unfulfilled affairs, besides the gifts and the yellowing letters of the general that she had kept in a jewel box. One evening, she sat on the porch of the house that the general had built for her and began to read the letters of the dead man. Surprised that some of the letters still smelled of the French perfume the general would sprinkle on them, she discovered the other bittersweet memorabilia of her escapades. Her reading of the dead man's letters was so painful she imagined that his bones were probably turning over in his grave, stunned that she was capable of contrition.

In addition to his letters, she discovered some loose military buttons, faded ceremonial photographs of the dead man, pearls turning obsidian, a fifty-pound note she had put away for life's rainy days, lapis lazuli and agate Fabergé jewelry that the general had spent good money on in Russia. Some ambergris and tiger-bone earrings had survived the ravages of the tropical rust in Malagueta, but she no longer had any use for them. She had arrived at a juncture in her life when she no longer felt like dressing like a wild, exotic malatta, but wanted to cultivate the charm of a discreet woman. That was because, after meeting Theodore Iskander, a man unlike any she had been to bed with previously, she had decided she wanted to spend the rest of her life with him. If anyone was going to be the father of the child she had always longed for and was now prepared to do anything to have, such as dabbling in the science of the "double eye," which she had previously had no use for, it had to be the bookish philosopher.

They had met by chance after her African gray parrot escaped. The bird was a notorious mimic privy to most of her secrets; fearing that it might spill them to the wrong ear, she went looking for it in the neighborhood and, drawn by its voice, found it perched on a branch of a guava tree in the philosopher's garden.

"It was fate," she said to Victoria, "that a mimic should bring me to a philosopher. Imagine what they would have been talking about if I had not gone there in time!"

Contrary to what many people thought, Habiba Mouskuda found it difficult getting over the death of her albino child. The reason was simple: she loved Theodore Iskander and wanted to prove to him that she was worthy of giving him a child. Although her life had been a willful onslaught on sex, fired by greed, lust, and an occasional appetite for scandal and eroticism, that was all in the past, a mistake bred by poverty, immaturity—for which she had suffered quietly. Now that she was older, wiser, she felt she should be given a chance to prove her worth.

She suffered terrible pangs of regret thinking that, with each relationship, she had failed to heed her mother's warning that she was heading down the destructive path trodden by mulatto girls. She had lectured the poor woman, now dead, with the serpent edge of her tongue, threatening to cut off the generous allowance she had been offering as a dutiful daughter.

"I shall say my piece," her mother would retort, "even if you don't like it. For I am not one of those mothers to keep quiet when I see something going wrong, just because you are feeding me!"

Being young and a malatta had always been great assets in Malagueta, what with the politicians and Corals vying among themselves for those girls, and it had seemed to Habiba Mouskuda that she was living in a golden age, dominating those stupid men.

Theodore Iskander was to change her outlook on life. As soon as they started going out, it was clear to him that she was quite intelligent, although she had stubbornly refused to further her education after she had polished herself a bit in secondary school.

"Who needs that," she had ridiculed her mother over the subject of going further in her education, "when all that will happen is that I shall end up being a clerk like you?"

With a philosopher's patience, Theodore Iskander set about discovering the fertile roots of her mind, and was determined to wean her away from the willfulness of her self-destruction and turn her into a good woman.

His patience eventually won her over. Soon she was visiting him regularly, sometimes bringing him wine. Occasionally, she would try to read some of his not too difficult books; most important of all, she brought him the gossip she had picked up from the politicians, about all sorts of schemes to milk Malagueta.

"You don't know how greedy and contemptible they are; always thinking about themselves; how fast they can get their children out of here in case of trouble, and about how much money they can steal while in office. They are disgusting," she spat, clearly regretting her dalliances with some of them.

But it was her forthrightness about her past, the stories she told without any embarrassment, that surprised Theodore Iskander. Habiba had prayed that, as a philosopher, he would be less judgmental.

"You don't mind, do you?" she asked one evening. "I had to unburden myself to someone, and it so happened that it was you."

"No, I don't mind," he assured her.

Given how careless she was about preventing pregnancies before she met Theodore, Habiba Mouskuda was not surprised that her womb turned out to be as prolific as a papaya plant; she became pregnant eight times in six years, only to abort the fetuses with the same ruthlessness with which she discarded the hapless series of men who trooped to her door. But after she had conceived of the possibility of having a child for Theodore Iskander, she bubbled with such excitement that when she lost the child, it was more than she could bear. Desperate to have his child, she turned to him for his understanding and support.

"It's all right," he said, swallowing his grief, for he too had thought of having a child. "You did not have to wait for me to say good-bye to my son."

He waited for the customary seven days of atonement to pass—death and mourning being rituals you did not rush in Malagueta—before going to see his mistress.

Although it had been a terrible period for her, Habiba Mouskuda understood his absence. With a gentlemanly patience that she had never experienced before, he began to guide her away from a descent into the madness that was beginning to shroud her soul. "Don't dwell on the loss of the child," he told her.

"Why?"

"Because pain is a prerequisite for the lasting attainment of happiness, and it is better for you to lose the child in the uncertainties of infancy than in his twenties, when the pain would be unbearable for you."

Habiba Mouskuda did not always understand his bookish words, but the warmth with which he said them was assurance enough that he was sincere. She was grateful for them.

Twice in one week he took her to one of Malagueta's isolated white, sandy beaches, where the noisy sandpipers, ravenous crows, herons, and scuttling sea crabs somewhat helped heal her soul. The ocean was beating its loud drums: it was glorious, and it was during one of those visits that he told her about how his illustrious ancestors had helped build the town, and that he was going to write a book about one of them.

"Which one?" she wondered.

"The poet Garbage Martins."

"I should have guessed," she laughed

"Why?"

"I may not have had much of an education, but I have heard about him. His fame; how he wrote revolutionary poems against the British occupation. And they say he was a great one with the ladies!"

Sometimes, for greater privacy, they would change locations, going further away to a marshy area of large mangroves, tall as palm trees, near a river that had begun its journey on Mount Agadi, which overlooked the city. The rains had almost drummed themselves out. Imposing in brilliant green and white against the golden sun, Tankor Satani's Xanadu loomed on Malagueta's hill, but the houses in the lowland had been pounded by the rain and needed repairs; the ocean was violent, and fish were very scarce in the markets. Even so, Theodore found ways to satisfy her desire for salmon, paying considerably for those caught in the raging ocean by some very daring midnight fishermen. On her birthday, they picnicked on roast chicken marinated in peanut butter, sage, and lime and sautéed with a good spread of basil and mushrooms. After his evening lectures on morality and the state, they went to his regular, dimly lit café to listen to the sweet harp of the kora and to laugh at the slapstick of the dwarf who was a regular performer there.

When the dwarf saw the pair come in one night, he stopped performing his tricks. His head resting upside down on a stool and his arms stretched out, he had been spinning like a top, uttering wild cries and, with the most amazing skill, pocketing the tips that the guests were throwing on the table.

The couple had just started drinking cardamom coffee spiced with coconut liqueur when the most extraordinary thing happened. With a flying leap, the dwarf landed on Theodore Iskander's back, wrapped his tiny arms round his neck, and told him, "She is beautiful, my friend, but a disaster; I see problems ahead for you if you don't give her up."

Calmly, the philosopher removed the dwarf from his back and replied with a dignified smile, "I know, my friend, but think of what people must have said to your mother when you were born? 'He is a disaster!' We have to make allowances for others."

He tossed a generous tip into the dwarf's donation plate and left with his mistress. She was quite shaken, but they did not say anything as they went into the street, where a small drizzle was falling. In time, he coaxed her out of her fear of midnight owls, which she had insisted were Hawanatu Gomba's friends, and of the thought that her dead lovers were really going to come for her.

"Look forward to being pregnant again, in spite of the ruin done to your body by those abortions," he said, over and over.

When they made love in the rain-drenched aftermath of the café, he was very calm, but went to her with his strong, bold strokes, hoping to bring her out of her fears, take her to a new island named *life*: one drenched in bright colors; and she, as though she understood what he was doing, opened up to him, a man she loved.

"Don't leave me!" she cried. "I shall be lost without you."

He slept over at her place that night and promised never to leave her, no matter what she did. He had come to the conclusion that, in spite of Habiba Mouskuda's air of toughness, she was as brittle inside as a branch of a mango tree. To his care of his mother, he had added the responsibility of caring for his mistress.

With her hair beginning to turn gray, Irene Iskander had become less concerned about aging than about what was really eating her up: the bewitchment of her son by the malatta. At night she would lie on her cotton wool mattress in the wooden house that her son, bless his soul, had remodeled for her, but was up first thing in the morning—a washerwoman's habit—even after she had retired. Singing quietly, she went out into the yard to feed the cooing doves and the cackling hens; or, at her leisure, tend the vegetables she was raising to keep her busy and to take her mind off what was happening to her son. Although he was providing her with a generous allowance, much bigger than the golden handshake the mean Corals had offered at her retirement, she was still unhappy about his relationship with that "Cor-raal!"

Irene was an uncomplicated soul, so it was easy for her to blame the vagaries of fate—her son's big "brain for book" and that "St. Jago," loose woman—for the fact that Theodore had not settled down with a good woman in a house to which Irene could come without having to bother about whether she had the right manners. Years of doing the Corals' laundry had left her with crooked fingers, painful knuckles, and arthritic knees that troubled her now and then, but that had not robbed her of her dignity, and her mouth did not have the taste of the brackish water from life's hardness, except for her dislike of the woman who had taken her son away from her. Radiant in her silk blouses and three-tiered plaid skirts, her ears studded with pearls that her son had given her, Irene went regularly to church, grateful for little mercies as she opened her heart to God, pleading that such manifestations of faith would serve as penance for whatever sins she might have committed. Back in the house, she read the Songs of Solomon, good enough for her simple mind that did not try to understand her son's worldliness, but she had deep longings for the wholeness of his soul, especially after its fission by Habiba Mouskuda. But when it eventually happened, it was not what she had been expecting.

CHAPTER EIGHT

The Unbearable Loneliness of Being Chief Justice

IT TOOK a while, but sometime after Victor Adolphy visited Tankor Satani to bring him the compromising sentiments of the judges, the president began to plan his revenge. One night, almost ashamed of how easily the idea had come to him, he telephoned the chief justice, disguising his true intention.

"Let us go somewhere nice, my lord, to discuss this terrible creep of old age that has not affected you, now that you have been given a new lease on life," he said, with what sounded like envy in his voice.

At fifty, with his widowed mother finally having joined her ancestors, Justice Atanasius Bama had immediately married his sweetheart of twenty years and was enjoying the sweet grapes of that union, not the least concerned that he had recently been diagnosed with fatigue and with what the most respected urologist in the country called a small inflammation of the prostate gland. Surgery was not necessary, the doctor had informed his patient; there was no cancer, but incontinence was an occasional embarrassment requiring the jurist to make several trips to the toilet during the day, for which the doctor had prescribed the medication Prazosin, 4 mg of which he should take once a day, before bedtime, so as not to affect his lovemaking. In addition, the doctor had ordered a total abstinence from the Black Label whiskey that the jurist always relished after a hard day's work. Based on his prognosis, the doctor had also imposed some other restrictions on his patient, although he did not expect the newly married man to adhere to such curative advice. Not when he had a wife waiting for him every night.

"Refrain from caffeinated drinks, citrus fruits, and lots of salt," the doctor advised. "Eat more fresh fish and vegetables, especially tomatoes and carrots. You should be happy, my friend. You have a new wife and a good many years to go."

It was not in the judge's nature to restrict his eating habits, and whatever ailment he had did not cloud his incomparable wisdom. Renowned for his impeccable integrity, which would get him into trouble after talking to his fellow jurists, he had expressed his dislike of politicians to them.

Although he was not overweight, the judge clearly showed signs of his culinary indulgence; but his large appetite was perhaps the only vice that could be pinned on a man so otherwise principled, and a great sportsman to boot. Tall, imposing, with a robust constitution and appetite and a razor-sharp intelligence, he was the youngest man to occupy the highest judicial office in the land. Born with an amiable personality, he was the scion of a distinguished family and belonged to a dying tradition of propriety and public service for altruistic reasons. After his wedding, he had moved into an official house with a cook, gardener, and watchmen, and was looking forward to making up for lost time after his devotion to his mother. Besides enjoying marital bliss, it was his intention to bring some form of probity to a notoriously corrupt judicial system.

Put on what he called a straitjacket diet by the doctor, Justice Bama accepted some of the restrictions with the dignified air of a man for whom life was really a series of enigmas. Crucially, he saw no reason why he should have been exempt from what was after all a small problem of the bladder; not when he was past fifty. Besides, there was the unexpected benefit that his medication was bringing him: a turgid erection every morning—the side effect the doctor had predicted—which was when the jurist liked to make love to his new wife, just before he went off to court.

When he received Tankor's call, the jurist had no reason to suspect he was walking into a trap. Recently, after consulting one of his sorcerers, Tankor Satani had decided that although the country was probably heading for disaster, it was still auspicious for him to finish the Xanadu. All the same, when the eunuch delved into the mysterious art for a second reading, he advised caution.

"Why?" demanded Tankor

"In dat matter, ah only give advice after what de mystic clouds tell me," he told the president.

For his part, surveying the mess he had to go through every day to get to his court, the jurist had come to a different conclusion. "Everything is collapsing around us," he told his wife one evening when they were sitting down to dinner: "the legal system, the schools, public morality, and even religion. So our marriage must have been ordained in heaven for it to happen now."

"And I am glad you never succumbed to his pressure," she said, referring to how some other judges had compromised their oath, sending innocent men to the gallows, just so that Tankor Satani could give the judges' children fat scholarships to European universities.

While Judge Bama was enjoying the fresh blossoms of marital life so much so that he seldom stayed late in the office, as was his past habit, Tankor Satani's own marriage seemed to have hit rock bottom, but had decided that with so many fronts on which he had to fight, the last thing he needed was a divorce. Yet, given his many mistresses and extramarital children, it was obvious to everyone that he was otherwise enjoying himself. Long ago, his long-suffering wife had concluded it was her lot to put up with the expected philandering of a politician; she had invested too much in that marriage, and the strain, even when she smiled, showed in her face; were it not for the fact that her children had turned out to be replicas of the old man—vain, avaricious and, in the case of the boys, great womanizers—she would have been a happy woman.

The courthouse was only a stone's throw from the presidential palace, and its colonial architecture of imposing white pillars, broad verandahs, Maroon latticework, and large windows to bring in light belonged to a bygone age, when life in Malagueta was taking shape in the middle of the nineteenth century and labor was cheap but very professional. That relish for beauty and pride in work and maintenance had been almost lost by the time Tankor Satani became president, which was why he had to depend on specialists to build his Xanadu. Everyone could see that the court building had not been painted in years. A thick blanket of moss covered much of its walls, and the garden of roses, hydrangea, and hibiscus beds at the front entrance had been allowed to die. Given the erratic supply of water, some of its toilets had broken down, and the ancient mechanisms of its ceiling fans had long ago given up the fight against the fiery breath of the humidity blowing six months a year. Yet, bewigged and pompous, it was to this hellish house that the lawyers went every day to trivialize justice.

Judge Atanasius Bama was aware of the perfidy in the legal practice and had been thinking of ways to excise the cancer. The disgrace into which a once-honorable profession had fallen was sickening, especially the way the government was interfering with court proceedings, the compromising lawyers and judges always willing to oblige the president. He took refuge in the books in his book-lined office and in his performances as a sideman in the "old boys'" orchestra of his high school. But it was being a knight at the Freemasons that really gave some joy to his spirit.

Most days he preferred to walk to the palace. Along the way he would pause with a "Good morning" to an old-timer weary of the age in which he was living, wanting desperately to die, or to an old lady off to sell the last of her trinkets for a meal.

"The learned fellow is very nice," they always remarked.

Today was different: the presidential car was picking him up. Soon he was riding with Tankor Satani through the maze of rusty, red corrugated-roofed houses in sections of the city, the warrens of lean-tos, over potholes, as the driver tried to avoid hitting a crazy drunk chewing on a chicken bone and the two o'clock worshippers running across the streets to their churches. Eventually he and Tankor were in the clear, wide-open hilly terrain of mansions, the gated communities where the privileged citizens lived, with their vast tennis courts, flamboyant gardens, and garages housing the Mercedes Benzes and four-wheel vehicles. As a newly married man, the judge was always happy just thinking about the joys of the marital bed, and he would have loved to stop for a moment to pick some of the exquisite roses growing in one of the gardens, to take home to his wife. Soon they were off the laterite roads, and as the car sped up a newly bulldozed road cut through woodlands that led up to the edge of the mountain, it dawned on the judge that they were on their way to the nearly completed Xanadu.

Even before they had turned into the circular road leading to the long driveway at the top of the hill, the massive edifice came into view. It was the first time that the jurist had really been up to the mountain to see the Xanadu, and his immediate reaction was shock. He felt angry, appalled by what he thought an extravagant project that had cost the country a bomb. Mounds of earth and burnt-out areas showed how savage the destruction of the rich flora had been to make way for it. He thought of the demand on the city's water supply and electricity to feed this monstrosity, not to talk of the lack of probity on Tankor's part, which the high office of presidency should have demanded.

"This is splendid, Excellency," the judge said, the censure in his tone undisguised, "but I wonder what our foreign friends will say about it."

Tankor Satani could not hide his irritation. "To hell with them!" he said. "Their criticism is not as important as what some of my own people have been saying about me."

"You mean you have received delegations protesting this extravagance?" the judge hastened to ask.

"Let's say I know some things I was not supposed to hear." The menace in his voice should have alerted the judge to what was coming.

Imperiously, Tankor Satani began to escort Atanasius Bama on a tour of the hilltop estate from the west side, which faced the ocean. From there they could see the old city, which the Maroons and Nova Scotians had built with planned elegance over two hundred years ago but which had now fallen into decay. But in spite of the city's disorder, some parts of it were still beautiful. The jacaranda-lined arteries leading to the beaches had not yet been destroyed and were struggling to hold their own in that old city of charmed decadence.

As the tour progressed, the judge heard the soaring invocation of *Allahu Akbar* from the loudspeakers mounted on the mosques' minarets all over the city. Now that he was convinced Tankor had brought him to the Xanadu on a not-too-pleasant mission, the sound of the ocean pounding those seafront shacks scattered along the rocky coast came as a welcome distraction. The waves were pounding the bays, and a regatta of colorful dugout canoes lay in one of those bays. In spite of the disquiet in his soul, there was no denying that the beauty of the view from the hill was breathtaking, and it occurred to him that this was why Tankor Satani had built his Xanadu on the hill.

Tankor Satani allowed the judge his contemplation. When he felt he had been sufficiently impressed with the vista, he scrutinized his face, hoping to read what was going through that legal mind, but was defeated by the inscrutability that the learned jurist had perfected after many years on the bench. Obviously ill at ease with one another, it occurred to Tankor that, except for when they were brought together for official reasons, they had seldom met, were worlds apart; men whose backgrounds were as different as goat was from sheep.

Given his lowly beginnings, Tankor Satani had lived in awe of, and with admiration for, the judge and his kind (though he would have denied it), drawn to but repulsed by their superior airs and self-righteousness. And he was aware, even though he was the president, that they did have virtues and that no matter how much he tried he could not fully comprehend them. For years, he had wondered how it was that men like the judge were able to look so satisfied with life: how they became that cut above the ordinary that made them such an annoying lot and feared even by those with naked power.

"You don't approve of the little retirement home that I have built?" he said to the judge, sensing his discomfort.

The judge felt sick. "It is not for me to approve, Excellency, but for you to be able to face your God and contemplate a life beyond his tolerance of our ways."

"Then what do you say about those who impose sanctions on others, even before God has had a chance to sit in judgment?"

"It all depends on when they see God's time coming," the judge said somewhat philosophically.

"In that case, let me show you something about 'God's timing.'"

Tankor Satani brought the cassette out of his pocket and inserted it inside the small portable recorder that he carried with him every time he came to inspect the work. A noisy crow had landed on a tree, and once again the pounding of the ocean could be heard as though it was near the hilltop, so Tankor Satani turned the volume up a bit. The enigmatic look on his face was that of a wounded leopard trying to act like a domestic cat. But he did not give anything away about how he had come to be in possession of the tape. Rather, he watched the judge beginning to sweat in the heat, hot around the collar, as anger and horror formed a bewildering map on the judge's face. He felt trapped in the pleurisy of someone's treachery; but given his legal training, his smile, although dark, was also inscrutable.

"You mean to crucify me?" the judge said after he had recovered something of his dignity and the old man had switched off the tape.

"No, my friend," Tankor Satani replied. "But from now on, you will bear witness to my ascension into the kingdom which you and your friends have kept me out of for so long."

When Atanasius Bama returned to his house, it was to the most miserable evening he had ever experienced. Noticing the troubled look on his face, his wife, Agatha, thought it was because of another bad day in court.

"Have a drink and forget about the country; what can one person do?" she tried to soothe him.

Rest for the judge, even when induced with a half bottle of whisky, was hard to coax. He went to his study to read a few lines from Corinthians and to pray for his soul. When he eventually fell asleep he dreamed he was dying, trapped inside his house in the middle of a turbulent ocean, and he saw a large barracuda swimming toward him, its huge jaws open in terrible menace. Just when he thought he was about to be sliced into pieces, a beautiful woman, half human and half fish, blocked the barracuda's path. With her powerful tail she lashed at the great fish and helped the judge, almost dead, to land safely on a quiet spot, where the glittering light from her tail revealed his house, brought up from the bottom of the sea with bamboo lights glowing in all the rooms.

"Leave that barracuda to me," the mermaid said before she went back to the sea. "I shall deal with him later."

A thick foam of sweat covered the judge's face when he woke up from his terrible dream. He was deeply shaken after his encounter with Tankor and assailed by the feeling that the room had become hazy and that it smelled of fish, but also of fresh gardenia. The dark rain clouds of the late afternoon began to move away, the sun came out, and he felt hot on his forehead.

When he finally switched on the bedside lamp, he noticed that Agatha was sleeping peacefully, unaware of the terror raging in his heart. But as if he was afraid he would disappear into the vortex of another strange dream, he woke her up and threw himself into her comforting arms, crying, "Hold me! I am afraid the light is about to go out of our lives!"

CHAPTER NINE

The River Between

IT WASN'T long before Habiba Mouskuda discovered that she was pregnant again. However, the enigmatic threads of a dream that she had one night tempered her joy. She was dressed like a bride in a white lace wedding dress, and her hair was done up in braids ringed with white gardenias. She stood alone near the oleander bush in her garden, an angel in an earthly paradise, and was surprised to hear someone calling her name, saying she had never looked as beautiful as she did on her wedding day. It was a brief, magical moment, quickly over, after which the foreboding image appeared. Straight ahead of her, she saw General Augustus Kotay, wearing his official military uniform, waiting for her at the entrance to the paradisiacal garden.

"I have come to marry you," the dead man said, "so that we can live together in my other house, because this one is crumbling around you."

Habiba Mouskuda's dreams had sometimes been so real they did not need an interpreter, but this dream was different. She woke up drenched in sweat, even though the air conditioner was on, terrified of the dead man's hieroglyphs, especially as the smell of frangipani that always accompanied the dead was pungent in the room.

Only the day before, she had swept her walls clean of the spiderwebs that the dampness of the rain had brought. Now she saw a large, gray spider climbing one of the walls, filling her heart with fear. She felt trapped, haunted, and imagined the sound of the dead man rattling the spurs of his boots in the room, making her feel she was going mad in that sulfuric air and that she could die any time now. She switched off the air conditioner and opened her windows to let some fresh air in. One hour later, running like a terrified cat, she went to see her friend Victoria to tell her about the dream.

"This does not sound good," Victoria said, concerned.

"Why?" wondered Habiba.

"To dream about getting married is not bad, especially if you are not wearing white, after all you have done! Don't get me wrong," the much older woman said. "But to dream about marrying a dead man complicates the interpretation. So let me take you to someone who can unravel the threads for us."

One week later, the first roosters had hardly begun to herald the dawn when the two women set out on a long journey by bus. After five hours, having left all the towns behind, they came to a region of unspoiled beauty, one not yet affected by the adzes of the greedy timber merchants who had been depriving Kissi of much of its forests. The plants gave off aromatic scents, and it seemed as if nothing had changed in that region for a hundred years. In the past only the dead and diamond smugglers going to the neighboring country of Bassa would have ventured this far, but the women were on a mission, taking a chance with death, so were very careful. A friendly oval moon had thrown its gentle evening rays on the trees, helping the women to avoid falling over the roots crisscrossing their path. In Malagueta the fumes of the traffic had killed off many of the birds; here the cornets of the forest birds calmed Habiba's soul, but her major concern was to get to their destination as fast as possible.

"I am a little afraid," she confessed about the eerie quiet they had entered.

"Don't be afraid now," Victoria said as they continued on the noiseless path. "I have not been here in years, but I can assure you nothing changes that fast in this part of the world."

She linked her hand with her friend's for assurance, and they walked for another quarter mile, both of them glad that the birds were still singing in the tall trees. When Victoria began to smile, Habiba Mouskuda felt the tightening in her heart relax and realized that Victoria had brought her close to the border with Bassa, the country run by a man descended from slaves in North Carolina; a man who had retained the natural rhythm of plantation speech.

Victoria was the first to hear the flow of the river. A small, reddish river ten miles long, it served as the border, and its flow was a meandering journey through a picturesque stretch of mangroves, wild lilies, and dwarf elephant grass. But it was as a source of diamonds that it had drawn the smugglers and other desperate men willing to kill each other, but who seldom succeeded in finding much in terms of fortune. Some form of life—a few huts, millet fields, barns, and cattle pens—was evident on Kissi's side of the border; men went from those huts to the river to pan for the diamonds, but sometimes found themselves sent to a quick death when its bed collapsed or when fierce battles erupted. Holding up the hems of their skirts, the two women waded across the river, carefully watching their steps so as not to sink into a muddy spot.

"How far do we have to go?" Habiba asked.

"Not too far."

The house of a sorcerer-eunuch was the first one across the river. For years, Pallo Yerimana had lived there and loved its isolation. Fate had given him that refuge, and he had been happy there. Except to those who came to ask for his help, he was a solitary man who guarded his privacy. He did his best to keep his power as a sorcerer hidden from most people, and his reserve in the hamlet had earned him the sobriquet "the silent crab." A refugee, like most eunuchs in the country, from the slavery in Mauritania, he had built the house some ten years ago. Ten years before that, when Pallo was only fourteen, a sadistic and brutal Mauritanian Arab had taken his knife to Pallo's manhood, allegedly for staring at his wives.

The pain had been terrible, but he realized afterward that nature had compensated him in the most amazing way: he could communicate with the creatures of the night. When he escaped from Mauritania, it was with his anguished soul and a few rags of cotton some kind folks had given to him. The only course open to him was to beg for a living in front of the mosques in the various towns along the way, offering his blessings to the pious, which was how he ended up in Kissi, brought there by some Senegalese Moors who had come to mine diamonds. On his first night in the border village, curled up on his mat under a baobab tree, he heard strange voices talking to him.

"Be quiet. Don't be afraid. We have come to give you the keys to the art of sorcery. We will also teach you about alchemy."

Even at that early stage, his patience was his greatest virtue, something that was to stand him in good stead when he became a big part of the lunatic household of Tankor Satani. After receiving his first lessons, Pallo set about building up the fire of his resolve to find answers to most human ailments, figuring how he could turn his tragedy to good use. Most nights an invisible hand would guide him as he roamed through the nearby forest, always with a hawk's eyes, a vagrant tasting the juices of wild plants while learning how to steal the toxins of snakes. After he had conquered the reptiles, he moved on to the tricky business of how to trap birds, especially hawks. Soon he had mastered the art of skinning lizards and digging out roots and scraping the bark of trees so that he could make the balm for some of life's bodily complications. When he felt hungry, all he had to do was to watch the antelopes plucking at some leaves and do likewise.

Sometimes he would watch the men as they came to the river from both sides of the border, and it would occur to him that written on their faces was the desperation of the age: terrifying, hungry, a message that life was short and death was preferable. This, he realized, was how later they were transformed into killers. He knew he could not stop them.

One day, when he thought he was on the right track to total sublimation, after he had not felt the need to eat, drink, or sleep for three days, he dropped off from exhaustion. In the cold grove that was his home, he began to shiver and felt as though death was taking him away, only to wake up later, his mouth refreshed with the nectar of sacred leaves and with an even greater prescience about sorcery. If his incapacitation as a man was the price he had to pay for this power, Pallo always returned from his odysseys healed in his soul.

"You have not changed much," Victoria remarked on the robust good health of the sorcerer. His dark body glowed with an ageless luster.

"On the plain of human growth, the first stage of old age is the arrival of anxiety. That is something that only people who fall in love experience," the eunuch said.

Five years earlier, when she had been on the verge of losing her mind over a forbidden love, Victoria had gone to see the sorcerer. On that visit, before she had even told him what had brought her to his shrine, he divined her torment. "Sacred hunger is one thing that we sometimes have, and love is beyond comprehension. But I shall cure your hunger, because your love is the kind that is bigger than your heart," the eunuch had said.

"How do you know I am here to talk about love?"

"I have never been in that territory, but nothing is hidden from sorcery."

He draped a white cloth over her head and sent her into a deep spell. As he had expected, she began to call, in a sweet monologue, her brother-in law's name, talking about their trysts now that her sister was somewhere in a foreign country selling illegal diamonds. Before visiting the eunuch, Victoria had been determined that however forbidden that love might be, she was not going to give him up, but Pallo had set about curing her of her confusion. "You may keep the man, but only for a while; then it will be you who will forget him," he said, and gave her a small bottle of healing lotion to help cure her.

Now the two women were waiting for the eunuch to unravel Habiba Mouskuda's dream, wondering why he was taking an unusually long time. While he was deep in concentration, Victoria looked at his hands and realized that even though he was a man, Pallo had the fine, beautiful hands of a woman: magical hands.

After what seemed like an eternity, he looked at Habiba Mouskuda and expressed his unhappiness about having to unravel the knots in her dream.

"Why is that?" she wondered.

"Because you hold in captivity the hearts of three dead men and carry the child of another, but there is the possibility that the father of your child may not have a peaceful end to his life. It is all because of your willful nature."

"But I love this man," she said, terrified of the omens.

"No! What you love is the idea of this man, but not his soul. Above all, you have made his mother unhappy, which is bad. What good is love if it brings misery to a man's mother? As for your dream, when dead men walk they are happy with their former lives; but when you dream about getting married to one of them it means that their souls are still riddled with anguish. And since you were not moved by their deaths, you can stop the traffic of the dead into your life only by atoning for past mistakes."

"And how do I do that?" the miserable woman, now feeling hot all over her body, asked.

"By giving them in death the love you did not have in your heart when they were alive."

It was with a disconsolate air that Habiba Mouskuda left the shrine. Unlike her friend, who was calm, Habiba Mouskuda was still inflamed from the fire that the sorcerer's words had lit in her. Some distance out of the man's earshot, she turned to Victoria, hoping the other woman's serenity held the answer that Pallo had not really given her. "Let us go upstream a bit," the pregnant woman pleaded, afraid she might drown with her unborn child.

An old canoe lay anchored near the bank of the river, and they climbed inside and began, clumsily, to navigate the river. When they had gone about a mile, Habiba Mouskuda suddenly felt like drinking the water so that she would be free of the hot brush fire growing inside her. The sorcerer had painted an uncertain future for her, and her torment, if not genuine remorse, about what she had done to her men was apparent to Victoria as Habiba leaned over to touch the river for a comforting feel, only to discover that the water was hot. Life, she realized, had suddenly become another country for her, a strange tapestry whose colors she had just discovered were different from any she had known in the past; a pastiche of worries, pain, and anxiety.

She thought of Theodore Iskander and began to imagine him already dead. It was horrible; he was so unlike the other men she had known, some of whom were now dead, those drifters into her life who had meant nothing to her. Filled with a deep foreboding, she prayed, slowly, the boat riding gently on what had suddenly become a rough river, as the child moved in her womb. For the first time in her life, she began to imagine the possibility of growing old without someone to care for her, her knowledge of the hand of fate limited, as had been her ability to give love in the past.

"Don't let him die," she cried in her pained heart, thinking of Theodore as the boat finally drew nearer to dry land.

"Do you think I am an evil woman?" she asked Victoria.

"When we don't love, a little sin is understandable," Victoria replied.

CHAPTER TEN

The Last Visit of General Augustus Kotay

WHEN THEY were almost near the bank, a rustle in the mangrove made Habiba Mouskuda very tense. Once again, as on that night when she had seen him waiting forlornly in the oleander garden, she saw General Augustus Kotay, dressed in his ceremonial military uniform, holding his hat in his hand. The moon that had guided the women on their way back had slunk under gray clouds, thunder was rumbling in the sky, and she began to tremble, dreading the reappearance of that apparition.

"I can't let you go through this all by yourself," Victoria insisted after she had got her friend home safely.

"It is all right, dear friend. This is something that I must face alone," the pregnant woman replied.

That night was the most miserable that Habiba had ever spent in the now haunted house. She combed out her long tresses and sat trembling in her bed as she waited for the dead man. She did not have to wait too long. Quite suddenly, she heard the familiar steps of General Augustus Kotay marching up and down in the living room. Aware that it was useless to resist when a dead man desired her, she lay trembling in bed, waiting for him to come into the bedroom, ready to surrender to his caresses, expecting his hands to fondle her breasts, his dead man's weight heavy on her, the way he had been when he was alive, after he had hurried out of his military uniform. But in spite of her fear and her determination to stay awake, she drifted into a half sleep. Still the dead man did not trouble her; it was as though, now that he had finally triumphed over her and could see how deeply distressed she was, he was content to sit in his favorite chair for a while, keeping time with the soft thud of his boots, looking at her.

"Go away and I shall give back all you ever gave me, including this house," the woman pleaded, in a hallucinatory voice.

"I don't want anything from you," said the sad dead man, "as you are incapable of gratitude."

"Give me one more chance and you will see what I am going to do."

"For all of us, or just for me?" the dead man wanted to know.

"For all of you, because I know the dead are tolerant."

General Augustus Kotay did not answer her again. Sitting in the same position in which he had been rattling his invisible boots, he reflected soberly as he looked at his former mistress. It was as though, determined to put an end to his wanderings, this was the last time his spirit would visit the house that he had built when he was under the cloud of confusion that he had mistaken for love of Habiba. With a pained look, he began to think of what remained of that obsession, his sometimes desperate wish to see her, and of the things that he had put in the house. By and large, her decoration had made the house worthy of some of the expense it had cost him, even if her taste in draperies was not to his liking.

However, save for the set of rattan chairs that he used to sit on, there was nothing left of his memory, of his passage through her life! Even if he had hoped to find some other evidence of his presence in this tormenting house, he knew, with that pristine knowledge acquired in the aftermath of death, that it was useless to indulge in that fantasy. She had cast him out with the termites, his old slippers, the empty perfume bottles, and the glossy magazines he had bought for her on his frequent overseas trips. He groaned, as only a dead man could, and said, "This was the house for which I canceled my annual leave, reduced the rations of beef, corn, and vegetable oil to my troops at the front, and inflated my per diem expenses when I went on that course on warfare."

When he was under Habiba's spell, the general had made a determined effort to respond to her most outrageous desires, sometimes taking some terrible risks. When, with her fickle mind, she decided to have an abortion, after she was the one who had wanted his child, the general had to appeal to a terrified doctor to perform it. This late in her pregnancy, the surgery could have killed her.

It was a terrible day for the general as he waited in his car imagining the worst. Three hours later, when he was allowed to take his mistress home, she looked like a fearsome ghost because she had lost so much blood. For the next two weeks he came to see her every day, bringing her not only the most ample supplies of medicine, provisions, flowers, and new clothes, but an intricately woven rug that, with brazen audacity, one of his Coral associates had smuggled into Malagueta, at his request, from Morocco.

Where were these presents now, if not in the trash heap of her memory? the dead man wondered.

Then it occurred to him that his wish to have her dead was illogical, cruel, and unnecessary: he would be tempting the hand of God, because he was willing to bet that eventually, in the labyrinth of her scheming woman's life, she would destroy herself. A sweet calm filled the soul of the dead man; for the first time in many years, the pleasant strains of a tune he used to sing as a cadet came to his lips. From the depths of his soul, he began to whistle its melodious cadence, and he thought he had never felt so free of anger, the anger he had carried all these years because of her. He got up from the chair not with the heavy martyrdom of a dead man, but with the pity he had not thought he could feel for Habiba Mouskuda. He touched her face. Then, as silently as he could, he left the house for the last time.

A light rain was falling as the dead man came down the steps lined with potted begonias into the garden, on his way back to his wanderings. Pausing for a while, he touched the leaves of his favorite oleander, smiled at a bittersweet memory, and turned up his collar against the rain. As if Habiba Mouskuda's other dead lovers had been observing what was going on, the drums of the rain suddenly became a crescendo—the end to a tragic love; a dead man's wish to clean out the debris in his previous life.

The rain drums were pounding the house when Habiba Mouskuda woke up and began to cry: so much rain in her soul asking for mercy that her tears could have washed the filth off of a swamp hog. She waited for the first light to dawn in her room, had a shower, got dressed, and, concerned only about saving her unborn child, headed for a bank owned by a Coral to withdraw all her savings from the bank, where General Augustus Kotay, at the height of their relationship, had advised her to keep her money, reasoning it was safe there from the government's hand. What she was going to do with five thousand dollars she did not disclose to anyone, but on that morning her face was lined with the worries of a woman badly in need of penance.

The Spanish Woman

Gabriel Ananias, the governor of the Central Bank, who was afraid for his life because of what he felt Tankor Satani would do to him for refusing to sell his beautiful house to the president, had been out that morning intending to withdraw some money from the same bank, with a view to escaping from the town. The sight of a beautiful woman on the streets of Malagueta that early in the day was not a rare phenomenon, given that some exotic Mandingo and Fulani women—deserters from Islam—had been attending the born-again church on the hill, run by a former beauty queen, and when they appeared in their splendid gowns and Malian gold jewelry, it drove even the most respectably married men crazy. During the sweet years as governor of the Central Bank, Gabriel Ananias's clandestine affairs had brought a bevy of those women to his philanderer's bed in the bungalow near the ocean. Prior to this morning, he thought he had slept with all the beautiful women in Malagueta, until he saw the malatta heading for the bank.

He stood riveted near his car and watched her as she crossed the intersection of Songhai and Timbuktu Streets, wearing an elaborate mantilla, with the mournful air of a bereaved woman that gave away the torment in her soul. The part of the city she had entered from her suburban house, ten miles away, was noisy with the usual riot of cars, *omolankes*—rickety pushcarts—intrepid beggars, some open gutters, and daredevil vendors: the typical street of vibrant music and colors, the hypnotic sounds of reggae competing with the gloriously sonorous beat of Congolese *soukous* and salsa, which took people's mind off the toil and grime of their existence as they shook their bottoms to the exotic rhythms. A pestilence of flies was buzzing about her as she walked past the decaying Odeon Cinema, where she had seen her first movie as a girl of thirteen. Hurrying to buy a matinee ticket, a boy pushed her out of the way, but she did not lose her incomparable dignity, and her disdain for the men who had been whistling all the time until she entered the bank was obvious.

Gabriel Ananias was still thinking about her when he went home to his disoriented wife, who was in the process of sorting out what to remove from the now hated house they were about to lose. After she had calmed down a bit, he told her about the most beautiful woman he had ever seen. "She must be a Spanish woman who has recently come to Malagueta to do penance for some terrible deeds," he said.

The thought of doing penance for whatever sin they might have committed that had led to their losing their beautiful house had been on Makita Ananias's mind . With the intuitive logic of a woman whose husband was a top banker and thus prone to all kinds of temptations, including beautiful women, she suddenly felt that her husband must have slept with the woman he had been describing and was trying to disguise his philandering with the excuse that she was someone he had only just encountered on the street. She gave him a long, searching look but did not try to probe his guilt, for she did not really want to know whether he had slept with her; it did not matter now, not when she was thinking about God, how life followed no written script, for it had dealt her a most cruel blow. She needed succor for the coming days of pain.

Not wanting to miss the four o'clock afternoon mass, she began slowly to tie a scarf around her head: a pillar of piety, poised, wealth having wrought a remarkable change in a former country girl. When she was at the door, and as though she could no longer control the soaring headache she had been feeling lately, she turned to her husband with a most inscrutable look, leaving him to fathom what was really on her mind.

"She is getting ready to do penance, all right," she said, referring to the woman in the mantilla, "but she does not have a single drop of Spanish blood in her veins. The woman you saw was the scandalous harlot Habiba Mouskuda, and if she has anything in her, it is the curse of the devil."

CHAPTER ELEVEN

The Fallen Angel

AMONGST TANKOR Satani's many victims—the chief justice, the innocent men who had a date with the hangman, those who were exiled or stripped of power and made to confess to crimes not committed—perhaps the biggest scalp was Gabriel Ananias's. Before his downfall he had been considered a man destined for great things with his extraordinary gifts: a sharp mind and wit, if a bit arrogant. Plus the story of his remarkable childhood had become the stuff of legend in the town. So no one expected him to fall for the cunning of the president. But in Gabriel Ananias, Tankor Satani found his most coveted prize, which left people stunned, mystified, and angry, when the young man became governor of the Central Bank. Even if it was no longer fashionable, given what the political class was up to, morality still counted for something, especially in the highly educated. When Gabriel Ananias went against that expectation, his downfall, six years later, brought some of the most caustic remarks ever heard in Malagueta: "What this goes to show is that pedigree is more important than wealth; if you don't know where you are going, know where you came from," said one of his own employees.

It was inevitable.

Years before he fled into exile, afraid that the presidential thugs were after him, Gabriel Ananias had renounced his belief in God. But for the unexplained arrival of some soldier ants and the divine intervention of a priest after an earthquake, he probably would have died before the age of ten. Yet, as though propelled by a tragic fate, he severed all connections to that childhood. His interest in entomology, as gratitude to the ants, had only lasted as long as he was at university, but did not survive the ravages of his soul when his unraveling began; proof to some people that being rich was not the same thing as having a soul. Those relatives that he had not known he had until they started turning up for favors when he was a big man were also sent packing as soon as he had helped them out of a difficult situation, which of course did not please them.

Had fate not taken a hand and brought him to the attention of Tankor Satani, he probably would have ended up following the wishes of the priest who had raised him and becoming a priest himself, or a professor.

Three years after meeting the president, Gabriel Ananias was appointed governor of the national bank. Six years later, unaware that Tankor Satani's radar had been tuned to all the goings-on in his life all along, the banker came crashing back to earth, where, as they say in Malagueta, "those that he left behind when he was going up were waiting for him." Of all his mistresses—those who had relished his expensive privileges at the bank resort and the golf club and the dinners at the Diners Club—the only one who did not forsake him was Jennifer Owens. He had not seen her in years, but she had kept in touch with him, reminding him of his duty to help others.

"You have been given a golden opportunity, so young in life, to help others. As a bank governor, use some of your profits to build schools, refurbish hospitals, and so on; the old man won't know."

Jennifer Owens was English and had briefly been Gabriel Ananias's mistress while she was crisscrossing the continent, in much the same way that a certain mystic named Sulaiman the Nubian, who had prophesied the founding of Malagueta over four hundred years ago, had done. A product of her class—upper middle, that is—Jennifer Owens was classy but unhappy with life and had attempted suicide after her Caribbean reggae lover had dumped her for an exotic samba dancer from Brazil.

"She drives me wild with that fire dance in a way you don't," the poor man confessed after the breakup.

When Jennifer Owens was planning her odyssey, she had meant it to be a soul-recovering trip, not one of those sterile touristy exercises. Thus she had been free to discover the unimagined. Armed with the images that she had seen daily on British television in London, she had expected to find mostly decay and squalor in parts of the cities and towns in the countries on her itinerary. The regular brownouts, whimsical children, dancing beggars, and, in some cases, the bare-faced officials trying to cheat everyone were part of her discoveries; but she had found Mali fascinating, discovering, in its marvelous antiquity and fantastic music by artists who were already the toast of the world, that she was in a very ancient land: poor but magical. In some of the old, dusty homes in the ancient city of Timbuktu, she discovered the greatest treasure of all: the seven hundred thousand yellowing manuscripts about literature and science, the astronomical and mathematical research by the professors during the golden centuries at the University of Sankore, and heard the poetry of the troubadours. In Senegal, she thought Dakar very "Frenchified," cosmopolitan, a "little Paris" in the tropics; but on those wide boulevards named after poets and philosophers, she saw the most dazzlingly colorful black women she had ever seen, walking in their splendid gowns as if they owned the world. "It was like a hundred versions of Mussorgsky's *Pictures at an Exhibition*," she wrote to a friend in London.

What had impressed her most was the beauty of the Dinka women in southern Sudan. When they were teaching her an intricate dance, she had, for the first time in her life, in that strictly traditional society, almost committed the ultimate sin of looking at another woman with desire. Awed by the vastness of the landscape, eating goat meat and drinking camel's milk, she had experienced, in one short month, a plenitude in her soul not hitherto imagined.

It was in Dar es Salaam, where she had been cooling off from her tour and buckling down to some "serious work as a correspondent," that she had met the banker from Malagueta at an IMF "Economic Restructuring" conference. Not only was she impressed with his view that it was the unjust economic policies in the world that were responsible for poverty and underdevelopment, she had offered her own opinion on the current situation of the continent: its village bumpkins had become presidents overnight, and were being helped by corrupt Western bankers to steal. "Hopefully, it is a teething problem; with time, everything will be all right," she concluded.

On his last day as governor of the Central Bank in Malagueta, Gabriel Ananias was sitting in his office thinking about her. Without relish, he smoked a cigar and drank a shot of whiskey to steady his nerves. He brought her letters out of a brown envelope, as though he hoped to find in them what he had lost: his soul, a direction in life, peace and fortitude, now that he was resigned to his fate. It was seven in the evening, all the other top officials at the bank had gone home, and, except for his driver waiting patiently in the Mercedes 350, he was alone. Dressed in immaculate green and white, the guards had begun their usual parade round the building, a whiff of the harmattan blowing in the November air making it a mildly cold evening. The central air conditioner had been turned off on the sixth floor, where his office was, as the air coming through an open window was pleasant. Now that thousands had been hatched after the end of the rains, the crickets had started to chirr on the hibiscus bushes, and his face momentarily seemed to lose the stress he was feeling in his heart. He went to the window and saw the distant harbor lights, the revolving cranes, and the ships of the various nations waiting to dock at the port, where so much of Malagueta's fortune and misfortune began. As soon as the crickets had lowered their chirring, the bats on the large cotton tree interrupted his solitude. With an eerie noise they had woken up to begin their nightly flight to other parts of the city. He suddenly felt lonely, terrified about the next day, thinking that life offered no planned route, no map to show how a man's destiny might play out from day to day.

Two hours earlier he had been to see Tankor Satani not in the Xanadu, but in the old house from where the old man would soon be hounded out by the ribaldry of the Russians and their exotic whores. Lately, Tankor had been going there to spend some time, "to get away from the nagging of my wife." Ostensibly, he had summoned the banker to talk about the state of the nation's economy.

"How are you, son?" the president greeted the banker in a friendly tone.

"Doing my best at the job, Excellency, sir."

They were in the dark wood-paneled study of the old man: some old faded copies of the *Economic Digest*, *Africa Confidential*, and other trade journals were displayed on an ottoman, showing that Tankor Satani was not an illiterate about the vagaries of economics. He let the young man make himself comfortable before offering him a drink, after which he began to prattle like a parrot about the latest collapse in the price of rubber and cacao on the world market and the slump in the price of coffee, which was bad for his country. The farmers could revolt; it was not a good year even for diamonds, what with the South Africans threatening to flood the market with the stuff, thanks to all that cheap black labor in their apartheid mines.

"It is not fair," Tankor Satani said with a note of rage, his sudden asthma attack sending him reaching for a pinch of snuff. "I do my best for this country, but some market speculators in Zurich or Johannesburg screw everything up with a stroke of their pen."

"That is the price we have to pay for our underdevelopment, Excellency, sir," the banker said, trying to give the old man a brief résumé of the vagaries of international trade.

"Underdevelopment, my foot! We are the producers but reap shit for our goods, which is why I put my trust in the only consolation that matters."

"In God?" the banker wondered.

"No. In the money I have saved, just in case the prices of commodities are wiped out. But that is not why I sent for you."

"What is it?" the banker asked. He thought it might have to do with another trip to Switzerland to see that the hydra of the president's account was breathing well.

"There are too many stubborn ghosts roaming around in this house at night, so I have decided to sell it to the state."

"But you have the Xanadu," the banker hastened to remind the president, thinking how ghastly it was for an old man to be chased out of his house by intrepid ghosts more pernicious than a bunch of drunken Russians and their harlots.

"Yes, yes," the president said, "but some new ghosts have begun to haunt the place; plus my wife nags me all the time. so I need another residence. I have thought long and hard about it, and I want you to do something for me, your father, after which I shall never ask you for another thing. Sell me your house and build yourself a new one; you are still young."

After this ominous, unexpected request, Gabriel Ananias felt his head spinning. Ganglia of pain and the memory of what had happened to Colonel Fillibo Mango seized his heart. But just when Gabriel Ananias thought he was doomed, the voice of a priest—a familiar note he had not heard in years—whispered in his ears with reassuring calm. "I shall save you this time, but you have lost your soul."

Thick, gray clouds sliced through the sky, leaving behind patches of darkness over the town, as Gabriel Ananias drove through the secluded diplomatic area to his mansion in the restricted Mansa Musa district of palatial houses. It was evening, the security guards were walking their guard dogs, and he noticed the police patrols deployed to see that no one other than the residents entered the gated community. On other nights, when he was being driven home, there had been nothing to fear besides the occasional armed robbers who were desperate to hijack some cars, but he had sent his driver home and was driving himself, wanting to think aloud. He might as well have been driving through a treacherous desert this evening, given the fear he felt in his heart. All he could think of was how to get to his house, to die in his own bed. But before he got there he had to take a detour, which was how he came to the intersection at Isatu Martins and Louisa Dundas Streets, where he almost crashed into a stationary TV van that was recording the latest confessions of a former beauty queen about the sorcery she had used to win top prizes during some past pageants.

"Confess your sins, just like me; God can see everything," she was going on; "repent or you will burn in the fire of hell."

"Amen" came from sections of the crowd.

If he had not been so troubled in his soul, he would have stayed to listen to the rhapsodic music of the gospel bands waiting to start playing. Buoyed by the testimony of the former beauty queen, a heavily pregnant woman was talking about "her miraculous conception" after ten years of barrenness "sleeping with all kinds of men," but Gabriel Ananias drove on, the conga drum rhythm of his own problems pounding in his head. To add to his pain, the aromatic blossoming of the seasonal flowers was bad for his asthma, as he had forgotten his medication at home: that house, the top prize of his life, which he was now in danger of losing. Suddenly the rich tapestry of life he thought he had sewn was turning out to be useless: his happiness, his standing with the president, and, worse, the thought that his mentor, Father O'Reilly, and the black ants had come back to haunt him.

Cold and biting, the Otutu had been blowing: a wind, like the harmattan, howling from Mount Agadi, its frivolous tongues scattering the dead leaves on the streets and sending some fashionable women hurrying home, doing their best to keep their calm as the wind created unholy havoc with their skirts, its voice rising to a high volume as it sent the caps of some bald men flying into the gutters. Grains of dust and sand whirled from building sites into his eyes, but Gabriel Ananias felt less threatened by the leaf storm than by the heat in his head. Scorpions scratched his throat and ate his confidence; he felt ashamed, forced to admit that Tankor Satani had deduced, with sly fox cunning and patience, that in spite of his earlier bravado, Gabriel Ananias was a boneless swine like the rest of the intellectuals, whose integrity could be compromised more cheaply than that of a penniless beggar.

He was not wearing a coat, and the cold razors of the wind were cutting deep into him, but he would have preferred to die of the cold than from shame; it was worse than how dogs were sometimes run over on the streets of Malagueta. What a horror it was to feel like rotten flesh, when all along he had thought he was a big and powerful barracuda feeding off the minnows that represented the sum of the lives of most men and women in the town. The ominous clouds now hanging over his future began to darken when a car pulled alongside his Mercedes, and he experienced a liquid terror when the windows were rolled down. Two of the occupants leaned over to stare and point at him, and he felt the worms in his belly tighten. Even more menacingly, the riders dropped shards of pots and glass, cowry beads, and ancient coins on the road, before tossing the headless body of a chicken at his Mercedes. Familiar with public religious rituals, Gabriel Ananias realized it was a *sara*, a sacrifice to drive away evil spirits but that could also be used to harm someone. A chill ran down his spine as he thought that the old man had probably sent his goons after him to bump him off the road, after which the president would seize his house with a presidential fiat. But then he heard one of the women in the cars singing a familiar Baptist song, and he was able to relax a bit. They were not out to kill him; the riders had just witnessed the soap opera, in which the beauty queen, in a final act of contrition, had made a donation of her luxury car, jewelry, and gowns to the church, and they were offering a sacrifice to help with the cleansing of her soul and to welcome her into the kingdom of the redeemed. All the same, he was in for a small shock.

"Get out of the car," one of the riders yelled at Gabriel Ananias as the car came to a complete stop, cutting him off. "People like you ought to be ashamed to use up so much petrol when others cannot afford one meal a day."

He came down from his car, pulled Gabriel Ananias out of his Mercedes, grabbed his coat collar and shook him up a bit, and was back in his car laughing, driving off before the frightened banker had recovered his wits.

Coming on top of his conversation with the president, such public angst hit him hard as he finished the last stretch home. When he reached his house, the guards rushed to open the massive gates, surprised that the banker was driving himself. Feeling as if he wanted to vomit, Gabriel Ananias got out of the car and rushed to one of the many bathrooms in the house. He was grateful to find that his wife was fast asleep and would not see the terror in his eyes.

A swarm of beetles creeping on the outside of one of the windows added to his fear that he was doomed. His lips trembled as he took a long, hard look at his face, lined with worries, tormented, cracked like a coconut shell, prematurely aged, although he was only thirty-eight: a man worn out, in spite of his wealth. Unlike the glossy black it had been only a few years ago, his skin was now a pallid brown; he touched his forehead and it felt rough; the lines of his brow were roots that he had not been aware of until then. His eyes were metallic disks smudged at the corners with a tragic arrogance: definitely a man who had lost his way in life but was desperately trying to find the route back to sanity. He let the water drip from a golden faucet for a while, and washed his face and hands before turning off the flow. Then, woodenly, he walked to the bedroom with a deep pain in his heart, the kind he had not felt since he lost his grandparents in an earthquake.

It was a large room, thirty feet by forty, with huge windows adorned with flaming gold and pale mustard African batik draperies. A built-in wardrobe of deep glossy mahogany took up twenty feet of space, and the floor was covered in an expensive arabesque carpet he had obtained in gratitude from a Moroccan whom he had helped with a most difficult proposition at the bank. The smell of slowly burning sandalwood in an urn rose in a soft mist. Unaware of the disaster that had crept into their house, Makita was fast asleep under an almond quilt in a huge four-poster bed of black and gold finish. Pine needles pricked Gabriel Ananias's heart as he stood for a brief moment looking at the woman he had married. He had always been proud of his wife's sense of decor, but now that the house was the source of his unhappiness, he thought he might as well be standing in a nest of vipers, spiders, and venomous snakes. She woke up slowly, obviously having heard him come in, rubbed the sleep out of her eyes, beat a soft spot on the bed, and invited him to sit next to her.

"It is over." Gabriel Ananias found the courage to tell his wife about their new situation.

"What is over?" Makita asked, shocked by the terror in her husband's voice.

"Tankor Satani wants our house."

"What for?"

"His vanity; to add to the others he has. It is either the house or my life."

"Lord have mercy," she said, "fate is ugly!" And began to cry.

CHAPTER TWELVE

The Mermaid's Comb

AFTER NOT dreaming about Henri Christophe for a long time, Tankor Satani was beginning to feel lost without the mysterious voice of the legendary king. It was one thing to have eunuchs practicing sorcery for him, some obsequious civil servants, an emasculated military, and his good friend Moustapha Ali-Bakr to call on, but they were mere mortals, unlike the dead, whose eyes went into realms unknown to the living, so Tankor had begun to despair that the old monarch had abandoned him for another chosen one. Increasingly he felt like a boat drifting on a turbulent ocean, tossed around like a small raft, and he missed what had in effect become camaraderie with a mysterious dead man who had risen from a two-hundred-year-old grave, "across two big waters," to navigate tidal waves, hurricanes, and tsunamis, borne on the backs of dolphins and whales, to come to where some former slaves had once done well but had now lost much sway. Given such an extraordinary journey, Tankor ought to have been suspicious of the old king, as he was probably using the visits to re-ennoble the descendants of the ex-slaves, but he dismissed the conjecture: the king was much too sincere to mislead a poor president, and was in fact the only one who had really looked into the depths of his soul. So when Henri Christophe reappeared a week later to Tankor Satani during a thunderous outburst in Malagueta, the president woke up feeling deeply elated.

On his previous visits he had appeared with his retinue, and later only with his harem, and had spoken of the mountain where Tankor Satani would later build the Xanadu. But now Henri Christophe was alone and had chosen an ocean without waves for this visit. He had landed at the extreme end of an isolated beach, over which a narrow moon showed the only sign of life: a woman sitting leisurely, with parts of her legs covered with grains of sand and with an aureole of fire blazing above her. Henri Christophe pointed to the stunning presence of the woman with his index finger.

"Go there," the old slave said to the president. "You will find what you have always wanted, but it will probably cost you your life; then you will have become me: so good-bye."

The dream left him completely confused, yet Tankor Satani was grateful when he woke up, happy that the ex-slave had not completely forgotten about him. A week later, convinced that he had in fact become Henri Christophe, he resisted the urge to go to church on Good Friday to pray for the damnation of the souls of the judges; instead, he went to what he thought was the beach on which Henri had appeared. The sky was brilliant blue, and a school of sandpipers was flying over the ocean. Leaving his guards behind at a great distance, Tankor Satani walked to a secluded area where he was certain no one was swimming. The enigmatic dream was still on his mind, and he thought of Christ walking on water, performing the miracle of the ten loaves and two fishes, but decided it was useless to confuse Christian beliefs with Henri's magical and enigmatic posturing. He recalled Henri's advice: "Don't confuse what you *see* with what white people think they *know.*"

He forgot about Christ and plunged deeper into introspection until a strange sight suddenly caught his attention. He focused his eyes intensely, breathing hard as he slowed down so that his approach would not be heard, and his tennis shoes were barely audible in the sand. Coming closer, he was almost blinded by a yellow translucence, and he felt his heart nearly leap out of his cage. Sitting in a languorous pose was a honey-brown mermaid with the luminous tail of a barracuda that some people said could kill a man with a single blow. Unlike Christ's crown of thorns on Good Friday, the yellow light haloed the mermaid with a luminosity that made Tankor Satani dizzy for a few seconds. Once he was certain he was not seeing an apparition, he recovered from the stunning presence, determined not to miss a chance in a million in a man's life.

Since time immemorial, people in the region had been talking about the mermaids: beautiful, elusive, all of them, ageless and enticing, although few people had actually seen one of those Mammy Watas; that is, except for the odd fisherman or two, or young men who, while swimming, according to legend, had been captured by the mermaids, who put the young men in a trance before seducing them. Tankor Satani had heard that the mermaids always had golden combs tucked into their hair. The mermaids always gave the combs to the men they had seduced: a magical thing that brought incomparable wealth and made the men the envy of those less fortunate. Sometimes the mermaids would come to the shore to relax, which was when daredevil men would sneak up on them to steal their combs so they would become wealthy. Tankor Satani was financially very well off, what with diamond sales rising, but felt that the years ahead of him could do with a fabulous addition to his wealth.

Doing his best not to be heard, he moved away from the blinding light of this mermaid's tail and went to hide behind a small growth of blue water lilies. Stunned by his discovery, he watched the mermaid as she combed her hair with a delectable air, her fingers, shaped like liana palms, weeding out ferns from her thick coils.

Like a condemned man awaiting execution, Tankor Satani felt his heart pounding quickly, but he remained immobile for a while, calling on the queen of fortune to smile on him. The mermaid's back was turned to him; feverishly he prayed that she would put down her comb. Time stood still.

As he had done on that memorable day when the foundation stone for the Xanadu had been laid, he began, quietly, to call on his mother to come from her grave, this time to grant him his last wish: to help him banish the terror and unhappiness of old age, which without wealth was like hardened alabaster clay not useful to anyone. The mermaid had finished combing her hair; but, like a tourist from a cold hemisphere, she seemed to enjoy being on the lonely stretch of white sand, relishing the tropical sun. Quite leisurely, she began to cornrow her hair. Tankor Satani's heart was about to explode, but he waited for a few seconds before seizing the moment that was to change his life forever.

Using a leopard's cunning stealth, he crawled toward her, keeping his eyes on the fire glowing from her tail. A lazy sea wave held the mermaid's attention; lost from their flock, some swallows were cruising in the sky looking for direction back to their sanctuary as a fire began to blaze from the mermaid's tail. Relaxed, transfixed by those migratory birds, she was unaware of the predatory feet of the man moving up on her.

Though aware that he could be flattened by a blow by that tail, Tankor Satani advanced quietly, determined to hedge his bet between dying instantly and living to an age when death would be mean, painful, and ugly. Between that moment when a man dies or is reprieved from the guillotine, he snatched the comb and just missed being silenced forever by the terrible whiplash of the tail. He turned and ran as fast as his feet would carry him, not daring to look back to see whether he was being followed, for at that moment the only thing that mattered was that he was leaving one world, however good, for something he hoped would be more fantastic, infinitely more joyous; moving away from the cacti and scorpions of his sixty-eight years. In the purple light of the evening, he saw the see-saw of pain and happiness on which he had lived much of his life beginning to disintegrate as, with the lightning sped of an untamed mare, he fled to where his car was parked.

"Drive quickly," he told the astonished driver before his guards, who had been smoking weed, realized Tankor Satani had returned from his solitary walk. He told the driver to head back to his house, terrified that something ghastly was about to happen to him, because a terrible heat was almost burning his pocket. "Step on the gas!" he yelled.

The poor man had never driven so furiously through the crooked and crowded streets of Malagueta, as he scattered the straggly chickens, mangy dogs, and *omolanke* pushcart drivers and almost crashed into a truckload of butane gas cylinders. When the driver was finally let inside the compound by the petrified night guards, Tankor ran out of the car, ignoring the guards, who had lined up, ready with the usual "Good evening, President, sah, how de beach, sah?"

The golden comb was now burning a hole in his pocket, and he barely had time to run into the small room near the study, where he kept his grigri, amulets, and other objects of sorcery that his eunuchs had given to him as protection against his enemies

It was an eerily dark place, a sorcerer's apprentice's magical den, where no one besides him had ever been, not even his wife. Hurriedly he opened a small black box and put the comb in it. After locking the door firmly, he rushed to his study, where he immediately fell asleep, deeply exhausted by his cheetah-like dash. When he woke up four hours later and went back to the small room, he was stunned by a terrible luminance. Even more incredible, an ominous female voice spoke to him:

"Give me back my comb," the voice said.

Tankor Satani was assailed by the feeling that the ocean had found its way to his house and that he was drowning after being miraculously thrown off his bed. He felt dizzy; violent waves were tossing him about, carrying him into abysmal depths, where galloping green-eyed sea monsters were rushing toward him. He heard the voice again: "Give me back my comb and I shall give you anything you want."

Tankor Satani regained his sanity and rushed out of the small room. When he was back in his study, he realized he had not been dreaming; a woman's voice had actually spoken to him. Nonetheless, thinking only of the enormous fortune that the mermaid's golden comb was supposed to bring him, he dismissed the thought of death, willing to tempt fate. Here, finally, was confirmation that he had indeed become Henri Christophe. In a pompous voice he said, "Not until I die will you get your comb back!"

Life had never been so sweet, so unimaginably wonderful for him.

CHAPTER THIRTEEN

A Ballad for Her Dead Lovers

SINCE COMING back from her visit to Pallo, the feeling that she was going to die from a capricious whim of fate had haunted Habiba Mouskuda. Assailed by the thought of her dead lovers visiting her again, she lost her appetite for lovemaking and began to eat with frightening gluttony. Thinking that they might be after her child, as she had not given any of them one, she decided to make her peace with the dead men, although she was not really afraid of death. At first she planned a large *awujor*—a feast, as old as the founding of the city, that the Yoruba people had brought from Nigeria and that had sometimes kept the dead temporarily happy. But she soon rejected its divination and eat-and-drink rituals for something dreamed up in the deepest recesses of her fantasy: the kind of grandeur she hoped would keep the dead men repose in an Arcadian afterlife. Two weeks after withdrawing her savings from the bank, she went to a boutique to buy a beautiful black designer gown. When she tried it on she looked very glamorous, if somewhat somber, and her allure was enhanced by the matching genuine pearls on her neck and ears and the silver brooch, inlaid with a small diamond, gleaming on her ample left breast.

"You look like a queen, Madam; any man will go crazy for you in dis dress," the boutique owner said gleefully, hoping for a good sale on what had otherwise been a bad day.

She left the house one morning with the regal bearing of an Italian diva to drive to the center of town, her allure and solemnity heightened by her black satin gloves, embroidered at the rim with a modest show of gold, and a small black handbag to match. The air was cool, and her rosy cheeks, flushed in the first flowers of her pregnancy, added to her allure. Even with her air of mourning she was stunning, wearing the same mantilla in which Gabriel Ananias had seen her. She parked the car on a quiet street and, as on the day when she had withdrawn her money from the bank, crossed the intersection of Samora Machel and Sékou Touré Streets, careful not to be squeezed in by the people walking in front of the haphazard mess of kiosks or the daredevil vendors selling everything from milk, cigarettes, candles, and soaps to antibiotics. The spread of those kiosks and sidewalk goods had turned much of the downtown into an open, crowded market, discomforting many of the old families who couldn't even get to their homes without having to walk over all kinds of wares in front of them.

A large crowd near the National Lottery building was fuming over the latest thievery of tickets by the officials as Habiba walked past them; the fricassee sellers were calling out "hot pepper chicken" to the workers rushing off to their respective jobs; and someone was filming the goings-on at the lottery with a Polaroid camera. Disgusted with the garrulousness of the Corals rushing off to the banks with large deposits of money, she crossed over to another side of the street, near the central Catholic cathedral, in front of which sat some blind beggars, into whose begging bowls she dropped a few coins "for your blessings."

With the beggars' chant of "Thank you, Madam, God will bless you" ringing behind her, she came to the basement of an old house built in the style of the American Deep South by the original settlers. Slowly she navigated her way through its dark vestibule. When she caught the whiff of formaldehyde, she knew right away that she was in the right place: the business of an undertaker. She walked in and daintily removed her gloves. If she was afraid of being in that dead men's den, with its unpolished coffins of dark wood in various stages of manufacture, she did not let it show; after all, she had not expected the place to be redolent of roses, bright and airy, and it was not unusual that she thought she noticed what appeared to be several bottles of half-drunk liquor, considering that making coffins required a stout mind most of the time. She sat on a stool, crossed her legs, wiped her brow with an embroidered handkerchief, and signaled to the undertaker.

"I have come to order three caskets, made of the finest mahogany, for which I am going to pay in full, to be delivered within a week. So make them look nice," she said.

The undertaker was a balding man in his fifties, puffy-eyed, clearly needing sleep, who had been napping in a chair when Habiba walked in, but at the mention of a full payment for a job of three coffins he came to her like a sprinting genie.

"What a great tragedy must have happened to you, Madam, for you to need three of these boxes at the same time, because in all my life I have never heard of anyone having to bury three corpses at the same time."

"That only goes to show how little you know about the power of love over death," Habiba Mouskuda replied, dabbing her involuntary tears with the embroidered handkerchief.

Why had he had not heard about the three dead people in the two o'clock afternoon obituary announcements on the government radio? the undertaker wondered. Given the way people would react to such a slight in Malagueta, the undertaker decided that the woman's suffering was so great she wanted to mourn in private, and that it had nothing to do with the incompetence of the radio announcers. With his years of dealing with grieving relatives reflected in his kind eyes, he felt a deep pain for Habiba and promised her he and his assistant would work four days and nights to have her caskets ready.

"For your great loss, madam, we shall choose the oldest wood: mahogany seasoned in carbolic acid that had been left to dry in the sun for years," the grateful undertaker said, trying to comfort her.

"Yes, yes," Habiba said, and was about to add, "don't forget that I am paying you good money," but decided it would be indecorous, considering what she was going to do with the coffins.

Over the next two days the undertaker and his assistant worked very hard on the wood to get rid of the pigeon and rat droppings encrusted by those annoying pests. Thinking of the stifling heat and the rapacious mouths of termites that were bound to finish off the wood in the grave before the bones of a dead man had even begun to disintegrate, they injected a half gallon of turpentine into the wood, and screwed four glittering brass handles into each coffin, reasoning that such a well-dressed woman must be burying high-society people who were entitled to a little chic in death.

As promised, the three caskets were delivered at the end of the week, when a van, its curtains drawn, pulled up unnoticed into Habiba Mouskuda's garage late at night. Out of genuine pity for her, the undertakers had brought six sawhorses on loan and offered to spend the night keeping wake with her, with a little rum of course, but Habiba Mouskuda rejected their offer. "This is a rite for which only one mourner is required," she said.

While waiting for the delivery, she had stripped her walls bare of the watercolors and African masks that adorned them, and an eerie feeling of grief permeated the house after she had replaced the flowery draperies with silk-laced white ones. Asked how the men should arrange the coffins so that it would be easy to put the corpses inside, she thought for a while before replying with serene dignity, "Put them side by side so that in death they would love me just as they did when they were alive."

She closed the door after the undertakers had left, drew the draperies tight, and put a match to some sandalwood in an urn; then she stripped naked and ran her long, delicate fingers over the small calabash of her pregnancy. Sitting in a straight-backed chair, she sought some comfort from the Pentecostal hymns spinning on her record player. Although the jewelry she had worn on the day she went to order the coffins no longer adorned her neck and ears, and her face was pale, she had never looked more stunning than she did now, visibly pregnant and naked.

A low rumbling noise in her stomach reminded her that she was hungry, but she did not feel the need for food except for the flanges of strength she needed to see her through the night. All the same, at nine o'clock, after she had eaten a bowl of chicken and celery soup, she did something she had never done before. In the amber light, she poured herself two jiggers of whiskey that she kept only for the purpose of entertaining Theodore Iskander when he visited her, but who, at that time, was abroad attending some philosophical seminar. When she began to feel the alcohol cruising through her body, she pushed an armchair into the living room and sat in front of the three coffins. Blood surged in her veins, and her face reddened a bit as her heart, set on this mystic journey, began to pour out the dark raptures of wine for her dead lovers. She touched the insides of the coffins and trembled at the feel of the red velvet trimmed with gold at the fringes, this being the first time she had felt how warm the inside of a coffin was: a strange discovery, considering that death itself to her felt cold and impersonal.

A longtime indulgence in make-believe helped her to create the illusion that the dead men were really there, and she imagined them rising in their coffins, wearing their best suits, reaching out to touch her, all of them stunned by her dramatic overtures. However temporary the moment was, she felt her dead lovers were happy, as her heart, filled with a sudden rush of love, poured out a rich, sparkling wine to transform their lives from the discarded scripts of her past life into the lives of men worthy of a whole vineyard, where they could drink and feel that their thirst had been quenched by the ambrosia of her full lips.

Inspired by her delicious fantasy, she raised her hands as though she was about to address a gallery of all the generous men who had loved her and other women like her. Slowly, with a crane's elegant neck motions, she began to execute a great ballerina's lyrical dance, her head thrown backward as she pirouetted round each of the coffins, urged on by a plaintive orison rising in her heart, her tall, beautiful figure casting shadowy whorls in the dark. When she parted her lips, her prayer, sweet like the song of a hummingbird, was transformed into a paean for Colonel Fillibo Mango, "*the sweetest of my lovers,*" and was assailed by the feeling that Colonel Fillibo Mango's broken neck had been made perfect again.

She looked as dreamy as an odalisque but was regal as she climbed into the coffin her heart had assigned to the gentle colonel and lay in a pose that, in spite of the gravity of the occasion, did not dull her glamour. She closed her eyes, and her hair was spread out like a wild bouquet of rich, black luster against the honey of her skin, from which oozed a sweet smell of grapes. With the alcohol's electricity rousing her, she asked the colonel to allow her some space in this home she had now built for him so that they could lie together, united forever. She expected Colonel Fillibo Mango, a good man, to tell her that he had forgiven her and that he had also overcome his despair over not being allowed to serve in the Foreign Service. Now that she had abandoned her gypsy woman's wild life, she told him about the books on love she had been reading, and the wine of atonement tasted sweet on her lips. She thought she had closed all the windows to avoid being seen, but one was suddenly blown open. Then it was that she heard a flock of evening orioles singing lyrically on the tamarind trees, so that it was as though she had touched the soul of the colonel and it was he that had inspired the birds to sing.

After a while she climbed out of the coffin, sat on a chair, and continued to speak to the colonel: "*Here is where your head is resting, Fillibo, next to my full breasts; here is where you always wanted me to caress you, between the penis and the balls; you unleashing that poet's passion that made you so charming, although I did not appreciate it then.*"

During the next two nights she performed the same ritual, climbing into the remaining two coffins and lying in the favorite position in which each man used to make love to her. The ripe, firm fruits of her breasts were heavy in her hands as she offered them to the dead men, in the desperate hope that now that she was giving them the love she had not shown them when they were alive, they would rest in peace. With General Augustus Kotay she was the most generous, since not only had he built a house for her, but he was also the oldest of the men and had left his wife and four children without a father.

She took her necromancy to unbelievable extremes, fasting for half of the day before the last night of her séance, drinking only enough fluids to keep her pregnancy nourished. Whereas for the others she had not worn anything, she put on a string of colorful glass beads around her waist and began to dance shaking her hips the way General Augustus Kotay had liked her to, to arouse him before they made love. Once again she was his desert whore, "*and you can do whatever you want with me, Augustus; but only for tonight, as I am no longer what I was, General.*"

Beads of sweat were running down her cheeks; in her delirium, assuaged by the feeling that she had really been transformed from the vixen the dead men had known into a cooing lovebird, she once again offered her ponderous breasts to the general, "*as this was how you liked them; always with a boy's hunger, in the milky way; me mothering you, you crying on my breasts, after those terrible afternoons spent listening to Tankor Satani raving about how the courts were tearing up his bills.*"

She was still lying in the general's coffin when sleep finally overcame her. But unlike her previously tormenting dreams, her dream that night saw her in paradise, her desert roses blooming alongside General Augustus Kotay's newly revitalized oleander. A military band was playing the beautifully haunting "Nimrod" from Elgar's *Enigma Variations*, which the general had liked a lot and had requested to be played for him in the event of a peaceful, natural death. At the first light of dawn Habiba Mouskuda woke up, fresh as carnations, to the early barbets singing in the black plum tree in her garden. Filled with a kind of bliss that she had never before experienced, she felt she had placated the angry spirits of her three dead lovers.

CHAPTER FOURTEEN

The Vultures of the Angels

FOR FIVE months, Tankor Satani had not been seen being driven in his custom-built limousine, with its top down, when his guards would create a laxative panic amongst the people because the old man had suddenly developed a prurient desire to watch the naked tourist girls sunbathing on the beach. While he was holed up in the newly completed Xanadu, lampoons had suddenly appeared all over the town crudely depicting him copulating with a nanny goat. Or sometimes it was a three-legged dog that was said to have caught his fancy, which went to show that although the poor people sometimes went to bed hungry, penury had not dulled their imaginations. Poems, written in a sensual style by Bafta poets, told of his living in a chimerical world where he had undergone changes to his form now that he was too busy to fly to Stuttgart to see the famous Dr. Wolfgang Benger for his regular transfusion of youthful blood, and to check on the latest line of Mercedes Benz cars.

His prolonged absence not only fueled the rumors about his health, it fed speculations that he was suffering from a horrible disease that could not be cured by any regular doctor. So it wasn't long before the deduction was made that someone had finally got close enough to "do him in": spread some *warapay,* the ancient Yoruba magical powder potent in sorcery, on him, or that he had made a mistake while reciting the arcane words to the genie they suspected he owed much of his wealth to, and that he was now in the final spasms of death.

"Debul done catch de president!" a drinker said as he sipped his palm wine in a baffa bar.

It was an illusion.

Tankor Satani's cabinet ministers knew otherwise: his death was unimaginable. Determined to quell any further rumors about a "devil catching the president," his special security unit hauled some of the rumormongers off to jail. After a meal of dried biscuits and bitter tea and countless hours of wakefulness in a room stinking of the stale odor of urine, they were forced to sign confessions admitting they had been put up to their diabolical acts by some underground opposition figures. In the same mysterious way in which they had appeared, the lampoons were removed overnight and hurriedly replaced with brilliantly colorful banners showing him alive and well, feeding on grilled barracudas in the Xanadu, safe in the mysteries of a wizened old man trying to cheat death one more time.

It was also at this time that Tankor Satani, as though convinced he was beyond reproach, unleashed his wrath on the publisher and printer of the house that had published the book by Colonel Fillibo Mango, who had been executed for his action. Carrying out the presidential order one morning, the prime minister, Enos Tanu, dispatched a truckload of the much feared security unit to the publisher's house. The truck driver turned into the street of the printing house with such speed that a large crowd came out to see where he was going. Before the troops had even alighted, the unfortunate publisher knew they were coming to his business with a most dreaded purpose. With an assortment of weapons—sledgehammers, crowbars, pickaxes—the troops smashed the doors of the publishing house open and began to demolish the printing presses. They stomped on the metallic plates, ripped the film negatives to pieces, smeared the dummies and engravings with oil, tore giant rolls of printing paper to shreds, emptied the large ink drums onto the floor, tossed the printers' types and other essentials out of the windows, and left the terrified publisher in no doubt about what would happen in the event of his publishing another offensive book about Tankor Satani.

"Next time we won't stop at the printing press, but will blow up your house," the leader of the troops said to him.

For a short while such tactics created the right amount of terror in some quarters of the city. But unknown to many people, there was one thing that had been troubling Tankor Satani's conscience for a long time, which was why he had not been seen in public during the nights of the lampoons: the latest batch of executions he had ordered had finally come to haunt him in the palace.

When completed, the Xanadu had a dozen bedrooms, but his favorite was the one that offered a grand view of what was left of the hitherto splendid forest, east of the palace. In the enchanting twilight, Tankor Satani would be seen gazing at the forest mushroomed with specks of iridescent flowers under membranes of dark clouds, sitting there as though he regretted the damage done to the landscape. When he was not in his study, it was in that room that he sometimes slept, to get away from "the nagging of this woman" over what Sallay felt was his insatiable hunger for material things so late in his life, or over how he had forced the banker Gabriel Ananias to go into exile, or over his executing the colonel and others. But falling asleep, even in that favorite den, had become difficult lately: much to Tankor Satani's shock, the angry faces of the condemned men, especially that of Colonel Fillibo Mango, had been coming to torment him.

One week before the colonel was executed, his estranged wife, Rikiya, had gone to see Tankor Satani to plead for her husband's life. "I know you are upset about his book, Excellency, sir, but don't send an innocent man to his grave when his mother still has black hair on her head."

Tankor Satani did not even lift his head from the comic book that he was reading before he replied. "He should have thought about that before he slandered me."

"Then think of his children, and spare his life for them," she cried, dropping down to her knees.

He promised he would think about it and said he might even consider dispatching him into exile as the ambassador to Washington, if her husband would confess. On the night before the colonel was executed, Tankor Satani allowed Rikiya a last visit to her husband because the president did not want it said that he had denied a condemned man's last wish to see his wife. When Rikiya saw her husband for the last time, she was struck by his incomparable dignity and stoicism, and his unbelievably cheerful mood lifted her spirit. He stood erect in his cell to show that months of being locked up had not dampened his spirit, and she thought he had never looked so noble and patrician. Still adamant about his innocence, but prepared for the worst, the colonel removed his wedding ring and gave it to his wife; then, calm and resolute, he kissed her good-bye, his last wish being that she would remember him for the courage with which he intended to die.

"Don't worry too much," he said, wiping her tears. "A man has to die, and I prefer to die standing up rather than think of you kissing Tankor Satani's bloodstained hands."

Rikiya left the cell thinking of her impeding widowhood and had to summon all of her dignity so that she would not collapse. On her way home, as she sat next to her driver, they drove in front of the prison, where the executioner was already oiling the ancient gallows on which her husband would be hanged. Thinking about the shattering effect that her husband's death would have on her, she saw a truck carrying a load of pigs on its way to the slaughterhouse, and was stunned as it crashed into the big Cotton Tree in the center of town and sent thousands of bats flying toward the hills. It was the first time in living memory that all the bats had left that tree in daylight: a sign to her that Tankor was about to hang an innocent man.

Colonel Fillibo Mango and eight other innocent men were hanged on a gray morning when there was not even a cloud visible. On the previous night, helmeted riot police had cordoned off the district near the prison with barbed wire; a noticeable gloom hung over Malagueta, and a thousand stars suddenly disappeared in the sky. It was March, always hot in Malagueta, yet it had rained all night and a mysteriously cold air was blowing from the ocean, sending a shudder through the veins of even the most hardened drinkers in the bars. On this night, unlike other nights, they were alone, because even the most intrepid ladies of the night, anticipating the event, had refused to go to the clubs.

"One of those men was my lover, and I don't want to see his face while I am with another man," a weeping woman said, and cursed Tankor Satani.

After the executions, and as though he dreaded public opprobrium, Tankor Satani remained in the Xanadu. To the handful of visitors allowed to see him, he gave the appearance of being at peace with the world, but nothing could be more false, for one month later, while he was sleeping alone in the study, he woke up shaking because a deep growling, like that of a deranged lion in his room, had disturbed his sleep. Even before he heard the footsteps in the hallway, he knew that the executed men had entered the Xanadu.

The heavy doors leading to the ballroom flew open, the metal windows rattled, and the furniture in all the rooms began to move as the dead men came into the corridors to unleash their wrath on the portraits hanging on the walls. His wife was spending the weekend with one of their children, and his guards were snoring away in another room, so only Tankor Satani was aware of the invisible entry of the dead men. Stymied by the knowledge that there was nothing the guards could have done for him anyway, because the dead were immune to bullets, he remained sitting on his bed in a state of fright, listening to the relentless feet parading in the palace, and he almost peed on himself as the stray dogs in the distant neighborhood began to howl that something was rotten in Malagueta. That was when the palace guards finally woke up.

"They are attacking de Pa!" they yelled, thinking that some disloyal soldiers were staging a coup. Thrown into frenzy by what sounded like wild stallions in the hallway, they rushed to Tankor Satani's aid, imagining that the horses were really soldiers; but when they opened fire, all they saw were griffon vultures flying out of the windows.

"It is all right," Tankor said to the confused guards when they finally got to his room. "Men who die before their time become angels and fly in and out of houses like vultures." He telephoned his wife for comfort, but Sallay cut him off before he had finished telling her about the mysterious vultures.

"That is God's way of punishing you for bringing those eunuchs to my house, stupid man! And also for the men you have executed. You see, the vultures came for you when you were alone," she said, and poured herself a glass of brandy with relish. He heard the loud noise as she slammed the phone.

Tankor Satani lacked knowledge of how intransigent the dead could be, so was unprepared for their persistent assault throughout the week. On those hellish nights when he sat trembling in a straitjacket position, drinking brandy and ginger to stave off his insomnia, they came back to taunt him. Laughing, the dead men filled the house with an operatic moan that shattered the chandeliers in the dining room. Sometimes, when he thought he had been given a break, he would hear their brazen legs strolling with an energetic stride only the dead could master. He listened to them as they slipped into every nook and cranny, like mongooses in search of snakes. The glittering fires of their angry marauding lions' eyes were trained on him when he entertained the diplomats from the Middle East, with whom he was discussing the expansion of trade; those stubbornly death-cheating men gave him no respite from their anger, making their presence known when he was busy with the speculators from Europe, working out what to do with the money he had stashed away in those Swiss banks to grow there like a bloated hydra in the event of his overthrow. A cold wind had been whistling on Mount Agadi for days, yet he felt so hot inside that he had to turn on the drone of the air-conditioning unit. But not even that could silence the locomotive sirens of the dead men or cool their hot temper from rattling the safe where he kept the Book of Secrets for all his holdings, which was more guarded than the cabinet's red papers of the country.

One evening, when he thought the worst had passed, he was disabused of that illusion when the palace began to shake to its foundation with a rumbling seismic tremor that frightened the pigeons away from their roosts in the eaves and gave Samson the chimp a case of severe hiccups in his cage. Mercilessly, the dead men went after the expensive art collection in the Xanadu, concentrating on the bronze statues; they smashed the porcelain Chinese jars, ceremonial Hausa swords, Shona bibelots, Mauritanian trunks inlaid with gold, stuffed animal heads, the alabaster collection of meerschaum pipes in the study, and the highboys in his bedroom. His favorite Hepplewhite chair, which the last English governor of Malagueta had donated to the nation, was lifted and sent flying out of a window before the dead men departed. On another night, as though the dead amanuensis's book had been turned into an orchestral suite louder than even the crescendo when September was giving birth to its wayward hurricanes, a terrible wind smashed the grand piano with such a fury that its keys began to play the mournful second movement of Beethoven's *Eroica* Symphony, marked *Marcia funebre.*

"Goddamn it," Tankor moaned in his torment. "I did not know the dead could be so relentless in their revenge."

It seemed he was heading toward a horrible end at the hands of those implacably nondead men. To die so soon after finishing the Xanadu, after snatching the mermaid's comb, deprived of the chance to enjoy the autumnal glut of his wealth in those Swiss banks, was a horror too ghastly to contemplate. He had never felt so vulnerable, so terrified, shocked that even his eunuchs' sorcery could not hold the fury of the dead men at bay. He racked his brain for days and came up with the fantastic idea of sending the dead men's children away to the best schools in England, a move he felt they would approve of, given their predilection for things English when they were alive. But while his diplomats were hurriedly contacting the right universities, another idea suddenly gripped him: he would arrange tax-free lucrative business deals for their wives and declare a moratorium on execution. It would leave the country wondering whether he was getting soft in his old age.

Filled with foreboding for their future if the dead men continued their assault on the palace, Tankor Satani also sent a distress letter to his old friend Moustapha Ali-Bakr, temporarily living in clover in Lebanon on the profits of his diamond business in Malagueta. "The graveyard is beginning to bite," Tankor wrote, referring to the belief in Malagueta that the dead do not sleep; they have "teeth" when they go to the other realm.

The news could not have come at a more inopportune time for the Coral, who was busy preparing for the lavish wedding of one of his daughters and had to think of the three hundred guests that had been invited. But a threat to his friend from the underworld, especially as it had been going on for a while, required all the help he could give to keep the dead out of the Xanadu. "Bastards, bastards," he exploded. "I can't allow dead men to ruin the life of my friend." Hurriedly, he sent a planeload of Tuaregs from Niger, men who were noted for their sorcery.

Wrapped in their customary black turbans, their faces veiled like most men of the desert, they arrived late one night in Malagueta and were quickly whisked off to the Xanadu in four-wheel-drive jeeps. When they saw the new arrivals, Tankor Satani's eunuchs were not too pleased about losing their influence, but considering that they had not been able to chase the dead out of the Xanadu, they kept their hurt pride to themselves. In a pitch as arcane as the dead had been using during their furious assault on the palace, the Tuaregs spent hours reciting copious medieval verses and sprinkling a powder made from the dried shit of camels and centipedes in a last-ditch attempt to drive out the wayward spirits of the dead men. But nothing could keep the implacable spirits out of the Xanadu, because it was a grove of the dead. Those who had died laboring to build it, those who had taken refuge there during the terrible currents of lightning, the lost souls of Malagueta's beginnings: all the voices would rise in a crescendo to give encouragement to the executed marchers as they went about terrifying the old man with their elusive assault.

"I am living in hell," he moaned.

Over the next three months the raucous voices kept coming, but Tankor Satani refused to succumb to the diabolical images in the mirror. His mind firmly on feeding on the hydra growing in those Swiss banks, he refused their call for him to do the decent thing and kill himself. It was June, and the rainy season was at its most volatile, making Malagueta a most miserable place, but there was the little business of attending the convocation at the university. Once that was done, he would take a holiday in Las Palmas, where he had bought a hotel. Hopefully, the dead men would not haunt him there.

CHAPTER FIFTEEN

Camwood on the Leaves

THE LAST thing that Gabriel Ananias did before he fled the cushiness of his office and home was to see Makita and their two children off to the safety of a trusted friend's house. Determined to rescue them later, after he was settled somewhere safe, he thought of all kinds of schemes to bring them out of Malagueta, but it was not to be. During the first months of exile in the neighboring country of Bassa, he was often assailed by such terrible omens about his future that he contemplated poisoning himself. For someone who had been rich, the indignity of living in reduced circumstances—in money, food, and accommodation—and listening to the same mournful music that the poor played in his neighborhood was terrible, especially after his Coral business partners, with whom he had exported squid to the culinary markets of Europe, swindled all the money he had salted away in a foreign bank under their names. He was just as humiliated when he tried to contact some of his old associates at the Central Bank and his friends with whom he had spent some great times at his favorite club after playing golf back in Malagueta. He was yesterday's man; they had forgotten about him. Besides Jennifer Owens, his other women had also forgotten him. But the worst indignity was that after waiting for two years for a word from him, his wife eventually took up with a Coral who had been a frequent guest at their house. Given how much he had invested in their marriage, Gabriel Ananias had not been prepared to be so humiliated. His pride was shattered, he missed his children, and he was determined to get them back from his wife, who was somewhere in the United States with her lover.

His suits were threadbare, he was down to a few button-down shirts, and his asthma when the pollen was out made his chest feel like hard leather. Thinking of the night when he had witnessed the confessions of the beauty queen, he wondered whether her purgatory had been as painful as his. But the more he thought about hell, the more it appeared as though it was destiny that had finally caught up with him, which did not in any way ameliorate the taste of bile in his mouth. For the first time ever, he felt trapped in the crepuscular mysteries and vagaries of life.

Then it was that he began to recall how his childhood had changed on the day a terrible earthquake had struck in his village when he was ten. He had emerged from the debris of the small house, the last breath of his dying grandparents slipping away, to be greeted by a white priest, the first such apparition he had ever seen in his life.

His name was Father Francis O'Reilly, but he was really a fraud. The priestly garb was something he still wore after he had been unfrocked by the bishop of County Derry, Patrick Kelly, for the crime of unbridled heresy, after O'Reilly had let it be known that he was intrigued by the teachings of a Bambara Christian convert who was passing himself off as the reincarnation of Donatus of Casae Nigrae, the fourth-century Afro-Christian bishop.

"Heresy will not be tolerated when we are trying to save the souls of pagans," the bishop warned when O'Reilly's interest in Donatus became obvious.

"I do not imply anything contrary to doctrinal teaching, My Lord," O'Reilly assured his bishop.

Nevertheless, the bishop eventually concluded that his subordinate was a bad influence on the order and that the only way to preserve monotheistic doctrine was to send O'Reilly to live among believers. He banished O'Reilly to Peru. Before sailing to Lima, O'Reilly's ambition had been to reverse the practice of teaching the principle of monotheism throughout the world by the European conquerors of distant lands, and he was undeterred by his banishment. As soon as he received his clerical duties from the bishop of the local diocese in Lima, he made an unauthorized trip to Macchu Picchu. During the sea voyage from Ireland he grew a long beard to shield his pale face from the summer heat of the Peruvian sun. The beard gave him a somewhat mysterious air. His voice, in the vast solitude of the Andean nights, would boom loud, while his bristling eyebrows glowed and the lines of his forehead widened into a most convincing picture of a man on a mission. If he was not entirely a zealot, the Indians nevertheless mistook him for a lesser god and taught him some Quechua in order that he might explain to them why they were having a drought that year.

When reports of such goings on eventually reached his bishopric in Ireland, the bishop was deeply upset. "That's it," he said. "His disobedience has gone too far, and he must be made to repent in some meaningful manner."

He thought the wilderness of Africa was just the place for a maverick to repent, and O'Reilly was dispatched to western Nigeria.

Secretly, after obtaining a rare copy from an old missionary, he began to prepare for his new mission by reading the Sixteen Corpus of Ifa, one of the most sacred books of the Yoruba people, who had stamped their great culture on much of West Africa and the Americas. He foresaw difficult times ahead, the phalanxes of unbelievers who would try to block his path, but he decided to go ahead, prepared to be respectful to the local people, knowing full well that the enigmatic Yoruba gods, conquerors themselves, demanded respect. He had been in Yoruba land for only a year when he began to send letters home detailing the eclecticism of its religious practices, the eroticism of its talking drum music, and the great artistic merits of its civilization. His eloquent letters made frequent mention of the generosity of their women, raising the suspicion of his sister that he probably had a woman among the "heathens," but she did not mind his 'going astray;' not when he had even managed to send a bronze figure home, which she proudly displayed on the mantelpiece for the bishop to admire on his regular visits.

Bishop Patrick Kelly had also formed the opinion that O'Reilly's exploits in Nigeria probably included having a "native" woman, so he ordered his wayward priest home. "We cannot allow any diversions from established doctrine, even by a freak," the bishop fumed during one visit to O'Reilly's sister. "Although this is not the age of the gun, when Christian enlightenment is supposed to be marching through the Dark Continent."

When O'Reilly was summoned back to Ireland, his bishop was determined to put out the bush fire of O'Reilly's apostasy. "I will not have you undermining the words of the Holy See and the power of our sovereign to rule over unfortunate beings," the bishop exclaimed.

"Is this the Inquisition?" O'Reilly inquired.

"No," the bishop conceded, "but you face excommunication from the Holy See if you do not confess your sins."

"Then I see God in my action and accept his divine justice."

Six months later, after he had been unfrocked, O'Reilly bade a tearful good-bye to his sister in County Derry and sailed third class on a freighter. Two weeks later, he arrived in Malagueta, still calling himself a priest. He came to a capital in chaos, jittery, the officials there trying to do something about a terrible earthquake fifty miles away. O'Reilly's deception went unnoticed by the authorities, who were only too pleased to dispatch him to the epicenter of the quake.

"It is the hand of God," O'Reilly said when he alighted from the Land Rover that had conveyed him to the site of the tragedy. He saw that the land had been scorched and that the cheap materials—wood, mud bricks, raffia palm—used to build the houses had been useless against the quake. Many houses had simply crumbled. From beneath the rubble he heard the inhuman howls calling out for help or a drink of water as death set in. It was a terrible picture everywhere: scrawny dogs feeding on the dead chickens and guinea fowls, the desperation of the burning people, the hideous noise of the farm animals, even the sizzling of snakes trapped in the flames of the raging fires created a picture of the imaginary toxins of hell for O'Reilly. With his piercing blue eyes, red hair, beard, and booming voice, he cut quite a distinguished figure walking around in his cassock, although there was something comical about the way he tried to shoo away the flies attracted by the smell of malt in his long beard; he had spent the previous evening drinking beer, which he had been assured by English veterans of the tropics was a good prophylactic against malaria. With so many people clearly marked for death, O'Reilly's concern was to see that they were baptized before they met God. He had just set about doing so when the miracle happened.

Many years later, just before he died, O'Reilly would remember how the young boy, not more than ten, had walked out of the rubble of his house through a roaring flame, without even a scratch, and haloed with a crown of ashes. For almost two hours the boy had been trapped between two heavy wooden planks, helpless, trembling with fear, watching his grandparents die, depriving him of the only relatives he had known. His howling, like that of a frightened bush pig running from a lion, had been drowned out by the wailing of the women frantically searching for their children in the rubble of their former homes. For water, he stretched his hand to grab and chew on a few tufts of grass his grandmother had been saving for a fever potion. He had almost given up hope of ever emerging out of that hell when he saw the column of black ants with eyes beaming like searchlights coming from a dark corner.

He lay transfixed, watching the ants as they came to one of the beams trapping him and began, as though miraculously ordered, to gnaw at it, their iridescent heads gleaming as they worked noiselessly. Almost two hours after the ants had eaten deep into the wood, he summoned all his strength, hauled himself up, and began gingerly to make his way out, conscious of how perilous his situation was. Two thousand people had died in the quake, but as the survivors were hurriedly burying their dead, he finally emerged into the late afternoon with his aureole of ashes, the ants leading him as though in a biblical tale.

It was Easter. When O'Reilly saw the boy emerging from the rubble, he immediately concluded that God had saved his life for a special purpose. He laid down the head of the dying man he had been tending, rushed over to the boy, and raised a small calabash of water to his parched lips. "Lord, I know I am a fraud, but have seldom asked for much, so save this heathen," he begged with eyes turned skyward.

He dipped his right index finger in some ashes, made the sign of the cross on the boy's head, and pronounced him cleansed of all earthly sins.

Noting that this strange white man, perhaps a doctor in the midst of dying people, did not have a goatskin bag like the others who had plied their trade in that part of the world, the boy took O'Reilly to be a spirit. But when O'Reilly did not disappear as spirits were supposed to, he assumed human proportions in the boy's eyes. The boy fixed a suspicious look on the Irishman.

O'Reilly admired his caution. "My son," he said, trying to reassure him, "I don't know whether you were baptized before I came, but I now pronounce you the bearer of light in the new enlightenment we shall build on the ruins of this place. What is your name?

"Moriba," the boy offered. He had received a few years of schooling.

"That won't do," O'Reilly replied. "You need a name befitting your new religion."

"I like my name," the boy said flatly.

"Henceforth you shall be called Gabriel Ananias because you have the face of an angel, and it was the archangel that saved you."

Never having heard of his biblical namesake, the boy asked for another drink.

The fire had risen in an intensity of terror and turned what remained of the houses into ashes. The dense vegetation was scorched, and the smell had traveled a considerable distance. Magnificently plumaged birds, which before the earthquake had been cruising above the town like magical dreams, were now flying helter-skelter, going nowhere. For the first time in his life, O'Reilly saw strange creatures with very large eyes moving frantically to avoid the flames: chameleons. The sibilance of the scorched snakes in the grass was not terrible enough to drown out the inconsolable moans of the men and women in the throes of death, still asking for just one last drink of water.

Aided by the boy, O'Reilly seized the opportunity to act as a priest. "First you give them some bread," he told the bewildered boy as he broke some crumbs.

"Why?"

"Because it is the body of Christ," O'Reilly replied, and brought some wine to the parched lips of the dying. "The priests do not do like this where I come from, but we are not in Ireland."

"Why you give them rum?" the boy wondered.

"Because it is the blood of our Lord and Savior Jesus Christ."

A week later, after the boy had been washed, fed, and clothed in the house where the priest had taken him, he went to sleep, his halo still above him. That night he dreamed that his grandparents had been turned into vultures. For the first time in his young but turbulent life, the boy sampled delicacies he had never heard of in the village: toffees, cabin biscuits, smoked herring, olives, pickles, which the once-a-week train brought for the officials, stopping far from the village in the outskirts of the town nearest to it, after which the priest would ride his bike to get his supplies.

Two years after the quake, O'Reilly had his greatest reward when the pillar of a new church stood on the very spot where Gabriel Ananias had been rescued. Every Sunday, its vesper bell brought converts, mostly orphans, to listen to the word of God, the new acolytes glad that they could hope for something to eat after the service was over. Although he was in a village, bereft of comfort, O'Reilly's enthusiasm was not affected as he went about his mission baptizing and feeding the orphans. Much later, after discovering that his ward was taking a deep interest in the regrown forest, O'Reilly's Irish soul found its musical high note when he would spend evenings singing the limericks he had learned as a boy in County Kerry. On a spring day, considering his work as a missionary almost complete, O'Reilly traveled all the way to the capital. With a considerable chunk of what was left of his savings, he enrolled his ward in a secondary school, after he was certain Gabriel Ananias's interest in entomology was genuine but that it would probably not interfere with a priestly vocation.

"Promise me that you will remember God's mercy to you," O'Reilly pleaded as the boy entered the school's compound carrying a heavy portmanteau on his head.

Gabriel Ananias stuck with God for a while, but when he was at university his greed overcame whatever resolve he may have had to honor a dying Irish "priest's" wish.

CHAPTER SIXTEEN

The Sorcerer's Hieroglyph

AFTER PERFORMING her séance for her dead lovers, Habiba Mouskuda lost her fear of death. Yet, recalling how the angels had visited the surveyor in her bed, she knew how intemperate they could be and hoped they would not come to visit Theodore Iskander when he was making love to her. The coffins were still in her living room, three candles burning near them. She changed the flowers every morning: a fresh smell of gardenia and geraniums permeated the place, and the feeling that her lovers' souls were now appeased had freed her mind of any guilt about how she had treated them when they were alive. The spirit of General Augustus Kotay had not troubled her that night when she had lain defenseless in his coffin, and for the first time in many months she felt she could go on living in her house.

However, one problem had begun to occupy Habiba Mouskuda's mind: what should she do with the three coffins?

"Keep them around for your entire life," a voice invading her sleep that night said; "that way you won't have to go around wondering where they are, since you now have them right here in your house."

She was up in the first flicker of light with a deeper clarity about her future, surprised at how easily she had closed the fissures in her past forever. Now that she was convinced she had a good man to love her, she radiated a form of bliss and could laugh, thinking of her wild days, at the Swedish tourists who, running away from their Scandinavian winter, had invaded Malagueta and were crowding the curio shops with their sturdy blond Nordic heads, buying up everything, or looking for transient loves. Several times late at night, with the heat down, the coconut trees swaying with fruits as their branches cooled the beaches, the beach police had surprised some of them as they made love to the local boys and girls, offering to take them to Europe from the hardship of Malagueta. That was a shame; it was such a beautiful place.

Things had turned out so well for Habiba Mouskuda lately, she thought of doing something special and different this coming Christmas: smoking ham, for instance, cooking some Jollof rice with a rich, thick stew of the fattest capon, sautéed in a ginger, thyme, basil, and tomato magic she would not divulge to anyone. Buoyed by the mood of the coming season, she thought she would open her house to anyone for a glass of tamarind-ginger beer, rice bread, goulash, kebab of venison, if the hunters went into the forest, and a rich Creole salad which had no competition in the world—everything washed down with some goat pepper soup, before they sang the Holy Child his birthday with a tot of good seaman's rum.

Besides thinking about the festivities, she felt it was also time to rid herself of some of the baggage that the mania of a reckless and loveless life had given her. So she went back to her trunk, intent on giving away some of the dresses she had accumulated to the women at the Cheshire Home to be auctioned off so some homeless children would have a good Christmas. One last time, she wore her jewelry and paraded, with an effulgence of spirit, in front of the ornate mirror that General Augustus Kotay had smuggled into the country in a case labeled "Military Supplies." Those gypsy skirts and Madeira blouses that had sometimes set the general's blood boiling were much too wild for the Society of Women of Charity, but she thought the women would find something in her collection to use, especially during the Christmas season.

A strong wind had been lashing Malagueta for days, the ocean was redolent of the great arrival of barracudas, the carolers had sent out their notices telling people they were coming to sing, and the lampposts were decked with banners advertising the latest plays of the various drama groups. This was the beginning of December, when Malaguetans would start a month-long season of festivities. Swept up by the lyricism of the times, Habiba Mouskuda was looking for an old program of one such play she had attended many years ago, when she saw the fifty-pound note turning gray at the bottom of the trunk.

"Holy Christ," she said. "Just seeing Queen Victoria looking so innocent in profile has given me an idea about how to go on being good."

Every Christmas, some rich Corals unable to face the New Year with a bad conscience about profiteering and smuggling would sweat over what to give to the government ministers and the city's poor. Habiba Mouskuda had one such relative. Using her most anxious voice for the concern of his soul, she called him over to her place and made him a good offer.

"I know you are not concerned about the poor because you have the big government fish in your pocket, but think of how much blessing you would derive from your priest by helping him to give the poor a good meal at Christmas, or a decent funeral when they die."

"How ah go get de extra blessing?" the Coral wondered.

"By giving your priest something for the poor to show that you are a good Christian."

"All right: but just dis one time," he offered.

Two days later, after she had arranged to sell them for a good price, she kissed the caskets good-bye, dried some new tears, removed the white lace blinds from her windows, and planted some fresh begonias in three pots: one each for the sweet soul of her dead lovers. With her eyes set on the day when the flowers would bloom and their scent would bring her the memory not just of how good General Kotay had been to her, but also of the good times with some of her other men, she turned her attention to more mundane issues, such as how she needed some form of protection, now that she was visibly pregnant, from the women who might not wish her well.

With some of the money she had received from selling the caskets, and now no longer afraid of crossing the border river, she made a secret visit to see the sorcerer Pallo, hoping he would receive her with less caution this time, for she was determined to lure him to the capital.

At first the sorcerer refused to consider her offer. He was not a man easily tempted by the prospect of living under the same roof with anyone, especially someone whose willful nature he had discerned only a few months ago.

"Go away, child, and leave me in peace to go on studying the eye of the serpent," he said.

Habiba was not a woman easily put off when she wanted something. "Think of the other things fate has chosen you to do," she replied, referring to his skills. "I have come to ask for a new reading into my future."

Pallo opened a small burlap bag and asked her to select two kola nuts—a red and a white—and drop them in a bowl of water. With his fine hands he washed them clean of all impurities; then slowly, in a clear voice, he began to recite sacred verses in a secret argot. He gathered the nuts, split the pods, and threw them onto the dirt floor, then closed his eyes and with a deft hand sent one red and one white pod so they landed on their backs. It was propitious. Habiba was going to be all right.

But while he had been reading Habiba Mouskuda's future, something incredible was revealed to Pallo. He saw someone waiting for him, a man who badly needed his counsel, and it occurred to the eunuch that God had merely sent Habiba as a messenger.

"He go die bad, bad, de way he acting!" Pallo exclaimed, opening his eyes to a startled Habiba Mouskuda.

"Who?"

"Tankor, and he big fool!" Pallo said as he collected the nuts.

He chewed on the white one and gave Habiba the red, smiling. "Give it to a beggar for good luck," he instructed the pregnant woman.

"Come to Malagueta and live with me," she pleaded. "Many people will come to see you for your help."

"I cannot live under the same roof with you."

Habiba Mouskuda suddenly had a brilliant idea. "Come and live with Tankor, then. I am sure he will pay you well."

Seeing that the eunuch was deeply insulted at the mention of money, she hastened to make amends. "I am sorry. I was just thinking of your comfort."

There was such earnestness in her voice that the eunuch eventually softened his long opposition to moving out of his hermitry. "Then go. I shall come to Tankor's house when I am ready."

Satisfied she had scored a major victory, Habiba Mouskuda went back to Malagueta.

CHAPTER SEVENTEEN

Hawanatu Gomba's Imaginary Lover

DISGRACED, LONELY, and miserable after being accused of witchcraft in the death of Habiba Mouskuda's albino son, Hawanatu Gomba had been in exile for three years in Bassa when she ran into a familiar face: Gabriel Ananias. He was just as happy to see someone from his guilt-ridden past, but soon discovered that she was unlike the other women he had known. Silent, wrapped in layers of reserve, she definitely did not give the impression of someone who would eagerly have gone to bed with him when he was riding high as a bank governor. Even in her poverty her dignity was obvious, and he was grateful for her silence, tired as he was of the clamor that had been part of his life when he was a banker. Back then, he had been in charge of a bunch of men who would cringe at his orders, and couldn't get to his office without some woman offering to spend a most memorable evening with him in his hideout. All he now wanted was to get to know this quiet woman, or, when she was not around, listen to some quiet music.

They had met by chance at a newsstand, and something mysterious in her eyes had impressed him: the strength that her soul was transmitting. He wondered whether, like him, she carried regrets in her heart about the past, pages of sadness, unwritten letters, humiliation, and the fear people had about being discovered lonely in exile.

"Let's meet at the small café near the post office next Tuesday," she said before she left.

But she was not there that day, raising his suspicion that she might be sick or the victim of a kidnapping, especially as he did not know where she lived. Then, when his worries were almost unbearable, she came to see him one windy evening, smiling, and shocked him with how easily she had found his place. She had dispensed with the severe spinster's frock that had so amused him the first time he had seen her and now looked lovely in a new flowery dress. Her eyes sparkled with mascara, but she still wore the old-fashioned wooden shoes of her inescapable Catholic upbringing and had brought him some fruits and cigarettes, in case he smoked, although she was not certain whether his landlady tolerated that indulgence in the rooms. Unknown to him—and she would have died of shame to admit it—besides the men that she served at the post office where she had found a job, she had not been this close to any man in years. Yet, after four days of thinking about Gabriel Ananias, she could still not put her finger on what it was that she found intriguing about this man. Perhaps it was because he looked so lonely, lost, a palpable sadness evident in him, even when he tried to smile. He reminded her of when she had first come into exile.

"There is not much in this place for a man like you," she began, using her good convent schoolgirl's voice to enquire. "So what are you doing here, unless you are hiding something big enough to make you prefer this place to being amongst friends?"

"How do you know I am not amongst friends?"

"By the way you are behaving: like a frightened rat."

Her prescience shocked him. Given his pain, he was a bit suspicious of such powers and wondered whether she knew more about his past than she was divulging.

"Let us say I have a lot of things to sort out," he said, hoping to put an end to that aspect of the conversation.

Hawanatu Gomba was not easily put off. "We all have our ambiguities," she replied. "It is just that some of us are given more time than others to sort them out, after we have been on the stage of the devil. So tell me, why have you come here bringing these magazines about the politics of the past that everyone here wants to forget?"

Soon after her unexpected entry into his room, her eyes had roamed over the dog-eared old magazines on the bedside table that he had been reading during the tenebrous nights of his exile. When there was a brownout and he could not read, he was often assailed by the thought that Tankor Satani's goons were probably closing in on his exile and were going to kill him, given how much Tankor could pay assassins. So, contrary to what Hawanatu might think, he was not a dangerous radical but a man afraid to die.

During two years of exile, besides his occasional fear of assassins, he had spent time thinking about when he was a nice little boy setting bird traps in his village before the earthquake. When the priest had touched his unbaptized lips with what he called the beatitudes of God, the young convert had felt a strange sensation; but at twenty-five, Gabriel Ananias started questioning his own pillar of strength when Tankor Satani tempted him. The corruption of his soul had started.

"What happened to you then?" Hawanatu Gomba wanted to know.

Gabriel Ananias had just commenced his university studies when, overcome by pleurisy, worn out by the tropical heat, Father O'Reilly died, once again leaving the boy without a family but with a sizable endowment.

In the penury of his exile, Gabriel Ananias was grateful for the presence of the woman staring in disbelief at him.

"How did you come to be in exile?" Hawanatu asked.

"It is a long story, one that requires more fortitude than I have had for the past two years. It started when you were probably too young to know about it."

Hawanatu Gomba kept staring at him. She felt he was still battling his invisible demons and that the loss of his pride in exile was almost unbearable; she imagined that stubborn ghosts visited him at night, intrepid ones he couldn't chase away even if he were to turn to God wholeheartedly now, start a new church, or do something dramatic to save his soul. His pain made her sad, but she realized he had clamped up, perhaps because the rest of his story was a descent into even larger whirlpools of pain: something he would rather not think about. The lines of his brow had tightened, the skin of his neck sagged, and his eyes—those of a man suffering the perils of exile and uncertain about the future—were misted over with regret.

She thought it prudent to let him save the rest of his story for another time; she would let him choose that day, at his own leisure. Happiness, she imagined, was a sensation he had not experienced in a long time, for she knew how illusory that emotion could be. She would be there when he was ready to come out of the web of his torment, to help release him from the shame that had almost destroyed his confidence. If he would let her, she would coax him to talk to her again, when his soul was not saturated with grief; she would have to be patient. The monkish sparseness of his room had bothered her the first time she came to see him, so she made a mental note of a few things she should bring on her next visit, not just to brighten up the gloom of that space but also to cheer up his soul.

She felt, shyly, like kissing him, wondering when he had last tasted the honey of a woman on his lips, but she was really not yet ready for that gesture, and perhaps, she imagined, neither was he. So she drained the last of her coffee and got up to leave, but not before she had unburdened her mind of a sudden intrusive thought.

"I have no business asking you this," she said. "But do you sometimes blame God for your predicament?"

"No, for God is only a symbol that we use when we need him."

Later in the evening, Hawanatu Gomba began to walk home to her own lonely room in one of houses in the warren hugging the city's limit near the waterfront. Membranes of dark clouds hung over the city, a piratical wind was blowing down the street, whistling about rain and threatening the shelter of some lepers who, seeing her go by as the first flurry of the rain was unleashed, thought she was a madwoman to be out in such inclement weather and offered to share their space with her to keep her warm and safe.

"It is not much, but we tell beautiful stories better than anyone," one of them said.

The sky was dark and the flashes of lightning ominous, yet she thanked them for their generosity and continued to walk. She felt the rain cruising down her skin, unaware that she was sharing the road with the zombies and the spirits of the tormented dead who would come out when it rained, looking for traces of their former lives. Lately, she had heard rumors of a coup d'état in Bassa. If true, the trouble could fan its flames across the border into her homeland. For some time she had been aware of the movement of troops leaving the capital to strengthen some of the frontier garrisons loyal to the government; the soldiers were uncouth, leering, always harassing women before boarding their jeeps. However, like Gabriel Ananias, she was holding off on returning to Malagueta.

Just as mad as Hawanatu, a stunningly beautiful whore dressed in cheap pastel, who did not seem to care about whether war was imminent, was hurrying off to board a rickety boat that would take a dozen of her kind to a Korean fishing boat anchored in midstream. Someone was roasting breadfruit on an open grill, and Hawanatu suddenly felt hungry.

A huge tree branch was blocking the road about a mile to her house, necessitating a detour on her route, which was how she found herself in a dimly lit street, keeping her eyes wide open for large potholes. Unlike the narrow horse-and-carriage streets constructed by the British in Malagueta, these were wide boulevards engineered by the fearless American resolve of the former slaves from North Carolina who had built this town to tackle the forest. But the houses, though newer, lacked the antebellum charm of those in Malagueta—no dormer windows and slanting roofs. The roads were slightly better maintained yet just as susceptible to the relentless pounding of the region's rains, the ugly fissures of peeling earth, and the freshets and spillover gutters during the rains in June. Adding to her misery was the fact that the town, being below sea level, was humid and damp, unlike Malagueta, where comforting breezes blew from the high plateau and the rugged terrain of Mount Agadi throughout much of the year.

Nonetheless, she liked the sound of the rain in this town. With her hair now completely wet, her dress pressed damply against her skin, she found herself thinking of Theodore Iskander and how his mother had carried her laundry bundles when it was raining. She wondered whether the good woman had ruined her knuckles washing the clothes she collected from the Corals—all that misery, only for her son to break her heart after his own heart had been lost to Habiba Mouskuda, ground up like alligator pepper.

The flashes of lightning had not let up. Skeins of ducks were coming out of the mangroves in search of safety under the houses, and large pellets of rain kept brushing Hawanatu's neck, but she kept walking, smiling, almost as though she were possessed. Rhymed couplets, inspired by the rain, rose in her soul, and a tremendous shudder gripped her. For the first time in years she felt giddy, and she experienced the sensation of wanting to be lifted up to the sky when some white egrets flew past above her. She imagined she was seeing angels, and just thinking of their beautiful faces was enough to make her feel free of her past misery.

She came to the intersection of Bokina and Mongo Streets, near the old slave district. Most people were hurrying to get home because the timpani of the rain had turned into a tropical crescendo. Felled branches of fruit trees and ripped trunks lay everywhere in the scary evening, yet she did not seem in any hurry. Perhaps it was because there was nothing for her to rush home to besides the same emptiness of unpainted walls, whorls of dark shadows, and the bad memories that she had lived with for the past two years. She really looked like a madwoman as she continued her leisurely pace, but after a while it was obvious to her that she was the only one walking in the rain. She paused only when she saw a window opening in a bungalow that was dwarfed by a large flame tree.

"You must be a witch to be out in this kind of weather," a woman yelled at her.

"Witches are afraid of the rain," Hawanatu laughed, "but I am not."

A few years ago, she had thought witchcraft a sign of being under the spell of the devil, which was why she had reacted so angrily to that ghoulish vilification by the Corals; but she felt so cheery in her soul that now she did not care what people said about her. She thought of how surprised the Corals would be if they knew about the changes that had happened to her since coming into exile. She was laughing and singing now as she pushed her fantasy to extremes. A sharp ripple of lightning sent her running. She imagined that the trees were giant men, and she was unwilling to go home until she had hugged all of them. As though possessed, she pressed her throbbing breasts against the trees and an unbearable hunger for love rose in her, the most violent she had experienced in a long time.

She was as wet as a barnyard fowl when she finally turned the key in her door, but drunk from the wine of being out in the rain, she did not go immediately to her bathroom to get rid of her damp clothes. She sat in a chair listening to the thunderous drums of the rain on her roof; then, her breasts quivering, she imagined a lover hurrying to her in the rain, desperate to caress those breasts. After the years of being without a man, she knew that she could die for the touch of one now as she closed her eyes, trembling, the drums of the rain continuing to pound her roof. How lonely she had been, she admitted; the rhythm of her breast so intense that she was unaware of the freshet under the building, no longer able to distinguish the rain from the music in her soul.

She drifted off to sleep but woke up two hours later still with the hunger to be taken. Uncertain how Gabriel Ananias felt about her, and alone in any case, she took a warm hot water bottle to bed, placed it between her legs, and picked up a good book to read. It was the longest torment she had suffered since leaving Malagueta, and trying to read merely added to her desire until, once again, she fell asleep and dreamt that a ferocious black bull was chasing her.

CHAPTER EIGHTEEN

Madmen and Specialists

MOUSTAPHA ALI-BAKR returned to Malagueta from his daughter's lavish wedding in Lebanon beaming with pride. Anticipating a cabinet reshuffle by Tankor Satani, he went straight from the airport to the Al-Hakim mosque in the center of town to thank Allah that the intrepid ghosts had finally left the Xanadu after relentlessly hounding the president for over two months. "Allahu Akbar," he said as he distributed the Friday alms to the lepers in front of the mosque after prayers, although he suspected it was probably the abracadabra of the Tuareg magicians that seemed to have driven the ghosts out of the Xanadu. He was in an effusive mood as he was driven in his Mercedes to see his old friend, thinking Tankor would be happy to see him.

"You have come at the right time," Tankor Satani said somewhat coldly.

Moustapha had brought a cane with a golden lion head for the president. Shocked by the old man's attitude, he felt his hand freeze on its handle.

His old friend was looking at him in a strange way, and the troubling thought hit him that perhaps the president was upset over a new ghoulish attack on the Xanadu by the vultures.

"What is wrong, Excellency?" Moustapha Ali-Bakr asked.

Tankor Satani cleared his throat before replying. "My people say that although you have been bribing every Tom, Dick, and Harry to make money here, you care very little for the welfare of the country that has made you wealthy. They say you have been sending lots of money to Lebanon."

Moustapha Ali-Bakr reacted as though he had been accused of treason. "Not true, President, sir," he said, and put out his large cigar. "Ah spend plenty money here, give scholarships to poor university students, big donations to party mammy queens. Ah keep soldiers happy with good-quality rice from Burma, and all my *pikin* are happy."

Tankor Satani's face had turned grave. "I know you provide generously for your children, send your daughters to finishing schools in Europe so that you can marry them off to your Lebanese business partners; but people say you are rude to their mothers, who are black. They say most Lebanese are racists, like the Arabs in Mauritania, Niger, and Sudan, who still keep slaves, rape black women, and burn the houses of their opponents."

"Double lie, Excellency. You forget me own mama black."

"Well, treat black people well, you hear? They are the ones who made you rich!"

While the old man was speaking, a small stream of perspiration had wetted the brow of the Coral. In the nexus of business and politics in Malagueta, he was the closest friend of the president, clearly the second most powerful man in the country, but was not stupid enough to take that friendship for granted. If there was any rumored damage in his relationships with his black women, it was a disaster. He had to attend to it immediately and pay less attention to his Lebanese brothers. For a not too dashing man, not more than five feet six, pudgy, freckled, Moustapha Ali-Bakr's sexual life had really been quite astonishing. In ten years, he had fathered lots of children by his African concubines and had seen his likeness in several shades of brown appear all over Malagueta, of which he was very proud. More than money, he felt children were assets, expressions of a man's worth; blessings, if they turned out well. By the time he was forty he was already a very rich man, and, after Tankor Satani came to power, had wasted no time driving out all the competition in the diamond mines: a ruthless operator who could afford to pay all the required bribes to corrupt government officials, hire thugs to threaten his most redoubtable enemies, and put himself beyond the reach of the law, even when he was suspected of having a hand in a killing.

Thinking he had reassured the old man about his decency to black women, he resumed chewing on his fat cigar and, choosing his words carefully, suggested to the old man that they should protect their interests with the right men in government. "Please, sir," he began. "Maybe you should think of putting one or two lecturers in the new cabinet. They know the book, but are so broke they will lick your boots to become a minister. I know what I have seen."

It was no idle boast by the Coral. He was a crude man whose indelicate mouth was feared in Malagueta, especially the way he would talk to most politicians, civil servants, even high-ranking military men and teachers who had made a habit of flocking to his office for handouts. But his worst contempt was for the academic class, a group he held in the lowest contempt, granting them less respect than what he grudgingly offered his drivers, whom he feared, and for good reason. Although he had no proof, he had begun to suspect that some of the chauffeurs hired by the Corals were sleeping with their neglected wives.

While their men were busy trying to control the diamond-smuggling business, while they were desperately chasing African mistresses in their expensive Mercedes and worrying about some unscrupulous gangs diverting truckloads of onions, mayonnaise, and whiskey from the quay, the Lebanese wives were reportedly seeking comfort in the arms of their drivers. If confirmed, the scandal would have shamed the cheeky Corals, but Moustapha Ali-Bakr was a businessman first, and in a matter such as this he kept his mouth shut. Moreover, he had always admired strength, the kind that had taken the Corals to the top of the brutal diamond world of Africa. He respected the drivers.

The impertinence of those drivers was all the more remarkable when Moustapha remembered that many of them were illiterate and smelled like village bumpkins, that they chewed kola nuts and drank cheap liquor; just the sort, it pained him to think, for spiteful, neglected Lebanese women to sleep with when their husbands were out chasing African skirts. After his suspicions were aroused about those goings-on, he began to notice that the drivers were walking around arrogantly, as though with huge secrets. One day he dared to challenge one of them. Coolly, the driver spat out his foul-smelling tobacco, laughed at Moustapha Ali-Bakr, and looked the Coral contemptuously in the eye. "Go to hell," he said, and grabbed and shook his manhood as though he were a proud bull.

Humiliated, Moustapha Ali-Bakr was driven to impotent despair by the fact that, despite their lack of education, the drivers had opinions about everything from world soccer to the frivolity of the devil, from the sexual hunger of Lebanese women to the relationship between the politicians and their Coral associates. On another day, when he tried to intimidate a few of them about being disloyal to their employers, he was met with a menace in their eyes that unnerved him.

"What you want, mister?" One of them threatened him. "We fit tell people 'bout all you tiff-tiff business if you not careful."

Afraid he might be poisoned, Moustapha Ali-Bakr did not press the point and never reported any loss of money to the police. Black magic, or the threat of it, was too potent a force for him to ignore in his position.

Dealing with the academics was quite another matter. A sad lot, they had begun to lose the respect people once had for them. But against all odds, such as their terrible salaries and the way the national university had crumbled while Tankor Satani was spending lavishly on the Xanadu, some of those professors had continued to uphold a fine tradition of learning. They lived in college digs where the water was frequently turned off and the electricity, at best, was erratic. It was painful to watch the most daring of them trudging off to some sorcerer for help in getting the ultimate plum of being named chairman of a department, which meant being able to travel abroad and save enough of his per diem to buy something decent for his family, such as a new TV or camera.

When Theodore Iskander had joined the staff of the university ten years earlier, full of a passion to teach and inspired by its illustrious beginnings, his intention had been to bring back a glorious age to a place that was once a leader in higher education but was now facing disaster. In those days the campus was a network of neat bungalows, a botanical garden, and private cultivations of rich, blossoming mimosa and jasmine, tended by gardeners in white uniforms. Dons and students wore black gowns to lectures, and there was magic and awe in being at the university. A lover of music, he recalled when the college chapel had reverberated with the heavenly notes of choral music: a program by the Malaguetan composer George Ballanta, particularly his operetta *Afiwa*, and Brahms's *German Requiem*, no less. Twice a year, plays by Shakespeare and the newly emerging Wole Soyinka had been staged in the auditorium; but the most memorable production had been of Julius Nyerere's translation of *Julius Caesar* into Swahili.

It was a bygone age that left him deeply saddened.

"What a mess we have fallen into since then," he said to Habiba Mouskuda one evening.

"That is Tankor for you," she said. "Destroying all the institutions, breaking men. But he couldn't have done so without the help of some of those shitty academics, lawyers, judges, and politicians."

The professors' salaries were not assured and were not enough to buy a decent month's groceries, fuel, and booze, so sometimes they appeared in the business district of Malagueta looking woebegone in their deadbeat suits. Often their cars had to be pushed because of a dead battery. It was easy for Moustapha Ali-Bakr to prey on that lot: particularly one of them.

Dr. Komba Binkolo was English-educated, well-spoken, bespectacled, a professor of political science. He had joined the faculty at the same time as Theodore Iskander and had not seemed like the kind to be seduced by the overtures of Tankor Satani and Moustapha Ali-Bakr. He had the air of a savant and the bearing of a chieftain, but it was a well-guarded secret that he had in fact started life in a rat-infested dark room in a slum under the Portuguese slave steps near the ocean.

Since leaving that area in his childhood he had not been back, and those who could recall that childhood but were reluctant to talk about it did not envy the professor his escape from its hell; for in truth, he came from a proud race and had, with the dazzling gift of his brilliance, risen above that slum genesis to the peak of academic respect. Like Theodore Iskander, he had at first given the impression that he was inspired by altruism to teach for a not too substantial reward, thereby earning the respect of his students. Over green tea in each other's homes, he and Theodore Iskander would spend time in heated conversations, always with erudition and marvelous diction, about what could be done for the country—Dr. Komba Binkolo cautioning patience and Theodore Iskander, with the volatile blood of the founders in him, only able to think of a complete change of direction in Malagueta.

When they were not engaged in academic banter, the two men would discuss their women, aware of what people thought about malattas, because each of them had a Coral woman, although Dr. Komba Binkolo's wife did not have the ravishing magnetism of Habiba Mouskuda.

"You are lucky, my friend," he said ruefully one evening, the crevices in his forehead revealing that all was not well at home.

"What is troubling you?" Theodore asked, concerned.

"You may not understand."

"Try me."

"As academics, we must all strive toward honor, but traditional values weigh some of us down; they stymie our resolve to choose between our integrity and family responsibilities. No one is putting any pressure on you to do awkward things because of Habiba Mouskuda's ancestry, whereas in my case, the Corals want me to tone down my attack on Tankor Satani because I married one of their own. My malatta gives me hell all the time, saying I am too proud to ask for assistance. Life can be very lonely for some of us."

Theodore Iskander listened with a mixture of concern and pity. "We all have our worries because of our Coral women," he said, trying to comfort his friend. "You should hear what my mother has to say about Habiba Mouskuda!"

As with everything in Malagueta, Moustapha Ali-Bakr had made it his business to find out about Dr. Komba Binkolo's predicament. At the first opportunity he hoped to become better acquainted with the professor, preferably through his Coral wife.

Moustapha Ali-Bakr's mansion not only rivaled Tankor Satani's Xanadu in size but was more splendidly decorated. It was built in the heart of the idyllic lower region of the forest overlooking Malagueta, and the first things that visitors saw upon entering it were imported Persian carpets, stolen Czarist icons, Impressionist paintings (he was a philistine but knew the value of art) and the heads of oryx and tigers. On a trip to China he had acquired a Ming dynasty porcelain vase and thus begun an association with Gao Bin Zhong, a merchant in Shanghai, for the export of sharks and tuna from Malagueta. In an atrium of exquisite beauty that opened into a garden of exotic tropical plants and birds stood the Italian sculptures, which, with the other items, showed to what expense the Coral had gone to make the place the most talked about in Malagueta. After being in the enchanting atmosphere of the garden, it was not unusual for people to say that they had been in paradise and did not mind dying right away. But the Coral's most outlandish display was a priceless collection of elephant tusks he had brought in from Bassa, where he not only sold diamonds but had a vast underground operation exchanging local currencies for dollars.

Unlike Tankor Satani's Xanadu, which could only be reached by a drive on a private mountain pass, the Coral's mansion was accessible by public transportation, but closed-circuit television and a vast private army, aided by members of the regular army moonlighting for extra money, made the place more impregnable than Fort Knox. Yet, grandeur aside, it was a mirage for people to admire and gawk at, because, as though he feared the sun as a blistering enemy, Moustapha mainly used a small room with its pastel curtains always drawn, while the rest of the house was always closed. The tiles in that room were of Moroccan ceramic arabesque, and the floor was covered not in Persian carpets like the other rooms but with a simple rug of camel hide. A depression at one end testified to where he did his duty to God, if not five times a day, at least three. After his first ablution, he would emerge from that room with a peaceful mien to face the world and dispense favors to the thirty or so people always waiting in the guest room where he held court as the unofficial associate president of Malagueta.

"Give us something to do in your empire, a contract to survey an as yet unexploited region of the country, a paper to write about the epic journey of the Arabs to cross the Sahara before settling here. Anything, Master."

People in Malagueta always say that if you were answering the call of nature in a dark alley and saw a Coral coming, you should halt your business with mother earth, put your pants on in a hurry, and disappear, because next day it would be in the papers that you were doing something different from what the Coral had witnessed. So when Dr. Komba Binkolo made what he thought was a surreptitious visit to Moustapha Ali-Bakr, he should not have been surprised to find it public knowledge a week later.

Having anticipated a furious response from his students and opprobrium from his colleagues if news of his visit to the Coral was leaked out, he had prepared the ruse that he had only gone to interest the Coral in investing in a salt mine in the far-flung regions of the country. Over and over, he would repeat that he had not really compromised his soul with the devil, but no one bought that story. His burnished brow now radiated a sheen of wealth, and his newly acquired suits and expensive Italian shoes further augmented the nouveau riche air in the way he walked with a sprightliness in his steps to his classes from his new car. Plus, for two weeks, trucks bearing gifts from the Coral were seen pulling up into the professor's garage in the middle of the night.

A Moslem, like the Coral, he celebrated the next Eid with the blood of a large bull, the fattest capons, and several gourds of rice pap, but the stress of his betrayal showed. In the cloister of his house, he sometimes took a discreet drink or two to calm him down, now that he had fallen from his students' grace. But he was still arrogant, rude even, to some old people: a terrible insult in Malagueta.

"What a terrible shame!" some of his students raged. "But of course, he has no pedigree."

Tankor Satani was the first to recall that the professor had been one of his severest critics after the execution of Colonel Fillibo Mango, so he gleefully welcomed the "book man's" transformation and smiled thinking that, aside from his problem with the mermaid, things were going well for him.

"Only the devil could have written this new script for me," he said to Moustapha Ali-Bakr.

Three months later, Tankor Satani dropped a bombshell on Malagueta. "I am reshuffling my cabinet, and have decided to name you the new foreign minister," the old fox said after summoning the professor to his office.

With a turnabout seldom seen in Malagueta, Dr. Komba Binkolo lost no time getting into the groove of his new appointment. Soon he was making a spirited defense of the recent executions, chastising the press for continuing to insist that the executed men had been framed. He dug into their private lives for dirt to contaminate their honor, and finding nothing salacious, he doctored his enquiries to make the poor men look bad.

"That academic male prostitute had something to do with my husband's death," Colonel Fillibo Mango's wife grieved. "He was one of the few men in the country who could have pointed out to the president that what my husband had written in that book was innocuous."

Except for Habiba Mouskuda, she lost all respect for the wives and mistresses of the academics, spoke about them with a snake's bile, and began to treat them like dung, especially as, like a pack of hyenas, these bejeweled women wearing new gowns and shoes could be seen going to their children's schools and brazenly trying to bribe the hard-up principals and teachers so that their darling little girls and boys would be able to march on prize-giving day in spite of their poor grades.

"Don't you feel bad about this?" one reluctant teacher asked another.

"No. As we say in Malagueta, 'You should ask for a head, and forget about which school you attended.'"

Theodore Iskander was so furious with his old friend, he couldn't even bring himself to mention his name after the appointment. When he saw the large van pulling up in front of Dr. Komba Binkolo's digs to transport his belongings to the new political quarters, it occurred to the philosopher that, more than the quality of an education, what really counted in life was pedigree: knowing where you came from, if not where you were going. Although all men and women wanted to be free of the burdens of pain, guilt, and poverty, one burden one should always carry was that of shame: it ennobled us. Given what he had been able to confirm—that the place where his old friend was born was really a hovel down on the fishermen's steps—he was not surprised that the new foreign minister lacked that distinction; but that did not ameliorate the contempt Theodore now felt. But his disdain had only just begun, for it became as though the educational system in Malagueta had finally come under siege when several other professors began to hope they too might be called upon to serve in Tankor Satani's cabinet.

Those were hard times in Malagueta. The country had been rocked by a drop in commodity prices and a hike in petroleum prices, and tempers were red-hot everywhere. People lost the liens on their houses to the wise speculators; fruits were left perishing in the orchards in the country, thus allowing the Coral importers to make hefty profits on produce brought in from Lebanon. The national railway stopped running, and it was a sad day for many of the old steam engine drivers when they saw the old locomotives being loaded onto the ships at the harbor after Tankor had sold them to Moustapha Ali-Bakr as scrap. He made a healthy profit when they arrived at their destination.

With most of the academics now in his pay, Moustapha Ali-Bakr should have been happy, but events three thousand miles away threw some sand into the *garri* of his happiness, as they say in Malagueta. War had broken out in Lebanon: the Israelis were battling the Palestinian guerrillas, bombs were raining down on Sidon and other cities, and the Litani River was blocked, causing him quite a good deal of concern because of his business there. So he turned his attention to buying up all the foreign exchange in the banks in Malagueta to help the cause in his fatherland. One night, disguised as a turbaned merchant, he went in a small car to see a great Timbuctan *maulana* in the poor section of the Arab district of Malagueta for a proper reading of the Koran.

"Good evening," the Coral said to the holy man.

"Bismillah al-Rahman al-Rahim: you are a Moslem, Moustapha, so you must greet me accordingly."

"Forgive me, Master, ah forget; but make you nor hide anything from me now," Moustapha said.

"As Allah is my witness, I shall tell you straight," the wizened man replied with an incomparable dignity. Then he opened his Koran and began to read the right verse, which he had selected from Surah 11.

> And incline not to those
> Who do wrong, or the Fire
> Will seize you; and ye have
> No protectors other than God,
> Nor shall ye be helped.

The reading left the Coral deeply perplexed. "Now, make you read me some words of comfort."

The old man fixed an inscrutable look at the rich Coral, then randomly opened a page in *Thinkers of the East* by Idries Shah. In a mellifluous voice he read the words of Sayed Sultan: "'If you pray, and feel satisfaction at having prayed, your action has made you worse. In such circumstances, cease to pray until you have learned how to be really humble.' Go and do likewise," the maulana advised Moustapha Ali-Bakr.

He thanked the holy man, who refused to accept any money for his reading but watched what he hoped was a chastened fool leaving his room.

Three years later, the war at a stalemate but with his eyes set on recouping his losses in the Middle East, Moustapha Ali-Bakr was preparing for a long stay in Lebanon. "Things are slowly shaping up in Beirut, Excellency, sir," he said to Tankor Satani. "The debris is being cleared, the Kasbah is filling up with tourists and European prostitutes, and the once-veiled Arab women smelling of aromatic perfumes have gone back to wearing miniskirts. This is the right time for us to triple our investment."

"Go, my friend, and bring me my share of the profits," Tankor encouraged him.

CHAPTER NINETEEN

Occasion to Dance

EVERYONE WATCHING Hawanatu Gomba, not too long after she had paid Gabriel Ananias a visit, was convinced she had either suffered a case of the nerves or come into some money, because she had started behaving strangely. The regulars at the barbershop opposite the post office where she worked were the first to notice the change in her. She looked different. Gone were the stiff taffeta blouses with the ruffles at the sleeves, the calico skirts cut below the knee, and the raffia handbags. For the first time that they could recall, she was wearing a watch, "as though she has a date with destiny." A whiff of lavender mist rose from her breasts when she went shopping for groceries. She bought gardenias at the florist and inhaled the sweet smell of their white blossoms, and with the sudden unruliness of her heart the days were magical. A few years ago, when she lost what promised to be a paradisiacal life with Theodore Iskander, she gave up the illusion that doing good was sometimes rewarded with an entry into paradise on earth. The enchanting bouquets of marital love or even the bliss of having children might well have passed her, but in the high noon of her new happiness she felt she could once again eat a meal of grilled barracuda to celebrate her contentment with life. She thought of how the sauce might taste.

She stopped doing her hair at home and went to a beauty salon, where she sat for four hours having a tightly entwined Senegalese coiffeur. She replaced her granny glasses with stylish ones, got rid of the cheap copper earrings, the convent shoes, and the floral scarves bought at the flea market. As though she had suddenly woken up to the idea that her eyes were her best asset, she gave up the pernicious habit of applying a thin layer of carbon from the bottom of her pots to her eyelashes. Poised, stepping out with a new confidence, she went early into the post office every day, whereas previously she would trudge in at nine or even later. Yet, as she had done in the past three years of exile, she kept much to herself, thereby furthering the suspicion that she had come into a large fortune she was secretly hiding somewhere, or that she was being kept by a big-shot man. One of the regulars at the barber shop opposite the post office dared to speak to her once on a most personal matter, in the hope of winning a bet he had made with his friends, who considered her a stuck-up, bitter woman.

"You are looking like a new flower in bloom, Ma'am," he ventured. "Somebody must be taking good care of you."

She turned on him like an iguana whose tail had been stepped on and gave him the full fury of her tongue. "I don't need anyone to look after me, but a jackass like you needs looking after."

Her visits to Gabriel Ananias were now fairly regular, so he was not surprised when she turned up at his room one Sunday evening looking radiant in her new outfit. On her first visit she had brought him only fruits and cigarettes, but now, after dusting the table and spreading a tie-dyed tablecloth depicting galloping horses, she produced a bottle of Madeira, some fresh mangoes and June plums—both out of season then—and a casserole of lamb, eggplants, and sweet potatoes she had baked the previous evening. "I have not cooked for a man in a long time, so I hope you like it," she said with a schoolgirl's shyness.

Clearly she was a resourceful woman who was experiencing a mischievous mood in her soul, which she couldn't hide.

While she would come to see him, he had not been to the post office for two weeks, for he was afraid he might be detected if he went there to mail the letters he had been writing to friends in the United States to help him locate his wife and children. The book that he planned to write about his fall from grace was still only a vague idea, one that would be full of his regret for departing from his "good Christian upbringing" and abandoning his entomological interest; full of his disgust with himself, it would be devoid of sentimentality.

But he did not feel up to the task yet because the contrariness and hardship of his present life still distracted from the concentration needed for such an endeavor. Moreover, it meant bringing up bitter and sad reminiscences and ganglions of pain over having been so vain as to be attracted by the shimmering light of the Xanadu. The shame he had suffered since he had last seen his family was unbearable. In addition, writing was a ritual he had never been keen on, and the only ritual he now observed was that of taking long walks to toughen the frailty of his body and help him overcome the brooding insomnia he had been experiencing lately. On those walks, full of rage and shame that his wife had taken up with a lowlife but wealthy Coral, he thought bitterly of her. And he dearly missed his children.

It was eight o'clock when Hawanatu Gomba and Gabriel Ananias finally sat down to the casserole. After they had finished the meal, she ambushed him with what was really on her mind. "You have not finished telling me about how you came to meet Tankor Satani when you were a student."

Gabriel Ananias recalled that when Tankor Satani visited the university as chancellor for the first time, some students had assailed the old man with such a tirade of insults that he later sent a truckload of thugs to beat them up. In gratitude for the thugs' fidelity to him, he immediately rewarded one of them with an ambassadorship and put another in charge of the rice distribution company in the town. "That will teach them respect for government," Tankor Satani said, satisfied with the beatings.

The sweltering heat of March was harsh on the larynx and on cold-blooded reptiles. Business being slow in the shops, there was no "dash" to be offered to the police checking to see whether the Corals had inflated their prices, and the weary-eyed clerks were dozing off in the customs house after lunch. In the courtyard of the national Catholic cathedral, the lepers had also fallen asleep, and the two o'clock hookers had put off going to the Korean boats that came to fish for tuna in the waters of Malagueta. At the convocation, Tankor Satani was dripping with sweat in his chancellor's gown. After hearing what had happened to the chief justice, the professors had finally invited the old man to assume the new office. But his discomfort in the heat was not helped by what he felt was the ingratitude of the students in that powder keg of a university. "They owe its existence to the special contributions that I am channeling to them from the sale of the country's timber and diamonds," he fumed.

Angrily he turned to the vice-chancellor for an explanation of the presence of the wayward coeds he had ordered expelled after they had tried to humiliate some of his ministers in front of their wives in public. "What are these harlots doing here, professor?

"We had no choice, Excellency. Their boyfriends, your ministers, pleaded for them to attend."

The presence of the papal nuncio and other foreign diplomats that Tankor Satani had allowed into the country, "against my better judgment," he often said with regret, tempered his anger. With impressive dignity, he sat through a tirade from a student leader about the lack of good food, books, scientific equipment—all the et cetera of "bad things" at the college. He made it right to the end of the ceremony.

When he was returning home to the Xanadu and was free at last to curse as he was wont to do, his anger reached boiling point when his motorcade was delayed by the appearance of a masquerade to honor the memory of Colonel Fillibo Mango. It was then that the truth hit Tankor that he had gone to the university without first appeasing the "voice" that he had imprisoned in the dark room. So when the day dawned for the second convocation, he left nothing to chance. But the preparations he made were of course very private.

When it was time for him to approach the dark room, he wore a simple white gown and stood trembling in front of the door. Slowly, so as not to make any mistakes, he began to recite the thirteen sacred words: Here I am, Mammy Wata, the queen of the dawn of my fortune. He had greased his forehead with a small ball of ointment that he always carried in his pocket. Yet he waited for another minute before opening the door to the dark room, where he immediately heard the movement of the presence in the black box, its sibilance more threatening than that of a trapped python. He stopped trembling, shook his head to revive his spirits and waited for the voice to speak. He did not have to wait long for the voice of the woman trapped against her will.

"When are you going to set me free?" she hissed.

"Not until I die!" Tankor replied.

"But death is not yours to receive, as you have defiled its beauty."

"The only beauty about death is to die rich," Tankor said emphatically.

"What do you want?" the voice asked, somewhat less threateningly.

"Not money, as I have enough. All I need is for you to prevent those whores from returning to insult me when I go to the convocation at the university."

"You don't need me for that, because you are the son of a whore," the voice said angrily.

Gabriel Ananias was in the back row of the assembled students when Tankor Satani arrived accompanied by his usual retinue of military men, the six enchanting orphans from Niger that he had rescued from the jaws of prostitution, and the sorcerer-eunuch Pallo. Many years later, sitting in his small, unpainted room pouring his heart out to a fellow exile, Gabriel Ananias would recall what happened on that fateful day.

A small commotion by some troublesome students had almost marred the occasion, but they were quickly ejected. Wearing a gold and blue gown, Tankor was finally crowned a Doctor Honorarius, chancellor of the university: the visitor who confers the degrees on the students. He was just about to make his inaugural speech when he saw the hand of a young man rising in the crowd of students. "What is it, my son?" the old man asked.

"You have no right coming here, Mr. President, to lecture to us about the need for sacrifice, after you have spent all that money building your castle on the other side of this mountain."

Two blue-coated officials rushed to the young man and tried to pinion his arms behind his back, but the old man stopped them. "Let him be," he said. "What is your name, my son?"

"Gabriel Ananias."

"I don't have to make a speech to someone like you, my son, because you are the namesake of an angel," Tankor Satani said. "And I can certainly benefit from your advice in matters pertaining to divine providence."

When the furor had died down, everyone felt that, because of his name, Gabriel Ananias must have cast a magic spell on the old man for him to be so compliant. Some enterprising cartoonists even drew lampoons depicting the young man lecturing him, and the conclusion was drawn that there was nothing like a man with some book learning to drive the fear of God into Tankor Satani. After such a promising start, the editorials concluded that Gabriel Ananias was heading someplace in Malagueta.

Even when he was busy with other matters—the Xanadu, worrying about fluctuations in commodity prices, the threat of war in the neighboring republic of Bassa—Tankor would spend a lot of time thinking about the bold young man, wishing he had a son like him. Surprisingly, he did not send for Gabriel Ananias right away, leaving it to fate to bring them together again.

Now that he was the chancellor of the university, his "people"—workers, peasants, taxi drivers, party mammy queens, etc.— came to hear him speak at the second convocation in the amphitheater. He cut quite a distinguished figure in his dark suit, white shirt, and maroon tie and looked very somber when the gown of the university was draped over his shoulders, and he was more comfortable this time to be among the academics.

Besides his wife and aides, he had also invited his new friend, the Coral lawyer Victor Adolphy, and, to show that his heart was in the right place as far as children were concerned, those magically gifted children, versed in the art of talking to djinns, that he had rescued from prostitution and who had insisted on sitting on the floor close to his feet.

Falling back on their habit of making music with the oud in the desert, they began, slowly, to chant his praise in their sweet boyish voices. One brought out a *tama*, a small drum that he had hidden under his gown, and started to beat a rhythm as though they were at a Nubian wedding. The professors were not amused. On top of everything else that they had to put up with, this was a lack of decorum that did not go well with the ceremony, especially after they had welcomed the old man with a speech infused with a little Latin and Greek. What other proof did they need to confirm that, in spite of his high office, the old man was a philistine? Imagine him bringing those heathen kids to a dignified occasion. But they knew well to keep their thoughts private.

The kids were allowed to sing and dance for another five minutes, and they let loose with some more Moorish fantasies on the *tama*, to the obvious discomfort of the professors, before Tankor signaled them to stop. The heat had risen, and the dignitaries were wiping their brows before they settled comfortably into their seats to begin browsing through the program, which was printed in italics. After the professors had finished murmuring about "the terrible kids," a decrepit Protestant bishop and a turbaned imam rose, one after the other, in the timely fashion of the day, to say prayers, calling on their versions of God to be present that afternoon.

Right on cue, a military band began to play "Legends of the Sea," which was Tankor Satani's favorite tune; he was a man intrigued by the voice of the sea.

Although he was among "book men," whom he considered harmless, the old man had taken the precaution of asking Pallo to bring his bag of abracadabra, which the sorcerer-eunuch had hidden under his large gown. If anyone was thinking of spraying the old man with witchcraft powder, he knew he could rely on the sorcerer to protect him. And just in case Tankor felt like resting during the ceremony, the vice-chancellor had taken the precaution of outfitting the VIP guest room with new sheets, while the air conditioner had been adjusted to room temperature, a new spittoon was placed under the bed, and a case of Star lager was chilling in the fridge for when the old man woke up.

Those circadian student-whores who had so riled Tankor on his previous visit had been expelled from the college, taking their frivolousness somewhere else: that was the nose and tail of things in those days. To show his disgust at the way things were going at the university since Tankor became the chancellor, Theodore Iskander had decided to skip the rigmarole of the ceremony, not wanting to have to listen to the old man.

Tankor had let it be known that he expected to see all the judges there. He was not disappointed, because there they were, roasting in their red ermine in the stifling summer heat. He heard them coughing like poisoned chickens, some bringing up phlegm, now that they were obliged to do his bidding after he had tamed all of them.

Defiance danced in the eyes of the chief justice, but Tankor Satani was not worried: he still had the tapes with which he had compromised the distinguished jurist. As soon as the military band had finished, Tankor Satani adjusted his huge frame into the imitation Louis XIV presidential chair, convinced of his immortality. None of the problems crippling the college assailed his thoughts. He felt he had become immortal sitting amongst those academics: he who had never been to college, except for that period spent attending the trade union course so many years ago. When the convocation was over, the playing by the police band of old folk tunes from a bygone happy period added to his levity. But as he got to his car, as though a long summer of forgetfulness had been erased from his mind, it occurred to him that the one person he wanted to see at the convocation this time was not there.

Lying between the legs of a vivacious woman in his dorm, Gabriel Ananias had slipped out of the convocation before the end. "So it was at the first convocation that you met him," Hawanatu Gomba said, touching Gabriel Ananias's arm.

"Yes," he replied reflectively.

The light rain that had been threatening to spoil their enchanting evening had petered out a bit, and the mild November air was sucking up the wet grass by the time he finished his story, but the mosquitoes had left the swamps and were buzzing in their ears. High up in the trees, the weaver birds had settled down to a dark, slightly humid night, and the chimp kept as a pet by the roominghouse owner was thumping its chest, inspired by a woman in the next room singing about her lover on board a ship. A beautiful woman in a peony skirt, she brought the nectar of her song out into the yard with her honey-sweet voice. Buoyed by her own song, she started to dance round a table, grateful that, after six months on a Panamanian-registered ship, her man was coming home. More than his love, she was looking forward to the barrel of salted pork and bacon he always brought after being away from her. It was good to be alive after the end of the rain, her voice said.

Hawanatu drank the first glass of the Madeira and, feeling her spirit fired up by the voice of the singing woman, closed her eyes and imagined the ship on which the man was hurrying home to his lover sailing on a peaceful ocean. She was certain there were flamboyant birds singing on the ship's deck.

"Do you like poetry?" she asked Gabriel Ananias.

"For many years, I read only materials that put money in my pocket. But I too have been consoled by a poet's words now and then."

Hawanatu savored the taste of the wine—a not too expensive one, given their penury. But she knew very little about wines and smiled when Gabriel Ananias began to talk about tannin, bouquet, robust flavors, and the sweetness of some dry wines, South African Riesling in particular, observing that his eyes were misted over with memories of his sumptuous days as a bank governor and of his time with his English mistress, with whom he had enjoyed some rare vintages from the then-pariah nation of apartheid.

More than the other memories of his past wasteful indulgences, that period was too painful. As though sensing his pain, Hawanatu took his arm again to let him know that his reduced status in life would not affect the love in her heart for him. He was grateful for her generosity of spirit in offering him a new lease on life. She took another sip of the wine and in its sweet rich flavor felt a languor she had not experienced in years. Slowly, she loosened the coils of her thick African coif and was assailed by the strange sensation that angels had entered the room, and couldn't help thinking they were the ones that might have danced for her on her wedding day had she married Theodore Iskander. The peony woman waiting for her sailor to come home had stopped singing and had put a sweet ballad on the phonograph. It told of how, in spite of all the hardship of life, love was still the antidote for all of life's ailments.

Hawanatu Gomba was inspired by the music. "Teach me to dance," she said to Gabriel Ananias, and stood up to be led by him.

She wrapped her arms around his neck, plastered her hungry body against his chest, and felt the rumblings of her hunger for love in her soul as they began to dance. Slowly, clumsily at first, they took the long, cautious exit out of the labyrinth of their intolerably miserable years, staggered by how much they had missed Malagueta and the taste not just of good wine but of the wild strawberries of love. After a while, she brought her head to rest on his shoulder and felt very happy. Thinking of the symbolism of his angelic, if misused, name, her lips began to move, and it was she who finally kissed him after so long, wishing that the two of them would one day return to Malagueta, where, because of his name, he would get back on the road to heaven, pardoned by the archangel, just as she knew God had forgiven her for her bitterness against Habiba Mouskuda. Then, because she had been so hungry for love all these years, she took his hand and brought it to her breasts and closed her eyes. In a faraway place, brilliantly lush, clearly the green hills of Malagueta, she saw a dark, svelte woman looking at her before disappearing into a gray mist: a phantom from her past telling Hawanatu that a woman had to learn how to love again after being jilted.

A startled bird's cry escaped from her lips and pierced her heart as Gabriel Ananias, realizing that she was ready, lowered his hand and searched until he had found where she had not been touched for years: a place that was soft and warm.

"Be gentle with me, it has been so long," she said as she opened up to him, a rain forest flower urging him to drink her nectar, as his fire, hot and throbbing, began, in the enchanting, if simple, room, to rise inside the radiance of her dark essence.

CHAPTER TWENTY

First Canto of the Mermaid

WHEN HE was forced to think about his children and reflect on how useless so many of them were, there were times when Tankor Satani felt some of his women had doubled-crossed him. Of his twenty children, ten definitely looked like him, with the deep rings in the neck and the sly, drooping lower lip; and they shared his passion for ribaldry. Like him, they were fairly tall. Remarkably, five of them also cursed a lot like him, and one of his daughters, so the rumors went, could drink the devil under the table, while another had been known to fly off the handle like a deranged cat if provoked. Her servants had also let it be known that she sometimes beat her weakling of a husband a lot when he was drunk. But Tankor Satani's other ten neither resembled him nor had any of his characteristics. Some of those kids were small, fine-boned, thin-lipped, and not given to rudeness. Two of them disliked politics and were very polite, which of course confirmed his wife's suspicion that they were not his.

"Foolish man," she would berate him occasionally, "unbuttoning your trousers everywhere, but not sure what your women have given you!"

She at least had given him one son of whom he was very proud and who he hoped would succeed him, "so that all I have worked hard for is not confiscated by the state after I am dead and gone." His name was Modu. A confirmed lecher like his father, and charming, he was the most intelligent of the children by his wife, even though he was really a failure in all senses of the word. As a teenager, before his father became president, all he did was play craps, and as soon as the bulge in his pants was evident, he began, quite frequently, to sleep with women, some of them double his age. When Tankor Satani became president, deeply concerned about how his enemies would seize on the peccadilloes of a wayward son to attack him, he shipped him off to a Russian university. Unprepared for the rigors of academic life, all the young man ever did was smuggle icons to Germany from the lightly guarded churches in Novgorod and Pskov, after bribing the old agnostic women guarding the churches with imported butter, blue jeans for their sons, and cheap malachite necklaces for their daughters, brought into town in his country's diplomatic bags.

Things were about to come crashing on Tankor's head, because the last time Modu tried to buy an icon from an old woman willing to risk losing her Hero of Soviet Labor medal for a couple of blue jeans her son wanted, things went awry. A guard of the Young Communist League had been watching her; she was arrested and sent to a labor camp, while Modu was put in "diplomatic detention."

Informed through diplomatic channels about his son's plight, the old man thought first of how to keep the news out of the foreign press. His wife had a contrary idea. "Let them jail him so he can learn how to be a man!" Sallay yelled at her husband.

Tankor Satani ignored her. Diamond sales were doing well, so he paid a huge bribe for his son's freedom, with the implied threat, when news of the deal began to leak out in Malagueta, of severe punishment for any write-up in the local press. Quietly, he brought his son home and quartered him for a while in the Xanadu.

The young man had spent most of his life on harebrained schemes paid for by his father, and there was no denying the soft spot the old man had for Modu, especially as he was his spit. Now that Tankor had begun to suspect that the Coral Moustapha Ali-Bakr, was cheating him, he voiced his concern to his son one evening when the young man was with him in the study.

"My bank account is healthy in the Swiss bank, but I am worried about my investments in the islands," he said confidentially.

"Which islands?" the young man asked.

"Las Palmas and Cape Verde, where I have two small hotels."

At the mention of the two hotels, Modu's eyes widened like a finalist's in a great black Jack contest. Looking into the future, he imagined that he might inherit one of the hotels: just the right place, away from home, for him to go scuba diving and engage in a little gambling and womanizing: the pleasures he had not been allowed to relish in Malagueta, so as not to offend the sensibilities of a watchful public since being expelled from the Soviet Union. But he checked his excitement: a dangerous thing when you were one of twenty children, with so many mothers waiting to lay claim to Tankor Satani's wealth after he was dead. He did not want to do anything stupid to raise Tankor's suspicion that he wanted him dead any time soon. But if Moustapha Ali-Bakr was double-crossing his father, Modu felt it was up to him to take care of the Coral. His future might depend on it.

"Give me the okay and I shall have him bumped off the road," he offered.

"Don't worry," Tankor said. "We have some unfinished business in Beirut. But keep an eye on him."

When his son had gone, Tankor stayed in his study for a while and began, in the evanescent evening, to imagine the dynastic line Modu might continue. Increasingly, he had come to think of himself as an emperor and not as a lowly president, and he would have to see that the young man was married to a good woman: someone with class. As usual, he felt unhappy about his other children. They had not really turned out well, and he surmised that it was like a Greek tragedy, given what he knew about men and their destinies. So, in spite of Modu's obvious imperfections, he stood the best chance of continuing his father's legacy. But it was not to be; he would cause Tankor the greatest pain.

One evening when Tankor Satani was thinking that the mysterious vultures had not been flying in and out of the Xanadu for some time, there was chaos on one of the beaches: a dead man had been washed ashore. It was May, when the sea was usually calm, and the drowning spelled a bad omen for Malaguetans, especially as it had happened not far from where some birds-of-paradise French girls had been sunbathing. Stark naked, they screamed as the dead man washed up on the white sands.

"Now de gods really mad with all dis foolish nakedness going on here," a boatman said, watching the girls flee.

The drowned man was fully clothed and, with his dark black hair seemed too young for the hand of death to have claimed him. His face had the pockmarks of a week's stay in the ocean, and his eyes had been eaten out by the savage rubbing of the ocean's salt. He had a gold band on his ring finger, although it was not clear whether it was in fact a wedding band. Giant cow flies were buzzing above his head, his jaws were stiff, and the insipid pallor of a leper was already evident on his face. As the news began to scatter that an angry ocean had thrown up a drowned man, a large crowd rushed to the scene, their faces smitten with horror.

Out of respect for the dead man, they were quiet at first, but soon a few voices began to wonder whether it was a mermaid that had claimed the man as her lover, even though his body had been returned to the world above. Some women began to wail, imagining, in their anguish, the name of the dead man and wondering what had happened to the other men who had gone down in the luxury boat, for it had become clear that the ocean had also claimed the life of a poet and stopped the hearts of a geologist and two engineers on a trip to a small island across from the capital.

Until he himself died, Pallo was to remember the look of the dead man thrown up by the turbulent current. While everyone was wondering who the drowned man was and why the other men had not been washed ashore, Pallo cleared a path so that he could examine the drowned man's face. It took the sorcerer-eunuch only a moment to discern the tragedy that had happened.

"It is all right," he said, bending low to touch the face of the dead man. "De others are lying peacefully in Allah's arms, but ah don't have de mouth to tell de fader of dis one 'bout his loss."

He had just recognized the face of Modu, Tankor Satani's favorite son.

It had been a week since Modu had disappeared during an outing. Fearing the worst, Tankor Satani had spent the past two days waiting for news about the fate of his son and the other passengers. Anxiety reigned in the Xanadu, yet he steeled his heart against the possibility of tragedy, and although he had grown noticeably old overnight, he was resolved not to bend to the will of some incomprehensible force.

"Life has no manual in which one can read the future," he told his wife.

In her grief, Sallay was now completely disgusted with him and had withdrawn into an impermeable silence. When he persisted in consoling her, he was shocked by her reply.

"To cheat life when you are young is one thing, but to go on tempting fate is quite another thing when you are almost at the doors of death. And in case you have forgotten, God is greater than all the generals who wage wars, not to talk of the presidents who order them."

"Then God will give us the strength to recover from our wars," Tankor replied lamely.

He had barely said that when Pallo walked in, his face grave with the confirmation of what Tankor had already anticipated. "Master, you have to come and see what ah not fit tell you me self," the sorcerer said.

The Xanadu was soon full of people who had never been there before: simple folks mixing with the rich; everyone who could make his way to the palace. While his other sons were receiving the notes and voices of condolence, Tankor Satani sat alone in the pitch-black solitude of his study. It was ten o'clock and, unlike that evening when he had listened to the music of the Arab singer as he was thinking about the hydra in Zurich, there was a disturbing silence in the room. From the warrens and crooked streets not too far away, he heard the stray dogs barking plaintively, as though they were aware of the grief in the old man's soul. He also heard, melodious, but intermittent, the warbling of the birds that had not gone to sleep. Then suddenly it was very quiet everywhere. It was then that Tankor Satani heard the menacing voice from the black box in the dark room, a voice as angry as the sound of ocean waves.

"That was only the first sign of my vengeance. Who knows what colors of my hands I shall show you next time if you don't take my comb back to the ocean."

"Not until I die," Tankor Satani moaned in pain.

CHAPTER TWENTY-ONE

An Empty House

MODU'S CORPSE had so decomposed that it was a hastily arranged funeral that sent him to his final resting place. The mourners were denied a final look at him, but were allowed to build a pyramid of flowers on his casket in the courtyard of the Xanadu. Even with the several bottles of French perfume sprayed on him, the corpse still smelled bad and the grief of the people was overwhelming. Many of them had trekked more than twenty miles across Malagueta to get to the Xanadu, and they camped outside under the eucalyptus trees, from where their lamentations rose like sirens in the night to the study where Tankor Satani was holed up in his grief. The common bond felt by the crowd for the dead man was real because, while Modu was pawing his mistresses scattered all over Malagueta, he had been generous to some of the people now in the crowd, for which they began a public discourse about life. Being simple people, many of them had a positive relationship to death, even if the victim claimed by the ocean was not one of their own. Moreover, in spite of the fear that Tankor Satani had begun to instill in their hearts lately, it was true to say that besides what they felt for the son, what had brought them out to mourn was the pity they felt for Tankor.

"To bury your child is painful, but to do so when he is a grown man is a bitter pain," one of them said, and daubed her eyes with a handkerchief.

Two days later, lines of that pain creased Tankor Satani's face as he sat next to his weeping wife, his head bowed, in the front pew of the National Cathedral during the unbearable torment of the crowded service. He looked more gnarled than an old baobab. Blood was almost clotting up in his head because this was the closest he had been to the doors of death since the death of his mother. All the same, he drew from his last reserves of strength to fight the pine needles of his pain. With what was left of the iron in his soul he suppressed his tears. But he was unable to concentrate on the sermon, which was too long. After a while, though, he started listening, not without discomfort, to the bishop intoning on the nature of sin, the faith with which the bereaved should mourn, and an et cetera of things Tankor should do so that God would forgive him for any sins he had committed.

"Those thirty pieces of silver we seek; are they worth the price we have to pay to the devil?" the cleric thundered.

When the service was over, Tankor Satani thanked the bishop for the sermon. The angelic bells were pealing for the last repose of the dead man, and not a bit too soon, as far as the old man was concerned. Although the stained-glass image of a suffering Christ, glorified with his crown of thorns, behind the altar should have given Tankor some comfort about how souls are redeemed, something about the church had riled his soul. That sanctuary, with its plaques of good parishioners now long dead, felt like a cold place to him, a catacomb of dead people, miserable, when what he needed was a warm place—not the warmth of fire, but of peace and tranquility—plus a chalice to cool his lips, whose trembling at the unimaginable tyranny of death he was having difficulty controlling. He needed some fresh air away from so many dead people, their faces sculpted in stone and bronze: deceased sons and daughters whose relatives, with a new pain in their hearts, were now wailing for his son. Slowly he walked through the throng of mourners, thanking a few, before hurrying into his car thinking of how he was going to survive this calamity. As though he had discovered a new idea, it suddenly seemed to him that all men and women were united in the frailty of their souls and in the closeness of death, even those favored for a time by the brush of good fortune.

How cruel a station in life a cemetery is to reach.

Although he had been prepared for some time, given his refusal to return the mermaid's comb, to accept whatever life might dish out to him, the loss of his favorite son was really not what Tankor had expected. He walked in front of the cortege and the mourners entering the cemetery, the flames of a fire roasting his insides continuing to burn. Life—this terrible ambush—suddenly felt like the weight of an elephant's head that he was being asked to carry deep into the eternity of the grave, an eternity clearly beyond the dust that his son was soon to become. With his right hand resting on his golden cane, Tankor Satani looked at the hungry mouth of the grave waiting for his son and realized he had never felt so alone in public, so mortified by the cruelty of fate.

Sallay Satani did not go to the cemetery after the funeral service but went back to the Xanadu, where she shut herself up in her room. For the next month, except when she allowed her other children to bring her food, the world outside was meaningless, a harsh and cruel mirage, a parchment of blurred images that bore no relation to what she was feeling. All day long she sat in front of a picture of her dead son, mounted on a small table and festooned with a wreath of white frangipani. At night, deaf to the pleas of her other children to try to come out of the cloister of her grief, she would recite the only verses she had bothered her head to learn, the psalms of David, drawing from their poetry the same constancy of strength that had kept her going throughout her troubled marriage to Tankor Satani. Her other children, all grown up and living in their own homes, did their best to remind her that she still had them, but as though the death of her oldest son had canceled out her claim to motherhood, she was unresponsive to their voices.

Long before the tragedy, Sallay had come to hate everything that Tankor represented: his power, his ruthlessness, and worse, his greed. Moreover, she was aware that he was hiding *something*: something that made him afraid, although she could not say for certain what it was. She was aware that his fear had always tormented him, even after the interludes of his victories, such as when he had come home boasting about what he had done to the chief justice. But the worst thing about the fear was that it was undefined, always striking indiscriminately at him, entering his body like a scalpel and tearing at the base of his heart. At other times, it seemed to Sallay that Tankor was hiding a stubborn tumor, one that was cancerous, growing in his head, making him distrustful of people. Most painfully, it had deprived him of the ability to give love and had pushed him, shamelessly, to vanity and avarice. Having found no other way to overcome the paralysis of that fear, he began to surround himself with needless toys!

Somehow she couldn't help thinking she was partly to blame for her unhappiness. She recalled how she had allowed her husband, when he came to office, to put out the bogus claim that he had been born into comfort, whereas he was really from nowhere.

Tankor Satani's insecurity, she recalled, would come up quite frequently during their marriage, the worst manifestation of it being that even after he had built the Xanadu his avarice was not checked. "This is insane!" Sallay would yell, but was powerless to stop him.

She watched in silence as he was overcome by the fantasy that he should own a car of every make. To her horror, he set about building a huge garage to house seventeen cars, and magnified his vanity further by his craze for a house in every suburb of the city. The vanity of a possessed man played havoc on his juvenile old man's craving at a time when she thought he should grow old with dignity. How could she not have seen that there was that horrible side to him? she wondered.

But after he confiscated Gabriel Ananias's house and forced the banker into exile, Sallay decided she had had enough of his madness and left him for a while so she could have some peace of mind.

"Life was much happier when you were a dogcatcher and we had very little. Now that you are the president and we can have anything we want, it stinks! This is not the way to get rich. I feel so unhappy sometimes, that it is as if I am living in a prison," she yelled at him before leaving.

She came back because of her son's death, but after she had waited the obligatory period for the repose of her son's soul, she announced to her husband that she was leaving, this time for good. "I don't know about you, whatever secrets you have been keeping from me. What you and your lunatic eunuchs have been up to. But I am not waiting for all the trees I have planted in the garden to start dying to know that another death is going to happen in this house."

"Where are you going?" Tankor Satani asked lamely.

"Back to the same place where you picked me up: amongst people who do not tempt the hand of God."

Dressed in a large, white gown and wearing cheap rubber sandals, she left that night without any formal ceremony, a sign, if Tankor needed one, that she was already shedding her life in the Xanadu and in the previous homes she had shared with him.

She sat quietly in her own small car driven by her own driver, an incomparable dignity plastered on her face. After more than thirty years of marriage, all she took were a few gowns in a suitcase, her Chinese fans, and a handful of jewelry pressed inside her handbag. "Is that all you are taking?" Tankor Satani asked, powerless to stop her leaving him for good.

Instead of a reply, she gave him a long, pitying look, one that would have wounded a hardened criminal or helped to age palm wine on a tree. After she had gone beyond the walls of the Xanadu, she did not even turn back for a final look at its imposing structure; she had never felt comfortable in that monstrosity. A week later, back among people who would help her heal, she began to tear the final threads of her husband out of her life with a brutality that surprised her. She canceled out all the years she had spent with him. The smell of his clothes was quickly forgotten, and so too was his favorite cologne. She suppressed the image of how he had knotted his ties, even of the aroma of his tobacco, which she had liked. All she was looking forward to was this peaceful retreat in her village, where, for the rest of her life, she was going to wear the white calico of a mother for whom the wind had gone out of her sail.

When Tankor Satani realized he was alone in the vast rooms of the Xanadu, he came to the painful conclusion that he had not really loved his wife, nor had any of his remaining nineteen children brought him happiness. Old age was lonely, painful, useless, if wasted on regrets, losses, grief, and failures, he reflected. At that stage in life, men should be able to transform their tragedies into strength; pain must somehow lead to equanimity. He had to go on. That was why he was holding on to what life's mysteries had given him.

Slowly he began to walk to one of the many verandahs that ringed the Xanadu, and in a vaguely distracted manner watched the line of cars snaking through one of Malagueta's main arteries. A forlorn figure, he imagined it was a lonely world down there as he pictured broken men living unattainable dreams: men drunk most of the time, beating their women and cursing their children in their powerless rage. More painfully, he also imagined the women worn out from giving birth too many times, and felt that perhaps now that an older daughter was the right age and had begun to attract men. she was the one providing for the family. He forgot about that hard world, sniffed the jasmine, and began to pace up and down; then, after stopping near the pots of gardenia, he moved on and realized that the geraniums needed a little bit more sun to keep them from dying. Having known so many deaths—his mother's, men's in the mines, and now his son's—he felt that nothing should be allowed to die again, even though he had been tempting death recently himself. Night was falling and scattering its luminous stars over the restless city. Finally exhausted, he sat down and began to brood in the capsicum of old age, thinking about his life and that of his dead son. Whatever future he might have wished for Modu had all but vanished by the time the youth turned sixteen, and Tankor Satani belatedly realized he was partly to blame, as he himself was inadequate in some ways.

Much as he would have denied it to his sorcerer, he had always been haunted by the fear that no one loved him or respected him, not even those factotums who slaved every day to carry out his orders. He thought of the enigmas he had read in the faces of his people, those tortured masks which, however much he tried to forget about them, haunted his nights with insomnia. Moreover, he would have been surprised to know that, long before she left him, his wife had come to the same conclusion about the prevalence of his fear. How shocked he would have been to learn that this simple woman he had plucked from a rural background, this woman who seldom had an opinion about anything, was the one person who best understood him! In her view, his vaingloriousness and madness to acquire things—houses, cars, money—was not because he was another corrupt politician, but because he had a deep void in him: a fear that he might fail in life, that he could slip once again to being a mere cog in the wheel of human development. No, he was not corrupt. It was worse than that. He was an empty shell of a man, someone driven by an uncontrollable passion to possess people, to control them.

When he was alive, Modu Satani had not seen his parents in a setting pregnant with love. On the contrary, his memory as a boy was full of the unhappiness of his mother: her silences, those monologues about "a woman's lot," the sadness that would creep into her eyes as Tankor Satani was planning his strategies to prolong his stay in power.

"My son," she cried one evening when she could no longer hide her grief, "I am only putting up with this hell because of my children and also because the shame of leaving your father would kill all the trees in the yard. But I am afraid of death."

When he thought about his dead son, Tankor Satani admitted he had fathered a monster. Suddenly the truth struck him that all his power, money, and possessions were only substitutes for the love he had not given to his children, nor dared admit he himself needed.

The Xanadu had never seemed so empty and cold: a waste of the national treasury, he was beginning to admit privately; a place perpetually haunted by a dead amanuensis and other ghosts that had refused to disappear permanently, its vast space, ugly and soulless, as miserable as a mortuary after Modu's funeral and the departure of Sallay.

"What is the use of a palace without people, emptied of love?" Tankor thought one evening, and shook his head, sipping a goblet of brandy as he assessed his present predicament.

After a while the eerie silence in the palace began to prey upon him. For the first time since the death of his son, he stopped to reflect on what had been foretold by the mermaid when he had not bothered about her threats.

Missing his son dearly and wanting to be near him, he went to the enormous garage one evening. He was alone, having waved away his driver, and he opened the doors of two of the expensive cars, mindlessly looking for something to remind him of his son. The cars had not been driven since Modu died, and in them there was a rancid smell of dried vomit, brandy, and cologne and the odor of his numerous women. Through the prism of Modu's death, Tankor Satani began to imagine he could see his own future unfolding.

He was past seventy, a crucial age for a man obsessed with immortal longings but who was now surrounded by the shadows of death. For the first time in his life he thought he might not make it to that threshold because the journey suddenly detailed in front of him was on an aimlessly scary road, not much of it clear. He wished he could be given back his youth or a few more good years to make amends for his faults. Desperate to make something of what was left of his life, he once again turned his attention to the events at the first convocation, where he had encountered Gabriel Ananias.

His own children—the trees of his life—had not matured, but there was always another one to be planted. Once again, he thought of how Gabriel Ananias had stood up to him. He liked that in a man and would make a son of him, because there was still some iron left in the soul of an old man to raise a real son.

Not until he died should they consider him finished!

CHAPTER TWENTY-TWO

The Not-So-Discreet Charm of the Bourgeoisie

THEODORE ISKANDER was so overjoyed when he discovered that Habiba Mouskuda was pregnant again that he went out and got really drunk one evanescent evening. As the rum wetted his lips, he felt the first signs of dizziness, and it occurred to him that it was his first feeling of inebriation in a long time; in fact, since his last encounter with Hawanatu Gomba, the woman his mother had hoped he would marry. He still thought occasionally about Hawanatu and hoped she had forgiven him for leaving her. For better or worse, he felt destiny had driven him to the Coral he would probably spend the rest of his life with, in spite of her famously tempestuous nature. Yet he was thrilled about becoming a father, although he knew Irene was still deeply convinced that the wily malatta had fried his heart with some raw plantains in a witch's brew and fed them to him. How else could she explain the madness of his son's choosing such a disaster, when there were so many nice gals from good families to choose from?

"What do you expect from a woman like that, Reverend?" she complained to her pastor when the cleric happened to drop by one morning for a cup of tea. "After she has slept with every Tom, Dick, and Harry, she now wants my son to give her *respect*! I know it is witchcraft."

The cleric had a contrary opinion. "Your son is undoubtedly a brilliant man, But in matters of the heart, all men are fools," he said with mischief in his eyes.

For his part, Theodore Iskander did his best to assuage his mother's doubt that the malatta genuinely loved him. "Things will turn out well with Habiba, so stop worrying."

Irene gave him a long look that spoke volumes about what she thought of the relationship, but kept her peace.

After rejecting the idea that Habiba might have used a love potion on him, Theodore Iskander went on with the business of preparing his notes for his university lectures. Deeply concerned about where Tankor Satani was taking the country, he saw to it that, in addition to their required texts, his students were reading Amilcar Cabral, Nyerere, Soyinka, George Padmore, and the only book of the imprisoned Nelson Mandela: all of them illustrious sons of Africa. When he was alone in the privacy of his small study and overwhelmed by the fragrance of the jasmine in the garden, the enigma of how he had come to love a volatile woman of such undeniable allure would sometimes occupy his mind. But he soon gave up trying to analyze the relationship, deciding it was a waste of time to understand the vagaries of human emotions.

"Passion is a violent bird!" he groaned.

Until he met Habiba Mouskuda, he had not really given the impression that he was a man who could be driven to the extremes of passion by women. And before his relationship with Hawanatu Gomba he had moved from one woman to another, avoiding any commitment, always reminding those stubborn women, who would use all kinds of tricks to trap a man, not to leave their slippers and nightgowns at his place, and not to cook for him, thank you, his mother was doing that just fine!

Wrapped up as he was in his political and philosophical thoughts, he had always avoided a long-term relationship. That was until Georgina Nandi-Thomas breezed like a fairy into his life.

She was a linguist with a spurious aristocratic air that he found amusing. She was twenty-eight, not exactly beautiful, but sparkled with an ebullient mischief and had been raised, since childhood, in an old-world culture. Tall, with lips that moved with a sorceress's intent, she was "copper-colored," two shades lighter than the dark-skinned philosopher. The second of three children in a family notorious for its pretensions, she lived under the thumb of a domineering social-climbing mother who felt her daughter deserved the proposal of a successful doctor, or at least a promising lawyer, even though Georgina's virtue, as far as those double-standard men were concerned, had been compromised by the number of men she had slept with by the time she was twenty-six. She had the bourgeois taste for brandy and the playfulness of a spoiled child, and her mind was as unsteady as a wind. Moreover, although she played a Chopin mazurka or two on the piano now and then, and had been educated in Malagueta and Europe, those accomplishments did not compensate for the fickleness of her heart or her lack of self-esteem, as Theodore was to discover after they started going out. So by the time she was twenty-eight, rather than being a top-notch professional woman desired by a surgeon or lawyer, she was still floundering in the waters of uncertainty as far as her choice of a mate was concerned.

Soon after her birthday in March, the air in Malagueta was tinged with the fragrance of its exotic flora. She had taken to wearing colorful skirts and exquisite jewelry, and looked very lovely when her path crossed Theodore Iskander's. In spite of her reputation for being fickle, and for having passed through the hands of several doctors, he came under her provocative spell. He did not share the bourgeois sentiment about a woman's past; if anything, he felt her experience of men was an asset. She should have learned a lot from those failed relationships, and hopefully was wiser, making her just the kind of woman he had always wanted to marry.

Although he lacked money, he thought his integrity was his best asset, and surprisingly, for the very first time in his life, he was seriously considering the possibility of living with a woman. It was not to be. The relationship lasted a brief three months, partly because their futures were sailing against each other like east and west, the Kremlin against the White House: his toward a deeper political involvement in Malagueta, while so many others were afraid to speak out. While hers? She was too much a part of her class, those who were always going on with their heads in the clouds, not wanting to dirty their hands in politics and finding ephemeral comfort in their supposedly superior standing in society. So it wasn't long before it became clear to Theodore Iskander that her life had to conform to the script of her interfering mother.

"He is just a lecturer, when you could still hope for a doctor or lawyer," she cautioned her daughter.

"Open your eyes, mother! There are not too many of them left unattached. And I am lucky that Theodore wants me."

The two lovers seemed to enjoy each other's company for a while, going to parties, the cinema, and concerts, where, with her spurious aristocratic airs, Georgina would sometimes act like a prima donna. But her limitations in music were so glaring, Theodore Iskander sometimes felt like laughing. She knew nothing of the *messa di voce* refinement of Montserrat Caballé or the classical lyricism of the great kora musician Toumani Diabate. All the same, he continued to see her, considering that she did have some virtues; but when, after two months, he had not mentioned the magical word "marriage," she was the one who broached the subject one evening, after they had just finished making passionate love.

"If I get pregnant, will you marry me?" she asked.

"I shall marry you whether you are pregnant or not, but will not marry you simply because you are pregnant," he replied, trying to put her in her place.

All the same, one month later, they were making plans for a simple wedding: one without the outlandish parade of her antediluvian aunts, who, sweating under the weight of their artificial jewelry and copious gowns, would be competing with her uncles in their black Venetian frock coats and Saxon shoes. Grudgingly, Theodore Iskander agreed to the postnuptial goombay music at the girl's house, but not to the other we-must-do's in that crazy place: all that highfalutin drama that would have driven a saint mad. And he was definitely not going to wear a suit! "I am not going to parade like a peacock in a frock coat to please your family," he told her bluntly.

"Then you don't love me!" she cried.

He was unrelenting. However, given how obsessed with decorum and God her family was, he held his agnosticism in check and was prepared to suffer the one-hour church service, wearing African attire, after she had pleaded with him and they had drawn up a list that allowed her thirty guests while he was left with twenty. Irene was not happy with that agreement; she had numerous friends she wanted to invite to her only child's wedding, even though she did not like the "aristo airs" of the girl.

"I can't stand her moder either," Irene confessed to her caterer.

"But de gal is your son's choice, so leave everything in God's hand."

"What a choice!" scoffed Irene.

Three weeks before they were to tie the knot, as though God's hand had moved the wrong way, Theodore began to notice that Georgina's eyes were not the sweet gems of love that he had known for a while. Something had changed about her. She had neither her usual cheerfulness nor the playfulness that was always waiting to burst out. Rather, she seemed to be laboring under a strain and avoided looking straight at him when she spoke. And as though searching for something far removed from Malagueta, her eyes had a vacuousness that troubled him, so that she seemed to him like a lost Titania responding to some wayward fairies. When they made love, it was without her usual sensual voracity. She offered him only the tepid surrender that she felt her duty required, leaving Theodore wondering what their marital woes would be like in the future after they were both tired of sharing the same bed.

For a while, Georgina continued to pretend that nothing was wrong. But Theodore was not fooled.

"Come down to earth," he said to her. "I can only make love to a woman, not an idea."

One day she did something that confirmed his suspicions. They had just finished another imperfect hour in bed. While Theodore lay smoking a cigarette, she opened his wardrobe as though intent on a robe to drape her nakedness, but instead began to examine his clothes. She counted the handful of trousers, his meager collection of shirts, the four pairs of shoes, and his vests. Since he did not own a suit, the exercise was quickly over, and her face told Theodore what he had suspected: he was not a big-shot lawyer and would probably not be able to keep her in style.

Matters came to a head one week later when he was lying in bed trying to fight off a bout of malaria, and she arrived with some fruits and juices. He was almost delirious from the effects of the malaria, yet his senses were acute to her responses, and he could tell she was merely going through the basic rhythms of administering to his needs.

"What is wrong with you?" he demanded.

"Nothing. Don't talk; you are not well."

"I know there is something on your mind that I want to hear, even if I am going to die tonight."

She avoided his eyes and took a deep sea cow's breath. Then, as though recalling a lesson she had learned but did not know how to repeat, given its taste of castor oil, she blurted out what had been troubling her. "My mother wants us to postpone the wedding indefinitely."

Theodore sank into a terrible depression for days. Thinking he might not recover from the malaria, Irene spent the next three weeks fighting it. With the vigor of a frantic mother, she put two hot water bottles on either side of her son to steady his neuralgic fits. She cooked pepper fish soup with thyme and basil and made strong ginger tea. Even though she knew her son was not a practicing Christian, she read the Twenty-Third Psalm to him and prayed for his soul, staying up all night when he seemed to be at the doors of death. Watching him drift in and out of the delirium of cerebral malaria, she trembled with rage that any woman would try to break the heart of her son, and she swore that she would henceforth have a say about the next woman he showed an interest in. The thought that her only child might die from a broken heart filled her with such horror that she went to the cemetery at one o'clock in the morning, bringing a live chicken and rum as offering to the dead. The moon was shining its bright watchman's eyes, and Irene was grateful for the its luminescence on the frangipani shading the nearby graves as she slit the throat of the bird and tossed it to the head of her mother's grave before spraying the grave with a good splash of rum, after which she lay at the foot of the grave and begged the dead not to take her son from her. "I shall die with him," she cried.

A week later, a strong concoction of forest herbs supplemented with a copious amount of bay leaf pepper soup, coupled with her prayers, eventually worked its magic, and Theodore's fever finally broke. And as soon as she felt he was strong enough to listen, Irene was forthright in her views about Georgina.

"Ah knew dat foolish aristo gal was not good for you, my son; so full of herself, and wit' dat crazy moder to boot; but you were so much in love ah did not want to interfere. After all, I am only your moder. But from now on, ah shall have something to say about any gal dat you want to marry!" She wiped away her joyous tears over his recovery from the illness and the fate of marrying "dat woman."

Three months later, when Theodore seemed to have got over what Irene called "a sickness of de heart," he received a letter from Georgina Nandi-Thomas posted from a northern European capital, where she had accompanied her mother to a women's congress—more to see the splendor of the city than to recover from the thwarted relationship.

"You will thank me one day, child," her mother said, "for saving you from a union with a penniless philosophy professor."

"He was probably my last chance at getting a man. You have ruined my life, mother!" Georgina cried. It was the first time she had ever contradicted her mother.

In her letter to the philosopher, written in beautiful cursive, she expressed her profound sorrow for what had happened and asked him to take her back, blaming her fickleness on a tyrannical mother hell-bent on choosing her daughter's suitor.

"In the deepest resources of my heart, I regret what happened," she wrote candidly.

It was too late.

While she was waiting for him to rescue her from her tyrannical mother, Theodore Iskander had spent the last two months analyzing what he had found fascinating about Georgina to the point that he had wanted to marry her. Now that she was away and he could think straight, the enormity of what she had done began to weigh heavily on his mind. It was while he was trembling with a bad case of malaria that Georgina had revealed how fickle she could be; what would she be like under other circumstances? His going to jail, for instance: would she have the strength to rally people to his defense? His mother was right: he would have made a terrible mistake marrying Georgina. For once, in the matter of common sense, he was willing to concede that Irene had won.

Years later, when he began secretly to go out with Habiba Mouskuda, one of his close friends came to warn him that he was making another terrible mistake. "She is a woman who has eaten the hearts of her past lovers: a bad woman who could destroy you."

"That is all right, my friend," the philosopher said. "I have been with a good woman before, and she was a disaster."

To the disbelief of his other friends, who would have kept Habiba Mouskuda hidden somewhere for the sole purpose of sex, he brought her out into the open and showed her off at diplomatic parties. He watched as her willowy, trance-like air sent some of the Western diplomats searching for the right verbs to express their desire for her when they thought he was not listening. But she only had eyes for him and kept him happy before and after he retired to his study to read Marx, Rousseau, and Nkrumah, ensuring that his head was not lost forever in reading those men's theories about social conditions in the world.

She was not unaware of what some of his friends thought about her, but dismissed their slurs as sour grapes because she had refused to go to bed with them. Now and then she would tease Theodore about how good it was for him, a philosopher, to have an exotic, nonbookish woman like her to take his mind off the complicated world of philosophy and politics.

"You know I have had a surveyor, a colonel, a general, and enough businessmen to give me an idea of finance. But you are my one and true love, my soul mate, Theodore," she cried one night after they had made passionate love.

"It is all right," he said. "I have always preferred *La Traviata* to virgins."

"Who was she?"

"It is an opera about an unchaste woman."

"There must be many of us," she said softly.

Momentarily transported to her past escapades, she left him to his own deep thoughts.

CHAPTER TWENTY-THREE

The Times They Were Living In

THEODORE ISKANDER spent almost three months brooding over the betrayal by his erstwhile friend, Dr. Komba Binkolo, after the latter joined Tankor Satani's cabinet. Afterward the philosopher seemed emptied of some of the bliss that being an academic had brought him. A dark cloud of uncertainty hung over him, and besides the pleasure that his woman was giving him, the only light about him was the occasional spark when he went down to one of the ghettoes to talk to some restless youths who had been railing against the government. One day one of the youths came all the way to his office to caution him.

"Be careful, Professor," he said sheepishly, feeling a bit out of place in the college surroundings." Tankor Satani probably has a spy down in my ghetto, and I don't want anything happening to you, like what happened to that colonel."

"Don't worry too much about me," Theodore Iskander said, and thanked the youth. "Tankor Satani has more pressing things to worry about after the death of his son."

Yet clouds of self-doubt continued to shadow the philosopher as he delved deeper into metaphysics, which he felt was contrary to the conditions of human beings in a deeply unequaled world. In a mix of politics and poetry, he would sometimes call to mind the leadership of the fiery young nationalist soldier named Thomas Sankara in a nearby country, while the voice of his ancestor, the poet, was uncannily urging him on with his work. He thought about the rumor, now gaining currency, that it was a mermaid that had drowned Tankor Satani's son. But after pondering on the tales about mermaids, nymphs, gnomes, and genii, Theodore Iskander decided there was nothing concrete in their subterranean world, beyond a certain fascination with the mythic, so he quickly dismissed the belief that a vengeful mermaid had assailed the old man. "It is another ruse to trick us while he is plotting something more terrible than the last round of executions," he decided.

A few weeks earlier he had embarked on a major writing project. After several failed attempts, his paper on politics, wealth, and morality had started to take shape; when published, it should stand him in good stead for a promotion in his department. That was something he had hoped for, but it now seemed irrelevant. He missed his mistress.

He stayed away from her for days, riding the crest of the illusion that he could go for a long time without wanting to sleep with her, wondering how many pages he had to complete before he would find some satisfaction in his work. In the clutter of his study, a light burning into the night, he buried his head in his work, drinking cup after cup of black coffee spiced with cardamom, and was sometimes carried into an Italian idyll by the sweet, burnished voice of Leontyne Price in Verdi's *Il Trovatore.* He was almost forty-seven, but still full of dreams about taking Malagueta back to a golden age. Yet he felt that, except for his lover and, perhaps, Irene, no one understood what he was trying to do; but he still had to convince his mother he had not been bewitched by "dat malatta."

Even with the inspiration of the great poet Garbage Martins, Theodore Iskander continued to feel lonely, especially as he had always felt like a lone traveler trying to do good in the face of so much evil in a country run by greedy men and speculators who did not give a damn for his altruism, which they found strangely amusing in a not too well-off philosopher. In a small city, it was easy for him to recognize those men by the way they spoke with contempt for the less fortunate, the pittance they would throw to the poor under the great cotton tree where they had taken to sleeping, unmindful of the vultures and dog-faced bats shitting on them.

"But that is not as bad as what is going on at the campus, professor," his favorite student—one who was deeply worried about him—offered during office hour. "Terrible things are happening right here to the girls."

"Such as?" the philosopher asked.

"Some of them are going to bed with the cabinet ministers and top civil servants, and even with some Corals, although the girls say they hate their guts."

"Why do you think they are doing that?" Theodore inquired gravely.

"The lure of fast cars; greed; and for money, so they can shop at the expensive Lebanese shops and go to the beach hotels where everything is expensive."

After the student had gone, Theodore Iskander was driving home in a small downpour, guided through the narrow streets by the weak bulbs barely gleaming from a few porches in the usual city blackout. He had been away from his mistress for almost two weeks; now he suddenly had the urge to see her.

She had been waiting for him to come so she could tell him about her plans for their future. Now that they were expecting a child, her dream was that he would move in with her; she would have the house painted mustard cream, his favorite room color, and would convert the third bedroom into a study. In the peace of that room, he would listen to his beloved Franco and the O.K. Jazz Orchestra, his operas, and the music of Orquesta Aragón of Cuba while she watched American soaps in the living room. But first she had to come to terms with the image of her dead son that had been appearing in her dreams. Once again, she went to see Pallo to unburden her soul of its torment. The sorcerer listened patiently before replying.

"Dat child not born properly," he offered.

"What do you mean?" Habiba asked.

"Being born is 'bout love; how de *pikin* go come to its moder; how de moder go love am. When your first *pikin* born, you nor love am. And, big mistake you make; you nor give am chance to love you. Dat make you bad moder; so he nor born proper."

"How can I make him love me as his mother?"

"Dat's not for me to tell you," the eunuch replied. "Ah know 'bout medicine, but ah not know 'bout daddy bisness."

Thinking of the mysteries of the world, especially the one growing in her womb, Habiba drove back to her house. She had always found Pallo's pronouncements enigmatic, and this one merely added to the cloud of confusion under which she had been for so long. Yet no sooner did she enter the house than she was resolved to push everything to the back of her mind and not to tell Theodore about the dream cycles she had been experiencing, or about visiting the eunuch. The cool breezes of the harmattan had begun to whistle in a low drone through the city, scattering a thin membrane of dust from the Sahel, which reminded people that December was approaching. In the amber evening, she sat looking at the clouds and heard the thunderous ocean throwing up great schools of minnows, on which the sandpipers fed furiously. Rising from the eastern edge, the city air smelled of breadfruit roasting on open fires as people waited for a good meal. but a freakish storm was soon rocking her windows and throwing dust in her face, so she went inside. Going from room to room, she closed the windows but left one open, reasoning she needed the fresh air in those anxious hours as she was about to move from the enigmas of a sorcerer-eunuch to the power of her virile lover. As the wind blew its melodic notes, the wide jacaranda branches kept the house safe from that force.

She had a long shower, soaped her armpits, breasts, pubic hair, and began to sing, in a soft voice, an old folk song about a catfish that fell in love with a wandering pigeon. The spikes of the ocean winds bore into her bones, but now that she had discovered how beautiful being in love could be, it was as though she had been transformed into the catfish and was waiting patiently for her wandering bird to come to her. She would see to it that he went nowhere else. When she heard her lover's car turning into the driveway, she toweled herself and waited. The naked warmth of her advanced pregnancy glowed in the jade light. But rather than jumping into bed with her right away, Theodore Iskander began to unburden himself of what had been troubling him since his conversations with his student.

"Are you aware of what the women are doing for their children in this country: sleeping with disgusting men?"

"Yes, but we have all done it for one reason or another," she said, certainly not prepared to go into that territory again.

Sometime in the middle of the night, as they lay naked, they heard the renewed *pata pata* of the rain on the lee of the house, quite loudly for that time of the year. But she did not mind.

"Oh, good," she said; "now you don't have to think about leaving first thing in the morning to go and pretend to your mother that you had slept in your own bed."

She snuggled up to him, and the sweet blossom of her passion, intense and warm, unleashed in great spasms now that she was quite heavy, rose and fell with the rhythm of the rain, her rich juices oozing out, so that her lover was glad of her radiance as the cold sauntered in through the window. Before this night he had not really noticed how her pregnancy had changed the contours of her body. Its beauty was stunning, the black of her nipples contrasting with the brown of the rest of her body. Honey was pouring out of her as he began to respond to her after she had made his penis hard again. At the first crack of dawn, happy but worn out by her, he got out of bed, dizzy from being kept busy like a young bull all night long. Finally able to leave the bed and stand by a window to inhale the air from the garden, he admired the bristling life of the topaz butterflies beating their luminous wings on the hibiscus, oleander, jasmine, and croton.

The rain came to a sudden halt. Streaks of golden light polished the room as Theodore Iskander, looking like a bronze god standing against the white walls that Habiba had painted, pushed the curtains aside. He felt tired but happy; how else could he explain what he had experienced that night, in the heat and passion of his mistress, listening to the rhythm of the rain?

"Come to bed and hold me again," Habiba said.

She had woken up from the peaceful dream she had been having about a journey they had embarked on. Coming after so many nights of being haunted by the spirit of the albino, this was a pleasant dream. In it, she and her lover had gone to live on an island, away from the volatile politics in Malagueta, sick of its scandals, the rubbish on the radio about the politicians. Shoals of the blue fish and lobsters that only the Corals, potbellied men of the collar, politicians, and tourists could afford to eat had swum in her dream, but she had not been interested in the marine life; her happiness had more to do with this man of bronze, a proud descendant of a great poet, than with what any island could offer.

"Do you sometimes wonder what is going to happen to us in ten years' time?" she asked.

"Not really; and it is not because I do not contemplate a future with you."

"And you have no regrets meeting me, even though I am a terrible malatta?" she laughed.

"None at the moment; so let us leave everything to fate to determine what is going to happen to us. For now, I feel we shall be together until my teeth begin to fall out and the lines of your neck have collapsed into a mass of slackening flesh."

"You say such beautiful things; it is one of the reasons why I love you."

"You seem to forget that I am descended from a great poet," he said.

CHAPTER TWENTY-FOUR

Between Two Women

WITH THE harmattan shimmering through the coconut trees on the beaches, December was when the oleander bloomed in Malagueta. Now that the rains were over, you could feel the tempestuous ocean rhythmically beating her drums: those magical sounds of a generous woman spewing an abundance of large barracudas that, when caught, some young men would march up and down the city's streets trying to sell. The air was sweet and the leafy seaside palm groves were cool, just the right temperature for outdoor celebrations. After wearing blouses and pants during the rainy season, many of the city's young women now looked stunning in African gowns—*bubas* and *lappas*—strolling leisurely on those crowded but enchanting streets, smelling of the erotic perfumes of Marrakech. Large golden earrings drooped from their lobes to enhance their exotic look, and after they had painted their lips with henna and sat for six hours for spectacularly elaborate hairdos, their eyes set on a "good" Christmas, they went off to their sugar daddies to collect for past favors.

The horror of Tankor Satani's drowned son had receded into forgetfulness, and the talk in Malagueta now was all about love, the sweet harmonies in people's souls, how the baby Christ was singing in their ears. Most nights, people went to bed and dreamed about chariots of gift-bearing angels, new lovers, and jobs: specters of hope that they would embellish next morning with all kinds of make-believe stories, clinging to them for the rest of the week. Money was short, but young men and women, brazen in their ripe sexuality, would crowd inside the bone-shaker vans, with all kinds of pastries, roast pepper chickens, fricassee, coconut oil–cooked crab meat, goat meat pepper soup, and drinks, singing and laughing as they headed for the beaches—those long-suffering people—where they would hold moonlight picnics and end up making love with inebriated passion under the palm trees bedecked with garlands, before the French and Scandinavian tourists arrived in droves to take over the white sands.

It was during this period of unbridled happiness that Tankor Satani stunned the nation with a most unexpected munificence: a pay increase of 25 percent for all workers.

Firecrackers had illuminated the sky from the Xanadu's windows that morning. In the music room the desert orphans, deeply touched by his generosity after he had ordered new suits for them, had resumed their rhapsodic carousals from the previous evening, when their drums and castanets had kept the eunuchs up all night, interfering with their prayers. After being caged up in a barn for a whole month, during the period when Tankor Satani was being eaten up by grief, the Abyssinian roosters had almost lost their beautiful plumage. But with the first signs that Tankor was coming out of the season of his grief, the servants brought the birds back to the henhouses, where they crowed so much that it was easy to feel, at least for now, that the siege of death had been lifted over the Xanadu.

Although he was ready to appear in public, Tankor nevertheless asked Pallo to consult the stars.

"It is good time for you to go to office," the great eunuch said effusively.

At ten o'clock one Friday morning, Tankor Satani came out of mourning. He emerged from the Xanadu with a dignified air, wearing a white suit, crocodile leather shoes, a pastel tie, and a Panama hat. A fresh gardenia in his buttonhole confirmed that he had woken up early and gone into his garden to get some flowers. His steps were brisk and confident as he waved a white handkerchief and gave a victory sign, and he smiled broadly to the small crowd that had gathered outside of the Xanadu to wish him well. Then he was driven off to his office in downtown Malagueta. He was the first to greet his ministers in the cabinet room, the first such meeting he had attended in two months, and he surprised them with his gaiety, making them laugh at his crude jokes. During his months of mourning, the ornate ballroom had been draped in a monotonous gloom, the lights turned off, and the curtains drawn. Now the great chandeliers were lit again, and a golden sun came through the open curtains, so that the curious folks, pressed together tightly but amicably in the gardens of the Xanadu, could see and break into clapping when Tankor Satani appeared at a window to wave to them.

"They made me feel as if they had also lost a son," he said, dabbing his eyes with his white handkerchief.

With a brilliant stroke, he had timed his generosity to coincide with Christmas, the time when the old folks and children were expecting their once-a-year presents from their faraway kin in Brixton in London, in Washington, turning tricks in the brothels of Rome, or laboring in the vineyards in Spain. Throughout the year, they worked hard at any menial job they could find in Europe or America to send food chests home for Christmas: boxes filled with ham, kippers, clothes, shoes, fruitcakes, Bailey's Irish Cream, scotch—all of which could be gotten in Malagueta but which they thought would be appreciated as coming from overseas. There was nothing to bring out the shine in an old woman's ebony face like serving her friend a tot of rum from a bottle stamped "For Export Only." "Go easy wit' dat rum, Kezia, 'cause ah don't know when next ma *pikin* go send me something dis good," she would say.

Shoppers—those with money in their pockets—thronged the colorful street markets looking for good bargains: clothes, jewelry, apples (apples!) from Lebanon, and, most coveted of all, the latest styles in the junks clothes bales, so that in church on Christmas day they would appear with dignity and raise their voices to celebrate the birth of the Messiah.

Lacking the easy rhythm of the Africans when they tried to dance, the pudgy Corals looked like baby whales out of the ocean, but that did not stop them going native and showing off their ungainly girth as they chased the black girls in the enchanting evenings on their own private beaches. Some calypso musicians, dressed like Moorish men, saw a chance to make a little extra money croaking the old songs that had kept people happy before the time of Tankor Satani. On another stretch of beach, temporary bamboo hutches had been erected, and the confectioners were doing a brisk business in groundnut cakes and peppermints. The bars had doubled their supply of liquor, this being one time of the year when God was supposed to turn a blind eye to inebriation. Christians as well as Moslems could forget about their religious strictures and become brothers and sisters over a bottle of rum or beer. Few were the poultry and pig farmers that did not triple their profits in that season. Tired of the stuffiness of their suits and ties, the men, like the women, changed their attire and went about in colorful tie-dyed shirts that had kept the tailors busy all week. The rich men looking very important in their Yoruba gowns and straw hats, such a glint of excitement in their eyes they could have been mistaken for people who had won the national lottery.

While Tankor Satani was coming back into public view during the fever pitch of Christmas, Habiba Mouskuda was thinking about the baby she was about to have. But one particular chapter of her checkered life had returned to haunt her. Once again, she had dreamed about her dead albino son.

She woke to a morning that was as cold as a dog's nose. Large mushrooms of dew were coating the ground, and the harsh Otutu wind was whistling like a disaster around her ears and frying the corn stalks in the fields. As usual, the barbets and orioles were lyrical in the trees and the stray dogs were fighting the fierce cats at the garbage dumps. Getting out of bed, her legs were as unsteady as those of a drunken catechist, but she threw a cotton shawl over her shoulders, startled by how pale she had become, even though she had been sitting in the sun determined to get a tan. She went into the flower-potted verandah hoping to decipher the mysteries of the dream, but she had suddenly lost what little skills she had at interpreting dreams and couldn't get past a few symbols. Before this new dream she had always slept with her windows open, after doing away with the pernicious habit of burning onion peels and hanging dried tapioca leaves behind her door to ward off any wayward lover she might have forgotten during her séance. Everything had been fine until now. It made her fret, not least because the dream threads had brought back memories of the scandalous way she had treated her lovers, whom she thought had been appeased by her contrition. Although she did finally decipher her dream, she was suddenly assailed by the one thing she was most terrified of, no matter what she had done to dispel that fear: General Augustus Kotay could come and go as he pleased in the house.

One evening when she was still shaken by the dream about her albino child, the feeling that General Augustus Kotay had returned suddenly assailed her. Sheets of lightning were raging in the sky, a breeze was rattling the shrubs in her garden, and she thought the dead man had probably come in, though she had not heard his feet. A whiff of his familiar French cologne made his presence obvious as he came into the bedroom, his walrus breathing rising, his hands reaching out for her pendulous breasts, wanting her to give him his own child.

"Go away," she whispered. "It is against nature for you to desire me in this condition."

She recalled how the general had always taken great pleasure in undressing her before they made love. But there would be no need for that ritual today: naked beneath her chemise, the trembling of her breasts intense, she waited for the invisible hands of the dead man to start caressing her. When it did not happen, it finally dawned on her that her imagination was really playing tricks on her. Like her other dead lovers, General Augustus Kotay was probably roaming in the gardens of Arcadia looking for a sweet, innocent girl! Habiba Mouskuda's peace had nonetheless been disturbed. Soon her days began to resemble ring circles of nightmares and curlicues of anxieties, her head filled with the chimerical images of how some dead men never really gave their lovers peace of mind: the bastards!

Her albino son had been dead for almost three years, but with so much guilt assailing her, Habiba suddenly remembered how rough his hair had been: sheep's wool hair. The squint of his eyes was pronounced, his nose was ugly between those eyes that stuck out like two small tomatoes on his pale non-melanin skin: eyes that had made his albinism all the more horrible to her. She wondered why fate had chosen to send her an imperfect child when she was not strong enough to accept him. Ruthlessly determined to enjoy life unencumbered by an albino, she had rejected him, thrown him away with a cold, heartless finality, ashamed to call him her son.

Now that he had come back to torment her, the twisted knots that she had sometimes felt forming in her stomach seemed to have come from the liquid fire glowing from the unhealed crimson wound she had inflicted on him, to remind her of what a terrible thing she had done. After her séance for her dead lovers, there had been a noticeable change in her personality. Incredibly, she even had a good word or two for Hawanatu Gomba. And to the surprise of even her severest critics, Habiba had been dedicated to Theodore Iskander, rejecting all other advances from much richer men. She seemed destined to spend the rest of her life with her bookish philosophy professor, sweet and loyal as Penelope, always waiting, in the dawn of a blue day of rain or looking at the golden sun, for him to return from one of those insane conferences only philosophers attended.

Two years into the relationship, in an effort to please him, she had embarked on a determined, if somewhat surreptitious, reading of the writings of Mariama Bâ, Wole Soyinka, and Toni Morrison, and had even shown an interest in Dogon architecture, Bantu mythology, and other nightmarish texts on his shelves. But after a while she gave up the attempt, not because she was incapable of reaching the highest penetration of the minds of those masters, but because she was convinced Theodore loved her for more than just her alluring beauty, and she did not have to impress him with her other attributes. "He has his territory, I have mine," she decided.

She too had heard the rumors about Tankor Satani's mermaid: how the creature had transformed herself into a beautiful woman named Death and had drowned the son of the president because he had snatched her comb one summer day on the beach. Grateful that she had been given another chance to become a mother again, Habiba quickly forgot about the mermaid, not wanting anything to do with the ocean or the primrose of death. Now that she was involved in a most delectable relationship with a brilliant man, life, even on a slippery promontory, had the sound of castanets ringing with exciting journeys for her. Having heard the voices of death in the past, she wanted to forget its song: those bones of her past lovers turning over in their graves.

The cold night was one of the most piercing that she had experienced, but the stars were shining like rose petals all over the land. After a while, the silence near the cove was replaced by the soft scratching movements of the animals that came out at night in search of food. A cat cried out, in fear for its life or howling for a mate. Lovesick cicadas chirped in the tamarind trees, turquoise moths crashed against the violet sunlight on the verandah, and wall geckos tongued flies. Looking at their tongues, she imagined she was kissing the red, hairy lips of her son, asking him to call her mother.

"Forgive me, Lord," she cried. "I was cruel to him."

A deep sadness overcame her as she finished her tea. She bit her tongue, drawing a drop of blood, conscious of the unhappiness in her soul. But she was no longer afraid of crossing the next river, however deep it might be, and was grateful to God for Theodore Iskander's love, even if she had not completely found the elixir to convince his mother that his malatta was no longer a femme fatale bent on destroying Irene's good boy. It was a difficult task convincing the old woman, considering how disappointed Irene was over the way things had turned out between her son and sweet Hawanatu.

Sometimes the old woman would drop by her son's house to see whether he was eating properly, saying it was reasonable for her to worry about his health because, as far as she was concerned, he was not living with a woman.

"Ah know you are a grown man," she would begin, by way of apologizing for her "interference." "But ah am still your moder, and ah get worried when you don't come over so that ah can feed you. And remember dat although you know all de book, there is nothing like a moder's blessing!"

Not yet ready to surrender her son to another woman, especially not to the malatta, she had ignored Habiba Mouskuda's best efforts to make her happy. In fact, Irene was so concerned about her son's state of mind that she would sometimes take furtive glances at him, wondering whether the malatta had been experimenting with *atefor* love potion on her lover.

"Lord have mercy," she cried one day, "de things moders have to put up with from dese diabolical gals!"

But reasoning that it was in her best interest to develop a close relationship with this daughter of the hated Corals, the old woman eventually began to think of becoming conciliatory to Habiba Mouskuda. For although she would have denied it outright, Irene was somewhat happy that Habiba was pregnant again. But she was still a little concerned that the Coral was not the sort of woman to make her son a good companion—not to talk of a good wife!

With her eyes fixed on that day when she had hoped to garland Hawanatu Gomba as her daughter-in-law, Irene had for years been putting aside a portion of her washerwoman's earnings. Deprived of her dreams—the chance to send a poor woman's Bible and ring on behalf of her son, dance to some goombay music at his wedding, and let the Corals see how, in spite of her poverty, it was from her womb that this good son—a philosopher, if you please—had sprung, she began, slowly, to transform Habiba in her mind from a vixen to a "we shall see what kind of gal she is."

One morning, smiling a bit, she showed up at the malatta's place. It was the first time she had done so, and she had something good to say to Habiba Mouskuda. "Ah hope your child will make my boy and you happy, especially if it is a son," she said, and went on to unwrap the bag of fresh fruits to satisfy a pregnant woman's craving.

Habiba was so shocked by this rare display of Irene's concern for her that she almost choked on the pig's foot bone she had been sucking. "Why are you doing this all of a sudden?" she asked incredulously.

"To be able to stand before God with a clear conscience when ah meet de Master, which, although you are not to blame for their sins, is something the Corals will not be able to do," Irene replied with unconcealed bitterness toward her former employers.

She asked whether Habiba was eating properly: "Good *plasas* stew, I mean; lots of vegetables, fish." The malatta was so skinny! "You should also do some exercise, child, to get rid of dem varicose veins," she said, and, slowly, as though from some other planet, moved toward and hugged the malatta, which brought tears to Habiba Mouskuda.

"Don't worry too much, Mama. I am determined to make your son happy," cried the malatta.

Irene had noticed that a rash of pimples had broken out on Habiba's face. "People say dat young women have pimples when dey in love. You in love wit' my boy?"

"Forever!" came the bold reply.

"And you won't feed him *atefor* to turn him against his moder?"

"No, Ma! I don't have to feed him love potions."

Later that night, long after a somewhat satisfied Irene had gone, Habiba Mouskuda dreamed about the albino yet again. But this time the labyrinths were not so intricately woven. During her frequent bouts of insomnia, which was when the albino would appear to her, crying, Mama, Mama, cold and miserable in the tangled web of roots, she had seen a lonely child asking her to look at his face, which was burnished by the eucalyptus balm his guardian angel had smeared on it. The sores on his lips had healed, she saw that his skin had browned like dark berries, and she trembled imagining him sucking on the roots of the tree, which she interpreted as really a wish for her breasts. After two miserable weeks, she was finally able to sleep. On the next morning, she threw a shawl over her shoulders and went to the albino's grave to ask his forgiveness for her lunacy.

"I love you, my child," she cried, genuinely moved by what she had done.

She felt much better after crying, and managed to get through the rest of the day. Later in the evening, unaware of how she had got there, she found herself in the enchanting petunia and geranium verandah and leaned against a trellis post, dazed, and inhaled the aroma of guavas and overripe plums. Surprisingly, although it was not the season, a trickle of rain was falling. Just listening to the small drums helped to untangle the knot in her heart as she let herself be soaked by the downpour. Even if it meant risking a cold, she was not going to dry her head afterward. She felt she needed to be washed clean of her sins. Never had she relished being in the rain so much.

And, thinking that after she had given Theodore a new son, an event she knew would please Irene, she would try to convince him to move in with her, she began to smile. His college digs were not suitable for a child to run around in, and were too close to his neighbors. She continued to smile, contemplating the prospect of unleashing her passion in bed. In spite of his bookishness, Theodore was not a complicated man. That was probably why he had forgiven her for the way she had treated the albino, and would forget all the heartache she had caused him. Now that she felt she had assured his mother of her fidelity to her boy, there was a new song ringing in Habiba Mouskuda's garden, one more enchanting that all those Christmas carols now heard all over Malagueta.

CHAPTER TWENTY-FIVE

Such a Long Journey

ONE EVENING when the sky was aquamarine over the city but less brilliant over the ocean, Pallo set out on a mission to the college on the hilltop. The giant turtles had finished laying their eggs on the beach, and Pallo had timed his departure with the turtles' constellation wisdom as he set out to meet Gabriel Ananias at Tankor's behest.

On the previous evening the eunuch had almost canceled the trip when Tankor Satani had brought up the idea of offering money to Gabriel Ananias so that he would come to the Xanadu.

"I know you have your own way with women, especially that malatta you have been helping with a difficult pregnancy," the president began. "But they are less stubborn than men. The students in particular. So here, take this with you, just in case all else fails to convince the young man to come."

The sorcerer was not the least surprised that Tankor Satani knew so little about the enigmatic hand of God or the compelling power of sorcery, or that everything had a monetary value for him. He smiled disapprovingly at the president. "If you doubt de word of God, don't cloud his powers with irrelevance," he said with a dignified shake of his head as he declined the offer.

"You will persuade him to come?" Tankor, now humbled, asked.

"It is my intention, Master."

After the death of Modu, Pallo had become Tankor Satani's companion in the almost empty Xanadu. When the sorcerer thought it necessary and was not engaged in some study of the medicinal properties of plants, he would leave his simple room and walk over to the main house to commiserate with the president over his recent loss. "Look at what de cruel Arab people done do to me, Excellency; but, with Allah's help, ah overcame it. We all get heavy load to carry sometimes."

"You are a great companion," a grateful Tankor would say, pleased to have the great sorcerer in his service.

After praying for the president during his time of grief, the other eunuchs had returned to their usual hermitry in the Xanadu and embarked on a project of the highest ingenuity: the development of a powder that they hoped would be more powerful than *warapay*, the Yoruba hunter's powder. When sprinkled on the skin, it should cause terrible blisters and drive the victim insane. Tankor Satani had requested it after his recent tragedy.

"I have all kinds of enemies, above and under water," he said. And stopped at that.

Pallo was not taking part in the development of the new powder. Delving deeper into the powers of sorcery, he had raised his expertise to the higher goal of proving that not only was it possible for humans to achieve a new level of levitation, but the same was likely true of other animals. He spent weeks mulling over this fascinating idea and became excited about the prospect of the same results in alloys, minerals, and vegetables. It was his belief that sorcerers all over the world, but especially in Africa, had made a startling discovery: groundnut shells, mollusks, and minerals, held together with alburnum, could float unseen in the air. But he did not divulge his conclusion to anyone. Instead, he stayed in his room for days, almost ruining his eyes in the fervent belief that it was only in crepuscular silence and peace that he could perfect his theory.

Unknown to him, the drunks in the rundown seafront bars had been circulating colorful reports of how some French women tourists, newly arrived in town and convinced that he had miraculous powers, had gone to the Xanadu to meet the sorcerer. Dressed as gypsies, the women had bribed the guards and sneaked inside the grounds of the palace. As soon as the women were in Pallo's room, they had immediately taken off their clothes, and the eunuch had miraculously whipped his penis back to life and made love to them. Not a bit disturbed by such wild rumors, or by the idea that he was now a very wealthy man with a most envious notoriety in those bars, Pallo smiled and seldom left his hermitage. "It only goes to show that sorcery is the oldest means of making people happy," he smiled when Tankor Satani told him of the rumors.

Usually robust, the eunuch was phlegmatic when he came out of his cloister one morning for a bit of sunlight. His broad shoulders drooped from the hours spent trying to perfect his concept, and he looked like a praying mantis and was badly in need of sleep. When not engaged in testing the limits of gravity, he thought occasionally of his life in that distant place near the border with Bassa, where there were bloody fights amongst the diamond miners in the river. What he missed most were his solitary walks in the forests, his undisturbed life; the longer he stayed away from his roots, the harder he found it to forget the nights when the zombies would wake up to disturb his concentration.

He was thinking about those creatures as he went on his mission to the college. To avoid detection, he was riding in a Land Rover and not in one of Tankor's Mercedes. He wore a simple, unobtrusive blue gown rather than a white, flowing one with golden embroidery. Recently he had shaved and oiled his head, "to let some breeze blow on it." To complete his disguise he felt it prudent to cap his head with a fez, and he wore a pair of nondescript sensible leather sandals instead of the white Moroccan halfback shoes he had taken to wearing since coming to live in the city. A tall man, although his height was not as commanding as Tankor's, he had to be careful not to be seen going through the vestibule of the dormitory.

The driver, whose name was Abu, was not of a talkative nature and seemed interested only in getting to their destination before it was too dark. "Why you going to de college," he finally asked, "where all de students do crazy things to make de president mad?"

Pallo conceded the students were a troublesome lot, but otherwise kept his prudence. "Nothing important," he said.

"De Pa send some warning against more student rudeness?"

"You ask plenty questions," the eunuch said, and was quiet for a long time.

After ten years of driving Tankor Satani, Abu was looking forward to his retirement from the Xanadu. Lately he had begun to hear that some strange happenings had been observed in the palace: a three-legged dog walking on the verandahs, men with pig's faces prowling in the garden. After a six-month lull in their assault, the griffon vultures had reappeared one night, flying in and out of the presidential bedroom windows. He liked the old man, but was a simple man afraid of the enigmas shrouding Tankor Satani's life; he did not want to be around the president much longer.

They were journeying south, and the drive to the college snaked up a winding mountain road in woodlands, near where some hikers had made a col, and there was a tarn where wild guinea fowls and ducks sometimes came to drink water and lotuses flourished. After a while the landscape was less enchanting. It was mostly rock, and a loose formation of crags hung perilously above a road on which snakes sometimes came to sun, so the driver progressed with particular care. Soon they were in an area where the forest was dense and mysterious and the foliage healthy after the rains, and Pallo immediately began to relive memories of his previous life. In such a paradise, he thought he might find fresh growths of ginger, eucalyptus, and cassia, which were crucial to the magic of a sorcerer. He got down from the jeep, plucked a eucalyptus leaf and sucked on it, smiling, then spat out the pulp. The early evening sky was a deep purple over the forest, and the owls had started their devilish night calls to witches: an indication to the sorcerer that the zombies were preparing to come out with their clay feet. Glad to be reliving the memories of his past life, he returned to the jeep.

"What you thinking 'bout?" he asked Abu, breaking his long silence.

"Nothing," said the driver; "just 'bout life; working all de time for Mr. President."

Being in the service of the old man had not been without its reward for Abu. He had a little nest egg, put away, or, as they say in Malagueta, his "old age umbrella." With the addition of his retirement money, he was looking forward to opening a corner store, where he would sell all kinds of provisions to the poor. But his greatest asset was that he had a good wife: a stout, pleasant woman who was an expert cook and from whose hands a delicious crab soup would sometimes materialize at their simple dinner table. After the politicians and the Corals had taken their share of the huge catch of barracudas in Malagueta, people like Abu and his wife would eat, with contented bliss, the rest of the catch. Their chunks of the great fish were always small, but spiced with parsley and thyme, roasted over a coal fire, they always tasted delicious.

The journey through the woods was making Pallo dizzy. It was a strange sensation, considering he had once been a woods dweller, but since moving to the Xanadu he had somehow lost his primal knowledge of those trees. It seemed as though the spirits that lived in them had abandoned him and deprived him of the gift of talking to them now that he smelled like a city dweller. His head was spinning, and he was saved from a spell of sneezing only when he brought a vial of medicine out of his pocket and applied some to his nostrils. Just when he felt like settling into a few peaceful minutes of napping before they got out of the woods, a sputter from the engine jolted him out of whatever sweet dreams he was contemplating.

Abu was not unduly worried. When he was in the British army in Burma, he and two other African conscripts had once dismantled and repaired a military jeep's engine. Moreover, this was a new Land Rover that had only recently been serviced. But they had hardly gone another mile when another sputter came from its muffler pipe and the radiator began to hiss hot water.

"It is a sign from God dat something strange go happen," the eunuch declared.

"What is dat?"

"When medicine talk, machines go to sleep."

Dark clouds now completely shadowed the trees, adding to Abu's worry about whether he had enough light to examine the vehicle and fix whatever problem had brought the engine to a stop. As soon as the hissing had died down a bit, he lifted the hood and was almost blown off his feet by his discovery. "Master," he said, signaling shakily to the great sorcerer. "Come and see de ting way done happened."

Pallo's movements were always those of a cautious man who weighed every step that he took in life. Alighting from the jeep, he walked in an unhurried manner, bringing the wide folds of his gown together. Noting the fear on Abu's face Pallo recited a few sacred lines to ward off any impending danger. He brought his great bulk close to the hood of the car and leaned over. Quickly he recoiled from the danger staring at him. Heaving in heavy spasms, its distinct green-and-black markings those of a mamba, the most poisonous snake of that region was coiled around the engine, a terror to even the spirits of the night. A false move by Pallo could have been his last.

Abu had been taught as a child that the only good snake was a dead one, stretched across the road with its head crushed by a large stone. By nature he was not a killer of snakes, but his ancestral instinct overcame him. "Make ah find big stick, en kill am," he offered.

The eunuch stopped him. "Leave am to me. Dis is de sign ah been expecting."

He raised his head to the heavens, and although it was still too early for the stars to come out, he searched until he had found one not yet named but known to him. After he was satisfied he had made contact with the right forces, he walked briskly toward the nearby bush, plucked some leaves, and rubbed them in his huge palms. He chewed on the leaves, sucked the juice, and spat out the pulp. Quietly, using even more caution than before, he approached the snake and aimed his spittle at it. A powerful spasm rocked the maddened serpent in its confined space. Indicating what a real danger it could be when not trapped, with what was left of its great strength it tried, in one great jerking movement, to break free, but Pallo was ready for it. He struck the snake with another well-aimed jet and watched as, in a final, powerful spasm, the mamba gave in to the throes of death.

For a snake known more for its venomous bite than for its size, the mamba was quite large, so the two men had to work hard to uncoil it from the engine. Pleased with his discovery, Pallo was inspired. Once again he raised his eyes to the heavens. Then, with a slow precise movement, he lifted the head of the snake and severed it from the body with the dagger he always carried. He let some of the blood of the snake flow freely, wetting the thirsty grass, but he was careful not to lose the poison in the duct, which was elemental in his treasured art. With an almost reverential patience he wrapped the head in some green cacao leaves.

Abu watched in silence as the sorcerer went about his task. Being a practical man, he did not understand the magician's cantrip and definitely had no need of mysteries, especially those in the coils of snakes. With the engine now free of its impediment, he gave it a try and listened as its familiar revs started going again.

"What you go do wit' rest of snake?" he asked the eunuch.

"Dat is for you, my son."

For the rest of the journey back, the sound of money was ringing in Abu's ears as he thought of the dry chunks of snake meat his wife was going to sell the next day.

CHAPTER TWENTY-SIX

Arcadian Eunuchs and Willful French Nymphs

After spending a night at his lover's house, Theodore Iskander was driving toward the center of the city under a sky decked with a golden sun when he saw the Xanadu looming over Malagueta. With its radiance of magic, it had people dreaming about what was going on there now that Tankor Satani had come out of mourning. As usual, Theodore did not want to think about that monstrous house, but rather about what Irene had said when he had first started to stay overnight at Habiba's house.

"Let her come over to your place, because you don't know when de man who built dat house will come back from the dead to remove the mattress from under her."

The thought of being thrown off the bed by a dead man when he was making love to his mistress brought a small smile to Theodore's lips as he steered the small car into a slow run. He stayed away from the shoulder of the narrow hilltop road, on which many motorists had died. Some hungry children had dropped half-eaten green mangoes, and he did his best to avoid skidding on them and going over the precipice on the other side of the road. Aside from the pain that his death would cause Irene, he was really not afraid of dying, not even in his lover's bed as Irene feared. In the past, he had sometimes felt troubled in the quiet of his soul, worried that his life was losing some of its threads; but he had to stay alive because of Irene's "Ah don't know what I will do, son, if anything happens to you!"

Getting closer to the city, he stopped thinking about death, certain he was making some people happy and that if you put aside the unfortunate incident with the albino, his life, in general, had been good.

He left the treacherous hilltop road and was soon driving on a narrow road that was a pedestrian's chaos for a few yards, before he turned into a detour that eventually ballooned into a wide parkway crested with a median of statues and shorn bougainvillea. Always cautious on that stretch of road, where the potholes were large enough to break the axle of a small car, he slowed down a bit as he passed the crumbling mess of the national radio station, where a huge electric generator was belching out thick black smoke. Some trucks that had been cannibalized for parts and a small mound of garbage took up one corner of the compound, not too far from which a dog was pissing on an untended flowerbed, killing the bachelor's buttons, already stripped of their blossoms. A group of children was riding see-saw on old cannon left there from the colonial days, and he felt that if the decay in that compound was anything to go by, Malagueta was like an abandoned pirate ship, in spite of all the prayers said for progress and prosperity in the churches and mosques.

To avoid going up Jomo Kenyatta Street, where there were three girls' schools, he took a different route to his digs at the college. The students at those schools were not known for their modesty, and, today being Friday, he was certain some willful girls might try to flag him down. He did not relish that prospect, as he had enough on his plate. Resolutely, he drove on Amadou Komba Street to get his mail at the post office, a detour that took him past the museum, which was holding an exhibition of the works by the Nigerian painter and sculptor Ben Enwonwu. When he was five blocks away, Theodore Iskander slowed down a bit because the sky was now a dark blanket of flapping wings, the blood-sucking bats that lived in the enormous cotton tree in the center of the town having started flying helter-skelter. A nun who, perhaps sensing a blasphemous act or two, was making the sign of the cross caught his attention. Cars were hooting their horns, and an excited crowd had begun to gather around the huge cotton tree a few meters from the museum.

"What is going on?" he asked a young man in a checked red shirt.

"Something not good for the eyes to see, Professor. Not unless you are one of those French tourists that take pictures to exhibit back home in Paris."

He parked his car near the museum, removed the radio from its carriage, dropped it into his briefcase, and went to find out what the excitement was all about. Picking his way through the crowd, he saw Tankor Satani's eunuchs dancing under the cotton tree, sometimes exposing themselves, with their eyes closed, and swaying to an Arcadian melody. They had oiled their bodies and painted their faces with camwood, and, as if they were bandits, had tied red bandannas round their heads and wore necklaces of cowry shells. If they were aware of the crowd that had gathered to watch them, they gave no indication, lost as they were in another world. It was as if the only thing that mattered to them was that they were experiencing a gratification not understood by anyone in the crowd.

Two scantily dressed French girls had pushed their way to the front of the crowd to get a better view. Over the objection of some women, who thought the whole thing scandalous, the girls had started taking pictures of the dazed eunuchs.

"Why you taking de picture?" demanded a heavyweight woman.

The French girls froze at her size then quickly moved away before replying. "Because we want to tell our friends about the sensational eunuchs of Malagueta."

"Gimme dem cameras," barked the big woman. "You want to sell de pictures back home, shame my country." The girls dodged her onslaught and found a safer spot to indulge in their bizarre pleasure.

It was their last day in town after a two-week holiday, and they had been on their way to confirm their reservations out of the country. On the previous night, both of them had experienced the most unbearable depths of pleasure making love to a very virile fisherman on one of Malagueta's numerous beaches. Prior to that, all the girls had done was to sit in one of the beach houses owned by a bunch of Corals, smoking hemp and listening with irritation to their vulgar boasting about how their African maids were cheap for a lay. "De women all cheap, cheap. And all de men are tiff man," the Corals said, smacking their chops and thinking of how they did business with the politicians.

While being waited upon by servants, sampling badly cooked Lebanese lamb chops instead of the fricassee, spicy chicken, goat meat soup, and other wonderful delights the tourist's brochure had said were part of the great cuisine in that region, the French girls had wished they were somewhere else. The holiday, for which they had saved for three years in Paris, was turning out to be a most boring affair, without drama, especially as the Corals, who would pay anything to sleep with a white woman, had turned out to be useless in bed.

A thirsty desert was burning in the heart of the girls, and it was with a most contemptuous good-bye that they rose from the beds of the Corals. The girls rejected with contempt the Corals' offer to drive them back to town. "What for? So that you can ask a big boatman about how to light our fire?"

And as though it had been foretold in the stars, it was while the girls were walking all the way back to town on the beach that they came across the fisherman.

He was the most beautiful man they had ever seen, and his raw magnetism gave him an aura of magic. Stripped down to his waist, he was singing as he hauled the morning's first catch in from the ocean. In the eyes of the girls, he was an ebony god who reminded them of the profile of the almost-naked Nubian wrestlers that had fired their erotic imagination in *National Geographic* when they had been studying the peoples of the Sudan in their Lycée. He was about six foot three, and his blue-black skin, in the golden morning light, shimmered with the radiance of a black constrictor. Had he chosen to leave Malagueta to seek his fortune somewhere else, the girls felt he could have graced the pages of the most expensive haute couture magazines in Paris or Dakar, and they thanked God that he had not done so, as that would have deprived them of the opportunity to meet him. Unable to stop admiring his impressive torso, they began to imagine his prowess. Each felt a small volcano rumbling in her stomach, and they exchanged glances, fired with scandalous intent, while some sandpipers were trying to pry open the net of the fisherman. Against the fisherman's protestations, the girls insisted on buying all the fish in the net, paying for it with some of the cash the Corals had lavished on them. When they gave the fish away to some urchins who had come alongside the boat into which the net was being hauled, the fisherman was dumbstruck.

"Why you doing dat?"

"The boys look hungry," said the mischievous girls.

It didn't take the fisherman long to deduce the reason for the girls' generosity. Seeing how the sun had bronzed their youthful bodies, he agreed to meet them that night on the beach. For the rest of the day, the girls were unable to still their lustful hunger. As the hours dragged on, they suffered excruciating torment, especially after the miserable time they had spent with the Corals, dreaming of a hedonistic evening with the fisherman. They spent part of the day eating roast snails, fried fish, and *akara* bean cakes bought from the women who were roasting those delicacies on their charcoal grills on the street: all the "dirty things" the Corals had bad-mouthed, but which tasted like aphrodisiacs to the girls.

When the moon came out that evening, it was lapis lazuli over the ocean as the girls, now completely in transport as they waited for the fisherman to come, drank the two bottles of cheap Algerian wine that the Corals had given to them as parting gifts. Intent on the highest level of intoxication, they also smoked some marijuana, which they considered better than the Turkish stuff available in Paris. Like a long-gone sailor returning home, the fisherman emerged from the ocean, where he had been swimming, and his ebony torso looked even more impressive in the evening light than it had in the morning sun. He shook the water from his hair, sat next to the girls, and took the plastic cup of wine they offered him. He saw the languorous look that betrayed the hunger in the girls' eyes. They waited until after he had taken a few sips, and, not wanting to waste any time, began playfully to stroke his beautiful arms. But he was a patient man who had always relished the long-drawn-out rhapsody of lovemaking, so he held his deeply aroused penis in check.

"Make you nor hurry," he said magisterially; "we get time."

The ocean had changed its tempo. The lovesick crabs came out of their holes in the sand looking for their mates on the beach, and he smiled as their claws began to entwine in the oldest lovemaking position in the world. But even then, he did not allow his own strong tumescence to rush him into the unknown straits of French passion, and it was not until the cascading cool breeze of the ocean was fanning his back that he began to smear the bodies of the two girls with some lavender oil. Then, in a rich baritone, his voice was sweet as he serenaded the girls with the calypsos that some of Malagueta's sailors had brought back from their nights with the Spanish prostitutes in the bordellos on the island of St. Jago. The aphrodisiacs had already made the girls giddy, and his voice merely added to their desperation, but he still kept tormenting the two exasperated creatures.

"Give it to us," they cried in desperation. Frantically they pawed at him, ripping off his pants. When they saw his majestically aroused sex, they gasped and cursed the insipid Corals for wasting a whole week of their holiday, and the world had never seemed so beautiful as when the fisherman began to make love first to the young flaxen-haired one, then to the older, gypsy-looking brunette, with a zeal that matched their own willful nature. They felt as though, after a quiet interlude, the Atlantic had changed its mind and the tempestuous music now tearing at their insides was really its pounding as they thrashed on its waves, like two sea cows coming to the surface to breathe.

Next morning, it seemed to the girls that the evening with the virile fisherman had only been a dream that had to be experienced all over again, for they had never before felt so much passion. Hailing a taxi, they went back to the beach, hoping their lover might be lounging there, but they were disappointed. For the rest of the morning they went around amazed at how daring they had been, and it was with that feeling that they found themselves, half an hour later, in the crowd in front of the cotton tree, where something even more enchanting than their previous evening's tryst was happening.

Tankor Satani's three naked eunuchs had got the crowd screaming. Determined to take pictures of them, the now aroused French girls summoned up their Gallic courage and forgot about the elephantine woman as they fought with other women similarly fired up. Quickly they clicked their cameras, certain that their contents would be worth more than the price of their tickets from Paris after they had been developed. Though the penises of the eunuch were flabby, they were still the largest male weapons the girls had ever seen, and the injustice done to those men brought tears to the girls. In a trance, the eunuchs rubbed their dicks, sending the crowd wild, and it dawned on the French girls that although life was hard for most people, Malaguetans had not really lost their capacity for magic since the fantastic days of Alusine Dunbar, about whom they had read before leaving for their vacation. Tears flowed freely from their eyes as they clicked their cameras for a few more photos of the eunuchs.

Pallo was the first to come out of his trance. He stood proudly, like an emperor, bringing into view the raffia belt adorned with cowries and small mirrors tied around his waist. With a grace unusual in a man his size, lost to everything and everyone around him but responding to something that came from the torment in his soul, he began, in a slow gyrating rhythm, as sleekly as a cobra responding to a charmer, to dance. Unwilling to be left out of the dance, the two French girls joined him. One after the other, using their hypnotic power, the other eunuchs drew the rest of the crowd into the dance, sending the women wild, moaning "Lord, Lord" as they advanced on the eunuchs, pressing their bodies against those delirious men working their magic. Willfully, the women touched the belts of the eunuchs. In the ornamental handiwork of glass and beads worn by the eunuchs, they tried to discover something that normal men had not been able to give them—something erotic, seminal; something they could feel at the back of their throats!

The release of their own depravity was so palpable that some of the women began to cry. For it was as though, for the first time in their lives, they could admit in public what they had been ashamed to before now: how dissatisfied they were with the insipid men they had married.

Theodore Iskander left the scene bewildered. All he could think as he walked back to his car was that he had witnessed a great carnival put on by the eunuchs at Tankor Satani's behest. Recalling his mother's suspicion of the influence that Pallo might have had on Habiba Mouskuda, he wondered what Irene would say if he told her about the afternoon's event. But there was not even a flicker of doubt in his mind that his mistress was above such legerdemain. All the same, he felt a bit uneasy about the evening as he drove on the mountain road back to the college under the heavy downpour that had begun to fall, scattering the crowd under the cotton tree. The blood-sucking bats gave off a raucous noise as, in their thousands, they flew back to their tree, over the head of the nun, who, hurrying home from the depravity of the women in the crowd, had opened her Bible.

Raising her head to the sky, as if she had divined the presence of God in the galaxy of heaven, she said, "Satan, Satan, get thee hence from this town."

CHAPTER TWENTY-SEVEN

Finally, a Child

EXCEPT FOR her soft cries when she was wet, Yeama Iskander was a quiet child from the moment she was born. Left in her bassinet to play, her mood varied from long bouts of silence to playful periods of baby antics, such as when she was trying to put a big toe in her mouth. Having waited so long to have a child, Habiba was alert to any sign of discomfort in her baby, and just watching Yeama was magical. The baby was quite dark, like Theodore Iskander, as though the dark essence of the philosopher's genes had completely neutralized the blood of the Corals. Irene had spent the last month feverishly preparing for the birth of her grandchild, as though she were racing against her own dwindling mortality, or getting ready for the renewal of it, which she imagined the birth might bring. Ignoring her rheumatic knees, she went shopping for feeding bottles, towels, mouth comforters, gripe water solution, and *ori* ointment for the baby's navel, thinking that Habiba might have forgotten to get these items. "You can't trust dese young Coral gals to do anything right," she said.

Just in case the envy of other women decided to visit the pregnant woman, Irene went to an herbalist to buy the accoutrements to fight it off. Her bones had started to creak from her descent into old age, but that did not stop her going to see her own Alpha Murray, a wrinkled old diviner, to ask him to throw his cowries and bones on the floor for greater illumination into the unknown. He gave her a cornucopia of ancient tortoise bones, alligator peppers, coral beads, dried cashew nuts, and the hairs of a Barbary goat. "Bury dem in de garden of de pregnant woman," the herbalist advised. "No witch man go come near de house then."

God, in his Christian incarnation, was never far from Irene's thoughts, so she dragged her old bones to the vicar's at her church to ask him a special favor. "Ah want you to turn up at Habiba's house a day or two before her delivery, to say a prayer to Master Jesus for her."

It was August. The thunderous drums of rain had been falling on the city, and the roofs and trees were slimy as the water cascaded down on them and onto the treacherous roads. The downpour left people in a bad temper and made the dogs miserable that they could not explore the garbage dumps. Calculating that her grandchild might arrive the same week that she turned seventy, Irene saw a good omen in the coincidence. "Perhaps God wants me to finally accept dis woman for my son," she mused.

One evening when there was a lull in the rain, Irene baked a simple cake flavored with turmeric on her coal pot. To amend for her past dislike of this daughter of a Coral, she took the cake early the next morning to Habiba's house, when the chattering blackbirds had only just woken up. "Ah know ah have not been too nice to you," she said almost sheepishly to the pregnant woman. "But ah want you to know dat as you go to de hospital next week to have my grand-*pikin* you have ma blessings. Don't let anyone tell you otherwise!"

"You don't know how much your blessings mean to me. And I want you to know that I love your son the way I never loved any of my previous lovers," a grateful Habiba said, and began to cry.

Then it was that Irene began, very slowly, as though the memory was still fresh and she had not gone past the threshold of that pain, to talk about

Theodore's childhood: how his father had died in a freak accident when Theodore was only ten, gored by a stray bull on the day he had been promoted to stationmaster at the railway corporation, where he had worked for twenty years. "Death took my man when his son needed him, and everybody blamed me for de accident; they said I was a witch who done pay off the debt I owe to my genie wit de poor man's soul."

Habiba Mouskuda was shocked that such a nasty thing could be said about such a good woman.

"It is true," the old woman continued. "So ah know what it is like, child, to be accused of killing someone: de pain, de bitterness; all de bad eyes people give you, as if you are Lucifer himself! But wash your heart clean of any evil for dat other woman, Hawanatu Gomba. Let people know your heart is clean."

It was the one and only time she had referred, ever so obliquely, to what Hawanatu Gomba had suffered at the hands of Habiba Mouskuda over the unfortunate albino.

There was sprightliness in Irene's steps when she left, feeling happy that she was finally about to become a grandmother, although she could still not think of her son marrying the Coral. Thinking of the good catfish soup garnished with a generous amount of sweet basil, bay leaves, and thyme she was going to cook from her secret washerwoman's recipe, she smiled. One day, God willing, she would pass it on to the Coral.

The heavy rains of August continued their fury. That night, as the torrent continued to pound the roofs, a moon-faced woman brought a satisfied grandmotherly smile to Irene in her sleep. In her dream, she had been transformed into a catfish with white whiskers, and since the water spirit was female, it was as though Irene had also become a powerful old woman. Sitting in her verandah on the other side of town, Habiba Mouskuda was also smiling, thinking about the old wives' tale that children born in August cried a lot. She did not mind having her baby born in that month: a child that cried was a healthy baby. Besides, she saw another beneficial side: the tears could calm the spirit of the albino. After all, Leo was a cardinal sign, full of love, generous, like her; even if many people had thought her hard and selfish. She would show them another side of her.

Her feet were now so swollen that her varicose veins looked like the roots of a coconut tree, but she could still move about. Irene had told her it was bad for an expectant mother to stay idle, as she could end up having a child prone to a morose outlook on life. "He could be born with talipes, uneven teeth, like a fowl's claws," said Irene. Like many women of her generation, Irene knew a lot of old wives' tales.

Habiba Mouskuda was determined to be awake when her labor pains started and had refused to lie in her bed that night. "I feel very relaxed," she said almost dreamily to Theodore Iskander, with a sense of déjà vu. "Everything has been cleared up in my head."

Wearing only a loose gown of flowered organdy, waiting for the first signs of labor to come, she lay on a sofa looking like a study by Gauguin. Theodore was sitting by her side and holding her hand, as though they were at some rite where happiness was assured only if they promised to go into that territory together: it was the way they felt they were going to be from now on, the lyrics of the barbets trumpeting their happiness.

"When I come down from this mountain," Habiba began, dreamily touching her belly, "I am going to see to it that we are always together; you will move in with me. We shall harvest the fruit trees, and when the sun has fallen asleep, we shall sit on the stones in the garden. When . . . Oh, God, it is coming!" she said, as she felt the oldest anguish of woman welling up deep from her insides, where a small river was getting ready to hurry her home to motherhood.

With an old maternal instinct that only women with children can possibly have, Irene was the first to sense the impending arrival of her grandchild, and she did not exhibit any sign of anxiety when Habiba Mouskuda began a low moan on the way to the hospital. Cradling the pregnant woman's head in her lap, she wiped the beads of sweat from her brow and stroked her face.

"Don't worry about anything, daughter. Ah know God is with you; ah prayed to him last night. You are going to put your load down without any complications, believe me."

The two women had been drawn closer together now, as shown in some clear signs of endearment, such as how Irene would plait Habiba's luxuriant black hair, give her a massage in the morning, and oil her pregnant woman's flanks to relax her varicose veins. It was during one of those close encounters that Irene finally concluded that although Habiba was tall and full-breasted, she was too thin—unusual in Coral women, who were mostly fat—but that she had the blessing of a wild mare's hips and pelvic bones arched so finely the child should come down the shaft without too much pain to the mother. Such a view was of course just what an old woman, suddenly aware that her grandchild was really on its way hours before she herself was about to turn seventy, would use as confirmation that God was responsible for the happy coincidence.

A month after Yeama was born, Habiba once again examined her features. The mysteries of genealogy would remain strange to her, yet she was happy that Yeama bore some resemblance to the albino buried at the foot of the almond tree, realizing that any signs of reincarnation need not necessarily spell disaster. As soon as she felt she could expose her baby to the wind, she took Yeama to the grave of the albino. Theodore was at the college, and she had not told him of her intention. This being her first day out since having the baby, she wore a blue-and-white gown of exquisite cut, embroidered around the neck in gold. The sun was throwing soft rays of light on the tree shadowing the grave, and white lilies were growing around the edges, bumblebees droned above her head, and butterflies were feasting on the nectar of a blooming hibiscus.

It was almost November, and the rains had petered out a bit, but the ground was a bit damp, maintained in that state, perhaps, by the guardian angel keeping her son cool in his grave: a view reinforced when she saw a pair of egrets perched on the branch of the tree: birds that some old people called *Malaika*: the messengers of angels. Under their watchful gaze, she spread a rug of coarse wool near the grave and made Yeama comfortable in her bassinet. Attracted by the smell of fruits she had brought, some flies were buzzing nearby, and she lit sandalwood incense to drive them away. She uncapped a bottle of water and split a kola nut. Then, holding the two pods, she leaned over a large rock and began to talk to her dead son.

"Say hello to your sister, Akim." Akim was the name of her favorite uncle, and she had settled on it for the albino.

She poured some water at the top of the grave in the same way she recalled seeing Pallo doing it. Right away the egrets began to flutter their wings and croak. With a steady hand she threw the pods on the grave, retrieved the upturned one, and chewed on it: a sign, as Pallo had once told her, that she was communicating with the dead.

Yeama was fretting a bit, so Habiba fetched her from the bassinet, loosened the top buttons of her blouse, and brought the infant's hungry lips to suckle at her breasts. Irene had been right about one thing: Habiba had breasts that were plentiful with milk, and she could have nursed twins easily. No sooner had she begun to think of what a wonderful period lay ahead of her and her baby than she was surprised by the unexpected arrival of Irene.

"You shouldn't come here so early, child," the older woman said. "It is bad for your baby. The sun is hot, all de dust in de air, and you don't know who comes here during the day. They will think you are mad bringing a child this young to a grave. Besides, you did not bring some food for the dead, only dis cold kola nut. You will have to do it all over again when de time is right."

There were lots of things she had to teach the Coral.

Later in the evening, Habiba Mouskuda was mulling over whether to tell her lover that she had been to the grave of her dead son, when Irene came into the living room. It was something the old woman seldom did, preferring to stay in her room most of the time. Saying that she had mislaid her needle and thread, she began a somewhat cursory search, raising Habiba's suspicion, because although she was a Coral's daughter, she knew that the black people considered needles the devil's instruments, bringing bad luck to the house, and not even the most insane unbeliever like her man would dare use them at night.

Concluding that Irene had come for another reason, Habiba watched the old woman going into every nook and cranny of the room, tarrying long enough to shoot a warning sign to Habiba while Theodore was reading. She felt grateful for the lesson the old woman was giving her about things left unsaid between women, just as there were places where only women walked, leaving men perplexed. From that moment on, Habiba knew a new bond had been sealed between the two women.

CHAPTER TWENTY-EIGHT

The Stallion of an Old Man's Twilight

GABRIEL ANANIAS had been out in the woods near the college, widening his study of entomology, and had just returned to his room when Pallo arrived. He was not surprised to see the great sorcerer. "To what do I owe this visit?" he said.

"De bright star on your forehead," the eunuch replied.

"You mean to the serpent of my mouth?" he said, certain that Pallo had come on behalf of the president.

"You speak big word, young man, but you get plenty sense to know why ah come here."

Gabriel Ananias could still recall his encounter with the president but had not spent any time mulling over it, not even when he was idle. When he was not busy studying entomology or sleeping with coeds, he preferred playing the guitar that he had recently acquired to pass the lugubrious hours of darkness after the brownouts at the college became somewhat routine. As far as he knew, the president was doing fine.

Offered a seat, Pallo took a quick glance at the student's digs and came straight to the point. "De president lonely."

"That is none of my business," Gabriel Ananias said impertinently. "He has his cars and houses to occupy his thoughts. What does he want to do with all of those things anyway?"

"Listen, make ah talk!" the eunuch interjected, trying to be patient with this impetuous young man. "When his *pikin* die, dat leave big hole in Tankor's heart. It make am poor, like church *arata*. But 'e like you, en want for do good for you."

Wrapped up as he was in the intensity of college life, Gabriel Ananias was not easily swayed by such a request. Considering what they had to put up with on the campus—lack of electricity, crowded classrooms, and second-rate science equipment—a good deal of creative brilliance was demanded of the students for their day-to-day survival. Besides the usual student angst about his "diabolism," Tankor Satani did not feature in their equations.

"Let me think about it for a while," he said, hoping that was the end of the matter.

"Dat is good, young man," the eunuch said, and bowed with grave dignity out of the young man's digs.

Ah, the Feel of This Power!

Back at the Xanadu, Pallo did not immediately go to Tankor Satani's study to report on his trip to the student. Instead he hurried to his room, closed the door behind him, and shut out the rays of the sun. Then he unwrapped the head of the mamba. As he had expected, there had been no color change in his trophy, but he was thrilled to find that the snakehead had grown to one and a half times its original size. Although the snake had been dead for two hours, the eyes shone like topaz. Such a phenomenon could only mean one of two things: the snakehead contained remarkable medicine or the eyes changed color in the heat of the leaves. Relying on his instinct, Pallo preferred the first explanation.

He made a hot concoction of alligator peppers, dead beetles, ginger root, bitter kola, and agidi leaves; then, with the skill of his sorcery, spiced the snakehead and lit the small charcoal burner in his room. After skewering the snakehead, his eyes closed, he began to chant in a magician's argot. His great frame shook when the snakehead, now fired up with his magic, began to turn first a deep red, then gray. He opened his eyes. With his eyes reflecting a deeper mystery, he began to prepare the head for a most remarkable transformation in his life.

It was Friday. Instead of unfolding his prayer mat, he stripped naked and with a serene smile began to dance in the same way he had under the cotton tree. The neper of his sorcery— those inexplicable electric currents that he knew so well—coursed through him as he rubbed the head of the snake on his penis, and a terrible spell—half woman and half man—overcame him. He felt the electrical surge in his loins. What he had just discovered was that he could cure himself of the curse of impotence, because he could feel what had not been there since the morning, many years ago, when the Arab had attacked him—a swelling of his penis! Two small stones had grown in his scrotum, and although the spell lasted only about fifteen minutes, he thought he would die from his discovery, from such fantastic happiness! When the surge ended, he knew exactly what he was going to do.

He kept his discovery secret for the time being, cautious not even to smile about it as he went to see the old man to give him a report about his visit to Gabriel Ananias.

A week later, Habiba Mouskuda took Yeama to see Pallo. She could tell by the way he was smiling that something miraculous had happened to him. He was not his usual austere self: he was lying on a goatskin mat, whistling a tune and munching on dates. "You are not the same," she said.

"No," he replied. "And some oder men never be de same again," he said with an enigmatic smile.

She was trying to solve that riddle when her quick senses were alerted to an immediate danger: a black snake had slithered from a curtained section of the inner room, where the eunuch kept the accoutrements of his sorcery, and was making straight for her feet. Its gloss was beautiful—she thought she had never seen anything so luminous—and mesmerized by its rapid movement, she was unable to think of a quick response. Mercifully, the snake continued past her and came to rest at the feet of the eunuch, where it formed a ball, breathing in slow, even spasms.

"You get clean heart," the sorcerer said. "If not so, dis snake go bite you."

She came out of her stupefaction and watched the sorcerer as he stroked the snake. The smile in his eyes conveyed to her what power he held over such creatures, but he did not give away the true nature of his happiness. All she could think was that it had to do with some magical discovery, which she hoped, given how close they had become, he would reveal to her in due course. For the first time since meeting him, she suspected that he was aware of her past as a whore. Though somewhat frightened of him, she did not think there was any reason to feel that he now thought less of her. She checked her fear, reasoning that he was a eunuch, after all, and not interested in women.

Terrified of snakes, she left his room as soon as she could. It was only when she was driving out of the visitor's driveway of the Xanadu that she remembered she had also wanted to see the Abyssinian roosters in the henhouse, which the emperor of Ethiopia had recently sent to Tankor in time for his birthday.

Monologues of a Lonely Man

For a whole week, Tankor Satani had been mulling over the results of the eunuch's visit to Gabriel Ananias. Convinced that it wouldn't be long before the student came to see him, he experienced his first happiness after two weeks of terrible ennui. During that period, he lost his appetite and went without a bath for as long as three days. He smelled like a pig and had deep nightmares. One night, after all the lights in the Xanadu went out due to a massive failure of the private generators on the property and he could barely contain himself, he yelled for Pallo. The blue flame in the dark room where the power was had never seemed so bright, but when the lights came on again, Tankor Satani dismissed the decision he had made only that afternoon to finally unburden his heart to Pallo about the mermaid.

Feeling a little better, he resumed his evening banter with the eunuch, not to ask his advice about divine providence but simply because he needed companionship. Always circumspect, Pallo never once let on that he knew the reason why Tankor Satani had never invited him inside the dark room. Their conversation took on a philosophical aspect, with the old man expanding on the twists and turns of politics, his useless children, what a shame they were, the peace he now sought after he had tamed the judges, hinting that he was thinking of retiring, the only problem being that he was not convinced of the fidelity of his prime minister, Enos Tanu, who was a bloodthirsty man too hungry for power!

"He gives me goose bumps," he said to the eunuch, "every time I think of the kind of leader he would make. As for the other one I am considering, the chairman of our party, he will be on top of a woman when the soldier boys find their way to the armory to stage a coup against him after I have died."

"Master, make you not worry too much 'bout de prime minister," the eunuch advised; "ah done see his future, and 'e go die bad."

At other times, Tankor Satani's monologues were quite long. Then he preferred to be alone, pacing on the wide verandah, inhaling the aromas of the plants, a large unlit pipe in his mouth, as he watched the traffic snaking through the city below, the crisp air keeping the mosquitoes away. Removing his pipe, he would inhale a pinch of snuff to clear a blockage that was making him sneeze. Sometimes his radio was tuned to a foreign station that he preferred to listen to instead of the local ones he had ordered regulated. The news about Africa was hardly worth listening to these days: all about military insurrections and riots, goddamn it; the same things that would be happening in Malagueta if he had not already moved against the restless generals, taking away their fearsome arsenal, bringing them into the cabinet, giving them a cut from the national corruption, and keeping their shameless harlots happy! Elsewhere, the news was just as bad: Europe was becoming a fortress, keeping Africans and some Asians out. Now that Mao was dead, the new leader had taken the capitalist road. He switched off the radio.

Although he was locked in a private war with the mermaid, he still thought of himself as someone heading toward immortality. Occasionally, he even thought of Henri Christophe, the immortal in La Citadel; reason enough for Tankor to conceive of the idea that he could buy—this being the land of Marabouts, djinns, witches, and sorcerers—something to bring about his own apotheosis, and unaware that Pallo had come to the opposite conclusion: that the president was doomed.

The heat in the verandah was making Tankor sleepy, but his siesta was troubled by the noise from the warren that had mushroomed at the foot of the hill below the Xanadu. He made a mental note to have the place raided. Not in the least displeased with the world at that moment, he stretched his legs and yawned. Wrapped in a gold-embroidered gown, he felt safe in the grandeur of his power, very much a man of his times, convinced he could survive even the most complex *warapay* poison he suspected his enemies were making for him.

Considering how he had come to this pinnacle, he felt his triumph had been nothing short of miraculous, determined as he was to become an immortal. The noise from the nearby warren was really a bloody nuisance, so he gave up trying to sleep and went in to drink a small jigger of rum to clear his throat. He felt at peace with himself, and although matters of state were pending—the peasants in the north of the country were restless, and a rebellion was feared—he thought that could wait until he had figured out how to deal with a little personal matter that was coming up on his anniversary calendar. His son had been dead for three years now, and Tankor Satani longed to communicate with the soul of the dead man.

Because his wife had left him and he felt she was the one the boy had really loved, Tankor Satani was at a loss about how to perform necromancy effectively.

"You for take 'nother woman," Pallo advised him when Tankor Satani brought up the subject the next day.

"Who would want this broken canoe?" Tankor said. "Ah too old now, my friend; besides, a woman will just suck me dry. Rock me left and right, and feed me to the hyenas afterwards!"

He was right.

Occasionally, when he felt the need for a woman, he would send his guards to bring one of his old mistresses to the Xanadu, only to discover, in spite of the woman's most seductive efforts, that there was very little powder left in his gun! In fact, he was now completely impotent but was keeping his secret intact because he did not really relish being torpedoed by the fake passion of some turgid bosoms, just for the sake of having a woman around. Considering how good these women were, in his experience, at spreading rumors and using potions to finish a man off, he dreaded the prospect. He was past seventy so was not unduly bothered by his condition, especially as his oars had not always been useless. When he was not brooding in the autumnal fires of his life, he would recall that he had fathered a lot of children, relishing the rhapsodies of his bacchanalian nights, a couple of years ago, with women less than half his age: blacks, mulattoes, whites, Asiatic-Indians, Chinese, Burmese, Arabs, and even some naughty Polynesians, who were a bit too fat for him, but so what? All of them had been drawn to him because of Malagueta's diamonds.

He smiled, thinking about those glorious days.

Now his reminiscences were all that remained of his sexual conquests: how sweet it had been to be a president listening to the cat meows and groans of some uppity women who had previously looked down on him. To have these beautiful memories, especially now that he cared very little for the song of some willowy woman who might want to bring back his manhood in bed, or about the fate of his country once he was no longer there, looming larger than life, was even better than a good orgasm. Only one woman now mattered in his destiny: the mermaid about whom he dared not talk.

"Ah get something for you," Pallo said, interrupting his thoughts.

"What is it?"

"Something to make you feel fine, Excellency."

Like two war veterans reconnecting after losing contact for more than thirty years, they went to the privacy of the study, where, after the curtains were drawn, the eunuch instructed the president to lie on a couch. "Make you nor 'fraid, now, Master; you go like dis."

With meticulous care, knowing how suspicious the president was of enigmas, Pallo began to examine Tankor Satani's dick. Except for the circumciser who had done a not too neat job on the president when he was seven, no other man had seen Tankor's manhood. He would not even allow those German doctors to go there: it was none of their business what the dick of an African president looked like. There were things there, which was precisely what the eunuch was looking for: juju by some women. Given that Tankor's former virility could be measured by the number of children he had—twenty-three in all, though he had not acknowledged some of them—Pallo was also looking for signs of gonorrhea, warts, herpes, or other sexually transmitted diseases.

"Sorry, Mr. President, but dis ting done know many 'oman dem; you nor know what damage dey done do to you," the eunuch said.

The examination lasted another five minutes. With the expertise of a diamond valuer deciding the carat of a stone, the eunuch felt Tankor's scrotum. He wrapped his hands around it, squeezed it a little, and stretched the wrinkled skin out; then he pronounced it clean. Methodically, he rubbed some *ori* made from goat fat on the flabby dick and made a quick note of its size. "Master, dis ting, when 'e get power, 'e fit reach eight inches; good for big man like you."

"You should have seen it in my prime!" the president boasted.

When he felt that Tankor's penis was ready to receive the power of sorcery, the eunuch brought the head of the mamba out of some leaves. Slowly, murmuring incantations to ignite its now recognized fire, he rubbed the fetish on the crown.

"Ah done do me own part," Pallo said, concluding his rite. "Make you find 'oman en try am now."

That night, much to Tankor Satani's surprise, considering how dry his gun had been for some time, he woke up with an uncontrollable erection. Incredibly, his old tobacco leaf of a penis was charged with a tumescence all iron and fire, eight inches long. Its vigor was like that of a black snake stirring from a deep sleep in the swamp; rising in his ancient loins with a terrible intensity, and awakening in his heart the hope that he could once again father a son. A man was never too old for that business!

Pallo had responded with moderate excitement to his discovery, but Tankor Satani went wild. "Fuck the mermaid!" he said. He was not going to die anytime soon, not when his penis was trembling with the sensation that it had just been injected with the power of a swamp crocodile! For the first time since his wife left him, he felt that the beauty of old age was the ability to keep his mind thinking young, refusing to age, fighting off the ghost of grief, his heart fired with sexual desire.

Briefly he thought of sending a conciliatory letter, sweetened with some money for a new wardrobe, to Sallay, asking her to come back to the Xanadu. A president needs an official wife, even if he can have his pick among the women in Malagueta. Yet given the way she had left him, without even a kiss, his pride would not let him sink to such an indignity. After all, he was the president and had not forgotten that she was a mere greenhorn of a girl he had plucked from the dozens available and turned into a respectable woman; he was the man who had taken her away from the backwardness of a hard rural life where children walked around half naked, sleeping sickness was killing off the cattle, and the men were more broken than soldiers coming home from a war. Why send for her?

In the autumn of his life, and with the promise of renewed sex frying his brain, Sallay would not respond to his needs. She was already past the threshold of pleasure, dried up mourning for their son, her eyes shut to the beauty of life after the transience of death; moreover, he was certain she was through with him, bitter about her years with him. After she left him, he had spent some time thinking about those years, trying to recall their rhapsodic evenings together, but gave up, reconciled to spending the rest of his life without a good woman in the castle of his solitude. Until now, his long monologues on the verandah had spoken volumes about his loneliness.

Feeling much better than he had done in a long time, it was little wonder that although he knew very little about galaxies, space travel, planets, and other such things, he was aware that some Western men and women had mysterious longings to travel to the distant unknown. His own horizon was more limited than those galactic reaches, but it was more real and much easier to ascend to. He needed a new woman for companionship: definitely a young one who could match his new ardor. After he had chosen her from among the dozens of women a president could have, she would see to it that his frozen balls were brought out of the icebox every night and that his cold, dead manhood—a condition put on him, no doubt, by the mermaid, just as she had taken his beloved son who had let his own balls go wild to his head—would be a thing of the past.

He was so elated that he could once again have an erection that he dismissed all thoughts of the mermaid and relegated her to the ocean, where she should be "until I die!"

Sharp as needles, the harmattan had been blowing from the Sahel, biting into his bones. He had left the windows open, and he could hear the wind tearing through orchards of young fruit, loud and frightening over the houses, racing toward the ocean, as though aware that the dead leaves in an old man's soul had been revitalized, and that old age—that terror for most men—had been conquered. He had never felt so robust. When the gray parrots began their mimicking of his voice, he smiled, thinking that even caged birds desired to be out of their aviaries.

Buoyed by the new music in his soul, Tankor Satani did something he had not done in a long time. He shaved, showered, and splashed French cologne on his cheeks, for the first time in weeks and gave up the pernicious habit of spending long hours brooding in the tenebrous cloister of his study. His steps were brisk as he left for the servants' quarters, hidden by a high wall at the far end on the grounds of the Xanadu. With all the music in his soul, he almost tripped on the increasingly threadbare hallway carpet as he came out and walked through two ceremonial lines of presidential guards, who greeted him with "How are you, President, sah?" Standing at attention as he commented on their brass buttons, the new tassels on their berets, how well they held their swords, the guards felt that something remarkable had happened to "de Pa."

With a wave of his pipe he dismissed them, and a perplexing smile spread on his face as he strolled over to a neat garden patch near the servants' quarters to talk to the women harvesting a healthy growth of cabbage they were planning to sell to the Corals and black aristocrats who ate such things. Not he. He preferred his potato leaves stew, black-eyed beans, and rice, thank you. As though his renewed zest for life had suddenly restored his interest in his animals, he remembered his dogs and hurried over to the kennels, where two Rhodesian ridgebacks were copulating: a good thing, because he would make a present of the puppies to some of his Coral friends to keep burglars out. Leaving the dogs to their insatiable happiness, he stopped at the henhouse, where the musically gifted urchins were feeding the Abyssinian roosters they were raising for his next birthday party. "How are the fowls?" he asked the boys.

"Good, sah; except dat dey getting too lazy on dis good life, not knowing when dey will be in your pot."

He was elated.

Surprisingly, the power in the black box inside the annex had been quiet for some time. Their dead roots revitalized, the begonias were blooming again on the verandahs, and the griffon vultures, called back, he hoped, to the pathways of the intrepid ghosts, had stopped attacking the palace, giving Tankor reason to believe that his old executed enemies were probably tired of tormenting him. He started heading back to his study, but not before he had stopped in front of the dark room, as though to challenge the irascible power that had so often tormented him. Back in the study, he sat in his favorite chair, smiled, and admitted that right then he could die for the body of a woman. It was there in the color of his eyes: the irises that had turned a bit red, as the citizens of Malagueta knew so well, when things were not going propitiously his way. For a brief moment he heard a voice in his head telling him to get rid of the mermaid's comb before it was too late, but his reply was emphatic: "Not until I die!"

Early next evening, relaxing after a hectic day of lectures, Gabriel Ananias was in bed with a vivacious woman at his dorm when he heard the whinnying of a horse in the distance. It was puzzling, because the bloodsucking tsetse flies had exterminated the last Malian stallions in Malagueta a long time ago. All the same, he got out of bed and went to the window, where he heard the nasal sound of the horse again, its voice cutting through the air like the shrill note of a runaway train. Even more incredible, he saw that the sky had become a colorful image of red, gold, orange and pink: agitated by the noise, the flamboyant Abyssinian roosters had broken out of their cages in the Xanadu. The stallion was really the old man at the paradisiacal moment of orgasm, and the birds had fled because, after such a long time without a woman, Tankor Satani was fucking his heart away in his study. The flying roosters had brought a large crowd out into the nearby streets, not to celebrate because the old man had found his *stallion* in the twilight of his life but because, bloody hell, they were finally getting something for free from him as they jostled to catch the fowls descending back to earth. Thinking that a miracle had indeed happened in the Xanadu, Gabriel Ananias smiled at the coed, whose eyes were misted over at the sight of the flying roosters, her heart green with anticipation at what this might mean for her lover as she pulled Gabriel Ananias back into bed, making him hard again.

With a woman's sensibility, she could discern from his smile that at that moment, turning his fate upside down, forgetting the promise he had made to Father O'Reilly about walking the straight and narrow, Gabriel Ananias had decided to do what he had sworn never to do: pay Tankor Satani a visit in the house of mirrors.

Book Two

Passion and Immortality

CHAPTER TWENTY-NINE

The Gadflies

THE GROUP of men who met one evening in a house on a pleasant street in downtown Malagueta was made up of three very different personalities: the philosopher Theodore Iskander, the banker Alpha Samory, and the doctor Sidi Samura, men from good families but of varying ages, each of whom had risen to distinction in his profession but was nevertheless unhappy. If they had one thing in common, it was that they were among Tankor Satani's fiercest critics.

To Dr. Samura, the combination of Alpha Samory's short height—5ft. 5in.—and his weight of 190 pounds was cause for a good deal of concern. Only recently, the doctor had discovered that the stout man had been suffering from angina pectoris for some time, caused mainly by exerting himself too much, forgoing his sleep and tennis, in trying to save the crumbling economy in Malagueta. Only forty-five, Alpha Samory was carrying on his shoulders what people had begun to refer to as the "elephant's load" in the country: the governorship of the national bank.

"Take a holiday, my friend, resign," said the doctor. "What can we really do about the mess in this country? You are merely killing yourself. And remember, you still have young children and a beautiful wife."

"I can't, Sidi. We have to stop the old man ruining the economy with his mad plans." He was referring to the widely circulating rumors among the politicians that Tankor Satani was planning the largest convention ever held in Africa, Versailles style.

Like the doctor and the philosopher, the banker belonged to a stubborn breed: he was one of those men who cared deeply about the nation and had been thinking of ways, short of a massive uprising, to stop the old man from finishing off a glorious experiment on the continent. With the same determination with which his legendary namesake, Samory Touré, had fought the French occupation of the neighboring country of Bakazo in the nineteenth century, the banker, more than even the philosopher, was prepared to confront "the latest political scourge on our heritage." Encouraged by his wife, he turned a deaf ear to any impending danger to his health, and continued with his elephant's load.

"Go with God. He will give you the strength to keep carrying it, and you are not dying anytime soon," she said.

In five years as governor, he had been trying to stem the flow of capital from the country by the politicians and their Coral associates. He blocked the shipments of natural resources—fish, kola nuts, bauxite, gold and iron ore. Recently all the profits from diamonds had been turning up alternately in Tankor Satani's and Moustapha Ali-Bakr's Swiss bank accounts. The banker was determined to put a stop to that.

Armed with some compromising documents, he went to see Tankor Satani in the Xanadu one evening. "Diamonds from Kissi are famous all over the world, Excellency. They have a clear brilliance that brings a sparkle to the eyes of all the merchants who trade them. Women go crazy in their desire for these diamonds and will sleep with any man to have them, but the people here are not reaping a penny from those gems."

"What are you hinting at?" said Tankor Satani.

"Excellency, your bank account is profiting from the sale of diamonds, but the World Bank governors are fuming because our treasury is almost empty and the peasants are getting ready to revolt up north. Now you are thinking of holding a costly convention."

Tankor Satani finished his brandy and ginger, fuming. "Who are you to tell me what to do?"

The banker was not put off. "I have stuck by you during difficult times, Excellency, but I won't let you use up the country's reserve on an expensive adventure. Moreover, there are other matters about which the nation is worried."

Tankor heard this as an oblique reference to rumors that he has gone back to spending lavishly on his mistresses now that he had regained his manhood. "To hell with the other things!" he said.

"History will judge you harshly, Excellency, if you leave a terrible legacy of debt to your people," the banker said with a professional defiance.

He left depressed. As he had always done when he could take some time off from his job, he stopped at the house of his good friend Dr. Sidi Samura, where he found Theodore Iskander having a drink with the doctor.

"You have come from the madman," the doctor said, reading the worry on the banker's face.

The soft strains of kora music from the doctor's study steadied the uneven palpitation of the banker's heart. He downed the glass of orange juice proffered by his friend.

"And how did your meeting with the tyrant go?" Theodore Iskander wondered.

"It was like talking to a wall. He is determined to ruin this country."

Two weeks later, the electricity in Malagueta went out one night. That in itself was not unusual, but strangely, the standby generator did not immediately come on at the substation serving the expensive hilly suburbs. In the darkness, two masked men, dressed in mourning black, came out of a bush and moved stealthily toward the banker's beautiful house on the hilltop. After another frustrating day at the office, the banker was sitting in his verandah, relishing the darkness with a glass of orange juice and listening to the crickets chirping on the hibiscus, not realizing it was the last time he would enjoy that simple pleasure. Early the next morning, attracted by the buzzing of large mango flies, one of his guards found his bloodstained body lying spread-eagled under a mango tree in the garden. His head had been crushed by a terrible blow, his eyes, bright like sea corals, were wide open, his teeth were smeared with blood, and he was clutching some papers. The guard let off a scream loud enough to wake the dead in broad daylight. While the dead man's wife cradled his battered head in the garden, Malagueta was shocked to hear on the national radio that he had been killed by one of his cronies over a corrupt deal.

"That is a lie!" fumed Dr. Sidi Samura. "He was the most honest man ever to hold that office." That day, the doctor determined that though others were silent, he could not be any longer. He hung his stethoscope on a wall and, with a fiery pen never before encountered in Malagueta, became Tankor Satani's most persistent critic.

Over thirty-five years, the doctor had perfected his routine of practicing medicine between eight in the morning and one in the afternoon, followed by a nap at two, after which he would return to the surgery at four for another two hours. Just before he had his dinner, he would be heard playing some Chopin on the piano, usually the *Grande Polonaise* or the *Raindrop Prelude*, or a Scarlatti sonata. After a good meal, it was usually off to his study to write plays and short stories until well after midnight. He would sometimes fall asleep in his chair until his wife came to rouse him and take him to bed. He was sixty-nine and, for the last twenty-years, as a community service, had been visiting a poor section of Malagueta to deliver babies, lance boils, suture wounds, dispense malaria tablets, and attend to outbreaks of measles. It was also an opportunity for him to listen to the Jelebas playing exquisite melodies on the kora and balanji. As an illustrious descendant of the great Malinke Empire, he did not use the word "griots," which was what the French called the oral poets, historians, and musicians of that heritage. When he was not listening to the Jelebas, he would watch the masquerades and street dancing that were part of his background so that he could infuse his writings with an authentic veracity. Since he was one of the top doctors in the country his friends and associates were mostly men and women of the bourgeois class, so his forays into the poor neighborhood were opportunities for him to "stay in touch with reality." His brilliance was a reminder of the old days in Malagueta, when learning was treasured. Sharp-witted, with a dry, almost English, sense of humor, he was a very taciturn and private man who was also an agnostic.

While tending to the poor, he had, with the utmost discretion, also been seeing a mistress, although one of his daughters was aware of the relationship. The woman was a Moslem from the same illustrious Mandingo background as the doctor's, but far from being a relationship based on any emotional need unfulfilled at home, the truth was that his mistress served a deep professional purpose. She was worth more than her weight in Mandingo gold to the doctor, for over the years he had been carrying out a secret experiment in a room at her place.

Long before DNA studies had shown that malaria may have helped topple the Roman Empire, Dr. Samura had been at the cutting edge of another line of research. In his small laboratory, he had set about proving a hypothesis about a particular disease common to the region. He closed himself up in that room for hours, emitting not a sound, which worried the poor woman, considering that his eyes were weak and he, a small man, was going without food for hours. She wondered whether he was getting tired of the huge platters of lamb kebab and couscous he had only recently relished from her kitchen.

"What are you trying to prove?" his mistress asked in despair one evening.

"That it was the invasion of Abyssinia by Italian bandits that led to the scourge of trypanosomiasis—sleeping sickness—among cattle and the people on the Horn of Africa and elsewhere on the continent."

He examined dust samples that had been preserved from the boots of Italian soldiers in Ethiopia after Field Marshal Rodolfo Graziani, who was fighting for Mussolini, had reportedly used chemical weapons in the massacre of thousands of Ethiopian troops and patriots, in contravention of the Geneva Convention, in the 1930s. "The Duce will have Ethiopia with or without the Ethiopians," the field marshal had remarked.

After the war, Field Marshal Graziani, also known as "the butcher of Fezzan," was tried and given a long sentence, but served only a few years.

The dust samples had been sent to Dr. Sidi Samura by an old associate at the Institute of Tropical Hygiene in Ethiopia. Furious about the bestial actions of Field Marshal Graziani against Africans, Dr. Samura pursued his work, by examining small fragments sent to him of the skeletons of Ethiopian officers and their prostitutes from that inglorious period. He read the manifests of the ships that had transported cattle from Italy to Ethiopia, and he carbon-dated the clothes of both races of the same period, sent to him by a colleague in Milan. Just as important were the crops, porcelain, jewelry, Coptic parchments, and animal bones found before and after the Abyssinian invasion. He used recently discovered scientific methods to fully understand the digestive habits of the cattle and new techniques to look at burial rituals and ceremonial shrouds. After more than three years of hard work, he was able to prove, emphatically, that not only did the Italians have a case to answer for the massacre of Ethiopians, they were also probably responsible for one of the greatest scourges in Africa: the spread of trypanosomiasis. Five years after he first started his mad research, the doctor published his findings in the *Journal of Tropical Medicine* in Malagueta, giving him an unassailable medical status in the community.

"Now we know that the people who gave us Julius Caesar, Latin, and Puccini could also have given us their diseases!" he remarked to Theodore Iskander.

But it was as a gadfly that Dr. Sidi Samura would achieve his greatest following. With Theodore Iskander he had been among the small group of men to criticize the excesses of Tankor Satani, and it was not unusual for people to line up to buy the newspaper in which the doctor's articles regularly appeared. With his sharp wit he would lambaste the stupidity of the politicians, writing that although he had known many of those creatures, he had never encountered an honest one. At first, Tankor Satani dismissed the doctor's anger as that of a raving intellectual concerned about his legacy as he approached his seventieth birthday. "At that age, it is not uncommon for some of us to start thinking of immortality," the president said.

To show what he thought of the likes of the doctor, Tankor Satani made one of his most spitefully controversial appointments, now that he had coerced the judges, by naming a former tally clerk to the estimable position of speaker of the parliament.

"It is like dressing Caligula's horse in purple robes and bringing him into the chambers to sit with the senators," the doctor wrote with derision.

Spearheaded by the foreign minister, the former academic Dr. Komba Binkolo, the government-controlled press had launched a campaign to discredit the banker Alpha Samory. They tarred his memory with the brush of corruption, insisting that he had committed suicide by jumping from his terrace because he was about to be arrested. Dr. Samura would have none of it and expressed his rage. In a blistering article he asked: "How did a man so heavy manage the difficult task of climbing over the walls of his verandah? This is a slander on a good man's name."

Tankor Satani finally lost his patience. A month later, at midnight, when he felt that the doctor's neighbors would be asleep and not present any challenge to their authority, the police turned up at the doctor's house, only to discover that he had been expecting them.

"You don't have to wake the neighbors up," he said. "The door is open, and you can come in. I have already packed my midnight bag."

If Tankor had hoped to silence the doctor, his nemesis turned out to be a very tough prisoner. Quartered in the old colonial prison for three months, his spirits were unbroken. His cell was near the gallows on which Colonel Fillibo Mango and others had perished before they were taken to their unmarked graves. Although the doctor sometimes thought about how near he was to that machinery of death, he was not afraid of suffering that fate. He was concerned more about the future of Malagueta, as he hastened to finish a play entitled *The Brutal Folly* on paper smuggled in to him by an admiring guard. Some nights the screams of the condemned men languishing on death row after Tankor Satani had declared a moratorium on hanging would keep the doctor awake. Although he was an agnostic, some verses from the scriptures found their way to his lips for the souls of those men. When he was released from prison, a small crowd was there to greet him. "Don't let Tankor frighten you, Doctor," an old woman said, giving him a kiss.

That was all the encouragement he needed. He resumed his blistering attacks on the president for the death of the banker, the collapse of the economy, and the profligacy of his cabinet ministers. But rather than a second jail term, the only sanction against the doctor, something that deeply hurt, was that, terrified of Tankor Satani's thugs, many of the doctor's friends stopped visiting him. They took to driving at high speed on his street, scattering some poor woman's stray chickens, sometimes almost crashing into trees. At the cathedral where his wife worshipped, they avoided meeting her eyes. Shamelessly, some of them even put off coming for their annual checkups, and they would hurry to hide their faces behind their papers, embarrassed, if they chanced to see the doctor in the barbershop. He took it all in stride, reasoning that the best that could be said about those men was that they had a sense of humor greater than their shame. It was not a moral quest that motivated his actions, but the feeling that on the road to God, each man was responsible for standing up for himself. And as though to prove the doctor right, Tankor Satani showed up unexpectedly at his house one evening.

"Let bygones be bygones, old friend," the president said. "I respect your integrity and what you have done for the good of this nation. I have made mistakes. But you must not put simple politicians like me in your class; I have to do what is right to maintain order."

Dr. Samura studied his old friend for five minutes: this was the only politician for whom he had ever addressed a rally, in the days when Tankor Satani was campaigning against the previous sectarian government. How terrible it was, he thought, that although Malagueta had been blessed with riches, it had not produced a single honest politician. He smiled wryly, thinking how little Tankor Satani knew about the ephemeral nature of power: the pointers—in the wrong direction—that hubris was the mark of a small mind. Hearing his wife, who had been taking a nap, walking to the bathroom, the doctor wanted to bring this meeting quickly to a conclusion, man to man. He took a long, searching look at the president and pitied him as he would have done a mangy dog, because he could see, in Tankor Satani's eyes, fear; never mind that he was the president. The doctor felt good to have received his old friend, and now he sent him packing. "Go to hell," he said. "Your friendship was not worth the price of a dog's leash."

The Twinning of Hearts

Not long after the dead man's family had finally given him a decent burial, the suspicion that Tankor Satani might have had a hand in the killing of the banker began to circulate in the town. Immediately after the ceremony, government bulldozers had been used to clear large swaths of land for the villas a Moroccan architect had designed to house the visiting presidents at Tankor Satani's pending convention. There was great unease in the hearts of the old Malaguetan landowners, who feared they might lose their holdings. Anticipating a run on land, Habiba thought it was about time she bought some, especially as she was worried about Theodore's future. Once again she sought Pallo's advice, and was glad the sorcerer offered to come to her place rather than have her visit him in his private quarters in the Xanadu.

"Ah know you don't believe in de sorcery business too much, but make ah see what de leaves say 'bout buying land," he offered.

She sat on the floor with her legs stretched out in front of him, a position she found difficult, as she had not been exercising much after giving birth. While he went into an inner room to perform some prerequisite to divining her future, she removed her dress and wound a wrapper just slightly below her belly button. He returned after a while and sat on his folded legs opposite her, so that he had a clear view of the blue-purple stretch lines from her recent pregnancy. Then he said a few arcane words, spat into his palms, and rubbed them on his forehead. Closing his eyes, he reached out gently until he had found and touched her belly. A strange feeling overwhelmed her as the sorcerer's hands moved in circles on her belly. Besides Theodore and her doctor, she had sworn never to let another man touch her that way again. But this was her sorcerer: he had no need of her.

After a while Pallo removed his hands from her belly. The sunlight in the room had dimmed a bit, and now threw a soft yellow hue on the sorcerer. In the pocket of his gown he searched for a box of matches and brought a speck of flame to the charcoal brazier that he had requested from her. When he had emptied his goatskin bag, the room smelled of seasonal wildflowers mixed with the sweet scents of dried spices and decaying leaves, and of the bewitching fragrance of dry tapioca leaves, basil, cloves, ginger, and alligator peppers. The fire glowed pale red: not the right color. Slowly Pallo stoked the coals to produce a blue hue, and sifted the ashes from the coals before he passed a few tapioca leaves over the fire until they turned brown. Then he waited for them to cool a bit. His intention was to send the woman into a trance. Habiba Mouskuda leaned backward, closed her eyes, and did not move even when Pallo touched her forehead. As he had expected, she was warm, which meant that she was not yet completely relaxed.

"Don't think about anything; I want to hear what your soul is saying," the sorcerer said.

When he was satisfied that she was finally relaxed, he drew some circles on her stomach with camwood, then wiped her perspiration with a cancellated bone sponge from a baboon that had died of natural causes. He closed his eyes and grunted. Inspired by the seminal gift that he was receiving, he murmured in his strange argot again and began to transfix her with the wonders of his sorcery. She felt a ripple in her stomach as though it were once again her water, long the source of life springing from women, that was about to burst, as when she was giving birth to Yeama. A slight tremor shook her stomach and electrified her quivering breasts; tears welled up in her eyes until, finally, her face broke out in rivulets of peaceful sweat. It was the sign that Pallo was looking for so that he could capture the message her soul was transmitting to him.

"Ebrything right, Habiba," the eunuch said as she came out of the trance; "no harm go come to Yeama; forget 'bout de past, and, yes, you for move close to waterside, next time you build house."

Habiba was shocked that he could be so clairvoyant when it came to divining her wish to live near water. Exhilarated, after he was gone she decided to go for a walk, as Irene had been after her for some time about her putting on some weight. "You have to exercise, child; all dat potato leaves stew you been eating is bad for you!"

It was a long walk, well beyond her immediate vicinity, and the quiet, unpaved road on which she lived merged into a laterite one, on which there was some traffic. She was just about to turn back when she was startled by a car that pulled up alongside her. The driver, who wore a suit, looked familiar. A top civil servant, no doubt; one of those pathetic creatures she used to torment with the brazenness of her eyes who was prepared to cook the government's ledgers, inflate contracts, cut corners in the running of their offices, just so they could please her.

He offered her a ride, which she accepted, and as soon as he felt he had her attention, launched into an impassioned desire for her. It was something he had wanted to tell her a long time ago. "I am prepared to look after you," he said, in a torrent of sweet words. "I can wait for a year, if necessary, for you to respond. Meanwhile, I shall open a bank account for Yeama. What are you doing with that philosopher who 'eats only books' and cannot provide for a woman like you?"

Three years earlier, determined to prove to Theodore that she was as good as any well-bred woman, Habiba had begged God to dull the sharp knife of her temper and to help clean out her lowlife mouth. But there was no telling what she might do if Theodore deserted her, and no one should blame a woman if she let loose a volley of poisonous arrows against desertion. But to hear insults about her lover from a gecko of a civil servant was enough for her to ask God to release her from her pledge, just this one time, so that she could defend his honor. Her eyes turned magenta as she went back to her old, sassy vocabulary, spiced with red pepper. She called the civil servant names that would have skinned the hair off the back of a baboon, and shot him with enough venom to put a harridan to shame. If his mother was alive (the poor woman!), Habiba sent him back to her with a fiery stew of ridicule for not having raised this gecko properly. She asked him how long ago he had started wearing his ill-fitting suit, who was it that taught him how to knot his ridiculous tie so that he looked like a brass monkey, and did he know that he smelled like rotten fish?

Finally, exhausted, thinking Irene might know the unfortunate mother of this wretch, she demanded to be let out of the car, slammed the door, took the number down and continued the rest of her journey home on foot. The cheek!

CHAPTER THIRTY

A Pasiphae, So Late in His Life

AFTER NOT having been heard for a long time in the Xanadu, the honeyed voice of Salma Aboudi, the dervish diva from Lebanon, was serenading Tankor Satani with her lovesick ballads one evening in the study. As he drank his usual brandy and ginger, the music filled the hallway long deserted by the ghoulish vultures.

With the first set of Abyssinian roosters now gone into savory stews in the kitchens of the lucky citizens who had caught them after they bolted their coops, Moustapha Ali-Bakr wasted no time replacing the birds.

"Make de servants put dese ones in strong cages, Excellency; we are looking forward to you eating them on your birthday."

Good food had never really counted as one of Moustapha's pleasures. Yet he had always suspected there was a connection between Tankor's cuisine and the way he made love to his women. The same, he felt, could be said about how he conducted his commercial business.

The musically gifted orphans had been left with nothing to do after the roosters bolted, besides their impromptu carousals with their tambourines or playing football behind the servants' quarters. Sometimes, when they were extremely bored, they would shock the cooks' wives with ribald stories about how camels copulate, or recall the marvelous art of falconry during their childhood in the desert, or the pestilence of locusts. They spoke of how they had lost their parents to unexplained sickness, and how, but for the intervention of Tankor during his visit to Niger, they might have ended up as boy prostitutes, or worse, as eunuchs guarding the harems of Tuareg or Arab chieftains.

"Dem Arab people bad to black people," the boys said then, almost crying.

With only twenty-four hours to go before Tankor Satani celebrated his seventy-fifth birthday, they finally had a chance to show their ancestral wizardry with a knife. Early the next morning, the shrieking roosters flayed, coughed, beat their wings, scratched, and drew blood from the boy's wrists, fighting for dear life as the boys slit their throats with a professional skill that impressed the servants. "If dey kin kill fighting chicken like dat, ah fear for sheep!" one of the servants offered.

The Xanadu came alive like a pirate ship later that evening. Fireworks lit the sky amid a rousing cacophony of traditional dancing and acrobats leaping like dervishes on the palace grounds. For the next three months, Tankor Satani's servants would recall, on their days off in town, what had gone on that night: how boisterous the drinking had been, and the scandalous eating by some very well-dressed guests who were making their first visit to the Xanadu. Gallons of whiskey, rum, Campari, wine, and stout had disappeared into the dry mouths of those guests. With ravaging gusto, they had attacked the platters of chicken and ground their teeth on roast goat and sheep.

One of the servants suddenly remembered an important detail. "But make ah tell you 'bout how de Coral people behave dat night," he said to an attentive audience. "Dey empty plenty champagne bottle inside de president swimming pool. Den dey begin swim naked wit' dem foolish black 'oman dem."

"God go vex for dat kind waste en foolishness," said a shocked listener.

The permutation of hunger observed in the Xanadu that day was nothing new. But it had previously been seen only in the poor, not in the privileged. Not content to gorge themselves, Tankor Satani's guests displayed scandalous voracity by emptying what remained of the platters of food into plastic bags, before going off to strip the bathrooms of towels, bars of soap, and toilet paper, and the hallways of light bulbs. It was an orgy of gluttony that shocked the lowly servants, many of them illiterate, as citizens they had previously thought respectable let loose their deprivation, daring Tankor Satani to stop them from ripping off what they felt was rightfully theirs; inebriated, they could express what they really thought of his rule. God help him if he tried to stop them; they were hungry, and had learned well the rapacious cunning he had taught them.

When they began, drunkenly, to strip some of the palace windows of their levers, one of the servants decided they had gone too far and complained to Tankor.

"Leave them," he said to the underling. "Like the grass near your house, there is too much food here; and, as we say in this country, the cow eats the grass where it is tethered. These people are hungry cows."

Smiling mischievously, he had been wondering how long it would take some of his hoity-toity guests to lose their pretensions and start acting like the remoras he knew some of them to be.

"It is a great milestone," he said to Moustapha Ali-Bakr, "so let them enjoy it."

Intent on enjoying a most virile night later in bed, as soon as the guests had gone Tankor urged the servants to take what was left of the feast. With a large swath of the crab, goat meat, chicken fricassee, pork, and chunks of grilled barracuda off of the platters, the servants were soon in their quarters, where their extended kin had been waiting.

"Let them also enjoy this day," the old man said.

Somewhat jaded, but still buxom in middle age, two of his old mistresses, Yebu Soko and Memuna Sillah, had been waiting for him to decide which of them was going to sleep in the presidential bed that night. When, unexpectedly, he had sent them some new jewelry a month earlier, it was obvious that he had regained his manhood. Now he seemed to be having a hard time deciding which of them should be his birthday present, but was enjoying their anticipation as they eyed each other with poisonous heat. But before he could decide, one of his caged gray parrots fluttered its wings and whistled a licentious tune, making Tankor turn around. Right away he forgot about his aging mistresses because, at that moment, as if an angel had sent her, Jenebah Djallo had entered his life.

She was a mere bird of a girl, but her frailty did not hide her most potent weapon, which she was displaying with a brazen air: the dusky pastoral beauty of Fulani odalisques, which had been known to cause cardiac arrest in some men. In the breathtaking aura of that loveliness, she looked like one of those creatures on which God must have been happy to work overtime to achieve perfection. She had the eyes of a gazelle and the long arms of a long-distance Masai athlete, and as soon as Tankor Satani saw her the air went out of his windpipe and his sexual clock began an erratic chime; she made him confuse Greenwich and Arabic times and almost choke on the pepper chicken he had been eating. Right away he knew that this was the girl he wanted to die in bed with that night! She was incredibly tall, almost as tall as he was, and a shade lighter than mahogany. Leaning against a trellis pillar, she was pursing her full, hennaed lips in disgust as she watched the last stages of the scandalous gorging taking place in the compound. Meanwhile, the parakeets and cockatoos, as though they could sense something mysterious about her, also began to whistle. Aware that she had created a seismic eruption in Tankor Satani's heart, she trained her hypnotic eyes on his seventy-five years with a sinewy wickedness, enjoying his discomfort as he tried to stare her down with his imperious presidential conceit, which failed to hide the torment in his loins.

Without blinking, she glared mischievously back at him, unsettling the old man so much that his dentures almost fell out of his mouth. Although the nymph was younger than his youngest daughter, it was obvious she had been preparing for this mature role for a long time, helped by the stars. A low décolletage revealed her majestic breasts, and the allure of her almond eyes was enough to drive any full-blooded man crazy. While Yebu Soko and Memuna Sillah were still eyeing each other, getting ready for a ferocious pas de deux, Jenebah Djallo's eyes were fixed firmly on their prize—Tankor Satani's heart! And as though she knew the celestial angels had heard her wish, she smiled, then turned her back on him, pretending she was talking to one of the caged birds, as Tankor Satani approached her.

"You have no business coming here to torment me so late in life," he stammered.

"And you have no business getting hot over your grand-*pikin*, old man!" she shot back.

Whereas his middle-aged mistresses had been dreaming of taking Tankor Satani to the heights of sexual gratification that night, hoping he would reward them for their skills before he reached his dotage, that was not the intention of Jenebah Djallo. For her, the heavenly bodies of the stars, where she felt the old man's restored virility had not really been tested, were her destination. Before beginning to torment his soul, she had put him on her scales and believed she knew what he really wanted. She smiled thinking he would not be surprised to learn that her ambition matched his: to get as much out of life using all available means—this old man should have been dead long ago, or at least his gluttony for young women, money, and cars should have been sated by now. She was sure of one thing: her eyes were just the right gems to create the last tremors in Tankor Satani's heart!

For the first time in a long while, considering how suspicious he had become of women after a few had saddled him with dubious pregnancies, Tankor Satani did not even bother to investigate the background of this one. How she came to be at the party was a puzzle to him; he did not recall inviting her. But it did not matter, not when the woman looked so divine. Just imagining what a night with her could do for his restored manhood was magical. He forgot about any breach of protocol that had let her come in, sized her up, and decided she was the best gift for the autumn of his life and that he couldn't wait for the opportunity to have her in his bed.

"Who are you?" he finally asked, his voice unsteady.

"Jenebah Djallo, sah."

"Where are you from? Who are your people?"

"You know how we Fullah people are, Your Excellency. We come from all places; cow people, merchants; we have no passports; just beautiful people free like our cows. So don't worry. Relax."

"Now we have Fullah bankers, teachers, and doctors," the old man said.

"Yes, sah; we Fullah people can do anything."

She looked at the old man with such a seductive smile it dispelled any suspicion about her intention. But it was obvious to Tankor that Jenebah was not a greenhorn and would not jump into bed with him for the simple pleasure of adding her name to the list of presidential conquests. Although she was so young, it was clear that life had ripened her. It was there in her eyes, those of an experienced woman who was there to show him that a man lives and dies only once, but should be allowed the choice of his demise. "Lord, Lord!" he said, unable to control his torment any longer.

Then he said something sweet to her that made her laugh, and the birds, which had been watching them the whole time, let out lewd whistles as the old man led Jenebah Djallo into the Xanadu.

CHAPTER THIRTY-ONE

Flames on the Streets

LIKE HIS old friend Dr. Sidi Samura, Theodore Iskander was appalled by the killing of the banker. In his lectures, given without any concern for his welfare, he was dismissive of the statements put out by his former colleague, Dr. Komba Binkolo, the new foreign minister, who had been trying to absolve Tankor Satani of all blame for the banker's death. "He is lying through his teeth, and he knows it," the philosopher raged.

Not surprisingly, his lectures electrified his students. He delivered them with verve, after preparing them meticulously. With great patience, he probed the depths of his students' minds, trying to bring out their best. Perhaps it was because his own tutors at Cambridge University had thought that, as an African, he lacked the rigor to delve deeply into the abstractions of European philosophy, and had dismissed his interest in Kant and Rousseau. Angrily, he had argued with those bigots and shamed them with the acuity of his mind. Now he was urging his own students to demand a lot of their professors. Besides his students and the occasional visits to the ghettoes to tutor peasants, Theodore Iskander had no life, other than that with his family. Unlike some other men, he knew he had left fatherhood until too late, but he was determined to be a good father now that Irene had softened her opposition to the malatta. He visited the doctor frequently, the two men being drawn even closer after the death of the banker.

"I sometimes wish I had been born in the old Southern Rhodesia or in Soweto," Theodore said one evening.

"Why?"

"For one thing, I would probably have gone to jail or been shot for my obstinacy; that is assuming Ian Smith had not cooked up some trumped-up charge to hang me."

"Yes, yes, the tyrants of this poor continent," the doctor said, somewhat sadly.

"Like our own," Theodore conceded.

"How strange it is," the doctor said, "that Mother Nature gave us one of the most beautiful countries in the world, only for it to be ruined by some of the most despicable politicians in the world."

Theodore Iskander reflected on the doctor's comment for a while before replying. "Yes. And some of the crudest."

Putting aside his occasional poetic endeavors, which he showed to no one besides Dr. Sidi Samura, he felt his writings had been useless. Just looking at the puzzled faces of his students confirmed his suspicion that his lectures were sometimes too serious. All that his scribbling might do was to ennoble him in a wishful future, for which some more practical men were already writing a different script.

His greatest pain, the depths of which had furrowed his brow, was that as the descendant of the illustrious poet, even if his own mother had been raised poor but was now fairly comfortable, he saw how difficult it was for a lot of people to wake up every morning, to face life. He took stock of his years of teaching; the students he had turned out—some good, others hopeless cases. Sometimes he went for long walks on the campus, only to be assailed by proof of how things had degenerated: the untended gardens, the broken desks littering the fronts of the classrooms, from which the handles on the windows had been removed by unpaid workers. Then he would feel that if they came on a visit, the ghosts of the founders of Malagueta would die of the stench coming from the environs. Feeling restless, he thought of asking for a sabbatical so that he could travel to the island of Gorée, the point of no return for some slaves sent to the New World; or to Timbuktu, to research the epics in the great manuscripts written during the time of the emperor Sundiata Keita. Perhaps he might even go to Ashanti land, where kings had lived and continued to live; there his soul might be inspired to write a book. If it happened, it would help to heal the hurt he had felt lately for all the people betrayed by his fellow academics after they were bought over by the Corals and Tankor Satani. He did not consider himself a martyr, but viewed his suffering as payment for the privilege of having been born into a noble family, so he stopped dreaming about an escape and came back to reality—he was going nowhere. Malagueta was too much in his bones, and he had a ravishing mistress to remind him of that reality.

Just when he had made that decision about his future, and as though some spirits had heard him make it, fate confirmed his choice.

A violent protest over the death of the banker had sent some students spilling out of their classrooms on the campus on the hill overlooking the city. Not wanting things to get out of hand, Theodore Iskander came out of his office as the students were smashing up some cars and unfolding banners denouncing Tankor Satani as a murderer. The students could not have chosen a better day to vent their anger on the government, because the mayor of the city, a flashy old dame, had come to the campus riding in a black Mercedes, and her presence was like a red flag to a bull. When she saw the burning cars and the lines of the advancing students, she tried to make her getaway in the sleek limousine, but a volley of stones halted it and a flaming torch just missed setting it on fire. Her guards quickly rushed her into another, less provocative car, just in time, because a fuel dump had been blown up, setting off the police sirens. Horrified, recalling how Tankor Satani had dealt with the last uprising, three years ago, when he had executed another set of "troublemakers," Theodore Iskander saw the helmeted troops of the Bakazo brigade coming out of their barracks. They were gendarmes that Tankor had requested long ago, when he could no longer trust his own soldiers, and Theodore Iskander cringed as they marched toward the students in their green fatigues.

On their commandant's order they began clubbing the students with their batons. When that failed to subdue the angry mob, the soldiers hurled teargas canisters at the crowd. A cloud of orange smoke, thick with poison and having a sickly odor, rose high in the air, and as the choking chemical began to immobilize some of the students, Theodore Iskander saw the surrounding plants wilting and the discarded furniture twisting like serpents in the flames. But not even that could contain the students' anger. It was then that Theodore Iskander heard the first shots ring out. Besides the twenty-one-gun salute on Memorial Day, it had been years since anyone had heard the sound of gunfire on Malagueta's streets, and Theodore Iskander thought he was dreaming when the wails of the students pierced the sky as the bullets came down. The last thing he remembered was the cold, dull sensation of the bullet that had found its mark in his leg, and that his lips were quivering with rage, not just at the unbelievable turn of events but also because his stomach was wrenching out of him, his blood flowing freely as he passed out.

Habiba Mouskuda was potting in the garden when the telephone rang. A light of iridescent gold had been in the sky all day and was reflected in the beautiful garden. Even so, she had been thinking about how much longer she could go on living in a house in which, at times, she couldn't help seeing the face of the man who had built it before he died. Suddenly all was gray, she felt cold in spite of the heat, and even before some students came rushing with the news that Theodore Iskander had been shot, she had an intimation that what she had feared for some time—his arrest or death—had finally happened.

She did not even wait for the students to finish describing the flames in the streets before she grabbed the sum of money she had put aside for an emergency, saved from selling those coffins. Crying, she rushed to her car and put it into high gear. The distance to the hospital had never before seemed so long. Given her agitation, she did not even realize that, in order to get to the hospital, she had to drive in front of the mortuary where, many years ago, she had dumped the surveyor after he had died on top of her.

Theodore Iskander was lying in the emergency ward, but the smile on the professor's face checked the horror she had dreaded for so long: that it would be hopeless and she would be left all alone.

"He is a strong crocodile, and there will be many more rivers for him to swim in if he is lucky!" the doctor said.

The doctor had made a tourniquet to stem the bleeding in Theodore Iskander's leg, and he was hooked up to an intravenous drip, giving him a chance to fight the pull of death. Seeing him lying there, Habiba realized she had never loved the mad philosopher as much as she did now, when he was so close to death. She held his hand and felt how warm it was. If he died, she could not go on living, even with Yeama there; she would not know where to turn, because he had changed her, just as much as she imagined she had changed him: this crazy man, bold and daring in all that he did, free of class bigotry in loving a woman despised by many of his type. When he squeezed her hand with a strong confirmation that he was going nowhere, not when he had done something meaningful for the first time in his life by being with his students when it mattered, it was clear to her, just looking at his eyes, that it would take more than a soldier's bullet to extinguish the fires of revolt that being the great-great-grandson of the poet Garbage Martins had lit in his blood.

"I am very proud of you," she said.

Terrified more than ever that because General Augustus Kotay had built her house with state funds, Tankor Satani might use that excuse to confiscate it, she resolved to sell the house.

CHAPTER THIRTY-TWO

When the Banana Plant Is about to Die It Produces New Suckers

TANKOR SATANI and Jenebah Djallo hardly left the grand presidential bedroom for the next six days. Except for the lights on the verandahs and the fluorescent lights in the hallways, the light in the Xanadu was a purple glow. It was a sorcerer's den of cat meows and moans as, fired by lust, the old man came very close to the relish for which some people had nicknamed him the son of Satan. He forgot about matters of state, even forgoing the already irregular visits to his office in downtown Malagueta, and gone was his fear that his prime minister, Enos Tanu, was always plotting against him. In fact, he even put the prime minister in charge of the government: something that Enos Tanu found out only when Tankor Satani's press secretary relayed a brief presidential fiat on the national radio.

Enos Tanu was deeply perplexed. What the hell was going on? he wondered.

"Maybe he is testing you to see how desperate you are for him to die," his wife said, advising him to be cautious.

Those were scandalous days of debauchery in the Xanadu, when the only report people had of the old man was after his guards had let on that they had seen him lumbering like an ox out of the bedroom three times a day, an enormous towel wrapped around his waist, as he made his way to his favorite verandah for some fresh air. At other times, they had also seen him and his nymph eating whatever meal the cook had prepared.

"In ten years of cooking for dat man," the cook marveled, "he never eat like dis before."

"Like how?" asked his assistant.

"Like big hungry man!"

Using her advantage of youth and coquetry, Jenebah Djallo almost succeeded in drowning Tankor Satani in the tormenting river of his unfulfilled longings. Brazenly, she stripped him of his oars and made him lose all his presidential pretensions, while she enjoyed his futile attempts to cling to his sinking canoe. One evening she threw him into such a delirium after she had danced naked for him that he thought she was a new mermaid—but one without a comb. At another time, she closed up like an ammonite shell and refused to come out until he had promised her a sizable share of his wealth. When he did, she let him mount her like a horse. But soon she was using a new wile: forcing him to grovel for her attention. As though she were a sea cow, he kissed her breasts and sucked her fingers, the irresistible mystique in those breasts urging him on. One night, because of the fire in his loins, his breathing was so labored that Jenebah thought he might die on top of her and deprive her of the promised share of his wealth, as he had not yet signed his will. But she was soon cured of that delusion when he began to light the mythical fire of the salamander somewhere raw in her womb, stifling the air in her throat, making her thrash like a Portuguese man-of-war barely able to float, and emit such wild cries that the gray parrots fluttered their wings and let off a singsong of obscenities they had learned from the old man, until the servants rushed to silence them.

Two days later, the midnight guards patrolling on the front verandah heard Jenebah screaming as though the untiring horns of a randy bull were charging her. Once again, her wails almost drove the birds crazy as, with the strength of a swamp crocodile, Tankor Satani rode her high sea, battling a tropical wave and taming the wild horse in Jenebah Djallo. This job of being a president had never been so sweet!

"Lord have mercy," the young woman screamed. "Before now, ah think say you are old dog, Tankor; but you get de horns of de debul!"

Tankor Satani smiled with the satisfaction of a man who had come home after a long journey exploring the world. "Child," he said, "you saw an old, drenched leopard but made the mistake of thinking it was a domestic cat."

Afterward, Jenebah lay like a beached whale with her flippers clipped, berthed on sand so hot she was sweating profusely. The palm trees were rustling from a seaside breeze, but it was not cool enough to dampen the heat that the salamander had ignited in her womb. She took a long, hard look at the seventy-five-year-old president, all fire and iron.

Later that week, when Tankor Satani was having a drink and smoking his pipe, his idyll was unexpectedly disturbed by the arrival of a trio of women: his estranged daughters. Unlike their mother, they were women of the world, very ambitious and cunning like their father. As they had married useless men, who could not take care of them, Tankor Satani represented their future, and for almost two years they had been waiting for word from him that he had forgiven them after they had sided with their mother when the poor woman fled the Xanadu. Recently, the scandalous goings-on in the Xanadu had finally reached their ears. Enough was enough; they were determined to throw the "Fullah cow" out.

"Shame on you," they yelled at their father. "You are like a banana plant almost ready to die, but are thinking of producing some new suckers!"

Tankor Satani glared menacingly at them. "Say that again and I won't leave you a penny in my will."

Not for the first time, his daughters shriveled from the thunder in his voice and beat a hasty retreat. Convinced that the "brazen little harlot" had succeeded in doing what no other woman had been able to do—give Tankor something to think about besides money, power, and cars—the women bared their teeth at Jenebah as she came into the verandah and took Tankor Satani's hand. And as though she were the lowest trash ever to be seen around their father, they glared at her with murderous contempt and swore they would find a way of getting rid of her when he was not looking. "Get all you can from him with your Fullah magic, you harlot, but know that we shall come for you."

Something in Jenebah's eyes was so menacing, so full of the mysteries of the ocean, that it frightened the women. Hurriedly, they left with a deep sense of foreboding about how the relationship might end.

The relationship was now public knowledge. To the shock of everyone, Tankor Satani not only installed Jenebah Djallo in the Xanadu, not the least concerned that she was fifty years his junior, almost illiterate, and had to be taught how to speak well to impress his guests, but let it be known that her word was his. Just before she came to his birthday party, the ghoulish vultures had attacked the Xanadu one night. Lacking the attention of his wife, the great house now looked like a sad, desolate ghost of its former self. It needed a good coat of paint, and smashed windows had to be replaced, new blinds put up.

"I am putting you in charge of renovating this house," Tankor Satani told his new mistress one morning. "Go to the Ministry of Finance and ask the accountant general for anything you need."

Soon, especially considering how young she was, she had redecorated the outlandish ballroom in the palace, changed all the carpets, and, with a list of which Coral businessmen to contact, had put in new light fixtures, toilet soap dishes, cutlery, and other items to replace those that Tankor Satani's birthday party guests had stolen. Taking charge of the day-to-day running of the place, she ordered the henhouse moved farther away from the servants' quarters, because the smell of chickenshit was dulling the aromas of the potted begonias and geraniums at the entrance to the palace. But her most important duty was to keep an eye open for Tankor Satani's daughters.

"If they come back, you have my permission to eject them," he told his new mistress.

For the first time in weeks, the sun came into the enormous hallways of the large house, the expensive rugs were hoovered, and the potted plants were refreshed with new soil. Dutifully the Horticultural Department dispatched a blue-robed crew to dig up the old lawns and lay new ones. Each day brought a sparkle to Tankor Satani's eyes, and he was no longer irritated by the smallest infractions by his subordinates; ah, the happiness a new woman had brought him! The buoyant mood was even extended to Samson the chimp. Terribly lonely and neglected in his cage after Tankor's wife left, he shrieked and thumped his chest one morning when a group of people, including a vet, came to see about his well-being. They began with a round of shots and an examination of his stool and urine, after which he was shampooed and groomed and left with enough bananas and toys to make up for all the deprivation he had recently suffered.

Interestingly, though, it was during this eurhythmic season that the students rioted, reminding Tankor Satani of when the banker Alpha Samory had arrived that evening, determined to tell the old man that the country could not afford the expense of holding the political convention that Tankor had been thinking of lately.

"This is the trouble with being president," Tankor Satani said after the rioting was quelled. "I cannot even make love to my new woman without having to bother about the state of the nation."

CHAPTER THIRTY-THREE

Rumors of a Magic Plane

FOR A while, it appeared as though the fire in Jenebah Djallo's eyes had deterred Tankor Satani's daughters from making another attempt to extract some money from their father. Yet they refused to give up on what they felt was rightfully theirs. "To us, she does not exist!" they said as they planned their next move against the "witch." Determined to get rid of her, they went public about what they thought was going on in the Xanadu, the most lurid detail being that the nymph was practicing witchcraft on their father. In addition to the scandal occasioned by such an unnatural relationship with that "Fullah cow," Tankor Satani's daughters also let it transpire that it was also possible Jenebah had been spicing his meals with hot capsicum and molding his brain with some *atefor* love potion.

"Dat's why 'e behavin' like fool man, after dat woman done feed am dat poison!" one of the daughters said angrily.

It was electrifying the way people reacted after hearing about the latest woman, very young at that, to capture the president's heart.

"De old goat sure knows how to pick dem," mused an old-timer while drinking his beer.

The daughters found a ready audience for their suspicion. For although the Fullahs were strict followers of Islam, Jenebah, they insisted, belonged to a renegade sect: low-class nothings, worse than infidels, whose members practiced sorcery. Everyone knew what hold they had on politicians—whether Christians, Moslems, or atheist—who would pay a lot to have a diviner of that sect in their corner. How else could Tankor Satani's daughters explain being chased out by their own father?

As though to lend credence to their story, the chimerical vultures had recently resumed their assault on the Xanadu, talking like enraged humans as they flew in and out of the haunted rooms. Sometimes Jenebah Djallo was seen running around naked, chasing them out of the palace with a broom, a huge belt of animal hide adorned with talismanic cowry shells and small mirrors dangling from her waist (the witch!), after she had spent hours taxing the old man's heart! She had put on some weight on her belly, raising the suspicion of Tankor Satani's daughters that she was pregnant, which was probably why she had been chasing the vultures. As messengers of the dead, the vultures could see through whatever evil scheme she had planned for their father.

"Between us and de vultures, we go get rid of her," the oldest daughter said one evening.

When Theodore Iskander, recovering from his wounds in the hospital, heard that the old man's daughters were seeking public support against their father, he laughed merrily. "What a dysfunctional family!" he said.

Fearing further loss of life among the students, he made an appeal from his sickbed for calm that was broadcast on the radio, but the tension on the campus would soon spread to the town. Banks closed their doors, and some foreign journalists who happened to be holidaying in Malagueta filmed reels of the pitched battles between gangs of protesters and the police on Tankor Satani Street. Under a hail of bullets, terrified women ran to the schools to fetch their children from the burning streets littered with the debris of crude weapons—empty oil drums, car tires—and the market tables smeared with the blood spilled after so many years of resentment. Using large tree trunks as battering rams, groups of unemployed youths broke into some of the Coral stores. Those were unstable times in Malagueta, and a burr of anarchy rang through the streets as the ground shook from the pounding of young men looking for anything to steal. While some diplomats stayed put in their offices, sending cables reassuring their governments that everything was all right, the Americans—not ones to understand the rage—dispatched their wives and children out of the country. Afraid that they might be killed on suspicion that they were taking diamonds out of the country, the three-piece-suited Swiss businessmen, who were the most discreet—always riding in black limousines with tinted windows—had taken the precaution of not sleeping in the same hotel. Rival street gangs continued to fight pitched battles. They smashed cars, hijacked goods, burned a paddy wagon, and threw flaming canisters of teargas back at the police. Not until military reinforcements arrived hurriedly from Bakazo was calm restored and a curfew put into force.

A week later, a somewhat inebriated servant told the guards on night duty at the Xanadu gatepost that he had seen a three-legged dog pissing into a pot of Tankor Satani's beautiful marigolds in one of the verandahs. After copiously spewing over the flowers, it had walked with a sagging posterior like a hyena's. In the dim light, the servant insisted he had made out the unmistakable thickness of a boar's neck holding the small head of the dog, but the most disturbing thing about the animal was that it had two bullfrog's eyes, very close to its ears. The dog was striped like a zebra. A most hideous creature indeed, but it had a very pleasant voice.

No one knew how the dog had arrived at the palace, but its presence was one more mystery shrouding the Xanadu, and some of the guards suspected the dog was acting as a spirit medium for the old man to communicate with his dead son. It wasn't long after that a woman with bleached skin, definitely not a spring chicken, came to the gates to talk to the guards on night duty while they were engaged in a game of snakes and ladders. Thinking she was a spy sent by the old man to check on their loyalty, they put the game away. "What you want?" they asked.

"I have been trying to get the old man to buy me a car, with no success. But I am not coming to the Xanadu again, because I have just seen a big, strange-looking plane landing on the grounds of the palace."

At first the guards took a dim view of her words, especially as, in her attire, she looked like a woman of easy virtue. Her eyes were hennaed, which was why one of the guards suddenly remembered her. On a previous occasion, she had whispered to him, in not too strict confidence, that she had been trying to have a child for the old man but he preferred to think of money.

"I don't think he can get it up these days," she said spitefully. Obviously she did not know that Pallo had worked wonders with that snakehead. And that was surprising, because now that he was back to his old ways, the spring of life flowing from Jenebah's thighs, it was no secret that some of Tankor Satani's old mistresses were busy cooking up all kinds of love potions to drive her from his bed. But the truth was that even before the arrival of Jenebah Djallo he had always preferred money to women, and even to his children, save for the one the mermaid had fed to the ocean.

Suspicious of the woman's intentions, the guards dismissed her as a slanderous wench and sent her away agitated. A whiff of cheap perfume—Bint el Sudan or some other aromatic wild-grass perfume that she had sprayed all over her body to entice the old man in case she was able to see him—hung in the air long after she had gone.

Yet, as soon as she was gone, the guards began to reflect on whether the strange plane was really a figment of her imagination. They did not dismiss its existence outright, especially as the president had a sorcerer who they knew was trying to prove that the nature of gravity was still open to all kinds of definitions, as far as sorcery was concerned. Most likely the eunuch had devised a hard-to-detect mode of transportation that Tankor Satani had used to conduct reconnaissance flights during the riot. In succeeding years, aeronautical engineers might speculate on whether the magic plane was a precursor of the Stealth Bomber or an invention known only to the high priests of sorcery. But for now, the guards, all of them illiterate, had some trouble weighing the value of science against the veracity of sorcery. When it came to the matter of making an old man happy in the invisible hours of night, they finally concluded that "de white man's science" would fail because the plane, built by a sorcerer, could be inflated and shrunk down to cope with any weather or radar detection.

Soon the rumor about the plane was firing people's imaginations. After they came off duty in the palace, Tankor Satani's servants would report that they had seen it hovering over the Xanadu, a soundless contraption shaped like a crane and dimly lit. Hard-luck women added a little salt-and-pepper relish to the rumors while they haggled over the price of minnows or vegetables in the marketplaces. It was daylight robbery the prices some vendors were charging these days, they would complain, promising to report that practice when they saw the old man any time he left the Xanadu. Men in rum bars—good places to hear mother-of-pearl gossips, especially if some peppery fish went with the stories—kept the rumors alive. Eventually they reached the ears of the old man himself, who did not seem to mind that his castle was the source of a good deal of fantasy.

"That is one reason why I chose this site for my house, so that I can have the pleasure of giving people something to talk about, besides the hardship in their lives," he said to Pallo when, as usual, the sorcerer brought him up to date on what was going on in the staff quarters.

CHAPTER THIRTY-FOUR

A Man of the People

PALLO HAD been holed up in his quarters in the Xanadu during the unrest. Intent on determining the degree of weightlessness of mollusks, groundnut shells, and tortoise shells in space, he did not let the events affect his experimentation. Occasionally, when doubts about which minerals might best suit his experiment defeated him, he would come out for some fresh air. Aware of the rage of Tankor's daughters over the "foolishness with that harlot," he smiled, wondering whether the president's mistress was pregnant; for she was beginning to eat raw mangoes. Pallo soon dismissed that suspicion: Jenabah's eyes lacked the sweet confidence of a pregnant woman who had fried a president's heart with sorcery. Yet, with a prescience found in few humans, the sorcerer had suspected for quite some time that Jenebah was there for another reason. There was something troubling about her dusky beauty, not only in the way she would flaunt her divine figure to torment the young guards at the palace, but in how the color of her irises would change from topaz to jade within two hours when she felt no one was observing her. When she was alone in one of the verandahs, she would stare at the ocean, and the lines of her young face would become mysterious, unmoving, almost inscrutable. Sitting near the pond in the garden playing with the floating lotuses or teasing the carp, tilapia, and other species put there to take care of the mosquitoes in the shimmering light of evening, she sometimes appeared lost to all that was in that garden, as though she were in a world removed from the Xanadu: one, as far as Pallo had observed, that was perhaps more magical than the palace, a terrifying place of retribution.

Knowing how obsessed the president was with his nymph, Pallo did not bother to convey his suspicions to him, especially as the flames that had almost torn the city apart had been occupying the old man's mind lately. Even more worrisome was how the events had affected the business community. Always thinking about stability, Tankor Satani was determined that there not be another instance of anarchy in the town. It was then that he made a most fantastic move: he decided to throw the gates of the Xanadu open to the "common people."

Although it had been completed a long time ago, not too many people had actually been to the Xanadu. From the moment construction began it was the talk of the town. No matter where you were in Malagueta, it was easy to see this huge castle towering like an obelisk. Being inside the Xanadu was a dream akin to going to heaven; just thinking of that ascent sometimes brought some people to desperation. They would have killed to see it, and there were mothers who would have prostituted themselves or sold their daughters.

When Tankor Satani was building the Xanadu, its grandeur had affirmed the excesses of his mind, and until one of his brother-presidents built a huge basilica in the Côte d'Ivoire (the things you can do with cocoa money!), this monstrosity in Malagueta was the biggest example of presidential architectural madness in the whole subregion. Theodore Iskander had surmised that it was the dream of a mental case, a mind bordering on the infantile. But that view was in the minority. It was the glass house of many people's dreams.

"Why are you doing this?" Jenebah Djallo asked, aghast, after Tankor Satani told her about his plan to throw open the gates to the common people.

"For the same reason that I put you in my bed and not some intellectual high-class harlot: to keep in touch with my roots."

Jenebah Djallo saw some logic in the old man's decision, though in her vocabulary "intellectual" was a big word best left to those young grammarians at the university.

It was in a carnival mood that people advanced toward the Xanadu on the day Tankor Satani threw its gates open to the public. The crowd had started marching in their flip-flops from all corners of the city as early as eight in the morning; some had even forgone their meager breakfasts, not wanting to miss this opportunity. They created the greatest traffic snarl ever seen on the narrow colonial streets that the English had built for horses and carriages, and not for the Mercedes-Benzes, Mitsubishis, Toyotas, Peugeots, and other gas-drinking monsters, not to talk of the *omolanke* mammy wagons, choking up the streets. The sun had risen high, and the old vehicles were belching out fumes that almost killed the trees. Dressed in bright motley colors, the people were making their way in their thousands, and the men were removing their colorful tee shirts to wipe their perspiration. Although the party was not until two in the afternoon, the streets really came alive with the revelry of the cobblers, tanners, and blacksmiths as early as ten in the morning. No one could find a porter to carry a load on his head that day; members of that guild had gone on French leave. Gaily dressed fishmongers mixed with the crowd, the dogcatchers gave the dogs the run of the city, letter writers closed their ink bottles, and wake-keepers, deciding that the dead could wait just this once, were singing, "Happiness is a good bottle of rum at Tankor's place!"

Theodore Iskander had been released from hospital and was trapped in his car on a street near the largest open market in the town. Knowing that all the main arteries would be congested, he relaxed and took in the spectacular event. Some young harlots who had come out of their hovels down at the bay near a boy's school were adjusting their hairpins, fixing brooches on blouses, or using hand mirrors to help them wipe off rouge and face powder. "We can't look like harlots. Not when we want to kiss de Pa!" a young woman enthused.

Above the rise of the houses, pitched high like those of morning birds, were the sweet voices of some people who had waited so long to see what their money had built, because everyone knew that Tankor Satani had used state funds to build the Xanadu. Roadside mechanics, hoping to see whether there were any scraps left over after this great engineering and architectural feat, came with their tools hidden inside their pockets; the schools closed down, and the kids had to avoid getting crushed by the large throng of fishermen that had come from the wharfs: tough men accustomed to catching barracudas and sharks but determined not to miss this opportunity to see "God's wonder!"

As the large crowd came up the hill toward the gates, singing boisterous songs, some even breaking branches from the prized eucalyptus trees to use as musical instruments, Tankor Satani's guards began to fidget with their rifles. Fearing a great crash on the gates, one of the guards fired above the heads of the people and was almost lynched.

"You done craze?" one of his colleagues asked, mortified.

Whether they hated Tankor Satani or liked him, building the Xanadu had really changed some poor people's opinion of him. If their own dreams were seldom fulfilled, they liked a man whose dreams bore substantial results: bold and daring and gleaming in the brilliant flame trees lining both sides of the boulevard to the Xanadu. The poinsettia had bloomed scarlet and, with the imported Australian eucalyptus trees, their leaves saturating the area with their enchanting and medicinal smell, had got some of the people thinking a most disturbing thought: whether it was true that Jenebah Djallo was mixing them in whatever condiment of love she was suspected of feeding the old man.

"With her hands; Lord have mercy on him!" said a woman incredulously.

Several months earlier, when Tankor Satani's big-shot guests had come to his birthday party at the Xanadu, they had limited their curiosity to particular sections of the house. Some had merely wanted to stand on the verandahs, with their breathtaking view of the ocean; the more daring had wanted to enter the bedrooms; the learned had wanted to see the study; while some of the more inebriated had wished to see the cage in which Samson the chimp sometimes played with his dick.

The peasants had different expectations. As soon as the invitation was broadcast on the national radio, the only thought that rose in most hearts was how fantastic it would be to stand in the garden of the Xanadu just once. Now that they were there, they broke loose, like a herd of wild animals, with stupefying passion and began the long fulfillment of that dream, forgetting, once they were in that magical world, how miserable their lives had been for years. Pressing and sweating against one another, they touched the alabaster statues and plants in the garden, sat on the benches, and climbed those useless non-fruit-bearing trees, wondering why grow them when you couldn't use them as firewood. Simple people, they did not understand that the enormous carp, swordfish, and tilapia in the fishponds were never going to be eaten, or that the wild hyacinths, lilies, and lotuses growing in the ponds were not vegetables. As for the geese and peacocks preening themselves, what a waste of fowl! Goddamn it, those birds belonged in the pot!

Some lanky youths who knew a thing or two about how to hit a ball stood for a while near a fenced-off area, marveling that the tennis court alone was as big as four fish markets combined. They went to the garage with its seventeen cars, eager to see the grand Mercedes and the silver Jaguar, their windows open and their leather seats still smelling of stale sperm from when Modu Satani was sleeping with his women. Trying to imagine how the old man decided which car to use on a particular day, they opened the doors of the other cars, fidgeted with the driving controls, and turned the lights on and off. Then, as though remembering something more primal, the greatest comedy in this theater of amusement, awe, and disbelief, they gave Samson a case of nerves in his cage, disturbing the poor creature's afternoon siesta and provoking him to hurl dollops of his shit at the human horde.

When sections of the crowd finally arrived at the henhouse to have a look at the Abyssinian roosters, Tankor Satani was there to show them around. He looked quite happy, not the irascible old man those slanderous newspaper critics had been portraying for so long. Who could be irascible when you had a nymph in your bed at seventy-five?

At a command, several servants emerged with large trays of drinks, and, incredibly, it was he who started serving the people and shaking their hands. His smile was as glorious as that of a well-fed cat as he told them, "Drink all you can, because today is your day."

When they were fairly inebriated, some of the peasants burst into songs from their youth, singing about the sweetness of women, the power of money, how important it was for a man to have his mother's blessing, or the blessing of having good children. Yet some slanderous details pertaining to Tankor Satani's mental state suddenly made the people quiet. But when they began talking among themselves again they dismissed all the talk about his propensity for monologues when he was alone in one of the verandahs as the hogwash of his enemies.

"Dey jealous of de Pa!" said an old peasant.

The late afternoon heat had gone down a bit, a cool breeze was fanning the people, and after a lot of drinks they were completely transported and hoped they might be allowed a look inside the palace. But the guards kept them out, which was a shame because there were so many rumors floating around about their president. One in particular that the peasants wanted to confirm was whether Tankor really had a pet lemur that was so tame it had been sleeping in the presidential bed until that "Fullah cow" drove it out of the bedroom!

"Dat is de trouble wit' women," someone remarked. "Bring dem to your house en dey start changing your life!"

A faithful lemur, this import from the Malagasy Republic reportedly followed the old man everywhere and had been observed watching his master's surreptitious visits to the dark annex. But when it tried to sneak in one day, Tankor Satani dispatched it with a swift kick, after which the poor creature developed a case of homophobia.

Other rumors had been circulating (Malaguetans were famous for their gossip).

"Dey say de old man get beautiful Mammy Wata?" asked one incredulous woman.

"Dat's why he so rich!" a clearly envious man commented.

"Keep quiet! It is Papa God who give am!" said the woman.

Tired of being cooped up in their air-conditioned hotel rooms on the wind-swept coconut-tree-lined coast, some well-heeled tourists had changed their attire and gone in with the peasants, only to leave disappointed. "All this sweating in the tropics," one of them complained, "and we didn't even get to see the dark room where the comb of the mermaid is supposed to be."

"Be careful 'bout what you say," an old peasant warned. "Dat is a secret."

All too suddenly, sooner than it took to contemplate how to get back to town in the dying light, the party was over. Like a slow train emerging out of a fairyland, the crowd began the long journey home, and Tankor Satani went to bed satisfied he had nothing to fear from his people.

CHAPTER THIRTY-FIVE

Finally, the River

THE PIECE of land that Habiba Mouskuda bought was dull: a grayish-brown strip of fairly rocky ground sloping into a river. It was a precarious joining of hard and swampy soil, on which cultivating a lawn was not going to be easy. Part of the river was really a brackish inlet from the ocean, banked on one side with mangroves, among which iguanas and snakes were sometimes seen lying quietly, waiting to catch the bullfrogs beginning their night song. A few solitary genets and some squirrels and iguanas lived near the mangroves, and land crabs, dragging succulent leaves and fruits scattered by the wind, were sometimes seen borrowing into their muddy holes. This stretch of land had never really been explored before, so when Habiba first saw it, it was as though she were entering a Cockaigne dreamed of in one of her languorous moods. The land was so beautiful and unspoiled that it reminded her that she was finally severing all connections to General Augustus Kotay; going to a place of her own where she hoped he would not come to torment her.

After a weeklong heavy downpour the grass had grown so high that she had to hire six men to cut through it with cutlasses to get to the river. She stood watching them sweat in the heat, their backs bent in the fiery midday sun, as snakes scurried to a more verdant home to avoid the fury of burning grass. When their labor was over, the men left some of the grass to brown on the ground so that people could use it to make mattresses.

Two days later, the last blade of grass having been cleared away, Habiba Mouskuda yielded to Irene's insistence that the land be "blessed." "You don't build a house near a river without first talking to de spirit who lives dere," the old woman insisted.

Pallo was invited to perform the blessing. He came first thing one morning, before the sun had risen in the sky, to prevent any clouding of his blessing. He wore a gown of elaborate blue brocade ringed at the neck with golden embroidery, like those worn by some of the local Moslem men on their wedding days. With the added splendor of a large silver chain, he cut quite a majestic figure and exuded a quiet dignity that came both from the advent of old age and the veneration of his profession. He walked slowly, slightly ahead of Irene, Habiba Mouskuda, Yeama, and Theodore Iskander, who had hurried from his lecture to be there. Pallo began to pace up and down on the riverbank, admiring the land and looking occasionally at the sky while stroking a clump of plants here and there. Quietly he murmured some incantatory verses to tame unruly spirits, because he knew that nothing in that world was accidental to knowledge. After a while he stopped at a spot where some animals had recently watered. He closed his eyes, faced the river, and offered a quiet category in sorcerer's argot. Its meaning was lost on the three people, as these words were meant for the spirit of the water, feared landlord of that stretch of God's land, but also the protector of all the creatures there.

When he was satisfied that he had made proper contact with the spirit, Pallo poured a tot of rum into the river and made a little speech about human relationship to spirits.

"We don't want to make him drunk," said Irene, "in case he go sleep and forget to answer our requests."

She had brought her dog, Tiger, a shorthaired mongrel of indeterminate breed: an old bitch, feisty for her age, who had lost part of her tail when she attacked a big snake at Irene's place. Allowed to roam about, Tiger dived into the river in search of conger eel; Irene always fed her conger to make her vicious so she would keep burglars away from her house. Such a dog, she figured, would make a good guard when the new house was built, but she wondered whether Tiger would still be alive by the time the house was finished.

While Tiger swam, Irene said a prayer, combining, as usual, Christianity with sorcery. Then she buttressed her prayer by singing, while clapping and dancing, one of her favorite hymns, "How Sweet the Name of Jesus Sounds in a Believer's Ear." It was seldom that she was seen to enjoy herself like this, however fleetingly.

When Irene was done with singing, all five of them—Pallo, Theodore, Habiba, Yeama, and Irene—stood for a while to admire the beauty of the land, drawn together in the spirit of their love and thinking of the future they all wished for Malagueta. Yeama was listening quietly as the river began to rise in a loud melody that touched her soul. Large flocks of herons, egrets, and kingfishers were flying in the sky as Tiger continued to dive deeper and deeper, trying to catch fish, without much success.

Now that the land had been blessed and he was leaving the university, Theodore Iskander finally started to contemplate a future with his mistress and Yeama. He was resolved in his decision to quit, but had not yet handed in his resignation. When that was done, he was certain he would be given time to look for other digs; his stay at the college had been a good one, and there was no reason to believe the authorities did not appreciate that. In fact, he was more troubled about what they would say about his leaving them than about the length of time he would be given to pack up.

Unlike his mother, he did not believe that spirits existed in the unfathomable depths of rivers and held sway over people's lives. But she had seen to it that he listened to her stories of how certain beliefs had kept her generation sane, strong, and prosperous during the days of hardship after the Corals and their ass-licking black friends had made Malagueta a hell, so he was intrigued by the ceremony he had just witnessed.

Tiger eventually caught some fish, but none of them was her favorite conger eel. His task done, Pallo refused a ride back to the Xanadu, saying he preferred to walk, and began to make his way home through the nearby bush on rough-hewn stone roads, while Theodore, the women, and Tiger drove off to Habiba Mouskuda's house. Irene had moved in with Habiba after Yeama was born. "You kin do with some help," she had said, and as soon as she was in her room had unpacked a small portmanteau filled with a jar of *ori*, that ointment of goat fat, because "dis is de best thing to heal dat navel of yours"; black soap, wrapped in leaves, "to wash you clean" of all impurities; three bottles of consecrated water her priest had blessed for Habiba to drink in the first days of her postnatal recovery; and a lot of other condiments for the well-being of mother and child.

Somewhat unsure of how he should prepare for fatherhood, Theodore had confined himself to the business of just being there. Now that he was not busy teaching, he had been spending a lot of time learning how to be a father. He was filled with happiness about his family, yet that feeling conflicted with the troubling mood in Malagueta, which sometimes made him sad.

Occasionally, he would think of what he was going to do for a living, unaware that his practical mistress—who had turned out to be a pillar of strength, especially after he was shot—had saved some money. General Augustus Kotay's house had fetched a good price for Habiba Mouskuda, half of which she had received, and the rest of which would be given when she had moved out of the house in six months, during which time she should have built the new house.

One day, with very little to do, Theodore Iskander went to a club near the ocean, where he was made to drink a few glasses of burgundy by some old colleagues eager to toast the joy of fatherhood he had finally achieved.

"How is Yeama doing?" one of them wondered.

"Fine," said the philosopher.

"Children are a blessing, if they turn out all right; I know that," offered the other man.

It was a sphere where many of them had been, but they were intrigued, almost envious, he could tell, that he had tamed a shrew some of them had previously thought beyond redemption, but had nonetheless secretly desired. In their eyes was the admission "How different he is from us." He finished his last drink in a mood of bliss, said good-bye, and left his friends glued to their barstools. As soon as he was out of view, he turned to watch them, anxious to discover whether his departure had brought a change in their demeanor. But what he saw was resignation furrowed in the brow of men who were already defeated by the boredom and rituals of their daily life: the office, golfing, church, funerals, Freemasonry, and membership in other institutions where, in the estimation of their wives, they had achieved an apotheosis of success. He walked to his car humming "Che gelida manina" from Puccini's *La Bohème*, realizing he had never wanted to be one of those men. But he was much better off than the tragic poet Rodolfo in the opera, although he liked his role. He gave a generous tip to the parking lot attendant. "How wonderful it is that I can love like a poet," he thought.

Unlike some of his comrades at the college, he relished the challenges of his age and felt sad that they had allowed their sanguine youth to be consumed by middle-life burdens. As the music of Puccini coursed through his soul, he wondered whether any of them would understand its rhythm, or its bel canto was like a river surging in his heart. Most likely they would have failed to recognize that, or realized that in the singing river that is in every man, not just the lucky ones, the chance is given to be free.

As soon as he was home, he parked the car in the garage and hurried into the bedroom, where Habiba Mouskuda was reading a novel in bed. With the last note of Rodolfo's plaintive cry of "Mimi, Mimi" in the closing bars of *La Bohème* still ringing in his head, Theodore Iskander got into bed and planted a kiss on the lips of his mistress.

CHAPTER THIRTY-SIX

A Savant Goes to the Xanadu

ONE MONTH after entertaining the "common people," Tankor Satani, convinced he had tamed the beast of revolt, turned his attention to what, in the autumn of his life, was his real obsession: holding his own Versailles

Conference of West African leaders. Remarkably, it was at this time that he also received a visit from Gabriel Ananias. The old man had longed for it to happen but had not been in a hurry to invite the young man. It was as if they were playing a game of cat and mouse; Gabriel Ananias had delayed asking to be received by the old man until he was convinced Tankor would be so exhilarated to see him that all other matters would be canceled. The visit could not have been more opportunely timed, because the waiting had given the old man the jimjams, making him behave erratically lately, in spite of the joy of seeing the peasants enjoying themselves on his lawn. A week earlier, Tankor had succumbed to his usual bouts of insomnia and was agitated. He displayed a cantankerous streak that left Jenebah Djallo wondering what had happened to the man who had so determinedly cured her impertinence in his bed.

He was as prickly as a harmattan announcing its arrival, cursing and ranting about everything. It made him look like the son of Satan. Although he issued orders to the various departments charged with preparing for the convention, he canceled the regular cabinet meeting, kept the new papal nuncio waiting for an audience, and even put off a trip to his Swiss bank, all just in case the savant decided to visit. His agitation was so unsettling, Pallo dared to ask whether he had become a clairvoyant.

"Don't worry, Pallo; you and I use different methods to achieve our objectives. So believe me, I know when the son of man is coming. And it is tomorrow!"

He skipped his breakfast the next morning, but drank two cups of black coffee and a glass of raw eggs mixed with brandy, then took a pinch of snuff to clear his head of a small cold. Although the ominous noise from the dark room was becoming a nuisance and was always on his mind, he did not feel threatened by the mermaid. Rather, later that day, instead of having a nap, he did something he had not done in a long time: he went to the kitchen to talk to his head cook, Koko.

"What brings you here, Excellency?"

"Today is a special day, and I want to see what is being prepared."

The white-coated cook shook his balding pate in amazement and scratched the back of his neck. In the evanescent light, his face showed that after the new madam had moved in and claimed the president's attention, all the servants, including him, had begun to feel a loss of influence over how the Xanadu was run. He swatted a fly pestering his face and cursed the threat of rain, thinking of his wife in their leaking-roofed house out in the countryside. He had just started to chop some onions and had not had time to add salt to reduce their potency, and salty tears were streaming from his red eyes before the old man came to the kitchen.

Koko had been in Tankor Satani's employ for five years and had discovered that great cuisines did not matter to Tankor's unsophisticated palate. Whereas his predecessors had liked a breakfast of kippers, tomatoes, baked beans, tea, butter (all that colonial stuff!), the cook would soon discover that Tankor Satani preferred his *akara* cake in the morning, day in and day out. He finally came to the conclusion that the president must really miss his dogcatching days. The paradox was that since Tankor Satani had sent the last Rhodesian ridgebacks to guard his Coral friends, he had a chimp, and those crazy cockatoos in the aviary, but no dogs roamed the grounds of the Xanadu, except for the rumored three-legged beast.

Koko was nearing retirement, and his aching bones had gone brittle and tired in his old white coat. When not afflicted with salt, his eyes were sad gray films reflecting his smoky toil. Had the president's visit happened earlier, it would have mattered a lot to Koko. He would have asked Tankor how he liked the special dish favored by the men in the town where the two of them had both been born. After many such attempts to please Tankor, with no favorable response, Koko had felt sad, especially when word had leaked out that after Jenebah arrived on the scene the old man seldom even ate his food, his mind being occupied by more sumptuous matters than the gastronomical specialties one country boy was cooking for another.

In search of support, Koko complained to the sorcerer, who, everyone knew, was the old man's eyes and ears. But after his years of service, Pallo's tongue had mastered the dry leaves of circumspection.

"My friend, you all alone in dis matter," the sorcerer said, to the disappointment of the cook.

Koko went back to his chores, hoping the pain in his heart would be healed when his wife received him with her ambrosia of love after he had retired, worn and washed out. Until Tankor paid his unexpected visit, Koko had given up waiting for a word of praise from the president. In the manner of a man used to serving his superiors, he lowered his head and read, in a stuttering voice, the day's menu: catfish stew, banana and crab fritters, a plain salad, and cassava cake.

"Add something else to the menu," Tankor Satani said.

"What you want me to add, Excellency?" Koko asked, mystified.

"Add some pepper chicken marinated with ginger, thyme. and sweet basil; sauté everything in olive oil; make some rice pap and spice it with tamarind juice; and cook a pot of cassava leaves stew, but with not too much palm oil. Grill some fish—groupers, if they are in season, or snapper. And make the salad more interesting."

Koko had not anticipated such an outlandish request. After all these years, when he had appeared to lose the esteem previous heads of state had granted him, he felt he was listening to the wrong man.

"You must be entertaining de new madam, Excellency," he said with conspiratorial modesty.

"No woman is worth this much attention from me," Tankor Satani said, cutting him off. "I am entertaining my new son."

Left to ponder who this new son was, Koko checked his speculation. Timidly, he thought of raising the subject of his long-suffering wife in the house where the roof leaked. "Master."

"What is it?"

"Nothing, Excellency," he replied, losing his courage. "I am just happy that you look after your servants so well."

Tankor Satani was sure Koko had really wanted to ask a favor, which he would have granted. But it was up to a man to behave with forthrightness, even to a leader, so he not only left the underling in a stew of confusion but placed him in difficulty to find another chance to ask for his favor: a headache that was nothing like the one Koko would have when he tried to get some fresh fish at the market the next day.

It was raining hard, and a lot of fishermen were afraid to challenge the ocean, so the only fish available in town were the frozen ones in the Lebanese shops, which were seldom considered good by the old African cooks. After all his years as a cook, Koko could tell the freshness of a fish by the color of its eyes. Considering how underutilized he felt, the president's request had not caused him to have a change of heart about his position. On the few occasions when Tankor Satani entertained important guests, he would have the meals catered by the Jacaranda Hotel near the ocean, where the cuisine was mostly Armenian, which was not really what some of the guests wanted.

In Koko's opinion, minnows were the finest things for fishcakes, but his gnarled fingers had also produced fine pork roast, tender bits of lamb and couscous, goat cheese, and porcupine fillet when he had cooked for the colonial governor, before Tankor Satani. With pride, Koko would think of the many times he had offered his cuisine to his friends who were cooks in other households. Given the impromptu request of the president, time was short but Koko was determined that when Tankor Satani sat down to dinner with his new son tonight, it would not be the president's last visit to the kitchen, God willing.

Contrary to what his cook thought, Tankor Satani was not really a village bumpkin when it came to the culinary art. In fact, he had an exquisite palate, thanks in part to his now-broken friendship with Dr. Sidi Samura. When the old man was alone, the loss of that friendship brought him great pain.

Besides Tankor's carefully disguised relish for good food, he also liked fine wines, a secret that only a few of his ministers knew about. They suspected that he had a concession from Spain as part of an agreement with that country's ambassador, under which port wine, rose apples, grapes, and codfish were imported for the sole pleasure of the president's guests. In exchange, he gave the ambassador a license for the export of chimpanzees, turtles, squids, sharks, oranges, and bananas.

Those arrangements, maintained with a secrecy unusual in Malagueta, had begun with the inspiration that came to Tankor Satani one evening when he was watching some crabs scurrying on the beach as he contemplated how to deal with the mermaid without giving up her comb.

After snatching that golden treasure, Tankor Satani had not gone back to the ocean for a long time. But recently, when he was tired of being in the Xanadu and felt the need for a change of air, it was off to the beach, on visits that left his guards asking why the ocean had such a fascination for him when he couldn't swim and the salt hurt his retinas.

One day as he sat looking at the bellowing ocean, his chest became hard, as though his decrepit soul was beating an irregular rhythm. The waves surged, and their terrible noise, as though the ocean was boiling, was enough to remind him that, although he could have an erection three times a day, the mermaid could still put a jinx on him.

Several months before coming upon the mermaid, he had found a favorite spot to sit in a beach chair and think. It was a craggy stretch of sand not heavily pounded by the ocean, where he would watch the crabs come and go as he delved deeply into how much longer he wanted to continue the rigmarole of being president. At first the crabs avoided him, until it dawned on them that he was probably a lost soul, one of those land creatures uncomfortable with their own species. Then one day the crabs miraculously started crawling up to him, allowing him to touch them, even becoming a little playful with him. And from watching those crabs he derived a new idea about how to become even more duplicitous in his dealings. His absences from the office, blamed on illusive illnesses, became even more regular.

Moustapha Ali-Bakr was the only one allowed to visit the castle during that period. Sometimes Tankor would be seen playing a game of backgammon with him, leaving his servants wandering how a president could sink so low as to play a simple game with a garlic-smelling Coral. But lately he had begun to suspect that the half-caste was double-crossing him, so he was ready to welcome the one person he felt he could trust: that impetuous young man from the university.

A few months before he died, Father Francis O'Reilly had instructed Gabriel Ananias on the importance of eating a good meal, however cheap, before going to visit someone in high office. "You don't want to go there and act as if you have been starving all your life," he had cautioned his young charge. "The first thing that an official looks for is how to corrupt the stomach, if not the mind."

Impetuous, cocksure, and brilliant, Gabriel Ananias still carried ambitions of a scholastic future and was sometimes mystified by how easy it had been for the president to win over some of the academics. The fat growing around the necks of their wives not only testified to the changes that had come over them, it fed his contempt for the way they lived off their husbands' directorships in companies, the reward for silencing their criticisms of the old man. Within months, the old tatters of the wives' gowns were replaced with designer wardrobes, and the red earth, turned over so that new houses could be built by their husbands, testified to the old man's success. With disdain for public opprobrium, the wives of the academics were sometimes seen in their shiny new cars snaking through the crowded streets on their way to the fashionable boutiques to buy the latest fashions from Dakar, Paris, and Milan.

Not surprisingly, Tankor Satani always had something to say about their husbands. "Yesterday they were quoting from Nyerere and lecturing to me about human rights," he scoffed to Moustapha Ali-Bakr. "Today they only live for the glory of everlasting wealth. Have some more brandy, my friend, and let us drink to the superiority of common sense."

After compromising the chief justice, Tankor Satani had surprised everyone with a hefty salary raise for the judges; he built new quarters and gave them bigger limousines. When Pallo asked why he had done that, he paused for a while, rubbed his thick fingers around the nape of his neck, and, with a benign smile, polished over the years of dealing with simpletons, replied.

"In life, it is better to play hopscotch with your enemy than to dance the foxtrot with an angel."

In spite of his name, Gabriel Ananias knew he was not an angel. Not yet, at least. That was why, after listening to the horse's whinny on the night when Tankor Satani was fucking, he had concluded it would be disrespectful, if not dangerous, not to respond to the old man's invitation for a visit. At first he thought of waiting six months before going to the Xanadu, but the student riot hastened his decision.

On the evening he came to the gate of the fabulous house, dressed in a blue suit, gray tie, and white shirt with cufflinks, he was immediately assailed by an asthma attack brought on by the aromatic blossoms of the surrounding plants. Chewing on some guava leaves that he always carried dilated his bronchial tubes. He hoped he might be lucky enough to see the vultures of the illusive dead men attacking the palace, or the rumored three-legged dog, or, perhaps, the eunuch's magic plane. Calculating that the old man preferred holding audiences in the evening, Gabriel Ananias had timed his arrival for when he felt the throng of Corals to the Xanadu would have left. He thought he might bypass the guards, sneak in through the visitor's entrance, and go straight to Pallo's quarters; Pallo would then take him to Tankor Satani. But a guard stopped him halfway, thinking the young man was one of those troublesome rioting students coming to the Xanadu to unfold a provocative banner denouncing the president.

"What you want?" the guard inquired.

"I have an appointment with destiny," Gabriel Ananias answered pompously.

The guard, who had not had much of an education, took a dim view of this supercilious air and swore at him.

"De only destiny you get is in guardroom, where we go feed you dry bread and water till you tell us why you done come here." Brutally, he began to drag Gabriel Ananias across the lawn. Trampled by all the common people who had come to the free-for-all party, the damaged lawn was slowly being brought back to greenness. As Gabriel Ananias was dragged past the Sahelian children playing hopscotch in the dwindling but still rosy light, he saw the three young men in clerical garb and of a most happy disposition—the result of a generous donation to their order by the president—emerging through the heavy wooden doors of the main entrance. At Tankor's invitation, the clerics had just offered evening prayers for the old man, sunset being the best time, they felt, since the devil in the hearts of the students would be resting. In view of Tankor's recent loss of a son, the clerics' intention had been to bring the president closer to their God. Contemptuously, they had dismissed Pallo's sorcery, saying it could not explain the workings of divine providence, or prevent it from working on Tankor Satani.

Not the least afraid that the clerics might try to supplant him in the president's favor, Pallo had just gone to a window to wish them a hellish return to their abodes when he saw the guard coming across the lawn with Gabriel Ananias in tow. The sight of the young savant so obviously discomfited filled Pallo with an incandescent triumph. He forgot about the clergymen and, convinced that it was his miracle-working sorcery that had moved the young man to come, he raised his head to his own image of God.

He felt elated: sorcery has a primal hold on all men, and its merits are indisputable. He began to dance as he had not done since that memorable afternoon with the other eunuchs under the cotton tree. Conceding, however, that the young man, unruffled by the guard, had the face of an angel, even though he did not believe in angels, Pallo waved to Gabriel Ananias.

"Release am at once," he yelled to the guard. "He done come to bring happiness to de president in his old age."

CHAPTER THIRTY-SEVEN

A Rooster for the River Man

ONE DAY when his daughter was six, Theodore Iskander picked Yeama up from school and realized that the child had been crying. Red-eyed, Yeama immediately went to a corner of the backseat in the car and refused to talk, causing great concern to her father.

"What is it?" he asked in a gentle tone. Yeama did not respond, and Theodore waited for a few minutes before pressing her. "No matter what it is, you can always talk to your parents. We are there to help and to try to understand."

"What is a harlot?" the young voice finally asked.

A chill ran through Theodore Iskander's heart. From the day that Yeama had started school, soon after she turned five, he had wondered when the inevitably malicious tongues would start wagging about Habiba's checkered past. It was not as though Habiba was the only one who had been down that road. He would see to it that Yeama was not destroyed.

"Where did you hear that word?"

Yeama sniffed into her handkerchief before replying. "We were playing a game in class, which I won. Then this boy said, 'You may be smart and your father is a professor, but your mama was a harlot.'"

"And then?"

"He laughed a stupid laugh that made me cry, so I told the teacher."

"What happened after you told her?" the philosopher asked.

"I saw a bad look in her eyes. She took the boy to the headmistress, and she wrote a note and sent him home. His parents have to come to school tomorrow because he had said a bad thing about my mother."

Habiba Mouskuda was livid when she heard about what had happened. "I am not ashamed of my past, as I have begged God to forgive me; and the only people who matter, you and your mama, do not hold that against me. So I won't have a boy, whose father is probably one of those arse-licking ex-academics, making my daughter's life miserable."

Theodore Iskander had to use all his powers of restraint to stop Habiba from going to the school to find out who this boy was. "What good would that do? Today it was one boy; tomorrow it will be a girl, and then another. The poor boy was probably put up to it by his parents. It is a terrible but common thing in this society, where malice is deeply rooted. As the Corals discovered a long time ago, Malaguetans can be mean, vicious, backstabbing creatures, especially one's own relatives and neighbors. No one but them should get ahead in life. It is going to be tough, but for all they might say about you, they cannot match your honesty. We will just have to let our daughter know about what circumstances forced you to do. Meanwhile, let us forget about it. Soon the rains will be here, and that will affect the building of the new house."

From the start, building on the land created some unforeseen problems for Habiba Mouskuda. When finally cleared of much of the grass and shrubs, the land was much rockier than they had thought at first. The river sometimes washed its debris onto the land, and the lot was narrow for the kind of house that the architect had drawn, although it was long enough for two houses.

Asked what kind of a cottage he would like, Pallo had been circumspect. "I only need two rooms: one for myself to sleep in, and one for my friends." Considering where he had started life, and given the simplicity of his taste, the cottage would be quite a luxury. He had never really felt at home at the Xanadu, in spite of the comforts that Tankor Satani had offered, and Pallo was looking forward to being away from all the goings-on at the palace, which sometimes defied the interpretation of sorcery.

Habiba was likewise looking forward to putting as much distance between the confusion of her past life and the new script she was making for the future. Beyond the basic measurements of the rooms and the size of the verandah where she would grow potted plants, sit, and watch the flow of the river, she knew very little about how houses were laid out, so was open to suggestions. Moreover, although Irene had been hinting lately that she was thinking of going back to her own house, now that Yeama was growing up, Habiba was determined that the old woman should not only stay with them but be part of the new house.

Theodore thought likewise, but would be respectful of whatever decision his mother might arrive at. "You are an only child," his mistress said when they discussed the matter. "A dutiful son at that. Having your mother living with us is a small price for me to pay for the love and happiness you have given me."

Habiba and Theodore's dreams for the new house were altered by the builder. "These architects may know all de books, Madam," he began, "but dey get no sense. De land too steep to hold a big house; when de river overflow it will come to de garden and threaten de foundation of de house. Whichever way you look at it, Madam, it will cost too much money to build a massive foundation and a retaining wall to hold back de water."

"Then what do you suggest?" Habiba wondered.

"A split-level house, with a hanging verandah. We go plant trees near de retaining wall. The house go be smaller dan dis one, but cooler; we go put ventilation on all sides. So let de architect redesign it; make de house slope from the high ground in de back, where de land is solid. After de pillars have settled firmly into de ground, we go turn de space in between into a small flat."

"How small?" Theodore asked, thinking of Irene.

"Big enough for a young couple to start life, or for de old lady to spread out in style."

A year later, the house overlooked the river. It was not as large as the one that General Augustus Kotay had built for Habiba Mouskuda, but its architecture was charming: high-vaulted ceilings, French louvered windows, round Moorish columns, arched stone doorways, semicircular verandahs, and a stone-walled living room. Its white outdoor finish blended well with the green of the trees and the mangroves throbbing with seasonal animal life. Huge landfills and stone terracing had checked the erosion of the sloping land, but had not affected the canopy of coconuts, mangoes, almonds, and acacia towering above the roof, which kept the intensity of the sun from scorching the struggling lawn. It was a house in harmony with its elements.

Irene had decided to stay because Yeama wanted her grandmother nearby. "I like hearing you talk about the river, Granny," Yeama said.

As soon as she was comfortable in her surroundings, Irene would spread a mat under the mangoes so she could keep an eye on Tiger as the dog chased after the lizards and crabs in the yard. With the first harvest of fruits, she had made almond cakes, sold baskets full of mangoes to the market women, and distributed some with a generous hand to some kids who came by, attracted by the bats flying in and out of the branches of the mangoes. Close by, near where the land narrowed into the river, Pallo had moved into his small bungalow, although he still went back now and then to his room at the Xanadu, Tankor Satani having appealed to him not to desert him. The rains had been light that month, and some kingfishers and other birds—egrets, herons, and marabous—would come to the river and wait, in the gentle flow of its tide, to feast on the fish swimming just above the pebbled bed.

Prior to selling her old house, Habiba had experienced a terrible twinge of sadness looking at the splendid garden she had cultivated with so much care. "I know leaving here is for the best," she told Theodore, "but I have been here so long, I feel as though I am digging up a part of myself that has taken root."

"Then bring a transplant of the oleander with you. It will do just as well in the new land."

Over the years, Theodore had observed that just being near the oleander and touching its flowers always had a calming effect on his mistress, no matter what was troubling her.

She recognized, in his thoughtfulness, not only the good man she had come to love so much but the generous, unselfish lover thinking about what had made her previous lover happy: the oleander she had planted for General Augustus Kotay. It should do well with the crotons and hibiscus in the new land so close to the river.

They had been living in the house for a year before it began to feel like a home. Furnished with the big dreams of these two people who somehow, until recently, would not have given themselves a chance at love, it was a nice home. Sometimes the philosopher would go alone to the river to reflect on whatever it was that held them together, beyond love, that emotion that was too easily lost in the whirl of irritations and in the stale habits living together inevitably brought; experiences exacerbated by the daily grind of life, not necessarily theirs, but definitely affecting them. Perhaps their bond, he decided, was in their spirits; not bound by the ludicrous stuffiness of many people in Malagueta, they had put their mistakes, regrets, and sins behind them. Given the beauty of the daughter they shared, they were determined to stay together, no matter what it took: that was why they had built this house. And besides the ghost of a lovesick general, who might come now and then to smell the scent of his transplanted oleander, Habiba and Theodore were left alone to care for Yeama, with a lot of help from Irene.

Happily watching Tiger as the dog slept, Irene would sometimes smoke an old meerschaum pipe, now that she had to admit there were reasons for her to be happy. Besides her granddaughter and dog, the one thing that fascinated her was the river as it meandered from the mountain to join the inlet from the ocean, right in front of the house! Late one night, with Tiger trailing behind, she headed toward the river holding a red rooster in her left hand. *Langa langa*, which was what people called snakes at night, sometimes came out in search of frogs, but she felt no fear in her soul this night: Tiger was there to protect her. For two weeks she had been watching the flow of the river, aware that its water was drying up, making it hard for the birds to fish. The grass had withered on both banks, and the plants, roasted by the sun, had lost their aromas.

"The water spirit is hungry," Irene decided. She was not one to speculate too long on premonitions, because her faith in God gave her strength. All she knew was that there was something sacred about this river. Spirits lived in it, with their riches, mysteries, and narratives—things that only time and patience reveal to the lucky few like her, as she stood ready to feed the Man of the River.

With a swift snapping movement she broke the neck of the rooster, tossed it into the river, and murmured a few sacred words as Pallo had done. In an instant, she had the feeling that a hand had come up from the river to receive the rooster and that everything was going to be all right for the new residents in the house.

CHAPTER THIRTY-EIGHT

Jewel of a Long Summer

SEASHELLS ILLUMINATE a city of glass. There is harmony in the depths of the ocean; all the creatures appear to live in peace. Dramatically, the scene changes: a three-legged dog is swimming in a river toward a man who is drowning—a powerful artist, that dog, but it is unable to save its master. Afraid to die, the man begins to shout for his sorcerer, famed for his magic, who had been working hard on a magic plane, an invention unknown to the Americans. The scene changes again: the sky is pitch dark, the streets of the city are emptied of trees; all the dogs and bats have died, vultures are feeding on the dogs. Next the streets converge into a tenebrous cul-de-sac. Pushed there by a raging tornado, the man is struggling not to enter that cavernous darkness. Suddenly there is a burst of light, but it is from a mermaid combing her luxuriant tresses on a beach; her eyes are luminous coals. The man is filled with a terrible fear because there is a noisy flapping of wings; the bats have come back to life in their thousands, and their faces remind him of real people he had known; they are coming toward him. Using the only defense he can think of, he throws a small parcel of priceless diamonds at them, but they keep on approaching. The mermaid laughs. "I am doomed!" the man cries.

Tankor Satani woke up one morning with the face of a man who had just dreamed he was dying. He was dripping with sweat and shaking like a bedraggled vulture waiting for a burst of sunlight. He yawned and tried to read the augury in his dream, but, after a shot of brandy, dismissed the experience as the effect of a large dinner he had eaten just two days ago. He steadied the uneven metronome in his heart, resisted a drift toward melancholia, and thought it was about time he went to see about what was paramount on his mind, besides the mermaid: how the construction of the villas for the convention was going.

Before his enigmatic dream, there had been good reason for Tankor Satani to be happy. Only two days ago he had enjoyed dining with Gabriel Ananias in the library of the Xanadu, an intimate room where Tankor sometimes had celestial dreams about his alter ego, Henri Christophe, the immortal Haitian monarch. The room was well furnished with ceramic jars and large sofas embroidered in Arabic motifs—gifts from Moustapha Ali-Bakr. In contrast to the heavy carpeting in the other rooms, the floor was covered in rugs of the most luxuriant artistry: Afghan, or perhaps Moroccan. Under a ceiling of Turkish arabesque, paintings with a common theme—the sea—hung on three walls, contrasting with sea-blue and yellow prints and batiks on the fourth wall. Wooden masks, carved in various styles of naturalism and grotesqueness, competed for attention with the paintings. When not tormented by the implacable vultures attacking the palace, or pulled away by the provocative appeals of his nymph, Tankor Satani read quite a bit, as evidenced by the books opened at select passages on the ottomans and filling the large bookcase of prime mahogany. He was not yet tired of his mistress, far from it; but thinking about his convention had checked his passion for Jenebah Djallo. A mobile bar took up a corner of the library, from where the old man had a breathtaking view of the ocean. He and his friends always enjoyed this vista when they got together to drink a toast to their mothers for this good life.

Given his proclivity for new things—he had an eclectic collection of cameras, cars, meerschaum pipes, gargoyle-headed walking sticks, TVs, and even a sailboat—the strangest item in the library was an old-fashioned German Grundig radiogram, a holdover from the days when Tankor Satani was quite poor, on top of which, as if to remind him of how far he had come, sat an expensive Sony transistor radio, its dial always tuned to the BBC so that he could hear what those Brits were saying about rulers like him.

The dinner had been going well until Gabriel Ananias caught the scent of a dog, although there was none in sight. "What is that smell, Excellency?"

"Nothing; just the smell of stale cigar smoke on the sofa."

The minutes ticked away. The two men were silhouetted in the glow of three candles. Thinking of his immortality, the older man was trying to push back his age, while the other was thinking that his youth made him innocent. It was a private affair, just the two of them, Jenebah Djallo having been dispatched to learn flower arrangement at the School of Contemporary Etiquette so she could show off her skills during the convention. The servants were in the kitchen, and the sweet lyrics of Congolese music came from the record player they sometimes listened to when they were resting.

Tankor Satani served his guest a big ladle of food and filled his glass with expensive Beaujolais. Under the influence of the Irish priest, Gabriel Ananias had developed a taste for wine, but he ate judiciously. He knew, from his study of biology, that the digestive system was not only a function of enzymes but also a tool with which to enjoy a good meal, but was also aware that Tankor Satani was enjoying himself watching the young man for signs of gluttony. After a while, Gabriel Ananias thought of bringing up the rumor that had been spreading in Malagueta about the three-legged dog, but decided discretion was called for during dinner. Then, unexpectedly, Tankor Satani ambushed Gabriel with a direct question.

"How is life at the college, my son?"

Gabriel Ananias laid his silverware on the edge of his plate. "It all depends on what you want to know, Excellency."

"Everything, my son."

Although it was rather unexpected, such cordiality did not seem contrived, so Gabriel Ananias allowed the old man the indulgence of calling him "son."

After the bank governor was found dead, Gabriel's first impulse had been to write a letter to a newspaper in protest. But when he recalled how Tankor Satani had dragged his critics off to jail and the gallows, he was circumspect.

The death of the banker and the rumor that Pallo was experimenting with gravity to test a magic plane had come just after the reported sighting of the three-legged dog in the Xanadu and had put the students at the college in a bad temper. Gabriel Ananias wondered what had happened to the rumors of that other creature: the mermaid.

When those rumors began to circulate, Gabriel Ananias was not the least interested in them. With only a year to go before he received his diploma, he had other things on his mind, topmost of which was that he was looking forward to a job at the Institute of Science and Technology. Hopefully, his study of entomology would put him in an advantageous position. Through years of patient and methodical study of the species, he had acquired a rare collection of ants. Some were native to the region, others were alien species the British colonial officers had brought with them when they were seconded to Malagueta from Southeast Asia. In an erudite paper that would form part of his final thesis, he had argued that the "Asian plague" was not only killing off rare species of plants and crops but was a deliberate attempt by the officers to infest the plants in West Africa. "Look at what they have done here," he wrote. "These people always accusing us of taking our diseases to them."

The publication caused a stir not only because he had written with the persuasiveness of a scholar and environmentalist, but also because he had argued that, as far as he was concerned, entomological damage was the first step in the chain of zoological disasters facing Malagueta. Rare birds were disappearing, their loss blamed, wrongly, on the appetite of voracious snakes. Primates had been reduced to dangerously low numbers and were turning up, caged and drugged, at foreign airports, destined for Western zoos. The disappearance of the forest preserves was alarming, but that was nothing compared to the scandal of teachers using imported textbooks to show African kids what some endangered species looked like.

Some Corals who had listened in disbelief as the article was explained to them by one of their paid academic lackeys saw a threat to their livelihood. A week later they met one evening in the house of an old smuggler to think of a counteroffensive. The cups of black Turkish coffee they had been drinking somehow tasted like aloes as they decided that something had to be done quickly if they were to retain their stranglehold on the export of wildlife, timber, and gold. One of them said spitefully about Gabriel Ananias, "He get de name of angel, but him mama is a whore!"

"Bastard: he wan mess up our business after de Fullah people done take bread out of our mot in de car market," the host agreed.

Tankor Satani heard about the smugglers' meeting when Moustapha Ali-Bakr led a delegation of his associates to the palace to remind the president of the time when the planeload of Tuaregs had arrived to help chase out the ghosts haunting the Xanadu.

"Do something about dis boy, Excellency," Moustapha Ali-Bakr appealed to the old man.

During the dinner, Tankor Satani had been thinking about how to bring up the subject of the paper, but it was clear to him that Gabriel was also wrestling with his own private thoughts. "There is anger over the death of the banker and the amount you are spending to host your convention," Gabriel said, with respect but determination in his voice.

Tankor Satani studied his guest for a while before replying. "You don't understand how things work, my son. Nasser was condemned for the Aswan Dam. So too was Nkrumah for building the Akosombo Project. But like them, after I am dead and gone, all that I have done will be viewed favorably. People like you will write about this glorious age. So have a drink and tell me about yourself."

"Not until you have told me how the banker really died, to assuage my doubts."

"It was an accident, my son," Tankor said.

"No one believes that story."

Before Gabriel Ananias came to visit him, Tankor Satani had thought he had mollified the rage of the dead man's relatives by arresting a well-known hatchet man and hauling him off to prison on the charge that he had been hired to carry out the dastardly deed by some disgruntled enemies of the dead man's. But the action was quickly dismissed as an official cover-up. The sibilant voices of angry women would greet Tankor Satani when he dared to go to his office, and he came under a barrage of insults every time his motorcade drove along the fish market road, where, in broad daylight, it was not unusual to see women, armed with large cutlasses or heavy clubs, hacking away at sharks. Even when his windows were wound up and his guards were riding alongside his car, those angry women were not deterred from waving their weapons in the air, cursing him, or banging their enamel cups for measuring entrails in disgust. Trying to placate the foreign emissaries who had called for an independent investigation into the banker's death and hinted that further aid to Malagueta might be delayed, Tankor Satani created an independent tribunal to look into the death. At the same time, he whipped the police into action, urging them to improve on their woeful fingerprinting expertise and come up with real evidence about the "suspect," who had allegedly been in the garden of the banker on the night of his death.

During Ramadan, he ordered the front of the bank building draped in a white banner for thirty days. On Id-ul-fitri, he slaughtered the fattest rams he had received as presents, even though he was not a Moslem, and gave large chunks of meat to the beggars and lepers who had come to the gates of the Xanadu to greet him. His hope was that such manifestations of public regard for the poor would put an end to the belief that he was a ruthless ruler. Using an old political wile, he went as far as offering an all-paid scholarship program for the banker's three children to attend university anywhere in the world, but his gestures failed to convince his domestic critics. Moreover, the public continued to agitate for the real culprits to be brought to book. And as far as his social life went, although he did not give up his penchant for sitting on the beach playing his whimsical games with the crabs, it was clear from his demeanor that Tankor Satani was unhappy.

Incredibly, as hungrily as he had relished getting his sexual prowess back, he suddenly lost all interest in sex and found all kinds of faults with Jenebah Djallo as excuses for not getting into bed with her. After tolerating it for so long, he began to criticize her habit of spitting into his beloved potted plants on the verandah, and he yelled at her for feigning pregnancy as she walked around looking lascivious in a tight wrapper and a blouse. Her mannerisms were so provocative, the guards had a difficult time keeping their attention focused on their security details.

"Harlot!" Tankor yelled at her one day, although it was clear she was not the real source of his anger.

"You used to like me like this," she protested coquettishly.

Even more disturbing, when the agitation over the banker's death refused to die down, there were times when he felt as though an atom of worry had been split open in his head. His nightmares played snakes and ladder while he slept, and waking up, he would imagine all kinds of explosions taking place in the Xanadu. Even with his music turned up high, he could still hear the power in the box in the dark room. With his legs caught inside the thick folds of his pajamas, all he could do then was imagine how the power might choose to act. His conjectures left him horrified.

Using her most seductive voice, Jenebah Djallo would sometimes try to comfort him. "You should forget about your problems; otherwise you will die before your time."

She would hold his hands as they sat on his favorite verandah some nights, she drinking mango juice and he, needing something to steady his nerves, drinking copious amounts of brandy and ginger, once the favored drink of the old gentry. Then she would kiss him on the cheek, ruffle his hair, and give him a sweet smile. Unknown to him, in the dim light of those intimate hours, the color of Jenebah's eyes would change from green to magenta, brown to amber, and her smile, as Tankor ranted about the first canto of the mermaid—the way she had dragged his womanizing son Modu down into the Hades of her spirit world—was mysterious.

One night he was so miserable that he almost divulged his greatest secret to his mistress: how he was keeping the comb of a mermaid in the dark room, where no one had ever been. But when he turned to look at Jenebah, the strange anticipation in her eyes made him realize that after he had gone so long without trusting anyone with his secret, it was unwise to let it out now. After all, she was a woman, and there was no telling when she would leave him like the others! Determined to achieve immortality, thinking that he needed the comb's magic to replenish all the expense the Versailles-like convention would cost him, he was obsessed with holding on to it.

That was why, in spite of all the questions that Gabriel Ananias was asking at the dinner, he was really pleased the young man was there.

Tankor Satani stopped his reverie and came back to the present. Looking at his guest, he ate the fruit dessert with a perfunctory air and slowly sipped his brandy, as though trying to forget his own subterfuges as he studied the face of the savant sitting opposite him. Determined to convince the young man of his sincerity, he suddenly remembered a popular adage. "You know what the old people always say, Gabriel: 'Common sense is better than book learning.' Do you agree?"

"I don't get your point, Excellency."

Tankor Satani did not reply right away. He knew he was being disingenuous and that he was offering the young man a lot of crap to muddle his head. Although he was trying not to let on that he was worried about the anger still boiling over the banker's death, he had been going to bed lately wondering whether a lot of people had discovered his secret hand in the killing.

Only the other evening, finally yielding to the suggestions of his sorcerer, Tankor had slaughtered two Barbary rams as a sacrifice to keep the banker safely reposing in heaven and stop him from inspiring the generals always plotting against Tankor to risk a coup, not to talk of giving ideas to the presence in the dark room. The narrow gutter behind the servants' quarters had streamed with the blood of the rams, and Tankor wondered whether Gabriel Ananias had seen evidence of the sacrifice when the guard was dragging him across the compound.

Cautiously gauging his move, when he thought it was prudent, Tankor Satani placed his right hand on the young man's shoulder and said in a fatherly voice, "Son, believe me, it was an accident. And I want you to do something for this old man."

"What is it?" Gabriel Ananias wondered, convinced it was something conspiratorial.

"Have you thought of doing something very important for the country?"

"I am doing that already, Excellency: alerting people to the depletion of our natural resources."

"That is precisely the point I am making," Tankor Satani said, seizing the opening he had been offered.

"I still don't get your point, Mr. President."

With a calm, unblinking stare, as if he were in another sphere, Tankor Satani began to spell out the future he had envisaged for Gabriel Ananias, one that only God or Lucifer could have inspired in him, full, as it were, of unimaginable blessings and celestial temptations. Offered in that indelicate margin between "knowing the book and using your common sense," it was so tantalizing that, until the day the old man's gobbling appetite for cars and houses reminded Gabriel Ananias of how far he had strayed from his scholastic ideals, he would never get over how unprepared he was for the ambush. The temptation the old man had offered him was so large, Gabriel Ananias immediately thought of the temptations of Christ. He wished, at that moment, for a sign from Christ, or from his biblical namesake, on how to respond, but none came. Without realizing it, he had lost his advantage over the old man.

"You who are so concerned about the future of this country, living only for your principles, which I admire, are just the right man to entrust with the second-most important job in the country, after the office of president,"

Tankor said. "Spend some time with the ants and your plants; read some more books. But what I have dreamed of, and hope you will accept, is that one day you shall become the governor of the Central Bank. As you know, the office is still vacant. I shall appoint a temporary head until you are ready to take over."

Gabriel Ananias felt his head spinning. The glittering lights in the Xanadu, which hitherto had not fascinated him, now appeared like a galaxy of unreal stars. It was a brief moment, but he thought he was one of those dancing mirages he had always imagined in those stars. The first cicadas had begun to chirr on the oleanders, and he was left speechless with disbelief, shocked by the old man's cunning. Then, incredibly, as though fate had sent her to help Gabriel Ananias make his choice, it was at that moment that Jenebah Djallo walked in, with the provocative fires of her youth, bubbling with the lessons she had been learning at the School of Contemporary Etiquette about flower arrangements for the convention.

It was the first time Gabriel Ananias had seen her. Unable to resist her allure, he looked at her for a brief moment and noticed that her eyes seemed to be telling him that, if he cared to talk to her, there were lessons she could teach him about how to avoid the fascination of the house with the dancing mirrors.

A few years later, when Gabriel Ananias fled his position as governor of the bank because Tankor Satani had designs on his house, he wished he had paid more attention to the message in Jenebah Djallo's eyes.

CHAPTER THIRTY-NINE

Tankor Satani Meets Gilchrist Obango

Soon after Gabriel Ananias paid Tankor Satani a visit, bulldozers went to work on a densely forested part of one of the hills overlooking Malagueta. All day long the machines were heard churning up the land so that Tankor Satani's contractors could start building the beautiful bungalows for the guests coming to attend his convention: forty-seven in all. The air was cool, a strong wind was blowing wood chips and nails everywhere, and mud and concrete cakes filled the chasms in the earth's surface. Mosquitoes had started breeding in the stagnant pools of water, and some street urchins had appeared from all over town to beg for the scraps of bones and bits of bread tossed to them by the Corals in the work camp. Predictably, the Corals had won the bidding to build the fifty Moroccan bungalows designed by a French-Moroccan architect. In the heat, they were pushing their black workmen like coolies, trying to have the buildings ready before July, when the fury of the rain would turn the ground into a huge quagmire.

Except for a few who would drink from the same water jug with the workers, eat *akara* bean cakes, smoke the same cannabis joints, and engage in man-to-man crude jokes with them, the Corals always acted like overseers from another age. They drove to the site in their four-wheel-drive vehicles and were always quick to bark insulting orders and curses at the workers for being lazy and for an etcetera of other imagined faults. A makeshift camp had grown under the few remaining canopies near the construction site, where some women sold fruits and delicacies cooked in coconut and palm oils. At night, while the crickets chirred, some of those women would come back in a variety of colorful disguises to offer discreet sexual pleasures in the shacks, after the men had paid the right price.

The smell of rich cooking during the day had already attracted a pack of stray dogs to the fringes of this temporary life. Although some of the animals eventually moved on to other places in search of food, a few decided to stay, and sometimes their barking was so loud it had a terrible effect on the men enjoying their pleasure. Half naked, they would rush out of their shacks with clubs, yelling at the dogs to go to hell. It was as if, in those dogs, the anger of sprites and other unfriendly spirits over the destruction of the area had found expression. "Must be de dead people complaining," surmised one of the angry lovers.

One afternoon, when he thought the work should have reached a satisfactory stage, Tankor Satani showed up at the campsite. He was wearing a sea-blue shirt, baggy trousers, and a broad Panama hat to keep out the heat of the sun. An unlit pipe gleamed between his teeth, and his right hand was tightly clasped on the gargoyle-shaped silver crook of his cane. Far from being satisfied with the work, he began to complain about its progress.

"You are way behind time," he told the terrified Coral contractor showing him around.

"No, sah; de wuk goin' fine, fine, like you want am."

"Not good enough!" Tankor Satani raged. "You still have to roof the bungalows and install the air conditioners. Why do you think I am paying your fat Coral arse all this money?"

Some unemployed workers had found jobs to earn a little bit of money in other parts of town, although not as lucrative as the work on the bungalows.

The convention was only about a year away, and there were potholes to be filled, municipal buildings painted, cemetery walls whitewashed, police and school uniforms made, even a facelift given to the prison, just in case some of the troublesome journalists from those highfalutin Western newspapers decided to write about the conditions there. A week earlier, Tankor Satani had ordered all the old graffiti on government buildings painted over with political slogans to fire the optimism of the people. Driving to the cenotaph to the memory of World War II veterans to see how it was being spruced up, he saw that fresh flowers had been planted on its edges. And later that day there was a carnival atmosphere as some old-timers came out with a flourish of harmonicas and guitars from a bygone age, demanding they be given shovels and pickaxes to help clean out the filth in the gutters for the price of a good drink every evening.

"If an old goat like Tankor Satani is going to celebrate his seventeen years in office with a convention, he will need all the help he can get from his contemporaries," they joked.

For the next three months Malaguetans were gripped by the same kind of frenzy as when the Xanadu was being built, yet nothing had prepared some observant citizens for the unusual shock in a town accustomed to the bizarre. One morning, as the old-timers were busy cleaning out the gutters to a song from the good old days, they saw ten prisoners descending from an open truck in front of a petrol station. It was not too far from a roadside market near the beach, where women sold confectioneries and alcohol to the old-timers on credit. The prisoners were not handcuffed and looked well fed; malaria had not turned their eyes yellow, their teeth were alabaster, and their feet were firm on the ground as they crossed the street laughing with their guards, heading toward a compound where some mechanics lived and worked. It was not unusual to see prisoners on the streets, which was not to say that Malagueta was a prison camp. Sometimes they would be seen offloading bags of rice or bundles of wood in front of a superintendent's house, or walking along Old Maroon Hill Road from the courthouse back to the central prison, prompting many people to surmise that there was no gasoline for the Black Maria.

No one bothered with this lot until fifteen minutes later, when one of the old-timers who had seen the prisoners alight earlier from the truck thought that if the sudden transformation he was witnessing was true, angels must live in Malagueta. "Lord have mercy," he said, "I don't believe what I am seeing!"

Four of the prisoners had changed their jailhouse garb for civilian clothes. They looked like strange tourists who had entered a Forbidden City. Instead of the prison-issued car-tire sandals that all prisoners wore, they were now wearing brand-new tennis shoes and tee shirts with American university logos. Imitation gold chains dangled from the necks of the most outlandish of them. Still wondering what was going on, the old man watched as they disappeared in the crowd of people hurrying to catch the nine o'clock bus to the Ake Murray district in the city, where some artists were preparing masquerades for the convention. Capitalizing on the mood of the times, some enterprising people had already started selling all kinds of bric-a-brac, including the new souvenirs that had only recently been printed for the convention: buttons, medallions, flags of all the nations whose leaders were attending, key rings, a long-out-of-print history of the founding of Malagueta by Thomas Bookerman. Even reproductions of William Blake's etching of Nebuchadnezzar, that masterpiece of terror with which, hung on their walls, many Malaguetans had kept their children on the straight and narrow path, went on sale, after not having been seen for quite a long time in the town.

The old man recovered soon enough from his startling discovery. It was as though he had just witnessed that performance of the eunuchs under the cotton tree everyone had been talking about, which he had missed, being down with malaria that day. Images of the transformed prisoners still fresh in his mind, he went to his regular pub, ordered a drink, and said aloud, "Bloody hell, with this kind of crazy government, even the monkeys would love to go to jail."

When the bartender discovered what was making his guest hot under the collar, he laughed boisterously at the old man's naivety. "My friend," he said, "God helps those who help themselves in Malagueta."

"You can say dat again," the old man agreed. And took a big swig of his beer.

The rains were fast approaching in small drizzles at night, making the ground soft, and the Coral contractors were having a difficult time completing the bungalows. Terrified of another outburst from Tankor Satani, they did something they would not have contemplated a month earlier: they asked Gilchrist Obango, one of the best African contractors in town, to oversee the rest of the work.

"I accept the task on one condition," he said.

"What is it, my friend?" the chief Coral contractor asked.

"That I am given a free hand to hire more laborers and twenty additional plasterers, masons, and plumbers."

"Please, anything," the Coral said plaintively. "Do something before de Pa begin to cuss our moders."

Putting aside their wizardry in the diamond-smuggling business, and although a moneyed class, the Corals were not really known for their professional skills. The additional labor cost them a lot of money, but it was worth the hypertension and stress, checked with copious amounts of ginger, opium, and other cures they had in plentiful supply, that they suffered when Gilchrist Obango discovered the terrible blunders that their journeymen brother electricians had made, especially in the wire circuiting of four of the houses.

"This would have sent some of Tankor Satani's guests to hell," Gilchrist said, shaking his head over how much had been spent for such a shoddy piece of work.

Under the supervision of this talented black man, the work progressed without a hitch for the next three months. Gilchrist Obango was big, pleasant, but very imposing, with a no-nonsense attitude about him. His presence checked the sassiness of the Corals and stopped their tongues wagging about African women, whom they had always regarded as cheap. Quite regularly, when they were sick of their own baby whale women, the Corals would be seen chatting up black women for a quick tryst. If, as sometimes happened, the black girls became pregnant, they were paid off with a little bit of money, nothing more, which was why Malagueta had so many street urchin malattas without a father's name.

Nonetheless, in terms of goodwill, the Corals knew a thing or two about how to ingratiate themselves when their objective was money, and as soon as Gilchrist took over the supervision of the work they started bringing Middle Eastern delicacies to sweeten the lips of the black workers. They watched in awe as Gilchrist created a sublime beauty, meticulously handling the timber, mortar, and spools of electric cable with a familiarity born out of the patience and love of work he had learned many years ago. Little by little, he coaxed the stubborn iron nails into their right journeys, chiseled uneven planks into straight two-by-fours, and corrected the crooked lines of walls with tiling that dispensed with machines. The results left the Corals' tongues hanging out in shocked admiration at the grace and elegance that the black master could bring to the bungalows.

Marrying Moroccan architecture to Malaguetan wizardry, he intended to demonstrate that he was doing a job not just of work but of dignity. In years to come, he felt, his reputation would rise and flow in the marvelous harmony he had achieved in the short time he had to show that he and his workers were men with remarkable gifts. Even though the men had to take time off now and then, when the wind from the hill or the terror of rain delayed them, the work, except for bits of plastering and landscaping, was finished three months ahead of schedule.

Two weeks later, Tankor Satani came on a final inspection. Informed ahead of time, Gilchrist Obango assembled his men to greet the old man, and to see Tankor's reaction after he had learned of the contribution they had made to the bungalows. Here, when it came to the joy of work, they were above the hastiness of the Corals. Faced with such a dignified group and stunned by the elegance of their work, Tankor Satani shook the hand of Gilchrist Obango and held it for a while. "Forgive me," he said. "I have let my own people down."

"Anything for you, Excellency," Gilchrist Obango replied. "We are a proud people and are happy to be part of your celebration."

On his way home an hour later, Tankor Satani saw the unused clearing made by the savage teeth of the adzes that had felled the trees for his grand project. In the wide expanse of the sky, the mist of the November morning had spread over the land, but it was not dark enough to hide the hawks circling above the rise of the houses in search of prey. All the same, his driver found it hard driving through the usually crowded streets, and his security detail had to yell at people to stay on the edges of the streets. Deeply moved by his encounter with the talented contractor, Tankor Satani's mind went back to those bygone days of his unfettered dreams when, inspired by the ghost of Henri Christophe, he had imagined how good it would be to build the Xanadu, as the reincarnation of the great emperor! "It was the work of a genius," he marveled, thinking of the bungalows that Gilchrist had completed.

It was a long time since Henri Christophe had first inspired Tankor to start thinking of immortality, and he was certain he was almost there. So he decided he would hire Gilchrist Obango as chief government building contractor and increase the salaries of all the government workers in Malagueta by 35 percent, if he made the profit he hoped from the commercial business he was anticipating after the convention. Later that night, after having neglecting her for so long, Tankor Satani crawled into bed with his "Fullah cow," and the gray parrots, which had not heard her screams in the last three months, went wild in their cages as the old man, thinking of how he was about to be crowned with the jewel of his long summer, began to create a long, tempestuous rhythm on the sea of Jenebah Djallo's daring.

CHAPTER FORTY

All the Pretenders

AS SOON as he was released from prison, Dr. Sidi Samura sent an urgent message to Theodore Iskander and a handful of really trusted men who had swung to the doctor's camp during his incarceration. Concerned that he might be detained yet again, the thought of the men coming to the house to discuss the affairs of state did not please the doctor's wife, Nemata.

"You are getting old!" she cried. "When are you going to stop the lunacy of trying to do something for this crazy country no one really cares about?"

"When the crazy fool who is in charge stops acting like God," the doctor replied with a rare show of emotion.

"I give up. You are as stubborn as the goat that you are," Nemata said in exasperation; her husband's astrological sign was Capricorn.

Throughout their long marriage they had suffered a lot, the most painful tragedy being losing a beloved son. Even then, Nemata had been amazed by how stubborn her husband could be. Whereas the doctor was reserved and distinguished with a formal bearing, Nemata had an air of happy serenity and was warm and generous of spirit. When they were forced to sell one of their two cars after her husband's practice was ruined by Tankor Satani, she did what she had not done in over twenty years—ride in the crowded taxis to and from the school, where she taught kindergarten music, thus earning the grateful respect of her principal for what she deemed her unnecessary sacrifice. Yet those rides, far from being mere hindrances for her, were beneficial, for it was then that she would hear hilarious tidbits about what people really thought about Tankor Satani, especially about his "Fullah cow." As much as she despised the president, it was with not a little amazement that she thought of him, at seventy-five, with such a fantastic mistress!

Unknown to the doctor's wife, he was already in possession of a secret pertaining to the president, more considerable than anything the public dreamed of. During his incarceration in the Central Prison, when he was not working on his latest play, Dr. Samura's thoughts had been focused on a more pressing matter: Tankor Satani might be dying. After the lights were turned out in the prison and he could not write, the doctor's mind was as active as a beaver on a log. He did a regular round of calisthenics to maintain his health, but he thought less about the possibility that he might never leave prison alive and more about what he knew of Tankor Satani's health. For although he was not the president's personal physician, Dr Samura was privy to a private diagnosis about the old man's health that had been smuggled to the doctor in the prison from a personal source in the neighboring country of Bassa after Tankor Satani had undergone a series of clinical tests in Germany.

The physicians in Bremen had not thought it wise to reveal their findings to the president, but the truth was that after a thorough checkup, including forcing the old man to undergo an MRI scan—a device he playfully said always reminded him of a girl in a miniskirt—they had discovered that Tankor Satani was suffering from potentially fatal brain damage, which might explain some of his irrational actions.

In the strictest confidence, the German doctors had relayed their findings to Dr. Klaus Schmidt, their former classmate at the Medical School in Tübingen, Germany, who was now the personal physician of the president of the neighboring African republic of Bassa. Ironically, while he was unaware that his own health might be endangered, Tankor Satani was concerned about the health of Bassa's President Kongoma, to whom he had only recently given three million dollars in diamonds for safekeeping, now that he was convinced his Coral associate Moustapha Ali-Bakr was double-crossing him. "I have learned too late that you cannot completely trust these Corals," Tankor Satani wrote in his secret diplomatic note, "but I have to keep this one by my side, because, as we say in Malagueta, he has his finger in my nose."

Ten years earlier, it so happened that before embarking on his quest to prove that it was the Italians that had spread trypanosomiasis in the Horn of Africa, Dr. Samura had spent a summer doing research in tropical medicine at a German university. During that period, he had made the acquaintance of Dr. Klaus Schmidt, after which a beautiful friendship had blossomed between the two physicians. Long before Dr. Samura's practice folded, the two doctors had paid each other visits in their respective countries, enjoying what each had to offer. Both men being opera lovers, they had attended a performance of Wagner's *Lohengrin* in Bayreuth and drunk good Bavarian beer afterward.

"For a genius, Wagner was a vicious racist," Dr. Schmidt said with genuine anger. "He hated Jews, blacks, and Gypsies."

Dr. Samura smiled understandingly at his friend. "Don't feel guilty for the sins of others, my friend. There are Jews, blacks, and Arabs who are vicious racists."

When it was the turn of Dr. Samura to show his friend his Africa, he introduced the German to the great epic poem *Shaka* by Thomas Mofolo; and the German, always one for archeological masterpieces, was stunned when they visited the ancient stones of Monomotapa in Zimbabwe. "In the worst example of revisionist history and racism, the white Rhodesians, many of them British, had the gall to say that black people could not have built this masterpiece," Dr. Samura said proudly.

Later they went to the slave ruins on Bunche Island off Malagueta, and further cemented their friendship with trips to the Seychelles and Zanzibar, where Dr. Schmidt, a skilled diver, hunted octopus while Dr. Samura, unable to swim, like many of his generation, spent his time writing unabashed poetry about the alluring beauty of the Swahili-speaking women. The two men not only had a high regard for their respective intelligence but shared a common interest in the future of the region. So when he was asked to serve as the personal physician to the president of Bassa, Dr. Schmidt jumped at the chance, thinking it would give him the opportunity to follow at close range his Malaguetan friend's newly discovered passion for political dissent.

For three years, Dr. Schmidt had treated President Kongoma of Bassa for all types of real and imaginary illnesses, sometimes in the white stuccoed palace on a hill in Bassa's dusty and humid capital, sometimes in a variety of sealed-off villas and bungalows in other parts of the country, where the president had given concessions to the American rubber barons and his privacy was guaranteed by ferocious German shepherds and armed guards from Texas. After a while, the relationship between patient and doctor took on the aspect of a father trusting his medically trained son with his secrets. Dr. Schmidt's assurances to the president that he was destined for a long reign, notwithstanding his high cholesterol level, did little to ease the greatest fear lurking in his heart: more than a military putsch, what the small, bald man feared most was that he would die suddenly, without a chance to remove all the amulets and fetish charms against evil that he wore under his presidential suits.

"Promise me that if I die on your table, you will destroy all the amulets to save me the ridicule of my wife, who has never witnessed me getting dressed for the office."

"Your secrets are safe with me, Your Excellency."

When Dr. Schmidt first received the diagnosis on Tankor Satani's health from the physicians in Germany, it was with the understanding that the findings were safe. But medical ethics soon gave way to what Dr. Schmidt felt was an even greater moral obligation: Tankor Satani's health was something he had to share with his illustrious friend in Malagueta, thus giving Dr. Samura the one piece of ammunition he knew he could secretly use against his erstwhile friend.

"The old fool has set his eyes on immortality, but he is as good as dead," the doctor remarked when he received the secret diagnosis in prison.

Dr. Samura did not hang up his stethoscope after he was released, although his practice had dwindled after Tankor Satani terrorized some of the doctor's patients. "Poor, small fool," the doctor said, pitying the president yet again. He was not bitter about losing his patients; he rented his surgery to a young and upcoming lawyer to augment his savings, and one day a week would treat the handful of his former patients who had refused to be cowed by Tankor Satani.

"We are right behind you, doctor, in this fight," an old woman said as she counted her widow's mite to pay the doctor for his services.

"All I need is your blessing," the doctor laughed, politely refusing her payment.

"You have that because, unlike the cutthroat doctors that I know, you have put your humanity before the profits of medicine," she replied with a dignified air.

Later that night, concerned about who might replace Tankor should the president die suddenly, the doctor went to bed thinking of how to invite his friends to his house.

The harmattan came early that year, and its breath of spring was cooling the air after the hot, lingering sun of June to October: a period made worse by the balding mountain's lack of a breeze, the toxic fumes of the ancient vehicles on Malagueta's roads, and the roaring fires spiraling from the shanties, all adding to the humidity. With only a few months to go before the convention, a frenzy of late activities had gripped the town: flags were hoisted on all the electric poles, and not just on Independence Square, leading to Malombo House, the official presidential palace, as in normal times. Spurred on by a sense of patriotism, even if they disliked the old man, engineers at the National Broadcasting House were trying its new, powerful transmitter to see how far its FM range would reach. One morning, to the enchanting rhythm of Congolese music, a tidal wave of women was seen shaking their bottoms in the compound of the Governing Party League of Women as they rehearsed some new dance steps for the convention. When they were tired of dancing, they began to stitch buttons to the shirts of their kids, who would line the main arteries of Malagueta to welcome the illustrious guests from abroad. In a spectacular burst of excitement, the Kam

Bay and Otamba ghettoes, where sweltering humanity occasionally fought over water, sex, and prostitution, but seldom over theft or murder, came alive every night with the deafening sound of rumba music, indicating that, no matter how expensive it was, some people in Malagueta wanted to be part of the old man's carnival in the twilight of his life.

Predictably, the Corals had given generously of their money and goods for the event, but their generosity was meant for the government. Fearing break-ins in their stores, as had happened during the students' riot, they lowered the prices of Java and Ivorian prints, bags of onions, evaporated milk, castor oil, groundnut oil, lard, butter, pilchard sardines, and those barrels of imported salted pigs' feet no respectable feast in Malagueta could do without. For an entire week, starlight and firecrackers illuminated the verandahs of the Corals, who had learned from past mistakes that the one thing that would get people in Malagueta hot under the collar was for those Arabs and their half-caste cousins to show disrespect when the common people in town wanted to celebrate, no matter what the occasion. The national brewery doubled its production of beer after Tankor Satani had granted the promised increase to all workers. Bars stayed opened late, and the chasm between unhappy couples grew wider, but who cared to remember what was said in the heat of passion or rage, when the liquor flowing in your head had dulled your memory? Amazingly, Tankor Satani achieved an incredible triumph when, much to the disbelief of the people of the town, Malagueta's most famous singer, the Raw Bonga King, who had been living in exile in the Côte d'Ivoire and whose lyrics were not-too-veiled criticisms of the government, arrived to perform at the grand opening. "It is a matter of national pride," he told a press conference.

During his now occasional forays into the heart of town, Dr. Sidi Samura had been making a note of all the preparations, and he was amazed by the fickle minds of some people. The same people who, only a few months ago, had been critical of the expense of holding the convention were now in transport about the event, possibly because they hoped to profit from it. As he no longer owned a car, he usually walked, despite his increasing age. But when he felt a bit tired of trying to solve one of life's greatest imponderables, he would rest on the steps of the monument to the poet Garbage Martins and offer some groundnuts to the sparrows that crowded around the statue. With the studied attention of a scientist, he would watch the pecking order of the birds—all eventually got some nuts, in spite of their different sizes. Then it would occur to him that as far as the desires of men and women were concerned, regardless of their creed or race, all aimed at some form of equanimity of spirit, and that no one wanted to be left out of life's occasional sweetness, never mind their places on the rung of the ladder; there was just so much each man and woman could stand in times of pain.

Given the excitement that so many people felt about the coming convention, the doctor decided it did not matter whether men and women danced in its masquerades, got drunk in the gutters, or peed into the newly regrown rose bushes in front of the law courts building and vomited afterward. What mattered was that they wanted, occasionally, in the harshness of their pain, or even in the iron of their souls, to dream of a world that was larger than theirs, incomprehensible. With the right opportunity, all men and women wanted to make love on expensive divans and not on grass-stuffed mattresses; have children who would dream of becoming great soccer stars like Pelé or successful pop stars like Michael Jackson. These were the only dreams that mattered, not the intellectual ruminations of men and women like him. Not at that time; tomorrow, perhaps, after the song and dance of the convention had ended and the wind and fire of the tropics had come back, unrelenting in their fury, to awaken Malaguetans out of their dreams of forgetfulness.

All the same, he was not unhappy. In fact, he had never been happier. A few days later, using the excuse of attending a musical evening in the doctor's study, the six men, including Theodore Islander, whom he had invited showed up at Dr. Samura's house. Mindful of the watchful eyes of the guard that Tankor Satani had stationed in front of the house, the men held, for all to see, the dog-eared music sheets of the compositions they knew were part of another world the guard did not care to understand, and thus he would not bother them with trifling questions about the reason for their visit.

With her usual grace and incomparable charm, Nemata welcomed the men to her house, displaying not the slightest hint that she was worried her husband might be heading for prison again. Considering his age, he might not survive, but she was prepared to back him to the hilt if need be. Ten minutes later, the men were in the study, ready to discuss the future of Malagueta.

Asked to stay by her husband, Nemata amazed him with the clarity of her thinking, if not with its logic. "What kind of egg is the crocodile going to lay that has not already been discerned in the riddle of the sand?"

She left the men in a stew of confusion, a state made even more enigmatic when, from across the study, they heard her, after she had sat down at the grand piano in the living room, as she began to play the first "Promenade" from Mussorgsky's *Pictures at an Exhibition* with impassioned elegance. As the glorious lyricism of the music filled the house, her husband left the men in the study and came to stand near his wife.

"How well you see these things," he smiled. "We are all on exhibit: Tankor, these men, myself; but the real picture is the one we cannot really paint, as that must be left to the next generation. Hopefully, it will be better than ours, and will save Malagueta from all its present pretenders to its future."

It was unlike the doctor to think about God when he was depressed; he was an acknowledged agnostic who had not been to church in a long time, since the death of one of his sons, when the doctor had bowed to the wishes of his wife for a "fitting" service. Yet after saying good-bye to his friends, he was filled with contrary emotions as he reflected on the disastrous situation in the country. The evening vespers at the National Cathedral were ringing, and he felt drawn by the chimes. But thinking of some of the Christians he knew—some of whom had so much vitriol in their souls that the devil could have walked naked in broad daylight without being ashamed of competing with them—he was suddenly assailed by the notion that perhaps there might be a God after all, one less abstract than he had imagined when he was a younger man: real, humane, and not so intolerant of the vices of his Christians.

He tried to envisage a greater manifestation of that God but failed. He sat down and opened a page of a three-year-old newspaper, in which he found the name of a journalist who had written a blistering attack on the president. It was then that something else caught the doctor's attention: a two-column article about Gabriel Ananias, perhaps the worst pretender of them all; the piece sent the doctor suddenly back to his agnosticism. If it had been that easy for vice to wean that young man away from the beatitudes of God, then who in the country was genuine? the doctor wondered.

Next morning, he was still thinking of the banker. The sun had risen beautifully, and it was a holiday, so Nemata had a free day from school. After she was through with some difficult chores she could not trust to their servant, she once again sat at the piano, not to remind her husband of her concern for his safety but to give him some pleasure, for she chose to play a polonaise by Chopin, one of the doctor's favorites. It was a peaceful idyll, and the doctor had only to listen to that beautiful music to forget about Tankor Satani. Normally he would have done some writing after his lunch, but the sun was so inviting that he thought he might go and see his oldest surviving relative. He took a bus to get to the wooded area on the hill on the south side of the Xanadu, where one might occasionally be lucky enough to see a wild guinea fowl and most of the houses were old wooden structures that the early

Maroons had built after they came to Malagueta following the defeat of the Haitian revolutionaries by Napoleon Bonaparte's forces.

"Nothing has really changed in this part of town," the doctor observed as he began to walk through the idyllic maze of history.

For his age he was quite strong, but after walking for another quarter of a mile he was tired and decided to rest for a while in front of a modern house that was strangely neglected. Then, as though he had entered a world of fantasy, unlike any that his scientific mind could dare imagine, it occurred to him that this was the once-splendid house of the banker Gabriel Ananias. It had lost much of its grandeur after one of Tankor Satani's sons had moved in; the rains had washed the paint off, lianas of moss grew on the walls, its roof was rusty, and plastic bags were strewn all over the neglected garden. But what surprised the doctor beyond belief, considering that the banker had fled years ago, was that a swarm of black ants was eating what remained of the plants in the garden. It seemed to the doctor as though they were eating the last of the ruinous pride of the young banker: it was the endgame of a story that had started well, in the heart of an Irish priest determined to save one soul, but that was to die in the heart of a misguided young man tempted by the mirrors of the Xanadu. It was a real tragedy, the doctor felt, shaking his head as he continued on his way, the sun still gentle on his face, to see his eighty-five-year-old aunt.

When he was back home, three hours later, he sat down to write, as usual, very late into the night. Two weeks later, he sent a note to his friend Theodore Iskander, asking him to come to the house to discuss a personal matter of literary importance to the doctor. Essentially a private fellow, the doctor would not have opened his heart to the philosopher if he did not have the highest esteem for the acuity of his vision. After years of writing plays that had been gathering dust in his drawers rather than being submitted to the indecent assault of the philistines who made up the censor's board, Dr. Sidi Samura had turned his creative energies to his memoirs. He was approaching seventy-five, still full of an anarchist's fervor, a trait greatly admired by his small circle of friends; everyone had heard about how he had sent Tankor Satani packing when the president came to make his peace with the doctor. With the same exquisite discretion he had observed through a relationship that had blossomed into twenty-five years of friendship, the doctor went to see his mistress regularly so that they could continue their exploration of the mystical world of the Mandingoes, whose pedigree they both possessed. He usually took a taxi, but once in a while his grave, dignified figure was seen strolling through the botanical garden, where he paused to touch the lotuses in the pond before turning into the warren of houses on the street where his mistress had a fine home, in which he was assured of the greatest privacy. Old age was something that he seldom worried about, not when he was too busy finishing his book on the spread of sleeping sickness by the Italians. He thought occasionally about death, only because his wife had begun to worry that he might die suddenly, as, surprisingly for a doctor, he cared very little about his own health and refused, in the molecules of science, but also in those palisades where as a doctor he had seen so much suffering, to believe in the existence of a divine being, leaving it to his wife and to her God to explain why so many evil men were living to a ripe old age.

Some mornings when the doctor woke up not intending to write, he thought he might do a few of the things he had been prevented from doing in his youth, but which he wanted to experience before he died; such as learning how to swim or improving on his game of *warri*, now that he had finally bowed to his wife's pleading to give up what she saw as a thankless fight to save Malagueta from ruination. Since the last time he and his friends had gathered in his study, the thrill that Dr. Samura had derived from those fiery articles he had dispatched to the press was no longer there. His fiery pen may have gone into desuetude, but there was no mistaking how he felt about some things, and he hoped, not with arrogance or any abrogation of duty, that he had been able to do a bit of good for the country in mixing with all kinds of riff-raff, much to the surprise of many ordinary people who had always thought he and his kind were elitists, especially as he always seemed to be wrapped up in his own secret dreams. When he came to think about his life, he couldn't help being bemused about how he had sent his old nemesis packing; in the battle for the soul of Malagueta, the doctor felt, he had gained a greater reward than Tankor Satani's.

"Look at this scribbling," he said to his young friend as he and Theodore Iskander sat down to tea in the doctor's study. "These are the real 'Confessions of an Albino Terrorist.' One day you might feel like editing them for publication."

CHAPTER FORTY-ONE

Sorcerers and Poets

ONE EVENING when the ocean was emitting a greenish vapor and the air smelled of poisoned sea turtles, some cheaply perfumed doe-eyed whores were coming out of their rooms in the Otamba ghetto down at the bay as

Theodore Iskander was limping toward his car. He had parked it near Dr. Samura's house, and as he got close to it, it dawned on him that the armed sergeant with a walrus mustache in front of the doctor's house had been replaced with a phlegmatic policeman, whose only weapon was a club resting in his lap as he slept. He looked a bit drunk, or as if he did not think the doctor was subversive enough to merit constant observation. Cicadas were chirring in the hibiscus bushes, and even though it was late, a brilliant sun gleamed orange over the city. Theodore Iskander knew a bit about planets, so he thought that the sun was an indication that Jupiter was in the ascendant, but he only had to look at the cluttered street to be reminded that he was on earth. He paused to light a cigar, and when he looked at the sun again the orange light was fading.

He was near the State Lottery building, a few feet from his car, and the pulse of the street was volatile; for there was some form of trouble brewing near the building because a woman had got into a fight with her no-good husband, who had gambled away his entire month's salary on a losing ticket. The melee brought expressions of consternation from some nurses hurrying home from their thankless duties at the rundown government hospital.

"Dis is what dis country has become: useless politicians and useless men," said one of the women. "May God save us from dem!"

"Amen, sister!" said another. And spat into the dust!

Melodiously sweet soukous music came from the boom box at a bistro adjacent to a nearby gas station. Business clearly was thriving. After dodging the daredevil taxi drivers, some stray dogs were waiting patiently for scraps of food, especially for a good leg bone. The sun's yellow radiance had finally disappeared, and the clouds were beginning to spread their night's shroud, while the tin lamps of the fricassee sellers were flickering in the soft hue of evening. As the philosopher walked past a group of women roasting meat on charcoal grills, one of them recognized him and called out, "Hello, Professor, buy something from me."

She had run out of veal, which was his favorite, but engaged him in some syrupy talk until he bought some chicken that she wrapped in some old newspaper, giving him an extra spoon of pepper. "It is good for you, Professor, if you know what ah mean," she said, smiling conspiratorially. The barbecue was hotter than any he had ever eaten, and as soon as he got into his car he drank copiously from the jug of water Habiba Mouskuda had always insisted he carry to cool him down when he was stuck in traffic.

Sometimes in traffic, at the cinema, or at sports events, but more likely at a funeral, which was always colorful, he would see some of his former colleagues. They would exchange handshakes, engage in desultory talk about their children, or, when he was pressed into it, would have a drink at a bar. At those encounters, it was obvious to him that they had grown worlds apart and he wished they would not trouble him, but he had not reckoned with their determination to use him. So one day he was surprised when his erstwhile friend Dr. Komba Binkolo, now the foreign minister, ambushed him at a sports event, where he had taken Yeama. The former political science professor came straight to the point.

"I know you think I have betrayed the ideal you and I once stood for, before I joined Tankor Satani's cabinet. But by being there I have probably checked some of the excesses of the old man."

Theodore Iskander could hardly contain his anger at this dishonesty. "You must be a worse fool than Gabriel Ananias, who thought he could find in the house of mirrors what he had not been prepared to seek in the house of God."

"Let us leave God out of our precepts. We have free will to make mistakes and to correct them with humility, which is why I am here. If you join some of us to plan the future, you will have honored the names of your illustrious ancestors," the politician pleaded.

Theodore Iskander was full of pity for his former colleague but did not spare him his disdain. "Don't waste my time," he said. "I have better things to do." He hurried to his car with Yeama in tow.

When he had stopped choking from the pepper, he thought about what Nemata Samura had said when he went to see his friend; how in her wisdom, offered with an economy of words, she reminded all the dreamers about Malagueta's future that the most refractory thing about this beautiful country was its volatile politics and despicable politicians.

Such contrariness was not new to Theodore Iskander. Even more insidious was that a worse form of racism, something more pernicious than that of white against black, was practiced in the country. One night he brought this up with his friend Dr. Sidi Samura.

"How can the politicians and their people call this place 'one country' when they have land tenure laws that bar Malaguetans from owning land in 90 percent of the country? It is revolting for black people to discriminate against fellow blacks, when they are only too willing to sell their lands and sometimes even their daughters to the Corals."

Dr. Samura studied him for a while. "Poor you; you do not understand the mind-set of some of our citizens. Like the ancient Troglodytes, they can only think in crude ethnic terms."

Given his love for the country, Theodore Iskander found that deeply revolting. "I had always felt that, when confronted with matters of morality and love, we would rise to the challenge of brotherhood, especially as this country is so small, only five million people. After our colonial experience, I had hoped that our selfishness would bend to the interest of the country. But it would seem that we are just as brutal to ourselves as the British, Portuguese, and Belgians were to the people they conquered."

Dr. Samura saw how deeply pained his friend was. "Don't let the disasters in this country destroy you. The incredible thing is that some very vicious and determined people are taking it back to the bush, all in the name of regional dominance.

Back in his student days, when he had depended on gas fires with coin slots to keep him warm during the bleak winter months in England, Theodore Iskander had missed Malagueta. Just thinking of its climate sometimes made him homesick, so he would seek out other students from home, only to be shocked that some of them preferred to find comfort in their separate ethnic lineages and not in a national ethos. He had cringed when some of those men would appear at a dance with some English tarts in tow, the men looking sheepishly pleased that they had netted their first Anglo-Saxon birds—pale, short-legged creatures that could not hold a candle to the exquisite beauty of the majority of Malagueta's women. But who was he to complain? As they say in Malagueta, "When there is a fire in a man, he can put it out with any kind of water."

He was still a few yards from his car. A burr of wind touched his face, but his legs were steady on the ground. Then, perhaps because the manager of the National Lottery, where all the commotion had now died down, was a Russian-trained economist, Theodore Iskander suddenly remembered that he had heard that the man might have some marital woes. Everyone knew that some of the most miserable men in Malagueta were those who had come home with Russian and Ukrainian wives, pale women with an ethereal beauty that refused to tan in the tropics, because they were really creatures of the tundra. For the most part they had good educations and were modest in the beginning as they tried to settle down in the new country, but they were fickle birds of adventure, and their spirits, when exposed to a little hardship, was not as strong as the poplars of their region. Such women were easily weaned away by temptation; many of them had used the chance of marriage simply to escape from their unbearable lives.

Less than two years into their marriages, some of them started revealing a self-destructive streak no one had suspected they possessed, and the ease with which they fooled around shocked their mothers-in-law, who, unable to control their rage, would ask their sons whether they were fools, where was their self-respect?

"You are behaving as though you were nursed on goat milk and not by me!" one angry mother said, lashing out at her son.

"I shall talk to Svetlana so she can start behaving properly," he replied, somewhat sheepishly.

"Talk to that harlot?" His mother asked in consternation. "Get rid of her, or, in the same way that I brought you into this world, I shall disown you!"

He did as advised, but that was not enough to appease his mother. Soon she was launching a campaign to encourage other mothers-in-law to do likewise, especially as some of the Soviet wives had come under the influence of Lubianca Muchenko, a shameless, dried-up blonde from Kiev that some idiot had brought home to his parents.

As soon as she had deduced the possibility of making some money as a high-class prostitute, Lubianca Muchenko threw all notions of decency to the wind. She bought a new wardrobe of outrageous miniskirts and organdy blouses too tight for her age and embarked on a most disgraceful adventure. Flaunting her shameless wiles, she dismissed her mother-in-law as no better than an illiterate cow because she could not read, and then threw her wedding ring into the dustbin to further insult the old woman.

"And you can tell your son that I have torn up my marriage certificate," she hissed at the old woman before storming out of the house with a list of some Corals willing to pay for what remained of her dwindling sexual assets. An economics graduate, she knew how to market those assets. "I did not exchange one miserable country to come and suffer in another," she told the first man she took up with as she began her new life.

With no concern for their marriage, she set about teaching the Russian girls how to drink heavily, and soon they were all dependent on vodka. She poured scorn on the husbands—those papier-mâché men—and dangled the tempting reward of easy money in front of the wives. That promise, even to the handful who were dedicated to their marriages and hesitant about embarking on a lowlife adventure, eventually found its way to their hearts, given Lubianca's inspiration.

Although she was aging, Lubianca clearly had no intention of submitting to a one-night stand in the bed of any man simply because he could pay for her services. With a cold, steely, demeanor, she always insisted on her dignity "like my Ukrainian ancestors always did, even when facing adversity."

Her reputation for weaseling like a gypsy in bed and for demanding gifts of diamond jewelry and uncut stones as insurance for her old age soon became legendary, and few women would deny that, with her alabaster skin and tempestuous breasts, she was capable of leaving some men (mostly Corals) with their tongues hanging out. And from them she expected some form of fidelity. Aware that what they really wanted was to sleep with the young Russian women who were under her tutelage, and that the Corals would pay anything to sleep with any white woman, she treated them like dogs and mocked their crudeness.

"I am not a charity case like an illiterate black woman that you can toss a few dollars to," she would taunt them. "Besides, you all smell of garlic, so pay me for the displeasure of inhaling your scent."

Driving home, Theodore Iskander was thinking about the unfortunate Russian women who had committed suicide after being despised by their in-laws. Soon he was thinking about other things: Tankor Satani's convention was near, and there was panic at the national electricity station because the generators had failed. The streets lay in an eerie darkness, dogs were roaming in packs, and Tankor Satani was fuming on the national radio about saboteurs. "I shall hang them if they do not fix the problem right away!" he thundered.

The thought of a new round of executions horrified Theodore Iskander as he kept his eyes open on the dark street to avoid hitting one of the dogs. Suddenly, as much as he hated what that house stood for, he was grateful when the luminous floodlights from the Xanadu came on and glowed brightly over sections of the city, even as far as the ocean, making it easier for him to drive. Still miffed over the expensive convention, it occurred to him that the next ruler of Malagueta was going to need all the help he could get to repair the damage occasioned by the extravagance of the convention. He finished his cigar and shook his head over the way he had begun to soliloquize, as he sometimes did when assailed by a difficult problem.

His journey home was on a winding hilltop route in the expensive diplomatic and high-society black area, redolent of bougainvillea and mimosa gardens. At the top of the hill, he checked the drift of his mind toward all kinds of philosophical thoughts. He was not really a practical man, he decided, if practical meant having the common touch. He had been trained to see things through the telescopic lens of his profession: and his view was narrow, defined by his own interest, full of elliptical visions, unclear in its objectives. Given the convolutions and great dramas of life in Malagueta, he was too much of a dreamer, someone who belonged to a lost world.

Driving under a hanging canopy of mangoes, almost home, he was not prepared for the shock when a huge vulture darted from a branch and flew across his windshield. Even though he did not dread the conjecture of a vulture's appearance that late, it was all he needed to feel that Malagueta's politics had better be left to those practical men, good luck to them, who were waiting in the wings.

Habiba Mouskuda was relieved when he arrived home just as the rain began to fall, for she was always worried about his limp. Yeama was asleep, but Irene—those African mothers—was waiting up with Habiba Mouskuda, drinking ginger tea. "You should not be out dis late, my son," she piped. "My heart wouldn't be able to take it should anything happen to you!"

"Don't worry too much, Mama," he said.

Now comfortably ensconced in the new house, Irene was always worried that her only son would be taken away from her, whether by some woman, whom she would be ready to fight, or by the pull of politics, which she disdained. Like her ancestors, whom she had been teaching Yeama about, she was fearless, but one thing she was not going to stand for was Theodore getting mixed up with all that politics.

Long ago, she had come to accept that even if she lived to be a hundred, her son's world would always remain an enigma to her. There were times when she could see that he was lost in that world and behaving strangely, but she was proud that he was continuing a family tradition of scholarship and caring for others. Later that night, after he had gone to bed and Habiba was still up doing chores in the kitchen, the old woman came up from her flat to appeal to the woman she had taken to calling her daughter-in-law.

"Don't let anyone talk him into going into real politics, she said. "It is dirty."

"Stop worrying, Mama; it won't happen. With his temperament, he won't last one week."

Incredibly, the Coral—that previously scandalous woman, cold and calculating in her dealings with men—had turned out to be good to her son. Habiba manifested it in ways that Irene had not anticipated, making her think that there were people who grew into goodness only after they themselves had suffered a lot, been bitten hard by life, and after God, in whatever incarnation, had spoken to them. And there was no denying the dedication that the Coral was giving to Yeama and the old woman as well.

Small, sprightly, and strong as a tree, Irene had always had simple needs. She ate very little, her constitution was robust, and she slept lightly; she was the first to respond to the dawn calls of the sparrows so that she could take Tiger out for her morning toilet. Later, insisting she needed the exercise, she would walk Yeama to school, about a mile away.

"You don't have to, Mama," Habiba would protest. "Her father can always drive her."

"Yes, I know," the old woman would counter, "but walking to school with Yeama gives me a chance to see all my old friends also taking their grand-*pikin* there."

It was Irene who thought it wise to educate Yeama about her mother's past. "You know, child," she began one evening when the two of them were the only ones at the house, "some people do not like your moder."

"Why, Granny?"

"Because she did some bad things when she was young, and had no experience. But she is not a bad person, and God has forgiven her."

"What kinds of things?" Yeama was curious; she had not forgotten the word "harlot" that the boy at her school had hurled at her about her mother.

"You know," the old woman continued, "she had many men before she met your daddy. Some were good, some bad. She made many mistakes because sometimes God can test all of us. I hated the Corals, but look, now you are my grand-*pikin,* so I do not hate them. Your mummy loves your daddy, so God has forgiven all of us."

For a long time afterward, Yeama would imagine her mother with those men: faceless creatures whom Habiba had not talked about, but who were nonetheless men who had known her the other side of womanhood when she was immature or, why not admit it, wanton. That knowledge of her mother's unsavory past, as Yeama was beginning to imagine it, would pain and anger her sometimes. But it was not in her nature to be confrontational, so she pulled back from wanting to hear firsthand from Habiba about those men. Then she began, slowly, to build the necessary pillars of strength that she could lean on when she was attacked in the future about her mother's past. Increasingly, as she learned more about her parents, she came to see her father in a new light, one brighter than the horizon called courage, for it took more than that strength to live with a woman so tarnished. She wondered how her father had coped with it, especially as she was aware that he had never hesitated to argue a point of principle, whether about politics, the church, or moral rectitude. In a way, she realized, it was her father loving her mother enough to get past the unsavory nature of her life and live with her that was the greatest manifestation of moral good. Not having been there when Habiba was a "bad woman," Yeama realized she could learn from her father's strength to understand and love her mother.

Those were happy days for the three women, when it was clear to Irene and Yeama that the Coral was not putting on an act, because Irene would have seen through it. Whatever she might have felt about Habiba Mouskuda in the past, Irene had to admit that the malatta had always spoken to her from a naked heart, even to the point of telling her things about her past that should have damned the malatta in the old woman's eyes. In time, just looking at her granddaughter, she gave up worrying about whether Theodore had made the right choice in his woman.

With the money left over after building the new house, Habiba Mouskuda was determined to show her lover that she had learned a thing or two about decorating a home. With Yeama assisting, she started with the study, the room with the splendid view of the river and of a narrow strip of the dirt road that came up to the house. When the house was being built, the trees where the study faced the river had merely been trimmed, so that bright shafts of sunlight came into the room through their branches.

It was quite a large room, the second largest in the house, with huge windows, an airy place, into which Habiba had poured a good portion of her savings as she tried to figure out what would please the philosopher and keep him happy.

With the growing awareness that her father's lineage was important and that he was writing a book about his great-great-grandfather, Yeama had suggestions of her own about how the study should look. "He needs a nice warm sofa, Mummy," she said. "And hang all the pictures from his old office so that he will not miss being at the university."

Theodore had not wanted an expensive study, but Habiba finally wore down his objections, insisting that he deserved the best. She continued her decorations with a warm rug, an armchair, and such manifestations of a woman's touch as pottery, soapstones, and plants that she felt would complement the darker, more somber essence of leather and wood. "In this room, you should not only be able to write, but you should have pleasant dreams in these unpleasant times," she said to a bemused Theodore.

The only sad point about the new place was the unexpected death of the parrot that was responsible for bringing Theodore and Habiba together. The bird was almost thirty, a mature age for an African gray, but it could have gone on living a few more years, dazzling the household with its mimicry. Sadly, unable to adjust to a new environment with too many noisy birds that had formed the habit of perching on his cage and pecking at him, the bird simply gave up the ghost. Habiba, heartbroken, went around for days imagining she was hearing the parrot mimicking. Everywhere she turned, it was as if the bird were there, taking her back to those days of her unbridled escapades with men, before she met the philosopher. She thought she might hear it forever, but after a while the voice stopped talking to her, and she decided to get another bird. But she did not need to, because the house was soon filled with the noises of wild parrots along with numerous other species of birds, whose names she was trying to learn from a book on birds that she had bought. She got Theodore to build feeders for them on the verandah; then, after they had lost their fear of humans, she watched as they came to the jasmine trellis to sing. Very soon the house was transformed into a magical aviary, and Habiba had never felt so wanted as when Theodore Iskander told her she had succeeded in doing what the first pioneering woman, Jeanette Cromantine, had done for her brooding husband: making a pleasant home for him.

"You are quite a woman," he said.

In addition to the singing birds, the house was soon saturated with the fragrant odors of wildflowers. Habiba was allergic to many of them, but she controlled her discomfort with natural vitamins and guava leaves, which Irene insisted were more potent than folic acid and any antihistamines you could get at the pharmacies.

"Those things are bad for your system, child; they foul it up and kill you before your time."

The natural vitamins did Habiba some good; the pallor of her cheeks soon turned rosy, healthier than the color of most Corals. She went back to decorating the house, draped the windows in soft burgundy, and lined the living room walls with ceremonial Bambara and Dogon masks. With a glint of mischief in her eyes, thinking of how she liked to inspire her lover, she installed Chinese lamps in the bedrooms and hung brilliant, elaborate tapestries on the walls. Finally, thinking that a man needs to have a few things of his own choosing in his den, she gave Theodore enough money so that he could collect paintings by young, starving artists who badly needed patrons.

"What a woman you are!" he said to her one day. "And to think that some of my friends thought you were a lowlife woman with no taste, unfit for a philosopher, when I started going out with you."

"The only thing lowlife about me was that before I met you, I had not yet found the right man to love, and who in turn would love me for what I am. Those stuck-up academics and money-throwing politicians were too dumb to try to wean me away from my lustfulness. Besides, they lacked the gift of patience."

When he was restless in the house, Theodore Iskander would sometimes go for long walks on the nearby beach, depending on how far his limp would take him. That was how one day, after walking over a mile, he came to the black rocks where he used to take Habiba when she was distressed over how she had treated the albino. Absentmindedly he walked for about another mile, whistling a tune, lost to all around him, until he discovered some cormorants, rare in that part of the world, nesting near some gorse bushes. The moment was magical: he watched the birds feeding their ravenous chicks while the waves rose tempestuously, making him forget about the state of the country. When he was back in the house, he realized he had lost some of the tiredness in his bones. The unexplained depression of recent weeks was gone.

He was approaching fifty and was looking forward, in the peace and quiet of that beautiful house, to writing his book, while enjoying being a father. When he was not engaged in his writing, he read extensively from the great classics to Yeama, taught her how to fly kites and play chess, and was surprised to find that she was interested in the workings of the internal combustion engine.

"Since you don't have a son," she said one evening when he was changing the spark plugs in his car, "you might as well teach me."

"Girls are just as good at scientific projects these days," he reminded her.

"But not all fathers think like you."

He was proud that his child thought he was liberated from traditional norms.

Now that Yeama was old enough to appreciate what he had been working on, she helped him throw out the academic papers he had embarked on at the university with an eye to promotion.

"I think you would enjoy writing the book about my great ancestor," Yeama said, recalling the details of the poet's life that Irene had told her on those evening when they sat on a rock watching the flow of the river.

With a passion he had not known he possessed, Theodore Iskander began to delve into the outlandish details of the poet's life: the breezy bohemianism of his childhood, his contempt for the colonial regime, and his numerous romances. Deeply impressed by the poet's nationalist fervor, Theodore Iskander finally found the peace that teaching had not given him in recreating the period of that illustrious son of Malagueta, helped by hours of listening to music. Because of the fascination of most Malaguetans for things foreign, Theodore had always found it difficult to acquire recorded African music. It was one of the great conundrums about life in Malagueta: almost as if they were ashamed of being black, the disk jockeys had to be begged to play African music in the bars—the expensive ones, that is. It was crazy.

The radio stations were just as bad, spinning cheap disco music, real trash from other parts of the world. Theodore Iskander had long ago stopped listening, especially after a visit to Germany, of all places (Beethoven, are you listening?), where he had discovered the gorgeous melodies of the Malian albino Salif Keita, whom he considered a genius.

In spite of his limp, the only time Habiba Mouskuda had seen her lover lose all of his inhibitions, outside of their bedroom, was when he was dancing to the soaring lyricism of the great albino. On those rainy days, when he was listening to the soulful blues of Ali Farka Touré, it was evident to his mistress that the philosopher's study had become a den of sorcerers and musical poets.

Sometimes drawn into the spell, Habiba Mouskuda would coil up on the sofa to read the poems of her lover's illustrious ancestor. In the glare of the fire lit to keep out the damp, the curlicues of sandalwood incense would make the study magical, transporting her to the glorious time of the poet, just as her lover, in the effusive poems of Garbage, had finally discovered the spellbinding sorcerer's world of the vagabond sage Alusine Dunbar.

Surprisingly, of all the women that Theodore Iskander had dated, including that stuck-up Georgina Nandi-Thomas, Habiba Mouskuda had turned out to be the most avid reader. She spent days reading a vast array of books by female authors about the struggles of women. But what really tore her up and brought long lines of tears to her eyes was James Baldwin's *Another Country*. She felt that the life of Ada, the heroine in that book, was a metaphor for her own youthful indiscretions of the heart. In the cozy atmosphere of the study, her reading of Garbage's poetry was very incisive, and she was prepared when her lover asked her to recite some stanzas by heart. She came up with the illuminating perspective that it was not only his revolutionary verses, written with a fantastic passion for Malagueta, that made him such a romantic figure, but his life being the stuff of legend, something she could not imagine being repeated.

"I can see why all those women loved him. He was one hell of a word wizard, besides being a very virile man. I would have gone to bed with him myself had I been born during his time," she said with a glint of mischief in her eyes."

"You are doing that already," Theodore Iskander replied, "by reading his erotic verses."

"But I prefer you, because you are also a poet at heart, and remember I had to fight off some tough competition to get you."

There was no mistaking the seductive tone of her voice after she had succeeded in getting him to take a break from his writing. Using her allure, she would begin a song to inspire his soul:

> Fire, fire, fire, ma baby dey come.
> I want to see ma lovin' boy,
> Lovin' boy I want to see,
> Fire, fire, fire, ma baby dey come.

In the irresistible aura of her presence he felt something more glorious than the warmth in the room. Lost in another sphere, mystified by the dreamworld of the poet magnified in the enticing irises in Habiba's eyes, he did not resist as she stretched her arms out to him, and he came to the couch, this lucky man, to be seduced in the poetry of the never-ending rhythm of their river-inspired music.

CHAPTER FORTY-TWO

Second Canto of the Mermaid

WITH SO much money spent preparing for it, Tankor Satani's Versailles-like convention was an unqualified success. The glittering hall of the Convention Center overlooking the ocean was refurbished, there was a new five-star hotel on the splendidly rugged coast to house the legions of journalists expected, and all the broken-down monuments were restored to their colonial elegance. The presidential palace had a new gloss, its ornate ballroom glistening like newly polished silver, so that the old man could feel very proud when entertaining his guests. To the disbelief of its citizens, Malagueta's erratic electricity stayed on twenty-four hours a day, and in the usually neglected botanical garden, now whitewashed in time for the convention, there were new beds of flowers blooming.

On the first morning of the convention, in the presence of fifty-five heads of heads of state or their representatives, three Christian ministers and three Moslem clerics, dressed in the splendid robes of their faiths and solemnly invoking their gods, performed the ceremony that Tankor Satani had dreamed of since that morning when the ghost of Henri Christophe first appeared to him to tell him to "finish my work that was aborted by that damn Napoleon." Church bells tolled across the country, drums and gongs thundered in the courtyard of the mosques, and Malagueta's small fleet of helicopter gunships began a dramatic flyover at precisely the same time that the sirens of the ships anchored off the coast let out a bellow the likes of which had never been heard before in the town. "Emperor Tankor Satani!" the clerics proclaimed as they placed the gold crown on the president's head.

"Let there be peace in the region," Tankor Satani told his guests in his maiden speech as emperor.

Later, in order of rank—emperors first, presidents second, prime ministers and military leaders last—they all signed a declaration establishing free trade in the subregion and canceled all visa regulations, sending a strong message to the Western nations that small African nations were tired of the unjust international trading system and that they were demanding a fairer price for their produce.

The most beautiful pageant of masqueraders ever to appear in Malagueta came out to wish Tankor Satani well after the coronation. Back at State House, still wearing his golden crown, he saw the fabulous *agogo* dancers choking up the triumphant arches on Independence Avenue as they made their way to the gates of his official residence. Five years earlier, in one of his Byzantine moods, he had banned all masquerades, worried that his enemies would turn the boisterous street revelry into an occasion for demonstrations against him. Nevertheless, masquerades still occasionally took place, and given how mysterious some of those cults were, his police had not dared go near them for fear they might wake up in the middle of the night with vipers and scorpions in their beds. Tankor had only recently lifted the ban for the convention and had not really expected such grandeur in his honor as he stood on the balcony, the evening sun radiating through the flaming trees.

A small wind was whirring around the flagpoles of the many nations represented at the convention; the Tomb of the Unknown Soldier had been spruced up, and fresh flowers lay at the foot of the monument to the great national poet, Garbage Martins. As the wind blew gently on his face in that magical world of his happiness, Tankor realized that the most extraordinary skills had gone into creating the costumes worn by the masked devils that were leaping about like dervishes. Masqueraders with large ornamented mirrors on their heads that marked them out as members of a secret sect seldom seen on the streets of Malagueta performed an exotic dance. Dazzled by so much artistry, Tankor Satani tried to imagine how long it had taken the revelers to arrange the magenta medicinal bottles, cowbells, goat horns, and cowry shells on the animal carapaces stitched like humps to their backs and at the other adornments—onions, stalks of dry pepper, and swishes of animal tails—that completed the artistry.

Some of the masked devils had a "leader" who at intervals would dip a tassel of grass into an herbal medicinal bowl and apply it to the back of the devils, sending the mask dancers into a frenzy.

Urged on by their black mistresses, there was a group of Corals in the large crowd. Given their roly-poly girth, they were dripping with sweat in the steamy heat of the tropics but waving their fat hands all the same to make Tankor Satani notice them. Cheap rum, offered freely by the Corals, had made the crowd wild, and they danced to the music of the Raw Bonga King as if they had no bones in their bodies. Tankor Satani was enchanted by the spectacular garlands and papier-mâché masks from all corners of the country hoisted high in the air. His heart could not help being moved, especially after the merengue drummers started pounding out their mesmerizing rhythms behind masqueraders whose exotic names made demands on pronunciation: Talabis, Abansholas, Alikalis, Egungun, mammy queens, and fairies. But no masqueraders could match the party women in their large *ashobi* gowns and canvas slippers. Brilliant in their colorful outfits and rather drunk, they brought tears to Tankor Satani's eyes as they competed with the masked devils. He fished a white handkerchief out of his pocket and waved it happily at the women, astonished that, at least on this day, his past crimes had been forgotten.

Later that evening, in the lush gardens of the seaside Tropicana Hotel, from where the guests could see sharks bobbing up from the blue depths of the ocean, the waiters were busy serving mouth-watering dishes such as ox bladders cooked with pineapples and white wine, porcupine breasts, pepper alligator tongues, barracuda fillets, and chicken kebab. Jollof rice, *plasas*, couscous, almond and berry cakes, and spectacular chargers of salads from every region of the subcontinent completed the fare. The bill for beer, wines, and liquor—brandy, champagne, whiskey, and rum—could have bought a new scanning machine for the general hospital, but that could wait. Today, Malaguetans were celebrating the coronation of Tankor Satani.

That was why, when four days later, incredibly, fate dealt him a most unexpected blow, he felt, rightly, as though a poisonous snake had bitten him.

Given how he had just been crowned an emperor with the finest jewels in Malagueta, the autumn of his life had really turned out to be a cruel mistress.

"Life is a bitch!" he groaned, and would repeat that sentiment again and again.

On the previous evening, as he brought the convention to an end, he had seemed headed toward the immortality he had spent years dreaming about. Exhausted, determined that there should be no hitch in the conclusion, even in the smallest details, he had not responded to Jenebah Djallo's plea to come to her arms that night. It was a good precaution, because the color of her eyes had undergone a remarkable change while she was waiting for him, shimmering from violet to green, sometimes glowing with a magenta fire. All the same, she knew he could not resist her allure for long and that it was only a matter of time before he would come to her bed to celebrate the jewel in his crown. In preparation, she took an exceptionally long shower, combed out her tresses, and saturated the room with aromatic blossoms of fresh lavender. She spread rich silk damask on the bed, and her eyes were green as she perfumed her breasts with the enchanting aroma of patchouli, which she hoped would bring out the fire in the old leopard. Around midnight, surprised he had not yet come to bed, she drifted off to sleep and dreamed of a storm carrying the Xanadu into the middle of the ocean.

That unimaginable horror was far from Tankor Satani's mind as he said a brief adieu to his guests, kissing the cheeks of their wives or mistresses in the Moroccan villas and pressing small wrappings of gold dust and gem diamonds into their palms to thank them for coming to his coronation. Suffused with happiness, he left them to enjoy the view of the ocean and urged them to stroll through the enchanting gardens and what was left of the nearby forest teeming with exotic plant species. Soon he was back in Malombo House, his official residence, where he began to dictate what he thought was important for posterity about the convention to his new amanuensis, a timid former professor who, although proud, had the imagination of a donkey.

"This is what I want to be remembered for," the old man insisted, "and not for the fact that I built the Xanadu."

They had finished almost three pages of the report when Tankor Satani's ADC came into the room, looking as though he had won the national lottery. "Your Majesty, sir, you have to come to the balcony to see what is happening."

Driving home with Yeama from his regular weekly checkup after his gunshot wound, Theodore Iskander was trapped in his car around the same spot where, many years ago, there had been a traffic snarl. It was for the same reason. After not appearing in public for a long time, Tankor Satani's eunuchs had come out to give a performance under the giant cotton tree in praise of the old man, sending the bats into a panic. To the glee of a wild crowd, the eunuchs were repeating the erotic gyrations that had enthralled the French girls and sent a nun scrambling for the right pages of the Bible to pray that such a "pagan thing" would not torment the souls of the founders of the town buried at the foot of the tree.

"At least we got a chance to see the wonderful eunuchs," a jubilant youth cried.

Around midnight on his way back to the Xanadu, the jubilant rhythms of the dancers were still resounding in Tankor Satani's ears. His immortality seemed real; it was inconceivable that he could die after his spectacular triumph. Inspired by that illusion, when he was back in the castle, catching some fresh air on the verandah, he missed the foreboding signals that his reign was coming to an end. He failed to notice that the potted begonias and geraniums had withered, or that the smell of poisoned sea turtles, like the one that had pervaded Malagueta not too long ago, was now permeating the palace. It was as though he had lost his olfactory faculty. As he was very tired, he did not make love to his mistress that night. Early the next morning, when he was more or less half awake, he failed to read the second augury when the new set of Abyssinian roosters in the henhouse did not rouse him with their crowing at the same time that the muezzins were calling the faithful to prayers. A thick mist hung over Malagueta like a bad omen, the velvety green of the hills had turned gray, but Tankor was unaware, for he was still at the height of his grandeur, and his head was swollen with grandiloquent contentment. When eventually, late that night, he was ready to make love to his mistress, he drank a glass of brandy saturated with three raw eggs, to which he had also added crushed alligator peppers and bitter kola for extra potency. Proudly, after thumping his chest, he stood, all fire and iron, in the nakedness of his glory, holding his eight-inch protuberance for Jenebah to admire.

"Let us do it like gorillas," he said, fired up by her youthful allure.

The lavender in the bedroom had lost some of its scent, and the patchouli on Jenebah's breasts was less arousing than it had been on the previous evening. Nevertheless, Tankor Satani sailed with the fury of his newly crowned importance, smelling of the erotic cologne he had splashed on. Half an hour later, he derived a sweet heavenly pleasure when Jenebah's screams set the cockatoos hiccupping in their cages and mimicking her; it was as though it was a satyr that was making love to her as she did her best to respond to Tankor Satani's unrelenting thrusts. So intent was he on not ejaculating too soon that he failed to hear the throat-piercing yelp of the three-legged dog, sounding as if it was being attacked. It was midnight. With an eerie noise that had not been heard in a long time, the ghoulish vultures suddenly reappeared, flying in and out of the Xanadu, but not for Tankor to see them. The smell of turpentine coming from the dark room did not alert his senses to anything amiss, for he was in another world, on the high seas of passion, enjoying the immortality he had spent years dreaming about, the tiring girl doing her best to keep up with the bull on top of her. "You really are the son of the devil," Jenebah said.

But just when it appeared that the fury of his lovemaking was one long cyclonic tearing up of the poor girl's womb for the sins she might have committed against her previous lovers before she graduated to his bed, it was all over. From beyond that unknown world where fate is always waiting to surprise us, Tankor Satani momentarily saw the image of a lovely woman emerging out of an aquamarine ocean, waving to him. Then, as though he had been shot, he heard his lower vertebrae collapsing. His face began to lose its human form, until he looked like a wild beast with fearsome eyes; like Satan.

Jenebah was not the least terrified of the metamorphosis. Smiling, she did not think that Tankor was going to die on top of her and did not show the slightest surprise when his lips began to spread like two patulous slabs of flesh. She was as calm as an executioner who had performed many hangings, and when Tankor Satani tried to move his damaged lips, she laughed with the satisfaction that what had just happened was what she had prayed for all along, from the first day she came to the Xanadu: to bring Tankor Satani completely under her power.

"Look at you," she said, smiling at the wreckage on the bed. "My wild boar has finally been tamed!"

CHAPTER FORTY-THREE

A Little Matter of Conscience

IRENE HAD not only served as an accoucheuse on the day Yeama was born but was determined to have a small say in the rearing of the child. "Ah got to teach her 'bout her family and de old ways before ah die."

Most nights when Yeama slept in her grandmother's room, she was regaled with the details of that genealogy. Like her father, she was dark, but she had Habiba's long, wavy tresses and oval face. It was from Irene that Yeama first heard the stories about the presence of a spirit in the river and about how it could be elusive, generous, but, when provoked, vengeful. "Dat's why de river so sacred child. Remember dat."

Patiently, she tried to explain to Yeama the cryptic world inhabited by sprites and djinns, and insisted that devils were not a figment of the imagination.

"Dey all alive, like real people; but de face of de real debul is something no one has seen. You are innocent, so de debul go come to you one day."

Some evenings, Irene and Yeama would be seen sitting on one of the large, flat rocks near the river. It was then that an indescribable serenity would radiate from the old woman's face, and it was easy to surmise that this grandchild with the blood of the Corals in her was probably part of God's overdue reward for Irene's days spent in another river doing the Corals' laundry. She had never looked so content with life, especially when, along with Yeama, Tiger was there.

Unlike Theodore Iskander, Habiba Mouskuda was not really happy. It had nothing to do with those ghosts of her lovers or her dead albino son. Using her instinct, Irene was quick to discern that something serious had finally assailed Habiba. She chose the right time, when her son was building sandcastles on the beach with Yeama and the two women were slicing avocados for dinner, to reach out to Habiba about her problem.

"You are thinking about de other woman, right?"

Startled by Irene's clairvoyance, the malatta nodded. "That business about whether Hawanatu Gomba had a hand in the birth of my albino has always been with me, but not in the way you think. She had nothing to do with it, but I was too blind to know that in those days."

"We all make snap judgments when we are young, child. Look at me; ah couldn't stand you, but now you are a blessing in my old age, so do not take any bad heart business to God. Go to church and beg his forgiveness."

"I have been thinking about going to see Hawanatu," the malatta said. After five years in exile in Bassa, Hawanatu Gomba had quietly returned to Malagueta to prepare for when Gabriel Ananias could come, as soon as he felt safe enough.

Stunned by her daughter-in-law's words, Irene nicked her finger with her knife. It was not what she had been expecting Habiba Mouskuda to say, but she said it with such sincerity that Irene had no doubt she had been thinking about this for a long time. The incredible lengths to which Habiba had gone to make those around her happy were perhaps the best proof for Irene that the mysteries of God, when they involved separating the damned from the healers, were hard to fathom. She marveled at the transformation of this daughter of the Corals and thanked God she was not too old to learn from her. She was ready to admit that you can't judge based on its parentage what a child would turn out to be. Finding it almost incredible that she should be thinking along these lines, Irene wondered whether Hawanatu Gomba, her first choice for Theodore, would have turned out to be so humble, bearing in mind that it was only after one had suffered that one could talk about the wholeness of life. If she were to die tomorrow, she felt she could do so happily.

She was not one for the gestures of hugging and kissing other adults, but with a grand sweep of her arms she squeezed the malatta to her breasts. "You have a good heart," the old woman said sincerely. "But let me go with you when you are ready to visit Hawanatu."

"No, Mama. It is a matter of conscience, and I must clear it alone."

CHAPTER FORTY-FOUR

An Amazing Gift!

PALLO HAD not performed with the other eunuchs during their appearance under the cotton tree to celebrate Tankor Satani's coronation. After his marvelous discovery of a cure for impotence, which no one other than Tankor knew about, the sorcerer had turned his back on any erotic public displays. Recently, he had moved into the bungalow that Habiba Mouskuda had built for him on her property, but he still had a room in a private wing of the Xanadu, and had been there during the entire period of the convention, after Tankor Satani had told him he valued his sorcery more than ever at this time when he was about to be crowned an emperor.

"Many of the guests have their own sorcerers and do not wish me well, my friend. So I need you to keep an eye on them."

On the night that Tankor Satani had his stroke, Pallo had not had any difficulty foretelling it. For two weeks he had been trying to get a large boil on his groin to ripen so that he could lance it. He applied a magical potion of palm oil, dead beetles, and camwood, but it did not work. Then, in the middle of the night, he felt pus running down his leg.

"The mangy dog has killed the leopard!" he exclaimed.

While finally relieved of his torment, he had discerned that a terrible disaster had happened in the Xanadu. He came out very early in the morning and was not surprised that the hieroglyphs in the clouds merely confirmed his suspicion.

"When it comes to our actions, God can see everything."

He walked through the newly tended gardens and saw the three-legged dog lying under a guava tree, but he did not have to consult his talismanic beads to figure out what had happened to the president. The smell of fresh blood had attracted some voracious red ants to the dead animal, and they were eating its eyes; flies were buzzing around its mouth, and its tail was splintered into fragments of cartilage, as though a hammer blow had smashed it. Even someone as familiar with the hand of tragedy as the eunuch could not recall seeing anything looking so horrible in death, except the drowned son of the president.

"Poor dog," he said. "What a tragedy it is to die for his master's crimes!" Then, his lips quivering, he began to work his worry beads and went back to his room muttering one of the great adages of the Sufi mystic Abboud of Omdurman: "To be old is to have less time before you and more mistakes behind you."

Soon he was in the presidential suite and almost tripped on the carpet in the hallway on his way to Tankor's bedroom. He had brought his goatskin bag, in which he kept the curling stone and other miscellanea of his art. Other than Jenebah Djallo, he was the only one allowed direct access to Tankor Satani's private chambers, so he breezed unchecked into the bedroom, where he was immediately assailed by the smell of frangipani, as though all the dead souls with a bone to pick with Tankor Satani had finally turned up to mock him in his agony.

Dumbstruck by the sight of the clearly paralyzed president, Pallo shook his head over the crimes he knew Tankor Satani had committed. Yet those crimes, terrible as they were to him, were dwarfed by the willful expenditure of the coronation.

"Even kings are weak," he mused, "but God has no patience with their arrogance."

Pallo's lips were still quivering as he went to a verandah and raised his eyes to the sky in search of prophesies in the stars about the future of the president. In the constellations, he saw that all the things that had been foretold about the future of Malagueta by that vagabond mystic Alusine Dunbar three hundred and fifty years earlier always came to pass, especially that its leaders would be terrible and that the lure of diamonds would bring disaster to the area. He pitied the broken man lying on the bed.

The Capacity to Walk on Water

Considering that she had just watched Tankor Satani suffer a massive stroke, Jenebah Djallo's composure shocked the eunuch. She had been expecting him, and contrary to what he might think of her, his presence, grave and dignified in a splendid white Moslem gown, suddenly brought back images of her childhood. She thought of those evenings in her village on the Fouta Djallon Mountains, when her father had tried to teach her and her siblings about the arcane mysteries of alchemy and about the mystics and dervishes of the Moslem world, lessons that Jenebah had treasured and had used with lesser effect on other men. However, given the devastating nature of her beauty, before she was even fifteen she had stubbornly refused to be confined in her father's or anybody else's cloister. The dazzling lights and golden promises of Malagueta had beckoned her away from his hearth until eventually, she arrived, ripened, wise, and cunning, in the Xanadu. When she thought about how the dervishes of the Moslem world always portrayed women, and of what had just happened to Tankor Satani, she came to a most startling reappraisal: the Sultan never really understood Scheherazade.

"She was not a sex kitten," Jenebah thought, "but a woman with a first-class brain, and she must have inspired me to keep this old fool dreaming for so long."

Pallo watched Jenebah smiling enigmatically, before he examined Tankor Satani. In stunned admiration he said: "Woman, you have succeeded where sorcery and coups have failed!"

On the second most important night of his life, just after he had been crowned with the jewel of his long summer and thought he had achieved the immortality he so desperately wished for, Tankor Satani had not only suffered a stroke that crippled his arm and leg but, as though to confirm that he had been born with the most incredible fate imaginable, it had left him with a most amazing gift: a permanent erection he was never going to use!

Amazed, the eunuch turned the president over on his back so that Jenebah Djallo could see his gift. But she did not show the slightest surprise, making the eunuch suspect that what she had been feeding the president about her ancestry was really hogwash. Looking at her eyes, which had changed from brown to green, Pallo thought he saw a mermaid in one of them.

"This is not the work of an ordinary woman," he challenged her, looking her straight in that eye.

When Jenebah replied, it was in the words of the Sufi mystic Rabia al-Adawiyya, crystalline in their purity.

"I have the capacity of walking on water." Then in her own words, she said, "And that is where a great fish is waiting for Tankor Satani."

Over the next three weeks, she watched as Tankor Satani writhed in pain from the absurdity of his permanent erection. She took all kinds of erotic liberties with him, such as bathing him in a tub of lukewarm water, guava leaves, dry sea sponges, alligator peppers, beeswax, crushed anthills, and particles of armadillo plates.

"This should bring down your erection," she said one evening as she rubbed balsam oil on his penis before wrapping it with dried banana leaves. Playfully, she held the terror that had tamed her youthful ardor in bed, but there was not the slightest hint that she was reliving any of those memories of when she had felt its power in the presidential bed. Rather, she looked at Tankor Satani's eyes and wondered whether they would light up with the same eagerness as in the past, when she had enticed him with "Let us fuck, Mr. President. Life is not just about money and cars, as you should know, my sugar daddy." Sometimes a cruel look would creep into her face, but it would quickly disappear, as though she felt a momentary pity for the wreckage of the man now so completely in her power. At other times her mock endearments would allay Tankor Satani's suspicions that she was up to no good now that he was confined to a wheelchair. His right leg and arm were virtually useless and his speech was slurred, but Pallo came often to rub some goat fat or *ori* and termite balm mixed with monkey urine on his tongue, and after a while the old man regained some of his ability to speak.

"Don't dwell on your condition all day long," Jenebah said one evening. "Being sick is sometimes like making love; you can't feel the same emotions all the time."

One afternoon, when the sharp needles of the humid weather were not cruel to Tankor Satani's bones, Jenebah found enough strength in her small frame to wheel him into the breezy air of the verandah. "It is my duty to see that he is comfortable in his new condition," she told the guards, dismissing their help.

Except for the tempestuous waves of the ocean brimming with tuna, it was a windless afternoon in Malagueta. Mischief was glowing in Jenebah Djallo's eyes, and she had a leer on her lips thinking of when she had carried

Tankor Satani on the past oceans of lovemaking, rocking his canoe with her legs, going along with his delusion that she was giving him pleasure. Yet now that the turgidity of his sex was so painful and he could barely move his right arm and leg, she sat patiently listening to him as he recalled, sometimes with surprising lucidity, the summer rhapsodies in the drawing rooms of his former glory.

"That was when the Arab sheiks, Swiss bankers, diamond speculators, African presidents, Asian diplomats, and others used to come to Malagueta for fun," he said, as though thinking of another century.

"In the good old days," Jenebah smiled, "when you were really a man of the world!"

A week later, a low harmattan was blowing throughout Malagueta, and large ravens and flocks of egrets flew out of the path of its needles to nestle in the trees as the old man and Jenebah came into the verandah to drink some coffee. Anyone seeing them sitting there would have sworn they were an ordinary couple whose happiness had weathered many storms. After a while, he said he had drunk enough coffee and asked to be wheeled back to his room, He had started to drool, so she wiped his snot with his handkerchief, stroked his damaged hand, and told him to close his eyes and dream.

"I am going to tell you something very sweet," she said with a beautiful smile.

It was not the same immortal laurel that she had insincerely whispered in his ears to inspire him in the past, but was just as important for his well-being. Watching to see what kind of effect her words would have on him, she began to sweeten the bitter cup of his misfortune with the saccharin that the leaders of the neighboring countries had been so affected by his tragedy that they had each named a street for him.

"Really?" Tankor asked in disbelief.

"Yes. Even that highbrow poet Senghor," Jenebah insisted.

"How do you know he is a poet?" Tankor asked, clearly awed.

"I read his poem 'Femme nue, femme noire' in school," Jenebah said, smiling.

Boldly, with a panegyrist's tongue, she surprised the old man with a recitation, in exquisite French, of some lines from the Niger poet Oumarou Watta, a Fulani like her.

"Where did you learn to read?" the old man stammered. He had thought all along that she was an illiterate woman.

"In Bakazo, where I was born. But you see, like all men, all you were interested in was my body, which was fine with me."

Full of playful mischief, she sat in his lap, felt his jaws, and rubbed *ori* on them, then skillfully applied it all over his face so that he looked like one of the masqueraders that had been dancing for him on the "Avenue of his triumph."

"Why are you doing this?" he asked.

"For the same reason that you kept me here; to help you die without too much shame," she said, and began to undress him for bed.

CHAPTER FORTY-FIVE

What Is Left of This Life after Those Sweet Days?

TANKOR SATANI was not always in pain while confined to his wheelchair, but was always aware of his predicament, especially of his dependency on his mistress. Embarrassingly, he had to rely on her for simple rituals like drinking water, taking a bath, brushing his teeth, changing his clothes, and urinating; not to mention the big visit to the toilet. In his decrepitude he realized he was now an unwilling prisoner of a very young, mysterious woman, whom he now suspected of experimenting with sorcery. Sometimes, he found himself thinking about his wife, Sallay, who had once loved him without wiles. He imagined her growing old in the faraway village of her youth, living in perpetual mourning for their wastrel son. Tankor Satani was certain she had heard about his stroke, news of which he couldn't keep from leaking out; not when all the newspapers and radio stations in the subregion had been reporting it.

It had been a long time since he had heard any noise coming from the dark room. Not surprisingly, given their private tussle of wills, Tankor Satani began to suspect the hand of the mermaid behind his infirmity but was unwilling to grant her credit for it. Then one evening, as if to confirm his suspicion, he heard a noise in the dark room, the voice of the elusive mermaid ringing with the sound of the ocean in his head, as she mocked him for being so stupid. "Hello, Tankor," she said, and paused. "How did you like my gift to you?"

All night long he lay in terrible agitation, sweating profusely, as though in the latest stages of cerebral malaria. So intense was the fire in his head that he thought he was finally dying, when it was that his piercing screams were horrible. When Jenebah put a cold towel to his forehead, he felt calm, but rather than expressing any gratitude to her, he searched her eyes deeply for any knowledge pertaining to the mermaid but she gave him only a blank stare.

"Death is not ready for you yet, Your Majesty," she said calmly, "so stop thinking about it."

Tankor looked at his mistress as though he were suddenly privy to when death might come for him. But with the same concentration with which he had planned how to deal with his enemies in the past, he became allegorical and began to think about how his stroke was in fact emblematic of his and the country's fate. Both had risen and fallen in seventeen years. This was probably how fate had outlined his life: his dreams had been fulfilled and, mermaid or not, he was not yet dead. Moreover, as painful as it was, his permanent erection sometimes had the ludicrous effect of making him recall some of the fantastic details of his extraordinary life. One evening, when Jenebah was sitting near a pond in the garden, Tankor Satani began to drift into the thrilling lagoons of his past adventures. Deliriously he recalled the seductive blonde frauleins stripping for him in the orchid fragrance of the presidential suites in the expensive hotels, during his regular trips to Germany for his blood transfusions to keep him young. He saw the faces of the sensual Susu women, on his visits to neighboring Bakazo, slowing him down with "not so fast like a rooster, Monsieur Excellency, when you can do it as strongly as a bull." His navigation in the tempestuous waters of the giggling Asian girls who were brought to the Xanadu by the Korean businessmen made him smile, and he had not forgotten the profuse orgasms of the brazen Arab Aphrodites on the frenzied nights of his Tangiers holidays.

His wife had left him, it was true; but he could still remember the first happy days of their marriage, when he had been broke—God, those were good times! But the more he thought about his present condition the clearer it became to him that, after making him rich, the mermaid was really out to get him! He wondered whether Jenebah knew why he had been going to the dark room.

"Life is a bitch," he groaned once again, trying to work the mechanism of his wheelchair, as Jenebah appeared from the garden to lend a hand.

Surprisingly, his old foes did not express any glee when news of his stroke leaked out of the Xanadu. Taking time off from his biography of the poet Garbage, Theodore Iskander even went to a florist to order some flowers for the old man, and sent them with a card wishing him well.

"Dat is how to treat your enemies," Irene had encouraged her son. "With kindness."

Dr. Sidi Samura was giving an injection for malaria to a fretful child when he received the news of Tankor's tragedy from an old servant he had once treated, who was now a gardener at the Xanadu. In spite of their old quarrels, the doctor was no less generous in his sympathy for his old nemesis, whose period in office he considered the saddest example of lost opportunities, a time when great things could have happened in Malagueta had Tankor not been so diabolical.

"What a great tragedy it is that this nation has not been blessed with a leader since the death of Thomas Bookerman, over a hundred and fifty years ago," the doctor said sadly.

The old gardener was more philosophical about Tankor's tragedy and thought Jenebah Djallo had done the nation a great service by crippling the president.

"She fixed him good en proper for his sins," he said.

He was a very devout man, almost simple in his belief in the efficacies of the scriptures. For that reason he was determined to look ahead, past the envisaged presidential demise, in God's time, of course, to the return of hope and joy in Malagueta. Surely this was the passing of a bad season, that most people of Malagueta had been expecting, and they couldn't wait for Tankor Satani to be dead and rotting in his grave. Given how useless his children were, there was no chance of a dynasty.

One day, quite early in the morning, as Tankor Satani was sitting in his wheelchair on the verandah, watching the crows in the valley, the physiotherapist Elijah Rokel arrived to massage his damaged arm and leg. Laden with desert sand, the harmattan was blowing crisply over Malagueta and it was too cold for the old man to be out. To keep from shaking and coughing, and to hide his erection, he was draped in an old fur coat he had received as a present many years earlier from the president of Romania.

"What are you doing up so early, Your Majesty?" Elijah Rokel asked in disbelief, wrapping the coarse woolen lapels of the coat into a ruff around the president's neck.

"This is where I slept, my son. The bastards left me here," Tankor said, referring to his guards, who had gone off to watch a blue movie after Jenebah went to bed with a headache.

"What a life, Your Majesty!" the physiotherapist said, stunned.

"A dog's life, my son!"

Still Tankor continued to live with the illusion that he was the emperor-president, because the infirmities of old age had never precluded leaders on the continent from holding on to power. And he had every intention of continuing in office until he died, for which reason he dictated instructions for the various service chiefs to pledge their loyalties to him, aware that because of the lack of unity in their ranks they wouldn't dare sabotage his rule.

"I shall hang all of them," he said, to the amusement of his mistress.

The smell of eucalyptus, jasmine, chamomile, sweet basil, and the other magical ointments with which Pallo had been treating the president gave the presidential suite the air of a small infirmary. It contrasted with the brightness of the Venetian flowery drapes on the windows and the fresh, aromatic blossoms of get-well-soon gardenias, roses, and other flowers sent by the Corals. The odor of so many plants eventually proved too much for Jenebah, who lost her patience one day and threw out everything.

"No one is going to be poisoned by flowers here," she said.

In the past, when the speculators used to come to discuss diamond and other business deals with Tankor Satani, they had ignored Jenebah. During the coronation, a delegation led by the American Ambrose Giles had contributed generously in the hope of getting preferential treatment at a new mine, one hundred miles from Malagueta. Anticipating a huge profit, Ambrose Giles had shipped water pumps, tents, generators, and drilling machines from Philadelphia, all of which were now sitting at the quay. When news of Tankor's stroke reached him, he was at the Paradise Hotel on the beach, drinking heavily and barely able to finish his usual dinner of barracuda fillet as he thought about the legality of clearing the goods from the port now that Tankor was incapacitated.

"Goddamn it," Ambrose Giles said unhappily, chewing on his cigar and thinking that his best bet was to appeal to Jenebah Djallo. "Diamonds are not perishable raw materials, but they are worth a man's time."

"And so is treating Jenebah Djallo with respect," one of his colleagues said. "Everyone knows the old man probably confided more secrets to her than to that Coral Moustapha Ali-Bakr."

While waiting for a chance to see the old man before he had his stroke, Ambrose Giles and two of his colleagues had been picking up the Fullah whores at the Voodoo Bar on the beach. Like most tourists, they were unable to resist the alluring beauty of those women. A great fear suddenly gripped him then that he had been taking a chance with his life. Any of those women could be a sorceress, like Jenebah Djallo, with the power to finish off a man. "Stop picking them up," he advised his friends.

A week later, Jenebah Djallo was surprised when the blond, ruddy-cheeked American came to the Xanadu to pay her his respects.

"Madam," he said sheepishly, "your beauty is legendary, but so are the exploits of your people. Please let us know if there is anything we can do for you, as we are friends of Emperor Tankor Satani."

Jenebah Djallo eyed Ambrose Giles with the studied eyes of a wise woman before replying.

"Mister," she said condescendingly, "Osman dan Fodio, the great Fulani conqueror of much of northern Nigeria, never needed anyone to do anything for him. Since time immemorial, the Fulani people have been masters of their destiny."

Ambrose Giles left the Xanadu thinking he had met the most remarkable woman.

After several applications of a powerful herb by Pallo, Tankor Satani began to show signs of improvement, although the sorcerer conceded it was too early to say whether the old man would ever be able to walk again. "Dat is for God to determine; we sorcerers are merely his messengers."

Yet it was enough for Tankor Satani to feel that he was still alive after cheating death in the bed of his ravenous mistress. Unsure of when he would be back at the office, he summoned his prime minister, Enos Tanu, and issued some presidential fiats.

"I am still in charge, and I hope that General Dan Doggo will see to it that there is no coup," he told the prime minister in a surprisingly strong voice.

"God forbid that anything should happen to stop you returning to office, sir," the prime minister said.

As soon as he was gone, Jenebah surprised Tankor with the directness of her question. "Don't you think Enos Tanu will be plotting against you?

"No! I have a real fool in the army commander; he won't go along with that serpent."

Good-natured, big, sunny, unassuming, with a voracious appetite for women, General Soriba Dan Doggo was Tankor Satani's dependable military chief. Over the years, people had formed one opinion about him: that if Tankor Satani asked him to jump out of a window, he would not only have been too glad to comply, but would have replied with glee, "Which one, Excellency?"

Putting aside a brief stint in the Congo during the tragically short reign of Patrick Lumumba, the general had never fought in a war. He had risen through the ranks of the army by virtue of his obsequiousness and being from the same region as Tankor Satani. Yet even those who found him idiotic would readily concede the general was a nice man. Enos Tanu's loathing for him was vitriolic, but the general otherwise seemed to have few enemies.

Long before Tankor Satani collapsed on Jenebah Djallo's chest, the general and the prime Minister had been locked in a silent to-the-finish struggle for the succession. And although it was Enos Tanu who received a presidential order to run the nation temporarily, it was General Dan Doggo who sent his troops to guard the hillside road leading to the Xanadu, with orders that the prime minister should not be allowed through without notice. That stealth was quickly noted by his archenemy, whose Marabout advised him that in all likelihood it would be a takeover of the official palace and not the Xanadu that would demonstrate who was the real successor. "Master, dis is big fight between you and de soja man, but ah go try to help you," the Marabout said.

The whimsical game continued as the general and the prime minister kept their ears tuned to any news of Tankor Satani's condition that Jenebah might release from the palace. Always quick to seize a situation that might be advantageous to them, the Corals sent delegations to pledge their loyalty to both men. And in what could only be described as a masterpiece of theatrical burlesque, General Dan Doggo started a brazen courtship of Jenebah Djallo, thinking that now that she had lost the vigor of one powerful lover she would be grateful for the chance to move to his bed.

"Anything you say, General," she replied calmly. "I like men with power."

He was greatly underestimating her, just as Tankor Satani had done. Although she had not been allowed into the dark room, her smiles sometimes suggested knowledge of what was kept there. Moreover, Tankor Satani would have been shocked to learn that she was not unaware of why the chimerical vultures had been attacking the Xanadu, and that when they came silently at night to the house she could see them, borne by the fury of those untimely dead men, and had been encouraging them.

Tankor Satani's erection was sometimes so unbearable he thought he would go crazy. Using all the skills known to sorcerers, Pallo had been making quick nightly visits to the nearby forest in search of new herbs to try to bring down the tumescence, but his most elaborate cure was to write copious Islamic verses on a slate, which he would then wash with water in a bowl containing some herbs, giving the potion to the old man. "Drink this," he said, "as everything must be tried to help you."

Inspired by the voices of some fleeting dervishes he could barely decipher in the night, Pallo went into a frenzied spell and chanted arcane tunes as he whipped the monstrous erection with a horsetail to bring it down. Just in case ice cubes might do the trick, he rubbed some on it. When that failed, he went back to the proven efficacy of sorcery. He ate some cassava leaves and spat his phlegm on the majestic phallus, but nothing could slacken the turgidity. The irony was not lost on the eunuch. Whereas a vicious Mauritanian Arab had deprived him of his own manhood and left him with no desire for women, he had other consolations in life. But this man, the president-emperor for life, had been given the largest erection conceivable, and his crippled arm and leg would not allow him to enjoy it!

"Man who wants to challenge God, go make mistake in life," the eunuch decided.

Trying to find some anodyne other than that offered by his eunuch, Tankor Satani finally decided that what he needed was to be out in the open, sitting in the sun, in the hope that exposing the monster to the elements might do the trick. Consequently, one afternoon he wheeled himself into the enormous hallway of the Xanadu, pushing his bemused mistress and guards out of the way as he headed for the door leading to one of the gardens. He had not played with Samson the chimp in a long time. Like him, the animal had entered the autumn of his life; sad, stripped of his dignity, he would pelt the guards with his shit when they disturbed him. That was what the president would really like to do now: throw his shit on those responsible for his embarrassing condition. He really needed to talk to Samson about the unbearable weight of solitude. But as he labored down the hallway, straining his back in this foolish endeavor, something about the walls suddenly caught his attention. If he needed any proof that he was on his way out, thought of as dead or incapable of ruling, it was there on those walls. Just looking at them brought horror to his heart.

On those walls, where not so long ago, showing how vain he was in his inestimable power and glory, his gilded portrait used to hang, there was nothing! Not a single presidential portrait, no gilded mirrors or tapestry!

"I am not dead yet!" he raged, looking to his mistress for an explanation.

"It is your guards, Excellency," she said ruefully. "They have been selling off some of your legacy. Or, as we say in Bakazo, what is left of your sweet life."

Book Three

Paradise, Bad News, the Houris, and a Turquoise Ocean

CHAPTER FORTY-SIX

This Island Now

MOUSTAPHA ALI-BAKR was out of Malagueta during the coronation. Although he was Tankor Satani's right-hand man, the Coral knew when prudence was called for, such as not being seen too much in public when Tankor was hosting his foreign African guests. It wasn't too long ago that the students had rioted against Tankor Satani, destroying property. During the riots all kinds of phantom enemies appeared in Moustapha Ali-Bakr's sleep. In one nightmare his son was hijacked by some of his employees, and in another an old woman he had fired as a cook threatened to turn him into a monkey. After dismissing sorcery all these years as black magic, he was suddenly afraid that the woman might possess some knowledge of it. Though he did not fare too badly during the riots, he was terrified of the premonitions in his dreams, and thought it prudent to replace his guards with men chosen from among the most fearsome warriors in the Boma district of the country. For greater assurance he brought in a new cache of arms, installed closed-circuit television in all of his properties, and began to spend long periods outside of Malagueta. Good communication in other countries would allow him to conduct his international business more efficiently, after all. Yet he had barely got over the thought of those phantoms when, during what had been a pleasant holiday, the even more shocking news about Tankor Satani's stroke reached him.

Before that, there had been bad news on another front for Moustapha Ali-Bakr: an oil crisis in the Middle East. Listening to the radio announcer, Moustapha trembled with rage thinking that it was his own Arab brothers who were partly responsible for the fact that he might have to revise the high profit he had hoped to derive from Tankor Satani's Versailles-like extravaganza. He had supplied much of the materials, equipment, food, and other necessities for the convention; now the bills had started coming in thick and fast for the German limousines, Cuban cigars, Italian marble tiles and golden bidets for the Moroccan villas, and the three hundred cases of Georgian champagne that, after being popped open, were left only partly drunk, since many of the old man's guests considered champagne a woman's drink, preferring whiskey. With the oil crisis cutting deeply into his profits, Moustapha Ali-Bakr realized he would be lucky even to break even, especially as many of the contractual agreements had been based on a stable oil market and the sale of diamonds.

Unraveling the knots in the agreements took some time and taxed the fastidious minds of the best Sicilian Mafia lawyers that Moustapha had brought in for that purpose. The legal obfuscation that Tankor Satani had entered into when he mortgaged Malagueta's future for his coronation was such that the lawyers marveled at the cunning of the Coral. The oil crisis was growing, and before the news of Tankor's stroke leaked out it did not take long for people to realize that things were now back to normal after the expensive coronation. The shops were now capacious spaces full of empty shelves, and the owners were charging the devil's price for the few items on sale. It was a nightmare, those long lines for gasoline snaking through Malagueta after the oil supply ran out. Unleashed by a new hunger, the winds of uncertainty began to blow ominously from morning to evening. But the biggest worry on people's minds, after the news about Tankor Satani's stroke finally began to circulate, was who would succeed the old man.

After living for so long in his shadow, being bullied by him, succumbing to his charm or devilishness, most Malaguetans could not think of Tankor not being there. To be able to live well, many of them had sometimes betrayed one another for his handouts; but with the first hint that he was not after all immortal, the realization that not even the best magician in the world could cure his stroke finally began to take hold.

For the Corals, the thought of his death was something too horrible to contemplate. During the riots, many of them had taken a cue from Moustapha Ali-Bakr and hurriedly closed their shops before the students brought their mayhem down the hill from the campus. As the crisis spread, those among the Corals who could afford the fares had sent their families home to Lebanon and put up their shutters. They had not forgotten, though it was many years ago, how Hawanatu Gomba had transformed herself into a menacing bird at night to frighten them. In truth, they had also done well during the coronation, having offered goods to the government and people for promissory notes, hoping, like Moustapha Ali-Bakr, to make a huge profit. Suddenly everything was turning out to be a mirage, and it was too much for the Corals. But they were businessmen, and somehow they had to recoup their losses. That was why they had raised their prices, though they knew it would infuriate the people.

Worried they might be poisoned, the Corals kept a close eye on their cooks, and they went to bed with their lights on, their illegal guns loaded. But they hardly slept, spending most nights in dread of all kinds of legerdemain by their servants, drivers, and washerwomen. However, more than their fear of the blacks, they felt betrayed by one of their own. Strangely, just when they needed his help to ease their anxiety, and as if the blacks had finally worked their terrible magic on them, their leader, Moustapha Ali-Bakr, was not in Malagueta.

He was two thousand miles away, vacationing in Cape Verde, where the Portuguese bandit Pedro Almerado used to water his ships on his way to the Americas during the hellish days of slavery. Unaware of what had happened to his friend in Malagueta, Moustapha Ali-Bakr was taking a respite from his many worries, especially about the oil crisis in the Middle East. He was really enjoying himself until he went against his own resolve not to read the international morning papers flown in from Europe or to make any calls back home. But when he opened the *International Herald Tribune* he came face to face with some disastrous news. It was the second day of his holiday, and he was sitting on the terrace of the hotel Quatro Sete Melo, which he had bought many years ago with money provided by Tankor Satani. It was a nice colonial building that peered out on an unruly stretch of the Atlantic lashed for six months by hurricane-driven winds, but in the pleasant climate of summer it was a favorite of tourists, mostly Senegalese, Scandinavians, and Portuguese.

On the first morning, some mournful clouds had kept the other guests holed up their rooms, but Moustapha Ali-Bakr, undeterred, had risen early to go for a swim. Except for the seagulls, trumpeting loudly as they fed on fish brought to the rocks by a small tempest, the beach was deserted. He liked privacy—he owned his own little stretch of isolated beach in Malagueta—and surprisingly, for a man who was short and pudgy, he swam with the sublime grace of a dolphin. When he emerged from the water, he was covered in velvety sheets of seaweed that made him look like a mermaid. Soon after arriving on the island that morning, he had gone strolling, arm in arm, with Rufina Solomon, his favorite black mistress, on the cobblestone promenade named after the Guinea-Bissau nationalist hero Amilcar Cabral. Moustapha Ali-Bakr had never really been keen on black revolutionaries. In fact he blamed them for the fact that some Corals had been chased out of a few countries in the subregion. But bowing to the insistence of his mistress, they had spent time admiring the murals honoring the illustrious son, who had waged an unrelenting war against the Portuguese colonialists. Aware that they were tourists, a flower seller had come up to them, and to show how independent a woman she was, Rufina bought a bunch of roses and placed them in front of one of the murals. "From all the women in Malagueta who admire you," she said, blowing a kiss to the mural of the great man.

Her steps were brisk as she dragged the Coral to go shopping in the Mercado da Epifina, an open-air market famed for its good bargains in African jewelry and Brazilian art, and where marvelous species of caged parrots always sang lewd love ballads they had learned from the visiting sailors. When Moustapha and his mistress returned to their room, they had a short rest because the sun had risen over the island. Later, when the sun had gone down, they went to the most exquisite dinner that they would eat together: a menu of avocados, *acaraje* fritters, squids, grilled vermelho (red snapper), coconut rice, plantains, pawpaw, and lemon pie, finished off with *batidas*, a Brazilian cocktail. That they were dining under the dwarf palm trees on the hotel terrace restaurant made the meal all the more memorable and the evening enchanting.

A well-dressed man with a Middle Eastern profile and a mulatto woman sitting at a nearby table had been eyeing them for a while. The man, obviously recognizing Moustapha, smiled and came over to their table. "We are from the same country, and it is an honor to meet you here. And you too, Madam," he said with a courteous bow to Rufina.

"This is one of the best places to be if you do not want people sticking their noses in your business," Moustapha said in a cold voice that did not encourage the man to continue the conversation.

"That was not nice," Rufina rebuked Moustapha when the man had gone back to his table.

"We are here for holiday, not for business talk. Believe me, I know his type," Moustapha replied.

The ocean breeze had cooled the island a lot, and the sun was now a mild disk of glorious mauve, pink, and orange hanging low over the city, and Moustapha and Rufina felt they could see the uninhabited atolls about a mile away. The air drifting from the center of town smelled of the sweet aromas of recipes made by the street vendors, and the flamboyant trees in the gardens bristled with the chattering of the spectacular birds on the island.

"Let us take a walk on the beach," he said to Rufina; but a waiter brought them another round of *batidas*, courtesy of the bartender. He was a mulatto from Guinea-Bissau with a quiet demeanor, and his smile resembled that of the head of a novitiate. After many years of watching people, the bartender had learned to tell the difference between lovers on a secret tryst and married couples on a vacation. It was all a matter of how much they embraced. "Lovers smile and embrace because they want to savor every minute of their holiday, while married couples spend too much time arguing about the menu and their children."

As if to inspire Moustapha and Rufina, he put on "Sodade," the poignant love ballad about homesickness by the celebrated barefoot Cape Verdean diva Cesária Évora. Moved by the music, Rufina immediately began drumming her fingers on the table. If she and Moustapha were thinking about Malagueta at that moment, neither of them said anything. But with the synchronized movement of old lovers whose hearts had always responded to the music of their homeland, they went to their suite. The fire of the cocktails was coursing through their blood, and like two teenagers on their first adventure they smiled and opened the windows to let in the cool breeze. After hurrying out of their clothes, they made love until the sound of the sparrows had died down in the trees.

On the second day of their vacation, just before he broke his own resolve and read the paper, he was waiting for her to join him on the terrace.

He loved coming to this hotel with Rufina because she spoke Creole Portuguese with what he called a "charming" accent, an asset that he found useful for business. But her best claim to his heart was that she was a tall, cocoa-brown, svelte beauty of thirty, twenty-five years his junior, and definitely his favorite of the three black mistresses that he kept in Malagueta. Before he read the papers, a sultry voice speaking Creole Portuguese had announced on the bar radio that the afternoon weather forecast called for calm blue skies after the early morning clouds. Pleased, Moustapha Ali-Bakr thought he might go snorkeling later with Rufina, the only one of his mistresses who was a good swimmer. That was another reason why she was his favorite, for it was common knowledge that although Malagueta had some of the most beautiful beaches in the world, only a handful of its citizens could swim well. "It is as if they are all afraid of water spirits, unless they are Mammy Watas, which most men spend hours looking for to get rich," Moustapha once said to Rufina.

Over the years, he had developed a peculiar routine for reading his papers; starting with the sports pages, then going on to enjoy the comics and checking the business pages before scanning the front section. It was a formula that he found healthy, as he always had constipation if, after reading the front page first, it was all bad news. He drank his orange juice and ate his fried fish, tomatoes, and eggs. Just before he turned to the front page, he had a queasy feeling in his stomach and knew that he was about to read about something terrible.

Rufina Solomon arrived to join him for breakfast looking radiant in a skirt dotted with pictures of birds, a white blouse, and snakeskin slippers. She would never forget the anguish on her lover's face as she approached their table on the terrace. "What is wrong?" she asked.

"It is about Tankor Satani. He done suffer stroke."

"Is it bad?"

"Bad enough for me to feel sick," the Coral replied.

Even in the gentle morning ocean breeze, Moustapha felt as if his heart were roasting and moths were crawling in his stomach. His mouth tasted of vinegar, and he was at a loss to know what to do. But then he was roused, as always happened when disaster was hovering above him, by the thought of going to Mecca to pray, after first sending his mistress home because she was a Christian. He had already been to the holy place twice but felt he could repeat his acts of penance one or two more times. Except that, given the state of his mind, he had forgotten it was not the season for the hajj. So it was the Christian woman who, laying her fingers on his oven brow, came to his rescue. "The best thing to do is to remain here until we know how the old man's stroke will affect your business," she said.

He kissed her hands, and right away the worried knot of his brow relaxed and the moths stopped gnawing at his entrails. Like a man who had been told his cancer was not terminal, he began to think of the changes he would make in his lifestyle, starting with reducing his intake of high-cholesterol foods. He would cut down on his cigars and exercise a bit more to bring his weight down. For reasons he could not explain, he suddenly felt that although she was a kept woman, Rufina Solomon had always carried herself with incomparable dignity, and that unlike some of those shitty academics and politicians he had on his payroll, she did not live in awe of him. He thought that she must love him in her own way to put up with his occasional intemperate arrogance in public. Frightened by the thought that she might now leave him, he saw something in her eyes he had not noticed before: strength. It had been there all the time since they had started going out, but he had been unaware of it, or that she had probably anticipated this moment when he might need her, in the labyrinth of his nightmares, this side the end of an era.

For the rest of the day, although the bartender had been playing rapturous Congolese and Cape Verdean music all day long to entice the tourists out of their rooms, Moustapha Ali-Bakr stayed glued to his radio in a state of unrelieved tension. His worst fear was realized when a porter came to the door to inform him that a telegram had come from Malagueta.

"What is it?" his mistress asked.

"Rioting has broken out in Malagueta!"

After Tankor Satani's coronation, the Corals had increased the prices for basic goods. There were long queues for gasoline everywhere and major skirmishes at the pumps, with one death. In addition to attacking the shops of the Corals, the rioters had smashed the cars of government officials and raided the shops of their mistresses. Stones had been thrown at some government buildings, and Moustapha Ali-Bakr's mansion had narrowly escaped being torched because everyone knew it was he who was responsible for bringing in oil to Malagueta from the Middle East.

" Lord have mercy!" he cried.

The truth about his connection to that region was all about blood: his arrogant feeling, even though he tried not to let it show, that his Lebanese father's phallus was superior to his African mother's breasts, which had suckled him and eventually made him a rich man. Surprisingly, in his fifty-plus years, he had never thought of living in the Middle East, where he was really a nobody, that eternally volatile inferno of brutal tribal, religious warfare, in which children played with bombs and the hearts of Jews, Druzes, Christians, and Moslems were battlegrounds of hate and meanness not explained in whichever book of God they claimed to read. So his future, as he had always known, was really the one that Malagueta had made possible for him, and for his kind.

"Your worries will pass," Rufina said.

Now that his future seemed a bit bleak, Moustapha Ali-Bakr was grateful that he was with this black woman. He tried to convince himself that he had always treated her well. God knows he had never yelled at her, and the fear that he might become even more dependent on her brought a dramatic change to his view of their relationship; right there and then, he decided that when they were back in Malagueta, assuming there were no flames in the streets, he would build her a house, as Allah was his witness.

Rufina had always believed that the best medicine to conquer bouts of depression was to make love, especially if it was money that was responsible for the depression. With her usual elegance she started the delectable rite of undressing when they were back in their suite. "Don't think too much about things you cannot control," she said as she slipped out of her gown.

They tried to come together, but it was not with the gorgeous passion of the previous evening, when their lovemaking had been serenaded by the down-slurred whistles of "Oh, dear me" from the sparrows on the trees. Although the birds were back, urging them on, Moustapha Ali-Bakr was cold in his loins and shaking uncontrollably, as though he was experiencing the first signs of malaria, and there was a fire in his head.

Rufina knew otherwise. After her failed attempts to arouse him, she got out of bed and stood there splendidly naked, folding her blue-frilled chemise. Convinced that he could only make love when he was in control of the situation, not itself a bad thing in the past, she made a quiet resolution. Henceforth it was she who would choose the place and time to please him; so she settled for the reduced man that he had become. As she got back into bed with him, smiling the beautiful smile of a victorious woman, her magnificent breasts had never looked so alluring, and once again the birds started singing their "Oh, dear me."

CHAPTER FORTY-SEVEN

Of Mice and Men

INCREASINGLY, TANKOR Satani's thoughts were about the mermaid. Wondering what she might be planning next, how she might demonstrate her power, was horrible. But he also thought about his prime minister, Enos Tanu, and for good reason.

In his speech as well as his manners, Enos Tanu was not as polished as the president, and he lacked the raw charisma and bounteous gift of gab that had enabled Tankor Satani to disarm even the most implacable of his enemies. In fact, the image that the prime minister cut was that of a grumpy, middle-aged man, only passably attractive; not the sort for whom women would have gladly removed their kabaslots, or loosen their lappas or skirts. Except that, with the lure of his office as tantalizing bait, there was no telling what some uppity women might do behind closed doors. He probably would have told them to keep their panties on; he was not really interested in women.

He had been married to the same woman for over twenty-five years, a woman who was quite lovely, although the union did not appear blessed with happiness. He was deemed incorruptible, and not for him the hunger for houses, money, and cars, or an expensive wardrobe of beautifully colored shirts and designer suits. Unlike Tankor Satani, he did not have the swagger of a man of the times, and, as far as people could tell, he had only one house in the capital and another in his home province.

He pushed himself to extremes to distribute the party's munificence to the loyalists when he thought their support was lagging, always leaving them amazed at his energy for a man his age. Although not a lady's man like Tankor Satani, he was the most skilled at rallying the rural women behind the party. Yet, unbelievably, he was the least liked of the triumvirate of Enos Tanu, General Soriba Dan Doggo, and the secretary general of the party, Amadu Marampa, now vying to succeed the old man.

During those uncertain times after Tankor Satani's stroke, everyone felt that Enos Tanu had enough secrets on just about anyone to stir a hornet's nest. He was deeply feared. Ironically, it was General Dan Doggo, a man not known for cynicism, who came up with the best description of the prime minister. "People feel that in Tankor Satani we have the 'son of Satan.' I don't know about that. What I know is that we have an Agba Satani, the 'father of Satan,' in Enos Tanu."

Enos Tanu had long been preparing for his own future after Tankor Satani had died or gone into retirement. He felt his time was coming. Tankor Satani owed him a lot as someone the old man could point to as being more diabolical than he was. Much better still, Enos Tanu had served as his Pontius Pilate when the old man was debating whether he should hang Colonel Fillibo Mango and the other alleged insurrectionists.

"What say you about their guilt?" Tankor Satani had asked his prime minister.

"That is not for me to say, but if you don't execute them, think of the next ones who might want to overthrow you."

When, not too long after, the banker Alpha Samory had stood up to Tankor Satani, the president once again sought the advice of his prime minister.

A week after the banker was buried, and while Theodore Iskander and Dr. Sidi Samura were thinking of what to do about the "suicide," Enos Tanu went to the Xanadu to see the old man. Even before the unmarked car had driven up close to the gate, the guards immediately recognized him in his immaculate white outfit. As he was let through the gates, his smile, as usual, was cold, his face morose, and the guards knew right away that he had come on a vexing mission.

As soon as he was alone with Tankor Satani, he turned the full weight of his anger on the old man. "Now that you have let me do your dirty job, I hope you will be able to sleep, because I have been seeing his face every night."

Although Enos Tanu was regarded as a ruthless man who would not hesitate to liquidate his enemies, having the banker killed had not been his idea. The suspicion was that he had merely arranged the killing at the behest of Tankor Satani. Afterward, for a whole week, in an inner room of his house, he had prayed to Allah to forgive him. He tried to cover his hand in the deed by inventing those damaging details about the hidden trysts the banker was having with the wives of his underlings. There was talk of "illegal bank accounts" and of the banker having had a drinking problem, none of which was true.

Tankor Satani had trembled at the thought of having the banker killed, his public image already being damaged after Colonel Fillibo Mango and the other eight men were hanged. And he had not forgotten that the dead men repeatedly reappeared as vultures flying in and out of the Xanadu. Besides, he owed the banker a debt of gratitude. Tankor had never forgotten that before the ghost of Henri Christophe appeared to him in a dream and set him on his "immortal journey," times had been hard, especially in the days when he was broke and the judges were hounding him. It was the banker who had helped him out now and then with small loans. He respected the banker and was grateful to him. But a challenge to presidential authority was another matter.

"I can't kill someone who helped me during the rainy days of my life, so I leave it to you to decide his fate," Tankor Satani had ordered his prime minister.

After Tankor Satani's stroke, Enos Tanu was waiting for a call from the Xanadu. But first he had to deal with General Soriba Dan Doggo.

Always smiling, General Dan Doggo was the least intellectual in the triumvirate of men who might be president, but that did not really explain why Enos Tanu held him in such contempt. For eleven years, during cabinet meetings, the prime minister was aware that the general thought he was the devil's apprentice. The prime minister's own opinion of the genial general was that he was a tamed, faithful dog without a tongue to bark at anyone. When, without any provocation, Tankor Satani would insult the general, he would stare directly past the prime minister at the large map of the country pinned on the cabinet room wall. Or, smiling, he would fumble with the various medals on his chest.

"You are so stupid," Enos Tanu taunted him one day, testing how strong a challenge the general might pose to him in the foreseeable future, "Tankor Satani could squash you like a mouse."

Without losing his calm demeanor, General Dan Doggo looked the prime minister straight in the eye and shot back, "I know, Prime Minister; but have you forgotten what we say about a mouse? While it is gnawing at your soles, it is also breathing silently at them to keep you unaware of its true intentions." The prime minister felt a moment of terror. Never having credited the general with even a rabbit's little brain, Enos Tanu would have been surprised to learn that they had both had anguished nights after separately dispatching two bankers to their different exits. In the case of the general, no blood had been shed; all he had done was send his troops to surround the house of Gabriel Ananias, who did not even wait for Tankor Satani to pay for the house before he fled into exile, fearing the worst.

Great spasms of guilt had tormented General Dan Doggo's brain after that deed. Assailed by the belief that a man passes through life several times but has to make amends for his sins during his first life before he can experience the other lives, the general sought consolation in the two recipes best suited to his temperament: God and sex. He went regularly to church with a solemn air for a whole month, and his prayers were often long and rambling and accompanied by whale-like breathing, as if he had not yet reached the threshold of hard crimes but felt he might be in danger of doing so. To guard against that descent, he sought the forgiveness of the angels for what was after all not a terrible crime, as there had been no killing. He wrestled with the demons in his head, and even contemplated resigning from the army to become a man of the cloth. Observing how regularly the general was coming to church, the deacon, a genial man with gray, thinning hair and gentle eyes, decided to talk to him.

Unlike those in some other churches, this pastor was sincere in the duty of the Lord. He took General Dan Doggo's fat paws in his narrow hands after service and asked the general a forthright question. "Is anything bothering you, General, that you think might require a special prayer?"

General Dan Doggo paused for a while before answering. "It is not big enough to warrant special prayers, Reverend, because the Almighty already knows what a man is thinking."

"That may be true, my son," the pastor said understandingly. "But God is sometimes too busy to notice all of our sins. My house is always open if you need me. Have a good day."

Buoyed by that assurance, General Dan Doggo felt better for a time. But after a while he began to feel he had to be with someone besides his pastor or his wife. So he spent a whole week visiting his mistress, not exactly to talk about the pain in his heart, but to make love to her. Tita was not one to delve into the complications of politics and military honor in Malagueta, not when she was benefiting from that alliance. Besides, she liked the ample general, who, when he was not preoccupied with the "diabolical menace of Agba Satani," was good fun to be with. A woman could ask for no more from such a man.

The Last of the Mohicans

Amadu Marampa was the most liked of the triumvirate. His ready smile gave the impression of a man who went about life full of harmony in his soul and was not given to spite. Convinced he had nothing to fear from an assassin's bullet, he left his door always open to all callers, and took pride in the knowledge that he was perhaps the only one of Tankor Satani's ministers who could walk the streets alone in the dark hours of the devil without anyone bothering him. Such was his wide circle of friends that he was sure one of them would rush to his aid if he were attacked in a mix-up. He was a charming womanizer, and what he lacked in dedication to his work was amply made up for by his deep concern for people. He went to most funerals for the old-timers when they began to drop from the tree of life, and he, of all the ministers, was the one most likely to send a card to an old woman who had given money to the party during its bad years in opposition, or sent lunch money to him in his youth. At his best, he was everybody's favorite uncle, the only one seemingly not interested in succeeding the old man, which was not to say he did not have his supporters.

Asked one time by a friend whether he had thought of what might happen to him after Tankor Satani was gone, his reply exemplified his simple belief in fate. "We have seen today, but we do not know what tomorrow would be like." Content with his present condition, he went about his business always cheerful, and was only seen at the Xanadu when the old man was expecting him.

It was the low hours of the night in the Xanadu. Jenebah Djallo was fast asleep, and the place was very quiet for a change because for some time the chimerical vultures had not attacked the palace. Most important of all, Tankor Satani had not been assailed by the voice of the mermaid since she spoke to him soon after his stroke. For the first time since that tragedy, he found himself thinking about the three men he was certain were also thinking about him.

These Strange Birds

Working his worry beads on the terrace of the Quatro Sete Melo in Cape Verde, Moustapha Al-Bakr was feverishly thinking about how many months he would have to remain on the island before going to Mecca, and about which of the three men back home was going to be his next partner. For some unexplained reason—it was almost midnight, too late for them to be out hunting for carrion—nine vultures suddenly appeared on a nearby coconut tree. As they lowered their wings and turned to look at him, they seemed to be talking amongst themselves. Knowing he was not imagining things, he took a long, hard look at them. He had never liked vultures—their huge wingspan, their unbearable menace, that mystery in their eyes! Moreover, they ate carrion. He wondered what kind of birds they were, anyway, to be out that late.

CHAPTER FORTY-EIGHT

Three Million Dollars Lost, Just Like That

AFTER A siesta one afternoon, Tankor Satani felt so good, he hurled himself out of bed into his wheelchair and eventually made it onto his favorite verandah, where he was surprised to see Jenebah Djallo sharpening her teeth with a bone file.

"Why are you doing that?" Tankor Satani asked suspiciously.

"Don't worry, ole man," Jenebah replied with a smile. "They are too dull, and this is just in case I have to bite on something hard."

Tankor Satani experienced a deep instant of terror.

But in a lyrical voice Jenebah Djallo began to sing the same enigmatic songs about her childhood in Bakazo, embellishing them with assurances that no matter what might happen to him, even if his wretched children were to desert him, she would not pack up and leave him to die alone, "as though you have no one in the world to care for you, Excellency."

The moment was magical, one of the many they had been sharing lately, now that his injured pride at being cared for by this nymph was no longer a problem. Most of the time, except for the handful of guards keeping a discreet distance from them (except when they came to ask what should be done about Samson, whose excremental missiles were getting to be a problem), Tankor Satani and his nymph were left alone. That was when he began to teach her how to play cards and do the crossword puzzles in the newspapers.

At those times, thinking they were up to no good, the parrots would whistle lewd tunes that he had taught them. "Which one is whistling?" Tankor asked his mistress one afternoon.

"It is the Congolese gray, the same one I was talking to when we met at your birthday party," she said.

"That was a long time ago."

"And a lot of water has run under the bridge since then."

In an enchanting voice she continued to sing some more of those beautiful Fulani ballads for him, pastoral poems from that unnamed village where she claimed she had been born, though it could be found nowhere on the map of Bakazo. Her voice was so lyrical that he always asked for several repetitions. The songs had the desired effect on Tankor Satani, both on his soul and on his body, that there was less hint of the devil in his look in those days. He seemed at peace with himself, and, as though Pallo's sorcery had finally done the trick, his damaged lips had completely healed. Yet the mystery of why he couldn't get his erection down continued to bother him, and he wondered how tormenting it must be for satyrs to live always in a tumescent state. In the past month he had been sleeping quite peacefully, always in the same position, on his back, because of the discomfort of lying in any other position. With an amused smile but no hint of sarcasm in her voice, Jenebah would say hello to the phallic god. Some evenings, when the parrots were not mimicking them, the palace was so quiet that they could hear the deep baritone of the frogs in the nearby grass.

The Xanadu was now mostly empty. One day, to the shock of the handful of guards still loyal to the old man, Jenebah Djallo suddenly resumed her pastoral habit of walking through the hallway virtually naked, wearing only some beads round her waist, insisting that although she was not under a tamarind tree in the field milking her ancestral cows, away from the prying eyes of men, it was nonetheless a crime for a woman—especially one so divine—to imprison her breasts in a bra.

"It would be as though I should be ashamed of being so beautiful."

Although he could no longer make love to her, Tankor Satani readily agreed. "It is a pathological disease for a woman to be ashamed of her body, especially if a man derives great pleasure from looking at her."

She had also begun to talk about how she missed the sound of the ocean, of being near the sea lilies and the bulrushes in the rivers. In great detail, she narrated how she used to enjoy coming quietly up on the bathers, popping in and out of the ocean like a sea cow. As he had so often ridden her as though she were indeed a sea cow, she felt Tankor would have no objection to her fantasies. Yet, pained by his irreducible erection, Tankor Satani's mind in those days was miles away from the present.

It seemed as if their idyll would go on undisturbed forever, until General Soriba Dan Doggo arrived in his official green Mercedes-Benz one fateful morning with the air of a man who had just seen the face of the devil. It was a cool, pleasant morning. Tankor Satani had come out into the verandah, seemingly not caring about the cold. Lately he had been insisting, to Jenebah's surprise, on remaining on the large verandah with her until quite late, telling her that although he was happy now, very soon he might be losing the view of the congested town. Even for someone who had always ranted that not until he died would things change, it was obvious that old age coupled with the stroke were just too many reasons for him to go on believing he was immortal. Quietly he had been preparing for the unthinkable—the thought that the mermaid was about to claim her debt. And although he dreaded the conjecture of how he might die, he seemed reconciled to his fate.

Incredibly, for a man who had spent so many years in a mad pursuit of wealth, he had lately begun to give the impression that he was past worrying about what would happen to his treasured possessions of houses and cars after he was gone. He still had some diamonds hidden somewhere in the Xanadu, but was reconciled to the possibility that he might not live long enough to use them. In fact, ironically, now that the initial shock of his stroke was over, he was indifferent to the slow pilfering by some of his servants and guards, who had been stripping the Xanadu of its most valuable items, his outlandish collections of clothes, shoes, memorabilia, silverware, along with some not so valuable items.

"They are ungrateful sons of bitches," he lamented to Jenebah, "but it is all right."

In the autumn of his life, it had finally dawned on him that he was down to a handful of loyalists he could trust.

"That is in the nature of men," Jenebah said.

"They are like chameleons, always ready to change their colors for a new master," said Tankor Satani. "But it does not matter."

"What does not matter?" Jenebah asked, intrigued.

"The riddle in the sand."

Save Me from This Masquerade

Riddles were not on General Dan Doggo's mind the morning that he arrived unexpectedly at the Xanadu. Dismissing the startled guards, who had thrown themselves at attention, he breezed into the presidential quarters, panting like a long-distance runner on his way to the verandah.

"What is it, General, that makes you look as if you have just seen the ghost of my old amanuensis?" Tankor asked.

General Dan Doggo considered the reference to Colonel Fillibo Mango for a moment and dismissed it as frivolous. He was certain that once Tankor Satani knew why he had come, the president would stop all the tomfoolery with his mistress.

"Excuse me, Emperor, sir," he said, "but I wish to speak to you in private."

"You can speak to me right here," the president said. "There is nothing secret between me and my woman."

"So be it then, sir. I hate to be the bearer of bad news, but an army sergeant has just overthrown and killed your friend, President Kongoma of Bassa."

Tankor Satani froze in his wheelchair. In the dim light his face suddenly lost the peaceful resignation of the old man who had been enjoying some enchanting evenings with his mistress, waiting, it had seemed, for the right moment to surrender to his death without too much struggle, especially as she had promised him she would be there when it happened, holding his hand. An unblinking rage—one that would have killed anyone foolish enough to stare at its fire for too long—blazed in Tankor Satani's eyes, making Jenebah think that if Tankor Satani really had to choose between her and money, his idea of happiness was a fat bank account. It was there in the menacing eyes of a man experiencing a terrible tragedy that was tearing his guts, killing him. For the second time in less than a year, Jenebah Djallo was assailed by the feeling that the evil look on the president's face was really that of the devil.

General Dan Doggo wished he had not come with that piece of bad news, but it was his official duty. He too felt he had finally come face to face with the devil when Tankor Satani bellowed, "The bastard, he died with my three million dollars in diamonds!"

It was a staggering disclosure to General Dan Doggo, but he did not show the slightest sign of amazement. Rather, in a calm voice, he tried to pacify the old man with the caramel that he was still alive and could ameliorate his financial loss in spite of the shock occasioned by the death of his friend.

"It is not the end of the world for you, sir. You are still in command of all the resources in the country."

Tankor Satani was not appeased.

"You don't know how this one hurts me, General," he said, gripping the outstretched hands of the general for support. "Those diamonds were meant for my daughters, shameless harlots though they are."

General Dan Doggo's response was almost philosophical. "In the end, sir, it is clear that God is greater than the mightiest president or emperor."

"To hell with God," Tankor yelled.

Nonetheless, a week later he was in church in Bassa. It was the first time he had left the Xanadu since he suffered his stroke. He wore a loose gown to hide his perpetual erection and was propped up in his wheelchair. His entourage included General Dan Doggo and all the service chiefs, to prevent their staging a coup in his absence, and he had also brought three of the best doctors in town. When a small crowd saw the presidential cavalcade coming out of the palace, the irony was not lost on some people that the man now in the margin between life and death was on his way to mourn another leader.

The dead man was the great-great-grandson of freed slaves from North Carolina, so it was the American government that took charge of his funeral, after admonishing the new leader of Bassa for being callous. A few hours after the coup, his troops had tied up and then shot eighteen cabinet ministers on a naked stretch of beach. But after he had assured the Americans that he was not a communist and that their holdings in the country, particularly rubber, were quite safe, they decided to do business with him.

Surprisingly, in spite of his long friendship with her husband, Tankor Satani's condolences to the widow were cursory, almost miserly in spirit. His voice was barely audible, and although that was put down to his illness, it was really proof of how pained he was that he had lost such a vast sum of money in diamonds. As protocol demanded, Tankor Satani managed to go through the ceremony of viewing the coffin, uncomfortable as it was for him to be wheeled around with his enormously charged dick among the dignitaries in the National Cathedral. But he paid little attention to the vespers for the dead man and none at all to the embellished homage by the diplomats. Filled with a serpent's venom for the tasseled military band that had earlier played its mournful tunes for the dead man, Tankor Satani cringed when the goose-steeping barbarians of the reconstituted presidential guard came into the house of God to line up for their last respects to the assassinated president. But he was deeply moved when he turned around and saw the dead man's children trying to console their mother in the gossamer web of her grief, shielding her from the impetuous pressmen bent on getting an interview.

"What bastards," he groaned. "They have no shame."

Gabriel Ananias was at the funeral, sitting in the back pew dressed in the only good suit he still possessed and taking care not to be seen by either Tankor Satani or General Soriba Dan Doggo. Now that Hawanatu Gomba had returned to Malagueta, he was miserable in his solitary exile. Shocked at how decrepit his old nemesis looked, the former banker, ex-playboy, former disciple of a defrocked Irish priest could not help wishing that lightning would soon strike Tankor Satani dead and put an end to his exile.

It was not a forlorn hope, although at that moment Gabriel Ananias did not know how close he was to the mark. In that mournful crowd he forgot about his own tragic life for a while, wondering how Tankor Satani must be feeling about his friend soon to be fed to termites. He turned his head a few inches to where the old man was sitting, and saw a look in the old man's face as though Tankor would have liked to slap the puffy face of the new leader, for whom he felt a murderous contempt, if only he had not been confined to his wheelchair. Paralyzed, his pain too much for him to bear, Tankor Satani groaned softly: "*Jesus Christ, life is this drama, this travesty, that a pygmy sergeant, who was not even qualified to be a major domo yesterday, could brutally kill an elected president and then be recognized by the Americans because he is not a communist.*"

Having become able lately to read the old man's mind, General Dan Doggo was aware of his torment. He took his hand and whispered in his ear, "Don't worry, sir, nothing like this will happen to you while I am around."

The booming notes of the twenty-one-gun salute rang out against the setting sun to signal that, indeed, President Kongoma was being taken to join his ancestors. As soon as the service was over, General Dan Doggo rushed to wheel Tankor Satani out of the church, missing the lonely figure of Gabriel Ananias staring at him. One after the other the dark-suited diplomats rose from their seats with a mournful air, to engage in a little tête-à-tête about how to deal with the new situation. It was surreal. Solemnly, they went to shake the hand of the dead man's widow and assure her that their respective governments would do their best to look after her and the children. Each of them had known and dealt with the president for the greater part of four years and had admired his avuncular style, whether he was in his official regalia or entertaining them at barbecues on his ranch, when he would sing for them, in that dark, burnished cadence of his roots, some of the old blues of his childhood.

Concerned about U.S. interests on the Guinea Coast, the diplomats began, deeply, to lament the assassination. Besides being one of their own, the dead man had definitely been their right kind of leader for "stability and progress," until this tragic opera of African politics destroyed his life. It was not so much the brutal nature of his death that had put an end to their optimism about the region—they were aware of other brutal deaths in their own cities—rather, sadly, they were appalled that the one virtue they thought Africa would never lose—respect for old age—had been thrown aside by those young soldiers they now had to deal with, whether they liked it or not. The diplomats could have continued with their protestations of support for the dead man's widow forever, but they had urgent cables to dispatch to their home countries about the "dignity of the funeral."

Being in the sun had exacerbated Tankor Satani's condition, and when he was back in his guesthouse he sat on a bed mopping his brow. It was then that he heard the final rounds of the funereal cannons, and he had to summon all the restraint of his already wounded dignity not to say some unprintable things about those military barbarians.

An unbearable pain raged in his groin, and with his good hand he grabbed his dick and squeezed it hard, thinking he was going to die from that agony. He felt a savage anguish thinking that his mistress was probably at that moment naked and alluring, leading a young man into one of the rooms in the Xanadu, while he was at a funeral, sitting powerless in his wheelchair.

"Life is a bitch!" he said, as he was wont to do when in pain.

This was not how he had imagined the autumn of his life to be: a broken canoe battered by sea storms and pitied by people he would have liked to hang. At the funeral some women had whispered how old he looked as he sat there with a huge blanket thrown across his knees to hide his disgrace. But when he had got over his nightmare about what Jenebah might be up to in his absence, he realized that, while he could do without sex, he had always been a prisoner of a deeper need for the only beauty he had yearned for in all those years in power, just so that in old age he could feel comfortable in the warmth and luxury of that beauty.

"Give me back my three million dollars in diamonds and spare me this masquerade of a church service when I die!" he groaned.

CHAPTER FORTY-NINE

The Professor of Desire

IT WAS a very unhappy Tankor Satani who returned to Malagueta and was driven with a full contingent of guards, buglers, and dispatch outside riders back to the Xanadu, where General Dan Doggo said good-bye to him and wished him well. Later that night, as the general slept on his couch, where he had dozed off after drinking three shots of brandy to reduce the stress of traveling with an agitated president, he had a premonition.

He dreamed that his guardian angel had willed that he should succeed Tankor Satani. But when he woke up, there was still that disturbing feeling of guilt over how he had dispatched Gabriel Ananias into exile. As he took his bath, he felt very depressed, began to inveigh against his fate, and shocked his wife Monica with an unnecessary act of cruelty against their cat. After that night, he took to sleeping with a gun under his pillow, until she reminded him of the unforeseen hand of divine justice.

"If the avenging angels are ready for you, they will simply blow out your brains with an invisible gun."

He kept having the most bizarre dreams about being president. In one his installation was so perplexing it would have required two hours of divination by a Marabout to extrapolate some meaning from it. He was dancing like a midget to goombay music, which was strange considering he weighed almost 220 pounds and was having a difficult time keeping it that way. Rings of mauve fire surrounded him, and he heard the rattling of cowbells in his head. From a corner of the room, a man wearing a white mask, very tall and angular, suddenly appeared and waved a dead mouse at the general, laughing at him. When he woke up, terrified of that world of gnosis, General Dan Doggo felt lethargic, as if an invisible ogre had cast a spell over him. Considering the stiff competition he was facing from Enos Tanu, he had every reason to fear ogres.

All the same, General Dan Doggo was determined to maintain his sartorial bearing when he appeared in public, and decided not to consult a Marabout, at least not for now. Preoccupied with keeping law and order during those uncertain days of Tankor Satani's presidency, he tried to put the thought of his apotheosis completely out of his mind so as not to arouse any suspicion from Enos Tanu. Yet given his fastidious loyalty to the president, the thought of Enos Tanu becoming president was enough to produce goose pimples on the general. Finally he decided it was not sacrilegious to think that it had indeed been written in the heavens that he would one day exchange his green khaki uniform for a civilian suit, a transition for which he had been receiving lessons.

His tutor was Dr. Bemba Kelfala, an assistant professor of history with the roving eye of a Casanova but as poor as a Coptic novice. Usually he was so broke by the middle of the month that he had to rely on some form of charity from his wealthy students for cigarettes, besides the favors some of the coeds granted him in exchange for good grades. Most times his shoes were unpolished, and he wore the same shirt for days. Sometimes he had the aspect of a man who slept in his rumpled suits, and he smelled of stale musk, but his odor did not diminish the raw charm some women found attractive in him. Remarkably, given how paltry the contents of his kitchen and pockets were, he had resisted the seductive offers of Moustapha Ali-Bakr, not merely out of principle but because it was assumed he couldn't stand the crudity of the Coral. "I may be broke," the professor said, "but as they say here, respect is better than wealth."

Besides a lust for women, what General Dan Doggo and the professor had in common was a jolly-boy attitude to life that was not affected by their tribulations: they were two of a kind. One day, unable to resist the feeling that he was soon going to become president, and aware that he would need some advantageous tutorial for that estimable office, General Dan Doggo went to see the professor at the university up on the hill. As usual, the lights were out on the campus, rats were scampering out of their holes in the gutters, and the potholes almost broke the axles of the general's car. A palpable misery hung over this sadly neglected university campus; on this weekend, always a miserable time for the students, the only human activity was the lines of cars taking the coeds to their sugar daddies in town.

The professor was brilliant but lazy and was coming to the end of his tenth year in the same position. Many years ago, he had given up hope of any advancement in his career and was now doing odd consultancies offered by various agencies to bring in enough to buy beer and cigarettes. His spirits were a bit low at the moment, so it was not a good time for anyone to call. Unaware that his luck was about to change, his brain barely registered surprise when, for the first time ever, the green Mercedes of the general pulled into his compound.

The professor went out with a hurricane lamp to lead the soldier through the puddle in front of his digs. "What a surprise, General; sorry for the darkness, but you know how bad things are these days."

Although not a man accustomed to hardship, General Dan Doggo did not seem to mind the darkness, the damp smell, and the wretched conditions, or that his polished boots were smeared with mud. The only drink the professor had was some beer in his warm, disintegrating refrigerator, which exhaled a rank smell because of the severe brownouts. The general sat on a chair with some of its springs jutting through the upholstery, accepted a beer, and drank it slowly. Then he began to explain the reason for his visit.

"This is my reward for refusing to compromise my integrity," the professor said enthusiastically.

"Well, as we say here," the general reminded him, "a patient dog eats the fattest bone."

They started with the fundamentals. "You have to watch out for the very passionate admirers, General, especially the women. There will be many of them if things go well for you."

It was not without reason that, although he was always disheveled and sometimes stank like rotten onions, to the point of embarrassment, Dr. Kelfala's students still regarded him as a good professor and would have defended him against any unwarranted sanction by his superiors. In a week's time he had the general eating out of his hands.

"The first principle in military leadership is to master Shaka's tactics during his campaign to build the great Zulu nation," he told the attentive general.

"I am with you on that one," the general said. "But keep it simple."

"In politics," the professor continued, "especially in Africa, General, everything is about timing. It depends on cunning and stealth far more than on the best armored divisions to defend you."

There were a few trusted and exciting students that the professor was in the habit of having over. No sex was traded during those evenings, and the intellectual discourse, although not always sublime, was good for the spirits of all concerned. With the students as audience, the professor went into action, putting the general through the torturous task of reading a simple speech in public. "Try to image what you will have to face when you become president, General."

Anticipating that day, the professor concentrated his first lessons on getting the general to pronounce the treacherous consonants, stressing where he should modulate his voice, how to stress his vowels, and when to pause, ensuring that the general did not sound as though he had hot charcoals in his mouth when he spoke. He instructed him on how to deal with the slanderous press, and went over the various details of leadership until he thought the general was on top of the task. He gave him advice on how to respond to enquiries from abroad about all matters pertaining to the dwindling diamond reserves, the most troublesome aspect of that business being the pestilential foreign journalists always looking for a scoop. Time permitting, after they had been perusing speeches by such icons as Nkrumah, Sékou Touré, and Garvey—the professor was already envisaging a career along those illustrious lines for his friend—Dr. Kelfala would round up a few coeds to meet the general at the professor's place.

During those enchanting evenings, the professor would fondle the girls while the general drank his beer; yet it was evident from the look in the general's eyes that he was already contemplating what it would be like to have that bevy of women around him all the time: girls, he had been assured, who were among the most daredevil creatures in Malagueta. The prospect of paradise had never seemed so real to the two men as they looked at each other wondering how soon it would be before Tankor Satani did the right thing and kicked the bucket.

CHAPTER FIFTY

Enigma of a Name

AFTER A long period spent testing his hypothesis about the gravitational force of some basic minerals, Pallo was ready to test his plane. When it was completed, his plane was a great feat of engineering stealth and alchemic wisdom; small in size, it could be miraculously inflated at his command. It could sit two passengers in the cockpit and was streamlined like an anteater, elongated at the front, while guaranteed to fly in all weather. Unlike a regular plane, it had no rudder blade or engine or even a visible instrument panel. With the skills known only to the masters of alchemy, he had engineered it for both vertical and horizontal takeoffs. It had been two years since he had started work on it, during which time his hair had gone mostly uncombed and had coarsened into a brighter gray, and his eyes, focused on that contraption in the enigmatic world of sorcery in which he had done his work to avoid detection, were not the brilliant, translucent gems they had been on that first day when he came to the Xanadu. It was a long time since Habiba Mouskuda had succeeded in persuading him to move from his hermitry in the woods along the border with Bassa to the madness of city life in Malagueta. He felt a deep longing for that period.

One day he decided to test his aeronautical masterpiece. Chewing some alligator pepper and raising his eyes to the heavens, he said "Poco a poco" the way orchestra conductors do. But in his case it was a command to the deities that had always been at his service, hovering above him during his most difficult nights, guiding his hands when he was grappling with the enigmas and possibilities of magic. With the voice of a master alchemist, he repeated his command and watched as his invention began to inflate and then rise in his room, proving, as he had always suspected, that minerals other than metals were subject to gravitational forces not known to ordinary science: he realized he had achieved a great feat. Then, very carefully, he began to clean out the room, throwing out all the magical evidence, so as not to give away his formulae. Yet despite what he had achieved, there was no real happiness in his soul. He felt sullied: a terrible thing for a magician to admit, especially as he had not intended to make any profit from his endeavors.

"Ah solved one enigma," he lamented, "but ah done betray my calling."

The truth was that he had started his experiment to please Tankor Satani, who had requested the plane to test a myth in Malagueta that such an invention was possible if done according to the laws of sorcery. However, recently, mindful of the terrible things that he knew Tankor Satani had done, the eunuch had been assailed by a most disturbing thought: Who was Tankor Satani? Where had he come from? Why had he made such a mess of the country? Was he a true son of that land?

Pallo had always wondered why no other family in the country bore the name Satani. Those who had known Tankor in his lowly profession of dogcatcher and were prepared to risk talking about it had let it be known that there were no birth or baptismal certificates to authenticate his nationality; no one knew where he was born, or, for that matter, where he had spent his childhood. He had no siblings! The only writings, vague and unconfirmed, about Tankor Satani had been penned by a most imaginative journalist, who had written that, according to legend, Tankor Satani's father was a migrant who had come from an unknown country to work in the diamond mines. This was not such a strange thing in Kissi, considering that Tuaregs, Arabs, and Moors had been coming there over the last two hundred years. Fearing he might be killed for his audacity, the journalist had fled Malagueta.

The journalistic details were obscure, but a fine thread of the narrative had survived. Like all good narratives, it had been embellished over the years. But this was the version that Pallo heard from Habiba Mouskuda:

One night after arriving very broke, attracted by the smell of tamarind juice, a migrant decided to camp in an abandoned hut in a village; during his first week, lonely, viewed with suspicion by the locals, he would have gone round the bend but for the fact that he had a good voice and that, when he could not bear his loneliness, he would sing of a lost country, glorifying his heroic results as a miner. After a week spent singing his heart out, he finally fired the imagination of a young girl, whose soul was now in torment after listening to him.

Her name was Naima, a fearless shepherdess who found it hard to sleep after listening to the pastoral poet. Reasoning that a man who could sing like a shepherd deserved a drink, she disguised her beautiful face in a large veil of purple silk that fell down to her knees and set out with a jug of palm wine one evening, determined to discover the owner of that mellifluous voice. She was a seventeen-year-old virgin who had reached a provocative puberty and had never left her village. Three months earlier, she had turned down a dozen suitors on the grounds that they had the imagination of donkeys, as she gleaned from the fact that they had been willing to wrestle themselves to death on her behalf.

"Imagine them fighting over me as if I were some kind of property" she hissed, even though that was the custom in the village.

An hour after she went to discover who the owner of the voice was, she emerged, in the starless night, giddy, with a delicious smile, having given her virginity to the pastoral poet walking beside her. For a man with such a mellifluous tenor, he was a giant; but in her giddiness she thought she had seen, in the dim topaz light of his hut, something pertaining to gentleness in his eyes. Not surprisingly, for a man with his build, he was, she discovered, greatly endowed as a lover. When he took her, he started slowly; but, as he began to savor his conquest, she trembled at the power of that endowment, her bones creaking as he stripped her of her innocence with his bold, hard strokes. Afterward, he held the fascinated girl spellbound with the details of his miraculous birth, telling her how he had almost suffocated at birth because his umbilical cord had wound around his neck, but that he had not cried.

"My mother was terrified. She thought she had given birth to the devil," he told the fascinated girl. Fearing the worst, his mother examined him and saw that his features were those of a normal child. However, thinking that he might bring her bad luck because of his abnormal birth, she named him Satani and abandoned him to the care of his grandmother.

Held spellbound by his voice, Naima swooned at the fantastic story of his birth and was prepared, had he merely hinted at it, to run away with him to the next town, where there was some mining of diamonds to be done. She did not even bother to look at him. It was not until after he had taken her halfway home that it occurred to Naima to examine the face of the man who had seduced her. As if to enhance her discovery, the quarter amethyst moon that had been guiding them down the path became bright, and Naima thought she could detect the face of a woman in it: a face incomprehensibly sad. The poet turned his face sideways, away from the moonlight, as though he were afraid of the glare, but Naima could still see the outline of his profile, the deep depressions on both sides of his head near his ears, as he turned.

Unexpectedly, as though what had just happened in that hut was some nightmarish joke, she saw that the man had two small horns back of each ear. She had never seen another man like him before.

She opened her finely shaped mouth to scream but passed out, and it was not until a great Marabout had spent three whole weeks reciting Koranic verses to revive her that she regained consciousness, by which time she was pregnant with Tankor Satani.

CHAPTER FIFTY-ONE

The Splendid Mystique of Nine Dead Men

TRY AS he might, Pallo could not shake off his depression. The unnerving feeling that he—an alchemist with extraordinary gifts—had been working for a man he now considered "de debul" gave him a wretchedness in his soul. That he had compromised his gifts wounded him deeply. When he could think clearly, Pallo's major concern was whether Tankor Satani's brood had the debul in them; that drowned one in particular. Becoming an unwilling accomplice to the lobotomies of a mad president was not why the gods had given him the gift of alchemy. He had made a horrible mistake!

"Dat is not de reason God gave me de gift," he groaned.

For the first time since completing the work on the magic plane, he left his room and was immediately assailed by the smell of frangipani: the plant of the dead. A thin mist of its funereal fragrance dulled his senses, but he was still conscious enough to hear what he thought was the low moaning of a dog. It sounded familiar, and that was strange, considering the dog had been dead for some time. To hear that voice coming from beyond that vista was the first sign that something extraordinary was about to happen in Malagueta. Pallo was a simple man, born to peasants and destined since childhood to do good work with alchemy. Painfully, he wondered why fate had brought him to Tankor Satani's service, as he had never really felt comfortable being near the president.

He thought of the destinies of men, how ironic that it was a eunuch who, after receiving the powers of sorcery, was able to restore Tankor Satani's virility. He still could not believe how incredibly great his gifts were; but convinced he had sullied those gifts, he washed his hands in a bowl of water tinged with basil leaves and alligator peppers as a prelude to some form of meditation before his next rite. Then, miraculously, he had the strange feeling of sliding into a deep trance, going into an extraordinary sphere, one so mystifying it would have defeated his new discovery of the possibilities of gravity. As he slipped deeper into the mystic world, he felt it spinning around him, saw that its exotic flora and fauna were losing their colors, and could no longer smell any fragrance in the flowers. The feeling that the world really was going round in a vortex overcame him when a mystic light came on to reveal the incredible developments suddenly happening all over Malagueta.

In that transcendental world, men and women were waking up from the longest headache in living memory, something deep and terrifying that had lasted seventeen years but was now coming to an end. Stunned, he saw the last of the caged magnificent birds cutting at the wire meshes with their beaks and flying away from the courtyard of the Xanadu. At the same time, borne by their enormous wings, a large flock of vultures was swooping down on the Xanadu and waking up the dead with their eerie noises, although, ironically, the vultures were the agents of the dead and had been performing their rituals for a long time. Even more incredible, Pallo saw several funeral processions crossing the bridge between old and new Malagueta, and it occurred to him that they might be heading for the Xanadu.

He watched in awe as they entered its great hallways, and he saw the coffins opening up and the nine dead men stepping out—men who had never really been dead, because their graves were unmarked tracts of land on which Tankor Satani's goons, stupid enough to think that such sacrilege could blight their memories, had poured acid after the men were hanged. Awed by their splendid presence, Pallo watched the dead men going from room to room with their inaudible steps. He saw them as they began to sweep the floors with their long invisible brooms, furiously emptying that monstrous palace of all the crimes that had been conceived there after Tankor Satani was inspired to build it after an equally deranged two-hundred-years-dead ex-slave and emperor named Henri Christophe invaded his head.

The dead men looked so noble going about their business in that mysterious world that when Pallo came out of his trance, inspired by them, he said "Poco a poco" one last time to his great invention, wanting to be done with this chapter of his life. He watched as the magic plane responded to his command, taking off to where he knew Tankor Satani was sitting in the unbearable solitude of his autumn, and he saw a red light flickering like a comet at the tail of the plane, which was something he had not added to its design. Here, Pallo realized, was confirmation, if he needed any, that the end result of sorcery sometimes went beyond even the genius of its practitioners.

An obsidian cloud suddenly draped Malagueta. He got up and poured water into an enamel basin and added some balsamic leaves. Gravely he washed his hands one more time of all the impurities that had led him astray from the purest practice of his art, until he finally felt he had cleansed his soul and that the room in which he had lived in the Xanadu was also purged of his mistake. Majestically, as on the day when he had danced under the great cotton tree with the other eunuchs, he stood up and left the room. Without turning back for a final glance, he began to walk toward the woodland back of the Xanadu, on the track leading to his old forsaken world of reflection and quietness. With a deeper insight into the vanity of men, he was returning to his simple life, and nothing was ever seen of the great eunuch after that night in Malagueta. In a last symbolic rite, he had burned all the paraphernalia of his art: leaves, oils, spices, balms, the head of a huge snake, and eagle feathers, leaving no olfactory trace for even the most acute nose of a dog trained to sniff the presence of the most implacable spirits.

CHAPTER FIFTY-TWO

Last Canto of the Mermaid

TANKOR SATANI had been brooding a lot since returning from his friend's funeral. Early most mornings he would be seen sitting in his favorite verandah looking at the sprawling city, and the idyllic evenings that he had spent with his nymph before General Dan Doggo ruined them with his piece of bad news were now beyond Tankor's recollection as he sank deeper and deeper into depression. That suited Jenebah Djallo just fine: she slept a lot now, and sometimes had dreams about the Fouta Djallon Mountains of her origins. Around midnight one Friday, when Tankor Satani was brooding and stroking his enormous erection, he began to imagine he was making love to his mistress. It so happened that Jenebah Djallo was actually sleeping in the bedroom and was having a long dream in which she was carried into heaven by two angels blowing bamboo shepherd's horns. Mysterious, alien women suddenly appeared: they were the Houris and were examining Jenebah Djallo as she lay naked on a divan, a bit dazed, but not because she had lost her virginity at fifteen and was about to receive some form of punishment; far from it—bloody hell, that was not a crime these days!

She was ill and had to be restored to good health after spending the last seven years as the mistress of the "debul." With exquisite care, one of the angels was pouring goat's milk from a gourd into Jenebah's mouth to cleanse the taste of asafetida that the lips of the devil had left. Using equally exquisite skills, the other women rolled her over and anointed her breasts and flanks with oil they had squeezed from amaryllis—and were amazed that her breasts were still firm, in spite of how the devil had been pawing them. Then, after trimming her nails, they cornrowed her long tresses and haloed her with fresh daisies, as though she were a new bride.

She woke up feeling giddy, moved by the feeling that she was really in paradise and that the surroundings of the Xanadu had been transformed into a most enchanting garden of stunning arbors and trellises of gorgeous bougainvillea. Wild bunches of lush hydrangea were brilliant in the sun, and the old fishpond had been emptied of its carp. Inspired by what she imagined was the music of the rhapsodic parrots, she rose from her bed and began to walk under the flamboyant canopies, mystified by how freely she could breathe in the now refreshing air of the Xanadu after feeling suffocated there for the last three months. It was an illusion: her days of being a wild shepherdess were over; she had undergone a metamorphosis of her human form, and the last thing she remembered was succumbing to a spell that the Houris were casting on her as they began to prepare her for the role for which she had been chosen long ago.

A deep sound, like a whale's breathing, was heard in the Xanadu, and a sharp metallic noise in the dark room broke all the windows in the palace, jolting Tankor Satani out of his melancholia. During his brooding, the persistence of things remembered from before his stroke had given him a terrible headache. He had not properly digested his food that afternoon, and that was unfortunate, because it was the last meal he would eat.

The deep breathing of the whale became so loud that Tankor Satani was alarmed. During the worst periods of his brooding he would forget about his mistress, but now that there was an immediate danger in the palace he became deeply worried about her. Slowly he began the difficult task of wheeling himself from the verandah in search of her, but he soon lost consciousness of where he was, for it was as though the great house was moving, swept off its foundation on that sloppy hill where it had loomed for years, and was now sliding down to the lowlands of Malagueta, where the long-suffering masses lived, going toward the river along whose bank Habiba Mouskuda and Theodore Iskander had built their house, the river that was also the dividing line between the new and the old districts of the city. A huge tidal wave was surging inland from the tumultuous ocean to merge with the river, as though that great body of water was finally tired of all the instances of betrayal by some of the citizens, tired of the filth they had been dumping into it over the past seventeen years, poisoning it to the point that it was now angry and wanted to be paid back for all it had given to Malagueta and the rest of the country.

Tankor Satani's head was spinning when he regained consciousness. He felt quite dizzy and tried to shake off the feeling of disaster shrouding his soul, but it was then that he became aware of the rising flood and realized that the Xanadu was sinking. Horrified that he was about to drown trapped in his wheelchair, he saw the slow, seductive movement of a woman emerging out of an ocean that had once been the beautiful parquet floor of the huge living room, spreading and swelling swiftly, and he realized he was not dreaming, because the woman emerging from that great body of water was none other than Jenebah Djallo!

In the amber evening light, Tankor forgot about the approach of death. Deluded into thinking he could finally make love to his mistress after so long, he felt lust foam round his lips and he held his portentous weapon, hoping she would take it, but he felt the flood moving very fast, the great house sinking. Then, in the greatest horror that he had ever witnessed, and as though he had been living under the greatest illusion all his life and fate had dealt him the cruelest blow, he saw Jenebah Djallo undergoing a terrifying transformation: she was losing part of her human form, her legs were fusing together, and, horror of horrors, she was becoming a mermaid in the flood.

"Lord have mercy on me!" he moaned in horror. "I have been sleeping with a Mammy Wata all this time!"

All You Amounted to Was This Rotten Peanut

It had been seven years since he snatched the mermaid's comb, and two years to the day since his stroke. Now his glory lay in the inconceivable ruins of that enormous house, its mirrors no longer shimmering with the temptation for people to admire it in the night, as they had done for twelve years. Lit by floodlights, its grandeur had always been visible to Malaguetans no matter where they were in the city.

Not surprisingly, in what was the most lucid thought to come to his mind in years, Tankor Satani began to recall what Henri Christophe had said many years ago: be careful of the mermaid; no man has ever fathomed her mystery. But it was too late for this new emperor, and he realized it was the end of his reign, of a perverse life. When he heard the deafening noise of a crowd swimming in the flood to get to the vast, solitary, unoccupied rooms of that monstrous house, the truth finally sank in that he had always been a prisoner there; even when he was dreaming of his macabre version of immortality. He had always been at the mercy of the men he had executed, of their incarnation as vultures that could come at any time to torment him. Against their invisible armor, his coronation and wish for immortality had always been useless and laughable.

The mermaid looked very happy wriggling her tail, teasing him, giving him time to think, act. After all, he was still Emperor Tankor! Telephones were still working; a few guards might be there. But it soon dawned on him that he was all alone in that cursed house, he and his destiny, no more, no less. It was the way his fate had been written, which, had he been less greedy and destructive, he might have been able to change, given the tremendous opportunities with which he came to power.

Before breaking into the Xanadu, the large crowd of young people had set Samson the chimp free so that he would not die in the flood and could spend the rest of his days swinging between the trees in the adjacent forest. Noisily, once inside the Xanadu, they began to look for the diamonds they thought Tankor Satani had been hiding there. Invading every nook and cranny of the palace, with a fury that had long been pent up, they thrust their knives into the sofas, cushions, mattresses, pillows, thick rugs, and jars, determined to take back what they felt was really theirs, stripping that fantastic house of what the guards had not taken away: the chandeliers, sideboards, light switches, toilet fixtures, door handles, bolts, beds, frames—anything they could lay their hands on.

Trapped in his wheelchair, Tankor Satani saw that the mermaid was not making any threatening moves toward him. She was definitely enjoying his torment, and he realized he was in her power even with that portentous weapon projecting like a lance! Somehow, he managed to decipher the keys to his last dream—how to bring the magic plane that had been sitting on the verandah to his rescue. Frantically, he said "Poco a poco" and hurled his ruined frame into the cockpit. "Not until I die," he cried.

With the magic of fire and water in the Xanadu, it was an incredible sight that night as, far from the cursed house, a crowd of people watched in awe as the magic plane took off. It was his last defiance, because what was really happening was the epicedium of a man witnessing his own end. His heart was beating erratically and he was sweating profusely as he manipulated the joystick of the magic plane, trying to cheat his fate by sending the great bird on a mad course to an illusory place in his mind, only to realize, when cyclonic winds started battering the plane, that it was taking him where he did not want it to go: to the farthest reaches of the ocean that for so long had been the beginning and the end of much of Malagueta's history.

Porcupine quills were darting from all sides of the plane in a forlorn defense of its pilot, but it was all in vain: the plane soon nosedived into the vast, boiling expanse of the dark ocean where the mermaid was queen, as Tankor Satani should have known on that evening when he stole her comb.

A deep turquoise light shimmering from the plants in its depths lit up the ocean to reveal the dugongs, flying fish, sharks, and butterfish surrounding the strange object that had crashed into their world, with the old man trapped inside struggling to break out. Overcome by the light from the plants, he realized that not only had he forgotten the code essential to break free of his entrapment, but rather than destroying the plane, the salt of the ocean seemed to be making it impregnable, as though, in a final act of mockery, Pallo the sorcerer had imagined this denouement all along and had wiped all knowledge of how to escape from the president's head. Unheralded, abandoned by the world, unable to breathe, Tankor Satani saw swimming straight toward him the largest barracuda he had ever seen, and he barely had time to remember that throughout his seventeen years in power amongst the human barracudas, he had never really looked at the teeth of an oceanic one, the way that great fish cornered its prey, until he saw this one: cunning, approaching with a menace terrible enough to make him shit the large diamond he had swallowed early that morning. With a crushing noise the great barracuda closed its saber-toothed tiger teeth on the plane. The sound was so loud it was heard all over Malagueta, but it was nothing compared to Tankor Satani's scream when the great fish, miraculously transformed into a mermaid, bit off the tip of his enormously erect phallus so that the trail of his blood streaked for miles in that ocean where he never stood a chance.

"What a terrible disaster you were," the mermaid said to him in the most provocatively sexy voice he had ever heard. "To think that all you amounted to was a rotten peanut."

Book Four

La Dolce Vita

CHAPTER FIFTY-THREE

An Unloved Polyp

AFTER BEING on the Cape Verde Islands for over six months, Moustapha Ali-Bakr eventually came to the conclusion that his holiday had really become a period in exile. The tourists were gone, and except for the seagulls and sandpipers the place was empty.

One evening, as he knelt down and faced Mecca to give thanks to Allah, a most horrible realization assailed him: his head had begun to stray into the tenets of a rival religion. Weighed down with his problems, he began to think of the flight of the Israelites from Egypt, and the drift of his mind was so bizarre he banged his head on his prayer mat a few times to get rid of his confusion and to ask Allah to forgive him so that he could concentrate on his Surah like a good Moslem. Nevertheless, for a whole week, he continued to drift in his thoughts to the wandering Jews. "Make ah nor drink dis cup too much," he appealed to Allah.

Every day he looked for a sign in the sky to tell him when he could go back to Malagueta, because it was almost unthinkable he would move his operations somewhere else. He was distraught and moody most of the time, angry over how Tankor Satani had died, and his heart felt like lead.

To make matters worse, that simpleton, General Soriba Dan Doggo, seemed to have outmaneuvered Enos Tanu and was on the verge of assuming power in Malagueta. It was not the succession that Moustapha Ali-Bakr had hoped for, but he was now determined to exploit it, especially as General Dan Doggo had leaked the details to some of Malagueta's now fearless journalists of how the Coral had cheated Tankor Satani over the purchase of the hotel Quatro Sete Melo. Afraid of going home for the time being, but longing to do so, Moustapha Ali-Bakr began to draw up new plans, for in the matter of progeny he was not as dumb as Tankor Satani had been. Whereas Tankor Satani's will was reportedly burned during the attack on the Xanadu, Moustapha's was tucked safely away in a Swiss bank vault, known only to his lawyer and sons.

When the large crowd had stormed the Xanadu, they had searched all the nooks and crannies for what they believed must be a complicated will, but it was all in vain. "Look like say de Mammy Watta done eat de paper," a man opined.

Of all the terrible deeds for which they hated the old man, the greatest was that, even in death, he had outsmarted them and had given Swiss bankers yet another unclaimed fortune beyond the reach of whatever government was now in Malagueta. "*Basta pikin*, dis stupid president. Idiot!" another angry man exploded.

Before he began to wonder about the Jews, Moustapha Ali-Bakr had made his trip of atonement to Mecca to thank Allah that his businesses in Malagueta had been spared during the recent riots. As he went round the Kasbah, it occurred to him that he had been remiss in his annual generosity, which was understandable considering he had been stuck on an island during that period, far from home. As soon as he was back in what was up till then a "temporary exile," he used the first opportunity to give a large donation to the Moslem Brotherhood, which was building a mosque in a country where the majority of the citizens were Catholics. He hoped that his largesse would lead to an end to his exile. Mostly he stayed glued to his radio, read with relish all the international newspapers printed in English, and grabbed at every scrap of passing news that visitors might bring, desperate for information about Malagueta.

He tried to relieve his depression with various elixirs, but his brain seemed to have gone dead when it came to new ideas about medicine; so it was understandable that one night, thinking yet again about the Jews, he went to sleep and dreamed he had become Moses waiting for a new tablet from God. "Now ah done sin, bad, bad!" he groaned.

His weight now drastically reduced because of his misery, he went through two prayer mats, half a dozen shirts, ten cartons of Evian water, and three baskets of Egyptian dates. He ate copious amounts of sugar cane and stained his best muftis with the regular cups of cardamom coffee he was drinking. And he was sick of mussel soup, which, with French bread, was the only meal his stomach had been able to hold lately.

But the most unbearable weight of his suffering was that he had lost his mistress. Tired of his brooding, homesick for Malagueta, Rufina Solomon stunned him one morning in a voice that left him in no doubt about how much thought she had given to the matter, six months into their exile. "I am going home," she said.

"Ah beg you, don't leave me here alone like a rotten canoe without an owner," he pleaded.

Her suitcase was already packed. "Don't try to get me to change my mind," she said.

"Stay with me and help me get through this unhappiness," he continued, "and I shall buy you the largest diamond necklace when we are back in Malagueta."

"You and diamonds!" she snapped at him. "Always thinking that all women want diamonds. In case you have forgotten, it was my country's resources that made you rich. Don't bother me. I have seen the light now."

Their relationship had soured lately after some misadventures at lovemaking. As happens with long-married people, an ocean of recriminations would flow from their failed attempts in bed, which left Rufina with an esurience that the Coral could not satisfy. She began to experience terrible nightmares, and was ashamed that she had sold her dignity for money to the Coral, "like a cheap harlot," knowing full well that, with Tankor Satani's approval, Moustapha was the most exploitative man in Malagueta. The smell of copious garlic on him, which she had always ignored, suddenly started to disgust her. They stopped making love altogether.

"It is useless. I can't sleep with you anymore," she said with brutal finality.

A week after she left, Moustapha Ali-Bakr felt so completely lost that the island began to lose its beauty to him. In truth he had never really cared for it, besides the fact that it was a getaway to the Middle East and his hotel was bringing him money. But that did not ameliorate his pain. Here he was, impaled on the spike of rejection, cast away. It was a most unusual feeling for a man who had never before experienced any form of rejection. Even in the brightness of the sun he was shaking with a fever. He felt he was becoming a newt, almost depilated, going bald. He kept to himself most of the time inside his room, a tumor-like pain growing in his head. More than the heat of the tropics, it was his loneliness that was roasting his entrails.

When he couldn't stand the long days of his anguish, he would come out of his room sometimes, a crab unsteady of limb, with yarns of loneliness knitted on his face. In the golden light of evening, intent on companionship, he would look for a friendly face; but it was to the jaw-breaking vowels of Creole Portuguese that he was thrown. Given the state of his mind, the last thing he could master was the grammar and vocabulary of a new language; he really missed the relish with which his mistress had guided him through that minefield. Save for the workers who had surmised that something must be wrong for him to stay so long, Moustapha

Ali-Bakr had no lasting contact with another soul: a terrible situation for a man who had always wielded power like a sheik and was constantly surrounded by servants, jesters, assistants, lawyers, academics, civil servants, politicians, and all the others who hung on his words. Before his mistress left him, he had assumed she would stay with him long into his twilight, if necessary. But during the year spent in exile, even on the days when there was sunlight and the sea was magical, and some tourists had begun, with the change in weather, to return to the island, he felt like an unloved polyp.

CHAPTER FIFTY-FOUR

After the Remains of His Days

A FEW countries away but on the same stretch of the Atlantic Ocean, General Soriba Dan Doggo had been at his mistress's earlier than usual in a secluded suburb, when the sight of what he first thought was a meteorite falling from the sky made him jump out of the bed where they had just made love. "It is a plane like nothing I have seen before," he said, "and it is heading for the ocean." Quickly he made the deduction that it was the much-talked-about magic plane, probably on a test flight by Tankor. "This is a disaster," the general said; "it is going to crash!"

He stood stunned by the sight of the fabled plane for a long time, then stared at the walls, his eyes blank and unmoving, looking as though he might go on standing like that forever, praying for a miracle to happen, unaware it had already happened in the Xanadu. Quick to discern what was going on in his mind, his mistress shouted at him, "You fool, your hour has come. Put your pants on and move fast!"

General Dan Doggo came out of his stupefaction. He put his clothes on hurriedly, kissed his mistress good-bye, and got into his car. But rather than driving back home, he set out for the military headquarters on Maroon Town Hill. After all the commotion that the crashed plane had caused, some noisy crows flying toward the ocean in search of fish momentarily unnerved the general as his car tore through the now frenzied streets of Malagueta. Even with his windows rolled up, the torrent of excited voices, loud instruments, and pounding feet celebrating Tankor's death assailed him. He saw parts of the badly neglected streets that had been transformed into patches of green, lovers' corners, drunk people embracing one another and dancing to rumba and Congolese soukous in the evening light. "Lord have mercy, we done free," they cried in jubilation.

The likelihood of being held up by the fiesta necessitated a quick detour on a bumpy road, but as soon as a straight road appeared, he drove hurriedly toward the old Maroon district, where the military headquarters were situated. Very much in transport, he went past the rampart of the parliament house, built by the Israelis, a solid edifice of granite and red stone. The thought that he might soon be presiding there was thrilling. A large man, he was perspiring as he hurried to his destination, even with the air conditioner blasting in his car, and his heart was beating a dangerous rhythm. He began to daydream, doing his best to keep his eyes on the road.

He imagined that he was already the leader; it was a surreal thought when he recalled how his mistress had borne his enormous weight only half an hour earlier, for which he would now have to compensate her double. But first he had to bypass the drunken revelry occasioned by the storming of the Xanadu. He was desperate to get to the military armory before it was too late.

Some girls, seeing his car coming, began to spread confetti at the intersection of Bookerman and Amadou Komba Streets. Not one to miss a chance to be serenaded by women, General Dan Doggo slowed down a bit, but he couldn't have chosen a worse spot, for it was where a quartet of dwarfs, dressed in wild, colorful costumes, was reenacting how the porcupine quills had darted from Tankor Satani's doomed plane.

"How you do, General?" said one of the dwarfs, leaping onto his car. "You nor go pass."

General Dan Doggo gave them some money.

"Make de boss man pass!" said the dwarf, and the general moved on, but not before he had kissed the cheeks of a few girls who leaned on his car and whispered the hope that they might soon be with him in paradise. Afraid that he had lost valuable time, he sent his car into third gear, and the engine roared as he tried to cover the remaining two miles. He was near the end of his journey when he saw a truckload of men rushing home with their loot from the Xanadu.

Once again he was recognized, but unlike the dwarfs, the looters waved frantically to him, making him feel even more certain that this was his moment.

"Go dere and take obah, General; we dey right behen you," they said.

CHAPTER FIFTY-FIVE

A Preemptive Move

GENERAL DAN Doggo did not have to be clairvoyant to imagine that, while he was driving to the national armory, his archenemy, Prime Minister Enos Tanu, must have been up to no good thinking of how he could outsmart him. The general might have had a slight advantage for the succession, given that he was the only one other than Tankor Satani who had the code to the national armory. But he was not really too bright and was not contemplating a massive military action. Yet, as he neared his destination, he was inspired, quite fortuitously, to act decisively by a piece of news. Turning on his radio to find out what was going on in the rest of Malagueta, General Dan Doggo had learned of an even greater crisis in the world: the Angolan government had launched a decisive push against the UNITA rebels in the long-running civil war.

Enos Tanu had other things on his mind.

To drown while trapped in a magic plane was not one of the exits from this life that he had envisaged for Tankor Satani. Being a good Moslem who believed in final funeral rites, the prime minister had ordered a search of the ocean for the remains of his longtime boss, but the body was never found; not even a shred of skin. However, a week into the search, two Spanish divers came up with an unexpected treasure: an old sea chest full of gold coins from the time of Pedro da Cinta, when the Portuguese bandit had watered his ships near Malagueta on his way to India in the fifteenth century. Crafty bastards, the divers hid their discovery from everyone, and after bribing some customs officers not to open their suitcases, took the first available flight out of the country and went to live off their priceless treasure in the Seychelles.

"What a terrible end this is!" Enos Tanu exclaimed. "It is as if man does not have much of a choice between being eaten by the sharks and the worms."

"Dey say God pay him for all his sins," his wife said sadly. Worried about her husband's soul, she added, "Make you go to mosque en pray now, if you get sin."

They were eating dinner on the evening when the plane plunged into the ocean: beans, chicken, white rice, and cabbage cooked by his wife the way he liked it, for he was a man of simple tastes. Still hungry after dinner, he chewed on the chicken bones as he meticulously worked out a plan to thwart General Dan Doggo.

Enos Tanu thought his wife was probably right and went to a mosque to pray. His own efforts might not be enough to please God, so he asked a good Marabout for his assistance with divine intervention. He felt a great pain in his heart as, involuntarily, he suddenly started thinking about the dead banker Alpha Samory. Even with the passing of years, Enos Tanu still found it hard to forget the way the short man had looked as he lay in his coffin, resplendent in a white gown. "Forgive me that terrible deed," Enos Tanu said quietly, looking at the sky. He decided to go to the mosque a second time.

Incredibly, it occurred to him, Tankor Satani had drowned exactly two years and five months to the day after the banker was killed; proof, as they say in Malagueta, that "de dead" do not sleep, but sometimes wreak revenge. With the fear of the dead ringing in his head he got up from his chair, watched by his wife, who had discerned his torment.

"Someone has put red pepper in my eyes," he explained lamely.

"What do you mean?"

"I now believe that God is greater than all governments," he said, chilled by the possibility that something ominous was about to happen to him.

"It took you dat long to realize it?" she said ruefully.

Enos Tanu urgently dialed the cabinet office, but the line was dead. He tried the house of the speaker of parliament, but the result was the same: all communications into and out of the city had been cut off, and his sense of a doomed script playing out was heightened when one of his guards came hurrying in with a piece of really bad news. "Excellency, sah, de street boys an' dem soldiers are smashing up de city," the hard-breathing underling said. "Dem crazy people are happy de president done die."

Here, if the prime minister needed it, was proof that General Dan Doggo had unleashed a diabolical maneuver to seize power. Determined to confront the general, Enos Tanu changed hurriedly into battle fatigues; although not a military man, he was fond of wearing that uniform to make him look tough and tenacious. His driver had pulled up in the driveway in a Mercedes, and he got into it with three bodyguards, after telling his wife not to worry about him. "A man dies only once, and I am not afraid to fight for this country."

The car charged out of his compound, followed by ten other cars carrying mean-looking security men. A black Mercedes, its windows tinted, presumably because it was carrying a Marabout, brought up the rear. Enos Tanu tried to get Captain Oumaru Konate, the commander of the Bakazo forces, on his walkie-talkie, hoping he could count on his loyalty in case of a showdown with General Dan Doggo, but failed to reach him. It was then that he saw the great topaz fire spreading from the remains of the Xanadu, and the shock of what had happened to that expensive house produced geysers of horror in the prime minister's heart. "Where was the general when all of this was taking place?" he thundered.

He did not have to wait too long for an answer.

General Dan Doggo had anticipated a power grab by his opponent. Inspired by the actions of the army in Angola, he was at that very moment leading the infantry of the Second Battalion of the armed forces of Kissi, on his way to the government-owned radio station to announce his assumption of power. His troops were tough, freshly armed, and determined to show their mettle, after not having been allowed much weaponry in the last ten years of Tankor's reign. But the general was still a mile away from the important prize of the radio station when his bush radio picked up the predictable signals that the prime minister and his guards were driving toward the university.

"Break into two files!" the general commanded. "Obey orders!"

Shaking off the image of a boy scout that had plagued him throughout his not-too-illustrious military career, General Dan Doggo made a preemptive move and sent the vanguard of his troops to block the narrow access to the mountain garrison, while he continued his advance on the national radio station.

Captain Oumaru Konate was sitting on a ridge that overlooked the city. He saw the change of government in Malagueta as an internal affair, one that his troops should not be involved in. Their honor was his first concern, especially as the military accords signed between the two countries were for the defense of the republic. To the captain, surrounded by his fiercely loyal gendarmerie, the idea of renewed fighting breaking out on the streets of Malagueta between the contending rivals was anathema; he was really a principled man.

His men had earned a reputation for ruthlessness after the way they had helped put down the student rebellion, so he was determined to dispel that image. To that end, he gave the order for them to start moving down the hillside road. At the approach to the sprawling city, the captain saw the frightened citizens boarding up their windows, shops being closed, and a scattering of daredevil drivers, fearful of losing their cars to unruly soldiers, racing home in a frenzy. The streets had the eerie feeling of a graveyard, and, unknown to him, some citizens were trembling with anxiety lying flat on their floors, anticipating the worst.

After a while, Captain Konate ordered his troops to stop their march on the city. Then, with the sartorial bearing of his French military training, he approached the leader of General Dan Doggo's advancing brigade and surrendered his pistol.

"*Mon devoir est d'honorer la République, et non la vanité d'un leader*," the captain said as he shook the hand of Lieutenant Markidi, the officer leading General Dan Doggo's men.

The lieutenant did not speak French, but understood the gist of what the captain had said. "I salute your integrity," he replied.

That night, after consolidating his position, General Dan Doggo made his first broadcast as president of Kissi and put Enos Tanu under house arrest.

There was great jubilation in the streets of Malagueta.

In the Castle of His Skin

Prevailed upon by Habiba not to leave the house, Theodore Iskander had spent some time in front of a TV watching the drama unfolding in Malagueta. Painful cramps in his bad leg made his limp more pronounced when he walked to the kitchen for coffee, and his mood varied from ambivalence to depression as he thought of General Dan Doggo taking over.

"This could be a disaster for an already battered nation," he said, thinking of the good-natured general's reputation as a simpleton.

"And I bet Tankor Satani must be laughing in his ocean grave," said his mistress.

"Leave everything to God," Irene interjected. "Dat soja boy may not be too bad after all. Remember, he wanted to become a minister of de church."

Theodore Iskander felt that anyone was better than Tankor Satani after seventeen years of his capricious rule, but his despair about the future was still great. He too had seen the fire spiraling from the Xanadu. Bored with the details concerning the new government, he switched off the TV in the living room and limped to his study, where he stood by a window with a view of the river, trying to make some sense of Kissi's terrible history. "Diamonds have been a curse to this country," he groaned.

"Don't fret too much over what you cannot change," Habiba Mouskuda said, surprising him; he was unaware that his mistress had followed him into the study.

Slowly she began to stroke his brow that was furrowed with worries, amazed that somehow his face was ageless and that, although his thick crop of hair was receding, it was still almost black, a remarkable thing in a man pushing fifty, still full of energy, both in his spirit and in her bed. She pressed his head to her breasts and felt a metronome ticking away in his heart, but did not have to say a word to reassure him she would always be there for him. He knew that already. His spasms had calmed down a bit, a relief to her, because she was worried he was becoming restless, trapped, unable to be out where he really wanted to be, in the ring of fire on the streets of Malagueta, witnessing whatever transition was taking place.

In front of the house, the river was flowing gently. As usual in the evening, there was a riotous assemblage of passerines on the branches of the trees along its banks, music emanating from their throats and their plumages golden collages in the waning but still rosy sun. Compared to the events going on in the town, this was paradisiacal, as if to remind them that their lives were not as turbulent and barren as it was for a lot of other people. Later that evening, while Yeama and Irene were fast asleep, Theodore Iskander and his mistress walked down to where the river had risen a bit and dwarfed the stunted bushes. With their feet submerged, they sat on a large rock and watched the river flowing with its mysteries.

The calm in his soul was evident to his mistress.

CHAPTER FIFTY-SIX

Show Us Your Penny, General

AFTER HIS tumultuous coming to power, General Dan Doggo's first day in office was anticlimactic. He sat at his desk in the Tankor Satani's old office but did not think about the dead man.

On his way there, General Dan Doggo's motorcade had driven past a horde of photographers, ordinary citizens, and some Moslem holy men. "Insh'Allah, God willing, dis one better dan Tankor Satani," said the holy men.

It was a beautiful morning, the sun was shimmering and, at seven o'clock that morning, wearing a blue suit instead of his military uniform, the general sat inside a white tent hastily erected on the grounds of his house to listen to an Anglican priest pray for him.

"God dey watch you, General; so make you go small, small wit' dis power."

"I know," the general replied.

At State House, he found some resplendently robed traditional chiefs waiting for him. They had traveled long distances to greet him, and when they had done him the honor of singing a little encomium, he got down to the real business of learning how to use the intercom, while the head of the civil service briefed him on the complex labyrinths of government. Later, in a brief broadcast relayed around the country, the general let it be known that he did not want to be called "His Excellency." "I am not a vain man!" he said. "Give me a chance."

After attending to the matter of what to do with the two-hundred-pound gifts that well-wishers had sent him, he went home late in the evening to a drink of scotch and a dinner of cassava leaves stew, after which he made love to his wife and then relaxed. Not a bad first day at all for a new president.

The center of Malagueta looked like a huge garbage dump: tons of rubbish and confetti had piled up during the celebration, and it was impossible to drive through the streets choked with fractured tree branches and empty fuel drums, with which the revelers had been carousing. General Dan Doggo understood such intemperance of the human spirit but was nonetheless afraid of anarchy. He ordered the military to clean up the mess and then banned further demonstrations. "It is the price the nation has to pay for years of denial and bottled-up rage," he confided to his tutor.

"Then you must make another broadcast apologizing to those who have lost their property," the professor advised.

On his third day as president, as the general sat at the large mahogany desk with the seal of his office, his mood suddenly changed from happiness to shock, after he had gone through the old cabinet papers in the Red Box. Even though he had expected the worst, given the profligacy of Tankor Satani's coronation, nothing had prepared the general for what he discovered. "The treasury is empty!" he lamented.

There was only two weeks' supply of oil for electricity, no oil tankers were on the high seas, and the grain silos were low because the nation's farmers had not planted enough, tired of being offered promissory notes for their efforts.

"This is not what I had imagined!" the general confessed to his tutor, Dr. Bemba Kelfala, who had been appointed to the office of minister of state for presidential affairs. "We shall show them you can carry this elephant's load," the former academic assured him.

Dr. Kelfala's old rumpled image of an impecunious professor was now gone. He looked smart in a light gray doubled-breasted suit that went well with a blue shirt and burgundy tie and shining black shoes. A distinguished aura hung about him as he was driven in a black Mercedes to State House. He waved to a bevy of young women blowing kisses to him from the visitor's waiting room near the security gates, and felt very pleased that his luck had changed dramatically, after many years of want, at no expense to his integrity. His office adjoined the president's; it was brightly painted and spacious, and its windows opened onto the luxuriant blossoms of a wild flame tree and had a splendid view of the ocean. With the added convenience of a connecting door, he could continue his tutoring of his boss in private and share a drink with him in the afternoons, when no one was around.

He was confident, with roguish charm, and was bubbling with as much energy as his boss and, in view of their importance, most mothers in Malagueta would have been proud to call them their sons. With a generous cash advance from his new boss, the professor had splurged on luxury items like wine, whiskey, butter, and expensive cigarettes, in addition to a new wardrobe. A powerful generator gave him regular electricity at his new ministerial quarters, and on the previous evening he had dined with and made love to his favorite girlfriend, relishing the cool humming of the air conditioner. "My new life is really good!" he said to her as she cuddled up to him.

One afternoon, he gave his boss his first piece of advice. "Schumacher: that is the man you should read, General!"

"Who is he?"

"A German economist who wrote a book entitled *Small Is Beautiful.* It is the bible about how poor nations should use their own resources for development."

General Dan Doggo reflected for a while before replying. "It sounds good to me. But I tell you what: you do all the reading and summarize it for me. That is why you are my minister of presidential affairs!"

Not normally one for torturous reading, General Dan Doggo sat down a week later in his study to digest the first position paper written by the ex-professor. "It is quite interesting," he said.

Full of detailed plans, the minister had suggested that tariffs be increased for the export of diamonds, coffee, cacao, and ginger, and that Malagueta's coastal waters needed better naval patrolling. "All of that should get the country going, as soon as they are implemented."

"How many months do you think we have before we begin to make an impression?" the general asked, and shifted his bulk in his chair.

"It depends on a few things, but more on how much pressure we can put on the business community."

"Which sector?" the general wondered.

"The Corals, of course."

General Dan Doggo smiled incredulously. Only recently, he had come to the same conclusion about the Corals. Yet although he was determined to bring them under his control, especially that loudmouth Moustapha Ali-Bakr, he still had to work out the nature of the relationship he wanted with them. The turbulent changes, coming so soon after Tankor Satani's death, had left the Corals sweating during the bitter nights in their homes, uncertain about their future. At such times they desperately missed the acuity of their chieftain to solve their problems.

When he thought of what the new government had promised to do—get rid of some of the draconian laws passed by Tankor Satani—Theodore Iskander's comment was philosophical. "It is a new version of *Great Expectations*," he said, not the least amused by their efforts. "Let's see what is really behind it."

CHAPTER FIFTY-SEVEN

A Woman of Esteem

MOUSTAPHA ALI-BAKR finally received a sign from Allah in the form of a letter from Dr. Kelfala telling him he could return to Malagueta. Relieved that his involuntary exile was over, he got on the first plane, before the new government had time to change its mind, and did not even bother to bring half of the wardrobe he had accumulated. The plane was full of all kinds of pale foreigners coming to speculate in rutile, gold, and diamonds. It was Friday when he arrived. In the rich tropical greenery the sun was mild. Without his past arrogant swagger, he walked slowly into the immigration room almost unrecognized, so trim had he become in exile. Forgoing his usual diplomatic treatment, he stood in line at the passport control for his turn. When, an hour later, he got off a helicopter after a fifteen-minute hop to the mainland, he found Malagueta now calm, the streets swept clean, the buildings painted, and new stalls rebuilt in the flea markets. He went straight to a mosque to pray, happy to be home. His wife and kids were safe in Lebanon, and he found that his house had not suffered too much from neglect except for a little peeling on the walls and rust in the windows and a door creaking here and there. His face lit up, and he really knew he had come home, when his four servants, middle-aged men dignified and smart-looking in their best white uniforms, swept him up in the wide folds of their arms. During his absence they had remained loyal, burning candles and offering *sara*, a form of public charity, for his safe return.

"Master, we glad you done come back safe, safe, after we pray to God so much for you!"

Tears ran down Moustapha Ali-Bakr's eyes. Afterward, in a Babel of tongues—Arabic, Creole, English, and some pidgin Spanish that they had picked up in Las Palmas—a handful of Corals and a mixed bunch of police officers and other officials came by to welcome him.

Yet when he was alone, his joy at being home was mitigated by how lonely he really was in a huge house, where the ghosts of past business partners had recently begun to appear. It was a quiet night, and bright stars beamed softly in the sky. Thinking that a bit of fresh air was what he needed, Moustapha Ali-Bakr went into the garden and walked around touching familiar plants now in bloom or grown too bushy while he had been gone. When he heard the distant barking of dogs and the owls screeching in the huge mango tree, it occurred to him that it had been a long time since he had experienced this mysterious a night. His loneliness was surreal.

He sat on a bench near his fishpond—many of them dead or eaten by his servants—listening as the crickets began to chirr in the sage bushes, the frogs trumpeting loudly under the hibiscus, and the lilies dancing to a small burst of wind. The moon was a blue-purple crescent that made the night even more mysterious and colorful, and he realized he had not seen this beautiful a moon, even though it was blanketed by low-hanging dark clouds, when he was alone in Cape Verde.

Strangely, the beauty of the moon contributed to his loneliness, especially as he had just started thinking about the death of Tankor Satani and longed for real companionship with someone tactile. But it was not for any member of his family that he longed. Rather, he missed the heart and hands of his mistress Rufina Solomon.

While he had been stewing away in exile, Rufina Solomon's esteem had gone up in Malagueta, for she was related to Dr. Komba Binkolo, foreign minister under Tankor Satani, who, in the game of musical chairs called politics in Malagueta, had retained that position.

It was the minister's Coral wife who had urged him to intervene on behalf of the diamond magnate. "Whether we like him or not," she explained, "there is no denying the fact that he controls the diamond mines, not to talk of the fish industry."

"And milked the old man of a large sum of money!" her husband retorted.

"That is precisely why he should be allowed to come back, so we can get some money out of him."

Rufina Solomon had been expecting a visit from her old lover for some time. But when Moustapha Ali-Bakr arrived, looking sheepish, at her new home, she refused to be seduced by anything the Coral had to say to her. "It is over," she insisted when Moustapha tried to buy her favor back with a large diamond bracelet and earrings to match. "Let your other women worry about you now."

"They don't have your brain and forthrightness to set me straight!" he pleaded.

"They have other assets!" she said, cutting him off.

"In the name of God, don't cast me out. It has been hard without you."

"You will just have to get along without me," she said, and sent him packing for the last time with a look that said she was past caring about the likes of him.

A thin rain was falling as Moustapha walked back to his car. He thought he might still have a chance to get Rufina to change her mind by appealing to her cousin. The foreign minister's wife soon rid him of that delusion.

"She is as stubborn as a mule when it comes to her esteem, and has taken up with one of the young radical journalists. So move on."

"Which one?"

"The one who used to attack Tankor Satani's genealogy."

"What does *dat* mean?"

"Oh, sorry, I mean his ancestors."

The journalist was a few years younger than Rufina but was mature for his age. Bold and confident, but not arrogant, he was a fearless crusader who had earned his laurels campaigning against corruption. Although he was dedicated to Rufina, he was also the idol of many other women. Moustapha Ali-Bakr remembered the brazen way the writer used to criticize Tankor Satani and was peeved that it was this young man who had won the bed of his favorite mistress. In the old days he would have paid a few thugs to administer the right punishment for such effrontery, but these were the nascent days of an untried government. He swallowed his pride, pained that no temptation of diamonds or a new house could win Rufina back.

CHAPTER FIFTY-EIGHT

The Same Potter's Wheel

HOWEVER, MOUSTAPHA Ali-Bakr would once again dominate the country's economy. One day, he received a message from the office of Dr.

Bemba Kelfala inviting him to State House for a chat. "Allah be praised," Moustapha exclaimed. "He wants me to forget Rufina!"

He went through the enormous gates of State House, and saw that some things had changed from when he was last there with his preferred list of ministers for Tankor Satani to consider appointing to the cabinet. The guards were no longer the straight-backed, red-tunicked elderly men who used to stand erect with an incomparable dignity at their posts. The new guards were fidgety youths with a hound-dog look in safari suits, and as Moustapha walked past them they blinked at him, expecting a generous hand after he had seen the minister. He had come alone with a large briefcase full of business papers and cash, and his head was swimming with new ideas for expanding coastal fishing rights.

He walked past the gun turrets positioned in front of the porticoes and noticed the untended mimosa and hibiscus gardens and the film of moss on the walls of the building, a sign of how the presidential palace had fallen into decay. After he was let through the massive wooden doors into the building, he began to mount the winding steps two at a time toward the fourth floor. There was no elevator in the building because, afraid of its potential use by insurgents during a coup, Tankor Satani had refused to install one.

When the Coral reached the third floor, he saw that the high-vaulted ceiling was peeling, its frescoes a bit stained from the dampness the rains had caused, but that the walls adjoining the winding steps had not been damaged by the pounding of the rains and were still hung with pictures of the former British governors and Tankor Satani. The governors looked imperious, buttoned up in their white coats, and Moustapha Ali-Bakr wondered why Tankor Satani had left their pictures to hang on those walls when he had been so hell-bent on destroying the remnants of that colonial banditry. The black servants looked bored sitting at the feet of the colonials on the lawn, and likewise wore white outfits, although of cheaper make. It was a different age, Moustapha reflected.

Continuing his climb, he recalled how, a long time ago, he had stood on Bookerman Street when the new monarch had come on a visit. During the visit, there had been a linguistic argument over what to call, in the local language, the aide-de-camp walking behind the queen. The literal translation was so sexual it sent Malaguetans into a frenzy of laughter, especially as they could not imagine Her stuffy Majesty understanding the joke. Clearly, it was not a joke now that the official residence could do with a massive restoration of its past grandeur.

Dr. Kelfala welcomed the Coral with a broad smile. It was the first time they had really met, and he offered his guest a seat and pressed a bell on his desk for an attendant to serve drinks to break the awkwardness.

"You are not the worse for having been in exile all this time," the professor began, trying to make his guest feel welcome.

"Ah thank Allah for dat," said Moustapha Ali-Bakr, remembering the giver of blessings.

"You can say that again," the ex-academic agreed, thinking of his own recent apotheosis. He studied the face of the diamond magnate, paying attention to the deep furrows in his broad brow above the hard brown eyes and Mediterranean hawk-like nose, contrasting with a mouth of medium width; just the sort of man he felt could become a menace when the Coral was barking out orders to his employees or minions. He saw that his skin was still healthy, almost glistening, thanks in part to what people say about the mix of African-Arab blood holding up well against the onslaught of old age and the battering of the weather, whether winter or summer, which made some men and women of Caucasian and other stocks over fifty look as if they were on the cliff of decrepitude in the tropics. Dr. Kelfala guessed that the diamond magnate was at the tail end of fifty, which would make the Coral a mere five years older than he was. In a country where age was respected, they were therefore equals and could talk in forthright terms.

"You must be feeling lost without the old man?" the professor continued.

"Well," Moustapha said, stuttering. "It was His Excellency's time to meet God. We all get for die."

It was the Coral's turn to study his inquisitor. Clearly the minister had been testing his mettle to see how much he would give away about the secret deals Tankor Satani might have entrusted to him. Although most Corals had a reputation for not keeping secrets, Moustapha Ali-Bakr knew when to be circumspect for his own good. A year was a long time to be away from his business, and much as he hated to admit it, a lot had happened in his absence. The previously itinerant cattle-herding Fullahs had not only developed a taste for the secondhand car business, but they had bought deeply into the real estate in downtown Malagueta with the profits from selling their cows. The shops of the old Arab traders and of the Maroon women, and the spice bazaars of the Aku people from Nigeria, had disappeared or been bought by this new business class.

Moustapha knew when to play ball. "Honorable," he began, "I am a businessman, but also a trusted friend to any government I have to work with. Tankor Satani, bless his soul, was a personal friend; no, almost like my fader; but that does not mean I cannot serve the new president."

"You will support whatever programs we have to implement?"

"Give me a few weeks," he asked. "As Allah is my witness, I shall be behind you."

"We are renewing all the mining licenses, and also those for fishing."

"I know!" the Coral enthused, and, seizing this glorious opportunity, added, "Which is why I have brought these new papers for your government to consider." He brought the sheets out of his briefcase and, with the practiced skill of a man accustomed to the secret intrigues of doing business at the highest levels of government, placed them on the minister's desk. He knew he was now on comfortable ground.

"And to show you how much trust I have in your government and want to support its small endeavors right away, here, with respect, Mr. Minister, is something that the Coral community wants to contribute. Make you take this and gee am to His Excellency de new president. We mean well."

He reached out and touched the outstretched hand of the minister, as if to suggest that men build bridges only when they are not afraid of one another and that self-respect need not be confused with vanity. The bold and the courageous among men know that circumstances, and not moral platitudes, are what separates the successes from the failures in the world. Pleased with his daring, he got up to leave. Then, as if he had suddenly remembered the most important bond, his hand flew into the briefcase to fetch a huge brown envelope that he placed on the minister's desk, confident that his gesture would not be rejected. "And this is something from us to welcome you to dis great office, Honorable. May God keep you in dis position."

That evening, when the minister had his daily briefing with General Dan Doggo, he thought it prudent to let his boss know about the gift from the Coral.

"He is up to his old tricks," the president smiled, "but we should keep it, especially as we are running out of cash."

Two weeks later, no one was shocked when the minister of presidential affairs was seen driving through the streets of Malagueta in a brand-new Toyota Land Cruiser, whose retail price was twenty-five thousand American dollars. "He done move from being poor bookman at university to big-belly man in gov'nament," someone remarked rather sarcastically.

CHAPTER FIFTY-NINE

In Praise of Virility

FROM ALL indications, General Dan Doggo seemed to have survived the initial challenge of his first six months in office. His stock was still high, he always arrived early at the office, and things were going so well in the town that people began to forget about "de bad days" of Tankor Satani. But they couldn't help noticing that the general was putting on weight, though he was already a heavy man. "Is all de good food his other woman dey feed am," the gossip telegraph hummed in Malagueta.

His marriage was still solid, but no one expected a head of state to confine himself within that institution, when even some members of the clergy did not adhere to a high level of marital propriety.

General Dan Doggo was soon tested.

One day a Fullah delegation came to congratulate him. The leader was a dignified Marabout, resplendent in a flowing boubou. As soon as he was seated, he looked the general straight in the eye and came to the point. "Excuse me, Excellency, but big man like you need 'nother woman: one who sabi talk our language!"

"But ah get wife," the general said.

"Dat is good for small chief; you are big chief now. We go gee you 'nother woman," said the holy man emphatically.

General Dan Doggo thought about what Tankor Satani had suffered at the hands of his "Fullah cow." But for all he knew, the holy man was not only feared for his mysticism but also probably controlled twenty thousand voters, among whom his word was gold during a Friday sermon. He dismissed Tankor Satani's tragedy as divine justice for his crimes against the state, and hoped his own future would not be like that.

After a crash course in Fulfulde, the language of the Fulani people, the general began seeing Mariama Tukulor. She was a stunning beauty who still spoke with the sweet cadence of her ancestral Fouta Toro Kingdom, without the pollution of the language that most of her folk had suffered after they had moved from there and the Fouta Djallon mountains to settle all over West Africa. Although most women would have considered it a privilege to be the mistress of the president, Mariama Tukulor always insisted on the utmost decorum when General Dan Doggo was coming to visit her.

She asked him to come always late at night, and definitely without all the trappings of power, such as riding in a limousine with his guards bringing up the rear in a blue car, its security light flashing and the sirens blaring to bring out her neighbors. "They don't like me and will be jealous of my good fortune," she told the general.

Unlike Tankor Satani's "Fullah cow," as people always referred to Jenebah Djallo, Mariama was not a sorceress in bed. However, before making love to the general, she would perform a ritual of oiling her breasts with cocoa butter, leaving the general stewing in torment. As he watched her anoint her splendidly golden breasts and then her thighs, in the soft light of evening, he couldn't have been happier.

Incredibly, as soon as she started sleeping with him, she appeared to have brought him some luck, and he could not help speculating that she had turned her own magic to good deeds. After the initial disappointment of discovering an empty coffer at State House, a small grant soon arrived from the African Union, with which the general flooded the stores with basic goods such as cooking oil, tomato purée, and evaporated milk. And his foreign minister talked the Chinese into giving more tools to the farmers. For a short while life was a great season, and gone was the fear among journalists of being locked up for voicing their criticism, as in the terrible days of Tankor Satani. "Dis Fullah woman good for de general," said the Marabout who had introduced them.

Six months later, General Dan Doggo made his first visit to a provincial town to see some of those troublesome chiefs, without his wife or either of his two mistresses but with a large retinue of party officials, diplomats, and religious leaders. It was a pleasant day, no dark clouds hung threateningly in the sky, and a large flock of sunbirds was flying in gold, blue, and yellow formations above the trees, lighting up the morning. Instead of riding in a helicopter, which would have taken only an hour, the general had insisted on being driven the five-hour trip on roads that were good for the most part but tricky on some stretches of thin tarmac and gravel ruined by the six months of rain. Soon the cavalcade was passing through orchards adjacent to small adobe homes. Goats and sheep, unnerved by the noise, and reckless children rushing out determined to have a glimpse of their new leader would stray in front of the leading cars, adding to the anxiety of the drivers. Standing up to their knees harvesting a new crop of rice in the swamps, some peasants were waving, and others had rushed from other forms of toil to the bluffs overlooking their villages, all of them driven by a desire to cheer their new leader.

Around noontime the sun was bearing down gently, and it was slightly cooler the further inland they got. When the general was at his destination, he discovered that his itinerary was quite a taxing one: the afternoon beginning with a meeting with the regional chiefs, after which it was off to inspect a school, open a new water supply, and listen to other concerns not hitherto penciled for discussion.

"I cannot be partial," he said. With the air of a trusted village chieftain, one clearly enjoying the power his presence and words had over the assemblage, he sat through an old simmering feud over water rights and finally got the contestants to talk peace. A young troupe of dancers and acrobats and a puppet show by colorful dwarfs had been invited to entertain the general. Later, exhausted from the long day's events, most of the general's staff and the diplomats eventually retired to their rooms for a quick nap before the dinner planned for seven that evening.

Sophie Burkham-Braun, the wife of the German ambassador, could not sleep in spite of the air conditioner cooling the cabin. Although she loved him dearly, she couldn't stand the bull snoring of her husband. A tall, svelte blond of about forty, she was new to Kissi, her first residence in Africa, and she was enjoying herself, finding the place challenging and mysterious after a boring tour of duty by her husband in Qatar. She did not mind that they had to use a generator when the lights went out in Malagueta or that her cooks were stubborn men who were polite but adamant about their dignity when challenged by a woman. Drawn to the simplicity of village life, away from the capital city with its copycat manifestations of Western life, she thought of how pleasant it would be just to be able to go for long walks through the quiet misty villages, at peace with nature, accompanied by a dog, without the phalanx of politicians and security men, and into the woods looming dark in the twilight, when she could imagine she was back in the Black Forest of Germany.

Their cabin was next to the president's, secluded from the others by a grove of large banana trees and a hedge of oleander, but the doors of the cabins faced opposite ends for greater privacy. She thought she would walk to the woods along a quiet path lined with brilliant poinsettias and wild hibiscus, have a cigarette, and come back in time for dinner. But she had barely gone a few steps when she saw a smiling General Dan Doggo in front of the presidential cabin. Sweating, with only a large towel wrapped around his huge bulk, he was bidding good-bye to a young ebony-black woman, a ravishing beauty who left Sophie Burkham-Braun breathless just looking at her. "The general must be a very virile man!" Sophie Burkham-Braun gasped.

She moved back into the shadows of the grove, amazed that after such a hectic schedule, the president still had energy left for sex when her own husband was snoring in his cabin. Momentarily, she thought of whether she should tell her husband about what she had just witnessed, but decided it was none of his business.

It was not until she had gone some distance and saw smoke rising from the fires outside of the huts that she remembered to light her cigarette, still thinking about the stunningly beautiful woman and wondering what it would be like to sleep with such a virile-looking man as General Dan Doggo!

CHAPTER SIXTY

The Children of Sisyphus

YEAMA ISKANDER turned sixteen three years after General Dan Doggo came to office. Although not as beautiful as her mother, she was a very attractive woman, quite charming and levelheaded, so Habiba Mouskuda felt her daughter was less likely to make the same mistakes she had made as a young woman. "If I have to ask God for anything when I come back in another life, it will be that I do not have the same beautiful face to torment men," she told Yeama.

"Are you ashamed of your past?" Yeama finally asked her mother.

Habiba had been anticipating this question from her daughter for years, not knowing how she would respond to it. "There are things I did that I had no business doing. Initially, in my callousness, I used to blame the absence of a father for my drifting away, for all the terrible hurt I caused men: those who wanted me for my body and to whom I readily gave it. But my worst crime was the pain that I caused the ones who really loved me. Luckily. I eventually grew up, and no one knew how I suffered trying to change."

One day, many years ago, before she met the philosopher, Habiba Mouskuda had felt so guilty about the "terrible things I have done to men," she drank a large dose of blue zinc oxide powder, intending to kill herself. Luckily the poison was not strong enough to kill her, but she bled profusely for two days, her stomach churning as she brought up what looked like green worms, before she collapsed. When she woke up, she was lying in her bed and her friend Victoria was sitting next to her with a large bowl of catfish pepper soup.

"Of all the terrible things you have done," Victoria said, "this is the most harmful and stupid!"

"I didn't want to go on living," Habiba Mouskuda said.

"Then you shouldn't expect too much out of life, because it is mostly about struggle and the courage to go on living."

Two weeks later, after she had not dreamed about Colonel Fillibo Mango for a long time, he appeared to Habiba. Of all her temporary loves, he was the only one who had really touched her; but, given that she had thought herself incapable of feelings back then, she had not realized it. How strange, looking back, to see that it was his gentle spirit that was making her feel how rotten she had been to men. She deeply missed the kind colonel, his poetic way with words and his gentle brooding. Not for the first time, she regretted that she had not gone to his trial, and had not been moved when Tankor Satani had him executed on a trumped-up charge. As though Colonel Fillibo Mango had discerned her torment, he reminded her once again of what she could do to assuage her guilt. "Devote your extra time to charity."

Next morning, shocked by what she was contemplating, she decided she would go to the leprosarium on the outskirts of town and volunteer her services. When, a week later, she was shown into the room where her first patient sat—an ordinary space with hardly any furnishings besides a bed and chair, the windows partly closed to keep out the light—more than the rudimentary conditions, it was the loneliness of the boy sitting on the bed that appalled her. He sat looking vacantly past her at a world that had blighted his future, a mere lad of ten, solitary, his face covered in welts, the terrible disease almost eating out his eyes. The ugliness on his face was frightening, yet he did not seem the least angry at his plight, and when he managed a smile, Habiba Mouskuda saw that he had fine white teeth. Then it was that the other feature of his disaster hit her: he was an albino. Gingerly she reached out and touched his face, and almost as though she were reliving a scene from her past, she realized it was her son that she was tending to, the one she had not looked at many years ago, when he had been born with multiple defects. Suddenly her heart could no longer stand the torment it had carried for so long. Uncontrollably, she began to cry for a life spent chasing mirages, for all the men she had treated badly, but more for herself, for her inability to give love. All at once, as though she had reached the deepest level of pain, she felt the great dam that had been locked inside her for so long burst, and she knew she would never be the same again as the boy wrapped his arms around her shoulders convulsed with her bitter tears. For the next twelve months she went, without fail, every Saturday morning to take care of him.

"He saved my life," she said to Yeama.

"How do you feel now?" Yeama asked her mother.

"I have learned to live with those ghosts. When I was young, life was not easy for women like me. We were sometimes terrible, but were also victims of a kind of vanity amongst men. Now I know that what a woman needs is not a rich man, but a kind and caring soul. I have accepted all my misadventures as my fault and hope you do not judge me too harshly."

"No, I don't. In fact, now that I am old enough I am beginning to understand."

In the widely held belief about an only child's life, everyone had thought Yeama would be spoiled or lonely, but she was neither. Like every other teenager, she was looking forward to her sixteenth birthday, and Habiba Mouskuda and Irene, just as enthusiastic that Yeama was approaching that magical age, had chosen presents to express their separate dreams for the young woman. Irene, who had never given up the hope that there would be a fine wedding in the family before she died, had spent the previous night going through her jewelry box for something appropriate for a sixteen-year-old. Now that she had finally accepted the malatta as worthy of her son, she had lots of crocheted materials, lappa and buba gowns, and pearls and other jewelry she would have liked to give to Habiba for her wedding. But after seventeen years of living together, the philosopher and his lover seemed so happy outside of that institution that Irene's only hope of dancing to goombay wedding music in that house was if Yeama eventually married. On the morning of Yeama's birthday, thinking that the tall, sweet, elegant girl would be awake, and because she wanted to be the first to wish her well and give her a present, Irene went to her granddaughter's room, where a shaft of light had come in through the trees.

"You are my joy, young lady," she began, "dat ah don't mind saying it over and over again. God works in mysterious ways to bring joy to people," she said, thinking of the Coral blood in her granddaughter. "Here, dis is what your granny is giving you on your birthday."

It was a pair of tiger's eye earrings studded with small gold stones. They had cost her much of the money saved from years of doing the Corals' laundry and from what her son and Habiba had been giving her since then, and she was happy to spend it. "Here, put them on," she said to the astonished girl.

"I know how much you love me, Granny, but these must have cost a fortune."

"Dat is nonsense, gal. If ah don't spend my money on you, who should I lavish it on before ah die? Now go back to sleep before your parents wake up."

Unknown to Theodore, Irene had paid for a coffin that was kept hidden in the attic at the undertaker's for her funeral; but although she was over eighty, death did not seem in a hurry to claim her. She was tough in spirit as well as in her bones, so she was not surprised when, one day, the children of a friend who had just passed away came to her with a most unusual request.

"Mama Irene, you are not yet ready to die, so lend us your coffin so that we can bury our moder."

Irene agreed, and over the next three years, the same request was made each time Irene bought a new coffin but showed no sign that she was ready to go to "de Master." However, when she bought a fifth coffin, she felt she had done enough lending and was determined to hold on to this one in case of a sudden death

One hour after Irene had wished Yeama a happy sixteenth birthday, the philosopher and Habiba Mouskuda came to their daughter's room beaming with their own wishes and to bring her presents. The philosopher had imagined that the women might give Yeama some jewelry, so his gifts to her were, selectively, a fine silver jewelry box and a metronome he knew she wanted, for she had started to measure the rhythmic notes of the various birds singing in the orchards by tapping her fingers. Long ago, he had not been surprised that she had shown a passion for books, and thus his most treasured gift was the collected works of the Senegalese writer Mariama Bâ, who had just died and whom Yeama admired greatly. With the hope that she and her daughter would continue to love and respect each other, Habiba Mouskuda gave her a beautifully embroidered gown and shoes to match. Since, surprisingly, in spite of all of her affairs as a young woman, Habiba had never been out of the country, it was her wish that her daughter travel as soon as possible, so she also gave her tickets for a holiday to any of the neighboring West African countries. Not-too-flashy pearl earrings and a necklace for Yeama's first communion completed her mother's gifts.

"And we are throwing a party for you, young woman," Habiba said, kissing her daughter.

"After all of this?" the sweet girl marveled.

"You deserve all of it," replied her father.

A Lack of Substance

The party was not a large affair, but it was colorful and celebrated with the frivolousness of youth by thirty of Yeama's girlfriends and boys, who danced to world music. It was the first time some of Yeama's friends had been to the house, so she gave them a tour of the living room with its beautiful collection of African sculptures and paintings by some up-and-coming Malaguetan artists. Later she took them to the study to see her father's vast collection of jazz and classical recordings. With her father's permission, they leafed through the manuscript of the biography he had been writing on his illustrious ancestor, the poet Garbage Martins, who had championed the pioneers of the city, and they looked at some other writings in that cluttered but tidy room full of old and new books. The aromas of an occasional cigar and brandy, and the busts of various icons of culture, philosophy, and music, added a sense of magic to the room, which was unlike anything many of the young people had experienced before that evening.

Among Yeama's friends were some budding poets who wanted to read some of Garbage's work aloud. Soon they were enthralled by the poet's world of fire and magic, imagining him reading his own poems aloud when Malagueta was a small, thriving town of wonderful dreamers. Two days later, although still a bit tired, Yeama went back to what she enjoyed doing best: reading, when the light in her room often glowed well past midnight. Her interests were in history, the environment, and geology; perhaps because the land was mostly of rocks—red and black granites—whose feldspars and quartz, when washed into the river, sometimes yielded rich potassium, which she was worried was toxic to the fish. But fish were plentiful in the river, and she had not forgotten how, when she was a child, Irene had taken her to watch the herons as they dived, and how one day they had seen a kingfisher come up with a fish twice its size, bash it on a rock, and eat it.

When Irene became too old to be trailing after the equally old but still feisty dog, it was Yeama who kept an eye on Tiger. As a young woman from an illustrious family, she had started to attract young suitors. They came timidly to the house and were always exceedingly polite, and after Irene had cross-examined them about their pedigrees they were allowed to stay and talk, always under the watchful eyes of Habiba.

"You are too strict with her," Irene observed once.

"I have to be," Habiba replied. "But it is not her that I am worried about, but that some no-good boy might slip into this family when we least expect. I don't want her making the same mistakes I made as a young woman, when my own mother allowed my indiscretions."

The boys that Yeama really fancied were those from what were considered renowned families, two especially: the last son of the estimable Dr. Sidi Samura, and the son of a Senegalese diplomat—a not-too-far-distant relation of the poet-president Léopold Sédar Senghor, who had dispatched the diplomat to Malagueta in recognition that the town had once been a citadel of learning. After the two young men had passed the strict examination of Habiba Mouskuda, she gave up worrying about their integrity.

They had been at Yeama's sixteenth birthday, but of the two boys it was obvious that it was the son of the celebrated gadfly that Yeama favored, and his competitor soon dropped out of the picture, which was a relief to Irene. Although she liked Pathe N'jai Tall, who was a fine young man, dark as rich ebony and with a noble bearing, she was worried about her only grandchild going to live amongst "those Wollofs, whose women are too fine, dey will make Yeama's life miserable for stealing one of their men. She would be lost forever to us," Irene cried at the prospect.

In contrast, Albert Samura was a pale figure, lighter than copper, and while he had none of his father's fiery revolutionary spirit, he was equally brilliant, frail like him, and bespectacled, but not effeminate. As if to dispel that last assumption on the part of anyone, and much to the consternation of his father, the eighteen-year-old was somehow interested in a career in the military.

"Of all the ways God could think of punishing me for not believing in him, this is the worst," the doctor remarked painfully about the twist of fate to Theodore Iskander when the two friends met one evening for their weekly session of chess, where they would be deeply unhappy together about the fate of Malagueta.

The philosopher tried to console his friend. "Perhaps in time, with lads like him to clean up the corrupt military, it will become an honorable institution once more."

"Not in our lifetimes, my friend," the doctor said despairingly, drinking slowly from his brandy goblet.

"So much the better; for then they will be honorable in their own time," Theodore replied.

Dr. Samura was in fact quietly pleased about his son's independence. It showed the boy had integrity and courage, especially given the doctor's loathing for the military. In reality, Albert had not really made up his mind about his career. His interest in the military had come to him after one particularly brazen incident, which provoked such rage in him that his normally gentle features were frayed when he visited Yeama one evening. As usual, he was dressed smartly, if casually, in a neatly pressed shirt and khaki trousers with brown shoes. He was always prim and proper, and would bring flowers for Yeama, unlike the other boys his age.

He was even more taciturn on that particular evening, and his seat could not contain him; he was as agitated as a hen calling a wayward chick to come home before a hawk found it. When he finally stopped pacing up and down the verandah and sat next to Yeama, it was clear to her that something awful had happened, perhaps not to him, but distressing enough to upset him. His face, as he stared at the river, was dark, with an intense gravity on it that Yeama found troubling. He cracked his knuckles and said, "Shame, bastard, son-of-a-bitch eunuch," disgust flooding his face.

"What is eating you up with such anger that you have not said anything all evening, except for the expletives so unlike you?" Yeama finally asked.

"The greatest disgrace ever to happen to the military since Tankor Satani corrupted them."

"Nothing could be worse than their pillaging of the country's resources when he was alive, or what is going on right now with this stupid General Dan Doggo and his ministers," she asserted.

"It is beyond belief," he said.

"So tell me."

"Some other time," he said.

With Moustapha Ali-Bakr back in favor, the stock of the Corals was once again high. As they had previously done when Tankor Satani was the president, they began to cultivate the top government ministers and civil servants of the new government, and were not averse to doing the same with foreign diplomats and airline personnel. Their inchoately chased tongues regained their uncouth argots, and they went back to savaging the black man's language, insulting people, and raining curses on their servants with a theatrical flourish. Even more disgusting, they resumed their sexual molestation of their children's nannies. To the chagrin of most Malaguetans, the discipline they had hoped for "with a military man now at the State House" had been short-lived. Without any warning, a rapacious horde of academics and politicians was let loose on Malagueta. It was rotten enough to make the dead turn over in their graves, as if a vengeful sprite had hurled a great stone on the children of Sisyphus.

"We thought it was terrible when Tankor Satani ruled us in the years of the barracudas," a distinguished retired academic said with disgust to his friend one night. "Now it is the time of the piranhas, and they are leaving nothing for us in the waters."

"But you have forgotten something," his friend replied. "They may have degrees in their subjects, but they lack substance and character. They are not the strong breed, and when it comes to stench, I would rather have a skunk near me than those academics-turned-politicians."

CHAPTER SIXTY-ONE

La Dolce Vita

Writing the biography of the great poet had kept Theodore Iskander holed up for weeks in his study, and his mistress was concerned about his health, especially as he was eating very little and drinking only cups of black coffee as he worked late into the night. "Come out for some exercise," Habiba would plead. "It is good for your leg!"

Yet when he took time off from his writing, it was to fume about the avalanche of Americans, Japanese, and Chinese that had suddenly discovered Malagueta. Brassy, manipulative, and arrogant, they were offering to buy up all that the new government was preparing to deregulate—electricity, the post office, television, and so forth—although it was in fact the lure of diamonds that had brought them to town. A new mine had been discovered, and the news had caused all kinds of excitement abroad. "Think of how rich we shall become, like the Belgians were in the Congo," said an American speculator as he shared the news with his wife. The excitement was not shared by the people down in the capital Malagueta. Kissi, but especially its capital Malagueta, was dying, it seemed. This city, built by free slaves, was losing its beauty and charm; its famed educational and legal institutions had collapsed; the citizens were losing the decency and humanity that had made them appear civilized. On its narrow streets, uncollected garbage would pile up for weeks, the botanical garden stank with the feces of the homeless, and large griffon vultures would swoop down from the historic cotton tree to feed on the dead dogs left lying on the streets.

One day, as Theodore Iskander was driving home, he was assailed by the feeling that the town was doomed. Over the weekend, long queues of the cars that not so long ago had been cruising the old districts had started forming for gasoline, some as early as four in the morning. The bakeries were running out of bread, and there was a shortage of rice and many other goods. A deep paralysis permeated the government as the last of the powerhouse generators packed up, food rotted in the putrid refrigerators, the kids had no ice cream, drinks tasted like molten lava, and clothes mildewed in the dark armoires of misery. In the wards of the crumbling hospitals, there were no drugs for the children of any small or large gods, or for the old, the dying, or the maimed. All day long, the hardworking doctors performed difficult surgery by candlelight; or when they were defeated by their task, left the untreated to die of their wounds and their pain.

"This is nightmare in paradise," one journalist wrote about life in Malagueta.

For the first time since the terrible riots by university students when Tankor Satani was president, Theodore Iskander felt the same was likely anytime now.

General Dan Doggo's response to the unfolding disaster was to feign insouciance and sleep most of the time. Aghast, his wife wondered what the hell was happening to a man who had initially wanted to wear the cloth of the church. She thought she had the answer. "You have been eating all kinds of stuff at your mistresses', so what should people expect?" she fumed.

That was partly true. But what seemed to have dulled the brain of the already not too bright general was his appetite for liquor. Increasingly, he was known to drink himself into a stupor, and would not leave a reception or party until he had drunk the last bottle of whiskey. Since coming to power he had added a few pounds, but he played tennis not to bring down his weight but to help with his gargantuan lovemaking to his women, one of whom had been awarded a contract to bring in a new electrical generator for the powerhouse. Ill-equipped for the task, knowing very little about electricity, she used the money to buy three fashionable downtown buildings. But such shocking indecency did not seem to bother the general and his cronies, as long as their pockets were being fattened.

The Patriot

The country was dying, but it was a golden period for the Corals and for some of the soldiers and top-ranking government officials. It was at that time that Albert Samura became so enraged that he thought of becoming a soldier, after an incident in the home of a Coral.

One evening, tipped off that a big-shot Coral dealer was about to smuggle a large gem out of Malagueta, General Dan Doggo dispatched his chief of staff, Brigadier Abu Karamoko, to the house of the dealer with instructions to stop it.

A short, pompous man, always nattily dressed, the brigadier was driven to the house of the Coral one evening. Unlike Moustapha Ali-Bakr's house, this Coral's home, although large, was a study in tasteless decorating: large, bland sofas; the usual plain Afghan carpet, without expensive arabesques; and a leather-bound copy of the Koran on a table. Artificial flowers sat in a pot containing sand, and there were hookahs from Turkey and samovars bought from desperate Russian wives living in the town. A hi-fi console took up a large space in the living room, a seafront breeze was blowing, and the low-hanging sea-blue chintz draperies were knocking against the windows.

"What you want?" the Coral asked impertinently.

"I have orders for you to surrender the diamond," the brigadier replied.

"Who give de order?"

"The commander-in-chief of the republic."

The Coral, whose name was Mamoud Khalil-Wahab, smiled contemptuously at the small man in military uniform, as though the brigadier were a minion, a chihuahua trying to act like a rottweiler. Earlier, as soon as the officer walked in, and even though the Coral had never done business with him before, he had discerned, in the chiaroscuro light shimmering in the living room, that the brigadier was a nobody. His smallness suggested he was not someone who, in the likelihood of General Dan Doggo being overthrown, the Coral would have to reckon with; he did not think it worth his while to even be civil.

"Go to hell," he said, with as much contempt as his voice could carry across the vastness of his living room. "De diamond not your business."

Brigadier Abu Karamoko rose from his seat. He took two steps toward the Coral and wagged a finger at him. "You are stealing from the country, and I shall report back to the president," he said, trying to salvage some of his dignity.

Like a shaft of lightning, one that almost erased his dignity, he did not see the slap coming from the Coral but felt it land hard on the right side of his face. A naked, ugly crack had opened on his face, and blood ran into his mouth.

"Who be you to give me order," the Coral barked at him, "when we done buy de commander-in-chief?"

Brigadier Karamoko lunged at him but tripped on the carpet. When he tried to get up, the Coral grabbed him and held him in a vise. Unarmed, and the Coral being a bit of a bulky fellow, the brigadier was at a disadvantage when it came to fighting back, so it was left to his aide-de-camp to defend his boss's honor. But when the underling pulled out his gun, intending to blow out the Coral's brains, the brigadier stopped him with a sharp command. "Hold your fire," he said. "If you kill him now, we won't know where he is keeping the diamond. His kind would rather die than talk."

"How did you hear about this horrible incident?" a shocked Yeama asked after Albert had finished his narration.

"From the son of the aide-de-camp, a classmate of mine."

"What a disgrace," said Yeama.

"The only one with any honor out of this disgusting incident was the aide-de-camp. He resigned from the army and was given a large pension beyond his rank of sergeant to keep the incident a secret," Albert said.

"May God help Malagueta," Yeama prayed.

While they were talking, the river had risen above the jutting rocks and begun to lash noisily against the retaining wall of the house. It was as though the deity living in it had been listening to the young man, who was shaking with rage. Yeama took his hand and squeezed it to calm him down. Two years younger than he was, she seemed wiser about the world, and as they bonded together, thinking of how low honor had fallen in Malagueta since Tankor Satani, and now General Dan Doggo, took over, she saw a large heron taking off, squawking loudly, as though it too had been listening and was sickened by this incredible story. Looking into the eyes of the courtly young man, she saw the fierce determination there, and she immediately understood how someone so clearly gentle and kind could have been moved to contemplate joining the military to restore a sense of honor.

The Best Whorehouse in Town

After a while, the complexities of being president began to tell heavily on General Dan Doggo. Drunk most of the time, he looked increasingly like a sad ghost of his old sartorial self in broad daylight and was regularly hounded in sections of the press as a glutton for young girls and an incompetent leader to boot. Having given him enough time to show his mettle, Dr. Sidi Samura and Theodore Iskander, with little concern for their lives, unleashed their contempt for the general in a series of articles published by the fearless journalist who had taken up with Moustapha Ali-Bakr's former mistress. In the articles, they railed that Tankor Satani had at least been trim, and that besides the Fullah nymph that he had taken to his bed (who, incredibly, had turned out to be a wily, vengeful mermaid), the old man had limited his conquests mostly to grownups! Inspired by the writings of the philosopher and the doctor, intrepid schoolchildren would laugh at the general when his cavalcade drove past their schools, and post lampoons of him drooling like an insatiable bull for young calves.

General Dan Doggo began to have terrible nightmares in which Tankor Satani was yelling at him from his ocean grave, calling him a "half-baked ignoramus!" These visitations came so regularly that General Dan Doggo began to dread falling asleep, fearful not only of the serpent's tongue of his former boss but of his wife's taunting during the few times she could stand sharing their bed. In all seriousness, he confided to his minister of presidential affairs that he was thinking of giving up the office of president, after only four years in power, for the priesthood.

"I am being roasted alive for being nice to everyone who comes knocking at my door for a favor," he complained to Dr. Bemba Kelfala. "But there is not enough of me to go around to satisfy all of them. So I had better resign."

"If you were to resign, it would spell disaster for all of us, General," said the former professor. "In the name of God, don't talk like that."

With his long days of penury at the university now behind him, Dr. Bemba Kelfala had almost forgotten how far he had come from the tedious grading of term papers and lectures on political theory. In those days he did not have enough money to even buy cigarettes most of the time, and the idea of losing the commercial ventures he had acquired since becoming a minister horrified him. Just as Tankor Satani had looked at the hills of Malagueta and envisioned the grandeur of his Xanadu there, the professor, for different reasons, thought of a descent back into penury; he saw himself in the deepest pit of Hades, where fiery demons were staring at him. It was then, with a stroke of brilliance, that it occurred to him that what the general needed was a new thrill: he would send some willful coeds to the general's bed. "It would be like sleeping with all the best brains and beauties in the town, General," he promised his boss.

He chose the most enchanting girls: tall, willowy, dark, light-skinned, ebullient, quiet, refined, or, occasionally, quite ordinary, but all of them bubbling with expectations and daring as they came to State House, initially in a trickle, usually in the late hours of the evening, then later in large groups, smelling of the exotic aromas of French or Arabic perfumes. If the General and his minister were working late, they would wait until both men were ready to retire to their secret lairs, with two or three women at a time, to satisfy their lust. Because it was in the center of town and easy to reach, the State House was more appealing to these girls than the Xanadu had been for Tankor Satani's women. General Dan Doggo and his minister were known to be generous—some might say reckless—with the nation's money, and soon a flood of women was streaming to the State House, as early as dawn, to "eat the country's money," breezing through the visitor's entrance to wait for the two men.

Malaguetans were appalled when they saw the parade of the girls. Some of them had university degrees they could have used in the service of other women. Others, though not so bright, were stunning birds of paradise who shattered all illusions about decency, their eyes glaring like luminous gems as they left the palace with handbags stuffed with cash. Beyond the incomprehensibility of how girls from good and not-so-good homes could be so cheap was the horrifying thought that it was an ex-academic who was pimping for the president.

CHAPTER SIXTY-TWO

The Serpent's Tail

MONICA DAN Doggo thought she would die of shame when she discovered that not only was her husband sleeping with many coeds, but his "pimp" was sampling the most beautiful ones before dispatching them to the general's couch. Long ago, given the complex nature of politics, she had accepted the idea of "shared property" as far as the general's taking of mistresses was concerned. "She has the wedding ring, but I have the man!" as one of General Dan Doggo's mistresses said.

But what was going on in State House went far beyond that; it was a disgusting scandal in flagrant violation of decency. Yet no court would have listened to Monica Dan Doggo, so she did not even contemplate a divorce. She blamed God and stopped attending mass, concerned that the priest of her order would impose an intolerable burden upon her soul by asking her to forgive her husband, when what she craved was the damnation of his soul.

She became a born-again fundamentalist Baptist and remained cloistered for a whole week in the guest room in their house, the door bolted to keep the general out, while she burned offertory candles for his damnation. Their two children were studying in England, and she was thankful they were not around to witness their father's debauchery. She also took some comfort in the realization that she was no longer in love with him anyway, what with the way he had let his bulk grow beyond the dignity expected of a military man. "Even Japanese sumo wrestlers look better than that fool," she said one evening.

They had seldom slept together since he became president, and although she still had sexual yearnings, she thanked God for giving her the strength to bear her lot. But nothing was as sweet to her as when she was apprised of a recent discomfort suffered by the man she blamed for her misery: the minister of presidential affairs, Dr. Bemba Kelfala.

Brushing aside the guards in front of the politician's mountain house, a leper, hunchbacked and disfigured, turned up one evening to beg for alms. He was not obsequious, but spoke with a strong, steady voice: "Just enough to see me through to the next day, Honorable," he said, relying on the minister's boyhood belief in Islamic almsgiving, if not the fear of a leper's curse, to elicit a generous hand of charity.

To show that his heart was still in the right place, Dr. Kelfala took the outstretched hand into his own. In anticipation of an immediate blessing from God for doing the right thing—giving the leper enough money to last a whole month—he raised his eyes to the sky.

"Let me bless you," the leper said in gratitude, and he held the minister's hand and looked him deep in the eye. Dr. Kelfala felt a sudden, unfathomable terror, as though he were really looking into the face of death. But after the leper had gone he was able to put the incident out of his mind, especially as he had a date with a shy new girl that night.

She was a dark, statuesque beauty with a finely chiseled face and nullipara's breasts that had tempted him the first time he saw her, while he was being driven home. Her lips were full, generous, yet she wore cheap clothes that made the professor feel she was from a poor but noble family. He told his driver to slow down for her.

"Come in," the minister said. "Let me give you a ride."

"I am from the same part of the country as you, sir, but the high cost of fertilizer has ruined my family's farming, so forgive my shabbiness, but remember that you have not visited the area once since becoming a minister," she said as soon as she got in the car.

When she was at his place a week later, she looked around the living room but did not appear awed by the furnishings. How commonplace his taste was became obvious to her after she noticed a goat tied to an old bench in his garage—clearly a parvenu, she decided. His meal and drinks were just as ordinary—beer instead of wine—and the entree was the routine that she could have had in any restaurant: half a chicken, beans, spinach, and white rice. As he watched her eat, he made the mistake of thinking she was enjoying it because her hunger seemed even more pronounced than her penury. It was a painful reminder of his own hungry days; but after she had taken a bath, she emerged looking very willowy, and as she walked toward where he sat on the bed, her regal dignity troubled him. He had never encountered a girl so devoid of wiles; not like any of those willful coeds.

"Leave the light on," she said as she began to undress.

Completely naked, she was even more beautiful than he had imagined, yet something in her eyes—a mixture of defiance, temptation, and daring—unnerved him. He tried to concentrate on her statuesque figure and voluptuous breasts, but noticed that her dark eyes were filled with what was clearly not surrender. What he saw was contempt for his kind: the academics and other intellectuals who had sullied their professions and betrayed the admiration she and others once had for them. Horrified, he was assailed by a feeling that she was not a normal human but the spirit of someone dead who had come to punish him for his crimes.

"Don't kill me, don't kill me!" he cried. He felt death looking at him, and like a whimpering dog he began frothing at the mouth. Because his head was slumped, he did not see the contempt expanding on the face of the beautiful woman, before he passed out in unspeakable terror. When he woke up with a livid fear in his stomach, two hours later, she was gone, but had left a piece of calico cloth impaled with a knife on his bed, as though to let him know that he was really dirt and that she could have killed him at any time.

When Monica Dan Doggo heard about the incident from one of the professor's servants, who was also her nephew, she rewarded him generously and had a most glorious evening for the first time in a long period of misery. "If he is not afraid of God," she exclaimed, "he has not yet heard about the serpent's tail!"

CHAPTER SIXTY-THREE

Of Heroes and Demons

SO SHAKEN was Dr. Kelfala after his brush with death that he did not go to his office for days, but stayed home drinking large glasses of whiskey. He stopped picking up women because any woman could turn out to be a sprite. And although he did not tell his boss about the incident, the debauchery at State House slowed down a bit. Then, as sometimes happens when tragedy has looked one in the face, he began to think of how to remedy what he felt was the deep emptiness in his life.

He toyed with the idea for a long time, thought about it when he was at his desk, even when he was driving back home, how he could regain some of his lost esteem as a man of learning, what, besides pushing for a raise in the deplorable salaries of his former colleagues at the university, he could do to show that his heart was still in the right place. When the inspiration came to him, it was after he had made a visit to some of the high schools to see for himself what they needed. As he was driving home one evening, the clarity of what he should do presented itself: he would commission a book about heroes to be distributed free of charge to the schools. For this venture, he turned to none other than his closest friend, the Hungarian historian Pukas Joachim.

Joachim was a dreamer. Six months earlier, in a not unexpected move, he had been kicked out of the university for insulting the head of the institution and had been living off the charity of his friend since then. A fat, presumptuous man, he had earned the contempt of his colleagues after boasting quite openly that he was the best teacher of history ever to enter the once venerable institution, which of course was arrant nonsense, given that Malagueta had some great historians who had continued to teach at the university.

His dependency on Dr. Kelfala made him the right choice for the job. "I came here to make a name for myself," Joachim said, his mouth dripping with disbelief, when offered a chance by his old friend to stop living from hand to mouth, "and I shall write the best book about heroes that has ever been written in this country."

Pukas Joachim was not a Jew, but his exploits on the African continent qualified as those of a wanderer, mainly for profit. He had been trained in Hungary and the UK as an academic but because of his intemperate language had failed to secure a permanent position at his preferred place of work, the School of Oriental and African Studies in London, where he and Dr. Kelfala had obtained their doctorates.

His curriculum vitae did not include his exploits in Chad, where some Tuaregs had chased him out after he tried to seduce their beautiful women, but he was quite loud about those in the Congo, where he had in fact taught at a Catholic university in Lumumbashi, which was where he first became interested in diamonds. While drinking in the bars of the lush, tropical city, he had heard that some Corals who controlled some of the exploit and smuggling of diamonds in the Congo ran a similar business in Malagueta.

"Go to Malagueta; de diamonds dere better dan dis here," one of his Lebanese drinking pals advised. "Also, de people nicer; dey speak English, and ah hear say all de beach nice."

Offered a teaching job in Malagueta, Pukas Joachim arrived with cash savings of five thousand dollars and with a grandiloquent claim, offered without any regard for the truth, that he had single-handedly done extensive research on a small group of pygmies in the heart of darkness that was the Congo. With slides and photographs, he explained, to small audiences, that these were the oldest people left unchanged by "civilization" in Africa. But when challenged for proof, his claim did not hold up, and he was thereafter regarded as a fraud, although he was allowed to keep his job because he had been given a three-year contract they couldn't break.

To be fair to him, he had some teaching skills, and he bonded admirably with the peasants. When his contract expired, the thought of going back to Hungary almost broke his heart. Depressed, he stayed in his house for days wondering about what to do, until he remembered the advice given him a long time ago, and ventured into diamond mining, hoping to make a quick fortune and retire to the south of Spain, where he had a small house.

"The Hungarian uprising against the Soviets failed, but I am not done yet," he said.

Contrary to what his Lebanese friend had told him in Zaire, he found the going rough in Malagueta, when his Coral partners doubled-crossed him with obsidian junk. Afraid that he might be kicked out of the country if he made a fuss about the affair, he obtained another teaching contract at a junior college, poorer now, having borrowed heavily from the teacher's pension fund for his wild ventures. For the most part, given his tendency to brag about his scholarship even after he had been dismissed by real scholars as a grasping fraud, the academic world shunned him, and his only real friend was another poor academic, Dr. Bemba Kelfala.

When it was published, *The Book of Heroes* provoked outrage in Malagueta. In glowing pages, Pukas Joachim wrote about the "greatness' of Tankor Satani, General Dan Doggo, and other "political pygmies," as someone dismissed them, yet he left out genuine icons, in the worst kind of biographical fraud imaginable. "This is what happens when you ask someone who does not know his arse from his elbow to write about us," an angry distinguished academic said.

Although Joachim was protected by his friend in government, howls of indignation went out for his dismissal from the junior college. Once again, it was his friend who came to his rescue. "I have the right job for you," said Dr. Bemba Kelfala. "One that will keep you out of trouble."

"What is it, my friend?"

"I am putting you in charge of a tourist resort on an enchanting island off the coast of Malagueta. A place where most people do not go."

"Why all the secrecy?" Joachim wondered.

"Because the waiters will be dressed in the costumes of nineteenth-century slaves, copied from drawings done at the time of Henri Christophe of Haiti. Except for provocative raffia skirts, the girls will be completely naked. The tourists will go wild seeing them while dining on grilled barracuda."

"You bet they will, Bemba."

"Stay on the resort as long as you like. Most Malaguetans hardly go there because it is beyond their reach," Dr. Kelfala said as he gave Joachim the keys to the main building.

"You don't know what you have done for me," Joachim said with gratitude.

"What are friends for, if they can't help each other?"

CHAPTER SIXTY-FOUR

Love and the French Lessons

ALL TOO sudden, General Dan Doggo became bored with his wild escapades. He began to spend his weekends at home reading his Bible, giving his wife the impression either that he was atoning for his sins or that God had finally touched his soul and the general was really contemplating what he had always wanted to do: become a man of the cloth!

It was an illusion. General Dan Doggo had fallen in love with a brilliant academic. They had met during the last university convocation, where Dr. Kelfala had introduced the woman to his boss. She was the kind that the general had not been interested in when he was obsessed with the coeds. Unlike those willful girls that the general had been sharing with his pimp, Madeleine Makassa was a professor of French and not a gorgeous bird of paradise parading down the promenade of easy conquest preening her feathers for aging men. After earning a doctorate at the Sorbonne, she had risen high in her profession and had only recently been widowed, after her husband, a highly respected economist, died in a car crash. Although his death had left her shattered, she soon bounced back at her work with remarkable courage, determined to go on teaching the poetry of Césaire, Senghor, Rimbaud, and Utam'si, and the novels of Cheik Hamidou Kane, Mariama Bâ, and Camus, with her usual passion.

Dr. Kelfala and some of her colleagues had paid for a bull so that she could perform the obligatory rites for the repose of her dead husband's soul. Afterward, Dr. Kelfala offered some advice. "Go abroad for a while, enjoy the bistros of Paris, eat in the pizzerias of New York, listen to the musicians at Covent Garden in London, or watch the flamingoes taking off in Nakuru Park in Kenya. I shall pay for anything you want. Try to dispense with the requirement of having to wear nothing but black for a whole year. It is bad for your soul."

Madeleine Makassa thought about it for a while but decided to stay. Her classes were too important. "I feel much better with my friends around than being lonely in a foreign country," she said.

She had another reason not to accept the offer of her erstwhile colleague, one to do with her sense of integrity. Although she was a woman not easily shocked, the sexual orgies going on at State House had left her wondering about the "home training" of those girls and about Dr. Kelfala's relationship with the president. A year after the professor became a minister, Madeleine Makassa had found it troubling that he now had a line of new four-wheeled vehicles in his compound. The expensive suits on the polyptych of the professor's previously trim frame had given him the aspect of a well-fattened bull, a grotesqueness that was beginning to compete with General Dan Doggo's own polymerous build. Even more incredible, she had heard that the professor had been buying up large sections of state land near one of Malagueta's most fashionable beach hotels, in addition to some commercial properties from the Gujarati traders in his hometown. Shocked by such extravagance, she thought it ironic that the prostitution of the mind was much more distasteful and profane than that of the body. As far as she was concerned, the former involved a doing away with principles, while the latter was sometimes a consequence of the terrible disasters that befall women: wars, rape, poverty, famine, and death—mostly the results of men oppressing women.

"Men are so unpredictable," she lamented, recalling that Dr. Kelfala had been one of the brightest stars at the university, whose mind she had deeply admired. She felt betrayed.

Built on a hill where there were still orchards of mango and orange trees, an unfinished house was the most important bequest in Madeleine Makassa's husband's will. It was one thing for Madeleine's husband to have loved her, but for him to have started building a house for her solely on his salary at a difficult time in Malagueta was proof to Madeleine's mother that she had married well. However, after he died, the reality of having to finish the house began to occupy her mind, and she was forced, painfully, to admit, while she was grading papers by the light of a Chinese lamp, that the one thing that gave her true independence—the house—was, ironically, an encumbrance on her freedom.

"God will find a way for you to finish it," her mother said, trying to help ease Madeleine's worries.

But with things the way they were in the town—erratic water and electricity supply at best, few jobs, a tight squeeze on money—there were no easy routes open to her. She was still grieving in her soul for her husband and trembled at the idea of falling into the hands of some grasping contractors, or of agreeing to cutthroat usury with the Coral-owned bank that was the only one lending out money for the kind of project she had. She felt handicapped, needed help: someone to guide her through the minefield of business deals, because, thanks to the behavior of those in the cabinet, the respect for academics was really low at that time. She was unaware that her life was about to change dramatically.

Dr. Kelfala came to see her late at night a month after the will was read. In spite of his libidinous escapades, he was a genuine friend, and she knew he did not desire her in his bed.

"What brings you here at this time of day?" she asked, aware that it was at a time when he was usually engaged with a woman either at home or in one of the fashionable restaurants on the rugged coast of the town.

"I came to see whether you needed any help," he said.

"You can say that I need some help," she conceded.

"Then I don't have to tell you that you can have any help you require. A loan or position in the government," he said, trying not to sound boastful.

After he was gone, she spent some time pondering what he had really meant, considering that he definitely had never made a pass at her. In the enigmas of their world, given that he was a political scientist and she had a doctorate in literature, it might have been thought they would easily understand each other. But she was left adrift, not any wiser for her education, a young widow wondering whether her mother had been right all along about placing one's trust in a gypsy woman's crystal ball. Only last week, the older woman had been to see one of the last gypsies left in Malagueta to have her daughter's future read.

"I see a fat man," said the gypsy. "Your daughter won't like him."

"Leave that to me," the concerned mother replied.

Madeleine could not help laughing at the idea of sleeping with a fat man when her mother told her about that. "Nothing is ever as they say," Madeleine said.

"But never say never about a road you have not walked on," her mother cautioned.

Notorious for the haste with which he had devoured the college girls and for the gluttony of his stomach, General Dan Doggo stammered an effusive pleasantry when his minister of presidential affairs introduced him to Madeleine Makassa at the university congregation. He surprised everyone by not immediately inviting her to visit him at State House. Given her high standing as a distinguished academic, she would have rejected his presumption outright. But he did offer, sometime later, strictly as a government loan, to finish her house, "so that you do not have to pay any usury. I don't get to meet brainy women like you, Professor," he said, obviously impressed with this blue stocking. "So allow me to help you."

For three months, one of his Coral contractor friends worked feverishly on the house before the impending rainy season, when the land would be mushy and work almost impossible. It was a task more demanding than it had seemed at first, as mistakes had been made in the original work: the large windows, originally meant to face the ocean and reconfigured to bring in a view of the forest back of the property, were crooked, and some doors were not aligned with their frames and would have to be completely replaced.

"Money is not a problem," General Dan Doggo told a worried Madeleine. "You are a good professor who deserves the best."

But even after the house was finished and the keys had been handed over to her, the general did not stop spending on what was now clearly an obsession. He made some secret enquiries about Madeleine's taste in furniture and saw to it that the house was furnished with stuff in keeping with her academic refinement: Danish sofas, Korean vases, Moroccan silver trays, Afghan rugs, Malian Bambara masks, and Malaguetan ornamental whiskey stools and tie-dyed draperies with the right motifs to match the rest of the decor.

Throughout all of this he was very correct with her. "Consider my help part of a long tradition of looking after the common good. Besides, your husband was a good man."

When Madeleine visited the general at the State House to thank him, he listened attentively and sought her advice on matters he felt she might have a better vantage point on than most of her erstwhile colleagues now in his cabinet. "They all want to become ministers, so will tell me what they think I want to hear instead of what they really believe," he smiled.

One day after she had been visiting him for six months as an adviser and he had still not made a pass at her, she began to wonder whether all the talk about his gluttonous binges with women was only the viper's venom of those he had not fancied. And she wondered whether he fancied her.

"Teach me how to speak French," the general asked one afternoon, as if to confirm that their relationship would remain on the level of simple friendship.

His grasp of the French language progressed so smoothly that Madeleine found herself liking him and was surprised at how easily that feeling had come to her. The more she got to see of the general, the more she discovered how really modest he was, a meek lamb. Given his refusal to be paid back the loan for finishing her house, she thought it was not a crime to accept gifts from him, when he had been known to help other women who were not his lovers. After almost nine months he still not made a pass at her, but remained really serious about perfecting his French.

"Why have you done all the things you have done for me?" she asked one afternoon when the lessons were over for that day.

"Because you are one woman that I respect," he replied.

"And you don't want to sleep with me?" she said, surprised at the ease with which she had come close to revealing what she had begun to feel for him.

"You underestimate your attractiveness, professor," the general said. "But I don't want to make the same mistake I made with my true love, which was a long time ago. I don't want to become irrational in love."

At thirty-five, Madeleine Makassa's body had begun to bloom with an alluring ripeness. Her soft curves and the delicate lines on her face were as though she had been fashioned by one of those naturalist sculptors that had studied at the Nok School of Fine Arts in Plateau State, Nigeria. Her loveliness was unmistakable after she had recently dispensed with the dark clothes of widowhood and started dressing in bright colors again. And there was no ambiguity in her eyes now that she had unsettled the general. She felt comfortable with him and really liked him, especially when he looked so meek during his French lessons. Her emotions having progressed from simply liking him to being tempted to see how he would respond to her allure, she pressed her advantage one day, after the lesson had ended, smiled at him, and she did not know what possessed her to do what she eventually did.

Perhaps it was the feeling, in the grandiose silence of the room, that this big bear of a man was the most uncomplicated creature she had ever known. When she looked into this sweet man's eyes, she was not the least amazed to find in them the unmistakable signs of wanderlust; they were the eyes of a man clearly not comfortable with his office, who wished he could be someone other than the president of Kissi. Then it occurred to her that, although not a product of an illustrious heritage, he was a good man, a cross between a milquetoast and a bit of a rogue: a character she had encountered in the minor novels of Balzac and the burlesque dramas of Wole Soyinka. The general was really a romantic who fitted the profile of a not too bright, but really harmless man, the kind that some women found attractive!

"Poor man," she said. "You have been giving me so much but not asked for anything in return." Slowly, with a provocative gesture meant to arouse the general, she pushed her chair closer to his, took his fat hands, and placed them on her quivering firm breasts. Not giving him a chance to resist, she unzipped his fly and brought out a fat, short animal graying at the scrotum and gasped at how different it looked from what she had imagined. As she began to massage the throbbing member with her right hand, she wondered which of her own students had held it in their hands? But it did not matter. "Allow me, General," she said as she moved from massaging to licking the crown.

She had not had too many men in her life and had not realized that some of them had such fat weapons. Yet once she began to put the icing on the cake, adding the caramel of her wonderful mouth to that otherwise tasteless fruit, she knew she could ask the general for anything she wanted: to give her the keys to the national treasury, or to renounce all further conquests of the coeds at the university, which she suspected he had not really enjoyed.

Hearing the deep moans of the general, she decided that all he had done in the past was to plow in the wet marshes of those willful girls. She knew he would do anything to hold on to her as she began to distill and to consume him in her alembic fire. General Dan Doggo forgot about his nightmares, the feeling that he wanted to give up being president lost forever.

As she began to move that joystick in her mouth into all kinds of unimaginably thrilling grooves, General Dan Doggo confessed that although the college girls had done the same repeatedly for him, they had been awkward beginners in a hurry, clumsy navigators only just discovering what it was like to traverse the phallic sea of man. What a difference it was to have a real woman giving him this blissful surge, coloring the crown of his animal into an erubescent fruit with her lips, so that when eventually the animal was so electrified, strong as stannum, the general experienced great spasms and was invited to enter Madeleine's warm, dark essence, he went on a shattering journey before landing on a seaweed beach, deeply spent.

"Stay with me forever!" he said when he was finally able to breathe.

Book Five

War and Those Diamonds

CHAPTER SIXTY-FIVE

A Different Kind of Coral

MADELEINE MAKASSA'S daring with the general was quite unlike her previous experiences with men, few as they were. But though amazed at herself, she did not feel she had been too forward with her new lover. For his part, General Dan Doggo, clearly in love, thought of making his first visit out of the country, bringing his mistress with him, but soon gave up the idea. "I prefer to stay here with you than to go to a conference in a strange place, even though I now speak a bit of the language," he said.

His insatiable appetite for her reached such a feverish state that he found it hard to stay away from her. He wanted to go to her place every day and take her to receptions and official functions, and seriously thought of reshuffling his cabinet and appointing her minister of children's affairs, but she balked at being so exposed.

"People will start talking, Soriba," she pleaded, trying to stop him committing a big mistake. But it was to no avail.

Now that his wife had retired into her born-again Christian cloister, where she had resumed lighting her candles to the avenging angels, intent on roasting his soul, General Dan Doggo eventually abandoned his empty marriage. He stopped seeing his other women, even Mariama Tukulor, the Fulani beauty, who had seemed capable of holding on to him forever. She had been tormenting him lately, refusing to sleep with him, even after he had built her a small house, until he had promised to bring down his weight. "You done fat too mos," she would complain during their lovemaking.

It dawned on her that she was losing him to his new mistress when, quite unusual for him, he did not come to visit her for two weeks. In vain she waited for his green Mercedes to pull up into her driveway, for her guards to greet her lover with "How are you, President, General?" when he arrived. Thinking of his gargantuan appetite, her kitchen smelled of sweet basil, thyme, mint, and *ogiri* as she cooked his favorite Saturday *plasas* stew, and she swore she would resist the temptation to nag him about his weight. But it was all in vain: he did not come. One night, feeling despondent over his absence, her tears fell and stained her beautiful gown as she burned incense in a silver urn, thinking of the hopelessness of waiting for him. In the dark wooden chest of drawers finished with ivory, the gifts that the general had given her sat like sad questioning ghosts of what she had done wrong. She had previously refused to consult any Marabout about her life, for she was a Fullah capable of reading the right Surah about divine providence. But now she asked a diviner to read some pages from the Holy Book for signs that the general had not grown tired of her.

The reading was not propitious. "'E done get book 'oman," the diviner said.

Painfully she heard about how General Dan Doggo's car had been seen at various times in front of Madeleine Makassa's house when the professor was not at the college. Given how well she had comported herself, unlike those scandalous college girls who had turned State House into a great whorehouse, Mariama Tukulor's humiliation was all the more painful when General Dan Doggo's most critical opponents thought he had finally shown he "get some class" after he started seeing the professor.

But just when the general and Madeleine were settling into what promised to be a period of bliss, their idyll was destroyed. War had broken out in Bassa after a rebellion there against Sergeant-turned-General Sey Warawara, who had overthrown President Kangoma, then gone on to rule with brutal force, finally picked up momentum.

"Life is a bitch!" the general exclaimed, borrowing one of Tankor Satani's favorite expressions, when he was told of the rebellion.

He was not the only one so dumbstruck by the vagaries of fate. Visibly aged in exile, badly in need of dental work, his skin taking on a sickly pallor, Gabriel Ananias had been rotting away in penury all those years but had been kept abreast of developments in Malagueta by the encouraging letters of Hawanatu Gomba. "Wait a little while longer until the dust has settled," she had written after the death of Tankor Satani.

Time and her willingness to forgive her enemies had not only healed Hawanatu's wounds but helped her forget her terrible loss of Theodore Iskander to Habiba Mouskuda. As she had done in exile, she found a job at the post office in Malagueta and, in her free time, was teaching a course on contemporary African women writers to the orphaned girls at a vocational institute, where she also taught needlework. "Learn all you can from these women, because you might need those lessons to help you survive in a world dominated by men."

Although she was by no means a born-again fanatic, she had found in religion a pillar on which to lean, and she would pray for Gabriel Ananias's return to Malagueta now that Tankor Satani was dead. From their correspondence she knew that Gabriel had even packed his bags to return home. But fate took a different turn.

One afternoon he found himself trapped in a stampede as people were rushing out of the way of the trucks carrying Sergeant-General Warawara's troops. Before the rebels launched their attack, the government had become increasingly hated. Its opponents had been disappearing in purges, and the soldiers, frequently drunk, would go to the shops and downtown markets to harass traders and demand goods from them, threatening to shoot them if they did not comply, and would feign all kinds of reasons to harass peaceful citizens. One day a large crowd of people stood on the main boulevard watching the troops leaving for the border. Many of the soldiers were hollering war cries and dancing boisterously up and down in the trucks taking them to confront the rebels. As the trucks rumbled through the outlying parts of the town, leaving behind a red dust, many cafés, banks, and shops shut their doors, and the sun, as though responding to the sound and fury of the trucks, bore mercilessly down on the city.

Quietly sneaking away from a small crowd in front of a newsstand, Gabriel Ananias hurried to his monastic room to reflect on his sad life. Just when he was thinking of going back to Malagueta, he was stuck in limbo, his fate once again uncertain. He felt, quite bitterly, that life had recently dealt him the cruelest blows, as when Tankor Satani had asked him to give up his house.

For a man who had lived in a mansion when he was governor of the Central Bank in Malagueta, his room in exile was quite small. Although it was not really a hovel, the paint was peeling off, there was only a single light bulb, and he had to share a communal toilet and shower with two other tenants. Always afraid of being killed by a disgruntled ex-employee who might also be in exile, he seldom left his single window open, and the air was stuffy, as in the houses of old people. Spider webs, the seasonal dampness, and the accumulation of old papers and magazines he had been reading to dull the boredom of exile added to the mustiness. But when he felt that he had reached rock bottom, his fate was somewhat changed. One of his old Coral friends, Faziz Haroun, who had made a fortune in diamonds in Malagueta before moving to Bassa, discovered Gabriel Ananias's circumstances and offered help.

"Not all Coral people bad; only wanting diamond, big Mercedes car, fine black 'oman and malatta *pikin* in Malagueta," the Coral said with genuine concern. "Ah sabi gratitude, de way you help me before, so, as Allah be me witness, ah go send you something ebry month."

"Thank you very much, Haroun," Gabriel Ananias said with gratitude.

Faziz Haroun kept his word. A week later, his benevolence allowed Gabriel Ananias to start living with some form of dignity after so many years of denial. He ate a three-course meal fairly regularly and even indulged in a bottle of wine now and then, a luxury that brought back memories of his spendthrift days as governor of the Central Bank in Malagueta. His wardrobe having become almost threadbare, he bought two new suits, shirts, socks, ties, and two pairs of shoes, a makeover that brought back some of his confidence and made him forget the humiliation of being a fallen angel. There was a noticeable sprightliness in his steps when he went out. For the first time in years, he began to imagine a future back in Malagueta, in which he might play a part, not in government, but, given his education, in some other sphere; perhaps as a social worker, a preacher, or, looking back to how he had been interested in animals, an environmentalist. He was still only in his forties, and it was never too late to start all over again. That future would, of course, include Hawanatu Gomba; they would live together and she, with her kindness, would help him to recover from the treachery of his wife. With the benefit of his experience in the banking world, he felt it was not impossible that they could have some level of comfort after he had come up with something to do. A new day was dawning, especially as the Coral had offered to give him some seed money to start afresh. Gabriel Ananias was looking forward to putting an end to his exile. But that was until he stopped to buy the latest magazines at his regular stand and saw the troops heading to the border.

They were mostly children, aged between thirteen and fifteen, conscripted by the government and given rudimentary military training to go and fight against the rebel leader, Judas Sampata, who was leading the rebellion in the north against Sergeant-General Warawara. To Gabriel Ananias, it was clear that in spite of their bravado some of the soldiers were too small for their uniforms and could barely hold their weapons. It was then that he began to think of his own kids and of the last time he had seen them. But for the benevolence of God, they could have been here in exile with him, rotting, lost, or perhaps conscripted, like the ones now on their way to an uncertain future. Hurrying home to avoid detection, he felt deep pain but also relief. Somehow, for the first time since his wife deserted him, he was grateful his children were safe somewhere in the United States.

CHAPTER SIXTY-SIX

The Long March

AT FORTY, Judas Sampata was a self-assured man, volubly eloquent, trimmed, and well-dressed, with a swagger and bragging tongue to match. His speeches were replete with slogans that he had picked up during his time spent training as a guerilla. He had a mercurial sense of his own importance and trusted no one, not even his own wife, because he was reportedly a deserter from U.S. justice, having escaped during a prison break outside of Knoxville, Tennessee, where he had been serving time for fraud. With the backing of some very rich opponents of the sergeant-general, he went off to an unnamed Arab country to receive military training and plan his rebellion. Not the least of his reasons for outrage was the rumor about how the president and his wife could barely write and read, were unable to use a knife and fork, and had to be taught how to flush the toilet properly. "They are bush people," the rebel leader fumed.

When he first started talking about a rebellion, few people took him seriously. Aside from the coup that had brought the sergeant-general to power, the region had been quiet for almost ten years. War was foreign to those people, and Judas Sampata was left brooding alone with his dream for a long time, finding it hard going from one sleepy village to another trying to sell his idea that Sergeant-General Warawara was a murderous tyrant who should be overthrown.

"I could have stayed in the Arab country and become a rich man," he said, trying to win over doubters, "but I couldn't stand being comfortable while that half-baked sergeant was destroying my country."

His first recruits were angry men who had always felt neglected by the government in the outlying villager. With the first fifty men, Judas Sampata advanced on the small towns. Soon they were marching through the backwoods of the country, but would sometimes come into vast empty spaces, with the occasional tree along the way being all there was to remind them of any growth, before they got to the next town, which was not different from the last. One day, after he and his rebel army had walked for well over twelve miles without encountering any life, a town suddenly appeared, and he was amazed that besides a school, church, mosque, a trading post, and a baffa or beer house, there was some other form of social life there.

It was evening when he and his troops halted behind what he thought had previously been a barn or grain silo. Huge mango trees and tall grass in the vicinity provided cover. Judas Sampata decided to explore the dead town. "Stay here," he said to his troops.

With three of his men he began to walk down the main street of the town. An eerie silence hung over the houses, and the ghost of a meager existence loomed large in the empty wooden stalls that stood in front of some of the houses. Some dogs had seen them as they approached and had begun to bark, but their alert did not bring anyone out of the small houses, where it was obvious people were awake because their hurricane lamps were lighted.

Further down the road the quiet lay of the small houses was the same, but now, as though the dogs were privy to other forms of unwelcome entry into the town, they completely ignored Judas Sampata and his men. They came to a house slightly bigger than the others, built of stone and finished with windows of steel, whereas the other houses were of mud bricks plastered over with dry cement. A huge gaslight flamed in the center of the house, and there was a billiard table and a dart board, but no one was playing. Rather, ten men or so were gathered in a circle on the floor, shooting dice.

"Let's go in," Judas said to his men.

The dice players stood up as the armed intruders came in. Only then did Judas Sampata realize that one of the players was in fact a very beautiful woman. Next to her was a man with a pirate's patch over his left eye. The woman was tall, very dark and svelte, and so beautiful that Judas could not help admiring her for a few minutes, which drew a sharp reproach from the man with the patch, who had just lost on a weak throw.

"Your eyes bodering you, dat you want dem fixed, man?" he asked.

He was a bitter ex-sailor with a temper as violent as the Atlantic Ocean that had been his mistress for over twenty years. It had brought pneumonia to his lungs and a persistent cough to his chest, after which he was paid off and sent home for good. But his body bore no sign of any weakness. Reduced to working on land as a carpenter, he felt cheated by life after that enormous challenge that was the sea, where he had sometimes felt like a conqueror on its waves and during numerous port calls had visited the brothels on the faraway islands of Madeira and Cape Verde to enjoy a few days of respite. He missed that feeling of freedom, and the only thing that kept him sane in his bitterness was the knowledge that he had a good woman. So when Judas Sampata stared at her, it set his blood boiling.

Not wanting to be distracted from his goal of recruiting more men, Judas Sampata thought it best to ignore him. But the man was persistent. "Ah axed you a question; your eyes bodering you?"

"I don't know what you're talking about," Judas said guardedly.

"You look at me woman," the bitter sailor spat out, and moved toward Judas.

"You must be drunk, man, so why don't you go home and sleep?"

Without any warning, the one-eyed man lunged at Judas, but with the same vigilance that had kept him alive in the prison outside of Knoxville, Judas saw the blade of the knife poised to enter his heart, quickly moved out of harm's way, and deftly delivered a sharp chopping blow to the man's neck, strong enough to take the air out of his windpipe but not causing any real harm.

"Let's get out of here," Judas said to his men.

A week later they were marching through some other small towns after he had recruited fifty additional men. But his small rebel army, although growing, was far from the minimum strength required to launch an attack on the well-heeled government forces. Then it was that he thought of trying the coastal town of St. Sebastian, where some Mandingo diamond smugglers sometimes hid and where the Portuguese slave ships used to water in the eighteenth century.

At the old neglected pier, he found a group of dissatisfied political thugs, high school dropouts, and escaped prisoners smoking marijuana. "I have a good job for you," he said.

"What sorta job?"

He tempted them with promises of a good life, including the beautiful women they could have in the captured towns and the booty they could take, and his numbers swelled considerably.

Two years earlier, when he had set out from the Arab country to launch his rebellion, he had left with a large cache of dollars. He now offered a hundred-dollar bill to each man that he recruited at the pier. "This is only the beginning, men," he said. "Once we start the rebellion, it will be all the way to the capital, where you will all have nice houses and sleep in warm beds, after we have overthrown those cannibals."

His persistence would soon pay off.

One morning, a dwarf tracker who had apparently heard about the hundred-dollar bill offered to any recruit showed up at the rebel camp on the outskirts of the town. "Ah know de terrain like de palm of me hand," he said after he had been introduced to Judas Sampata.

"And you will guide us to the capital?" the rebel chieftain asked.

"Trust me," the dwarf said.

Judas spent two weeks at St. Sebastian waiting for a cache of arms dispatched by an Israeli merchant in Hungary with his own diamond business plans for Bassa after the rebellion was over. Soon the dwarf tracker was leading the rebel army through bush paths along the coast, spying on government positions, picking up tips about the government strength. His knowledge of the terrain, as he had said, was great. Many times, when the rebels could have walked into an ambush, it was his keen canine sense of smell that led them away from danger.

Sometimes the sun was a merciless disk, the dust was terrible, and the road was painful for the young boys among the troops. "Slow down a bit and get some rest," Judas Sampata ordered after one hard day's march.

Next morning they were back on the move, but a sudden burst of rain slowed their progress. Nonetheless, desperate for additional men to launch his assault, Judas Sampata pressed on, not wanting to lose his momentum. But he soon realized that in some towns the men had fled to the safety of the high forests, where, after the rains, the tracks had been wiped out, beyond the knowledge of the dwarf tracker. "We will rest in the caves," Judas Sampata ordered.

They resumed their march not too long afterward. But once again the rain slowed their progress. Finally, almost a month after Judas Sampata left St. Sebastian, he launched his rebellion with about three hundred men. He chose a soft target, a town with fewer than a thousand people, where he received tactical support from some unlucky Malian diamond miners, whose fathers had fought in the bloody campaign to drive the French out of Algeria and who were prepared to fight for a profit. The capital was a good three hundred miles away. To get to it, Judas and his men had to march through some more sleepy towns and villages that made up 75 percent of that densely wooded country. When, finally, they were near the capital, they came through some picturesque hamlets, orchards of mangoes, breadfruits, and fields of wheat and homes with cone-shaped roofs, all with rows of small neat gardens, life being very orderly in that very beautiful countryside.

It was the wet season, and the rains continued to wreak havoc on the march. "Wait until de rains finish," the dwarf cautioned. "Snakes ebrywhere now."

"The gods must not be in my favor," Judas Sampata said. "But we should be in the capital in three months," he added, trying to reassure his troops.

It had been ten years since he had seen the coastal capital, but time had not blurred how he felt about that place: the way its beauty had been sullied on the day that Sergeant-General Warawara had staged his coup and then executed seventeen members of the last government; how those men had been lined up in only their underwear on a gray, windy day, the ocean raging behind them as they were shot; and how the brutality of the soldiers had set his blood boiling. Wars, he decided, were not about morality but about bloodlust, ancient feuds that men had always settled in one form or another. With his eyes set on reaching the coastal city before Christmas, he soon resorted to a desperate solution: the conscription of young boys, some of them as young as ten, who were brutalized into submission. There was a rebel who had had some training as a nurse; after he had injected cocaine into the veins of the young boys, they began to show the signs of derangement, and Judas Sampata soon had his killing machines.

"Now that you can handle rifles, bazookas, rocket launchers, and grenades with the same fearlessness as the older rebels, you have become the children of war," he said with a menace in his voice that left the boys in no doubt about his cruelty.

CHAPTER SIXTY-SEVEN

Naked Woman on a Fabulous Horse

ACCOMPANIED BY his new mistress, General Dan Doggo eventually took a holiday in the Senegalese town of Saint-Louis, where he was able to practice his French: "*Bonjour monsieur, bonjour madame,*" he would greet the waiters.

"*Bonjour, Monsieur le Président, et Madame aussi,*" the waiters would reply every morning, as the fat man arrived for breakfast, smiling at the professor.

Two weeks later, he returned to Malagueta early in the evening, determined to stop any rebel spillover from Bassa into Kissi. As his motorcade drove into the center of the city, the general saw the large, exuberant crowd on Amadou Komba Street yelling slogans and showing the flag. Crude banners depicting Judas Sampata as an uncircumcised dog that should be stopped were hoisted on trees; angry young men were demanding weapons to defend the borders. The inordinately nationalistic fever surprised the general, because Malaguetans were not really people for showing the flag. "This is serious," he said to his mistress as he waved to the crowd.

"And you thought you did not have public support," Madeleine said encouragingly.

Later that night, although they had no proof, a small crowd was seen combing some of Malagueta's outlying districts with flambeaux, looking for spies. The general did not approve of their action, but nevertheless seized the opportunity presented him. Next morning, he changed into his military uniform, and his chest was laden with the blue and brown medals that Tankor Satani had awarded him for loyalty, and when the sun came out it was bright on the gold medal of the Order of the Mosquito, the second-highest honor in the country. However, when the general tried to strap his baldric on his chest, it was too tight, and he realized that if he were to inspire his army to defend the nation, he would have to serve as an example by going on a diet. He recalled what his ex-mistress, Mariama Tukulor, had said: "He was too fat!"

Aware that his soldier's honor was on the line, he drank his coffee with a little dose of gunpowder dissolved in it, and his voice boomed a note higher as he addressed a large crowd at Patrice Lumumba Square. "While I have been too lenient," he said, "some fools have mistaken that for weakness. But I shall show them that I am in charge."

It was so unlike him that some in the crowd found it hard to believe his voice could be so thunderous. But, chanting war songs, some others immediately rewarded him, all the same, with a show of support. Exalted not only by the crowd but also by the thought that he had a woman who would stand by him, come what may, General Dan Doggo was effusive that evening when he visited his mistress. "I feel so good, sweetheart, it is as if I have been listening to rapturous music all day long," he said.

His passion for her that night was expressed with such tremendous power that she thought he was a dead man come back to life, reincarnated in the flames of war, in a hurry to make love before going off to fight again. Much later, still dazed from the fire of his colossus, Madeleine sat by a window and began to hum one of the general's favorite love songs, "Fire, fire, fire, fire, ma baby de come," while his postcoital snoring sounded as if it came from a bull that was sleeping in her bed.

As real as the threat of war was, it had not dampened the enthusiasm and preparations for Easter: bunting of the various churches hung all over Malagueta, paper kites were flying in the blue sky, and the wreath sellers were stitching their colorful artistry for the mourners planning to visit their loved ones at the cemeteries. Madeleine Makassa was not a practicing Christian, but with only two days to go before Easter she was assailed by thoughts of the strict Catholic education she had received and of what the nuns would say about her relationship with the general. Sitting partly naked, drinking her coffee, after the general had gone, she thought it was ironic that she should be thinking of the Messiah after making love. She began to imagine Christ in his terrible campestral agony, hanging naked on his cross, blood dripping from his hands and feet. Even more disturbing, as though he had been watching her become involved with General Dan Doggo, her husband suddenly came to mind as she thought of the image of the suffering Christ. "I am disgusted with you," she thought she heard her husband say in an angry voice.

She was mortified.

Perhaps it was this feeling that made Madeleine suspect General Dan Doggo's clarion call to war had a false ring to it, when the greatest danger to the country was the pillaging by members of the government. For the rest of the evening she was in torment. When she finally fell asleep later that night, she had a most unusual dream, in which General Dan Doggo had been turned into a horse that she, quite naked, was riding. This horse, she realized, was not an ordinary animal: it looked more like a centaur, and it was talking to her, asking whether she was sure she wanted to go where it was taking her.

She sent the great beast into an earthshaking gallop, and gasped for breath as she rode past the early Easter celebrants, the false-faced masqueraders and masked devils thrilling the student nurses hanging their laundry to dry on the porches of their training school. A long line of tired people was waiting near a fruit kiosk for the rickety *poda-poda* vans to take them home to their small rooms in the warrens in the east end of Malagueta. To relive the tedium of waiting for those unreliable vehicles, they had been tossing coins to a dwarf dancing on its head, hoping his famed magical powers would bring them good luck at Easter. They were not prepared for the sight of the fabulous horse that suddenly rounded a corner at a furious gallop.

"Lawd have mercy," someone said, "dis is a better horse dan dat donkey dat Christ rode on Palm Sunday. And look at dat naked 'oman!"

A brilliant sun was shimmering in the morning when Madeleine Makassa woke up from her dream drenched in a terrible sweat that left her in no doubt about where the horse had been taking her: to a place she had suddenly become afraid of visiting. She felt like a cheap woman and was grateful that General Dan Doggo was not coming that morning because of an important meeting he had with his commanders. She got dressed hurriedly and was soon driving to the cemetery, which was where she knew the horse had been taking her in her dream. Before going on her holiday with the general, she had paid the cemetery workers to tend to her husband's grave in time for Easter, but when she arrived there she was shocked at how neglected it looked. Thick grass had grown on the edges, a dead snake lay rotting on the tomb, and someone had put broken pieces of glass there.

"Forgive me," she cried with piercing anguish as she knelt down and began to weed out the grass. She swept the dead snake away with her hand, amazed at her bravery, but then became disoriented when dead leaves began to whirl in the wind and the dust near the grave rose in a thick powder, out of which she saw her husband emerging dressed in a white gown, looking very composed as he spoke to her.

"I built you that house so that you could stay in the circle of decent women, not for you to entertain your fat soldier boyfriend there."

She opened her arms to receive her husband and ask for his forgiveness, but he walked past her as though she had never existed, leaving her trembling with the irrevocable life sentence imposed on her by a dead man disgusted that she had been sullied by a corrupt buffoon. Rather than going home right away, she spent the rest of the day on a beach, throwing up most of the time.

General Dan Doggo had gone to her house at about four in the afternoon and was not surprised that she was out, assuming that like most people, even the nonbelievers, his lover had gone to visit her dead at Easter. Perhaps, he figured, she had decided to avoid the morning throng of mourners by going in the afternoon. A week ago, he had dispatched a battalion of soldiers under the command of Brigadier Tamu Malombo, the commander of the Third Infantry division, to the frontier, but his meeting with the other commanders had not gone too well; they wanted more ammunition to fortify the borders, which of course the government could not afford, and the soldiers had gone away without really believing him. Now he was waiting to make love to his mistress; she would take his mind off the fighting along the frontier with Bassa. He felt he deserved a respite from his problems.

He poured a drink and thought of the over three hundred women he had slept with since becoming president, and it seemed incredible, given how modest she had seemed at first, that the bookish widowed professor had been the one to really light his fire! You can never tell with women, he decided.

The sun had gone to sleep over the ocean, and the first chirring of the crickets was bringing in the evening. Down in the riotous city, the wicks of the kerosene lamps were beams of mushrooms flickering in the streets;

somewhere in that far-flung city the passionate voice of a muezzin was calling the faithful from the minaret of a mosque. The patriotic fever was still high in some sections of the city, and General Dan Doggo heard the distant booming of tom-toms; he smiled thinking that rum was definitely running high in those drummers' brains. Impatient for Madeleine to come, he smoked a cigarette, wondering why she was taking so much time talking to her husband, even though he knew that talking to dead people always took some time!

When he heard Madeleine's car coming up the driveway, he jumped out of his chair, ready to embrace his mistress. But he checked himself when he saw that the woman who had just walked in looked more like a ghost than an alluring companion: she was pale and downcast, almost as if she had been stricken by a sudden case of cerebral malaria. He held out his arms, but she raised her hands in refusal, and he had to stand and watch this stranger in front of him as she began to sob uncontrollably, like a woman who had just lost her only child.

"What is wrong with you?" the general asked, completely at the end of his wits.

"I am afraid I can't see you anymore," Madeleine cried disconsolately.

General Dan Doggo felt as though he had just been sentenced to death. "What do you mean you can't see me anymore?"

"There was a horse in my dream last night."

"And what has that got to do with me?" the general asked in disbelief.

"It was a strange horse: you. I was riding naked on it. The dream prefigured death for both of us if we continue to see each other. So please, go away."

General Dan Doggo had never been one for enigmas. For once, he felt Madeleine Makassa was confusing sorcery with the French dialectics she had learned at the Sorbonne, which he had sometimes listened to in the past but was now driving him crazy. He knew her well enough to be sure that no good would come from arguing with her when she was so clearly disoriented. Unable to make sense of why she had been gone all day, he rose and said a quiet good night to her, certain she would be back to her normal self tomorrow and would have forgotten about the unfortunate dream.

It seemed incredible, therefore, when he came round next evening, bringing a gift of a diamond bracelet for her, that there was no trace of her having lived in the house. It had been cleared of all of her possessions, the walls stripped of her watercolors, the chests of drawers and the long built-in wardrobes emptied. A piercing wind was blowing from the mountain, where some old vultures were now the only occupants of the abandoned Xanadu, and howling like a disaster as it entered the living room. The kitchen was as clean as if it had never been used, and the toilets had a powerfully disinfected smell strong enough to neutralize the foul odor of a field horse. All the enchanting aromas of Madeleine's perfumes were gone: it was as though the place had been cleansed by an invisible presence. But she had left all the furnishings that General Dan Doggo had ever bought her, and when he had recovered from the shock, he slumped into one of the sofas and felt his arteries hardening as though he were about to have a heart attack.

It was only two days ago that he had felt at the highest level of bliss, when he was making love to Madeleine. But this, it seemed to the general, was probably the worst day of his entire life. Early that morning, he had received a confidential report that the rebel war in Bassa had spread over the border and was more serious than he had thought. "Life is a bitch!" the general said, and not for the last time.

He was a very lonely man.

Frayed by this creeping war, General Dan Doggo's emotions were raw, so the last thing he was prepared for was to lose his mistress. Wondering whether the neighbors had seen a van pulling up late at night to load Madeleine's possessions, he had one of them brought to him by his driver.

"No, General," the neighbor, a student, said. "All I saw was a strange horse winged like Pegasus. By the way, General, it was the professor who first introduced me to that Greek mythology. And as far as I am concerned, anything to do with Medusa at this time is bad for the country."

As he was being chauffeured home, General Dan Doggo could not make up his mind about which loss was the most terrible: his mistress or, if it came to it, the country.

CHAPTER SIXTY-EIGHT

Bless You, Granddaughter

IT HAD been many years since anyone had come to Irene to "borrow" her coffin. She was quite old now, but she still did not seem in a hurry to meet her maker. On the morning that she turned ninety, although she was grateful for "dis long life," she felt somewhat lonely thinking about all of her friends who had died, and of her dog Tiger.

Now she was remembering:

Far from being gray and boring, she felt, the autumn of her life was all gold, although not the gold of money. But when she thought of her husband and his early death, her struggle to make a living, she wished he had been there to see how well their son had turned out.

In the last twenty years, she had, surprisingly, become addicted to Coca-Cola ("Ah should have a vice to take to God") and had lost some of her fine teeth, but she was otherwise quite fit, although she now walked mostly with a cane and wore cashmere stockings when it was a bit chilly during the rainy season and in the harmattan.

On that morning, the soft rays of the sun came into the room with an early shimmer of light, after a month of rain, and Yeama pushed the door to greet the old woman. "You have brought the sun, granddaughter," Irene piped.

"No, granny, you are the sun," Yeama said, and kissed the forehead of the old woman.

She studied her grandmother. The contentment on Irene's face gladdened Yeama's heart but also made her aware that it wouldn't be long before Irene was gone: gone with the enchanting smells of her magic recipes, her arabesque stitching of the antimacassars draping the sofas in the family room. Yeama would miss her grandmother's outlandish skirts, with pockets deep enough to hold large sums of money; she would miss seeing her make the patchwork for the beds; and Irene's narratives about the enigmas of the spirit of the river would come to an end.

Without Irene to guide her, Yeama felt that her world might become a little like a rudderless boat on the river. She was not really prepared for that day.

She tried to imagine sitting on the black rocks on the banks of the river without Irene; not being able to listen to her voice. Sometimes the river had been very quiet, when the only indication that another life was there was when Tiger would growl at some perceived creature in the nearby bushes, or bark teasingly at the silhouette of her father moving from his desk in the study to go and put on an album, or when her mother would come to the verandah to water the plants and wave to her daughter and Irene before settling down on the couch in the study to read quietly without disturbing the concentration of the philosopher. In the golden harvest of Irene's ninety years, Yeama was grateful she had been lucky enough to be part of the wheat.

That was why she was there in that room, and with a deep rush of gratitude welling up from her heart, she began to adorn her grandmother's neck with beads of onyx, the most luscious black she had been able to find, to contrast with Irene's golden skin. A smell of incense was in the room, because Irene had put some sandalwood to burn in the urn, just as she did every morning to ward off evil spirits. In the lush garden the white oleander was blooming, and Yeama had gone out quite early in the morning to pick some of its flowers so she could make a small bouquet for her grandmother. After giving it to her, she kissed Irene's spidery but very steady hands. Then, solemnly, Irene gave Yeama her blessing. "God bless you, child. I pray your children will be good to you in the same way that you have been good to your parents and to me."

"Thank you, Granny," Yeama said, and kissed Irene's hands one more time.

Yeama had always, in spite of her parent's abundant love, felt closer to Irene. She hoped she would be ready to accept the day, with gratitude, when Irene eventually died. "You have been good to me, Granny," Yeama said.

"You are welcome, child, but when are you and Albert getting married, so dat ah can begin to exercise my old bones for my goombay dance?"

"I have something to tell you, Granny."

The old woman saw what looked like mischief in her granddaughter's eyes. "What is it, ma child?"

"I am going to get married."

"Praise de Lawd! When is it?"

Thrilled that she was finally going to dance to some goombay wedding music, Irene began to imagine dancing with the shy Dr. Sidi Samura at the wedding of his son to her granddaughter. Even though her bones were old, she was determined, on that day, to drag the venerable doctor to the floor. Surely, given how well-bred he was, he would not refuse an old lady a dance. But Yeama's next words canceled out that wish.

"It is not to Albert."

Irene fixed her still-bright eyes on her granddaughter. "Tell me ma ears are not lying to me, child."

"No, Granny."

"Then who is it, my child?"

"It is Pathe N'jai Tall."

"You young people will never cease to surprise me! Now whatever happened to Albert?"

CHAPTER SIXTY-NINE

War and Poetry

AFTER THE early blossoming of their love, Yeama and Albert had, sadly, begun to find areas of disagreement that were hard to bridge. Their interests collided not so much on principles but on what Yeama called Albert's "obsessions." Painfully, they began, unknown to their parents, to drift apart.

It was not that the young people had stopped loving one another. Far from it; they still did, and Yeama had done her best to try to reconcile their differences. As proof of their love, she still had Albert's intensely passionate letters, written over a span of three years, and he had hers. In those letters, they had poured out their hearts not only as young people enjoying the first flowering of love but also as children conscious of their backgrounds, knowing that if they were married two fine families would be united. In the changing world of Malagueta, where there were not many distinguished families one could admire, such a wedding would have attracted a large crowd, even if the young people did not want one. An inveterate agnostic for much of his life, Dr. Sidi Samura had even secretly begun to contemplate having to go to church for the first time in over fifteen years, since the funeral for another son, to attend the wedding of Albert, who was a fairly regular churchgoer. He was the first to notice the sudden change in his son, but had not rushed brazenly to find out what was wrong.

It was inevitable.

After hearing about the disgraceful diamond incident, at which the Coral had slapped Brigadier Abu Karamoko, Albert was so enraged that the government did not do anything about it, he went around for days brooding like an impending storm. Convinced there was really no one to talk to about his disgust, he eventually decided that he and hopefully a few other young men had a mission to clean up the stain left on the military's honor. He put off visiting Yeama for some time and spent long hours reading the biographies of military men—Churchill, Nguyen Giap, and Shaka—but did his best to hide that obsession from his family. Quite frequently he went for long walks up the old Military Greens on Jamaica Hill overlooking the old slave jetty, a place rapidly losing much of its appeal as a hideout for lovers because the woods were thinning out. The cemetery for the British and Malaguetan officers killed during the colonial occupation was nearby. One day, as he walked past there thinking about that tumultuous period, his attention was distracted by the vegetable boats in the wharf. He stood for a while watching the women going into the boats to haggle over the price of fish and vegetables and to jab a finger at an insulting man, all in good fun, this type of life in Malagueta that he loved so much. Eventually, tired of his wandering and thinking he had not been to see her in a long time, he turned up at Yeama's.

It was nighttime. He sat down and took a book of poems out of his pocket, and read a few lines from a poem by Wole Soyinka:

> Your hand is heavy, Night, upon my brow,
> I bear no heart mercuric like the clouds, to dare
> Exacerbation from your subtle plough.

Yeama saw his brow tighten. "It has been a long time since I have heard you quoting from a poet," she said, knowing how fond he was of Pablo Neruda and Garbage Martins.

"I have had no time for poetry these past days," he said dryly.

Yeama was alarmed. "Why?"

"Because war will soon come here, and I have been preparing for it."

"It is as if you have said good-bye to the things that made me love you," she cried, twisting her handkerchief.

"I have not. It is just that everything has its place and time."

"Your place is here with me, not on some clouds on which you are not temperamentally suited to exist."

He had been raised to be exceedingly polite to even the most unimportant peasant, but it was obvious to Yeama that, in his anger, he was already beginning to lose some of those old courtesies, especially when he talked about the military. She listened as he referred to that institution as the place where he might find some worthy cause, regardless of the danger. But at so young an age, Yeama did not want to contemplate two deaths should Albert die in the first flurry of battle or be brought home to her, broken in his bones and spirit, just when she was preparing herself for or just getting over the death of her grandmother. It was an image too bleak for a twenty-year-old to imagine.

"The country is like a skiff going down the tempestuous rapids of change, and definitely not for the best," Albert said, looking very grave.

Yeama had a brave spirit but felt that martyrdom was best left to men and women who had had some experience of life and love, like her father and his friend, the estimable doctor. What she wanted was to marry and have a child, and then, yes, she would be ready to back her husband in any quest, however dangerous it might be.

"I love you, but if you insist on joining the army, you will be doing it all on your own," she said.

"Then you are rejecting me?"

"No, Albert, I am rejecting the madness that has made you blind to the reality that the military is already so corrupt under General Dan Doggo it will take an earthquake to clean it out."

"Yes," he replied, "which is why I want to join and help clean it up."

Heartbroken, but still in love with Albert, she turned to Pathe N'jai Tall for comfort, and the Senegalese was never so happy as on the day, a year later, when Yeama agreed to marry him, but on the understanding that they would stay in Malagueta.

CHAPTER SEVENTY

The Coming of Lucifer

INCREASINGLY, NEWS about the war on the border with Bassa had a ring of disaster to it. Jolted from the planet of bittersweet love, where he had been nursing his injured pride as a rejected lover, General Dan Doggo eventually turned his attention to the crisis. When he decided to move, his actions were shot through with a burst of energy as befitting a leader. The territory where the rebels had come in from Bassa into Kissi was mostly forested, although some had chosen to enter through more open country and were repeating their mayhem everywhere. Refugees were streaming across the border. As he read the dispatches from the war front, General Dan Doggo realized the situation was genuinely serious.

"This is a disaster," he said to his minister of presidential affairs, wondering who was behind the invasion.

"What shall we do, Excellency?"

"I shall order a general mobilization."

The stream of refugees from Bassa was unlike anything that the officer commanding the First Battalion of the Kissi army had anticipated. In contrast to other conflicts, not all of the refugees were the usual peasants in threadbare clothes. Some were professional men and women, doctors, lawyers, teachers, accountants, and surveyors, who had abandoned their pseudo-American lifestyle and comfort. As they fled down the treacherous paths, it occurred to them that the territory through which they were passing had not changed much since the days when the itinerant Tuaregs had come with their magical potions to Malagueta, over two hundred and fifty years ago. On the footpaths and bridges not washed away by the freshets of the rainy season, the flight of the refugees would set off a frenzied flight of birds in the clear blue sky. Some of the foot refugees carried huge bundles on their heads and eventually ended up in makeshift camps set up in the border villages. Others were luckier: days after leaving Bassa, their glinting Fords, Chryslers, Chevrolets, and Buicks, never before seen on Malagueta's narrow streets, streamed into the city, where the exhausted refugees searched for any relatives they could find or paid exorbitant rents to unscrupulous landlords, who were happy to kick out some of their old tenants.

Briefed about the flood of refugees into Kissi, General Dan Doggo finally called a meeting of his war council. "We have to declare a state of emergency to deal with this neighboring crisis," he said to his minister of presidential affairs.

"It is no longer a neighboring crisis, General. It is a national emergency for us!"

"What do you mean by a national emergency?"

"Excellency, sir, war has come to our country, and our towns have been attacked."

There was thunder in General dan Doggo's voice when he spoke. "How dare Judas Sampata export his war into our country?"

"He has, General, sir, but the man doing the damage for him is none other than Lucifer Kontofili, who, if you recall, was in the army with you many years ago."

The Mulatto Urchins

As most Malaguetans were soon to learn, Lucifer Kontofili was the closest they would come to the specter of the devil. To his own troops, he was a mystic figure whose hold on them bordered on the bizarre. Before he had attacked Kissi, fantastic stories had already been told about his elusive nature and extraordinary powers, painting a most fearful picture of the rebel leader. Few of the troops fighting in his name had actually seen him, but that did not stop them from talking repeatedly about his powers. Those who had come in contact with him had spread the word that he wore talismanic amulets on his arms, and there was a general belief that he was immune to bullets, or that his hands could deflect their trajectory. Most intriguingly, no one had ever seen him take off his shoes, and his beard, white and shaggy, had not been trimmed in years. The picture that many of the fascinated troops had of their mystical leader was of a fanatical prophet with red, fiery eyes set in a thick forest of hair, with a not too large nose projecting out of that growth. When he smiled, his face was one of cruelty, and his terrors would soon become the worst scourges ever to hit the country.

One evening, determined to test the story that there were small diamond rings on his toes, a beautiful female recruit came to his tent and offered to sleep with him, thinking that no man would resist the allure of such a woman. Lucifer had anticipated her intention.

He watched as she undressed. When she was completely naked, she felt that would bring him under her spell. With her long hands she removed his trousers and undid his shirt and was sailing down to his knees, stroking his legs, trying to remove his socks, when he stopped her with a brutal pull of her hair.

"Ah tink say you done come to test what people say 'bout me, heh?"

"No, I just want to make you happy."

"Ah go give you enjoyment, now, now," he barked at her.

When she left his tent an hour later, it was clear to the other women who had seen her go in that she was not the same woman. The dull beans of her eyes showed the bruising contest she had had with the devil, her legs were weak, her hands rested on her sagging hips, and her breath was labored. She smelled of the potency of the devil's perfume, for not only did Lucifer Kontofili have strange oddities in making love, but he was a ruthless beast in bed so that she could never sleep with another man.

"How was it?" one of her friends asked with a wink.

"He was so strong, so brutal, my sister, he has ruined me!"

For the next three days, in a bid to remove the stain of the devil, her mouth tasted a fiery concoction of ginger root, salamander tongue, ground beetles, and alligator pepper. She walked around like a zombie as the potion coursed through her, but rather than putting the other recruits off the devil, her experience merely served to excite them with the hope that they could not only unravel the enigmas shrouding him but tame the beast in him.

Preoccupied with war, Lucifer did not give any of them a chance to test his prowess. "Me not be stupid man," he said, aware of their temptations.

For all its mystery, Lucifer Kontofili's life was really a simple one of failures and bitterness. Extreme cruelty and savagery were part of his nature. As far as his troops could tell, he was about fifty, although no birth certificate existed to confirm it. Little disclosures fallen from his lips had led them to conclude that he had been in the same rebel training camp in the faraway Arab country with Judas Sampata, but that, unlike the failed Mandingo diamond dealers, he had fought alongside the former jailbreaker not for profit but for a more tantalizing prize.

"Help me to get rid of Sergeant-General Warawara, and I shall give you all the help you need to overthrow that buffoon, General Dan Doggo," Judas had promised.

Judas Sampata was closing in on Sedonia, the capital of Bassa, when Lucifer Kontofili decided to set out with two hundred men to attack the border town of Kanji. "Ah go fight now in me own country," he said.

"And you know I shall give you all the support you need," came the encouraging words of Judas Sampata.

That night, before crossing the crocodile-infested river between Bassa and Kissi, Lucifer Kontofili sat in deep contemplation on a large stone cushioned with dry grass, while his small band of rebels slept in a makeshift camp. He felt something moving under him and drew his revolver, but saw with relief only a small python slithering from under the dry grass and making quickly for a nearby bush. This was a propitious sign: pythons do not bite, but merely swallow their prey. And so he would swallow his prey. He sat down again and reflected on how far he had come from when Tankor Satani had incarcerated him in the cells of the central prison in Malagueta many years ago, where he had done seven years mostly in solitary confinement. He was an uneducated man, but arrogant and ambitious, and fancied himself as good as any other soldier. Although only a sergeant, he had expected to be promoted to captain.

Bitter after serving his sentence for insubordination he vowed: "Dey soon see what power ah get when ah return," as he left the country.

The two hundred men who had crossed the river with him had been selected mainly for their knowledge of the territory, but also because they had the same rancor in their souls as he and had been waiting, with a long-simmering anguish in their hearts, for just this opportunity to return. Many had spent time chasing dreams in faraway places and had vowed to avenge a shame worse than slavery for them, which was that even before Tankor Satani came to power, the riches of the land had gone mostly to a few people.

He raged as he recalled the conceit and arrogance of the various Arab, Israeli, European, and American diamond dealers puffing on their fat cigars in the luxurious hotels in Malagueta while they were waiting for some government civil servant or cabinet minister to bring diamonds to them. The most glaring insult, as far as he was concerned, was the way those "foreign exploiters" had looked at the waiters, as though they were dirt, and yelled impertinently at them. Then, after a good diamond deal, they had tried to treat the women like harlots. Some of the women had slapped their faces. "Go and treat your mothers like harlots, not us, you bastards!"

Lucifer Kontofili felt murderous hatred in his soul for the diamond merchants, but his strongest disgust was for their black lackeys who had made the exploit possible. "Look at what been happening here since de Coral people cam to dis country," he raged one evening as he surveyed the terrain in front of him. "Dey been raping our moders and sisters; dey smuggling de diamonds; our own black broders all ass-lickers taking bribes and selling dere daughters to all Tom, Dick, and Harry; de Corals paying dem for exploiting us. Shameless, our broders and some sisters."

Some of the boys who had volunteered to fight for him were the angry malatta urchins whose Coral fathers had tossed a few coins and cheap fabrics to their black mothers before going back to Lebanon with lots of diamonds to marry their partially veiled Arab wives. Always dirty and ragged, laughed at by their mothers' enemies, treated as outcasts, the malattas were easy to spot all over the coast of West Africa, where, for generations, the Arabs had been trading. Forever stamped with the shame of being sons from cheap unions, they were mostly uneducated and not equipped for anything useful to society, only for service in the underworld and ghettos. After he had stirred one group of those tragic youths to the point of boiling rage over how their mothers had been treated by the Corals, Lucifer Kontofili knew he had his most determined followers.

"Men, as dey say in our country, de time done come for you to show de Coral rapists and de black traitors dat your moders did not put milk in your noses to turn you into fool men."

CHAPTER SEVENTY-ONE

A Simple Wedding

YEAMA ISKANDER and Pathe N'jai Tall were married one sunny evening in the enchanting garden of the house in front of the river, and not in a church or mosque as Irene had originally planned. "The situation in the country is too dangerous; let us not take a chance with all the hooligans around," Habiba Mouskuda advised her daughter.

War was slowly spreading across the country, and it was unsafe for law-abiding people to move freely about. Increasingly concerned about whether the rebels had infiltrated the army camp outside of Malagueta, many young lovers had stopped riding the *poda-poda* vans to the now-dwindling seaside moonlight picnics. The dance halls were empty, and people no longer thronged the Coral cinema houses showing movies celebrating the exploits of Lord Rama and the beauty of the goddess Lakshmi in faraway India. Without the old men patiently nursing their glasses of stout, the smoky rum bars looked like silent ghosts of bygone days.

But after waiting for over fifty years just so that she could dance to goombay music at the wedding of either her son or granddaughter, Irene was not to be denied this opportunity. Even though her joints were not the best on that day, she came out into the glorious sun "on my own two feet," wearing a finely woven kabaslot gown, and sat in the comfort of a cushioned wicker chair. The warmth of her smile was almost as bright as the rays the sun was casting on the white oleander, and she watched as a Protestant minister married the couple. Like most Senegalese, Pathe N'jai Tall was a Moslem, but had not insisted that his wife should be married into that faith, because he did not think religion should come between a man and a woman. But the gown that Yeama wore was an expression of her own religious independence: a brocaded *buba*, laced round the neck in gold, usually worn by Moslems, whereas Pathe was attired in a suit, favored by Christians. To passages from Senghor and Garbage Martins and soft melodies on a kora, the wedding that had seemed unlikely only two years ago, when Pathe had dropped out of the running for Yeama's hand, was one of the few bright lights in an otherwise uncertain period.

Dr. Sidi Samura had hoped Yeama would marry his son but knew of their friendly parting, and was there to celebrate with his lifelong friend. "Yeama was already our daughter, so nothing has changed," he said, shaking Theodore Iskander's hand.

"And Albert will always be my son. So let us hope he finds some peace in his choice of career."

The full impact of the war was still far from Malagueta, but it had already led to a rationing of goods and services. Determined that all the guests should turn up, Habiba Mouskuda had seen to it that they could get fuel she had paid for at a filling station. She was approaching fifty but had lost nothing of her allure, and her dazzling cleavage enhanced her wonderful arrival into middle age. The décolletage of her dress was an ample reminder of what had once tormented Colonel Fillibo Mango and General Augusto Kotay into forsaking military glory for her, but there was nothing left of the sorceress's impulse in her heart. Her enchantment enhanced by the aromatic blossoms of the plants in the garden, she moved in a wonderful glow of admiration among the guests, a well-groomed lady seeing to it that they were well taken care of by the servants, all the catering having been supervised by her now very sophisticated intellect. When it was time for a bit of "bone-shaking," Pathe and Yeama opened the dancing with some Senegalese *mbalax*, which was a bit too wild for the older guests.

"Let us show these you people how to do the good old dance," Habiba smiled as she went up to Irene so that they could do the more sedate goombay, which made Theodore Iskander smile.

The goombay rhythm had drawn the other guests to their feet, and Habiba Mouskuda had finished dancing with the old woman and was putting away a tray when her face suddenly lit up. The person she had longed to see over the years was there. She gathered the folds of her gown and walked to the gate, for coming into the compound, looking splendid in her own golden embroidered gown and holding a beautifully wrapped gift, was the unmistakable figure of Hawanatu Gomba, and Habiba Mouskuda thanked God that such goodness still existed in the world to make possible this act of forgiveness.

"You don't know how much this means to me; that you could come to the wedding of Yeama, who could have been your daughter, is the greatest wine of forgiveness anyone could offer me."

Hawanatu Gomba's smile was so sweet that she left Habiba in no doubt that the now aging women were long off the trapeze of winner and loser. As if to seal a pact of forgiveness, they embraced, genuine emotions welling from their hearts, and cried tears of joy for the young couple. After all those years, their youthful fight over the same man was now lost in the graying of their lives. Both of them had learned, from those intemperate expressions of the mind, what it was like to suffer and forgive and to like each other afterward.

"I would not have missed this day for anything," Hawanatu Gomba said as she drank the glass of wine offered by her old rival.

Irene had seen Hawanatu Gomba come into the compound. Thinking of how she had dearly wanted that woman for her daughter-in-law, she was heartened that the two old rivals had engaged in such a public act of reconciliation. When nearly all the guests had left, but just before Pathe was to take Yeama away, she asked Hawanatu to stay behind. "Help dis old woman out of her chair," she said, winking.

She leaned on Hawanatu's arm, and they walked slowly together to the river to offer a drink to the Orishas and to thank the river spirit for "making me see dis day." Then, very slowly, as though she had suddenly remembered the numerous ways of invocation common among her generation, she raised her eyes to the heavens with this plea: "Thank you, Master Jesus, for everything. I know there will be some pain ahead for de young people, but let it not be too soon."

"Leave me alone now, daughter," she told Hawanatu, and on legs that appeared to have been made steadier by her invocations, Irene began to walk away from the river as though she were miraculously free of the pain in her joints that had threatened to derail her happiness only the night before. She came and draped her arms around the young couple. "You look very beautiful," she said to her granddaughter.

"Don't worry about anything, granddaughter. Pathe is a good man."

When Irene smiled, it was obvious that if the angel of death came that night she would be happy to go. But first, with a wry expression on her face, she looked Pathe straight in the eye and served him notice of what she could do beyond her grave. "If you don't take good care of ma precious little granddaughter, ah shall send another man to take her away from you. And remember, you are going to stay in Malagueta with her, so dat I can come to visit anytime I feel like it."

Pathe's dark skin glowed in the evening sun, and the light in his eyes was brilliant as he nodded in agreement. Not only had he married into one of Malagueta's finest families, he knew the old woman liked him. He was glad she had stayed tenaciously alive to see this day.

"I hear you, granny. I won't take her to Senegal."

"I shall hold you to dat promise," Irene said, now fully prepared to meet God "anytime de master is ready for me."

CHAPTER SEVENTY-TWO

The Last Song of Lieutenant Albert Samura

WHEREAS IRENE had made her peace with God, the same could not be said about General Dan Doggo, whose departure from office Lucifer Kontofili had been contemplating three hundred miles away.

On the day that Yeama Iskander was getting married, the sound of bazookas and AK-47 rifles bought from a Bulgarian arms dealer ricocheted on the hilly terrain of the eastern town of Kanji, when Lucifer Kontofili's rebel army had set out to capture the nearby diamond mines. He had timed his assault to start at midnight, when he felt the nearby military garrison would be lightly defended. His intention was not only to seize the prized mines but to march on to the next objective: the rutile deposits at Batonga. Those reserves contained minerals that the Americans were using in the manufacture of fighter planes, an old one of which an arms dealer had promised the rebel leader. His rebel army now fairly large, a column was advancing on the town after it had marched for days through harsh forest where reptiles and deadly scorpions crawled. The men looked very dirty, their feet ached, and their corns had become too callused to lance.

Lucifer Kontofili urged them on. "Four more days, men, and we go take dis town en make money."

On the outskirts of Kanji, they came across deserted market stalls, broken-down kiosks, and quiet homes on rough empty roads, in which most of the local citizens were hunkered under their beds, too frightened to come out. A sliver of good road ran through this town, which had a small government clinic, a school, and fields with ears of corn, cassava, and yams. Otherwise it was a miserable town, and other than the mines, thirty miles away, and a small nearby cacao plantation, there was not much else to advance its claim to importance.

"Look at dis town," Lucifer Kontofili said. "Nothing to show for de rutile."

Sacred Messengers

Brigadier Tamu Malombo, commander of the Third Infantry, had been sent to defend the town by General Dan Doggo. Anticipating the rebel attack, he had strengthened his front-line defenses with rolls of barbed wire as a perimeter fence, and a palisade of wood and heavy sandbags. A young lieutenant named Albert Samura, who had volunteered for the task, was in charge of an artillery column outside of the fortification to halt any advancing rebel troops. For someone only recently commissioned, his bravery impressed Brigadier Malombo. In three days of fierce fighting, the front line changed hands twice, and both sides had to call up reserves of men to hold their lines.

The rebels were fighting with brutal determination and were much better armed, with sophisticated weapons, and seemed to have the advantage. But when the dust had settled, twenty of them lay dead, while their comrades retreated into the bush to rethink their strategy.

Brigadier Tamu Malombo was a Sandhurst-trained infantry man, one of the last of that breed, and unlike General Dan Doggo was a trim man with a passion for golf and a fondness for sports cars. His no-nonsense approach to service was what had earned him the respect of General Dan Doggo. Until the recent battle, the brigadier had not imagined how brave his young bespectacled lieutenant was.

"You are a brave man, Lieutenant," the brigadier remarked with undisguised admiration, unaware of the torment in the young officer's soul.

During a lull in the fighting, some vultures had left their perch on a giant baobab in a ghoulish swoop for the remains of the decomposing rebels, while the lieutenant was surveying their burnt-out weapons. As the birds shrieked for favorable eating positions, the irony was not lost on him that while he was looking at the detritus of war, his former sweetheart had, in the blooming richness of her garden, married the refined Senegalese. On the night before he led the charge against the rebels, the lieutenant had been assailed by the persistent smell of wild forest flowers, which reminded him of Yeama's garden. He had prayed for guidance, but felt that perhaps she had been right to be afraid of his obsessions. For the downside was that at that moment, as he stood not far from where the vultures were engaged at their sinister task, the only smell around him was putrid, and he was tormented by the sickening feeling that he had led a group of young men sent to die for a cause, while the senior officers had remained down in Malagueta, fiddling with the rations meant for the soldiers. "Here we are dying for the nation," he raged, "while General Dan Doggo and his ministers are acting like vultures down in Malagueta!"

He finished examining the burnt-out weapons and went back to the large tent, where his troops sat in various positions of fatigue and helplessness, though a few were evidently still full of hope for the cause for which they had volunteered. He was the most educated among them, and he read in their eyes how for them, unlike him, the war was a journey out of their old, unprofitable lives, a hope that they might be emancipated. They had not had a bath or a decent meal in two days, for it had been three weeks since fresh supplies had reached them from Malagueta, so he relaxed the strict rationing, and after the cook had prepared the evening meal the men were given hefty helpings of the scant supplies they had. He did not smoke, but as he watched his comrades sharing their last cigarettes, he imagined that he could see, in their now more hopeful eyes, that they were once again capable of dreaming of a bridge that stretched far from the land corridor of the present conflict. The effect was surreal. While he was unmarried, bits of evidence heard from the lips of his men had confirmed their marital status. Occasionally they would talk about the families they had left behind; and sometimes, when encouraged, he would share memories of his childhood, quite distinct from theirs. That was the stuff that Albert was made of: he cared about other people, which was why he had volunteered to hold the first line of defense against the advance of Lucifer Kontofili. He liked Brigadier Malombo and was happy to be serving under him. But somewhat irritated by his own presumption in thinking he was destined for greatness on the battlefield, Lieutenant Albert Samura stepped back in time to figure out, with as clear a logic as he could muster given the convolutions now unfolding, what it was in their bones and blood that made some of the senior officers such weaklings and cowards, soft in their bellies and afraid to venture into battle. "It is a tragedy," he said. "The top military brass is shitty, just as mineral wealth has been a curse for the country."

Urged to rest for a while by his troops, later that night he fell asleep and was soon taken up by a dream in which the ghoulish vultures, no longer plucking out the eyes of the dead rebels, had landed on his chest and were dancing in a circle. Then, almost as though it were real, he saw the smudges of camwood around their eyes and felt the spurs of their talons as they dug into his chest, drawing blood, and the droppings of the birds were cold on his hands. It was ominous.

Two days later, the rebels had regrouped and were now some five hundred strong, more disciplined, and had brought two howitzers to the assault. With a fierce determination to take the military garrison, they launched a massive attack, and it was as if thunder was booming in the sky and an earthquake was raging in the ground as they struck, trapping most of the lieutenant's men, fighting with an equally fanatical courage, in a foxhole of surprise. The last thing that Lieutenant Albert Samura remembered, when he was hit in the chest, stunned that he had dreamed this denouement, was that the flow of his blood was hot, but that he felt no pain, because, under the image of those flying vultures, regarded by most Malaguetans as sacred messengers of the dead but also detested in some parts of the world as eaters of carrion, it no longer mattered to him which was the most painful way to die: on the battlefield, or knowing that he had given up an estimable woman who had not wanted him to die so young.

CHAPTER SEVENTY-THREE

Diamonds Are Not So Beautiful

IT WAS a remarkable rebel victory. With more than a quarter of Kissi now under his command, Lucifer Kontofili continued his advance on the eastern and southern fronts. Whereas only two years ago refugees were streaming in from Bassa, the reverse was now true. Long lines of people were heading toward Bassa and the French-speaking republic of Bakazo. The terrain was difficult all round, and the old and the infirm were sometimes left to die unburied on ground mired in bogs and misery. Sometimes there were long lulls in the fighting after the rains had made the hauling of heavy weapons hazardous, but that did not really stop the carnage. Soon more towns had fallen to the rebels.

Desperate to save their skins, friends turned against friends, sons against fathers, and daughters against mothers. But in one town, the young men, afraid the rebels would press them into their ranks or rape their women, had fled with the women into the dense groves of forest, hoping that Lucifer Kontofili would be satisfied with plundering their homes and not hurt the young children left in the care of some old people.

It was a terrible error in judgment.

The rebel chieftain always had answers for any eventuality. "Round up all de *pikin*," he said as he arrived in the lead Land Rover in a convoy of armored personnel carriers. "Bring dem near dis tree."

"General," one of his lieutenants asked with a shaky voice, "why you want all de *pikin* under de tree? 'E nor make sense to me."

"You go soon see sense," Lucifer replied.

At first the children refused to come willingly. To coerce them, they were slapped hard on the face or had their ears pulled. Regardless of age or gender, they were ordered to line up, and tears welled up in their eyes as some peed on themselves, while their pleading cries, even before any harm had been done to them, were gut-wrenching. Confined in their rooms, their grandparents could do nothing but pray for the unfortunate kids.

Lucifer Kontofili sat under a tree with cruel menace on his face. "Stretch you hand," he barked at the first child.

With horrific force, the first cutlass blow landed. The child's terrible scream rang through the valley and sent the gibbons fleeing deeper into the nearby forest. She was only ten, her legs crumbled like rotten wattles, her tongue came out, and her spasms were long and violent as blood-gushing, quick death ran out of her mouth. A few of the rebels squirmed uncomfortably in their boots, but watched as two brutal commanders readied the other children for a similar fate.

Fifty children had their hands chopped off that morning. When Lucifer Kontofili left the town, the vultures, drawn by the smell of blood, swooped down and ripped out the flesh from the discarded limbs. "Now people know we mean bisness when we talk 'bout fighting wit' us," he said, advancing on the next town.

Two days later, a thousand conscripted children were marching off to war barefoot or in the remains of flip-flops or whatever contraption could pass for shoes. It was obvious that they hurt deeply from the pain in their feet, but more evident, just looking at them, was that they had been damaged beyond repair in their souls and minds: kids who would soon become killing machines against other children after they had been forced to participate in other horrendous forms of barbarity.

They were victims themselves as they marched through villages looting and plundering. Those child-rebels experienced their first sexual pleasure raping some women, and, just as horribly, they went wild chopping off the hands of people, mostly other children. At times their minds were so deranged they could not even distinguish between day and night, between their own mothers and sisters, between towns.

When General Dan Doggo heard about the bestial acts of Lucifer Kontofili, it finally dawned on him that the situation was really desperate. In spite of the valor of more young soldiers sent to die as their comrades had under the tragic lieutenant, the rebels were now only sixty miles away from the hills of Malagueta, and General Dan Doggo had to contend with a new twist, something odious, repugnant, and terrifying.

For quite some time the press had been publishing articles about the appearance among the rebels of mercenaries from as far away as Ukraine and South Africa. These reports had come from young soldiers who had returned from the front to the capital, broken in spirit and seriously wounded. In addition to the tactical advice given by the mercenaries, the rebels were reportedly now augmented in their drive by the advanced weaponry they had purchased with monies received from the illegal arm of the international diamond cartels for the sale of the precious stones mined by the rebels. It had been quite easy to smuggle the diamonds variously in banana leaves, in the wide trousers pockets of rebel couriers, in tomato paste, or wrapped in handkerchiefs nestled in the bosoms of rebel women. Soon many of the gems were turning up uncut in the receiving houses of Tel Aviv, before being sent to the polishing centers of Bombay, Surat, and other Indian cities.

Bernard Tindermann, head of his ancestral diamond firm in New York, had never seen anything like the packet of uncut diamonds that came to his office one day from Malagueta. "These are the finest stones I have seen in thirty years of doing business in Africa!" he said joyously, jumping out of his seat in his midtown Manhattan office.

With the expertise of a master valuer, he looked at the flawless stones from the brutal war; he touched the exquisite gems, examined them with his piercing eyes, and felt that, besides the joy of finally being rewarded with such an unexpected treasure after years of not getting beautiful gems, he could finally dream of a golden retirement. He imagined, his eyes beaming with delight, how the diamonds, when cut and polished, would grace the necks of the bored menopausal wives of the city's rich businessmen, or of their mistresses. If his conscience pricked him at receiving those blood diamonds, Bernard Tindermann did not let it show. He was a shrewd businessman who could not let such an opportunity at great wealth pass him. But a week later, as though he wanted to assuage a minor feeling of guilt, he anonymously sent a check for half a million dollars to a children's charity somewhere in Africa.

Soon more parcels of blood diamonds were turning up in New York, Tel Aviv, Antwerp, London, and Johannesburg. In return, through his conduit in Bassa, Lucifer Kontofili received guns from Ukraine and lots of cash. If Bernard Tindermann and others could sleep at night, it was none of his business what they were doing with blood diamonds. As long as they could pay for them, the Westerners could have the diamonds. "Dat is white people's bisness," he said.

Yet one morning, as he sat listening to the BBC on his bush radio, his insouciance was disturbed by a most unwelcome piece of news. Some troublesome organizations in London had produced "incontestable" proof of a link between his murderous pillaging and the frequency with which the diamonds were appearing on the world market.

"Ah only answer to higher order," he raged, switching off the radio. "And dat one not from de Almighty God!"

He was disturbed, nevertheless, by the bad public relations, especially at a time when he had begun to feel that his long campaign against the forces of the government was almost at an end. Increasingly, spies and deserters from General Dan Doggo's army had been flocking to the rebel camps with reports of a feeling of panic in Malagueta, of shortages of goods, of gasoline rationing, and of foreigners leaving. Only some diehards had refused to be panicked. The evenings of celebration in the bars that were already down to a minimum were now things of the past; except for the fricassee, groundnut, and ginger beer vendors brave enough to come out at night, the streets were mostly empty. Not wanting any interruption in the sale of the diamonds, Lucifer decided to hire a lawyer to tend his public image abroad: a man whose articulate pronouncements were revolting, especially as he was being paid by a butcher who had chopped off the hands of children.

"Plunder ebryting; bring dem to camps," Lucifer Kontofili said as he spearheaded the rout of government troops from yet another town.

No Sweetness in This Town

After the valiant Lieutenant Albert Samura and other brave young men were killed, Brigadier Malombo, a highly principled man, finally came to the conclusion that he was unable to defend his garrison in the face of the terrifying rebel advance. His position was fragile, he was short of supplies, and before long, painful as it was, he gave orders for his troops to retreat from the garrison to a hill, thinking it best to save as many lives as possible. He had seen enough slaughter. But some of his men thought the rebels had bribed him with diamonds, turned their guns on him, and shot him.

"No one is surrendering," they said as they prepared to go on fighting until they had killed or been killed by the rebels.

Lucifer's supply of food was now vastly improved, and he was close to his next major prize in the interior of the country, the rutile ore plant owned by a consortium of American, African, and Japanese firms. As he approached the outskirts of the town, he saw the clear, wide tracks through the lines of mahogany trees for miles, the great chasms in the earth's surface, and the ugly excavations of red laterite piled everywhere. Dogs were playing on the huge mounds, and as the sun had come out, the vertical crusts or sunken beds were clearly visible in the shifting sands of the deep rutile pits. Depending on how often the mining company had sunk its giant machines into the bowels of the earth, to haul it to the surface where it was sieved for the precious minerals, the destruction to the environment was terrible.

To the handful of rebels educated enough to make a small assessment of the ruined land, it was clear that the ore had not been beneficial to the town: the locals lived a wretched life. But in the grandeur of its well-built homes, its terraced gardens, tennis courts, and offices powered by giant smoke-belching electricity generators, the mining compound looked like a transplant from outer space.

Lucifer Kontofili attacked it with a vengeance, only to discover that the staff had been evacuated a long time ago. "Take ebryting, ebryting," he urged his men. "De telephones, radios, files, and yes, all de telebision sets. What dey doing in de offices, anyway?"

"Maybe all de men watching blue movies during lunchtime," one of his commanders offered.

"You make fun of me, officer?"

"No, General; just talking 'bout strange 'abit some white people have for sex."

The rebels went to the various offices of the white and the handful of black senior officials, tossed aside the abandoned photos of families and homes in faraway places like Alabama and Florida, until they discovered that there were many "telebision" sets to go around. The sight of so many electronic items lent an aspect of generosity to Lucifer for his top lieutenants. They had been fighting a long and difficult war, and he was assured of their loyalty, so, feeling they had earned a respite from fighting, he ordered a halt to all activities.

He ignored his "funny" officer. "We go camp in dis mining compound for one week."

The showers in the senior quarters were still running, so he and his officers sponged themselves clean and looked forward to lazing around for a while. "Now we go watch telebision," one of them enthused.

"But how we go look telebision if electricity out?" asked another.

Eventually a bright one among them decided that in a town like this, with all the gadgetry left by the departing expatriates in the compound, there ought to be a local boy who could do something about the electricity.

They found a technician named Salifu Kimbana, who had been trained to care for basic equipment. Nothing fancy—oiling the generators, cleaning the filters of the air-conditioners, fixing the sewing machines of the bored wives, and so on. Frog-marched in his pajamas by the rebels, he came quietly. Thinking her husband was going to be shot for working with the exploiting class of people that owned the mines, his wife began to cry loudly, but the rebels quickly set her mind at ease.

"Don't worry, now. If your man finish dis job good and proper, 'e go come home wit' new telebision set for you."

Salifu was pushed into the room, where he was immediately assailed by the heat; low on oil, the last generator had stopped running. After some thought, he remembered where the diesel and engine oil were kept, and soon had a generator going. As the fans and air conditioners began to burr, the perspiring rebels settled down for some welcome relief.

With his professional eye, Salifu tried to assess the problem with the television sets, but he did not even have to touch any to find out what was wrong. He smiled. Looking at the faces of the rebels in the room, he noted the cruelty on some of them; others just looked like young men waiting to enjoy a quiet evening after a long period of fighting. Although aware that a quick gunshot could finish him off if he did not get the television sets going, he continued to smile, and then began to laugh. His audacity confused the rebels, for it was clear to him that there was no sweetness in that room. Not thinking about his life, he felt a sudden, unexpected surge of joy at discovering what mind-boggling illiterates the rebels were, and that even if it meant he was going to die, he knew he was superior to them. Triumphantly, he would be the one to tell them what arseholes they were.

"These are not television sets," he said. "They are computer monitors!"

CHAPTER SEVENTY-FOUR

Going Home to the Angels

UNTIL A government military delegation brought the body of his son home, Dr. Sidi Samura had not recently given much thought to death. With Tankor Satani long dead, the doctor had reestablished his practice, although he did not keep tiring hours, limiting his expertise to a handful of people, so that he had lots of time to read, play *warri*, and, on Friday, chess with his friend Theodore Iskander. Occasionally the doctor would think of his son at the war front, his face grave as he reflected on the terrible tragedy of the nation that had led to the present crisis.

"War is a disaster!" he told his friend one evening when they had sat down to drinks, "and for our Nero to be dining lavishly at this time is worse than treachery."

"Yes, my friend," Theodore agreed. "I sometimes wonder what terrible deeds the pioneers must have done for us to be reaping this hell."

"The men probably raped some women and turned their backs on them."

"Then again, some of those men may have loved some double-crossing women who saddled them with children that they had not fathered," the philosopher said ruefully.

"You mean like some of Tankor Satani's women?"

"We shall never know."

Two days later, the doctor had just finished writing an article lambasting General Dan Doggo when he heard a loud commotion coming up his street. Even before he went to the window to find out what it was all about, some sixth sense told him they were coming to his house and that he was about to receive some bad news. He was right.

The body of Lieutenant Albert Samura had come home in a military jeep.

"I bring you the respect of the commander-in-chief of the republic," the grim-faced major leading a team of six men said as he removed the white, blue, and green flag of the nation from the coffin of the dead lieutenant.

Not for the first time in his life, the graveyard had bitten the venerable doctor by taking a second son. He seemed to age instantly, and his shoulders, always held high even when he was in jail, slumped in despair. After the soldiers had opened the coffin, he touched the face of his son, lying with the same nobility that Yeama had admired. Trembling, the doctor touched the delicate mouth and the finely chiseled chin, the product of the genes he had passed on to his children. He stood for a while looking at his son, and his heart was filled with an indescribable pain for this wasted life—a musician, doctor, scientist, or artist in the future—killed on the battlefield of a corrupt, buffoonish general.

"Go away," he said to the soldiers as soon as he managed to find his voice.

It was with a wrenching ache that they watched him begin to climb the steps to his bedroom, where his wife, already concluding that a terrible disaster had happened, had begun to wail loudly.

Soon the rebels were closing in on Malagueta, and casualties were mounting among General Dan Doggo's troops. Yet he did not see any reason why he should reduce his gluttonous binges of wine and food. Only recently, he had returned to the bed of his Fulani mistress, Mariama Tukulor. Because of the anxiety brought about by the convolutions of the war and thinking she should not be left unprotected, she forgave him and did not mind that he was still a bit too heavy when they made love.

"*Ah* know say you go come back," she said, "because dat madam professor nor sabi make you happy like me, eh?"

Whereas there was scarcity in the shops, the general and his friends had not conceded an inch to discretion. They were still getting supplies from their Coral friends, who always had large hoards of goods, just in case. A wiser man when compared to the buffoon of a general, Moustapha Ali-Bakr, concerned about losing his powerful control of diamonds, went to the Coral community for contributions to the war chest of the government. "De government sojas using primitive guns to fight de rebels firing new rifles, bazookas, and American Stinger missiles dey buy cheap, cheap in Peshawar. We have to help de military; otherwise, Astafullai, we all finished!" He raged.

The reference to Allah prompted a digging into the considerable assets of the Corals. Six times a day, even among the nonbelievers, copious prayers were said to the Almighty. But for some Corals what had once been thought unlikely became a reality, as they began to make contingency plans to leave Malagueta, just in case the rebels came close enough to threaten their lives. They were not the only ones worried about the threat posed by the rebels. Western embassies, the Americans' especially, organized an airlift of "non-essential staff"—wives, children, and flat-out drunks—who had really been in Malagueta for the sun. The thought of going back to their small apartments in Europe or their mortgaged homes in the USA was a bitter pill for many to swallow. They thought angrily about losing their servants, swimming pools, and the incomparably beautiful beaches, and of how inconceivable it was for the bitter tongues of winter and gale storms to lash them after they had enjoyed so much sun in the tropics. Worse, after losing their chauffeured cars, they would have to drive their children to school on icy roads on bleak mornings. Away from their palatial homes in the sunny, fashionable districts of Malagueta, they would most likely drink themselves to depression!

This Side of Paradise

While the Corals and diplomats were losing sleep over the advance of Lucifer Kontofili's rebels on the capital, a life richly lived finally came to an end in the house in front of the river. It was an event for which Theodore Iskander and Habiba Mouskuda had been preparing lately.

Increasingly, although the family did not always talk about the impending rebel disaster, Yeama had sensed for some time that Irene was unconcerned about the war. It was clear the old woman was hanging onto the trellis of her long life for another reason, waiting, it seemed, until she had seen her first great-grandchild. One day, when her granddaughter came visiting without her husband, Irene took the hand of the young woman and looked beseechingly at her, then asked a pointed question: "What are you and your husband doing at night?"

Leaving her granddaughter speechless, she walked to her room, trailed by the scent of the geraniums. Then she came back with her Bible and with her fading eyes read slowly but clearly about a lamb being raised even during the time of the lions. Lately, she had assumed a tone of quiet reserve, and, as though she were finally sinking into the autumnal nights of her life, her chattiness was gone. In one way or another, she had been preparing for her demise, but still hoped that her last wish would be granted. In the cluttered nest of her room she had lots of memorabilia, amongst which were the items she had kept from her son's childhood, those summers that seemed so long ago, for Theodore was now approaching sixty-five. After hours of rifling through her bags and portmanteaux, the old woman came up with the bibelots she had kept all these years: the finely printed program for her son's confirmation, her trinkets and the blouse with the ruffled frills at the neck that he had worn. One evening she made a quiet gesture of handing over the icons to her son, when Habiba was out in the garden.

"Here," she said. "Ah have kept these for you. You will give dem to my grand-*pikin*, hopefully not too long now. Ah can't wait forever in dis worl'."

Theodore Iskander was quick to discern what was on his mother's mind. One day, he dared to ask the inevitable question about funeral rites.

"Have a simple ceremony, and bury me next to your fader," she said, smiling.

"And your coffin?" he asked with a little gravity.

"I don't want one of dem new bronze things rich people are dying to be buried in: all dat money spent for the eye-seeing of man. No, sir! Put me in a wooden coffin: we are bone people, not bronze. And ah already paid for one at the undertaker's."

Although he was aware of the several instances of people coming to borrow a coffin from his mother, he was nonetheless flabbergasted. "And before you go?" he asked.

Irene smiled sweetly before replying. "You mean, is there anything ah would like to have before de Master calls me home?"

"Sort of, Mama."

"A great-grand-*pikin!*" the old woman said, her smile still sweet.

Within two years she was gone, but with the happy knowledge that Yeama had given her a great-grandson. After having her baby, Yeama and her family moved in with her parents because Habiba was worried their lives might be in danger.

"We are safe there," Yeama had tried to assure her mother.

"Not in these times," came the mother's concerned reply.

Fittingly, given how close the two of them had been, it was Yeama who discovered her grandmother in death, when she came one evening into the old woman's room with her son. As usual, Irene had left her windows open for some fresh air, and as she walked in, Yeama was assailed by a permeation of exotic scents from the garden: jasmine and white oleanders and hyacinth, whose bulbs had newly opened up near the river. An enchanting sweet spell came through the window to saturate the room where Irene was lying in a quiet, final sleep.

She looked so happy that it was as though, in the final hours of her life, she had felt that, with all the gifts given to her, she had done her best for her son, and he for her, and that to die so close to the river that she and her granddaughter had loved so much, mystified by the enigmas of the water spirit, was propitious: she was going to heaven. Just before she started to drift into unconsciousness, Irene heard the singing orioles perched on the branches of the almond tree under which she had spent so much time with her beloved dog Tiger. In that long summer when Pallo had blessed the land and Tiger had dived for conger eel, Irene saw the face of the dog and knew that Tiger and the angels were coming for her this side of paradise, and she went home with them, her smile warm and peaceful.

Yeama closed her grandmother's eyes, then picked a pair of scissors from the old woman's sewing kit, clipped a strand of Irene's hair, put it in the palm of her son, and closed it.

"Good-bye, Granny," she said, as tears of gratitude welled up in her.

CHAPTER SEVENTY-FIVE

The Beasts of No Nation

AFTER A blistering attack on him by the philosopher in one of the now fearless newspapers, General Dan Doggo finally hired Gurkha soldiers from a British regiment to help defend Kissi. After two weeks of intense fighting, the Gurkhas seemed to have blocked the rebel advance on the capital at Kotokumbu, a strategically placed town thirty miles away by highway, between Malagueta and the rest of Kissi. During the lull, bandits would come out of the surrounding bush to waylay the government convoys, snatch vital goods, and kill the truck drivers.

Now that Irene was dead, Pathe N'jai Tall did not feel he would be betraying the old woman's trust by suggesting a change of country. The hiatus in the fighting was all that he needed to broach the subject of departure to Yeama. "Let us leave for Senegal," he said. "We can come back when this war is over."

Yeama would hear nothing of it. "I am not leaving," she said.

"Don't be stubborn," Pathe pleaded. "The rebels are closing in; the government is weak, corrupt; its troops are deserting; soon it would be too late."

Still Yeama was reluctant to leave. This land that sloped into the river was where she believed Irene's ghost sometimes came to visit. The signs were there. Although it was the dry season, the plants were green, the flowers had not withered, and the river was always high, its rhapsody sometimes rising above the plethora of bird noises on the trees. Yeama felt that it was Irene who was responsible for these unusual changes in the environment. Then one night, looking radiant in a long blue gown, and with her head crowned with an aureole of blue hyacinths, Irene appeared to her granddaughter in a dream, and when Yeama woke up, she made the decision her grandmother had whispered to her in the dream.

"You go ahead," Yeama said to her husband. "Take our son with you. I shall join you later."

Yeama's most difficult task was to convince her parents that they should also leave. After a long dry spell, rain had been falling heavily throughout the week, and not even the fire in the charcoal grill had been able to mitigate the feel of damp and mildew in the house. The pain in Theodore Iskander's leg, which had not bothered him for a while, had suddenly returned, and he now walked with a pronounced limp. Quite unlike his normal tenacity and endurance, he complained a lot about the cold needles of the harmattan biting into his bones, causing great concern to his family. With the hospitals running short of drugs, Habiba Mouskuda finally applied a poultice and made him drink some hog hock and parsley soup to alleviate his pain.

"You will have to see a surgeon out of the country," Yeama pleaded.

"It is all right," he said. "The pain is just a nuisance that old age brings to all of us. A little *ori* ointment should take care of it."

"Daddy, that goat ointment is all right for a minor fracture, but this was a major wound. You know there is no working MRI out in the country, and the one at the best hospital in town is unreliable. The standby electric generator could go out while you are being examined."

"Let me think about it for a while," Theodore said.

They had been talking in the living room, he with grave dignity and she with her eyes pleading. After a while, he got up from his chair and began to limp slowly to his study, where he sat at his desk and poured himself a brandy, lit a cigar, and leafed through the pages of his almost completed biography of his great ancestor, the poet Garbage Martins. To have done so much work on a glorious period of Malagueta's history, when the present one was rife with conflict and all vestiges of sanity were now disappearing, filled him with a deep happiness. Then, the present, as it always seemed to do, dwarfing the past, he thought of the tragedy of his old friend losing his son Albert. He felt a deep pain for the doctor and realized how much he owed to his friend for enlightenment.

"What a tragedy it was for Albert to have died so young," the philosopher mused, putting on an album by the great Ali Farka Touré, whose music he had always found pleasing to work to during the long hours of writing the biography. Suddenly, in spite of everything—his still alluring mistress, the river—he felt lonely.

At sixty-seven, he was completely gray now, bearded, but healthy, except for "this damn leg," and was surprised at how he had started to miss his mother more than he thought he would at the time of her death. With so many things on his mind, he felt a bit tired and was soon asleep on his couch. Habiba came to throw a blanket over him to keep the cold out of his injured leg.

Next morning, feeling prescient, as he sometimes did, about a tumultuous incident to come, he thought he should telephone the doctor's house to see how he was faring. Because of the acute fuel shortage in town, he had not been able to visit his friend in a week. But the lines were down; an underground cable had been chewed up by the dynamite some fishermen had thrown into the river to catch fish.

He stood near the window with a good view of the river, through which he could also see, though somewhat blocked by the branches of a tree, the road leading up to his house. As if to confirm his premonition, one of his old students came hurrying up the street, grave-faced.

"Dr. Sidi Samura is dead, Professor," the student said, unable to control his tears.

Because the doctor was not a churchgoer, the National Cathedral bells had not tolled for him as they would have for a distinguished Christian son or daughter. If there had been bells, Habiba, intrigued, would have informed the philosopher, just in case it was someone he knew.

"When did it happen?" the deeply shaken philosopher asked the student after the rivulet of the shock had sunk in.

"Yesterday, Professor."

It transpired that the doctor had died soon after a Bible-toting Pentecostal born-again proselytizer had visited him. Informed of the doctor's impending death by his wife, the cleric had come to the house hoping to get the old freethinker to confess his sins. When the doctor saw the woman coming in, dressed in a white gown, he did not even give her a chance to say hello. "Go to hell," he said. "If there is any defender between my God and me, it is God Himself, not your church!"

He died that evening with a smile on his face, and his wife, stroking his sandpapery face, thought he had never looked so peaceful in their fifty years of marriage.

Next evening, as his mistress was comforting him, the deeply saddened philosopher sat at his desk and wrote an impassioned, glowing tribute to his friend, entitled "Death of a Titan":

> *Sidi Yaya Samura, who has just died, would probably have been amused that his death occurred at a time when moral objections are being voiced against the scientific inroads into cloning man. Over the years, those of us who followed his career would recall that although he was trained as a doctor, a good deal of his active life was spent not in medicine but on more abstract issues like morality and free will.*
>
> *For those interested in astrology, it is worth mentioning that he had the same birthday as the great civil rights leader Martin Luther King Jr.: January 15. Throughout his life, although he was by no means a church person, Sidi Samura's response to moral and social issues was somehow expressed in religious terms. Religious in the sense that, when faced with questions of belief and obedience, he chose the path that upheld his individuality, even at the risk of losing his freedom and earnings.*
>
> *In his view, the moral imperative to speak out was best expressed in Paul Tillich's argument that "a moral act is not an act of obedience to an external law, human or divine. It is the inner law of our true being, of our essential or created nature, which demands that we actualize what follows from it."*

Many will recall Tankor Satani's failed attempts to silence the gadfly. He detained Sidi Samura at the central prison and reportedly offered the doctor various ministerial appointments and the ambassadorship to the United Nations upon his release. Not surprisingly, Samura laughed at him and asked the president out of his house. Although he lost two sons when they were young, perhaps the tragedy that wounded him the most was when some of his so-called friends, out of fear of offending Tankor Satani, stopped visiting the dissident, or making use of his great skills as a doctor. It was a sad reflection on those men. In an age of political pygmies and ethnic bigots, Sidi Samura was a Titan who will be greatly missed."

Returning from the doctor's funeral, after Habiba had used all of her connections to get some fuel so that they could attend, Theodore Iskander became aware of the deep grief in many sections of the town. Shops had closed, and there were lines in front of the offices of three newspapers that had published not only Theodore Iskander's tribute, but also the last scathing writings of the doctor. It was the early evening darkness, the lights of the fruit sellers were flickering, and Theodore Iskander realized that some of the doctor's admirers were chanting and singing festively.

"Long live the doctor's spirit," someone said, buying a round of drinks to honor the dead man.

Then, thinking the doctor's life should really be celebrated and not mourned, they broke into rhapsodic calypsos, holding their drinks as they went to drop flowers in front of the doctor's house. The day had been long, and there were dark omens on the horizon about the future of Kissi, but it did not matter. In the looming darkness of the times, it was clear that it would be a long time before the light of the doctor was allowed to go out in the memory of most people.

A stubborn insistence on being one of the pallbearers had worsened the strained leg of the philosopher, and he found it hard to walk for days. Eventually, bowing to Yeama's insistence that he go abroad, and convinced that he had to stay alive to continue the unfinished work of his friend, Theodore Iskander left Malagueta one rainy morning, accompanied by Habiba Mouskuda, Pathe N'jai Tall, and their grandson, Kounate.

On the evening before they left, Habiba Mouskuda thought about the years she had spent in that house; about how happy she had been there; of the caring and wonderful man who had become not only her lover but also the father of their wonderful daughter. Redemption, if that was what had happened in her life after her heartless past, had never been so sweet, so beautiful. Later that night, as the orioles were settling down on the mango trees, she urged her lover to come with her for one last look at the river.

"Come with me and let us taste its sweetness one last time, until we come back." Hand in hand, they walked to the bank of the river, and all that Habiba could think of was how lucky she had been in life, as the river began to flow so that it sounded like a melodious song of farewell.

"You will try to be safe now?" Theodore Iskander said to Yeama as her parents were about to leave their house for exile.

"Don't worry. The Gurkhas are very professional and will defend Malagueta to the last man. I shall be here when all four of you return soon."

Six months later, unaware of the danger facing her, perhaps because the government had been suppressing news about how close the war was to Malagueta, she went to the garden to stretch her legs. The high wall would keep her safe, she thought. As she was about to go back to the house to continue listening to Dizzy Gillespie, she saw the three men, armed with rifles, their heads wrapped in red bandannas. She tried to run to safety, but they chased her, cornered her, and threw her to the ground, leaving her in no doubt that if she did not surrender her body to them, they would not hesitate to use the cutlass, whose shiny blade one of them held in his arms.

More than five years after he first launched his attack on Kissi from Bassa, Lucifer Kontofili and his rebels had finally entered Malagueta. On the night that the rebel leader began his bombardment of the capital, the one man he would have liked to capture was not there. Two nights earlier, General Dan Doggo was at Mariama Tukulor's house when he heard a great commotion in the neighborhood.

"It is some hoodlums, and they are looking for the general."

Mariama Tukulor was the first to react. She saw the fear in the eyes of the general and pitied him, but felt nothing but hate for the rebels. "Here," she said. "Put this on and go through the back door; there is an exit through the maze of houses. A boatman will take you away."

General Dan Doggo had barely finished putting on his mistress's *grand boubou* before the hoodlums started banging on Mariama Tukulor's door. When they finally broke it down, they found her regal and composed, daring them with her eyes to attack her.

"Where is the bastard general?" one of them asked.

"He left a long time ago, dressed like a woman and accompanied by his long-term pimp, the minister of presidential affairs, similarly attired," said a boy of ten who had witnessed the scene.

"How did they leave?"

"Like beasts of no nation," the boy recalled the boatman saying as he quietly led them down a path toward the sea, on their way to the French-speaking nation of Bakazo.

CHAPTER SEVENTY-SIX

The Return of the Native

SOON AFTER saying their obligatory prayers one fine November morning, some recovering lepers sat in the shade of a tamarind tree working their deformed fingers into the meal prepared by the charitable sisters in the compound of Saint Ignatius Catholic Church. Bright blue clouds were moving across the sky as the lepers began to eat, at the same time that some vultures left their trees looking for more road kill on the streets of Malagueta. Concentrating on the few morsels of meat in their meal, the lepers did not notice the boneshaker bus emitting carbon dioxide fumes as it crawled to a stop near the post office opposite the church. The driver, whose stained clothes showed that he had traveled on some dusty roads before arriving in the city, came down with the melancholy air of a man who had not made a profit from the trip and could not wait to get rid of his passengers.

The first group to alight consisted of twenty-five colorfully dressed women. Some carried bundles of clothes on their heads; others, holding cages of noisy chickens and bags of smoked fish, hurried their children out of the bus, one of whom had almost forgotten his pet iguana. The last passenger to alight was a man whose skin had a sickly pallor. He took one last look at the bus, as though leaving a jail where he had completed a long sentence. He came down slowly and kissed the ground like the pope visiting a foreign country, although he was in fact a born-again Baptist who had been looking forward to his homecoming. His eyes were a dull, liquid brown and reflected a native son's gratitude as he dusted some feathers off of his coat, after he had suffered the indignity of riding on a bus in which women were taking their chickens to market.

The lepers had finished their meal and were dozing off, watched by the charitable nuns, by the time the vultures swooped down on some carrion. With a dull whistle, the wind was scattering plastic bags in the air and sending specks of red dust into the man's eyes, but that was the least of the bother he had experienced since he boarded the bus eight hours earlier in a frontier town. He wiped his eyes with a cheap cotton handkerchief and managed a thin smile; then, after a moment's hesitation, he said good-bye to the driver.

Gabriel Ananias, the former governor of Malagueta's Central Bank, had come home.

It was the end of the war, a force of regional troops had defeated the rebels, and Lucifer Kontofili was awaiting trial, charged with mass murder. After eight years in exile, Gabriel Ananias's first thought was to locate his girlfriend, Hawanatu Gomba, but he knew that would not be easy, given that Malagueta's population of half a million had risen to three times that number from the flood of refugees from the countryside.

"This is a disaster," he said, and picked up his suitcase.

He stood on Samura Machel Street, feeling a bit awkward in his ill-fitting suit but grateful to be breathing the fresh air of the Atlantic after not being near the ocean for so long. He saw the bats, with an eerie noise, returning to congregate on the huge cotton tree, and he noticed, almost in shock, that the jacarandas were blooming on the grounds of the National Museum nearby, when everything else had the pallor of the decay that had spread its hand over the city. The carrion vultures were making a most unholy noise near the cathedral, frightening away some young nurses hurrying home on the crowded street. Gabriel Ananias took everything in. It was as though he were staring at the face of some apocalyptic evidence that the earth had thrown up in a fit of rage. Where was the city that he had left? he asked, looking at the desolation. Briefly he thought of a return to the despair and uncertainty of exile in Bassa, but he was broke, having used up nearly all of his money to buy a cheap ticket to come home.

After Hawanatu Gomba returned to Malagueta, Gabriel Ananias was shocked by how regularly he had started to talk to himself, how close he was to losing his mind, which was why, as soon as he could, he got on the first chicken-feathered bus going to Malagueta.

When the women saw how pathetic he looked, they tried not to laugh at him, but it was impossible for them to control themselves. "Look at his suit," one of them said, trying to be discreet. "It is as if he don't have a woman to take care of him!"

"You can say dat again, my sister; it must be a long time since he slept wit' a woman," another said with mirth, especially as she liked men.

Gabriel Ananias walked to the top of Samura Machel Street, turned into Timbuktu Boulevard, the main artery in the town, and was immediately taken aback by the mounds of filth everywhere. But it was not until he was pushed out of the way by a group of ragged beggars and maimed children darting between cars to beg for a living that he realized he had in fact been standing in front of the charred remains of the Central Bank, of which he had once been the governor. Not for the first time since he boarded the bus, he had to dust off his suit, then continued his rediscovery of the city. In front of the once splendid Palace Hotel, now a rundown place for drunks and musicians singing sultry evening calypsos, he came across a bevy of women waiting for a group of United Nations officers, hoping the men would take them to their beds for the price of a week's meal.

"You should see them parading at night in front of the two hotels functioning in town," Hawanatu Gomba had written in one of her letters to him in the past year.

With the sweet smell of their perfumes, their dangling cheap brass-plated earrings, their Bint el Sudan powder, and the myriad colors of their *kan kan* skirts, those dainty whores on the streets of Malagueta looked beautiful as they went about their business.

"They are brazen but have a dignity," Hawanatu had continued. "Not like those shameless college whores and female lawyers who used to flock to the presidential palace when General Dan Doggo was the president."

Before boarding the bus for Malagueta, Gabriel Ananias had been thinking about those whores and of the prospect of opening a church where sinners like him could come to worship. As he was contemplating that prospect, a convoy of cars crawling up Timbuktu Street to the main courthouse, near the cotton tree where the dog-faced bats were shrieking, interrupted his thought. The convoy included an armored personnel carrier in front and three military jeeps in the middle. Four special security cars, a Black Maria, and another armored personnel carrier brought up the rear. The Black Maria looked as if it had been in the garage for remodeling: a whole steel panel had been removed from one side and replaced with long black bars, making it look more like a cage in which a fierce, demonic animal was being held.

It was a bright, sunny day, but not hot, and a cool breeze was blowing from the ocean. Wiping the sweat bubbles from their dark faces, the soldiers guarding the Black Maria were having a difficult time holding back the large crowd of people surging behind the convoy. Gabriel Ananias felt a chill running through him when the crowd started pounding the vehicle with their fists and screaming, "Beast, beast!"

The crowd did not feel menaced by the soldiers, and when the convoy was in front of the courthouse, Colonel Emmanuel Ariko, the head of the security detail charged with getting it there, had a difficult time bringing the situation under control. He gave the go-ahead for the armed soldiers to come down from their jeeps, and they took up positions. But the crowd surged forward, and, fearing a riot, the soldiers fired their guns into the air to disperse it. But it was futile; many Malaguetans had been waiting two years for this moment. "Hand the monster over to us!" they demanded.

The colonel had to use all of his powers of persuasion in appealing to the crowd to allow him to do his job. "There will be no kangaroo court," he said. "Justice will be done according to the laws of the land."

When the doors of the Black Maria were finally opened, a man came down, and the crowd went wild pressing forward to get their hands on him. He was bound hand and foot, his beard was wild, and his piercing, metallic eyes were vacant. He wore tattered clothes, and his wide mouth reminded some of the people in the crowd of the pictures of Nebuchadnezzar after he fell from God's grace. It was the first chance many of the people had had to see the man, after years of living with and suffering from his fearful legend.

The man took a quick, disdainful glance at the crowd and spat on the ground. He sulked as the soldiers pulled his chains, and showed his contempt for the angry crowd by scratching his balls. "Kiss dem," he spat out.

The crowd surged forward. Once again the soldiers had a difficult time holding it back, but after a determined attempt they finally managed to whisk the prisoner into the courthouse, and there was a deafening noise as the great metallic doors to the building clanged shut behind him.

After waging one of the most brutal wars in the world, Lucifer Kontofili had been brought to face justice.

On the previous night, in the deepest secrecy, and with not even his guards told where they would be taking him, Lucifer Kontofili had been brought to a rehabilitation camp, where a team of limb fitters, nurses, doctors, and parents were waiting to show him his armless victims. He was marched past the rooms where they sat, but his eyes did not betray any emotion. If the authorities had painted a diptych of all the horrors in the world, it would not have compared with the wretchedness in that camp. Some of the guards there had been in other conflicts around the world, yet the sight of those maimed children was harrowing enough to make them doubt for a moment the existence of God. They could comprehend natural disasters, the barbarity of one adult against another, but the pain in the eyes of some of those children not yet past the rites of childhood was wrenching and unnecessary.

Gabriel Ananias continued his exploration of the city, a forlorn figure lugging a suitcase, flummoxed by what had happened to Malagueta. Some of the people who had been yelling themselves hoarse when the prisoner was being taken to court were now returning to their various jobs. Thinking that the solitary man looked familiar, one of them was about to say hello, but decided he was probably mistaken. "After the war, this city is full of mad people," he thought to himself, and walked away, leaving Gabriel Ananias grateful for his discretion.

Gabriel Ananias's desire to see more of the old city took him to the Treasury Building. All that was left of the once-splendid structure the British had built was a burnt-out shell, in front of which an oleander bush was still blooming. Not too far away, he paused to stare at the famed National Hotel, where a great writer once lived, now bombed out and left standing like a dark, monstrous ghost of its old self. He felt tight in his throat as he thought about how Lucifer Kontofili and his rebel army had ruined the city.

CHAPTER SEVENTY-SEVEN

The Last Song for Mabinty Koumba

OPPOSITE THE Catholic church where Gabriel Ananias had kissed the ground was a rundown bar furnished with a few stools, some expired wall calendars, and pictures of Hollywood starlets from a bygone age. A beat-up phonograph was cranking out Congolese music, and some old-timers were drinking stout. Two of them had seen Gabriel Ananias kiss the ground. Intrigued that Gabriel Ananias had arrived light—a battered suitcase being his only luggage, a contraption held together with nylon strings—one of the old-timers sat thinking for a while about the stranger. His interest was deepened because of the clothes Gabriel Ananias was wearing, the suit hanging uncomfortably on him being of a cut long gone out of style.

"See dat fellow wit' de suitcase," the old-timer said to his friend nursing a glass of Guinness. "He looks familiar, like dat banker who used to run de Central Bank in de bad days of Tankor Satani."

"Can't be," said his friend. "He probably in America; where he done keep all de money he make on de side with dem Corals."

"Ah swear he is de one," the first old-timer insisted.

His friend licked his chops before replying. "Dat being de case, we soon find out. News travels fast in dis town."

On his walkabout, Gabriel Ananias had stopped in front of the monument to the poet Garbage Martins. It was badly neglected but was now being repaired. Some passionate lovers of poetry had recently put some fresh flowers there, but a wind was blowing them, and Gabriel gathered them up and weighted them down with a small branch. He felt tired but did not intend to stop his exploration of the city, now that he was not really worried about being discovered by some old friends.

The humidity was penetrating deeply into his skin, the salty sea vapors were thick over the rise of the city, and his asthmatic breathing was taxing his bronchial tubes, but Gabriel Ananias continued walking until he was back at the burnt-out Treasury Building. Hoping, perhaps, that the magnificent State House built by the British had been spared, he hurried up Jamaica Hill to have a look. The building had been saved but was covered in moss, grime, and soot, its massive stone walls showing the savage pockmarks inflicted by the attacking rebels. "At least the new government has somewhere to meet," he said.

For some strange reason, perhaps because he had dealt so often with him during the time when he ran the Central Bank but had not heard any news about what had happened to the Coral, Gabriel Ananias began to think of Moustapha Ali-Bakr.

He would soon find out what had happened to him.

Three years earlier, when the rebels attacked Malagueta, they had come through the hills overlooking the city thinking about the good life awaiting them. Their intention had been to take over the beautiful hilltop homes of the Coral businessmen, the army generals, politicians, lawyers, doctors, and preachers.

On the night before launching the attack on this suburban paradise, Lucifer Kontofili had assigned the task of leading it to his top commander, Ali "Scorpion" Marampa. "Make you go slow, slow wit' de attack; dis be big prize; all we fight for long tem. Only kill people if dey refuse to surrender house, money, and all de good tings like motorcar and women. You hear? Dat's why dey call you Scorpion, eh?"

"Leave ebrything to me, General," Scorpion replied.

Next to Lucifer's, Scorpion's brutality was legendary. He was six feet, three inches tall, lanky and somewhat ungainly, with a neck like a giraffe's and a devilish leer on his lips, and it was common knowledge that he had used rape as a brutal weapon of war again dozens of women. He seldom washed, and he smelled like rotten mangoes, but on the night before attacking the targeted homes overlooking Malagueta, he soaped himself clean in a nearby stream and urged his troops to do the same. "You nor want people to know we dey come to dem house."

His plan was to attack the homes when, except for the dull porch lights and the faint glow powered by the private generators of the rich, the area would be dark.

This time Moustapha Ali-Bakr had stayed put in Malagueta because he felt his presence would prevent the looting of his many properties. During the long conflict he had dished out a lot of cash to many rebel spies, and on the night before Scorpion launched his attack on the hill-top homes, a renegade soldier with contacts to the rebels had gone to warn Moustapha Ali-Bakr.

"Make you leave de house and go someplace for safety. Dey come and attack de house, but if you stay, dey not kill you. Dey just take all dey want; den you give dem some money and dey leave you," the renegade said.

Except for his eldest son, who was twenty-five, Moustapha Ali-Bakr had sent his family to the safety and comfort of a palatial house in Beirut. Built with money from his diamond dealings in Malagueta, the house was a carbon copy of his West African tropical mansion, except for the olives, grape vines, and apples that could not be grown in the tropics. Despite its splendor, however, he had never felt comfortable in that house and was willing, to the horror of his wife, to see the war out in Malagueta, which was why he had been so generous with his donations to the government war chest.

The hands of the clock were ticking toward midnight, and Moustapha Ali-Bakr sat waiting in the middle of his favorite room with his son. "Allahu Akbar," he said, hoping for deliverance if the rebels attacked. As he had been advised, his doors were open; twice he had counted the ten thousand dollars in cash that he hoped would check the ire of the rebels. He did not rule out the possibility that he could talk to them one on one, when he could offer to work with them when they became the new government. Although his father was an Arab, his mother was a black woman: that, he felt, ought to stand him in good stead with the rebels, although he had still not forgotten how the black woman who was his favorite mistress—the woman he now called a black bitch—had deserted him.

Earlier that day, after the warning from the renegade soldier, Moustapha Ali-Bakr had carted many of the valuables in the house to a safe place, but had left the house reasonably furnished so as not to raise the suspicion of the rebels.

As he sat working his worry beads, he looked anxiously at his son to see how the young man was coping with the anticipated arrival of the rebels, Like his father, the young man was sweating but was otherwise calm.

"Don't worry too much," the young man said. "The rebels are all high on cocaine and just want some money before they go off to rape some women."

Slightly past midnight, some rebels under the leadership of Commander Scorpion came as expected. When the much-feared commander entered the house of the Coral, he was surprised to find it open. "He get proper sense," he said.

"'E notto fool man," another rebel agreed.

They found Moustapha Ali-Bakr sitting, Buddha-like, on his prayer mat with his legs folded, his eyes, in the dim, mauve light of the room, soft, not betraying the fear in his soul. His son was sitting motionless in a chair about ten feet from him.

"Make you take all you want," Moustapha said to the feared commander. "Ah beg, nor kill me and my son; 'e nar *pikin*."

He showed the commander the "gift" of ten thousand US dollars and watched as Scorpion counted the bills—one, two, three, four thousand—until he had reached ten. Moustapha Ali-Bakr concentrated on the brutal lines of Scorpion's mouth and began to shake, thinking that the rebel commander knew he had in his hands the life of the second most powerful man in Malagueta.

"Dis not enough," Scorpion said after he had finished counting.

"Ah swear to God, dat's all ah get in de house," Moustapha said, trembling with fear. "Banks done close because of de *wahala* in de country; it is big trouble for man like me."

"'E lie," said a young, drunk rebel. "'E trying to fool you, Commander; de *basta pikin*."

After sitting quietly all the time, showing not the slightest emotion and letting his father do the talking, Moustapha Ali-Bakr's son sprang to his feet. "Don't call my father a bastard!" he raged.

"Sit down! Siddom, ah tell you!" Moustapha yelled at him.

Khalil Ali-Bakr did as he was told, but not before hissing his contempt for the rebels.

Calmly, aiming his revolver so that he would not miss, Commander Scorpion shot the impetuous young man in the mouth and followed with a quick second shot to the chest. He smiled with a sneer as thick and hot blood streamed from the young man's mouth, like the red water in the alluvial rivers that had made Moustapha Ali-Bakr rich. Fool that he was, shocked at how foolishly he had gambled away his life, the young man began to work his mouth in the last movements of his day.

"You killed me *pikin*, you killed am!" Moustapha howled, and tried to get up.

He never made it to the frontier where his son was curled up in the last spasms of an untimely death, unable to tell his father how much he loved him, a tragedy that Moustapha had not contemplated. Moustapha moaned horribly as he watched his son; he felt he was losing his mind, that the world was turning into a mosaic of ugly colors, unlike the beauty of his diamonds. Then, incredibly, sensing that he was about to leave this world, he thought about how he should have loved Malagueta not only for its diamonds but also for the fact that his mother, Mabinty Koumba, was a black woman. Like many of her kind, she had loved generations of Corals, only to be discarded like junk. Howling like a dog for the loss of his son, Moustapha Ali-Bakr banged his head against his chair, and then he began to sing, in Arabic and in Kilubu, his mother tongue, a last song of belated gratitude for his black mother Malagueta. "Allahu Akbar," he said as Scorpion fired a bullet through his heart, from which the smell of garlic began to permeate the room as Moustapha's blood spilled across the floor to join his son's in the eternity of death.

The Old-Timer Was Not Mistaken

Gabriel Ananias went back to the spot near the post office where he had got off the bus, unsure of where to start looking for her: Hawanatu Gomba, the one woman he knew would not mind taking care of his wretched soul, who would be glad to see him and take him to her breasts. Assuming she was alive.

His thoughts were disturbed then, as fate took a hand in his homecoming. "Ah not too sure am right; ah could be mistaken; but you look like dat fellow who used to run de Central Bank a long time ago," the old man who suddenly came up to him said.

Without hesitating, believing that, for the second time in his life, fate had intervened to save him, just as those miraculous ants had appeared to lead him out of the ruins of the quake, and that this was his only chance to get to Hawanatu, Gabriel Ananias immediately owned up to his identity. "You are not mistaken," he said softly.

"Goddamn it!" the old-timer enthused. "Told dat friend of mine dat me eyes not playing tricks on me, but he don't believe me. Come, son, let me buy you a drink and fill you up on all dat been happening in dis town since you left."

Gabriel Ananias picked up his suitcase and followed the old man. It had been so long since he left for exile. Now he had returned a much wiser man. If, in his youth, he had strayed from the moral plane envisaged for him by the priest, he felt he had paid the price for that betrayal. It is not a matter of how much we fall, but how determined we are to rise. He was determined, and felt it was not too late to make amends for his ways; he had a good woman waiting somewhere in the city for him. As God was his witness, he would work hard to make himself worthy of her. Never again would he go chasing mirages; there were none left in this city. He was glad he had been given a chance at redemption.

In the depths of his soul he began to cry softly, because, in spite of their poverty, people were still kind in Malagueta.

CHAPTER SEVENTY-EIGHT

The Sweet Reward of Integrity

FOR TWELVE years after he came home with a foreign wife, three lovely daughters, and a medical degree from a university in Eastern Europe that no one had heard of, when Tankor Satani was president, Dr. Farrar Aziz had labored in obscurity in a back-street office, trying to make a living as a psychiatrist. He was a kind man with a pleasant disposition and was mad about cricket, but the smallness of his office and the battered old car that he drove made it obvious the doctor was having a difficult time with his practice. He was not a bad doctor but had gone into a field of specialty most people considered useless in Malagueta. Five days a week his nurse would open his office doors, dust the old magazines and half a dozen plastic chairs, and wait for patients, but only the irregulars came. When the doctor treated them, it was mostly gratis and for ailments unrelated to his training

"This is a do-for-God kind of practice," he would say to his nurse, who greatly admired his humanity.

As was not uncommon for doctors in Malagueta, who were often called upon to cover all aspects of medicine, he sometimes had to treat ailments like disorders of the mucous membrane, colds, malaria, and ear, nose, and throat infections. He enjoyed his practice, but it was clear that the doctor was not happy at home.

Given the paltriness of his earnings, it was rumored that his wife had been secretly "trading" their three daughters so that they could have the good life the doctor could not provide. With a color that was almost golden, the girls had blossomed into beautiful young women by the time each was seventeen.

If he was aware of those rumors, the doctor chose not to let them bother him, at least not in public. He turned a blind eye to his daughters' new, expensive wardrobes, ignored his wife's unexplained spending sprees, and allowed her to hold her regular Tuesday afternoon tea parties for other women from Eastern Europe, occasions that were now sweetened with expensive cakes and liqueurs. One afternoon he came home tired, only to halt in his tracks, stunned, for there in his garage was the sleek big golden BMW sedan the oldest girl had been driving around the city, in flagrant disregard for her father's integrity, certain she had the backing of her ambitious mother. Their house, which for years had been a rundown bungalow, with a roof that leaked during the rains, was suddenly transformed, now that the second daughter seemed to have come into lots of money, into a bright, cozy nest, the furniture reupholstered, the kitchen gadgets replaced.

"You have turned our daughters into harlots," the doctor finally yelled at his wife.

"And who is responsible for that?" she asked, frightened by the unexpected anger in his voice. "We couldn't go on living the way we were."

"Some of you women from your part of Eastern Europe are a bad lot," the doctor said with disgust.

Pained in his heart but powerless against the four women, he went about his work, but there were days when he seriously thought he might kill his wife. However, given that he loved his mother deeply and did not want to cause her grief, he dismissed that option and sought solace in other distractions or private pleasures. He started cultivating geraniums, and, in the morning chill of the harmattan, to get away from the loneliness he felt in that now strange house, he went for long walks on the beach, as the early November mist draped the mountain behind him.

While waiting for his irregular patients, if there was electricity in his office he would listen to operas, especially to Mussorgsky's *Boris Godunov* and Rossini's *Il turco in Italia*, which were amongst his favorites from his student days.

Considering how disgusted he was with his wife, he had his doubts about his worth, although his eyes gave very little away about what was really going on in his soul. A man of few words, he was occasionally observed by some fishermen to press his palms on his chest, perhaps to suppress the murderous rage in his soul, when he was out walking on the beach. Yet nothing could completely shake his confidence in himself. It was as though in the quiet toughness of his character he had come to accept that every man must give in to divine providence for his doing or undoing. Which was how, one morning, when he least expected it, Dr. Aziz became the most important medical officer in Malagueta.

As one of only two psychiatrists in Malagueta, Dr. Aziz suddenly and incredibly become the expert who would unravel the utterances of Lucifer Kontofili when the former rebel leader was brought to court to stand trial for crimes against humanity.

"Forgive me for not believing in you," his wife said, shamefaced over what she had been doing with their daughters.

"As Malaguetans say, "God's time is the best,"" the doctor said, and looked at his wife with pity.

Tragicomedy, public rage, and melodrama, rolled into one messy script, were the cameos during the first week of the trial. Lucifer Kontofili had refused to shave since he was captured and was taken into the courtroom looking disheveled in prison garb, his eyes roaming all over the courtroom like those of a caged cat. True to his reputation, he proved a most difficult defendant in court. Fearing the anger of his victims, no local lawyer had dared risked his life to defend him, and the best intentions of the government to see that he had a fair trial became a test of wills. Pressure had come from Downing Street about the prisoner's "right to a fair trial," so a lawyer had been hired in Britain to defend the prisoner. But jeered at by the multitudes in the court and ridiculed by the prisoner, the Englishman found the atmosphere too much. He caught the first plane out of Malagueta and was soon back in London, where a tidy fee had already been deposited into his account, regardless of the outcome of the trial.

Every day the proceedings were marred by the tragic sight of victims of the war: the throngs of men and women and children who came to the courthouse with the stumps of legs or arms, graphic, horrific evidence of Lucifer's crimes.

One afternoon, aware that the eyes of the world's press were on the proceedings, Lucifer put on quite a theatrical show. He tried to strip naked in the dock and had to be forcibly restrained; he made faces at the judges, whistled lewd suggestions to women, and was quickly given a bucket when it looked as though he was going to urinate on the spot. At the end of the third week, his rambling from the dock was so incoherent that the government prosecutor was convinced the prisoner had really gone mad. Finally, bowing to the inevitable, the government hired the long-neglected psychiatrist.

The first session did not go too well between Dr Aziz and Lucifer Kontofili. "Ah talk to no one," the prisoner ranted in his cell when he saw the doctor come in, "only to de power bigger dan de court. Make you don't waste me time. Court is evil, but war sweet, like 'oman."

The prisoner had not counted on a wily opponent like the redoubtable doctor, a man known for his remarkable patience who had dealt with, and survived, the whims of a nagging wife. Dr Aziz had not only expected the rant, but had been given all the support he needed to get a proper diagnosis of his patient.

"Take all the time you need, Doctor. And may God help you with that devil," the prosecutor had said.

Provided with a brand new car, an office, and a consultant's salary and staff, Dr. Aziz came to visit the prisoner every day in his cell for three weeks. "You say you won't talk to me, only to a bigger power," the doctor always began his session. "What is his name?"

"Dat's not your bisness," Lucifer would say, glaring at him.

"Are you having dreams?"

"Plenty. Ah see people dancing for me. Dey all calling me champion: big chief, like Napoleon. You know he fight Russian people?"

"Do you feel like shaving?" the doctor asked once, curious why the prisoner had not changed his attire or trimmed his beard.

"No. Me Samson. Man wit' power. Ah wear same clothes so people fear me."

"And you smell like a pig," the doctor felt like saying, but thought that would merely enrage the prisoner.

Throughout the sessions, the doctor observed Lucifer closely. Quietly, looking at the prisoner's eyes, he made notes about how often Lucifer would roll them, searching, it seemed, for moments from the past, an illusory world unconnected to the courtroom or this cell. Now and then, Lucifer was quiet and would bite his nails or fold his arms. At those times the doctor felt Lucifer was close to being rational, giving him a chance to try to decipher the prisoner's mind. On two occasions, before going into the cell, the doctor had made a most interesting observation through a peephole. He saw Lucifer trying to stand on his head, thumping his chest like a gorilla, talking to himself. At other times, as though giving orders to his lieutenants, calling each by name, Lucifer would rant for long periods. The doctor was always mesmerized.

Finally he felt he had gathered enough evidence. It was contradictory in some parts, and he was aware that his conclusions could be challenged on several points, but that did not deter the doctor from expressing his opinion that, in addition to delusions about his own importance, given his reaction to the presence of his victims in the courtroom, Lucifer Kontofili was suffering from a serious case of schizophrenia.

"As far as I can tell," the doctor said, "he has been suffering from it for some time, since long before he went out and started chopping off the hands of hundreds of children and then attacking the diamond mines."

"I shall assume that is a medical opinion, one that can be challenged before God?" the prosecutor asked.

Dr. Aziz was calm as he answered this challenge to his expertise. "Science is not in competition with theology; it is only God who can explain his cruelty to children, the beastly maiming, his mindless bombardment of the republic, all the fantasies about orders coming from someone higher than God. From my prognosis, I have concluded that no purpose would be served by continuing the trial and therefore recommend that this madman be held in a mental institution for the rest of his life."

"That is too good for him!" the prosecutor raged.

"He is not my problem anymore," the doctor cautioned him.

"Then we shall think of the right place for him."

Dr. Aziz did not raise any objections. For years, Lucifer had remained an enigma. If the government wanted to create their own enigma about where they intended to hold him, the doctor did not want to know about it. He packed his bags and walked to his car. As he was driving home, he started thinking about the hundreds of patients he now had to care for, following the decision of the government to have them treated for the nightmares suffered during the war. At that moment, although not an arrogant man, he felt he was among those in Malagueta who had been right all along about how integrity would eventually win out over greed. Only a few months ago, he had almost gone mad when his wife and daughters had made him doubt his own worth. Now he could afford to smile.

His integrity was his diamond, and he was proud of it.

One week later, as dawn broke on the streets of Malagueta, the city came alive with thousands of people heading toward the giant cotton tree, not far from Malombo House, the office of the president. Under that tree where, not so long ago, Tankor Satani's eunuchs had danced in rapture, driving a nun to search for the right pages in her Bible to pray for God's deliverance, the people saw Lucifer Kontofili, trapped like an animal in a metal cage. The sun was shimmering on the colorful gowns worn by some of the people. Still sporting his unkempt beard, Lucifer Kontofili stood half naked, barking and foaming at the mouth like a mad dog in the last stages of rabies: a testament, some people felt, to that long nightmare that had been the war in the country. But it was also his life that had been wasted, and his eyes had the scared brightness of a wild, cornered animal unable to break out of its cage. Rather than feeling hatred for him, a few people in the crowd began to pity him. As he continued to bark his fury, unable to grasp what was really happening to him, it was as though all the terrors of that long, terrible war had been nothing but a bad dream. Tremendously affected by the sight of the once-feared rebel leader so nakedly exposed, most people realized then that he really was demented, and had probably been that way for a long time. Consequently, this was not the punishment of a court, but the result of the choices he had made a long time ago about how he wanted to live his life, and of the way he should be remembered: a man who had been born with a mad streak that would eventually kill him. In the naked contempt of the thousands of children he had mercilessly destroyed by maiming them, he was a monster.

"Dis is de best sentence for him," a one-armed child said, "because no prison big enough to save am from all of us."

Epilogue

When she could bring herself to watch, Yeama had been following the trial of Lucifer Kontofili on television. Many months earlier, when the devil's claws had touched her, she had felt as if her blood vessels had stopped functioning, but with a little effort she got her blood flowing again. She caught a strange scent and realized it was the forest odor the last man had left in the air, his shoulders hung low as he walked away into the dark mist.

In spite of the torture in her soul, Yeama found it hard to forget his face, with that look of a frightened animal that had hung about him. Judging by the smoothness of his cheeks and the mouse-like urgency of his steps, he was not much younger than she. A light wind rustling the trees disturbed her reverie. Revived by the wind, she recalled that when the devil's men had trapped her, the air in the garden had been still, noiseless, and that she had been able to hear her own heart pounding like the tremor of a conga drum. Pinned to the ground, she had lain on a cruel death's road, more used than a circus horse and opened to the devil's claws. She had not been prepared for this day when fate would show her its harsh, meaningless journey, full of rough stones hurled at her face and with no sign to warn her that a bend in her life was about to come. No, she had not been prepared for this horror. She had lived for twenty-three years and borne one son, only to have the sons of other mothers pinion and rape her. The rough bed of the earth on which she had lain and the torn-off fragments of what was left of her clothes drank the small trickle of blood from her back, her insides were churned out, she needed a drink, but at that moment Yeama's legs had the weight of a dead man mad in his coffin.

She thought of what the men had said about her mother, what Habiba might have been as a young woman, how many relationships she might have had with men, before she had settled down with her father. But it did not really matter, had never mattered. After the horror of what had happened in the country, she couldn't sit in judgment on her own mother, or play God—the past was another country! And she definitely had no intention of telling her husband or mother about what had happened to her.

Although her soul was shattered and her lips bruised, she tried to harness the bit of strength still left in her, determined to raise herself to her full height, resting heavily on the palms of her hands. How difficult it was to regain what was left of her dignity? When she was certain the sons of the devil were gone, she began to remove the particles of dust from her body and ran her fingers through her tangled mat of hair, trying to stay alive, in spite of the constriction in her heart. Until now, she had been certain that no one had witnessed the arrival of the devil's men, but when she raised her head in the twilight she had a shock. Her brush with the devil had not been a private affair, as she had thought, for high up on one of her coconut trees was a witness: a large vulture.

A speck of light just bright enough for Yeama to have a closer look brought the vulture into focus. Perched on a branch, it looked like an old woman. With a grave face she looked at Yeama, as if to signal that there was nothing here to clean up, because this was not the kind of transition from life to death that interested her.

For what seemed like an eternity, she fixed an understanding look on Yeama, trailed her wise eyes over the wide sweep of the verdure, and let out an ancient screech that echoed across the river as she took off with a great expanse of wings, borne by a sudden gust of wind.

Yeama stood for a while and watched the sacred bird ascend. Terribly sad, she realized she had not felt so lonely since her family had left for Senegal; fragile, so unspeakably in need of an answer about why she had been hurled this side of horror.

The bird had completely disappeared into the nimbostratus of the night by the time Yeama found her voice. Left with a miserable, empty feeling in her heart, she began to pray and cry that once she was back in the mysterious world of bird-women, the vulture would make some sense of her ordeal and send a message to her, perhaps in the labyrinth of dreams, about how Yeama was connected to what was going on in other parts of the country.

Yeama's legs were now less wooden, so she threw some dry leaves over the dead dog, a temporary rite until she could bury him. Then she walked back to the house from where they had dragged her, a clear hesitancy evident in her steps as she pushed the door open.

Still wondering why the sons of the devil had chosen her, she collapsed into a chair and thought of how strange it was that, in spite of the powers granted to the dead, her grandmother had not warned her about the evil wind that was blowing toward the house. Before the devil's men attacked her, Yeama had never considered the house unsafe. It was not the sort to attract rebels, surrounded as it was by a wall and a large orchard. But she had not imagined how easily the rebels would scale that wall. For almost six months after the departure of her husband, parents, and son for Senegal, she had felt safe and happy there. Most evenings, after a busy day, she would spend an hour or so reading paperback novels and books on animal husbandry, or simply listening to the river, before going to bed, where, under a warm quilt, she had long, baroque dreams about her son. She had thought herself fulfilled, independent, never in need of pampering by anyone; now she was badly in need of companionship.

Until recently, the war had been somewhere else, away from her, in the provinces, not in Malagueta. In the comfort of her home, she, like many of Malagueta's citizens, had lived with the illusion of being safe, having no other choice but to trust the pronouncements of General Soriba Dan Doggo's government.

"We were betrayed by that useless drunk!" her father had said bitterly.

She felt completely drained of spirit as she got up from the chair. Once, when she was young, her father had taken her to see cows calving. She remembered how exhausted, dry in the mouth, they looked. Her own mouth was dry, an arid desert in April; wondering whether this was how those cows had felt after their ordeal, she barely managed to walk to the kitchen.

It was Sunday, the day when she usually prepared a gourmet meal. When the sons of the devil had suddenly appeared and dragged her out of the house, she had been getting ready to cook a rooster: the one that had serviced the hens and given Yeama dozens of chickens. The rooster was a fine bird that had always outperformed the younger competition for the hens. Lately, though, he had begun to show disinterest in the hens, his comb was bent, and his crowing was losing its beauty. Sadly, Yeama had brought a knife to his throat, poured hot water all over to soften the skin, and plucked him clean of his feathers. Feeling deeply guilty, she cut him up into fine pieces and slapped a garnish of herbs and spices on them, not forgetting that the feet, neck, and head were to be reserved for the dead when they came to visit, just as her grandmother had taught her. Irene had also carefully instructed her on how to garnish domestic fowl and other homegrown birds so that they would taste better than the stuff they sold in those expensive supermarkets. "You cannot compare a rooster that has been raised on worms, ants, and corn and allowed a free run amongst the hens with those bred in hatcheries heated up with electricity and fed with the shit of other birds," Irene had said.

It was a chilly evening, but the air in Yeama's kitchen was hot. While the devil's men were attacking her, the uncooked poultry had started to attract flies, and their buzzing now caught her attention. But, as though she was paralyzed, her hands refused to respond to any sort of command. She finally managed to move her fingers a bit, and thought of throwing out the meat, but realized that would mean discarding the memory that was her wound. Yet she hesitated to cook and eat the meat, certain it would go down her gullet tasting of venom and shame and course through her blood as a reminder of how helpless she had been.

Then she had a brilliant inspiration. She could convert the raw blood of the rooster into a deadly, invisible weapon against those motherless men who had declared war on her. But first she had to rid herself of the smell that the crudeness of their manhood had left on her unyielding body. She went to her bathroom and searched in her medicine cabinet for the black soap that Irene had taught her to use during the long days of malaria, and for some aniseed oil.

The cicadas had started to chirr noisily on the plants. Still outraged over the loss of their rooster, the hens were getting restless, and she realized she would have to get them another one later to make her peace with them. Guided by the narrow moon, she walked to the orchard near her house to pluck some leaves from the avocado, lime, papaya, guava, sorghum, and mango, in the same way Irene had done in the past. When she had gathered enough leaves for the rite of purification, she went back to the kitchen, got the stove going, put all the leaves in a big pot of water, and watched, enthralled, as the cauldron began to make spirals of amber smoke. Then she went to stand by a window as the spidery hands of night began to spread their dark shadows, but she was still able to make out the outlines of the river lit up by the sparkle of gray stones just beneath the rise of the water.

After the cauldron had turned brown, the pungent smell of the leaves was sharp in the air. In spite of her pain, she began to respond to the song of the river, and it helped her resolve to go on living in what was left of that stretch of paradise. A week earlier, she had sat for eight hours on the verandah to have her hair done up in a neatly threaded braid, but it took her less than thirty minutes now to uncoil it in readiness for the act of purification. She touched the bruises on her back, where the grass had pricked her, and looked at her fingers to see whether her blood had blotched out. Her thick tresses fell to their full length on her shoulders as she studied her face in the mirror. The soft folds of her lips were sore, and although she was trying hard not to cry, she saw that blood rings had formed in her eyes.

When she thought the mixture in the cauldron was sufficiently brewed, she emptied it into a large bucket. Bubbles of sweat broke on her brow, and her nose was permeated by the smell of organic herbs. Naked except for the towel draped around her shoulders, she carried the bucket out of the house down a path to the river illuminated by the fragments of light from the azure moon. At other times, she might have been afraid of snakes, scorpions, land crabs scurrying out of their holes; but after her ordeal with the devil, there was nothing to fear. During those magical moments spent with Irene watching it flow, the river was what had bonded Yeama to her grandmother; a long, dark python it had seemed at times, snaking its way to the ocean, full of mysteries, whether those conjured by Irene or imagined in the mind of her granddaughter. Thinking of those moments, Yeama knew she could take her chances with the river.

She stood naked, close to where the river wetted the grass, and felt the touch of a breeze bearing down and pricking her wounds like a dozen needles. Throughout her ordeal the river had been singing, moving slowly; but its plaintive note was tremulous enough to bend the necks of the bulrushes. A bellowing noise, like that of bustling rapids, rose from its depths, as if the womb of the river was opening up and beckoning Yeama to enter, where she would be healed. Yet she remained on the bank of the river. Almost straining her back, she began to pull out some tussocks of grass, applied the rich scent of the black soap to them, and, ever so slowly, began to wash herself from head to toe, cupping the water from the cauldron in both hands. In tune with the river, she tongued the lyrics of a song, savoring the words as she tried to remember how Irene had soaped her skin when the bad days of malaria had stayed too long and had to be chased out of her life. Moving her arms in a rhythmic pattern, Yeama sang along with the river and rubbed the tussocks all over her body. In the nimbus of the clouds, she saw that the moon had widened a bit, casting its light on her ebony skin, at the same time that an owl was returning a witch's call. It was a good sign.

Yet as soon as she had emptied the pot of its liquid, she looked at the leaves, inhaled their aroma, and realized that her rite of cleansing was not yet over. Her insides needed cleansing.

Slowly, she began to chew on some of the leaves. Though they tasted sour, there was no doubt that their juices would wash her clean of the sacrilege of the devil. She felt a transformation in her soul as her dignity was restored, her reason brought back.

The moon was now a bright glow, adding one final mystery to the feeling of being reborn that Yeama was already experiencing. It was then that she heard a voice she had not heard in a long time. Death had carried that voice away some time ago, but it seemed to have come now from the moon shining above the trees. Yeama did not panic, not even when she heard the voice call her a second time, because even before she had looked in the direction of the trees, she knew it was Irene calling out to her.

"Yeama, Yeama," she heard the clear voice of her grandmother calling.

A great plenitude filled Yeama's soul, she felt calm and closed her eyes as she began to experience the sensation of the soft texture of a pair of hands transmitting healing, the hands of a woman familiar with the contours of her body. The sweetness of the healing was almost unbearable, No, she was not dreaming, not when she could see the face of the beautiful woman, who now spoke to her.

"Don't worry, my child. After tonight, the hands of the devil will be turned to ashes when you next confront him."

Yeama went back to her house. In what was left of the night, she cooked the rooster using Irene's favorite recipe, and nothing had ever tasted so good in her mouth. In spite of the horror she had suffered at the hands of the devil's men, Yeama admitted she had known some good men; that was why she knew she would sleep peacefully tonight, protected by the water spirit and confident about the future.

She had saved the blood of the rooster. Next morning, the sound of mortar fire resounding in the hills overlooking Malagueta did nothing to destroy her confidence as she poured the blood on the ground to wake up the soul of the dead. The river had not stopped singing, and was flowing toward the ocean. Inspired by the river, Yeama not only felt toughened but was determined to meet the devil on her own terms.

Now she was waiting for another sign from Irene.

After the dull six months of rain, she was also looking forward to some sunlight in November, just before the first, sonorous notes of the cool desert harmattan, when she liked to sit on the verandah to read, enthralled by the sweet scents of the geraniums, the wild gardenia bushes, and the thriving pots of marigolds, the fluorescent light drawing bumblebees to its glow.

Late one evening, except for the chirping of the red bishops returning home, the jostling of the orioles, and the tired voices of the thrushes with their tales of how far they had gone to catch worms, an eerie calm descended on her garden. Then, as though she were reliving an eternity of suffering, Yeama saw the large boat sailing down the river with three men and their cargo of looted goods—television sets, mattresses, sacks of rice, flour, and gallons of cooking oil. Even before she saw their faces, she knew who they were and recalled that dreadful evening when the sons of the devil came to the house. Having waited so long for this day, she raised her face to the moon, certain that at any minute Irene would appear to her.

A purple light appeared in the sky. Yeama rushed close to where the river wetted the grass and stretched her arms, and she knew she was not dreaming when, in the now translucently bright light, she saw her grandmother, resplendent in an expensive kabaslot, standing on the opposite bank of the river.

As on that day when she had first appeared to her granddaughter, Irene smiled, and the ground beneath Yeama's feet shook as an incredible noise raged in the river and created a powerful surge like none that Yeama had ever seen before.

"Don't be afraid, child," Irene said to Yeama. "The dead have not forsaken you." And then she was gone.

An awesome force immediately possessed Yeama so that she lifted her long, beautiful arms, and trembled as a second quake unleashed, all along the dark, raging river, a great, menacing ball of fire that smashed to smithereens the boat bearing the men. She shook with the force of a possessed woman as she went deeper into the river until she stood knee deep in it, from where she saw the men struggling for their lives. Yet she did not feel triumphant, but hoped that what was happening would somehow give thousands of men, women, and children in Kissi some peace and a place in Irene's galaxy. As though they had been cut into pieces by invisible knives, the men were bleeding profusely, and Yeama realized she had never felt so close to her grandmother. She smiled as she imagined Irene looking at her as she watched the attempt of this monstrous lot to get out of the river, knowing fully well that it was useless, because the scent of their blood had brought the crocodiles from the nearby swamp into the river to feed on them, as the river continued its furious, tempestuous music, the way Irene had told Yeama it could when inspired.

Next morning the crocodiles were gone, and she saw the river flowing quietly and the wilted plants revitalized in a shaft of golden light, while, walking noiselessly into the compound, glad to be home and prepared to surprise her, were her parents, husband, and child, refreshed from exile. After the horrible nightmare of a long winter, spring had returned to Malagueta, and in spite of what had happened to her, there was a stubborn hope in Yeama. Feeling happier than she had in a long time, she stripped naked and plunged into the river. With the ferns whose medicinal properties her grandmother had taught her how to use in the time of innocence, Yeama began to bathe, humming to the melody of the river, and couldn't help smiling as she recalled what Irene had told her that time:

> *There is something sacred about this river.*

Begun in

Sierra Leone,

1991–1993.

Written all over again in

Sweet Briar and Harrisonburg, Virginia,

Brooklyn, New York,

Springdale, Utah,

Las Vegas, Nevada,

June 1998–2004.

Completed in Pacific Palisades, California,

December 2005.

Revised at Cove Park, on Loch Long, Scotland, 2012.

Acknowledgments

A work this size, written during some of the most difficult and painful years of my life, could not have been completed without the kindness and encouragement of friends and the support of institutions. Consequently, I wish to thank the following people: John and Rita Hirsch, for their kindness and wonderful friendship in Sierra Leone and the United States; Debbie Shanley and her husband, Dan, and Betty-Ann Sittig, for friendship and dinners in Connecticut; Elizabeth Nunez, for telling me about the Virginia Center for the Creative Arts; Sunny Monk, Craig and Sheila Pleasant, and all the wonderful people who always looked after me at the VCCA; Peter Bergdoll and Magrit Luqman in Germany, for their friendship and kindness; Peter Karefa-Smart, for his friendship; Dr. Edison Jackson, for inviting me to Medgar Evers College, CUNY; Dr. Joanne Gabbins, for inviting me to James Madison University; Anne Francois and Debbie Ngozi Frazer, for helping me to survive in New York City, Wole Soyinka, for opening doors for me and for his kindness; Richard Wiley, Eric Olsen, and Chris Argent, for camaraderie at UNLV; Glenn Schaeffer, founder of the International Institute of Modern Letters, Las Vegas, for his generous support; Russell Banks, for changing the terms of my stay at the IIML and for putting me on to the agent; Kim Konikow, for inviting me to the MESA: An Arts and Humanities Center; Claudia Gordon and the staff of the Villa Aurora in the Pacific Palisades, California; my special "broda," Niyi Osundare; my hardworking and dedicated agent, Ellen Levine, who, with her assistants, was there for me, for believing we could do it; and all the others who, in one way or the other, saw my wife (now deceased) and me through those painful but very creative years. Thank you so much, all of you!

The following institutions invited me to teach or write. I wish to acknowledge their support:

Medgar Evers College, City University of New York

James Madison University, Harrisonburg, Virginia

Virginia Center for the Creative Arts, Amherst, Virginia

Hassayampa Institute, Prescott, Arizona

The Mesa Arts: An Arts and Humanities Center, Springdale, Utah

The International Parliament of Writers, Paris, France, for sending me to the International Institute of Modern Letters, UNLV, Las Vegas, Nevada

Villa Aurora Foundation for European American Relations, Pacific Palisades, California

Cove Park, Argyll and Bute, Scotland